KATHARINE SUSAN[...]

(1883-1969) was born in Fiji, the daught[...]
Her family moved when she was three [...]
Melbourne and Launceston. In 1904, at [...]
went to South Gippsland to become, [...] ..... Her father
committed suicide in 1907 and the following year she began her
autobiographical novel, *The Wild Oats of Han*, though this book was not
published for many years. Katharine Susannah Prichard made her first
visit to London in 1908 and returned in 1912, working as a journalist. In
1915 her first novel, *The Pioneers*, won the Hodder & Stoughton All
Empire Novel Competition enabling her to return to Australia to devote
herself to writing 'about Australia and the realities of life for the
Australian people'; her second novel, *Windlestraws*, was published in
1916. In 1919 she married Hugo Throssell and moved with him to a house
on the hills of Greenmount near Perth in Western Australia; their son was
born three years later. Meanwhile she continued writing novels: *Black
Opal* was published in 1921, followed by *Working Bullocks* (1926), *The
Wild Oats of Han* (1928), *Coonardoo* (1928) – winner, with M. Barnard
Eldershaw's *A House is Built*, of the *Bulletin* prize – *Haxby's Circus* (1930),
Intimate Strangers (1937), *Moon of Desire* (1941) and the goldfields
trilogy, *The Roaring Nineties* (1946), *Golden Miles* ((1948) and *Winged
Seeds* (1950). Her autobiography, *Child of the Hurricane*, was published in
1964, and three years later her last novel, *Subtle Flame*, appeared.
Katharine Susannah Prichard's novels have been translated into many
languages including Russian, Polish and Czech; she also wrote plays and
poetry and her short stories were published in four collections between
1932 and 1967.

A committed communist, pacifist and founder member of the
Communist Party of Australia, she visited Russia in 1933. In her absence
her husband committed suicide and, returning to Australia, she threw
herself further into political work. One of the founders of the Movement
Against War and Fascism, she attended the National Anti-War Congress
in Melbourne in 1934 and at the outbreak of the Spanish Civil War
organized the Spanish Relief Committee in Western Australia. In 1943
she became a member of the Communist Party's Central Committee.
Katharine Susannah Prichard was awarded the World Council's silver
medallion for services to peace in 1959. On her death at the age of eighty
six, her coffin draped with the Red Flag, she was given a Communist
funeral and her ashes scattered near her home on the slopes of
Greenmount.

Virago are to publish *Golden Miles* and *Winged Seeds* in 1984.

If you would like to know more about Virago books, write to us
at 41 William IV Street, London WC2N 4DB for a full catalogue.

Please send a stamped addressed envelope

THE
ROARING
NINETIES

*A Story of the Goldfields of
Western Australia*

KATHARINE SUSANNAH PRICHARD

WITH A NEW INTRODUCTION
BY DRUSILLA MODJESKA

Published by VIRAGO PRESS Limited 1983
41 William IV Street, London WC2N 4DB

First published in Great Britain by Jonathan Cape 1946
Virago edition offset from first edition

British Library Cataloguing in Publication Data
Prichard, Katharine Susannah
    The roaring nineties.—(Virago modern classics)
    I. Title
    823[F]   PR9619.3.R75

ISBN 0-86068-379-6

Printed in Finland by Werner Söderström Oy,
a member of Finnprint

To
B. S.

INTRODUCTION

The Roaring Nineties, first published in 1946, is the first in a trilogy of novels set in the Western Australian goldfields from the turn of the century. Written from the perspective of the miners and miners' women it draws attention to Australia's militant past and potential for a radical future. Women were scarce on the goldfields, but through the memorable Sally Gough they are given a central focus, holding the community together through harsh and often frightening conditions, from droughts to strikes. Despite the scarcity of women in early Australian history, and despite the continuing image of Australia as a man's country, many of the best writers have been women and there is a long tradition of women's writing that tackles that difficult set of relationships between the 'woman question', politics and literature. Katharine Susannah Prichard belongs to this and to a broader tradition of radical writing committed to democratic politics and Australian cultural independence. The complex and contradictory impulses of politics and aesthetics are deeply embedded in her life as well as her writing, and the threads of her commitment stretch back to her childhood.

Katharine Susannah Prichard dates her political awakening to the end of the last century when her journalist father lost his job and, 'ill and dejected', could not find another. She had been born on 4 December, 1883, in Fiji where Tom Prichard was the editor of the *Fiji Times*. The family moved back to Australia in 1886, first to Melbourne and then to Launceston in Tasmania and it was there that the family's fortunes were so suddenly reversed. The furniture had to be sold and the family was kept going by her mother's sewing. The pain for Katharine was that she could neither understand nor change her parents' misery although she recognised the injustice of the situation. She did what she could by putting herself through school on scholarships. By 1902 when she sat for her matriculation, her father was temporarily in work again and she hoped she could stay on to study for a bursary. But her mother was ill and there was not enough money for her and her brothers' fees; as the girl it was Katharine who stood down. She took a number of jobs, from governessing to journalism, all the while keeping up with what would have been her university reading in the public library at night.

In 1908 Katharine Susannah Prichard was sent to London to cover the Franco-British exhibition for the Melbourne *Herald* and in 1912 she returned, hoping, like so many talented Australian women of her generation, to find ways of living professionally and independently in the

vii

comparative freedóm of London. There were more opportunities for work there than in Melbourne, but the dynamics of 'independence' proved no less problematic. What London did offer her, however, was a systematic self-education. She was determined, she wrote in her autobiography, to work out the causes of social injustice. She explored the politics of Syndicalism, Guild Socialism, Theosophy, Christian Science and the Women's Social and Political Union; none satisfied her entirely, but they left her receptive to the impact of the Russian Revolution and with a good background for her subsequent study of Marxism.

By 1917 she was back in Melbourne. One of her brothers had been killed in the war, her father had committed suicide and her mother was alone. Besides, the war-time jingoism and the barbarism of the trenches had made her, as it had other expatriate Australian writers and intellectuals, sceptical of Europe's claims to cultural superiority and hopeful for the possibilities of social change and cultural regeneration in Australia. If nothing else, it was felt, Australia was not shackled to anachronistic and elitist cultural traditions and there had been no war fought on her soil. Furthermore, in 1915, Katharine Prichard had won the Australian section of the Hodder and Stoughton All Empire novel competition with *The Pioneers*. With £250 in her pocket, more than she was to earn from her writing for many years, she returned to Melbourne in February 1916, confident of herself as a writer and of the possibility of a broadly-based radical literature in Australia.

By 1920 Katharine Susannah Prichard was a marxist and, much to her family's surprise, married – to Hugo Throssell, a captain recently returned from France with the V.C., and, like herself, a socialist. They went to live in Western Australia, in the hills on the outskirts of Perth and there she bore her only son, worked for the establishment of the Communist Party of Australia (C.P.A.), educated herself on the major industrial and social issues of the state and wrote some of her best novels: *Working Bullocks* (1926), *Coonardoo* (1928), *Haxby's Circus* (1930) and *Intimate Strangers* (1937).

These novels combined a journalistic emphasis on social and political detail with a tentative exploration of modern, if not modernist techniques and ideas. At this time Katharine Prichard was interested in the relationship between sexuality and the unconscious and, influenced by D.H. Lawrence, in notions of the poetic novel and a romanticism that embraced the vitality of the natural world. These two impulses in her writing did not always sit easily together, but the resultant tension is one of the sources of energy in her writing during this period.

Before the Second World War very little Australian history or serious social comment was being written, and feature journalism was also rare. It was the writers, and particularly the women writers, who opened up significant areas of social debate: it was women novelists who wrote, in fictional form, the first Australian histories and opened to public debate the dreadful realities of race relations. Katharine Susannah Prichard took this documentary and political aspect of her writing seriously. She lived with the timber cutters in the south west for *Working Bullocks*, travelled with Wirth's Circus for *Haxby's Circus* and stayed on a station in the north for *Coonardoo*. Of the three, perhaps *Coonardoo* (1928) is the most significant in this respect, for it was the first Australian novel to portray Aboriginal characters with recognisably human emotions, intellect and sexuality. This in itself was bold in the climate of the 1920's. There was some university based research into Aboriginal society but *Coonardoo* was the first popular statement that Aboriginal culture, far from being primitive, was rich and complex; it was the first popular exposure of the exploitation and decimation of the Aboriginal population which was assumed to be primitive and backward and thus dying out. The official attitude was that white society could but soothe the pillow of a dying race; *Coonardoo* made such blandishments impossible. The dust raised by the novel took a long time to settle, not least because the Aboriginal Coonardoo has an affair with a white man, an idea which, in 1928, was more shocking than the novel's central point about the dispossession and destruction of an entire culture.

In her novels of this period, Katharine Susannah Prichard was becoming increasingly interested in the sexual as well as the economic and social oppression of women. It is at this point that the two impulses in her work came together, for it was in the area of sexuality and the unconscious that she was most influenced by modernism. This was as important in her work of this period as the more conventionally documented industrial, social and political issues, and it was approached, however tentatively, through streams of consciousness, shifting point of view and an extended use of metaphor. The inevitable result was that Katharine Prichard was forced ever nearer her own situation as a woman. *Intimate Strangers* is located in the experience of urban educated women; it dramatises the effect of the depression on a marriage when the man loses his job and resents but depends on the woman for survival.

Intimate Strangers was finished before Katharine Prichard went to Russia in 1933, a year of double trauma. First she had to face the disparity between the dreams of socialists in far-away Australia and the daunting realities of the Soviet Union at the end of the first five-year plan. Then on her way home news reached her that Hugo Throssell had committed suicide. The marriage had, it would seem, been under stress before she left, at least partly because of the pressure of her political work. There is some evidence to suggest that her time in the Soviet Union had made her reassess the priorities of the personal and the political. The bitterness of the moment was increased by her terrible fear that Hugo had read the manuscript of *Intimate Strangers* in which the bankrupt husband kills himself leaving his wife free for a more passionate lover. There is no evidence to believe that Hugo Throssell had read the manuscript; financial disaster and depression seem much more likely factors in his death. Nevertheless the doubts were real and it was a long time before she wrote again. *Intimate Strangers* was not published until 1937 and then its ending was changed. There was *Moon of Desire* in 1941, Katharine Prichard's only potboiler, written in the vain hope of film rights and an end to her remorseless financial anxieties. *The Roaring Nineties* was her next serious work of fiction and very different in tone.

During those years of silence, Katharine Prichard threw herself into the C.P.A., associating herself closely with Party politics and doctrines. When she began to write again she accepted more completely than ever before the strictures of socialist realism. The debate over this period of her work centres on whether it is a culmination of traits that were always evident; or a retreat from the poetic and sensuous which had enriched her writing but brought her perilously close to disaster. Certainly, by the time she wrote *The Roaring Nineties*, socialist realism had been enshrined as policy both by the Comintern and the C.P.A. After its brief flowering in the early twenties, modernism had been discredited in the Soviet Union. At home the confrontation in the cities between the militant left and pro-fascist paramilitary right during the depression and then the war had given her a renewed sense of political urgency. So it is not surprising that her writing moved in the direction of socialist realism.

It is significant that the novel opens with the dispossessed Aborigines, making the point she had driven home in *Coonardoo*, that white development had been at terrible expense. However she is less successful in her portrayal of the Aborigines than she was in earlier novels. There are only two Aboriginal characters of any substance, and despite the opening pages none of the narrative is told from their point of view. Indeed by directing the narrative through the point of view of the miners the text comes close to endorsing their patronising and even racist attitudes at the expense of her earlier and more subtle analysis. Nevertheless Kalgoorla is given symbolic importance for it is with her that the first volume opens and with her burial that the third concludes.

The use of the miners' point of view is much more successful in the historical and class analysis that forms the core of the novel. The goldfields were a fertile choice for a working-class Australian history. The Southern Cross flag had long fluttered over the mines and Eureka stockade in Victoria in 1854 and had come to signify, not altogether correctly, republican and even revolutionary struggle. The goldfields offered a symbol of a radical past and a focus for the analysis of its failure. *The Roaring Nineties* documents the economic, political and social history of the goldfields through the conflict between the alluvial miners and the large companies that came in the wake of the prospectors, buying up the

x

best mines, hiring the disaffected men as cheap labour and trying, eventually, to usurp the traditional rights of the diggers. It was a conflict centred on colonial as well as class exploitation as foreign capital poured in and drained the minerals and wealth out of the country. The issues involved in the conflicts over Australia's mineral resources and the dispossession of the Aboriginal population still reverberate with as much bitterness in contemporary Australia.

This broad historical perspective is interwoven into a rich account of life as it was lived on the goldfields. The novel unfolds through the richness of this social detail and through the personality of Sally Gough. The narrative moves fast and *The Roaring Nineties* makes good reading. In particular Sally Gough is a marvellous character, tough and uncompromising. She provides continuity and a central reference point not only for the novel but for the fledgling community, a source of moral as well as domestic strength. She is also the focus of familiar themes: of the struggle for independence as she battles to earn her living; of disappointment in love as marriage becomes routine and Morris fails, as husbands inevitably do, to live up to romantic ideologies. Strong and successful as she is, the desire to be swept off her feet remains but when passion comes her way it clashes irrevocably with her sense of duty and, more importantly, with her politics. The family remains intact as it ultimately does in all Prichard's novels, but ambivalently so.

Sally Gough provides a focus for Katharine Susannah Prichard's interest in the ways in which women are exploited as much for their strength as for their weakness. There was plenty of scope for exploitation on the goldfields: women were scarce and their favours dangerously in demand; there was little opportunity for independence and little to protect them from predatory or violent men. But Sally Gough is no victim. She maintains her integrity and her dignity despite appalling conditions. Rather the novel explores, through her, the price women pay for their strengths, taking on the load of the men while protecting them from knowledge of their weakness. The weight on Sally's shoulders is enormous and there is no relief for the very reason that she is able to carry it. Her pain comes from her strength and the knowledge that there is no one on whom she can lean. And so it is through work rather than love that she comes to terms with her own passions and 'the passions this lovely, sun blasted country bred'. Whereas it was sexuality that bound the characters in the earlier novels to each other and the strange power of the Australian land, in the trilogy it is work that forms that nexus with the environment. The sexual division of labour becomes central to the relationship between the sexes, just as it is work and the vastly different relationship to gold that irrevocably divides the miners from the owners.

Class and sex, love, death and the contradiction between the personal and political remain central to *The Roaring Nineties'* sequels, *Golden Miles* and *Winged Seeds*, which trace Sally and the Gough family's lives through the hard and varied years to the Second World War. They are also novels in which Katharine Prichard reworked her own uncompromising relationship to these issues in a period of cold war and personal isolation.

Drusilla Modjeska, Sydney, 1982

INTRODUCTION

In this story of the goldfields of Western Australia, I have tried to tell, not only something of the lives of several people, but to give also the story of an industry.

For several years, I gathered material, living and working on the goldfields, yarning to old prospectors, and hearing from them of rushes, experiences of the early days. I read all the old newspapers and almost everything that has been written on the subject; but the story grew from the reminiscences of two people I have called Dinny Quin and Sally Gough. The incidents of their lives are authentic, and other characters have their counterparts among pioneers of the goldfields, although for the usual reasons it has been necessary to avoid being photographic.

In providing names for the figures which move across such a vast background, it was difficult to find some which had not been associated with the goldfields at one time or another; but actual names have not been used, except when they have an historical, or almost legendary significance.

Particularly, in relation to the struggle for alluvial rights, the names of men who took part in it have been retained; and also some of their speeches, because these give a better idea of the feeling engendered than one would be justified in assuming.

The Roaring Nineties is planned to be the first book of a trilogy which will tell the story of Dinny Quin and Sally Gough, and of the goldfields.

I wish to express appreciation to proprietors of *The Kalgoorlie Miner* for the opportunities for research which they made available to me, and also to the records of John Marshall in *Battling for Gold,* Jules Raeside in *Golden Days,* and Arthur Reid in *Those Were the Days,* all of which contain much valuable, factual material.

KATHARINE SUSANNAH PRICHARD

CHAPTER I

SMOKE lifted high in the fine dry air. Like a sigh, the breath of
a living thing, it rose from a low hillside, over the outstretched
land wrapped in grey scrub to the far horizon. In the east, the
sky flashed to a luminous glare as the sun rose.

The blacks sleeping beside their camp fire stirred. A young
man knocked smouldering logs of the fire together, picked up his
spears and stood gazing over the vast wilderness of his hunting
grounds. Nostrils wide, scenting the morning air for the taint
of game, his senses picked up something alien in the atmosphere.
Naked body, taut and alert, his dark eyes searched the distance.

'Yukki!' Harsh and hoarse as the call of a bird, his warning
rang.

Heavy figures lying about the camp fire stumbled to their feet,
crowding round him.

Away to the south, across the sea of scrub packed closely
together, a puff of dust hung in the air, moved slowly. Voices
rattled to fear and excitement, as men and women watched that
smudge of dust, many miles away, creeping towards them.

A small family group, an old man, three or four full-grown
men, their wives and children, the aborigines knew that trail of
dust against the dim screen of the sky denoted men and beasts
coming to take possession of their hunting grounds. Men whose
fire-sticks spat death and who seized any native they could waylay to find water for them. Water, or gold—the magic these
white men sought, which lay covered with dust in the dry creek
beds, streaking the rocks of weathered hillsides. White men had
died on these plains and in the shingly ridges, because neither
their wits nor their magic taught them to find food and water
in a dry season.

More of them had come, these strange men and four-legged
beasts, emptying the water-holes, scaring away the wild animals,
tearing up the earth in their madness to find that yellow stone,
which the blacks feared because it brought this devastation upon
them.

In a few moments the women had picked up their coolamons
and children, the men their spears, womeras and kylies, and the
camp was deserted. The dark figures streaking away among the
trees, snap and rattle, and mulga fleeced with downy yellow

I

blossom, had the same lithe grace as the trees. They moved among the trees like their shadows, with the swift swaying gait of tough slender trunks bowed and driven by the wind.

The hunters went on ahead, scattered and disappeared. The old man, with the women and children, moved steadily towards the north-east, where a long low roller of blue hills lay along the skyline. By midday the party had covered many miles at an easy dawdling pace.

One of the younger women began to lag behind and an old gin fell back with her. The girl, heavy with child, followed the old woman when she turned away from the travellers, along a rough gutter torrential rains had made in the hard red earth. The girl walked slowly, and more slowly breathing hard. She clung to a tree and would have sunk down beside it, but the old woman looking back scolded and urged her on. When they came to a slight depression barred by huge boulders, the girl sat down and the old woman put her coolamon, little skin bag and digging stick on the ground. Her fire-stick she held carefully until she had scrabbled a few leaves and twigs together to cover it.

Then she climbed the rocks and peered anxiously over the edge of a weatherworn boulder. In a shallow hole on one of them was a small pool of clear water. With a grunt of satisfaction she scrambled down, grabbed her coolamon, the big wooden scoop for holding water and food, and climbed the rocks again, drank herself, filled the coolamon and carried the water to the girl. With her hands, she swept the earth of pebbles beside a bush of bright green mallee and cleared a wide swale round the fire.

The dry leaves and twigs had flashed to flame over her fire-stick and lay in smouldering embers. The old woman squatted over them, raking them together and feeding the fire with dry sticks. Then she piled green branches on the blaze and a thick aromatic smoke arose. The girl struggled to her feet and crouched down in the smoke. She sat back on her heels, gasping and straining. The old woman stood off from her, shrilling fiercely, scolding and singing, stamping her feet and beating her hands together. Presently an infant was crying in the silence.

The old woman tied the cord between mother and child with a thread of human hair-string from her dilly bag. She severed the cord with a sharp strong thumb-nail. The baby lay on the earth squalling lustily while she attended to the mother. Then she greased the child with reeking fat from her bag, smeared him with soft ashes from the fire and laid him beside the mother.

She pulled a long dry branch across the fire so that it would smoulder for a long time and stretched herself beside the mother and child. Soon all three were asleep beneath the bush which cast a shifting lace of black shadow on the hard red earth.

They were still sleeping, the quiet broken only by a shifting of leaves, the shy twittering of small birds, when two white men came through the trees in the late afternoon. The men stepped warily, revolvers cocked, led by the smoke of the fire to where the women lay; but the shingle slipped and clicked under their heavy boots. The old woman jumped up, screeching fiercely and clutching her digging stick, as she saw the men.

No man of her race would have dared to invade this sanctuary. Even the father might not see his child until the old woman and girl returned to the place where the tribe met beside a gnamma hole in the far hills.

These men were thirsty. They made signs to the old woman that it was water they needed: put the revolvers back in their belts. She knew well enough what their wild eyes, the dried sunken leather of their cheeks meant, the swollen tongues that could barely form the words they hurled at her. There was so little water in the gnamma hole, she was reluctant to show it to them. But they had to be got rid of, so she scrambled up the rocks to the water, and they followed her.

The men drank sparingly and filled their water bags. They brought their horses, scooped up the water to the last drop: gave the horses a drink from their felt hats. The old woman watched, muttering and growling. They laughed boisterously at her sombre rage.

Later they shot some of the bush pigeons which came down at the gnamma hole to drink. Roasted them on the fire, but they gave the old woman and the girl only some hard bits of salt meat from their saddle bags. The women ate, though their fear increased as the men camped by the fire for the night. The old woman warned the girl that they must be ready to run away with the first light. There was no water for miles and they would have to travel steadily all day to reach the next rock hole.

The white men asked about that: where they could find more water. The old woman pretended she did not know: would tell them nothing. They tried talking to the girl: she too was sulky and silent, hugging her baby and staring at them with scared, savage eyes. The men tied the old woman's hands and legs together. The girl tried to get away; but weak, and with a baby in her arms, could not run far. They caught her and brought her back, trussed her up too: then stretched to sleep undisturbed by the old woman's jabbering and the girl's shrill cries.

In the morning, all the white men could talk of was water. Where was the next water? Would the gins take them to water?

3

The old woman remained dumb and obdurate, but the girl was thirsty; made signs, pleading for a drink. The men fed her with more salt meat, and refused to give her a drop of water from their water bags, though they poured the water into a mug and drank it themselves before her.

The trick was a good one they knew. They had tried it before, fed a native with bacon or salt meat, and kept him without water, until, maddened by thirst, he led them to the nearest soak or gnamma hole. The girl understood what they wanted: would make straight for water, they believed.

One of the men lifted her on to his horse. She fought frantically at leaving her baby. His mate slung it up to her. They rode off.

'Gabbie! Gabbie!' (Water! Water!) the men shouted. The girl wailed and pointed to the broken back of a blue hill in the distance. She would take them there. The old woman vanished among the trees.

The prospectors had camped at the foot of that hill where a native well was hidden, when men of the tribe descended on them. Spears flew: a black rain in the dawn. After gold was found at Coolgardie, the bones of white men were discovered near the well.

The young gin, Kalgoorla, was an old woman when she told Dinny Quin about those white men. They were not the first she had encountered. The baby born that day had died; but Kalgoorla had another child, a girl, Meeri, born after she and two other gins had been stolen by white men on the track, years before.

All her life Kalgoorla clung to the ways of her own people. Although for many years she came and went among the scattered mining camps with men and women of her tribe, she never lost her fear and hatred of white men.

CHAPTER II

THERE was nothing Dinny Quin liked better than yarning about the early days.

An old prospector, tough and shrewd, with a gammy leg and a quizzical spark in his blue eyes, he had been a young man when he went out with the first team following Arthur Bayley's tracks from the Southern Cross to Coolgardie in September 1892.

The 'Cross was almost deserted that morning Art Bayley rode in across the salt lakes, his saddle bags stuffed with gold, Dinny said.

It was a fresh spring morning. Shallow pools, at the foot of the hill and the township, flashed silvery in the sunshine. White shacks and bat houses looked like a handful of shells flung down there in the distance. Most of them were empty and lifeless. The sheds and top hamper of the mines stood dumb and inert, their long spidery poppet legs raking the sky.

Yet the township on that dumpy hill in a sea of scrub was an outpost of civilization. An island in the unknown. Grey-dark, the scrub stretched under frail blue skies to the far horizon: a vast mysterious wilderness of stunted trees, shingly ridges and desert sand plains, for hundreds of miles in every direction.

Southern Cross! A few years ago it had sprung into existence like stars of the constellation on a dark night. Those stars had led a party of prospectors to water, and gold, so they called the place Southern Cross. It refuted prognostications that gold would never be found in payable quantities in Western Australia.

The Swan River Settlement was hard hit by an economic depression, following collapse of the land boom and a failure of banks in the older colonies of New South Wales and Victoria. News that gold-bearing reefs had been discovered at Southern Cross enabled Western Australia to weather the doldrums.

Soon prospectors, miners, storekeepers and speculators were swarming over the timbered ranges and widespread plains from the coast to the 'Cross. They tramped beside their teams and pack horses all the two hundred and forty miles, or loaded up at the railway which penetrated as far as Northam, the centre of a flourishing pastoral district, and trekked the rest of the way. The small fussy trains, few and far between, were quite unequal to coping with the rush of traffic to the new goldfields.

There were sensational rumours about this gold being found in the Yilgarn Hills, and men with the gold fever on them, took to the track, spending sometimes a month footslogging and camping by the way, rather than brook any delay in their chance of picking up a fortune. They dreamed of a new Ballarat or Bendigo lying out there in the vast, unknown back-country of the West.

Southern Cross grew in a frenzy of optimism. Prospectors kept coming in from the surrounding country with good reports. Mines were floated on rich crushings. The first bar of gold smelted in the blacksmith's forge raised hopes sky high, although that bar of gold disappeared mysteriously. Before long Frasers, Fraser's South, the Central and Central Extended, were employ-

5

ing two or three hundred men and the township had spread from a clutter of tents to the dignity of a street with rows of tin and weatherboard shacks, mud and hessian huts, stores, pubs and a warden's court.

But food and water were scarce during the long dry summer. The meagre supply of fresh water came from a few soaks near granite outcrops. Dams broached only salt water. Condensers had to be erected to make it drinkable for men and beasts. Salt water played havoc with the newly imported mining machinery: rotted the boilers and mucked-up the crushings. Fraser's yielded nothing but a black amalgam despite the promise of its ore.

Shares fell to zero and the slump set in. A new manager and new methods of dealing with the salt water gave the mines another lease of life. Good gold was extracted from the black amalgam, produced by the action of salt and refuse in the machinery. Crushings increased in value but costs of production rose. Wages were cut and the miners went on strike.

'A man couldn't live on what the mine-owners wanted to pay us,' Dinny said. 'The cost of food and water was so high—and don't forget Fraser's had been payin' dividends.'

The mines closed down, and almost everybody who could, left the field. A few miners hung on, hoping the mines would re-open, or that a living was to be made fossicking round about. At Hope's Hill, and on two or three shows, gold was still being won in payable quantities. Prospectors continued to trade their 'dwts' for stores and water. But for the most part only miners and prospectors who could not get away, and were waiting to pick up a job with a teamster, hung about the pub, gloomy and dejected, that morning Art Bayley rode in across the salt lakes.

As they kicked a football about the street, some of them scarcely noticed the solitary horseman. There was nothing unusual about a prospector coming in like that from a trip out-back, looking all-in himself and his horses just about knocked-up. And Art Bayley, slumped in his saddle, bearded and dirty, his horses as rough as bags, nobody recognized them until they had shambled on down the street towards the Warden's office.

Then something about the purposeful set of the man's shoulders, the way he kept his old felt hat pulled over his face, and never chanced an eye in the direction of the pub, aroused Speck Jones' suspicions.

'Who's it?' he queried.

'Well,' Dinny replied, 'I'll take my oath that's Art Bayley's ginger nag, though he's lookin' the worse for wear.'

'What's Art doin' passin' the pub, and old mates, without lookin' sideways?'

6

They watched the horseman pull up at the Warden's, yank off his saddle bags and stagger through the doorway of the rough shed.

'Great jumpin' Jehosaphat, he's on to something!' Bill gasped, and the boys gathered round.

'Went out along Hunt's track, four months ago, him and Harry Ford,' somebody said.

'Tommy Talbot reckoned he was on gold, when he came in for stores a couple of months ago,' Speck remembered. 'Tommy bought three or four brumbies, and got Harry Baker and Dick Fosser to go out with him to see what Bayley was up to.'

Eyes glittered: a quiver of excitement stirred sluggish pulses. In a few moments every man near the pub was sauntering down the street to the Warden's office. There, crowding in at the door, they saw what they had been dreaming about—gold in great lumps, gold stringing schisty quartz, hundreds of ounces of gold. And Art Bayley was applying for a reward claim one hundred and twenty-eight miles north-east of the 'Cross.

The town went mad when the news of Bayley's Find got round. Hell's bells, what a spree there was when Art Bayley had fixed up his business and began to celebrate, shouting all and sundry until the pubs ran out of liquor! Every man who could stand bought stores, tried to beg, borrow, steal horses, a buggy or spring cart, and packed his tools and camping gear. Store keepers put up their prices fifty per cent. You could have bought a horse for a fiver the day before, but that afternoon fifty pounds wouldn't buy one.

Speck Jones and Bill Garrity, better known as Bill Jehosaphat, with the shrewdness of old hands, who had been prospecting in the Kimberleys and on the Murchison, tackled Pat Murphy, the teamster, who had come in from the south. Pat was loading up to take the track for Bayley's Find on Sunday morning. He was charging a man five pounds to throw a hundred-pound swag on the wagon and swamp along with the team.

But Dinny Quin was broke. He had spent a lot of money on prospecting trips, in likely country away to the north, during the slump, and scores as long as his arm were registered against him at the store, the pub and Mrs. Gough's boarding house.

Nobody worried about Dinny's debts. Everybody knew he was a good prospector and an honest man. But money was short in the 'Cross that day: stores and gear changing hands for fancy prices. Dinny induced the storekeeper to stake him for a few pounds of flour and sugar, tinned dog and tea; but he was still shy of the fiver for Murphy when he went to see Alf Brierly, hoping that Alf might have a bit of money to spare.

7

Dinny never doubted that he would get away with the rush in the morning, even if it meant humping his swag every inch of the hundred and twenty odd miles to Bayley's Find. But he knew better than most men what prospecting out-back would mean; knew too the value of every minute lost when pegging on a new field was at stake.

It went against his bushman's and prospector's instinct to start behind scratch on a trip like this. In the crazy excitement of preparation for the track, however, it was every man for himself. A man who could not pay his way had to shift as best he could. Speck Jones and Bill Jehosaphat would have been willing enough for Dinny to fall in with them, but they too were short of cash: had just scraped up enough to square them for swamping with Murphy.

Dinny's last hope for the loan of a few quid was Alf Brierly. Alf was a fine lad; had been an accountant on Fraser's before the mine closed down. He boarded at Mrs. Gough's when Dinny, himself, was working on the mine and took his meals at Gough's.

Alf and he had been out on prospecting trips during the slump and got on well together: had brought in a few colours and made tucker now and then. Alf would be a good mate for the rush, Dinny decided. That was if he had any money to buy stores and pay his way.

Alf was packing his swag when Dinny found him at Gough's. He had stuffed a few stores into a gunny bag, rolled them up with his tent and blanket and was going to hoist them on his pick and shovel for the journey. He, too, was short of a fiver for Murphy: intended footslogging his way to Bayley's.

'Footsloggin's alright,' Dinny declared, gloomily, 'but it's no joke carryin' stores as well as y'r tent, blankets, and pick and shovel, over a hundred miles. Besides the mob'll beat us at the post if we've got to hump our dunnage. The ground'll be pegged for miles around'

'We're going all the same, aren't we, Dinny?' Alf asked cheerily.

'We're goin',' Dinny agreed. 'But if I could chew somebody's lug for a couple of fivers I'd feel easier in me mind.'

'Same here,' Alf admitted.

It was then Mrs. Gough came to Dinny with tears in her brown eyes.

'Oh, Mr. Quin,' she cried, 'Morris wants to go with the rush to Bayley's Find. And he isn't a prospector. Has no good mate like you to show him where to find gold. He'll be lost in the terrible desert country out there—die of thirst, or be speared by wild blacks.'

'Don't you worry, missus,' Dinny comforted her. 'He'll be alright, Mrs. Gough!'

Dinny had a great opinion of Mrs. Gough. She was a grand little woman, he said. Had worked like a navvy running a boarding house in the 'Cross when Morris lost his job on the mines.

He was the Hon. Morris Fitz-Morris Gough, it was understood, and had been appointed assistant-manager of a mine by way of inducing him to put money into its development. Knowing nothing about mining, and unwilling to exert himself to learn, he had been dumped when it was convenient. Mr. Gough was indignant at being deprived of both his money and means of earning a livelihood: threatened the company with litigation, but compromised on the promise of reinstatement as soon as the mines overcame the salt problem and increased production. They never did sufficiently to employ Mr. Gough again.

The couple were stranded and almost destitute when Mrs. Gough started cooking meals for men working on the mines. She was a good cook and her dining-room well patronized. After awhile she had two or three empty shacks moved into the yard and made them available for paying guests. The Hon. Morris was furious, ignored both her hard work and guests, although they enabled him to live fairly comfortably in the 'Cross while he was waiting to recapture his job.

'He was a lazy hound, in those days, Morrey Gough,' Dinny explained. 'I'd no time for him. He let Mrs. Gough do all the rough work of the place and keep him: never did a hand's turn to help her. But she thought the sun shone out of him.'

Mrs. Gough told Dinny why, that day she asked him to look after Morris on the rush. She was still a young woman then, it seems: in her early twenties, not very good-looking but brisk and bright as a bird, with beautiful brown eyes, dimples, and a smile which made it difficult for any man to refuse what she asked him to do. Least of all himself, Dinny confessed, because he owed her a good deal, one way and another.

'My father was a pioneer of the south-west, Mr. Quin,' Mrs. Gough said. 'So I'm an Australian born. Hardships don't matter to me, but it's different with Morris. He came to the colonies to go on the land and make a fortune. Of course, he didn't know how hard it is to work on the land, and he couldn't work like that, clearing and burning off, mustering and branding cattle. At first we had servants and stockmen, but they wouldn't stay. The cattle wandered away in the scrub and the blacks speared them. I tried to help Morris; but it was no use. The place went to rack and ruin and he hated the rough lonely life.'

9

Mrs. Gough was very upset, Dinny could see, and trying to explain why she wanted him to keep an eye on Morris.

'His father was so angry when Morris sold the station and put the money into the gold-mine, here, he cut off Morris's allowance. That meant we had to manage as best we could.'

She went on, the quirk of a smile at the corners of her mouth:

'My parents wouldn't give their consent when Morris wanted to marry me. And so we eloped. It was very romantic—but terrible, too. Papa and Mamma will never forgive me. And so there is no one to whom I can tell our troubles. Morris thinks if he goes on this rush he'll find gold like Art Bayley, and be a rich man and can go back to the old country. But he says I can't go on the rush, and I'm so afraid for him, Mr. Quin, because he has no friends, and won't know how to find his way about in the back-country.'

She had confided in him, won his sympathy, and was appealing to him for help, Dinny knew. He felt there was nothing for him to say but what he did:

'That's alright, ma'am. Mr. Gough can come along with Alf and me, if he's got a fiver to throw his swag on Pat Murphy's wagon—which is more than we've been able to raise, ourselves, yet.'

'Oh, but I can lend it to you,' Mrs. Gough cried eagerly. 'When the new manager and engineer for Fraser's came up, they stayed here, so I have a little money put by. But, please do not tell Morris. He wanted to play cards the other night, and I said I couldn't give him any money: hadn't a penny to spare.'

'You can trust me, ma'am!' Dinny assured her. 'And I'll fix it with Alf.'

Dinny needed money so badly that day he didn't care where he got it: would have robbed a blind man for his coppers, he said. Under ordinary circumstances he would have felt 'as mean as they make 'em, to be taking her hard-earned cash from Mrs. Gough. He owed her so much already. She had grub-staked him for a prospecting trip on more than one occasion, and he and Alf were indebted to her for bed and meals.

But Mrs. Gough had been very kind and good-natured; always insisted that they must eat and could settle-up with her when the strike ended, or they struck a few 'weights out prospecting. For that reason, as much as any other, Dinny could not refuse to take Mr. Gough in tow. Particularly when Sally put it more as a favour than an obligation.

'It's a loan I hope to be repaying with interest some day, Mrs. Gough, ma'am,' Dinny remarked, salving his conscience. 'And God knows a fiver's worth double the amount to me at this moment. I can never repay y'r kindness lettin' me have it. I reckon Alf feels the same way.'

'It's alright then?' Mrs. Gough queried, brightening. 'Morris can go with you: be mates with you and Mr. Brierly? Now, tell me just what you'll need. I can fix you up with food from my store cupboard and get Morris's clothes ready.'

Dinny was only too pleased to accept Mrs. Gough's offer. He explained that it would be best to pool their resources. They would be able in this way to make the most of their space on the wagon. He and Alf had the tools, tent and camp equipment, which would be almost impossible to buy that day in the 'Cross. Morris could contribute stores which were at famine prices and also almost sold out.

As soon as he told Alf the good news, Dinny went off as fast as his legs could carry him, to arrange for himself and his mates to throw their swags on Pat Murphy's wagon and swamp along with the team.

When he came back a couple of hours later, after having had several pots with Murphy, Art Bayley and a few other prospectors at the Club Hotel, Dinny was as drunk with the yarns Bayley had told him as with the beer he had consumed. But still sober enough to pack his swag. Morris took orders from him as a matter of course: was as excited and amenable as Alf, and both of them congratulating themselves on having such a good bushman and prospector to throw in their lot with.

Dinny gave them all the news of Bayley's Find that was going round the town.

'Art says,' he babbled gaily, 'the stuff he brought in weighs five hundred and fifty-eight ounces. And there's more where it came from. The whole country's lousy with gold. Tommy Talbot and his mates tried rattin' the reward claim, but Ford pulled his gun on them. He's up there now, shepherdin' the ore. It's the richest show he's ever seen, Art says, and he's seen plenty. There's goin' to be a big rush when the news reaches Melbourne and Sydney. Our luck's in to be ready to start and peg right away. Have y' got y' miner's right, Mr. Gough? Y' have. That's alright. The boys are mobbin' the Warden. He's done the hardest day's work he's done in all his born days, signin' up rights. Was scratchin' away all through his dinner and 'll be up all night the way things are goin'. I reckon we can do with one tent, and hang on to your ground sheet, Mr. Gough. I got an oil drum we can stow away for water; and if y' can spare that couple of empty kerosene tins I see on the back verandah, Mrs. Gough, they'd come in handy. We can pack stores in 'm and use 'm for cartin' water.'

Dinny checked over their equipment. He allowed Alf and Mr. Gough an extra flannel shirt, pair of pants and boots, though he had only a second shirt himself. Each man was taking his own blanket, water bag, billy, quart pot, tin plate, knife and fork. Dinny's dolly pot, pestle, and couple of panning-off dishes were carefully packed among the clothes. A hank of rope and bolt of wire went with the tools, picks, shovels, axes, flint and steel, all wrapped in the tent and tarpaulin, packed with bagging and firmly roped together. Flour, sugar, tea, a few tins of meat constituted the stores. Dinny added a bottle of pain killer. Alf's rifle and a box of cartridges were considered necessary to add to the food supplies and Morris was permitted to pack his revolver.

By midnight all the swags were neatly rolled and ready for departure of the wagon at dawn.

During the evening, Marie Robillard ran in and threw herself, weeping, into Mrs. Gough's arms.

'Oh, Sally,' she cried, 'my Jean is going on zis rush and 'e says I cannot go with 'im.'

'Morris is going too,' Mrs. Gough said hardily, 'and I've got to stay behind. We'll have to make the best of it, Marie. Mr. Quin says there's no danger, really. Other men have been out there in the wilds for months—Mr. Bayley and Mr. Ford, and Tommy Talbot and his mates. And Mr. Bayley says the blacks are quite peaceable, like they are around the 'Cross.'

'But, yes, I know,' Marie interrupted, 'Jean 'as been saying zis to me also. And maybe 'e will find much gold. But it is terrible 'e goes on a journey so far, and I must stay by myself here alone and cook at the 'otel. Always before I 'ave been together with my 'usband, and I am desolée for him to go away.'

'That's just the way I feel,' Sally's cheery common sense asserted itself. 'But we can't do anything about it, Marie. Every man in the 'Cross is crazy to go on the rush. We'll just have to wait and see how Jean and Morris get on. Perhaps they'll come back soon, or we can go to them.'

Marie was comforted by the thought. She told Sally that her Jean would be going to Bayley's Find with the yardman from the hotel who was an old prospector. Jean had been the boast of the Club Hotel, a French chef; but Jean was not a cook, Marie had explained to Sally. He had been a teacher in England, though he wanted to be a farmer, buy land and make a home for his old parents who had been driven out of France by political persecution. Marie, too, was the daughter of refugees, but her father and mother had died when she was a child.

Soon after they were married, Jean and she came to Western

12

Australia, hoping to find work and the good wages they had heard so much about. Jean had worked on a farm, hoping to save enough money to buy land and animals for himself. But the wages of a farm labourer were very small, and it seemed that he would be an old man before his dream was realized. So he had been attracted by the first gold rush to Southern Cross, and Marie had come with him on a spring cart from the Avon Valley.

Jean had tried prospecting without any luck and worked on the mines for a while. There were so few women in the 'Cross at the time that Mrs. Gough and Marie Robillard had met at the store and become acquainted. Even Morris was disposed to be friendly towards the young French couple who were so devoted to each other and a little like fish out of water in this strange country. But he treated them rather coolly after Robillard took a job as chef at the hotel. Which was one of the reasons why he resented Sally having turned her shack into a boarding house, she thought. Morris said Sally had shown an extraordinary lack of dignity and regard for his wishes, by doing such a thing.

'But we must eat, Morris,' she protested, 'and this is the only way I can think of being sure that we will, and have a roof over our heads.'

Marie Robillard and Mrs. Gough had seen a good deal of each other during those months when Morris was so moody and difficult: ignored the paying guests, refused to eat with them, or do anything to make a success of Sally's venture. Most of the day he spent lounging on the verandah with a book, or newspaper, and in the evenings played poker at the pub, making or losing a few pounds with any money he could borrow from Sally, or anybody else.

Always loyal and chirpy, Sally would not allow anybody to imagine that she and Morris were 'in quarrel' as Marie said; but Marie understood without a word being spoken when one was anxious and unhappy about one's domestic affairs. She was reserved and sensitive, herself: wore her black hair folded smoothly about the pale, rather plain oval of her face, and seemed a quiet, insignificant little woman until something roused her emotionally. Then the black silken lashes lifted from her grey-green eyes and she flashed to a vivacity which transformed her.

Morris said Marie was a woman of unusual intelligence. She discussed books and people with him as if she knew more about them than he did, which amazed Sally. But Marie had a demure way of deferring to Morris's opinion, and yet deriding it with a light witticism that delighted him. If Marie had been flirtatious, Sally thought, she might have been jealous; but Marie was not, and had declared her affection for Sally, with an impulsive foreign simplicity which somewhat embarrassed Mrs. Gough, although she appreciated this pleasant companionship she had found so unexpectedly. Many an evening Marie would come to sew and chat when she thought Sally might be feeling lonely and miserable; but after all, Sally discovered she developed as warm a regard for Mme. Robillard, during those months when Morris was so grouchy, as Marie had for her, though she could not express it as easily.

But that night before he left for the rush, Morris shook off his dour and sombre mood. He had put on flesh, while he was loafing about, looked fat and paunchy beside Dinny and Alf: rather absurd in his prospecting outfit, moleskin trousers and flannel shirt, with gold pince-nez pinched on the bridge of his aristocratic nose. But he was as excited as a schoolboy, talked and joked affably with Dinny and Alf, as if to assure them he realized a change in their relationship: was prepared to take orders and be the most agreeable of companions on the trip.

After all the packing was done, Dinny decided everything was in order, and that he and his mates were as well equipped as could be expected under the circumstances.

Alf and Morris swore they could not sleep. They wanted to sit up all night in order to get down to the wagon on time. Dinny hustled them off to bed.

'Y'll need all the shut-eye you can get in order to stand up to y'r first day on the track, me lads,' he chuckled.

Mrs. Gough was sure they would.

"I'll sit up and watch for the dawn,' she said. 'And have a good breakfast ready for you before you start.'

She did, too, Dinny remembered. And he was so grateful to her for making it possible for him to get away with the first team setting out for Coolgardie, that he forgot to curse at having the Hon. Morris tacked on to him as a mate.

CHAPTER III

AT dawn men were streaming out of the township. Men and horses surging down the broad white track to the salt lakes and disappearing into the dark scrub on the far side. Horsemen with heavily-laden packhorses. Men in buggies with a couple of brumbies playing up at starting, kicking and shying, rearing and snorting, threatening to smash the rattle-traps behind them. Men

14

in spring carts behind plodding old draughts. Young men and old, carrying their swags, pushing wheelbarrows with all their gear, picks and shovels, blankets and stores loaded on, or dragging makeshift hand-carts. Some of them had put a box or barrel on wheels, nailed a piece of wood on either side and harnessed themselves to the shafts. Such a hustling and commotion there was, with cursing and outbursts of anger, laughter and shouting, yells of: 'Good luck!' 'See yer at Bayley's!'

Swamping was a luxury that day. When Big Murphy bawled to his team, cracked his long whip and pulled out, his wagon was piled high with stores and camp equipment. The men whose swags were there walked off jauntily, thanking their stars they had only themselves to carry on the long march ahead: a hundred and twenty-eight, or a hundred and thirty miles, on rough tracks through the bush. But what did that matter? Nobody had any doubt of surviving and making a fortune on the new field, although Mrs. Gough and Mme. Robillard, who had gone down to the ford to wave good-bye to their husbands, climbed the hill again, weeping and wondering whether they would ever see them again.

Two other wagons followed Murphy's, with teams shanghaied, and swampers walking alongside. All day the exodus went on, as prospectors from outlying camps came in and stragglers hurried out after the vanguard. By nightfall there were only half a dozen able-bodied men left in Southern Cross.

The rush followed an old track blazed by Hunt, the surveyor, who had gone out in search of pastoral country, thirty years before.

Over hard shingly earth it wound, across low undulating hillsides, through forests of wodgil and morell, or salmon gum and mallee where columns of the delicately pink-stained eucalypts rose from moss-green of the wide spreading mallee bushes: through thickets of gimlet, dark-leafed, with a natural screw down their slim bronze trunks: across ironstone ridges, blue in the distance, on to the flat land where the freakish, light-limbed snap and rattle began, running into the mulga, sandalwood, thorn bush, and salt bush country. Every sixty miles or so huge isolated boulders, like sleeping mammoths, held gnamma holes. Soaks where water was to be expected lay at the foot of granite outcrops.

Heavy rains had fallen. It was a good season. There was plenty of water along the track: herbage sprouted in vivid green patches. The rush swung along under blue skies, stirring red dust. The days were hot with blazing sunshine, but the nights cold.

'There was not much time to sit yarnin' round the camp fires of an evening before we turned in,' Dinny said. 'Everybody was in too much of a hurry to get where we were goin'. And sleep? You could sleep like a log after trampin' all day. Y'd hear the chinkle of the horsebells in the bush for a while, doze off in the glow of the camp fire, and before y' knew where y' were, it'd be daybreak. Murphy 'd be rousin' hell out of Alf, or some other young chap, to help him bring in the horses. Young Paddy 'd have the billies boilin', and it was every man for himself gettin' a bite to eat, before we'd be off again.'

Alf Brierly would start singing 'John Brown's Body' as they tramped along, and everybody with breath to spare, though his voice was as hoarse as a crow's, joined in. Way down the track the men would catch on. You could hear them bawling any old song if they didn't know what Alf was singing. Every day he'd sing some love song or other for a girl he was fond of. He had come from Victoria when Southern Cross was booming, hoping to make money and get married as soon as possible.

'He was a fine chap, Alf Brierly, broad-shouldered and well set up, with an honest-as-the-day sort of face on him,' Dinny said. 'But—' and his blue eyes glinted to their quizzical smile, 'we were all fine chaps on the track. Full of vigour, and hope, and enthusiasm. There was never a finer bunch of men than went foot-slogging into Coolgardie with the first team.'

They were seven days on the track, walking all day and every day from sunrise to sun-down. Dinny hobbled along briskly, although the pain in his gammy leg was like toothache, and Mr. Gough groaned in his sleep, so sun-burned and footsore, he could scarcely move. They were up and off with Murphy's mob at dawn, just the same, plodding ahead of the team, and counting the miles till the first fifty were past. Then, elated to find the way a steady mechanical pace was eating up the distance, and each day bringing them nearer the El Dorado of their dreams, the men joked and yarned as they tramped along, or stretched for a smoke beside the camp fire after having snatched an evening meal.

'To give him his dues, he wasn't a bad mate on the track, Mr. Gough,' Dinny said. 'I've met worse. He stood up to things pretty well, and it was tough goin' for a man as soft as he was.

'Took a tumble bein' the Honourable Morris Fitz-Morris Gough wasn't goin' to be any use to him on the rush. We called him "Mister" at first, and were very polite; but let him take his turn makin' the fire and boilin' the billy. That was one for Mrs. Gough, because we'd seen her waitin' on him hand and foot, tryin' to chop the wood, and makin' a joke of it when Alf or I'd take the axe out of her hand. Mr. Gough had been off-hand with us in his own house too: almost insultin' at times—lookin' at us as if we wasn't there. But "Mister" hurt on the track when every man was Tom, Dick, or Harry to the rest.

' "Look here, you chaps," Mr. Gough says, one night, "if I don't suit as a mate, you've only got to say so; but drop the 'Mister' or I'll make other arrangements."

' "That's alright, Morrey," I says.

'Alf took the hint. "No offence meant, Morrey," he says.

' "There was offence meant," says Mr. Gough, "but I dare say I earned it!" '

They had a good laugh and got on well after that. Everybody else dropped the Mister.

'To tell you the truth,' Dinny went on, 'Morrey did his best to forget he was the son of an earl. I don't think he ever wanted to remember it again. He was a prospector like the rest of us. After a few days, looked as much of a scrubber as any man on the track: didn't shave, was dirty and footsore, but in good heart. He'd been sleek and dapper when we started out, with a bit of a pot, gold rimmed pincers on his nose, and a bald patch showin' through his fair hair. He'd walked the pot off of him, you couldn't see his bald patch for red dust, and broken his glasses, before we got to the end of our journey.

'Gambling was his weakness, though. Even on the track he couldn't resist takin' a hand with Frisco Jo and his mob, though I warned him what to expect. 'Frisco had a bad reputation in the Kimberleys, Morrey," I said. "You got to watch him."

"I'll watch him," Morrey said. They played poker beside the camp fire now and then. One evening Morrey drawled:

' "You're a poor hand at that trick, Frisco! I could do better myself."

'Frisco up and clouted him over the jaw. Morrey was about half his size, too short and flabby to stand up to Frisco, though he was game to try. Alf hopped up: "Here," he says, "if you want a scrap, Frisco, try me!" The men cleared a ring. Alf and Frisco shaped up. Frisco knew how to use his fists alright: was heavier than Alf; but, Christ, the lad was a pretty fighter. He could have laid Frisco out long before he did, got him dancing mad and blowing like a grampus before he let him have a dinnyazer that knocked him.

'Frisco never forgave Alf for that dust-up.' Dinny's fine old face, weathered and furrowed with wrinkles, lost the zest of his reminiscences. 'When he could have done Alf a good turn, he didn't. He was the only man I ever knew bore Alf Brierley a grudge—though there was nothing you could swear to. Years

17

after, Frisco laughed and joked about the scrap they'd had. Neither of them ever forgot it. There was many a time when they were well-to-do citizens, they'd have liked to take off their coats and have a go at each other, like they done that night on the track.

'He wasn't a bad sort, Frisco, one of these brummy would-be Americans, born in Ireland: liked to get round in a coloured shirt, high boots over his trousers, a big wide-awake felt hat, with a revolver in his belt. He'd got used to wearin' it on the Californian gold fields, and in Mexico, he said. But he had his good points like the rest of us. One of 'em was Paddy Cavan. He took the kid under his wing, as you might say, after Pat Murphy gave him the father of a hiding for pinchin' his tobacco and tradin' it with swampers down the track for a penknife, and odds and ends, Paddy thought might come in useful.

'He was a smart youngster, Paddy Cavan. Everybody laughed at his cheek when he joined the swampers tramping alongside of Pat Murphy's team. Paddy had no more than he stood up in, and a tucker box tied up in a bluey on his back. In a pair of men's trousers, sawn-off at the ends and tied round his middle with a piece of rope, a blue woollen jersey and a seaman's cap twisted front to back on his head, he cut an odd figure, standin'-up to Big Pat, when Pat wanted to give him a kick in the behind and send him back to the township. He wasn't havin' stowaways on his team, Pat.

' "What's y'r name?" he asked.

' "Patrick Aloysius Cavan," the kid says.

' "How old are ye?"

' "Eighteen last Christmas," the kid answers, slick as could be, though Pat Murphy had his doubts about that answer, and Paddy admitted later, he was thirteen or thereabouts, because the other age didn't tally with the rest of his story.

' "Where d' y' come from?"

'Pat Murphy roared laughing when he heard, and Paddy got a job helping him with the horses.

'Round the camp fire, one night he made Paddy tell us how he came to be at a loose end in the 'Cross when the rush started.

' "We're all mates, here, young'un," Pat said. "No one'll give you away to the police now."

'Paddy knew that all right. He was a red-headed, freckledy faced little devil, light-fingered and cunning as they make 'em; but for impudence and guts, you couldn't beat him.

' "Me, I was cabin boy on the barque *Annie Rooney* tradin' from New York," he says. "We was makin' for Bunbury to load hardwood. A day or two off the coast, every son of a gun on board was stowin' biscuits and tyin' up his things, ready to skip for the goldfields as soon as we got ashore. Everybody was tryin' to make out the lay of the land for Yilgarn."

' "The skipper knew that, and anchored a couple of miles off the jetty. He wasn't losin' his crew, Cap'n Hawkins; said he'd load up from a lighter and take in water and stores in the roads. The men was dancin' mad. But the Captain had to go ashore, see the company's agents, and somebody had to go with him in the dinghy.

' " 'Here you,' he says to me, bein' the youngest and most innercent lookin' of the lot, I suppose. 'Take hold of these.'

' "I grabbed the books and ship's papers and followed him to the side of the ship. I'd got some biscuits in me pocket and a few cents American money. The men knew they were seein' the last of me. One chap shoved a couple of biscuits into me hand. I dropped them into me trouser's pocket, got into the dinghy and we rowed off. There we was, me and Cap'n Hawkins, him all flash in white and gold braid, pullin' himself, and me sittin' in the stern, huggin' the ship's books and tryin' to keep meself from grinnin' at the men. You could almost hear them cursin' and saying good-bye as they looked over the side. I didn't know where the goldfields was, nor how I was goin' to get there. On'y that I was gettin'—

' "Cap'n Hawkins marched along the jetty up to the town, and me, I trotted along behind him. He looked like he was upholdin' the prestige of the whole American navy, with his bellhop behind, carryin' his parcels. 'Good-day!' he says to everybody we passed. 'Good-day!' affable and puffed-up as a turkey cock.

' "When we reached the company's office, the agent came out of his room, all smiles, and falling over himself to show he was pleased to see us. Cap Hawkins took the books and went into the inside room with him.

' " 'You wait here, my boy,' Cap says to me.

' " 'Aye-Aye, sir!' says me.

' "As soon as he was safely in that room with the door shut, I takes a squint at the street. A few country people about with their horses and carts, cows browsin' along the sidewalk, two or three shops, trees all round. I steps out, strolls along the street, turns a corner—and off! Hell, how I run! If you'd seen the way me legs travelled that mornin'.

' "Of course, it was no good to me wanderin' around the bush," the kid says. "I guessed Cap Hawkins would get a search party out after me, and he did right enough, but I managed to give 'em the slip. After a couple of days from a bit of a hill I see the *Annie Rooney* put out to sea. There's plenty of creeks down there, so I was alright for water. When I'd eaten me biscuits I wanted a feed: was too scared to go near the houses till it was dark. Hanging around and listening to what folks was sayin', I found out there was a lugger loading piles for the new jetty in Fremantle. I stowed away on her. A couple of nights after dropped on to the wharf at Fremantle and struck out along a big road leadin' up country.

'"Was pretty hungry, you bet. Been livin' on anything I could pick up for nearly a week. Then I see a chap camped on the road with a team of bullocks: was tryin' to make up me mind whether to tap him for a job or a feed, when he spots me and roars: 'Heigh you, where d'y think you're goin'?'

'"'Goin' to the goldfields,' says me.

'"'You are, are you?' says he. And laughs fit to kill himself.

'"'Well,' he says, 'I'd advise you to take off that cap—or you won't get far.'

'"And sure enough, there was me wearin' the ship's cap, with *Annie Rooney* starin' you in the face! Gee, how we yelled!

'"I told that chap how me and Cap Hawkins parted company, and he took me on to give a hand with the bullocks. He'd been a sea-farin' man, Barney: said he'd come ashore, himself, lookin' for the goldfields—but Yilgarn was bust. He was goin' up there: said I could go along with him and see for meself if I made meself useful on the track. That's how I come to the 'Cross. Jest arrived when Art Bayley rode in."

'He'd tramped two hundred and forty miles. It took over a month in those days for the teams to reach the 'Cross from Fremantle, and there he was takin' on another hundred odd miles, as spry as you please. Gaol and the cat for desertion was all he'd get in Fremantle, of course, so he had no intention of going back there.

'Oh, well, he's a great man, these days, Paddy Cavan. I had a suspicion he'd get where he wanted to, and not be too particular about the ways and means. But if you'd seen him trudging along the track, his shoes tied up with pieces of rag and bagging when they wouldn't hold together any longer, y'd never 've believed he'd be Sir Patrick Cavan and the power behind a score of mines on the Golden Mile, one day.'

There were fierce arguments, sometimes, as the men tramped along, about who discovered the first gold in Western Australia.

'My Dad used to say a convict first raised hopes about gold in the nor'-west.' Speck Jones had started the ball rolling. 'It was in 'sixty-four. A convict put up a tale of having picked up a handful of gold on the coast near Camden Harbour, when he was mate of a Dutch ship. She was the *Marie Augusta,* tradin' between Rotterdam and Java. Got blown out of her course by a storm: hove to in the bay for repairs. Was there for several days, and this chap swore he picked up enough gold in a couple of hours to sell to a bullion merchant in London for four hundred and eighteen pounds. He was celebratin' his luck when he got into a brawl. A man was killed and Wildman took the count with penal servitude for life.

'He offered to lead an expedition to the place where he'd picked up those nuggets, if the authorities would wipe out his sentence when the gold was discovered. His story caused a sensation in the Colony. Little or nothing was known about the nor'-west at the time, and the convict talked about the coast as if he knew it alright. So his terms were accepted.

'The government put up a subsidy of one hundred and fifty pounds. A ship was chartered—the *New Perseverance*—and she sailed, takin' a party of settlers, prospectors, natives and horses, with Police Inspector Panter in charge, to explore this gold bearin' country. The ship was nearly wrecked in a blow, but anchored in the bay, safe and sound. Wildman went dumb on the spot, though. Neither threats nor promises would induce him to show where he'd picked up his nuggets.

'After explorin' for twenty miles in every direction, the party returned to the ship, without findin' a trace of gold, satisfied the convict had been making fools of them. The *Perseverance* sailed south. Wildman tried to escape two days later in one of the ship's boats. He was recaptured and put in irons—ended his days in Fremantle gaol.

'Nobody paid much attention to yarns about convict gold, after that. The rumour about convicts who went out along this track with Hunt in 'sixty-five, havin' picked up gold, was squashed.'

Several old miners and prospectors remembered that rumour. They thought there was something in it.

'Four convicts escaped,' said Sam Mullet. 'And only three were caught again. They did have some small nuggets on them. A mate of mine knew a warder in Fremantle gaol, and this bloke told him. The convicts said they'd tell where they got the gold if they were given their freedom. The authorities wouldn't fall for that idea again. So no more was heard of it.'

Dinny said Art Bayley had told him, an old hatter up on the Murchison used to say there was gold in the country Hunt had passed through, east of the Gnarlbine Rocks. Macpherson, he called himself; but was always mysterious about how he knew. Ford reckoned he was that escaped convict, Bayley said.

Before Bayley ran into old Macpherson, all the same, Speck

argued, gold had been struck in the Darling Ranges, at North Dandalup, on the Blackwood in the south-west, at Mount Tallering out from Geraldton, at Serpentine and Roebourne. Gold, it seemed, was scattered all over the damned country, but not in payable quantities. Not until the big rush to the Kimberleys started did miners and prospectors from all over Australia flock to the west.

'My father was a miner,' Dinny said, 'one of the men who built the Eureka stockade at Ballarat in 'fifty-four, and put up a scrap for miners' rights. I came over when Hall's Creek was first heard of. Phil Saunders got gold there early in the 'eighties, but it wasn't until 'eighty-six the rush set in. God A'mighty, what a trek that was! Four hundred miles from the coast and mighty little gold when we got there. Men died like flies on the track out from Derby, what with fever, the heat, mosquitoes, flies, rotten food—and natives. Fierce as hell they were, and a man never knew when the spears 'd be whizzin' round him.

'There was two thousand men on the fields at one time, but yarns kept coming in of gold further south, on the Murchison and inland. Austin the surveyor 'd been talkin' of rich specimens at Mount Magnet and Lake Annean. My mate and I came down and did pretty well at Nannine; but the Yilgarn district was booming, so we took a boat from Roebourne to Fremantle, and made tracks for the 'Cross.'

Speck Jones had been early on the field. 'Yilgarn,' he said, 'was the native word for quartz, and there were likely outcrops all through those hills. A settler named Charley Glass was the first to see gold on the far side of the Darling Ranges. He took up land about a hundred miles beyond Toodyay: was digging a dam and came on a "floater."

'Colreavy and a partner went out prospectin' and found gold-bearing reefs at a place they called Golden Valley. Harry Anstey and another party struck good specimens at Lake Deborah. Soon after, Tom Risley discovered a rich reef thirty miles east of Golden Valley and christened the place Southern Cross. He and his mates 'ad been two days without water, and their bones would have been bleachin' in the scrub, he used to say, if Charley Crossland hadn't taken his bearings by the 'Cross, which led them back to a soak where they knew they could get water. Tom Risley picked up the first "slug" on the spot and located the reef.

'Hugh Fraser 'd been prospectin', up north, round Mount Jackson, but came in and pegged alongside Risley. The chances are Anstey or Paine, one of his mates, found the first gold in the Yilgarn district; but there's no doubt Tom Risley was the discoverer of Southern Cross—though Fraser got the reward claim, and Fraser's, Fraser's South, the Central and Central Extended started the mining industry. A year ago the Yilgarn produced more gold than any other field in the west. The mines would still be payin' dividends if the mine owners had given the miners a fair deal.'

Bill Jehosaphat liked to jeer at the 'experts' who prophesied that gold would never be found in payable quantities in Western Australia and that the back-country would be a deathtrap for prospectors.

'The fact of the matter is,' he would say, 'the government those days didn't want settlement of the country interfered with by rushes and the gold fever. The early settlers were land hungry. What they were after was land, and more land for cattle and sheep, wheat growin'. They were scared the discovery of gold would rob them of labourers: send workers scourin' the country for wealth that would make 'em their own bosses.'

'Bill wasn't far wrong either,' Dinny chuckled. 'When Hunt went out explorin' in 'sixty-four, he must've walked over the goldfields. But he wasn't lookin' for gold. He was lookin' for good pastoral country—and thought he'd found it. The government sent him out again, the following year, with a couple of blacks and a party of soldiers and convicts to make a track for the settlers. It was then the four convicts escaped and gold was found on them, though nothing was done about it.

'But after all it was the gold fields opened up the back-country, and the pastoralists had a tough time in these parts, though there's good mulga, stretches of salt bush, and after rains the whole blasted countryside 's a flowerin' wilderness.

'It was like that in 'ninety-two. Never seen the country lookin' better than it did from the Gnarlbine Rocks that year. And how we all gaped! We'd thought it was a desert we were goin' to, and there was grass and flowers everywhere: white everlastings lyin' like snow under the trees, and the mulgas yellow with blossom.'

Some of the horsemen, and men driving a pair in their four-wheeled buggies, were lost sight of after the first day, and from away down the track others caught up to and passed Murphy's team, every day. On the last stages of the journey some of the men became restive. Johnny Miecklejohn and George Ward decided to keep on walking at night. They took only a billy and water-bag, some flour for damper, a bit of sugar and tea, and went off, telling Pat Murphy they would collect their swags when he pulled in at Bayley's.

It was moonlight, and they took a risk of missing the track.

There were all sorts of will-o'-the-wisp pads made by animals in the scrub, and the stunted trees threw weird, misleading shadows. Alf was tempted to join Johnny Miecklejohn and peg a claim before the mob arrived; but Dinny knew better where to peg, he realized, and Dinny could not trust his gammy leg to carry him any faster. Morrey, too, was sure he would knock up if he tried to walk half the night as well as all day, so Alf stuck to his mates. He was one of the first with Pat Murphy's team to sight Bayley and Ford's camp and set the air ringing with his shouts and cheers.

Tommy Talbot, and miners from the 'Cross with him, halooed from their claim on the ridge to greet the rush. When the team pulled in on the flat, they were there to meet it and trade their gold for stores with Pat Murphy. Men fought for their swags, and in the wildest excitement, swarmed over the ground to measure off and peg claims on the flat, or alongside Bayley's.

Alluvial was rich on the flat, Bayley had told the Warden, fine gold in the sand as thick as specks of fly dirt on a window.

'That was why we called it Fly Flat,' Dinny said.

CHAPTER IV

COOKARDIE, the blacks called the rocky pool at the end of the long low ridge. The first prospectors didn't care what the blacks called it. Coolgardie was near enough for them. Some of them thought Coolgabbie was the native name.

Bayley and Ford were camped at the north end of the ridge. Tommy Talbot, Harry Baker and Dick Fosser, away to the south.

After the rush arrived, tents sprouted everywhere against the red earth: tents of weather-worn sail cloth, hessian, and bags sewed together, brand new tents of white canvas. Tarpaulins were slung over the branch of a tree. Scrub was cut down to build brush sheds. Smoke from scores of camp fires went up in the early morning. On the flat all day the dust of dryblowing rose in a tawny fog. From the ridge came the crash and rattle of men breaking their way through rough ground, shovelling dirt, the ring of picks on solid rock, the bark of axes clearing scrub. Shouts of 'Slug O!' and the surge from adjacent claims when a dryblower picked up a lump of gold, kept excitement at fever heat.

At sunset, finds for the day were compared, dryblowers showing off their slugs and bottles of dwts, while men on the ridge pounded ore in dolly pots, panning off before the light failed. The smell of damper and salt meat cooking over smouldering fires filled the air. Gossip and yarns were all of gold, and other rushes, when darkness closed in round the camp fires and stars were glittering in the evening sky.

Tommy Talbot, Harry Baker and Dick Fosser had a claim pegged south of Bayley's. The chief topic round the camp fires was Tommy's yarn of how Bayley and Ford had bluffed him and his mates out of the reward claim.

Dinny, and some of the miners who had been on strike at the 'Cross, knew Talbot, Baker and Fosser had gone out after Bayley and Ford, the first time they came into the 'Cross for stores. Tommy Talbot said he and his mates suspected Bayley and Ford were on something good when they went out across the salt lakes to the north-east with five pack horses and stores for a couple of months. Tommy and his mates bought four brumbies, pack saddles and bags, saddle and bridle, loaded up with rations and went out after Bayley. They had only one riding horse, so took turns to ride him, following Hunt's Track to the Gnarlbine Rocks.

Tommy Talbot is an old man now, grey and prosperous, but he still tells the tale of how he found the reef gold at Coolgardie, much as he did sitting beside his fire on the old camp.

At the Gnarlbine Rocks, Tommy said, he and his mates met Jack Reidy and three other men. Reidy said they were going back to the 'Cross: had got a bit of gold, but nothing worth making a fuss about. He told Tommy where Bayley and his mate were camped: put them on the track north-east from Hunt's.

A couple of days later, Talbot and his party struck a gnamma hole. There were fresh horse tracks round it, so Tom reckoned Bayley was not far away.

'Next morning, after going half a mile along the ridge,' Tommy used to say, 'I near jumped out of me skin, when somebody alongside of me said: "Good morning," and there was Art Bayley. I told him we were prospectin' and he said: "That flat's worth a trial." We were standing on the ridge a few hundred yards from here—'

Tommy Talbot and his mates camped near the gnamma hole and put in some time prospecting over the flat. They got a small nugget and over an ounce of gold the first afternoon.

'There was a big white quartz blow, near Ford and Bayley's camp,' Tommy said. 'Ford was working a small leader there, but it was about played out. He stayed in the camp and worked the leader while Bayley went out prospectin'. He prospected twenty miles out, as far as Red Hill and specked alluvial. We fossicked along the ridge, gettin' a bit of gold, here and there: then one morning, I picked up a rich specimen, followed traces up the hillside, and before we got to the top, there was the gold shinin' in the rock all round us.

'For a few minutes we went mad with excitement. The cap of the reef was all quartz and gold. We started breaking it off: pulled off our coats, tied up the sleeves and carried away as much stuff as we could: but we couldn't carry all of it. Dug a hole and stowed away about a sugar bag full of specimens. It was a bit after midday when we left. Somehow we got bushed on the way back to camp, the scrub bein' thick and us too excited to look where we was goin'—

'It got dark and we were knocked up, carryin' the gold and wanderin' round; but about midnight heard the tinkle of a horse bell, and made for it. Found our horses standing round the gnamma hole waiting for a drink. Watered them and turned in.

'Next morning we started out for the reef again. We'd slept like a log bein' knocked out when we got in, and were late gettin' a move on. Why didn't we peg when we found the gold? Gord knows. Went mad at the sight of it, I reckon.

'But when we got there, Bayley and Ford was peggin' our find. They said we was three young fools and all was fair when you were on gold. There was a bit of an argument and Ford took out his revolver; threatened to shoot if we didn't get off the ground. Bayley said: "Put away that gun. There's to be no shooting."

'Bayley would've let us stand in with him but Ford wouldn't agree. Bayley said: "There's going to be a boom here soon. If you fellows peg on to our pegs, south of our lease, you ought to make five or six thousand out of it. We've only pegged a short distance south of the rich shoot." So that's what we did. But Bayley and Ford kept the specimens we'd buried. Dollied some of 'em and took the rest into the 'Cross.'

Tommy Talbot was twenty-one at the time, a Devonshire man, a bit undersized, black haired and bright-eyed as a rat. Why had he been such a mug as not to peg his ground as soon as he sighted the gold? That was what old prospectors could not understand. But Talbot and his mates were miners on strike, new to prospecting. Ford and Bayley, old hands at the game, and to give them their dues, they had done all the pioneer prospecting of the field.

Most of the men stood to Bayley and Ford: agreed they were within their rights. Some of them maintained Talbot and his party didn't peg because they didn't know how to: hadn't even provided themselves with a miner's right.

Art Bayley was a likeable chap, genial and easy-going, a good bushman and prospector. One of the first things he did in the 'Cross, after the reward claim had been granted, everybody knew, was to send word to mates on the Murchison to come overland to Coolgardie and bring Macpherson along: but old Mac had disappeared. Nobody ever heard of him again.

Bayley's story about the reef gold at Coolgardie was different from Tommy Talbot's, and Ford's from Bayley's.

Bayley said: 'Talbot and his mates raided our claim, one night, picked off surface gold, and buried a lot of rich stone. I had my suspicions and went to see if things were alright next morning: found a hole had been sunk and a lot of gold taken. I went over to Talbot's camp and found one of his mates there. He said the others were out prospecting. "If they prospect again where they were last night, I'll put a piece of lead through them," I told him.

'I wanted to get away into the 'Cross to report the find. Agreed not to take action against Talbot and his mates, if they kept off our ground and left Ford alone. I showed them a place where they could 've done well. We got fifty ounces there in three days; but that didn't suit 'em. We went over the ground and showed them the pegs twenty times; but Ford had to order them off, over and over again. While I was away he helped 'em to peg four men's ground next us. That's how it was, boys, and that's all I've got to say.'

Ford was a regular hatter, it seems, surly and uncommunicative. He didn't like men poking about his ground, or showing them the gold he and Art were bagging to take down to the 'Cross. There was plenty of it: rich stuff. Dinny swore he had never seen so much gold lying about a camp. But Ford's account of the finding of reef gold and the pegging of Bayley's reward didn't tally with Bayley's.

Ford said he was taking horses to water at the gnamma hole when he picked up the first piece of gold on Fly Flat. That day, he and Art Bayley specked eighty ounces on the flat, a five-ounce nugget among them. When they had about three hundred ounces, they decided to make back to the 'Cross. The miners were on strike and things at a very low ebb there, lots of men hanging about and ready to rush any promising prospect.

Bayley and Ford did not declare the alluvial they had found on the flat that first trip; but made back with stores, saying they were going out to find what Jack Reidy and his mates were up to.

Reidy and his mates were camped near the gnamma hole. Bayley and Ford went down to have a yarn with them, told them they'd got colours, and asked Reidy to stop and prospect round a bit, then they could all make tracks together. It was a trick to put Jack Reidy off the scent, of course: but their stores were low, and Jack and his mates wanted to make back to the 'Cross.

'We threw up our hats when we saw the last of them,' Ford liked to say, with a grin on his sulky mug. 'It wasn't until we got back to Fly Flat, Bayley found a rich leader in decayed quartz, on the ridge. I prospected the big blow and got gold at both the north and the south ends. Struck more gold than we could handle. I started making bags to pack the stuff. Bayley went out to hunt up our horses. There was very little water and he had a job catching the horses.

'Three young men came along and camped down by the rock hole. They were always poking about our claim. One morning they asked me to show them the pegs. I pointed them out. We walked past where the gold was lying in the reef. It hadn't been touched. I came back to the tent and went on packing the gold we'd got.

'It was nearly sunset when Bayley got back. He asked if I'd been at the reef. I told him I was only down to show those chaps the pegs.

' "They've been at the reef and taken a lot of stuff," he said.

'Bayley went over to Talbot's camp next morning and they gave him some of the gold—but not all they took.'

Arguments raged round the camp fires. There were men who reckoned Tommy Talbot and his mates had got a rotten deal: were entitled to the reward claim. Others who held Bayley and Ford were within their rights, even if they had moved their pegs to include the rich shoot, because Talbot and his mates, on their own admission, had not pegged.

Dinny, Alf Brierly and Morrey Gough pegged a three men's claim on Fly Flat. They set to work shovelling dirt. Alf went mad with excitement when he specked a two-ounce nugget the first day. Morrey picked up three ounces the next. Every dish Dinny panned off showed a fat tail of fine gold.

Almost every man on the first workings was seeing gold, but water was getting scarce. The number of men and horses on the field grew every day. Prospectors, dryblowing to save water, poured the rubble and sand from one tin dish to another so that the wind blew off the dust and left the heavy specks of gold in the dish. The trick had to be practised with a steady hand. Alf learnt it quickly; Morrey, slower in the uptake but more careful, proved a better dryblower in the long run.

There was a sensation the day some men poking about on Bayley's lease struck a rich patch. Bayley and Ford had pegged a mining lease, and old prospectors contended that alluvial miners were within their rights fossicking below the reef. At any rate, a mob rushed the patch and a rough and tumble for the gold followed. Men rooted in the earth with their hands, fought and tumbled over each other in a frenzy to grab one of those nuggets of dusty red gold.

Bayley went for the Warden who had come up from the 'Cross with him. When Warden Finnerty arrived, the men put their case and obtained a decision as to the rights of alluvial diggers on a mining lease. Warden Finnerty ruled that the mining regulations in force at the time gave the leaseholders exclusive rights to any gold within twenty feet of the reef, but that alluvial claims could be pegged beyond the twenty feet surrounding the reef. As soon as he saw which way the Warden's verdict was going, Dinny slid out of the crowd, and stepped-off a claim just below the rich patch. He pegged and started work on the claim right away: had twenty ounces to show his mates, that evening.

'A lot of good gold was found in that ground,' Dinny said, 'and on the flat below it, called the Spud Paddock because several slugs picked up there were as big as potatoes, weighing four and five, even seven pounds.'

Every day brought more men, on horseback, in buggies and footslogging into the camp. Teams pulled in laden with stores and prospectors. Parties set out to scour the scrub in all directions. Dinny became restless. Alluvial had not much attraction for him. He was after bigger stuff: wanted to get out prospecting: locate a reef and take up a mining lease with some prospect of making big money. Alf and Morrey agreed to work their claim on Bayley's lease while Dinny went off into the bush.

Soon a coach was running from the 'Cross to Coolgardie. Camel teams arrived. The great unwieldy beasts with their Afghan drivers, lurching across the flat and standing out against the clear blue sky, gave the place a queer foreign aspect. Every nationality under the sun was represented among the miners, and prospectors, investors, company promoters, 'shanty' keepers, speculators in meats and groceries, who flocked to the rush.

The sale of alcohol had been declared illegal; but 'bum boats,' carrying supplies, contrived to elude the police. At first Constable McCarthy, who arrived with the Warden, kept a sharp look out for sly grog. He poured a consignment of rum into the sand; arrested a bottle as evidence, when a vendor was caught red-handed. The case was heard in Southern Cross and Constable McCarthy produced his bottle to prove that old so-and-so had been selling spirituous liquor to men on the rush. The bottle was opened. It contained water and the case collapsed.

'Somebody had done the constable for his rum,' Dinny chuckled.

By October there were four hundred men encamped on the flat, along the ridge and over rising ground to the east where the town began to arise on either side of a broad dusty track. The cost of living mounted. Water was several shillings a gallon and not much available: flour and sugar one and sevenpence a pound, tinned meat three shillings, butter six shillings a tin.

It was rumoured Bayley and Ford had sold out to Sylvester Brown for fourteen thousand pounds. Reports of new finds kept coming in, and of good gold on the Lady Forrest lease and at Mount Burgess.

As the mild spring weather passed into the blazing heat of summer, with bare blue skies clamped down over the dead dry earth, dust storms and the scarcity of water drove disgruntled diggers back to the 'Cross. Mining regulations as to the manning of leases were relaxed so that holders could leave their claims until the rainy season began. Men on gold, as a rule, remained, although the Warden advised retreat. Notices were posted, asking men leaving the camp to go in detachments so that water along the track would not be exhausted. Teamsters were required to obtain licences. News that the teams carting water from the Gnarlbine Rocks had to wait two days to refill and that the water was very low, caused a panic.

Typhoid broke out. Raeside, of the Water Supply Department, complained bitterly of the way Afghans and their camels were polluting the water by camping near the soaks and wells.

'Around some of the wells,' he said, 'the ground is like a manure heap, reeking with filth. The Afghans wash their dirty linen on the edge of the well and dirty suds fall into the water. Most of the camels are bad with mange and should not be allowed near any of the drinking places.'

The government placed a caretaker on every tank, soak and rock-hole, between the 'Cross and Coolgardie, to safeguard the water, dispense it only to men in need, and licensed teamsters who had to pay for what their horses or camels consumed.

Dust storms swept the camp, shrouding it with hot red sand: sand that hung in the air when the whirling wind passed, seeping into everything, leaving everything covered by a layer of grime. Thunder rumbled and died away with a few flashes of sheet lightning.

Miners and prospectors would turn out and yell to a dull, dirty sky clouded with red dust:

'Send her down! Send her down, Hughie!'

Often the storm passed with no more than a few spattering

drops to lay the dust. Men pulled in their belts, cursed, joked, and ate sparingly of their rations. They shouldered picks and shovels at dawn and went to work on their claims, tossed mullock and blasted their way through quartz and ironstone, toiling in desultory fashion until the fierce light waned. Then they flocked to the shypoo shops and shanties to slake their thirst with the beer that cost no more than water: or, after lighting a fire and boiling water to make the black tea which parched throats and empty bellies craved, lay off in the tattered shade of spindling trees beside their tents.

The earth glowed in garish light at sunset. Shadows sprawled indigo and purple on the ironstone pebbles. The sun disappeared in a disc of molten crimson. Crimson and gold flamed across the sky above the sombre wave of the surrounding scrub.

Before it was dark, crowds were swarming round the two-up rings on the dusty track: poker schools collected. The racket of gaffing over the spinning pennies, the cards slapped down with gay bravado, broke the hot stillness. Fierce and reckless was the gambling that whiled away the sultry nights when not a breath of wind stirred the air, and stars were dim in a sky like a sheath of dull metal.

Sometimes a cool breeze sprang up an hour or so before dawn, and the sigh of the camp greeted it, as men turned in their sleep and stretched to gulp at the freshness. But at sun-up the breeze would sidle away and the dry stagnant heat of another day begin, registering a hundred degrees before work was started, and soaring to one hundred and eight or one hundred and twelve by midday and until late afternoon.

A crew of scarecrows, withered and gaunt, grimy and ragged, men who weathered that first summer on Coolgardie never forgot it. Not all of them filled the nights with beer and poker, or the delirium of the two-up rings when a man might win a hundred pounds on the toss of a penny. Many stretched on the hard hot ground beside their tents, staring up at the stars and gasping for any breath of cooler air the darkness brought, or sat round, gossiping and yarning about teams on the road, the future of the field, whether that outcrop of gold-bearing quartz on Bayley's reward was an orphan, or whether there were other deposits, as rich, in the vast unexplored country, stretching for hundreds of miles on every side.

The yarns were all of gold: the fickle ways of the yellow siren they all followed: yarns of old rushes in the Kimberleys, on the Murchison, at Nannine and Cue. With the rowdy exuberance of men shouting and brawling round the gambling rings and shypoo shops came gusts of hoarse laughter and singing. From the camps, too, laughter streeled, as men swopped lies and jokes through the brief dark hours, often to the accompaniment of the blacks' wailing near their old gnamma hole, which some fool in his search for gold had destroyed with a charge of dynamite.

CHAPTER V

ARRIVAL of the mail coach, or the teams which brought stores, was the great event of those days. Every man on the rush would turn out to meet a teamster, hear news of the rest of the world, and try to buy a few stores.

Cracker Jack, an old mate of Dinny's, was one of the most popular men on the road. A big handsome chap, with a great laugh, and keen on his job, there was nothing Cracker would not do to get water for his horses if he was 'unlucky,' as he said, about obtaining a licence to travel. Many a time, he stared death in the face to make the trip from the 'Cross to Coolgardie that summer.

'Was travellin' on an old permit this trip, boys,' he explained once. 'Me horses was so tucked-up when I came to the Thirty-Four Mile, they had to have water. But the old bloke on the tank wouldn't be bluffed into givin' me more than a drink for meself. The water was reserved for the mailman and coach horses, he said. He'd got strict orders.

'I reckoned there was enough for me and my horses too. The argument was going, hot and strong, when he fell down in a fit. I was wonderin' what the hell to do with him, when all of a sudden I realize it was an act of God, him passin' out like that. I yanks the tank key off his belt, and yells to my boy. We fills our water bags at the tank and waters the horses. Then I goes back to see how the tank-keeper's doin'. He was comin' round nicely. So we lit out—to avoid explanations.'

The men were always ready to chuckle and applaud Cracker's yarns about how he used his wits to get water on the track.

Another time, he was going up from the 'Cross with a load of stores. His horses had been two days without water when he reached the government tank; but Cracker had no permit. The tank-keeper refused to let him have water for his horses although he had a good supply. Cracker was smuggling a consignment of grog with those stores, and decided to crack a bottle for the tank-keeper's benefit. But Cock-eyed Charley, as he was called, had a score to work off against Cracker, and even the sight of Cracker's rum wasn't so sweet as his revenge.

'Y're not gettin' round me, that way, Cracker,' he said. 'And y're gettin' no water for horses here, without a permit.'

Cracker went off to camp nearby, for the night, determined to water his horses; but not so sure Cock-eyed Charley would fall into the little trap he had laid. The native boy with him had made a fire, Cracker doled out the evening rations, and was settling down to his own meal, when a teamster, named Jim Ryan, pulled in from Coolgardie, his horses just about mad for water.

'Got a permit?' Cracker asked.

Jim, too, had been unable to provide himself with a licence to obtain water on the track.

'Well, Cock-eye says we're gettin' no water for the horses here without a permit,' Cracker explained.

'The lousy old bastard,' Jim yelled. 'I'll show him whether he can hang on to water when horses are perishin'.'

'Wait a bit,' Cracker said, not wanting murder on his soul. 'He wouldn't drink with a bloody water-thief, meanin' me, Cock-eye reckoned when I tried him with a bottle of rum, jest now. "Right," I ses! "I'll drink your share and me own." Swigs at the bottle, and goes on yarnin' and swiggin' for awhile. Got him worked up— and fair bustin' for a drink. Cock-eye reckons I'm shickered when I staggers out—forgettin' me bottle.'

Jim enjoyed the joke and sat down to have a bit of tucker with Cracker. They waited until it was dark. Then seeing no light in Cock-eye's hut went over to the tank. No use fossicking round for the key, Cracker decided. He tapped the tank to find the level of the water, and Jim shot a hole where it would pour out gently while Cracker held a bucket to catch the flow. They filled their buckets, watered their horses and moved off in opposite directions. Cracker's rum had done the trick with the tank-keeper: laid him out, while the teamsters helped themselves.

But Cracker's most famous exploit was when he was going down from Coolgardie to the 'Cross, and had to run the gauntlet of all the tank-keepers he had bluffed on the trip up. He was racking his brains, as to how he was going to water his horses at the first government tank, when he came on an English Johnny who had been prospecting, and was making his way back to the 'Cross, just about all in. Cracker gave him a lift.

The Johnny was wearing a pith helmet, 'one of these 'ere Stanley-in-darkest-Africa hats,' as Cracker said. And Cracker had a summons for travelling without a licence on the track to Coolgardie in his pocket. It was an official looking document with a large seal attached. The seal and that hat gave him an idea.

Cracker explained the position to his passenger.

'I've got to get water for me horses at the next tank, or we're euchred,' he said. 'And I won't get it unless we can work this scheme. We're a Water Supply Department outfit, see, prospectin' for water, and you're the officer in charge. I'll keep out of sight when we come up to the tank-keeper's hut. The nigger can look after the horses. Nobody 'll recognize him. All you got to do is, barge up to the hut and start rousing like a big bug, flash this seal at the old man—not lettin' him read the document by any chance. Get him all worked up, pronto, then push off.'

The Englishman agreed to play his part: did it so successfully that there wasn't a hitch in the scheme. It worked all along the track.

All through the long summer, Cracker kept his team on the road, and by hook or by crook, brought news and stores to the men marooned in that drought-stricken wilderness. Nearly always he brought a letter and box of food for Morris from Mrs. Gough: letters and parcels for Jean Robillard, too, from his wife.

Cheery and dauntless, prospectors derided the hardships they suffered. To groan and growl was held to be evidence of a poor spirit. Pessimists and cautious souls had left the field. The men who stayed prided themselves on their capacity for endurance. A reckless spirit of defiance kept them fighting for the fortune they believed lay waiting for them to pick up, somewhere, out in that grey limitless scrub, under the red sunblasted earth.

Good humour, and an indomitable will to survive and defy the sun, bound all sorts and conditions of men together through 'the drooth,' as Dinny called it. Now and then a prospector came in from the bush, a skeleton with wild eyes and ragged beard, almost insane for lack of food and water. There were tales of men having been forced to drink their own urine in order to survive: of a man who had killed his horse and drunk its blood to keep himself alive.

It was recognized that if he was starving, any man could take a feed from another man's camp. Tools lying on a claim indicated that the owner was sick, and woe betide any scavenger trying to jump that claim.

There was almost a riot when the water shortage was at its worst. A string of camels came in with two hundred gallons of water for Bill Faahan who had built an hotel, and contracted with an Afghan to bring the water in from a soak fifty miles away. Men fought like lunatics to fill their water bags, until Bill bargained with them to let him keep fifty gallons, and started to dispense the rest. An old man, in a frenzy to get a drink, leaned over the tank, overbalanced, fell in, and had to be fished out! He got more than his fair share of water that day, the boys swore; and Bill cursed at having his water flavoured with stinking old prospector. But curses and laughter were the order of the day. Nobody minded what happened, so long as food and water held out—till the rains came.

'When it rains—'

'When the rain comes—'

That's what everybody was saying. Gold for the time being was not so important as water.

The blacks had steered clear of the white man's camp while the season was good, hunting kangaroos, bungarras and emus on the plains and in the far-away hills. They came into the Gnarlbine Rock and their well at Coolgardie when the dry season began, to find them commandeered by the white men, almost empty with the drain of so many men and beasts. There were still soaks and rock holes they knew of in the outlying country; but the secret of these places was well guarded.

When the kangaroos and even crows were lying dead round the rock holes, and the natives learned that the white men had food, they congregated round the camp like flies, living on any garbage the storekeepers threw out: butcher's offal and the dregs in tins and bottles. Wine and tobacco! You could buy a native for either after a while. They would come from the bush, thin and hungry, with no more than a hair string belt round their middles, and the women, quite comely when they were young, stark naked. In no time, the same crowd would be skulking about in odds and ends of cast-off clothing, begging food and tobacco, bartering their women, though out in the bush, under the starry skies, you would hear them making corroborees for rain and wailing about the desolation that had come on them.

The natives soon learnt a few words of the white men's language and the white men a few words of theirs. A lingo sprang up which both blacks and whites understood. A wheelbarrow was a familiar object on the rush, so the blacks called the coach 'big fella wheelbarrow,' a horse and cart 'pony wheelbarrow.' They exclaimed at the first camel they say: 'Big fella emu!'

Among the white men the blacks maintained a sombre reserve: but among themselves, they laughed and made songs about the strange ways of the white men: their madness for the stuff called gold which no-one could eat or drink, and the way the white men burrowed in the earth like boudie rats, searching for it.

Many prospectors who were experienced bushmen cultivated friendly relations with the aborigines whose services they needed as guides when they went out prospecting. Others, to whom they were merely niggers, treated them like dogs, abused their confidence, stole their women, rough-handling and knocking them about on the slightest provocation.

'I never had any trouble with the natives,' Dinny said. 'Always treated them kindly and left their women alone. Any man who did was fairly safe. Though the blacks' idea of vengeance is different from ours. If one man of a tribe has killed a man of another tribe, it's any man of the guilty tribe vengeance must be taken on, according to tribal law. That's why, later, prospectors out east and to the north, were speared: had their camps raided. They were payin' the penalty for the rapes and shootings other white men had committed, though the blacks in the Laverton Ranges were always a wild, fierce lot. Between the 'Cross and Coolgardie they were peaceful and friendly—as harmless as babies.'

Dinny was for hanging-on at Coolgardie while there was any water to be got. A thunderstorm might blow up any day, he argued, when the water shortage was at its worst. He had come on likely country about twenty-five miles north-east of the camp and intended to make a beeline for it as soon as the rains came.

Alf and Morrey were satisfied to abide by his decision. They might be losing the chance of their lives by deserting Dinny, they agreed, and had very little to gain by returning to the 'Cross. Without money or work, what was life worth? They were prepared to risk their lives in this bid for a fortune: took turns, every night, to tramp thirty miles to the Gnarlbine Rocks and wait with other men for water to be doled out at dawn.

The remarkable thing about those natural rock holes was that though they might be empty during the day, at sundown they began to make water. All night the water seeped into them, and by morning there was a clear fresh pool to be drawn on.

'You don't worry about the heat and tucker while y're working,' Dinny said. 'It's better to keep goin' than hang round Tom the Rock's shanty, or lie about sweatin' your guts out.'

He worked and kept Alf and Morrey working all through the withering, pitiless heat of those long days. They had pegged a block south of Bayley's, when their claim on Fly Flat petered out, put in their time slinging the pick, shovelling dirt, and dollying a bit of stone in the late afternoon, to keep up their spirits.

For all the work they put into the ground, digging costeens and sinking a shaft, they had little to show for their pains. The gold was there, but nothing to get excited about. It enabled them to pay their way, that was all. While there were more promising shows, nobody was buying low-grade ore, and there was not much buying at all while the water shortage lasted. Dinny reckoned on a revival of the rush and the chance of selling to some new-chum investor when the rains came. The block was near enough to Bayley's to justify expectation of picking-up the lode at greater depth.

Alf slung his pick doggedly, became lean and hard on meagre rations. He burned the colour of leather, grew a beard. His eyes held fear and desperation, though he laughed and cracked jokes with Dinny and Morrey: went about singing his love songs and 'John Brown's Body' as he had done on the track.

The men teased him about the love songs, and the letters he wrote to his sweetheart, sprawled on the ground every evening at sunset. They knew her name was Laura, and that her father, a wealthy old politician in Victoria, would not allow his daughter to marry Alf Brierly until Alf had found some way of earning his living.

Alf's father had been well-to-do and lost everything in the land boom, it seemed. Alf came west to find a job, took his chance with the Fraser's Gold Mining Company and had been dumped when the mines closed down. Alf was stacking on striking it rich and going back to marry his girl, everybody knew. It was for that he slogged away through the heat: about that he dreamed as he lay on his back, gazing up at the stars, or watching the moonlight drip in liquid silver from the black pointed leaves of the scrawny trees, when men came round Dinny's camp to yarn in the evening.

Most of Dinny's pals, miners from the 'Cross, liked Alf well enough. A good-natured young chap, straight and sterling, they reckoned he was, though a bit of a wowser: kept Dinny off the booze too much. But Alf was a good mate, and that was all one man asked of another those days.

To give Morrey his due, he did pretty well also. Having got over his first bout of sunburn, bleeding feet and blistered hands, he stopped moaning and settled down to make the best of a bad bargain. Life on the rush had been hard on him. Soft, fleshy and short-sighted, as he was, he had more backaches and belly-aches—aches and pains of every description—than any man he ever knew, Dinny said. But Morrey got over talking about them after a while and set out to prove his mettle. He did that, though his blood boiled in the heat, and his smooth fat face turned the colour of raw ham under a crop of coarse bristles.

Morris had never gone unwashed and unshaven before. He loathed smelling like a filthy animal; but water was too precious to spare for a bath, or shower, or clean clothes. A dry blow, or lick-and-promise swipe of face and hands with a wet rag, was

all any man could allow himself. Morrey got used to dirt, and
the flies that swarmed in the shaft even, blowing his sweaty
flannel shirt with crawling maggots. They were nothing to the
torture he endured when barcoo rot attacked him. The great
sores festered on his back, hands and legs: his lips split and
were raw and bleeding.

Dinny and Alf made him lay off work for a while. They
bandaged his hands, dosed him with salts and lime-juice when
they could get any. Morrey groused more at having nothing
to do, once he had got used to working underground, than he had
done shifting mullock and dryblowing in the blazing sunshine.

It was as if he were afraid his mates might put something
over him: strike a rich pocket and keep it to themselves. Dinny
jeered at his fear of losing sight of a 'weight, although he didn't
believe Morrey imagined them capable of such treachery.

Men on the rush dealt drastically with any violation of the
unwritten law of loyalty between mates. The camp code was
scrupulously observed: the most serious crime on the prospector's
calendar to hide or steal gold from a mate: betray the mutual
interest of the diggers.

Now and then, there was a roll-up, a muster of all the miners
and prospectors on the field, to settle some dispute about a claim
or row between mates. The banging of a panning-off dish
summoned all and sundry. Whenever that sound was heard, a
digger was expected to leave whatever he was doing and attend
the roll-up.

Usually when the men assembled, the aggrieved person gave
his reasons for calling a roll-up. The men elected a judge and
the prospectors in a body acted as jury. The accuser stated his
case and brought evidence to support it. The accused was asked
whether he pleaded guilty or not guilty: could produce any
evidence in his defence. The judge then summed up, very ably
and impartially as a rule, and the verdict was left to the men.
A show of hands decided whether they considered the accused
guilty or not guilty, and whether the known penalty for infringe-
ment of the camp code should be carried out. This required
that the offender should be banished from the camp, with food
and water for twenty-four hours. The man became a pariah
wherever he went.

Dinny would talk for hours about the roll-ups. He said the
roll-up enforced the only law and order that had reality in a
community held together by a sense of justice common to the
men of all races on the field. It was a spontaneous organization
of working men which had to be respected; and acquired for

38

Coolgardie, in the early days, the reputation of being the only goldfield in the world where crimes of violence did not occur.

In the old camp there were Frenchmen and Germans who had fought in the Franco-Prussian war, Swedes, Danes, Poles, Russian political exiles, Englishmen and Irish rebels, Cockneys and Scots, men from the goldfields of California and Mexico, Jews and Afghans, although the greater number of prospectors were Australian born, bushmen and station-hands, farmers, stockmen, miners, shearers, clerks, tradesmen and shopkeepers.

Differences of nationality dwindled in the welter of races and creeds. A man was often better known by his nickname than any other. Everybody knew Cracker Jack, for example, but most men would have shaken their heads if you had asked for Mr. Johan Krakauer: said they didn't know him. French Fred, German-George-the-Swede, Camel Thompson, Larrikin Green, Pigweed Harry, Far-down Mick, Dynamite Dow, Speck Jones, Yank Boteral, Bill Jehosaphat, and Blunt Pick, Sam Mullet's mate, were well known identities, but few men could have sworn to their christian and surnames.

The search for gold and the necessity for preserving their existence in that out-of-the-way place, surrounded by hundreds of miles of dry, almost waterless wilderness, reduced all men to the fundamental necessity of human society, combination to safeguard mutual interests. The roll-up served that purpose.

A warden had been appointed to see that the mining regulations were complied with. If the world had been ransacked, a better man for the post than Warden Finnerty could not have been found, Dinny contended. Finnerty was in tune with the spirit of the place. He carried out his duties with a firm hand, but identified himself with the men and their code. Many a yarn Dinny told about Warden Finnerty.

Authority of the roll-up was not disputed. It was not invoked without ample justification. Decisions invariably vindicated principles of common honesty and fair play.

Mounted police were early on the scene, but they too adapted themselves to the unwritten law of the fields. There was a lot of talk about disorders and the wild life of Coolgardie, but Dinny declared the police had little to do in the early days. Might occasionally chain a fighting drunk to a tree for the night, and bring him before the Warden's court, held in a bag shanty, in the morning; or go out in search of missing prospectors, but for nearly three years no serious crime occurred.

Thousands of pounds' worth of gold was stored in canvas and hessian tents, and transported in an open buggy for seven days through the bush without an escort. But there were no hold-ups, no attacks on lucky prospectors going back to the 'Cross with a fortune in their saddle bags.

Not until the mines were sold and big companies demanded protection, did mounted troopers armed with carbines and revolvers provide an escort for the gold coach.

CHAPTER VI

FRISCO JO MURPHY added to his reputation over the roll-up that gave Pug Charley his walking ticket.

Frisco had struck a good patch soon after he arrived on Fly Flat, sold his claim and bought a couple of camels. He joined forces with an old prospector who had a pair of brumbies and they went off prospecting towards the south-east, with a black and his gin, and stores for two or three months.

When the dry weather started, Frisco came in with a tale of woe and only a few ounces of gold. The blacks had cleared out, and the bull camel had savaged his arm. When the wound was giving him hell, Frisco took the other camel and started for the old camp. George was following with the horses, he said.

It was two or three weeks before George appeared. Frisco was talking of getting up a search party to go out and look for him when George crawled into the camp, minus his trousers, and raving about a dirty trick Frisco had played him: left him without water and taken all the gold they had won on the trip. His horses had got away, and he had been bushed making his way in.

Frisco swore German-George-the-Swede, as he was called, was off his head. He had left George as much water as he had taken, and the condenser. Warned him to make tracks because water in the hole they had dug on the edge of a dry salt lake was low. He was prepared to lead any man to the spot where he and German-George had specked a few bits of alluvial. He had brought the gold along, as they agreed, and told half a dozen men he was holding George's quota for him.

No one could fault Frisco's statement. But George would have no more to do with Frisco. He was never the same man, a bit crazy and liable to run amok when he saw Frisco: start muttering about the gold Frisco had stolen from him out there by the salt lake.

It made no difference to Frisco. He was extraordinarily popular: carried on through the drought gaily, recklessly. A striking figure in his sombrero, coloured shirt, worn moleskins, with a revolver stuck through his belt. If anybody chaffed him about his gun, Frisco would laugh as if he saw the joke. 'She's my mascot, Maria,' he'd say. 'Never have any luck without her.' And show off some of his tricks, shooting pennies in the air, or spin lurid yarns of amorous adventures in Mexico and along the South American coast, where 'Maria' had extricated him from many a tight corner.

Open-handed and on easy terms with everybody, Frisco was reckoned a good sort, despite his brag and bluster. If he wanted to be thought cock of the walk and do the honours of the field, when any distinguished stranger, or wealthy investor arrived, nobody minded. Frisco would see to it that the new chum did his duty shouting drinks, and if he himself made a bit of commission on any deals he brought off, advising men to stick out for a higher figure than was offered, or urging them to accept less, when business could not be done any other way, no objections were raised. Frisco's gusto and vitality were a boon during the doldrums before the rain came: kept up the spirits of the camp. Through glaring days and sweltering nights, he could be heard, twanging his steel guitar and bawling lustily:

> 'She was a good girl, a decent girl,
> And her hair hung down in ringlets—'

Frisco took things easily during the dry spell, gambling at night, and lounging round his camp most of the day; but nothing of importance happened that he did not have a hand in. He hustled up a hospital committee to get a couple of hessian shacks erected for men who went down with dysentery and typhoid: took a turn with the volunteers who looked after the sick men, though the scarcity of water, the flies and dust sweeping through frail walls of the huts, gave the patients small chance of recovery. They lay on stretchers made of bagging and bush timber in their working clothes, often with their boots on, unwashed and delirious for days. The old man put in charge left the kerosene tins used by patients suffering from dysentery standing about, uncovered, and fed his patients with condensed milk. Most of them died.

Jean Robillard had a close call, that summer. He never would have survived but for the way his mate nursed him. Old Cow's Belly was a queer stick, Dinny said. A broken-down Englishman whose name was Cowes Bell, he had been prospecting round the 'Cross for a year or so before he got a job as yardman at the pub when Robbie was chef there. They stuck together on the fields, although Cow's Belly was a lazy, drunken old blackguard

41

who let the young Frenchman do most of the hard work on their claim. Yet Robbie owed his life to the way Cow's Belly had looked after him when he went down with typhoid: kept washing him with wet rags and feeding him with boiled water.

Cow's Belly's only idea had been to keep the patient as clean and cool as possible in his own tent; but the treatment had been successful when men were dying like flies in the hospital shacks. Alf and Dinny had given him a hand. Carted water and cooked his meals, taken turns to watch Robbie when he was delirious, thinking all the time of Mme. Robillard, and her grief-stricken eyes when she said good-bye to her husband.

Frisco aroused the hospital committee to apply to the government for assistance. This request was refused. The diggers cursed the government, subscribed for medical supplies, and held on, fighting the sun and the flies and fever as best they could. A fight—any fight—relieved the tension of those days. Frisco refereed many a bout with bare knuckles, and even dog fights, barging in to restore law and order when the betting got out of hand and the scrap became an all-in go among the onlookers.

It was he who summoned the roll-up after Pug Charley was caught ringing in crook banknotes at the two-up school. The muster gave Pug two hours to leave. Pug refused to budge from his camp, armed himself with an axe.

Frisco, backed by a couple of hundred angry men, faced him with his revolver.

'You've got to go, Pug,' he said.

'Who d' y' think you are, y'r bloody big bluffer,' Pug yelled. 'Y'r can't make me. Nor any man like you. The first touches me gets this axe.'

Frisco's bullet drove clean through Pug's hand. Pug dropped the axe. Doc Todd, who had some professional qualifications, but was trying his luck prospecting, stepped out of the crowd, sent for his bag of bandages and instruments, fixed up Pug's hand, and the men put him on the track with water and rations for twenty-four hours.

But for Frisco's action a nasty situation might have been created. The verdict of a roll-up had never been flouted. Frisco gained prestige: had upheld the miner's law and was right bower in the camp that night.

Young Paddy Cavan, who was here, there, and everywhere, when there was a row on, gave glowing accounts of Frisco's daring and coolness: his bull's-eye at first shot, and the way Pug collapsed when the axe dropped from his hand and blood spurted all over him.

Frisco threatened Paddy himself with a roll-up when he found the youngster pilfering from his tent: but Paddy ran at his heels whenever he got a chance. He had camped with Frisco when they arrived on the rush, made himself useful fetching and carrying water and stores, cooking for Frisco and washing his clothes when there was water to spare. After Frisco kicked him out, Paddy started doing odd jobs round the sly grog shanties and stores, sold papers when a batch came in on a team, made-up to any digger on gold, looked after him when he was drunk, cadged water and food if he couldn't buy them, and slept wherever he happened to be, in the dust beside a shanty or the butcher's shop.

He had built himself a humpy of boughs not far from Dinny Quin's tent, and busied himself collecting bags and tins to roof it before the rains came.

Cheeky and independent, the kid strutted about, never losing an opportunity to earn a few shillings. If only he were not so light-fingered, many a man would have been willing to take him in tow, Dinny said; but Paddy had no desire to be towed. He regarded himself as a man like the others, and was biding his time until he could find a mate and go off prospecting.

Meanwhile he did a bit of lousing on the dumps: picked up a nice little nugget now and then, and went scavenging round the camps for any odds and ends that might help him to furnish his camp. A clout over the ears, or a kick on the backside, was often the end of one of his forays. That did not worry Paddy. He bobbed up smiling just the same: continued to take what he wanted with an assumption of injured innocence and a gift of the gab, recognized for what they were worth, and passed over with good-humoured tolerance by the diggers. A shrewd urchin, game, but not to be trusted, they agreed.

Paddy looked after German-George when he was ill, and before long was talking of him as his mate: said they were going out prospecting after the rains.

'After the rains! After the rains!'

'Would it ever rain?'

That's what everybody was saying.

As the months went on the heat became a dead weight. Dust-storm after dust-storm tore at the tents and frail hessian shacks, levelling them with the ground, sending sheets of canvas flying into the bush, and passing with dry thunder, a crackle of lightning. The days continued under iron skies, in glaring white light.

Men cursed and tightened their belts, grinned and hung on, grim and determined to beat the weather.

At last, after a day of suffocating heat and whirling dust,

down it came, the blessed deluge. The music of rain splashing on tents and tin sheds drove men to an ecstasy of rejoicing. They turned out to cheer; lifted up their faces and opened their mouths to drink the bright drops; danced round, hallooing and shouting, getting drenched in the downpour.

Alf was one of the craziest: capered about hugging Dinny and Morrey; threw off his clothes and took a shower bath. When water was rushing through the tents and everybody had to sleep in wet blankets, it was treated as a joke. In the morning few men had a dry stitch to wear. It was still raining, raining, raining.

Rain filled all the dams and banks and potholes. Every gully was a rushing torrent: water lay flashing and shining in depressions on the flat land and away through the bush.

CHAPTER VII

WITH news of the rain, population flowed back to Coolgardie. A horde of prospectors, miners, investors and speculators arrived by every coach, with the teams, or on horseback and in buggies. Alluvial was petering out: few men on Fly Flat making tucker; but new leases had been taken up in the surrounding country. Prospectors went out towards the horizon in every direction, steering for any line of blue ranges or hill lumped against the sky.

Dinny sold the block he and Morrey Gough and Alf Brierly had been working south of Bayley's to an Eastern States syndicate for £2000 and a wad of shares. Dinny proposed to buy horses and prospect the country twenty-five miles north of the old camp where he had specked several small slugs before the dry weather set in.

Alf decided to stick to Dinny; but Morrey wanted his share of the sale in cash. There were rumours of rich prospects out Mount Youle way. Frisco had chummed up with a prospector who knew the track and Morrey was set on buying a couple of camels and going out with the prospecting party making for Mount Youle. The partnership was dissolved, Morrey going east with the rush to Mount Youle, while Dinney and Alf Brierly turned north.

They were out over two months before they began to see colours in every dish they panned off, and specked floaters in sandy rubble at the foot of a ridge where Dinny declared he could smell gold. Dinny went loaming along the ridge for several days before he knapped a rock that showed fine shotty gold. Further along he located the reef in weathered boulders whose broken face was cobwebbed with gold.

Alf's heart thumped at sight of the lump of quartz Dinny showed him. He could hardly believe what Dinny said, that the reef was about ten feet in length and he reckoned it would go ten ounces to the ton. That, for Alf, meant the realization of all his dreams, wealth and Laura.

They went off to the reef, pegged a mining lease, and packed a bag full of specimens. Alf rode in next morning to report and apply for the lease. With so many men roaming about it was too risky to delay, Dinny decided, although Alf's news would bring a rush on their heels, and clean up the alluvial.

Coolgardie had changed a good deal in those months. A town site had been surveyed. The camps spread out around it. There were four pubs along the main street; shops and houses of wood and corrugated iron were being built on either side of the wide dusty track. It swarmed with diggers and speculators when the teams arrived. Auctioneers bawled from their rostrums set up in the open. Goods were sold before they left the camels' backs. The crowd milled round Bill Benstead's tent which was butcher's shop and post office combined, or stampeded towards the warden's hessian shack when news of a new find ran like wildfire through the camps.

The town seethed with excitement as prospectors came in, their saddle bags packed with rich specimens, applied for leases, sold their gold or rights, and went on a spree, shouting all comers. There were reports of rich prospects along the Ninety Mile, and at Roaring Gimlet. At every rumour of a sensational find, men went out with camels and horses, tramping, wheeling all their tools and camp gear on a barrow, or strapped to a bicycle. Alf was mobbed for details of his and Dinny Quin's lease.

Over a thousand men and a few women were living on the field by then. Publicans had sent for their wives and barmaids were installed. Miners' wives camped with their husbands in the tents around Bayley's. Poppet legs of the mine straddled the blue sky. Japanese and Chinese prostitutes sat like painted dolls at the open windows of a row of hessian and canvas shacks in what was known as the Rue de Lindsay.

Capitalists and their agents, two or three English aristocrats, Lord Percy Douglas and Lord Charles Sowerby, put up at the pubs and bid for promising shows. The Open Call was packed with investors and speculators. Miners, prospectors and penniless adventurers thronged the streets at night and assembled to meet

45

the teams. All the crooks, parasites and swindlers who batten on a mining camp were there in force. A priest had arrived. White-robed Afghans, haughty and aloof, strode through the crowd.

A few blacks drifted about in odds and ends of cast-off clothing, a young gin, sometimes, wearing no more than a digger's dilapidated old felt hat, or white collar. Among the miners and prospectors in their dust-grimed dungarees and old trousers, flannel shirts and odd waistcoats, the toffs were distinguished at first by their 'colonial' rig out, new moleskins, blue shirts, and wide-brimmed felt hats. But these took on the colouring of the fields, before long: were as dust-raddled and grimy as the rest. Only the mounted troopers in their dark blue tunics, white riding breeches, and polished high boots, looked spick and span as they rode through the streets, or swaggered into a pub, with jingling spurs.

The agent for a Victorian syndicate offered £5,000 and the same value in shares for Dinny's and Alf's lease. Dinny wanted to hang out for a bigger price, although on fuller investigation the reef did not justify his expectations. The gold was freakish: came and went inexplicably a few feet beneath the surface, and prospectors were coming in every day with specimens and reports of rich finds. Alf, beside himself with happiness and impatience, wanted to sell and go off to be married. He wired his Laura that he had found a gold mine, and was sailing by the first boat leaving Fremantle to arrange for their wedding.

Dinny fretted because he thought Alf intended leaving the fields for good.

'Not on your life,' Alf said. 'We've got to keep our eye on the mine. Look after our interest.'

He proposed bringing his bride to Perth, letting her live in the city while he spent several months of the year working with Dinny.

The purchasers requested Alf to report to their principals in Melbourne. After signing up on the sale, he took a seat beside the driver on the next coach going south. The camp turned out to cheer as he drove off and Alf stood, shouting and waving, till dust swirling from the horses' feet and wheels of the coach hid him from view.

Dinny had been too sober and penurious while Alf was about, Speck Jones, Yank Boteral and some of his old mates considered. He was at a loose end now without Alf. Dinny feared that his luck and a wife would be the ruin of Alf, and was sore at losing a good mate. The boys led him off to the nearest pub to drown his sorrow in champagne. Nothing less than a champagne spree was expected of a prospector who had two thousand pounds to play with, and Dinny knew of no way to celebrate but to shout every miner and prospector in sight.

It cost him a pretty penny, that spree. He heard afterwards that he had asked a damsel in the Rue to marry him. She agreed if he would settle a thousand pounds on her. Dinny gave her a note for a thousand pounds and she had cleared out with it. When he heard the yarn a fortnight later, recovering from a bout of d.t.'s, it sounded like a fairy tale; but the amount was missing from his account at the bank—still a canvas hut on a rickety wooden frame—and a lot more money as well. As a matter of fact, not much remained to keep him in stores for the rest of the year.

He sobered-up then, started collecting and sharpening his tools to go out prospecting. By that time, Paddy Hannan had come in with reports of a rich find on the track to Mount Youle. Dinny wondered whether Frisco and Morrey were in on it. Every man who could was packing up and making for Hannans, thirty miles north-east of Coolgardie.

Dinny was tempted to go off with them, but Billy Frost and his mate Bonner came in and applied for a reward claim at a place they called Siberia. It was arid, open country, black iron-stone shingles over red earth, they said, but plenty of gold there. The rush started right away and Dinny went with it.

'That was the worst rush ever I was on,' he said, 'though the Mount Black was worse. I had a couple of horses, rode one and packed the other, but most of the men were foot sloggin', carryin' their swags and tools, or pushin' a wheelbarrow—and it was a seventy-mile stretch without water. There was very little gold, except on the reward claim, when we got there, and no water except in a soak, eight miles away. With between forty and fifty men on the field, there wasn't a dog's chance of the soak holdin' out. It was a case of get or perish.

'I got out, but had a tough time on the track. Me horses knocked up and I was jest about all-in. God knows how many men perished. I would've, if I hadn't met Renou of the Water Supply Department with a string of camels, takin' out water. He saved a good many lives on that trip. Two men I know were buried along the track. Nobody ever knew how many perished: but for years afterwards prospectors were findin' a heap of bones here and there in the scrub and givin' them decent burial.'

A letter from Alf was waiting for Dinny in Coolgardie. Alf wrote that he was married and that the directors had appointed him general manager of the Lady Laura, as they had decided to call the mine. He was returning early in the year with Mrs.

Brierly. Machinery and a mining engineer were being dispatched. Would Dinny give the engineer all the assistance he could and keep Alf informed as to the way things were shaping on the mine?

It took Dinny a long time to recover from his gruelling on the Siberia track. He felt dried-up and light-headed in the sun: kept seeing mirages and wanting to chase the water lying in tranquil stretches along the horizon. The long blazing days started again, so there was nothing for it but to take things quietly until his strength returned.

He was glad to potter about the mine during the hot weather. Men coming in from the bush told terrible stories of thirst and death in the grey interminable scrubs. On Hannans water was five shillings a gallon and hard to get at that.

A thunderstorm in December put everybody in good heart. Nearly two thousand men collected in Coolgardie from the surrounding camps for a gorgeous spree that Christmas. Celebrations were riotously merry for days. There were sports, Salvation Army services in the street, and a ball at Faahan's. Shops, hotels, brothels and gambling joints did a roaring trade. Shouts of laughter and singing resounded all night. The tinkle of Sister Agnes's tambourine and her voice crying: 'Are you saved, brothers?' 'Have you been washed in the blood of the Lamb?' mingled with delirious oaths from the two-up school. Now and then a miner flopped on his knees to keep Sister Agnes's side-show going, or a crying drunk confessed his sins to loud applause.

In boisterous good humour, the diggers thought it was only a fair thing to oblige Sister Agnes at Christmas-time. She was a good sort, worked at the hospital during the day. It was Frisco, himself, on his way to a rendezvous with Miss Cherry Blossom, who started the ball rolling by singing hymns with Sister Agnes and joining a prayer meeting on Christmas eve. Most of her penitents had every intention of being dead to the world before morning, but they dropped a few coins, or bits of gold, in her tambourine, and went on their way hilariously.

There were brawls in the small hours and reconciliations over the bars in the evening. The pace was fast and furious while the gold in a man's shammy lasted.

After New Year, revellers left for the outlying camps. Work on the claims and leases went on as usual. The town looked deserted. There was more excitement about the arrival of a donkey team from Esperance than about the erection of winding gear at Bayley's. Everybody crowded round to laugh and applaud the staunch little beasts who had pulled three tons two hundred miles from the coast.

Roaring Gimlet and White Feather were booming when the shortage of water became serious again. Men poured back to the old camp: but Coolgardie could not yet cope with the demand on its water supplies. The government bore failed to keep the condensers going and water at the Gnarlbine Rocks was almost exhausted. Exemptions were granted and an exodus to the 'Cross followed. From the 'Cross to Coolgardie the road was closed to teams, only the coach continued a weekly running.

But Dinny was as happy as larry when the mailman brought him word that Alf Brierly and his 'missus' were at the 'Cross. They were staying at Mrs. Gough's and would be coming through on the first coach after the rains.

CHAPTER VIII

THE coach that rattled into Coolgardie during April '94 was loaded to the roof with men and baggage. It had three women passengers as well. One sat beside the driver. The two others in the crowded interior clutched their bundles, gazing wide-eyed and aghast at the cluttered camps and fuming dust of Fly Flat, a string of camels winding through, with Afghans striding alongside.

A red and yellow carry-all, mud-splashed, mud caked high on its wheels, the coach swung up the main street between the rows of corrugated iron, wood and hessian buildings, as Big Mac let fly his long whip, sending the six jaded horses walloping along with a clash and jingle of harness, to make an impressive entry into the town. He pulled up with a flourish opposite Fogarty's Hotel.

The horses stood with dropped heads, sweating and blowing. Men in the street surged round, yelling greetings to Mac and mates on board. Shouts of surprise, a volley of cheers, resounded when they recognized Alf Brierly and realized that the girl sitting beside him on the box seat was his bride.

Alf yelled back, proud and happy in the spontaneous outburst. He helped Mrs. Brierly down from the box seat. She was a sight for sore eyes, plump, fair, dressed in white, with a light blue veil floating over her white sun-hat. Old mates crowded round to shake hands with Alf. He had a busy time introducing Mrs. Alf Brierly.

'Laura, this is Speck Jones—a good friend of mine. Mrs. Brierly, Speck!'

'Hullo, John! My wife, Mr. John Meicklejohn.'

'And Bill, himself—'

'Great jumping Jehosaphat, Alf, so you brought the wife along after all!' Bill exclaimed.

'She wouldn't be left behind,' Alf explained gaily. 'Bill Jehosaphat, Laura!'

'How do you do, Mr. Jehosaphat?' said Laura, and the crowd roared.

'But where's Dinny? The old devil—'

Dinny had to fight his way through the crowd.

'Give us a chance,' he shouted. As his hand locked with Alf's he gasped. 'God, lad, it's good to see you again!'

The men fell back as Alf introduced Dinny to his wife.

'This is Dinny Quin, Laura, the best mate a man ever had.'

Dinny made an old-fashioned bow over Laura's hand.

'Pleased to meet y', Mrs. Brierly,' he said.

In the excitement of greeting Alf Brierly and his bride, the other women were scarcely noticed as they descended from the inside of the coach. But some of the bystanders, who did not know Alf, enjoyed the love scene Robbie and Mme. Robillard gave them, as they met, hugged and kissed, radiant with joy and exclaiming delightedly. Robbie quickly extricated his wife from the crowd and marched off down the track with her on one arm and her portmanteau on the other. Mrs. Gough stood looking about her expectantly, as if waiting to be claimed and embraced also.

Dinny, and two or three of the other men did not see her as they grabbed Alf's baggage and the party surged over to Fogarty's Hotel, where Mr. and Mrs. Fogarty were waiting to welcome Mrs. Brierly. Greetings and inquiries mingled in an eager chorus:

'Hullo, Alf!'

'Glory be to God, but y'r lookin' fit, lad!'

'Welcome to the fields, Mrs. Brierly!'

'How's things up here?'

'Boomin'.'

'Any rain down below?'

'Got two inches one night in the 'Cross.'

'Y' don't say!'

'Teams bogged round about Bulla-Bulling.'

As she stepped daintily across the dusty track, the eyes of scores of men followed Mrs. Alf Brierly. She looked as pretty as a picture cut out of an illustrated magazine. They wondered how in the name of blazes she was going to fit into life on a mining camp. Mrs. Alf seemed delighted to have arrived: had a pleasant, friendly way with her: must have persuaded Alf she would make the best of things, it was agreed.

That was just it, Alf was explaining to Bill Fogarty and Mrs. Fogarty, Dinny Quin, Speck Jones and Bill Jehosaphat, as they settled down to a round of drinks in the dining-room.

'Laura insisted on coming,' he said. 'She wants to see what life on the goldfields is really like: said she'd rather rough it with me, than be a grass widow so soon—though, of course, she'll have to go down for the summer. I am going to put up a house. It's on the road now. We'll live near the mine until she's showing a handsome profit—we can stow away a few thousand for our old age, and take a trip round the world.'

A chuckle of applause went round.

'Things're not so rough on the field these days,' Bill Fogarty objected. 'Coaches runnin' and teams bringin' in stores reg'lar. Water's been down to eightpence a gallon, though it's gettin' a bit short again with the crowd comin' in every day. There's a bit of green feed about, too. Dick Lyons brought in a mob of bullocks this week. They're running out be the Rocks, so we'll have fresh meat for a couple of weeks, at any rate.'

'Best winter climate in the world, Mrs. Brierly,' Speck remarked encouragingly.

'Be a paradise on earth, Coolgardie,' Dinny agreed, 'but for the dust, flies, and the drooth.'

'How's Hannans?' Alf asked. 'There's a rumour over east that Hannans is going to be the big field.'

'Don't you believe it, me boy,' Bill Fogarty flared up. 'They've got nothing at Hannans to beat Coolgardie.'

'What are you givin' us, Bill?' Speck chortled. 'Dick Egan's struck a reef on the Croesus, as promisin' as anything on Bayley's.'

'And the Maritana's showin' the richest alluvial at nine feet, I've seen in all me born days,' Bill Jehosaphat added.

'I reckon Kurnalpi's got as good a chance as Hannans, of bein' the big field, Alf,' Dinny hit in. 'Couple of chaps I know got two thousand ounces there last week and Middy came in with a pair of nuggets went eighty-four between 'em. He says old Molyneux picked up a bobby dazzler, went ninety-eight ounces.'

'Alluvial's all right,' Bill Fogarty declared obstinately. 'But it takes a mine like Bayley's to keep a town goin'. Coolgardie'll be the big city of the fields, Alf. Why, they struck a reef in me backyard the other day!'

'Cripes!' Alf's eyes lighted to a restless fire. 'Do you wonder

I couldn't keep away, Laurie? It's so full of interest, the life here.'

'It is, isn't it?' Laura murmured. Her blue-grey eyes flittered over the dust-stained, corrugated iron walls of the pub, and across the big, bare shed of a room with forms and a few chairs beside the long tables set for a meal.

'Morrey had any luck?' Alf asked, looking round the familiar faces and missing the bland countenance of Morris Gough from the circle.

'Nothin' worth speakin' of,' Dinny said. 'He's workin' a claim at Hannan's with Frisco and two other blokes. Hasn't been in for the last two or three months.'

'What? Alf started to his feet. 'We brought Mrs. Gough up on the coach with us. She was expecting him to meet her. Wrote to say she was coming.'

'She won't know what on earth to do,' Mrs. Brierly said quickly. 'Do go and bring her here, Alf.'

As Alf walked away, Dinny joined him. The engineer from the Lady Laura held Alf up at the door. Dinny went on and found Mrs. Gough sitting on her tin trunk beside the coach, bags and packages all round her.

The horses had been taken out of the coach, and the crowd hanging about the new post office tent where the mails and papers were being sorted, stared curiously at Mrs. Gough's forlorn figure. One or two men strolled over and inquired whether they could do anything for her; but Sally, scared by their bold glances, or rough courtesy, repelled them with a digni-fied: 'No, thank you. I am waiting for my husband.'

Her face brightened when she saw Dinny.

'Oh, Mr. Quin,' she cried, 'where is Morris?'

'Well, ma'am,' Dinny replied gently. 'He's out at Hannan's —it's about thirty miles from here.'

'Oh, dear,' Mrs. Gough wailed, her eyes brimming, 'what shall I do?'

Alf left the engineer and walked across from Fogarty's.

'Come over to the pub and stay with us,' he said cheerily. 'Laura says you must.'

Mrs. Gough gathered up her bundles, two handbags stuffed with books, clothing, and odds and ends of feminine gear. The paper bag of grapes she had been nursing all the way along in the coach fell to pieces: the grapes fell in the sand.

'The grapes are melting and so am I,' she exclaimed ruefully, trying to smile.

'There now,' Alf picked up the grapes and rubbed the sand from them. They were to have been a special treat for Morris, he knew. 'You mustn't worry. We'll send word to Morrey and he'll be here, in a day or two—if not sooner.'

'If you would be so kind!' Mrs. Gough gasped, struggling with her disappointment. Dinny staggered off, her tin trunk on his shoulders.

Mrs. Gough was not such a pleasing sight, as Mrs. Alf Brierly had been, men in the street observed, as she walked across to Fogarty's. All they could see of her was a little woman dressed in black, with a woe-begone face and brown eyes, her hair drifting in wisps and tails from under a straw hat tied on with a red and yellow scarf; but there was something about her walk, the way she put her feet down on the sand and shifty gravel that interested them.

Alf's missus looked like a white butterfly which had flown into the camp and would drift away again; the other, as if she belonged to the country. She was like one of the brown moths that took on the protective colouring of bark on the trees and came fluttering into their tents, round the candle-flames and kerosene lanterns, on early summer evenings.

Alf reproached himself for having forgotten about Mrs. Gough in the excitement of arriving and showing off his wife. He felt responsible for Mrs. Gough's coming to the fields, although he had tried to dissuade her when first she told him she was going to Morris. Then Laura had been seized with the idea of coming, and he was satisfied to think there would be another woman about with whom she could be friendly. Very nice for Laura! But when Marie Robillard decided to come too, he began to have some misgivings as to how she and Mrs. Gough were going to fare if Robbie and Morris could not provide them with some of the comforts he planned for Laura.

Of course, Alf had taken Laura with him to Southern Cross, intending she should return to Perth and live with friends while he went on to Coolgardie. Staying at Mrs. Gough's in the 'Cross, waiting for the rains, he and Laura found Sally unhappy and worried about Morris. She had not heard from him for months. Cracker Jack and the mailman assured her Morris was alive and well; but Mrs. Gough had made up her mind to pay her husband a visit after the rains. Alf advised her to write and let Morris know she was coming, guessing that Morrey's appearance might be a shock to his wife if she had not seen him for nearly two years, and he was not prepared to meet her.

The two women had become quite friendly in the 'Cross: started to call each other Sally and Laura. Alf learnt more of Mrs. Gough's and Morrey's history through her confidences to Laura than he had ever known. He was so accustomed to see

Mrs. Gough drudging about the boarding-house, a chirpy, hard-working little woman, that he had not thought of her as belonging to the same species as his Laura.

He was sorry for Mrs. Gough: thought Morrey gave his wife a rough deal; but she was a sturdy, loyal soul. No one ever heard a word of complaint out of her.

Laura could not understand Mr. Fitz-Morris Gough. What sort of a man was he, she demanded indignantly, to leave his wife at a place like the 'Cross: let her work so hard, and cry her eyes out at night because he did not write to her?

'If you go away, looking for gold, again, how do I know it won't be the same for me?' she cried, voicing a secret fear. 'You've got the gold fever, too, Alf. I can see it in your eyes. I'm not going to let you leave me. I'm not going to be left behind and break my heart waiting for letters.'

'No chance of that, darling,' Alf declared happily. 'You mean more to me than all the gold in the world.'

He was remembering Laura's outburst, and damning Morris for putting his wife in such a predicament, as he escorted her to Fogarty's. Mrs. Gough was younger than Laura and charming when she cared to be. Had been as lively as a cricket on the way up: looked like a gipsy when she sat by the camp fire at night, a coloured scarf tied over her hair, and sang songs with the rest of them. It had been a good trip: a thrilling adventure for the women to camp out under the stars and sit round in the evening, listening to the men's yarns about gold and the fortunes prospectors were making out there in the wild dark country all round them.

When everybody contributed an item to the camp fire concert, Laura sang in a light, well-trained soprano, Sally with a gay natural joyousness, and Marie in a low husky voice, very moving, though nobody knew what she was singing about.

Marie was very happy because she was going to see her Jean again.

'Two years, it is a long time!' she sighed. 'And I have no joy to cook for the strange man. And lock my door at night!'

Sally was not so sure that Morrey would approve of her having come to join him.

'He'll say there are too many hardships. I should not have come,' she said. 'But he will be glad, all the same, to have me with him, I know. And I'll say, the hardships are not so great when you are there, my dear. It is only when you are away I cannot bear them!'

With Alf, himself, Mrs. Gough was still reserved and shy, as she was towards most of the men with whom she came in contact.

54

She had been a different person, on the track, blithe and fascinating in an ingenuous way; but dejected and unhappy as she was now, she looked quite plain and unattractive.

As Alf introduced her to Bill Fogarty, Mrs. Fogarty and the men sitting round the table, Mrs. Gough apologized for her distress. It was very foolish, she confessed, to be so upset because Morris had not come to meet her.

Everybody tried to cheer and console her, offering all manner of suggestions as to what could have detained Morris. The chances were Morrey had not got her letter, Bill Fogarty said. Perhaps he could not get a horse, or a lift in from Hannan's. Maybe he was out on a rush.

'Don't you worry, missus,' Bill Jehosaphat urged. 'Have a drink and you'll feel better. Nothing like beer on the fields when things go wrong.'

'Everybody's drinking our health, Mrs. Gough,' Alf said. 'You must wish us luck too!'

He put a thick glass before her and filled it.

Sally lifted her glass, smiling to him and Laura.

'Much happiness—and much gold,' she faltered.

The company laughed and drank.

'The same to you, Mrs. Gough,' Alf replied, and insisted on refilling the glasses so that everybody could drink to Mrs. Gough's health, happiness and prosperity on the fields.

A man came in from the bar with a letter for Mrs. Gough. He said a native had just come over with it from Hannan's.

'It's from Morris,' Sally cried eagerly, as she unfolded a piece of soiled paper.

There was dismay in her brown eyes as she looked up after reading Morris's note.

'He says,' she said slowly, 'he is on a good thing. He cannot get in to Coolgardie for a few days. I must stay here until he comes for me.'

'That's the men all over, dearie,' Mrs. Fogarty exclaimed. 'If you was dyin' and they was on gold, the gold's all they'd worry about.'

Sally struggled to restrain the tears welling against her will. Laura put a hand over hers.

'Could we go to our rooms, Mrs. Fogarty?' she asked.

Mrs. Fogarty bustled out ahead of them.

'Your luck's in, there was a rush on the Ninety Mile yesterday and I've got a bed to spare,' she said, 'or God knows where I'd 've put you. Alf should've let me know when you was comin'.'

CHAPTER IX

THE room Mrs. Fogarty showed Laura was small and stuffy. Two small beds, a dressing-table made of boxes covered with cheap cretonne, and another box cupboard on which stood an enamel basin and jug, almost filled it; but the beds were neatly made, had white covers, and there were strips of oilcloth on the floor. Sally's room was smaller, with the same makeshift furnishing.

'There now,' Mrs. Fogarty exclaimed proudly. 'They're not much to look at, but if you knew what it meant gettin' the comforts of civilization up here, and keepin' a place clean and tidy, you'd reckon this is luxury to anything else you'll find in Coolgardie.'

'They look heavenly after all those days on the coach,' Laura declared sweetly.

Sally was too familiar with the smell of stale beer, tobacco, and rank male sweat that permeated her room to bother about it. When Mrs. Fogarty left her, she closed the door, flopped down on the bed and wept to her heart's content.

A little later she heard Alf and Laura talking in the next room. Laura had opened the window.

'Lord, sweetheart,' Alf protested, 'Ma Fogarty 'll have a fit. The place will be full of dust and flies in no time.'

Laura's little laugh rippled.

'I've thought it all out, dear,' she said. 'I got used to flies and dust on the coach, and I'd rather have them with air than without.'

'Have it your own way,' Alf agreed.

'If you don't mind, dearest!'

Laura's voice dropped to a lilting murmur.

'Oh, Alf, I'm so glad I came! Think how awful it would be if you were here and I was somewhere or other in town, miles away. I won't mind the heat, and the flies, and the dust, so long as we can be together.'

'Darling!'

Through the thin partition Mrs. Gough could hear every word and movement. She knew Alf had taken his wife in his arms: that they were standing folded together. She could hear their kisses, the long-drawn breath and little laugh with which they separated. Their happiness accentuated her misery. It was so long since Morris had taken her in his arms and kissed her like that. She felt suffocating in the closed-up box of her room, but could not bestir herself to open the window.

Presently she heard Laura exclaiming as she peered into the water jug:

'Why, Alf, it's full! Do you think—do you really think I could have a wash?'

Alf walked across the room to gaze at the water.

'Bill Fogarty's doing things in style these days,' he commented gaily. 'And they tell me, in spite of the rain a few weeks ago, water's none too plentiful now, with three thousand men on the field. Never mind, we can pay for what we want. Try a cat wash, if you like, darling. Rub yourself over with a wet paw; but for the love of Mike don't ask for a bath just yet. Bill's as likely as not to inquire whether you'll have it in beer or water. It's a little way he's got of putting new chums in their place.'

'Oh, beer by all means, Mr. Fogarty. I always bathe in beer for preference!' Laura replied lightly. 'That's what I'll tell him, Alf—if the worst comes to the worst—and I must have a bath.'

'Ssh,' Alf warned. 'These walls are only hessian and paper. They can hear what we say all over the place.'

The sound of Mrs. Gough's quiet sobbing reached them.

'Poor little woman,' Alf whispered. 'It's too bad of Morrey not to have been in to meet her. Of course, he could have come, if he'd wanted to.'

On the other side of Mrs. Gough's room was the kitchen. She could hear preparations for a meal going on there: a clatter of dishes: Mrs. Fogarty moving pots on the stove. When her husband came in to know whether dinner was nearly ready, she was not in the best of tempers.

'No, it's not!' she declared wrathfully. 'And goodness knows when it will be. How in the name er blazes do you think I can cook, do all the work of the bloody place, and start receptin' flash dames? What the hell do Alf Brierly and Morrey Gough mean landin' their women on me? Do they think the fields is a health resort, or what?'

'Aw, go on, Lizzie,' Bill murmured soothingly, 'they're nice enough women, I'm sure.'

'Trust you to think so!' Mrs. Fogarty's exasperation increased with his attempt to mollify her. 'Presently, they'll be wantin' baths. You see. And you'd have me running me legs off cartin' water for the young ladies. Not if I know it, Bill Fogarty. You can give them baths if you want to, though there's over a thousand men comin' in from the Pinnacles. Speck says they near done a perish for water, and we'll be short in a week, if we don't get some more rain. You can tell Alf Brierly from me, the sooner he gets a shack for his missus the better pleased I'll be. As for Morrey Gough, the hound, what does he mean draggin' a woman up here and leavin' her in the lurch?'

'He hasn't done that, darlin'. He—'

'You don't tell me he couldn't have got in if he'd wanted to. Dinny says he gave her a tough spin in the 'Cross: had her slavin' her guts out runnin' a boardin' house and never did a hand's turn to help. Always the little gentleman. I got no time for Morrey Gough, Bill, and you know it. How much does he owe us now? A good bit, I'll be bound, and never got anything on his belt, if it's a question of squarin'-up—though he can always find a few ounces, or a couple of notes, for a poker game.'

'Shut up,' Bill growled. 'You don't want her to hear, do you?'

'If she doesn't know her own man by now,' Mrs. Fogarty grumbled, 'it's time she did.'

Mrs. Gough sat up, her cheeks flaming. She restrained an impulse to dash out and scream: 'It's not true!' Morris was not like that. He had not treated her badly. He hated her to work in the boarding house. That's why he was so surly about it. There was nothing else to do, of course. It wasn't Morris's fault there was not enough gold in Fraser's mine, and they had lost all their money.

These people did not understand Morris: how he had come to this country to work and make a new life; and how difficult it was for him, with all the good intentions in the world. He was careless about money, because it had always come to him easily. He could not realize how important every penny seemed to those who worked hard for their living. Men born with a silver spoon in the mouth were like that.

Her thoughts whirled in a confusion of misery and anger. It was insupportable that people should talk like this about her and about Morris. She could not endure their compassion. She would not, Sally decided. But there was so little money in her purse, she hoped Morris would come soon. Paying the bills for stores she had sent him from the 'Cross. and her coach fare, had left little over, and living at this hotel would be costly.

Mr. Brierly said Morris had shared some money with him and Dinny Quin when they sold their claim and dissolved partnership. Was it true he owed the hotel people much money: that he was playing cards again? The cursed cards were the cause of all his misfortunes. Why did he have to play? What was this mania for gambling which possessed him? Had he ceased to care for her? He had left her so long at the 'Cross without a letter or word about how he was getting on. That was what had made her so anxious. That was why she had decided to come to Coolgardie.

Mrs. Fogarty said: 'If she doesn't know her own man by now, it's time she did.'

Quite true, Sally agreed. She was loth to look at Morris except through the romantic glamour with which she had enveloped him when they ran away together and were married; but an instinct stirred, shrewd, critical and realistic. Of what use to blind oneself to facts? At the 'Cross she had begun to understand the struggle for existence: how one must throw all one's will and energy into it. She must not be a little fool: let her emotions run away with her now.

If Morris was like that: if he was lazy, selfish, unscrupulous about money, and his passion for her had faded, she must manage her own life without depending on him: be prepared to manage his also. She had no intention of allowing him to drift and forget his obligations as he had been doing. Oh no! And she was not going to allow him to use her as he had done. Her life with Morris was going to be a partnership in which her clear brain and energy should have a chance. She would not fail in her duty to him; but he also must realize her right to a policy in their affairs.

Her slim brown hands clenched to her thinking. Sally rose from the bed, went to the window and opened it.

It was true, she informed herself, that Morris had treated her shamefully, leaving her so long alone at the 'Cross and neglecting to write to her; letting her send him stores and pay the bills —while some of the time, at least, he had money: could have relieved her of so much worry and work. But no, he had played cards. He had spent his money in other ways.

That state of things could not continue. He must not gamble away her life and his own. She could provide for herself: open a boarding house for miners here in Coolgardie, or at Hannan's, as she had done at the 'Cross. But it must be understood between them that she was fighting for her own future as well as his.

Sally went to the washstand. The jug was empty. She opened her case and took out a towel. It was a sad, dirty face which stared back at her from the mirror on the makeshift dressing table. Tears streaked the red dust on her smooth skin. Her eyelids were swollen. She tried to rub off the dust: was still rubbing when Laura knocked.

'Come in,' Sally called.

Laura entered, looking as fresh as a flower in a white muslin frock.

'Oh, my dear, haven't you got any water?' she cried. 'Come into my room. Alf's gone for a drink.'

Sally felt there was nothing she needed so much as water to restore her equanimity. She followed Laura into her room. While Laura poured a little of the yellow tepid water into a basin, Sally threw off her dress.

'Bath is a word, it seems, we mustn't mention,' Laura sighed. 'But I'm simply dying for one, aren't you?'

Sally's smile glimmered.

'I've learnt to manage without. Can wash all of me in a tea-cup of water. On the 'Cross, often, we've had to be very careful, so I'll make the most of this opportunity, if you don't mind.'

'Oh, do,' Laura exclaimed. 'I'll watch the door so that Alf doesn't come in.'

Mrs. Gough stripped, and wetting her towel, scrubbed her slim brown body vigorously.

'It's a different world,' she cried, refreshed and satisfied to have wiped away all traces of tears and mental disturbance. 'I'll go back to my room and put on some clean clothes now.'

The brown silk foulard with a small hemstitched collar of finest unbleached linen, in which she appeared for dinner was not new and fashionable as was Laura's voluminous muslin, but it was well-made and becoming.

'She looks nicer in her old clothes than I do in any dress in my trousseau,' Laura exclaimed to Alf, later.

'Nonsense, darling,' Alf replied. 'You look lovely in anything.'

Mrs. Gough had worn that dress with the naive intention of exerting herself to inspire confidence; but not in Mrs. Alf Brierly. The dress was one Morris had bought for her when they were first married. She was wearing it, now, to impress Mrs. Fogarty with a sedate and entirely respectable appearance.

Mrs. Fogarty had a busy time serving the meal. Usually, Alf explained, Bill Fogarty ran in a couple of lads down on their luck to give a hand waiting on the tables and washing-up; but if a rush was on, not a man could be found to waste time and the chance of a fortune, on such a job. Sometimes Bill himself assisted by carrying loaded plates and cups of tea into the dining-room. He was busy in the bar, that day, and Mrs. Fogarty had only an old fossicker she called Wirewhiskers to help her.

Stout, middle-aged, full of energy, clad in a grease-stained dark blue print dress, bare feet in felt slippers, she bustled backwards and forwards from the kitchen to the dining-room, cracking jokes with the men, shouting imprecations at Wirewhiskers.

Mrs. Fogarty was a hard-doer, Alf said, good-hearted, but with a temper that blazed and roared like a bush fire. Sally marvelled at her performance. Now and then a man got up from the table, carried out a pile of empties, and returned with a relay of plates, piled with hot corned beef, onions and potatoes, plum duff, or dried apricots floating in a bright yellow custard. Cups of tea followed, although a few thick white china cups were reserved for distinguished visitors. Enamel mugs and milk tins served the purpose for regular customers.

The clatter of dishes and racket of men's voices retailing the news of the day, with laughter and boisterous oaths, resounded until everybody had eaten and was full enough to stroll with satisfaction into the street again. Sally made her way to the kitchen after the meal.

She found Mrs. Fogarty, sitting on a box there, having kicked off her slippers.

'Oh, me feet! Me poor feet!' she cried. 'It's the tortures of hell I suffer with me feet, Mrs. Gough.'

Sally exclaimed at the swollen misshapen feet with veins standing out in thick cords, Mrs. Fogarty thrust out for her inspection.

'Let me get some hot water for you to bathe them,' she begged, 'and then we'll rub them in methylated spirit. It's good for tired feet, I know.'

'There's the washing-up to do and tea to get,' Mrs. Fogarty objected testily. 'Wirewhiskers is so damned slow, wastes half the water.'

'I'll wash up, and you can rest a while,' Sally replied.

Mrs. Fogarty gasped her astonishment:

'Well, I'm blest! And I thought you was one of these flash dames would be expectin' me to run round after you.'

'Me?' Sally laughed. 'I've had a boarding house in the 'Cross, so I know what it means to do all the work in a place like this.'

Mrs. Fogarty thought she might as well try the treatment Sally suggested. She shouted to Wirewhiskers, who was deaf and having his meal at the kitchen table, that he could wash-up presently—'earn his keep for once in a way.'

Sally found a kerosene tin which had been cut in half, and filled it with hot water. Mrs. Fogarty soaked her feet, explaining with some pride that they were too small for the rest of her, and how vain she had been about them as a girl. She could remember compliments galore about her pretty feet.

'But I never thought I'd be weighin' sixteen stone and having those very-close veins, in those days, dearie,' she sighed. 'To say nothing of bein' head cook and bottle washer in a goldfield's pub!'

When Sally made a request to Mr. Fogarty for some methylated spirit, he brought her a bottle of overproof whiskey: said he didn't stock 'that rot-gut,' but maybe the whiskey would do as well. As Mrs. Fogarty was too fat and top-heavy to reach her toes, Sally rubbed the spirit into her feet while Wirewhiskers, getting on with washing the dishes, mourned such waste of the good stuff.

'Put it inside, not outside of you, missus, and it'll do you more good,' he implored.

Mrs. Fogarty said she felt a new woman as a result of Sally's ministrations and decided to rest for an hour or two. Sally sat with her while Mrs. Fogarty talked about the difficulties of catering on the fields: the scarcity of fresh fruit and vegetables, and how, often, she had only tinned stuff and salt meat to cook with. If the meat was fresh, it would not keep in hot weather. There wasn't enough water to run a cool safe, and the flies were fierce: blew even the butter if they got a chance.

From food, Mrs. Fogarty turned to gossip about women on the fields: the fortunes barmaids were making out of the gifts of gold lucky prospectors lavished on them for favours anticipated, or received. How decent the men were to a decent woman, but woman-starved and liable to run amok if a likely female gave them any encouragement. There had been a fight over a barmaid in the hotel yard only a few days ago, and a woman who was no-better-than-she-ought-to-be, had let the men gamble for her daughter at a rowdy party. Now and again there was a brawl in the Rue de Lindsay.

'The Rue de Lindsay?' Sally wondered why a street in Coolgardie should have a French name.

'There's a she-been there, kept by a woman the boys call Madame Marseilles,' Mrs. Fogarty exclaimed. 'She's got one or two French girls in the place. They're mostly Chinese and Japanese women in the other bad houses.'

All this was by way of being friendly advice, Sally realized. As a final gesture of confidence and esteem, Mrs. Fogarty lifted her skirts to show the varicose veins bulging in thick purple knots and contusions on her massive thighs.

'But it's terrible to suffer so much,' Sally protested, 'and be on your feet all day.'

'I'll last out me time, dearie,' Mrs. Fogarty remarked cheerfully. 'And it's no use worryin' about what comes after.'

She heaved herself on to her feet and trotted about barefoot, making preparations for the evening meal.

'While I'm here, I can help you,' Sally said. 'It will help me too, because then I won't fret until Morris comes.'

'Name your own wages, darlin',' Mrs. Fogarty agreed gladly.

'Wages?' Sally's finely-etched brows drew together. Then she smiled as if such an idea had not occurred to her. 'We need not talk about wages—yet,' she said lightly. 'Show me where to find things, and I'll set the tables for tea now.'

She knew that evening meal on the goldfields would be called 'tea.'

CHAPTER X

WHEN Sally appeared in the dining-room that night helping to serve the meal, most of the men took it for granted Mrs. Fogarty had got a waitress at last. Sally hurried about with plates of corned beef, of stewed apples and custard, and put cups and tins of hot tea beside them, as if she had done nothing else all her life.

'Oh, I say, Mrs. Gough, you shouldn't be doing this,' Alf protested.

'Why not?' Sally exclaimed gaily. 'I am used to it. And Mrs. Fogarty is suffering dreadfully with her feet.'

Alf was accustomed to see Mrs. Gough working about her own house and waiting at table. He was not so upset as Laura, who guessed that Sally had other reasons than Mrs. Fogarty's swollen feet for wanting to make herself useful.

'You mustn't do it, dear,' she said to Sally before they went to bed. 'Alf wants you to regard yourself as our guest till your husband comes.'

Sally smiled, stiffening a little.

'It's very kind of him,' she said. 'But I cannot allow Mr. Brierly to provide for me.'

'Alf says your husband wouldn't like you to be working in an hotel, here.'

'No.' Sally could be as obstinate as a mule when she chose, Laura told Alf afterwards. 'There's a difference, perhaps, to working in one's own house and in a public place. But Morris must understand, I can't sit still and twiddle my thumbs when it's necessary to do something.'

It was evident during the next few days, that her 'doing something' meant getting up at dawn to sweep and tidy, set the table, and be ready to fetch and carry for men wanting an early breakfast. It meant making beds, flying about all day, preparing for meals and clearing away after them, waiting at table, and washing dishes when Wirewhiskers had d.t.'s after a spree with old cronies who had sold a claim for a few thousands.

Laura was indignant.

'It's too bad!' she exclaimed. 'I can't bear to see you working so hard, Sally. Alf's sure Mrs. Fogarty could get a miner's wife or daughter to help her. There are several men with families about, now, he says.'

Sally's little laugh rippled.

'But I like to be a blessing to Mrs. Fogarty, Laura,' she said.

Every hotel on the fields was packed with visitors, it seemed. Every day more capitalists, mining magnates and prospectors arrived. Mrs. Fogarty was at her wit's-end where to put all the men and a few women, who demanded the best her rough and ready accommodation could afford. She turned out of her own room for the Hon. Mrs. Candy, and Sally gave up her room to two nurses who came on the coach that week. Even then one of them had to sleep on a palliasse on the floor, and before morning Bill put a prospector's wife with several children in with the nurses. Men were sleeping everywhere, stretched out in the dining-room, and on the ground, sheltered by the verandah. Sally and Mrs. Fogarty had a tent in the yard and Bill slept in the bar.

Mrs. Fogarty raged at having to feed such a mob, as she called her miscellaneous visitors. How she did it, three times a day, slapping about in heelless slippers, cursing and sweating over the cooking, and rousing hell out of Bill to find a slushy to help in the kitchen, was a miracle, Sally said. A miracle she helped to fake, Mrs. Fogarty replied jocosely: was loud in her praises of the way Mrs. Gough had set-to, and not been afraid to soil her pretty hands, doing any sort of dirty work to tide a body over an emergency.

'If ever the Lord did me a good turn, it was sendin' that little woman to look for her husband, and keepin' Morrey Gough out at Hannans, just now,' Mrs. Fogarty told Dinny Quin.

Dinny was not so sure about the good turn the Lord had done Mrs. Gough.

'Morrey wants a kick in the pants, not comin' in to meet her,' he said.

'No need to worry about that!' Mrs. Fogarty declared, emphatically. 'She's better off here than she'd be with Morrey Gough, if I know anything about it. Though Mrs. Gough knows how to take care of herself. I'll say that for her. She can take a bit of back-chat from the men and keep them in order.'

'That's right,' Dinny agreed.

'There's not a man would say a word out of place to her,' Mrs.

64

Fogarty chuckled. 'They know well enough she's not the sort they can shout a few drinks and carry on with, for a bit of gold —though I did have trouble with Big Mac, the other night.'

'Mac Darra?'

Mrs. Fogarty's fat jolly face creased to her laughter.

'He came in from Kurnalpi with a lot of alluvial. Sold it and started drinkin'. Thought he was on top of the world and could buy all he wanted. Come roarin' through the house; "Mrs. Gough! Where's Mrs. Gough? I want Mrs. Gough!" She was with me in the kitchen, as it happened. "It's all right, me dear," I ses, "I'll deal with him." And I did.

' "Now what the hell's the matter with you, Mac Darra," I ses, "comin' shoutin' after a decent woman like that?"

'And I give him the rough end of me tongue. You should've seen him get out of the kitchen with his tail between his legs, and next morning when he'd sobered up, he comes round to tell me he didn't mean anything insultin' to Mrs. Gough.

' "That's the worse of you randy devils," I ses, "when you've got a drop of drink in, you don't know how to behave."

' "For Chris-sakes, missus," he ses, "don't tell me I said anything amiss to Mrs. Gough. Fact of the matter is, I was goin' to ask her to marry me."

' "Marry y'r?" I ses. "She's got one husband, and not likely to take another." '

Dinny grinned. 'All the same,' he said, uneasily, 'if Morrey doesn't come soon, I'll go and fetch him. There's lots of men thinks Mrs. Gough's a widow and fair game.'

The days filled and fled for Sally. She was glad to be busy and not just moping and worrying about Morris. She began to feel quite at home at Fogarty's. Her self-confidence and sense of independence had grown. She could laugh and talk with men in the dining-room, be on quite easy terms with them, and yet maintain a certain touch-me-not-air they respected. But it was not easy, sometimes, waiting on hundreds of men, running backwards and forwards with piles of heavy dishes, and trying to be quick and cheerful all day. Her back ached and her head whirled. She threw herself on her bag stretcher at night utterly weary. And every night she wept a little for Morris. Why didn't he come? Why had he left her so long among strangers?

'It's gettin' too much for you, dearie,' Mrs. Fogarty said. 'And for me too. Bill's sending to Perth for a cook and a couple of waitresses, and we're goin' to build more rooms and a new dining-room and kitchen. Fogarty's 'll be a real flash pub before we're through.'

'Then I'll be losing my job?' Sally queried.

'Not if you want it,' Mrs. Fogarty assured her.

Laura went out with Alf to the mine and camped with him there for a few days. They asked Sally to go too, but she said she could not leave Mrs. Fogarty until the waitress she was expecting arrived. Besides, Morris might come and be disappointed not to find her waiting for him. But every day it hurt a little more that Morris had not come.

Alf and Laura returned from their camp beside the Lady Laura when a rush was sweeping the crowd out of town away to the south. Alf went along to investigate the new find. The hotel was almost empty for a few days. Mrs. Fogarty sat with her legs up enjoying a nap in the afternoon and Sally had nothing to do.

It was brilliant sunshiny weather, though cold still in the morning and at night. Sally longed to get out of the stuffy little pub and its atmosphere of stale beer, sweat and tobacco smoke. She wondered how Marie was getting along. Had not heard of her since they arrived, although old Cow's Belly frequented Fogarty's and Mr. Fogarty said he was sore with Robbie for bringing his wife to their camp.

'Where is it?' Sally asked.

'On the far side of Fly Flat,' Bill Fogarty told her. 'Robbie and Cow's Belly 've been on a good patch of alluvial, there.'

Sally decided to go to see Marie. Laura was delighted at the idea and at Sally's suggestion that, all three, they might take a walk in the bush, or have a look round the diggings.

They were not sure Alf and Morris would approve of their going for a walk in the bush, or round the camp, without a male escort. But she was a good bushwoman, Sally assured Laura, and not afraid of being lost in the scrub surrounding the township, nor of meeting with any misadventure among the scattered claims and mining leases.

All the same, men stopped and stared as they saw Mrs. Gough and Mrs. Brierly pass. It was as if these two quite ordinarily good-looking and well-dressed young women were apparitions, as they walked towards Robillard's camp, laughing and talking together, their figures in light, long-skirted dresses swaying over the rough shingly earth, and their heads topped by small straw-decker hats, bobbing about among the dumps and mullock heaps.

'Can you tell me, please, where Mr. Robillard's camp is?' Sally asked an old man rattling a shaker on Fly Flat.

'Spare me days if it's not Mrs. Gough,' he exclaimed, thrusting out a great, grimy paw. 'The boys were sayin' y'd come up from the 'Cross, missus. Goin' on to Hannans, I suppose. Morrey and Frisco Jo's been doin' real well there, they tell me. There's

66

some thinks Hannans is going to be the centre of the fields, but there's a lot of gold round about the old camp, yet. Why, the alluvial here was supposed to be worked out. But when the boys from the Murchison came along, they discovered the bed of a dry creek three or four feet under the old workings, and got a lot of good gold thousands of men 'd walked over.'

The fume of red dust was rising from shakers all over the flat, which was honeycombed with pot-holes and mounds of red and white rubble.

'They brought these contraptions along with them,' the old man gabbled happily, indicating his shaker, consisting of three or four trays of wire netting and a sheet of galvanized iron standing on ricketty legs. 'And a grand invention they are too. Brought us a bit of luck, this morning. Heigh, Wally!'

His mate dropped the long-handled shovel he was wielding languorously on the edge of a hole nearby, and strolled across.

'This is my mate, Wally Storrs.' Sally's unknown friend did the honours proudly. 'Mrs. Gough and—'

'Mrs. Brierly,' Sally added.

'Show 'em the slug we got this morning,' Wally's mate commanded.

Wally pulled a dirty shammy off his belt, unwound the string round it and held a fritter of gold, powdered with red dust, on the palm of his hand. Wally's mate picked it up, spat on it, and rubbed off the dust on the leg of his pants to show the gold.

'There she is,' he exclaimed, admiringly. 'Goes round about twenty ounces. A real nice little slug! Not as big as the one a bloke brought in from Hannans the other day. Went ninety-two ounces, she did. But this 'ere's the best bit of luck we've had after shovellin' dirt for nearly three weeks, missus, and we reckon there's more where she came from.'

'Of course,' Sally agreed, knowing what was expected of her, 'she's not an orphan. You'll be striking the rest of the family quite soon, and be rich men both of you. But we were going to see Madame Robillard—'

'S'elp me, I quite forgot!' Wally's mate grinned. 'Robbie's camp's over there be the bit of scrub. I'll take y'r across. The ground's a bit crumbly beside some of these pot-holes.'

He steered Sally and Laura among the dumps and fuming shakers, until Marie saw them coming and ran to meet them. It was too late that day to do more than sit and talk for a while in the brushwood shed her husband had built for her beside the tent. But Marie was delighted with the idea that they should go for a walk in the bush next afternoon. She was very happy and quite content to be living in a tent and cooking for Jean by an open fire.

'It is a second honeymoon,' she said gaily. 'And me, I learn to be the good prospector: 'elp mon mari when Mr. Cow's Belly is drunk. I waggle the shaker like so, and already find a little slug sitting back on the riffles when all the others jump away. I will show 'im to you.'

She went for a small glass bottle, half-filled with specks and fragments of gold; extricated a tiny slug and displayed it with as much pride as Wally's mate had shown over his.

'I 'ave wash 'is face,' Marie explained. ' 'E was so dirty you would not know 'e was a little bit of gold. And me, my face is just as dirty with red dust when I work on the shaker. The first time, my arms and my back, they ache, oh la-la! Never again will 'e let me touch the shaker, Jean 'as said. But now, it is not so bad, and I work with 'im every day.'

Sally was envious of Marie when she and Laura made their way back to Fogarty's. Marie was as happy and excited to be living and working with her husband as she would have been, had Morris come for her and taken her to his tent, Sally thought.

'That sort of thing may be all very well, now, while the weather's good,' Laura remarked coolly, and with some distaste. 'But in the heat and the dust-storms, Marie won't be able to stand it.'

CHAPTER XI

EVERY afternoon for the next few days, while Alf was away and things were slack at the hotel, Laura and Sally went for a walk in the bush. Sometimes Marie joined them.

The spring sunshine held a marvellous brilliance and everywhere vivid green herbage sprouted against the red earth. In the bush the wild flowers were out, and it was pleasant to get away from the ugly, ramshackle town for a while; to drink the keen air and exclaim at the clear blue of the sky: gather wild flowers, or sit among the slight innumerable trees, and gossip about their husbands, how they fell in love, and wonder about the future.

Mrs. Fogarty had warned them not to wander out of sight of the scattered camps and dumps of rubble flung up beside shafts and costeens. It was so easy to lose your way, get bushed in the scrub, she said. Even good bushmen did.

But Sally assured her that, born and bred in the bush, she knew how to keep her eyes open, and not ramble far from the winding tracks.

White everlastings lay in drifts like snow under the trees: tiny pink ones were tucked among the rocks and laced the damp ground near them. Yellow flowers with an exquisite fragrance showered tall straggling bushes, and desert pea, scarlet and black among its grey furry leaves, sprawled across a depression beside the native well. As light-heartedly as schoolgirls, these young married women gathered wild flowers and exchanged confidences that were to be woven into a life-long friendship.

They were not afraid of the blacks they met now and then. Poor, miserable looking creatures, trailing in or out of the town, clad in dirty odds and ends of clothing white men had discarded. The women and children were usually naked; begged sometimes for food and tobacco. But Sally avoided the camel pads, disliking the bold, curious glances of Afghan camel drivers and their jeering badinage. She was terrified of camels. Once a hobbled camel had chased her, so if they came across camels feeding among the trees, the girls fled to a safe distance.

Passing the big mine whose poppet legs stretched against the blue of the sky, they stopped, one day, to peer at the workings. Mr. Sylvester Browne, himself, showed them some rich ore which had been hauled from a new level in the mine. He pointed out the spot where the first reef gold on Coolgardie had been discovered, and presented each of them with a small quartz specimen threaded with gold, as a souvenir of Bayley's.

Marie often talked of Jean's father and mother who lived in London. They had been foster parents to her when her own parents died. She had lived with them in an apartment near the Tottenham Court Road: been apprenticed to a dressmaker and scarcely remembered her mother. Maman Robillard had told her about the persecution in France after the fall of the Paris Commune, and how her father had been killed in the fighting on the barricades. The grandfather of Jean also. He had been a goldsmith and a patriot who threw in his lot with the cause of the people.

It was an English friend who had arranged for the escape of the family and Mme. Robillard had smuggled Marie and her mother away with them. Her mother had died soon afterwards —of grief and the suffering she had been through, Mama Robillard said. Marie had always loved Jean; but they lived so like brother and sister in the same house, she was afraid when he became a man he would find a more attractive girl to fall in love with. Jean had studied at a university and gone away to teach in a big school; but when he came home they were affianced, and maman and papa Robillard said it was what they had always hoped for. So happy they all were, but so poor, and it was hard to live always in a London slum.

Jean wanted to make a home for his parents where they could have some peace and comfort in their old age. So he decided to come to Australia, and Marie had come with him. At first they met with so many misfortunes and disappointments in this country. She had been very ill when her baby was born and the doctor said perhaps she would never have another child. But she could not believe that. It seemed, now, as if all their dreams might be realized. If only they found gold, if only Jean found enough gold to buy a farm and send for his father and mother!

Laura said she hoped she and Alf would never have to live with her parents. She and Alf had been sweethearts while they were still at school and it was more or less understood that some day they would be engaged. Alf's father was supposed to be a rich man, but suddenly there was a dreadful scandal. It was said he had lost a lot of money in the land boom, and then embezzled trust funds. At any rate Alf was studying engineering at the university when his father came to him, gave him a five-pound note and said he must shift for himself.

The papers were full of Mr. Brierly's arrest and trial soon afterwards. Her father, who was a well-known politician, forbade Laura to have anything to do with Alf; but she had met Alf secretly, before he went to the west, and promised to marry him as soon as he got a job and she was of age.

'So of course,' Laura ended, happily, 'when Alf came back from the fields after discovering a goldmine, my father and mother had to make the best of it. They gave us a big wedding and—here we are.'

As Sally told her love story, ripples of laughter flashed among the grey-leafed trees. It was not that there was anything very amusing about the story, but she had such a droll way of telling it.

'My father was very proud of being a pioneer of the south-west,' she said. 'And mama, of course, never let us forget she was a Russel of Russelton, although she had gone out into the wilds with papa, worked hard, and brought up a large family. There were six of us, five girls and one boy, and he the youngest, younger than me. We were all very excited when a letter came from the Governor, Sir William Robinson, asking papa if he might send the son of an old friend in England to us for colonial experience. The Honourable Morris Fitz-Morris Gough, he said, was going to take up land and wanted to see how we ran a cattle station. Well, papa invited him to be our guest on Warrinup, and Morris came.

'Mama said he was a typical young Englishman, "so debonair and charming"; but how we laughed—at least Bob and I did—when Morris turned out in doeskin riding pants, long polished boots with spurs, a silk shirt and big felt hat, to go mustering. We gave him a bad time, I'm afraid, racing through the scrub. He lost his hat and got his shirt all torn the first day he went out with us: had a nasty fall too when his horse propped at a creek. Morris shot off into it. But he took his breaking-in very well, and was really a good horseman, so we rather enjoyed showing him round, teaching him to track and work natives.

'Papa used to call me his head-stockman. I'd worked out of doors with him since I was sixteen. It was hard to get stockmen in the south-west then, and I liked to think I could ride and track strayed cattle with any man. Mama did not object because it was necessary to help papa. Bob was two years younger than I, and we only had two native stockmen. She never thought Morris would look at me. I was such a hobbledehoy, brown and sun-burnt, her "ugly duckling," she used to say.'

'But, no, Sally!' Marie exclaimed. 'It could not be!'

'Well, mama hoped Morris would fall in love with Ceciley or Grace,' Sally continued. 'They were fair and lovely. So were my two other sisters, Fanny and Phyllis. But Grace and Ceciley had spent a summer in Perth, been to a garden party and ball at Government House. They had prettier clothes than the rest of us, because mama thought they ought to be married first. Of course they helped Fanny and Phyll in the dairy, and did their share of the housework, but mama fussed more about Ceciley and Grace. She made them put cream on their hands and wear gloves at night, wash their faces in buttermilk, and brush their hair for hours. Poor mama, she spent days furbishing up their dresses before Morris arrived. It was too bad of me to spoil her plans.'

'Oh, Sally,' Laura laughed, 'how on earth did you do it?'

'I don't know,' Sally's laughter chimed with hers. 'I didn't want to: was too surprised for words when Morris kissed me and said: "I adore you, Sally!" It was marvellous to be made love to like that. He was such a Prince Charming and I couldn't imagine why he had fallen in love with me. I thought it must be because he admired the way I handled horses and could give a hand yarding and branding stock. But Morris wouldn't hear of that.

' "My darling little Sally," he said, "I love your youth and daring. I love your turned-up nose, I love your colonial impudence. But most of all, I love you because I love you—and that's all I know about it."

'Of course, I fell in love with him, too,' Sally went on, 'and was afraid what papa and mama would say when they knew. Papa was very annoyed when Morris told him he wanted to marry me.

' "You can have any of the other girls," Morris says he said, quite bluntly, "but I can't spare Sally."

' "Neither can I," Morris said.

'Mama explained to me that it would be dreadful for my elder sisters if I was married before they were. Almost an insult to them. Besides papa needed me to help with the stock. I wept and wept: said papa could get a stockman if he paid decent wages. But it was no use. Mama and papa refused to consent to my marrying Morris. I was only eighteen, too young to know my own mind, they said, and they were afraid he was not the kind of man to whom they could entrust my future—although they hadn't thought of that when they hoped Morris would marry Cecily or Grace.'

'Why are parents so unreasonable?' Laura exclaimed.

'So Morris and I eloped, just rode into Bunbury one day and went round by boat to Fremantle, where we were married. Papa and mama never forgave me.'

'They are still alive?' Marie asked.

'Papa was drowned trying to cross the river when it was in flood,' Sally said, the brightness fading out of her face. 'Mama died last year.'

'But you're not sorry you married Morris?' Laura queried, wondering whether the gilt had worn off her romance for Sally.

'Oh, no,' Sally cried eagerly. 'We've been very happy, although things have been difficult sometimes. At first we lived at an hotel in Perth and Morris bought lots of clothes for me. I was such a country bumpkin, and he thought he had to teach me how to behave. Mama would have been horrified at the idea that any of her girls could not comport herself with grace and dignity in society. But Morris used to make me walk up and down to be sure I could manage the train on my evening dress, and I had to practise my curtsey to Lady Robinson, ever so many times, before we went to dinner at Government House. Sir William Robinson was cross with Morris for having outraged colonial hospitality, he said, and run away with the wrong daughter; but he was very kind to us. Morris quarrelled with him about something else. I don't know what it was. And then we went off into the country.

'Morris's father had bought a station for him beyond York.

72

Morris was very pleased with it, but I knew from the first that we could never make a success of the place. There was no water, workers wouldn't stay there, and Morris wanted to live like he did on an English estate. His father was angry when Morris sold Booingarra and put the money into a mine at Southern Cross. He stopped Morris's allowance, and, of course, we lost everything when Fraser's closed down. I had to do something to show we could earn a living, and so I started the boarding house. Morris was annoyed with me, but I hated to be always in debt and borrowing money.'

Sally's voice faltered, and a note of defiance crept into her distress.

'Morris thinks it's enough for me to be Mrs. Morris Fitz-Morris Gough, but I tell him that I am the daughter of a pioneer, too, and not ashamed to work: do whatever is necessary to earn a living.'

She jumped up and walked away.

Marie and Laura exchanged glances, as they rose from the rock on which they had been sitting, and went after her.

Sally turned and faced them, her eyes flashing.

'I'm not blaming Morris,' she said. 'It's just the difference in the way we were brought up, has caused all the trouble between us. I love him. And I'm sure he loves me—though you wouldn't think so, the way he has left me waiting here. Didn't bother to come and meet me even!'

She broke down and wept. But as Marie and Laura tried to comfort her, making excuses for Morris, and saying they were sure he wanted to come, Sally's sturdy spirit reasserted itself.

'How silly of me to behave like this,' she exclaimed, smiling through her tears.

And presently they were making their way back to the township, all three laughing and chattering as if nothing had disturbed the pleasure of their excursion.

CHAPTER XII

THEY were returning to Fogarty's, their hands full of flowers, the afternoon they came across a row of corrugated iron and hessian huts, with Chinese and Japanese girls sitting at the windows. Almost unreal, like dolls, they looked with their smooth painted faces and elaborately dressed hair. Marie stopped to stare and smile, Sally exclaimed in amazement; but Laura was shocked, wanted to hurry on. The Japanese girls stared back, their black still eyes unsmiling, as though they were merely pictures behind the wooden window frames of those drab little houses.

The street was almost deserted. Only one or two men moved slowly along its wide dusty length. A bigger house of corrugated iron with a narrow wooden verandah stood at the far end. On the verandah a stout middle-aged woman, tightly corsetted, and dressed in black, sat in a big chair, with two or three girls beside her. One of the girls was singing, listlessly:

'Au clair de la lune, mon ami pierrot;
Prête-moi ta plume, pour écrire un mot.
Ma chandelle est morte, je n'ai pas de feu.
Ouvre moi ta porte, pour l'amour de Dieu.'

At the sound of that familiar air and the lilting music of her own language, Marie exclaimed delightedly. It was such a surprise to find one of her own people in this out of the way place, that in a moment she was chattering eagerly to the girl who had been singing, to the woman, and to the other girls. They were chattering eagerly, gaily to her, laughing and almost crying, as if they were long-lost friends miraculously re-united. Nothing would do but that Marie and her friends should have a cup of tea with Madame and the girls. It was too early to expect visitors, Madame explained, and besides, everybody had gone to the rush. It was very bad for business.

Laura looked on, horrified. She tried to dissuade Sally from going into the house; but Marie was already on the verandah and Sally felt that she could not desert her. Laura, herself, was overcome by Madame's good-humoured cordiality and the girls' laughing attempts to reassure her.

Poor Laura, it was very embarrassing for her! She did not want to leave Marie and Sally in such company, nor yet hurt the feelings of those other girls by being gauche and disagreeable. She had tried not to look disapproving and ill at ease, taking tea with filles de joie in a house of sin. But how angry she was with Marie when they got away and were walking back to the hotel!

It was certainly indiscreet to have let an impulse run away with her like that, Marie confessed. Very regrettable, certainly. She should not have drawn Laura and Sally into association with those 'impossible women,' as Laura called them. But, Marie explained, she had quite forgotten who they were, what they were, when she heard Lili singing. Laura could not imagine

74

what a joy it was to hear one's own language and speak it—after not having heard it for so long. Also, the French did not regard prostitution quite in the same way as the English. It was considered an institution which safeguarded the family. Marie herself did not subscribe to this point of view. She had been taught to think of these women as unfortunates who were forced into a way of living no woman would choose for herself, because they were the victims of poverty.

Sally confessed she could not share Laura's feeling that these girls should be treated as unfit for young married women like themselves to speak to. It was horrible, she agreed, to think of that dark, serious Nina, and Lili, so dainty and lively, submitting to the brutal caresses of any stranger in order to make money for Madame Marseilles, but they did not seem unhappy.

Belle looked harder and stronger than Lili, more inured to her calling. She was a handsome woman for all that, fair and florid with eyes as blue as the sky, and heavy breasts. English, she said, and proud of it. Only living with Madame until she could get a house of her own. She had a client who promised to set her up as soon as Madame would release her. Bertha was German, a dull, quiet girl with a cast in one eye.

Lili had said Madame was very kind to her girls, already one of them had married a rich prospector. Madame was making a lot of money, expected to retire in a few years and become respectable: promised to find all her girls good husbands if they would work for her for three years. It was easy enough to find a husband on the goldfields. There were so few women.

Lili explained that she, herself, did not wish to marry again. She had been deserted by her husband, an opera singer, before she was twenty, and this was the only way she could earn her living. She was looking forward to the time when she could choose her lovers, induce some man with the big luck to take her back to Paris.

'The little fool, she's thinking of Frisco Jo,' Sally remembered Belle had said. 'And Frisco will not bother about her if he strikes it rich.'

Lili's little laugh and her gesture of indifference fluttered.

'If not he, then another,' she cried.

'Tiens, Belle!' Madame interrupted, brusquely. 'We do not speak of clients to the young ladies.'

It had been a very proper and polite little tea-party with talk about the weather, the strangeness of this unknown country, shocked exclamations at the black savages who sometimes wore a hat and nothing else to cover their nakedness, and much lamentation about the shortage of water and the difficulty of washing oneself. Lili had given an example of the prospector's bath, spraying a mouthful of water on to her hands, and rubbing it over her face and neck.

'It is the best way!' she cried, while everybody laughed at her gaminerie.

They had talked of the rush, too, and the fortunes people picked up lying about on the ground. Madame, herself, had found a small slug one morning after rain, near the wood-heap.

Marie was grateful to Sally for saying she could see no harm in their visit, although Sally agreed with Laura that it might be as well not to mention it to Mrs. Fogarty, or their husbands.

CHAPTER XIII

NEARLY a month had passed when Morris drove up to Fogarty's in a dusty buggy harnessed to a pair of lean, rough-haired horses. Bill Fogarty hurried in to tell Sally he had arrived.

Sally scarcely knew her husband when she ran out to meet him and he walked towards her. Morris! That brown-bearded man in moleskins, a rough-dried shirt and a dilapidated felt hat? She recognized his shabby brown tweed jacket first. Then his eyes, though he wore no glasses, struck a thrill to her heart.

'Morris!' she cried, and found herself clinging to the bearded stranger.

Morris kissed her perfunctorily. He would consider it unseemly to make a display of affection in public, Sally knew.

Men standing about outside the hotel greeted him in hail-fellow-well-met fashion. Morris replied with easy familiarity. He looked just the same as any other prospector or working miner, except that he held himself with a certain assurance.

'How's things out at Hannans?' somebody asked.

'Not too bad,' Morris replied.

'Gosh, you've struck it lucky in the old camp this morning, Morrey!'

'About time my luck changed,' Morris laughed, passing into the hotel. Alf, coming out to look for him, led him to the dining-room where Laura was finishing her breakfast. Morris sat down to talk to them while Sally flew off to bring him something to eat. As she put a plate of bacon and eggs before him and cleared away used dishes on the table, his eyes followed her. He was surprised, evidently, to find Sally so much at home and bustling about like that.

The Hon. Mrs. Candy, an Englishwoman who had come out to visit her son, prospecting on the fields, and had bought the Tatters Mine, stopped to have a word as Sally passed on her way to the kitchen with a pile of dishes. Mrs. Candy was very excited about rumours of a new find, Sally told Morris.

A digger with a hangover, at a table near the end of the room, called: 'Hey, missus, could y'r squeeze the pot for another cup er tea?'

'Of course, Charley,' Sally replied, blithely, and moved away to get the tea for him.

Morris's arm swung after her. He turned to look at the digger.

'How about getting it for yourself, old man?' he asked.

'But Morris—' Sally protested. She sat down beside him, realizing Morris was not pleased to discover what she had been doing in the hotel. She tried to explain that Mrs. Fogarty had been so busy, suffered terribly with her feet, and there had been so many people to cook for and serve with meals. After all, to help her a little was the least one could do, under the circumstances.

Morris was more interested in the new find. He went on eating his breakfast, asked Alf:

'What's the strength of this rumour: something richer than Bayley's, a few miles out of Coolgardie? I got it from a teamster on the track.'

'It's a bit of a mystery,' Alf said. 'All sorts of yarns 've been floating round for a day or two. We don't know yet who's got the gold, or where it's supposed to come from.'

Sally decided her explanation could wait until she and Morris were alone.

Alf and Laura tried to persuade him not to take Sally out to Hannans. Their house was nearly built, they said, and Sally could stay with them until Morris put up a shack for her.

'Thanks awfully,' Morris replied. 'I have already made arrangements for Mrs. Gough to stay at the boarding house.'

It was at that moment Bill Fogarty bustled up. 'She's a grand little woman, your wife, Morrey,' he said, breezily. 'My missus says you can leave her here as long as you like, and she'll pay Mrs. Gough any wages she cares to name to help about the place.'

'Mrs. Gough is not a domestic servant,' Morris drawled, after a moment's silence.

'God damn your eyes!' Bill's temper flared. 'Who said she was? Don't you go givin' yourself airs to me, Mr. Gough. You can't afford to. Your wife's a welcome guest whenever she cares to step into this house, but I can't say the same for y'rself.'

77

'I'm sorry, Bill.' Morris looked it. 'I can't help feeling a bit uppish this morning. If you hadn't seen Mrs. Fogarty for two years, I bet you'd be feeling the same way.'

Alf laughed boisterously to relieve the tension and Bill Fogarty joined in.

'Come 'n' 'ave a drink,' he said, 'and we'll let bygones be by-gones.'

The men went off to the bar, and Sally scurried about tidying up the dining-room. Laura helped. If it was necessary to appease Morris by showing him that she also was willing to give Mrs. Fogarty a hand, she would do her best, she assured Sally.

When Morris sauntered out from the bar, Sally took him away to her tent in the yard.

'Why have you humiliated me by waiting at table in this damned pub?' Morris demanded.

'But, my dear,' Sally protested, 'what was I to do? I hadn't enough money to pay for a room, and I couldn't allow Mr. Brierly to do that for me.'

'Why not?' Morris demanded. 'Alf's a rich man, now.'

'I prefer not to be under such an obligation,' Sally replied firmly.

'It may have been just as well to get on the right side of Bill Fogarty,' Morris conceded. 'I owe him a few pounds. But you might have been a little more dignified: remembered—with all these people from home about—that we have some social position.'

Sally's eyes sparkled.

'At least Mr. and Mrs. Fogarty will understand I was anxious not to impose on their kindness,' she cried. 'How absurd to talk of dignity and position when one is helpless!'

'Dick Egan, Camalleri and others have made a lot of money at Hannans,' Morris brooded. 'Hannans is going to be the big field, not Coolgardie. It's not alluvial but reef gold we're looking for, there. If this lease Frisco and I are on now comes up to expectations, we can settle up with everybody and live in comfort for the rest of our lives.'

'If—' Sally objected. 'Meanwhile I don't like people to say we borrow and don't pay back.'

'The fact of the matter is,' Morris exclaimed irritably, 'you should have stayed at the 'Cross. A man's got to live as best he can, on the fields—and forget everything else. It's no place for a woman: for my wife. But as you've come, I'm not going to leave you here, at the mercy of any blackguard. Oh, yes, I know I should have driven over for you before, but I just couldn't beg, borrow or steal a buggy.'

Sally's gaze disconcerted him. Of course, he was accustomed

'to her acquiescence with his wishes: an implicit devotion. Astounded, he heard Sally say: 'I would rather stay here and work for Mrs. Fogarty, Morris.'

'That's out of the question,' Morris said sharply. 'We'll leave for Hannans to-morrow morning.'

But they did not go to Hannans next morning. By midday the town was in a ferment with news of the rich find which had been a mystery for days. An old prospector had come in from the bush, the pouches heavy on his belt. He was sick, he said; but went on a spree, started flashing his gold about, and boasting gleefully of the golden hole he and his mates had struck.

'Who're y'r mates?'

'Where are they camped?'

There was not a hope on earth of the old man keeping his secret. The wildest yarns spread, and grew whiskers, as Dinny said. Diggers besieged the warden's office seeking details of the new leases posted there.

When it was discovered that Jack Mills and his mates had dollied eight thousand ounces, valued at £ 32,000, on a lease called the Londonderry, the town went mad with excitement. Men fought round the stores to get provisions. Every man who could get away, rushed off along the ten-mile track to the south.

Morris Gough lost no time harnessing his horses and threw a few stores into the back of the buggy. Men clamoured round him for a lift. Morris took Speck Jones and Bill Jehosaphat with him; loaded tools and camp dunnage; made a few pounds on cartage, and was off.

Fogarty's bar and dining-room were almost deserted that evening; but late at night, the agents of foreign financiers and big syndicates came back from inspection of the Londonderry, close-lipped and sceptical. They could not believe that the dazzling ore they had seen came from the workings shown them —a hole not more than four feet wide and three feet deep, which was all the sinking the prospectors had done.

No one denied that the hole literally blazed with gold on all faces. Most of the speculators were busy until nearly morning writing reports, arguing and quarrelling about the probable value of the mine. P. W. Armstrong, the dispatch-rider, went off on his bicycle, taking important messages to cable from the 'Cross. A fast camel, ridden by an agent of one of the big financiers, set out to race him. Two or three mining men saddled their own horses and rode off to get into telegraphic communication with their principals. An offer of £ 25,000 had already been made, it was said, and the prospectors had turned it down.

Bill Fogarty was cock-a-hoop because the Londonderry rush

79

promised a new lease of life for the old camp. It justified his belief that Coolgardie, and not Hannans, would always be the centre of any mining industry on these fields, and his pub the centre of that.

Laura and Sally went along to have a look at the samples of Londonderry gold, on show at the bank that Monday morning. They met Marie on her way there, too, and mingled with the crowd seething round the specimens. One big lump of dirty quartz weighed three hundredweights and was a third gold. Every other piece shone with tangled skeins of the bright metal. All sorts of men, shopkeepers, mining magnates, teamsters, Afghan camel-drivers, prospectors and miners, fused in a demented throng, exclaiming wild-eyed and with strange oaths at this new display of secret wealth which had been torn from the surrounding country.

The voices clanged in their hoarse excitement:

'God A'mighty!'

'Allah!'

'Mary, Joseph and Jesus!'

'She's the biggest thing since Bayley's!'

'Bayley's never put up such a bloody show!'

'And they haven't started to work her yet. Tons of gold where these beauties came from!'

'She's goin' to be a world beater—the Londonderry!'

As the three women walked back to the hotel, they were conscious of a vague depression; as if they realized for the first time the dread and sinister influence of gold: the madness it put over men like an evil spell.

'Why should it be so important—gold?' Sally asked.

'You funny little thing,' Laura replied lightly. 'Gold means wealth, power. That's why men are so crazy about it. They can get all the things they want, if they've got gold—enough of it.'

'I know that.' Sally frowned thoughtfully. 'But why should they have to depend for what they want on this little bit of metal in dirty old rocks? It isn't as useful as iron or copper.'

'The value of gold is a superstition,' Marie remarked, as if there were no doubt about it.

'For goodness' sake,' Laura exclaimed, 'don't let anybody hear you say that! Gold's the god they worship up here. Even Alf! I wish sometimes he'd never come to Coolgardie—though, of course, if he hadn't sold his mine we couldn't have been married for years. But he's different somehow. I didn't want him to come back—'

' "He has followed the yellow siren that sings in the wilderness," ' Sally murmured. ' "Never more will the tenderness of woman suffice, or the labour of cities and farms." '

'Don't say that,' Laura cried. 'It makes me feel as if someone were walking over my grave. To tease Alf, sometimes, I tell him gold's my hated rival.'

'The man they call Dryblower said it,' Sally replied, laughingly. 'He was drinking at the hotel the other night, making verses and reciting. Don't you remember?'

'Oh, yes!' A smile chased the fear from Laura's blue eyes. 'You can't complain if you're on gold, I suppose. But I'm going to make Alf leave the fields next year and get some enjoyment out of life. It's too awful to think of spending the rest of one's days up here in the heat and dust, isn't it?'

Sally agreed with her.

'Mon Dieu, c'est effrayant, un tel sort!' Marie exclaimed.

All day, and for days, men surged through the town from outlying claims, from Hannans, White Feather, Roaring Gimlet, Cashman's and Kurnalpi. They paused to cluster round those specimens at the bank, load up with stores, gulp a drink or two, hear the latest news of the rush at the pubs, and moved on in an endless procession of horsemen, buggies and spring carts harnessed to horses or camels: men, dusty, shaggy, and carrying their swags, tramping along, their boots tied on with pieces of rope, or riding bicycles, bundles and camp gear fastened round them.

The talk was all of fabulous prices that had been offered for the Londonderry.

'They say Beaglehole, the manager of Bayley's, has offered fifty-thousand pounds,' Bill Fogarty rushed into the kitchen to tell his wife. 'But Mills and his mates 're hanging on for a bigger price.'

Everybody was telling everybody else how Jack Mills struck the first gold on the lease. He had gone out with a party of five men, soon after the rains, all of them hard up and with only a horse and dray to carry their stores. They had been out for months, as far south as Lake Lefroy, without picking up more than a few pennyweights. Footsore, and downhearted, they were making their way back to Coolgardie, doing a bit of prospecting as they went along. Then Jack Mills stumbled into camp one evening with a bag of samples that changed the gloom of his mates to mad rejoicing.

'I'd been knapping rocks along a likely ridge,' Jack Mills himself told Bill Fogarty. 'Hadn't seen a speck of gold all day, and sat down to rest a few minutes about sundown. Was as miserable as a bandycoot; felt like chucking up prospecting and trying to get a job with a teamster, or on the mines. Started kicking at the withered moss on a boulder in front of me. All of a sudden, I noticed there was a gleam where I'd knocked off a bit of rock. Stooped over to have a squint at it. And, by God, there she was! I jumped up and began smashing into the rock all round. Every lump was lousy with gold.'

Early next morning, prospecting along the reef, the party located the richest deposit and started work on it. Afraid to bring other men about before they had exhausted the possibilities of alluvial shed from the reef, Jack Mills and his mates did not disclose the extent of their treasure when they applied for a mining lease. They hoped to strike a reef which might yield half an ounce to the ton, so they set up a small furnace for calcining ore and dollied out the gold with pestle and mortar. For seven weeks they had managed to keep their secret.

Some resentment was expressed at the way the Londonderry men had bluffed about their find. In the general excitement and rush for claims, that was lost sight of. But Morris returned at the end of the week, disappointed at having found the country pegged for miles on every side of the lease. There was very little alluvial, he said, and nobody had struck gold beyond the Mills party's pegs. All the honey was in the Londonderry hive. That was the richest thing he had ever seen: the rock, in shallow workings, ablaze with gold.

Dinny Quin and some of the Murchison prospectors had their doubts about a rich shoot in poor country for permanent values; but held their tongues, except among themselves. They thought Jack Mills and his mates were fools not to sell. It was rumoured the Londonderry men were nibbling at £100,000. Then Lord Fingall offered £180,000 and a sixth interest. His offer was accepted. With the value of all the gold they had taken out of the ground, Jack Mills and his mates stood behind greater wealth than any men had yet won in the West.

The Londonderry boom whetted the appetite of overseas buyers for gold-mining properties in Western Australia. Agents were offering fancy prices for promising shows.

As soon as he returned, Morris was in a hurry to get back to Hannans. He intended urging Frisco to stand out for a bigger figure than they had put on their ground, he said. Besides, he had borrowed his horses and buggy from the manager of Cassidy's Hill, and the chances were Charley Hunt would be wanting to come in from Hannans himself, to have a look at the Londonderry. The Golden Wonder of the World, it was being called.

CHAPTER XIV

Morris went off to buy stores after he came in from the London-derry rush. Sally did not know where he slept that night. She had seen him playing cards in the bar parlour during the evening: heard Bill Fogarty lock up for the night, and expected Morris to come to her tent. He did not appear until morning, then called to her from the yard, looking dishevelled, and groggy about the eyes: said he had 'dossed' on the verandah, was going to put in the horses, wanted to make an early start.

Before six o'clock, Sally was ready, standing in the yard with her hat and dust-coat on, her brown tin trunk, handbag and parcels beside her; but Morris had driven off to make a few extra purchases and did not return until long after breakfast. When he pulled up at Fogarty's again, he called to Dinny Quin, who was standing with a group of men outside the hotel, to tell Mrs. Gough he was waiting.

Dinny went off to find Sally and heaved her tin trunk on to his shoulder. She gathered up her bulging handbag and parcels, followed him through the hotel and out to the buggy. Morris stowed away her trunk, bag and parcels. Sally climbed into the buggy and sat on the seat beside him. Everybody came out to the hotel verandah to say good-bye.

'Don't forget,' Laura said, 'come in to see me whenever you can, Sally, and I'll get Alf to drive out to Hannans some day soon.'

Mrs. Fogarty and Bill stood in the doorway.

'You've got a good home here whenever you want it, darlin',' Mrs. Fogarty called. 'Bill'll even give you a bath—when we've had a drop more rain.'

'You needn't wait for the rain, ma'am, if that's any inducement,' Bill called.

'Damned cheek,' Morris growled, whipping up his lean horses, 'for two pins I'd drop the reins and go over and give Bill Fogarty a piece of my mind.'

'Good-bye! Good-bye everybody!' Sally cried, feeling a little weepy and sorry to be leaving these kind people, although she had known them only a few weeks. 'They're so good-natured, Morris,' she explained, soothingly. 'Only joking to cheer me up.'

'I find jokes of that sort, about my wife, in execrable taste,' Morris remarked coldly. 'You must not allow people to presume on your lack of dignity, Sally. A woman's reputation up here is not worth a straw if she permits any sort of familiarity.'

He would have liked to add, Sally thought, that he had been displeased to discover her laughing and chatting with two or three men, in the hotel dining-room, the evening before, when he returned from the rush.

Morris knew, of course, that women were scarce and she might have chosen from a dozen men, all of them woman-hungry, had she wished to console herself for his absence. Having cashed in on rich claims, they were willing to offer her anything she might desire, if, and when, she would sleep with them. Morris imagined probably that suggestions of the sort had been made to her and resented the idea. Refrained from mentioning it, perhaps with a sense of some culpability for the circumstances to which she had been exposed. A culpability for which Sally would not acquit him, he might guess. She could be quite stubborn and self-assertive, his 'darling little Sally,' he had discovered.

Poor Morris! It was a long time since he had been jealous, Sally reflected. Not since they had been living in Perth, as a matter of fact. Oh, yes, she had emerged from her chrysalis on their honeymoon. It seemed necessary to show Morris that she would not be an embarrassment in any society. And how delightful it had been to find people thought she was attractive! 'So witty and charming, your wife, Mr. Gough!' she had heard Lady Robinson say to Morris, and Sir William had been very attentive, sending a horse for her, and taking her for rides in the early morning.

Too attentive, Morris thought, when Sir William danced with her three times at a ball one night. Morris was very grumpy about it, objected to the gaiety with which Sally enjoyed this new way of life, and the flattering courtesies men showered on her.

'Your husband is jealous, my dear,' Lady Robinson had warned her. 'Don't give him any cause for anxiety.'

Jealous? Sally had never thought of that as an explanation for Morris's taciturnity, now and then. She had been concerned all the time to make him proud of, and pleased with, her social success.

But she thought Lady Robinson might be right when they went up country and Morris confessed he was glad to have her 'all to himself again.' What a shock and disappointment the station had been to him! He had been so pleased to own thousands of acres: an estate bigger than any in the old country, he said. Of course, he had been prepared for a certain amount of pioneering and roughing it, but the shortage of water and workers to help with all the clearing and building to be done, had been heart-breaking. To find the homestead on the station just a slab hut was a blow, in the first instance.

Morris had spent a lot of money having material carted for building a decent house, refusing to listen to what Sally said about the need for first repairing stockyards and digging dams. She knew what ought to be done. All her life she had heard the problems of opening up new country discussed. Morris was glad enough for her to work with him, but insisted on running the place in his own way.

That was the trouble. He did not understand why a cattle station in almost virgin country could not be run like a farm in the south of England. It was a mistake to order stockmen and rouse-abouts to do things without getting on a cheery and friendly footing with them. Particularly when they knew their job better than you did. Even the carpenter and stonemason had walked off before the house was finished. Morris lost nearly all his cattle that first year, what with a dry season and the depredations of natives. He had worked hard to save the stock when it was too late. Too late to save Booingarra also. He had begun to hate the place before long, and all the toil he put into it: could see no end to the struggle with drought and the debts which accumulated.

It was really the best thing he could have done to sell, although he got only a few hundred pounds from the stock and station agents who had sold him the property. Was lucky to get that, most people said, although it had cost his father several thousands to buy and stock Booingarra.

Everybody was rushing to the goldfields at Southern Cross just then, and quite naturally Morris turned to them as a means of making money. His father was furious with him for selling land to speculate in goldmines. Said he had squandered a fortune to give Morris a chance of making good in the colonies; but from henceforward Morris would have to shift for himself. Not another penny need he expect from the family resources.

Sally understood that there was something discreditable in Morris's past, which was the reason why he had been sent to Australia. Sir William Robinson hinted as much when he wrote to her father. 'The young man has got out of his depths, gambling and sowing the usual wild oats,' His Excellency had explained. Something to that effect.

But Sally thought it was unreasonable for anybody to blame Morris for the failure of Booingarra, or for investing in the Fraser Gold Mining Company. The proposition put up to him looked a sound one, offering a job and dividends. The job, unfortunately, had been only temporary: a bait, she suspected, now, to ensure that Morris would put money into the company.

Dividends ceased when the mine closed down and Morris was left plucked and penniless.

Something must be done and done quickly, Sally realized, if they were not to starve or become cadging derelicts. Morris had opposed the idea of taking lodgers into their house: would have nothing to do with it. There was no rousing him, though, from the gloomy apathy into which he had fallen, so she had been forced to disregard his wishes and let a room to Alf Brierly and a bank clerk who could not afford to live at the pub.

Later she arranged for two empty shacks to be moved into the yard behind the house, and could accommodate more men. Dinny Quin and another miner had occupied one of them then. Her boarding house had become quite a flourishing concern despite the slump.

Sally smiled as she thought of it. How her back and her bones had ached, though always she pretended to Morris it amused her to cook and be a successful business woman. She had tried to be brisk and cheery in order to keep up her spirits and his. Did he still resent that she had taken matters into her own hands and proved she could provide for them both? She had become very drab and unattractive, with all the hard work, no doubt. Just a plain, close-fisted little boarding house keeper. Only during these last weeks at Fogarty's, among people who liked and flattered her, she felt she had regained something of her natural gaiety. 'The air of the goldfields agrees wit' you, me dear,' Mrs. Fogarty had said. 'You look years younger than when you came up. And y've put on weight, if y' ask me. Wit' them dimples, and the laughing eyes on you, don't tell me you haven't been a rogue in y'r day!'

Was that what had disturbed Morris, her improved appearance? Why had he looked so displeased when he found her talking to some miners in the dining-room at Fogarty's? And objected to Bill Fogarty's rather crude sally? It was comforting to think so, at any rate, and that Morris still loved her, although he had seemed so unenthusiastic at seeing her, and so dilatory about coming to meet her.

Sally did not forgive him for the affront of that delay. Morris still had not offered a satisfactory explanation for it, she considered, and she had no intention of letting him pretend to be unaware of the embarrassing position in which his negligence had placed her. It ruffled her to hear Morris talk in that distant, lordly way.

'Did you pay my bill, Morris?' she asked, quietly.

Morris did not reply.

Sally went on: 'It is we who presume, then. We owe Mr. and

Mrs. Fogarty for my board and lodging, about twenty pounds, I understand. Even if I had let them pay me for the work I did, we would still owe them several pounds. You were playing cards last night, Morris. If you had money to play cards, you had money to pay Mr. and Mrs. Fogarty. Why didn't you?'

'Now, see here, Sally, if you think I'm going to stand this sort of nagging,' Morris exclaimed irritably, 'you're greatly mistaken.' He threw his whip out and the horses jerked themselves forward, stirring the soft red dust on the road, so that it rose in a fog round the heavy four-wheeled buggy. 'I'll send you back to the 'Cross if I hear any more of it.'

'No, Morris,' Sally said, the whisp of a smile in her eyes, 'you will not send me back to the 'Cross. You will not send me anywhere. I will go where I please.'

Mr. Gough glanced at her, amazed. Never before had Sally spoken to him like this: indicated such a complete disregard for his right to make decisions for her. She may have been wilful, gone her own way, occasionally, in Perth when they were first married, and in the matter of making their four-roomed house available to boarders in the 'Cross. But it had always been with cajoleries and apologies, implying a sense of delinquency in not conceding to his wishes.

Sally had been very staunch and loyal during their most difficult times together, Morris reminded himself. Never had she allowed him to blame himself for the misfortunes which had come upon them. Never had she given him any cause to regret the rash, romantic impulse of their marriage. He never doubted her devotion, even during that brief period when she had enjoyed playing the butterfly in colonial society. He had been surprised to discover how fascinating she could be to other men. Sally had been a trifle indiscreet, perhaps, but always she had accorded him that naive worship which made him forget his family regarded him as a black sheep and a good for-nothing. What had come over Sally that she could speak to him in such a way? Had she changed towards him? Was it possible his long absence and seeming indifference to how she was faring had wounded her so deeply that she no longer felt about him as she had once done?

Absorbed in his gloomy introspection, Morris made no attempt at comment or conversation. Sally and he sat, side by side, like strangers, looking out over the slowly jogging backs of the horses as they followed a rough track through the scrub.

On the outskirts of the town there were a few camps, torn earth and mounds of creamy-red gravel, windlasses over shafts.

A party of prospectors coming in from a trip up north hailed Morris for news of the Londonderry rush. Morris wanted to know where they had been: whether they had struck likely country. Nothing worth sticking to, the men said, and one of their mates had been speared by blacks. Blacks had raided the camp, cleaned them out of stores. The prospectors went their way back to Coolgardie. Morris and Sally drove on to Hannans.

Later they passed a string of camels and their Afghan drivers, padding slowly along the side of the track.

The hours and the miles went by: hours and miles of dry red earth overcast by black ironstone pebbles on which the thin bony trees stood, with tough dark leafage thrust against the sun, and flowing away into a grey sea in the distance: hours and miles of pale, ineffable blue skies, with the horses and buggy moving like some sluggish insect beneath them.

Once Sally exclaimed to herself and Morris looked at her as if he expected her to speak; but she had nothing to say. He saw she was sitting bolt upright beside him, looking young and tragic. Sally must be twenty-two now, he reminded himself. She was eighteen when they were married, and that was four years ago. What was she thinking to be staring out before her with such sombre eyes, the line of her mouth tight and unsmiling? Such a grave little mug Sally had drawn her face into!

What was the matter with her? It was as if she were thinking in a language of which he had only the most rudimentary knowledge. He could never quite forget that he was an Englishman and she a colonial—as proud of being the daughter and granddaughter of pioneers as if she were a princess in her own right. There was a difference in their outlook which irked him considerably.

Concessions must be made, of course, to the customs of a country, and conditions of existence in a new and strange environment: but Morris retained a secret allegiance to traditions for which Sally showed no respect. She had no sense that it was unseemly, for instance, for Mrs. Morris Fitz-Morris Gough to work like a servant in a goldfields pub. Morris could understand a reluctance and repugnance to do such a thing; but to prefer this work of a menial to accepting Alf's offer of assistance, was beyond him.

It was all part of Sally's attitude towards what he regarded as the privileges of gentlefolk. She thought it was absurd to claim these privileges in a country where so much work had to be done, and perhaps she was right, Morris admitted. He had learnt that as a result of his experiences on the land. And here on the goldfields a man had to prove his ability to work for himself on the same terms as any other man. Morris had shed many of his conceptions as to the proper relationship between master and man, though some prejudices still clung.

He could not yet accept democratic tendencies in the colonies as anything but a disease which had to be endured if it could not be cured. But Sally, there was a queer plebeian streak in her, which perplexed him. She seemed to live and move and have her being in tune with these tendencies, as a matter of course.

Perhaps her colonial up-bringing had something to do with it. Pioneering was supposed to foster self-reliance and independence, and, certainly, working on her father's station she had learned to be capable and self-willed. But John Ward had been a sturdy enough old conservative. The family was well-connected, and Morris could not imagine Mrs. Ward approving of any of her daughters asserting themselves and defying the authority of their husbands as Sally had done.

Of course he had been somewhat to blame for what had happened. Morris could not completely exonerate himself, nor explain his disinclination to go to meet Sally. He was ashamed of the despair and apathy into which he had fallen, and of having left her without news or means of support for so long. He had hoped to go to her, in triumph, with a fortune in his pocket: successful and recompensed for years of toil by the luck so many men had won. Ignorant fools who spent hundreds of pounds on booze and harlots.

Morris persuaded himself he had waited and hoped, until a week ago, that the lease he and Frisco were holding would be sold and he could meet Sally with good news: demonstrate to her he was not the rotten failure he felt, even at this business of prospecting. But, as a matter of fact, it was not until he heard men in the camp talking of the new waitress at Fogarty's and realized what Sally was doing, that a possessive instinct stirred and he had been aroused to go and fetch her to Hannans.

It had been disappointing to find her disinclined to accompany him. More than disappointing to discover Sally so different from the adoring wife he had left. He missed the melting softness with which her eyes used to meet his: the appeal of her mouth always ready to be kissed. There was no appeal about it now. All her features seemed to have taken a more definite line. And it did not suit her, really.

Sally was pretty only when she was laughing and lit up. She could not look solemn and tragic with that funny little snub nose; but there was no doubt she wished to impress him with the seriousness of what she had said. Was it possible Sally had ceased to care for him? That she would leave him if she pleased?

Morris could not contemplate such ideas. It amazed and shocked him to think Sally had spoken as if she might repudiate all wifely obligations towards him.

He would have been more amazed and shocked had he known what Sally was thinking as she sat beside him. Through her mind, gossip about Morris, of which she had caught fragments, at various times, reverberated.

'Damned shame to be taking that little woman out to Hannans. It's a rough camp. What Morrey calls the boarding house, a bunk-house with a couple of brush sheds.' That was Bill Fogarty talking.

And Mrs. Fogarty: 'What the blazes does he want her out there for? Why can't he leave her here with me?'

To which Bill had answered: 'What does any man want a woman for?'

'God damn his eyes——' Mrs. Fogarty's indignation crackled—— 'I'd like to have the handling of Mr. Fitz-Morris Gough.' Bill's reply was drowned in her gale of laughter.

Mrs. Fogarty began again: 'He's lookin' for trouble with Frisco floatin' about, and her the only good-lookin' woman nearer than the Rue de Lindsay, though Frisco's got a native girl hanging round his camp, I'm told.'

Alf's voice came muffled as though he were talking to Laura in the next room:

'Can't make Gough out, he's got breeding, manners and all the rest of it, but no scruples where money's concerned. Never dreams of paying a debt, or minds who he takes money from. Of course, up here we're pretty casual about borrowing and lending. It's the recognized thing if a man's got cash or credit, and another's broke, to fork out and trust the other fellow won't forget when his luck changes. A chap never knows when he may be in the same position, himself, and need a helping hand. But Morrey makes a welter of it—throws away any gold he's got, playing poker, rather than pay his debts. Dinny Quin, now he's one of nature's gentlemen. Never known him to do a mean thing. The drink's got him, of course, but I'd trust Dinny with my life —can't say the same for Morrey.'

All this Sally was thinking over, comparing with her talk to Morris, considering in relation to his attitude towards her, their life together and the illusions in which she had wrapped him. She did not doubt that she loved Morris. Her loyalty and devotion were unimpaired; but she was determined to take a more definite part in their affairs, so that they could hold up their heads: be worthy of some respect, even in this free and easy community.

Her meditation shifted to Frisco Jo Murphy. She had heard a good deal about Frisco, one way and another, and come to the conclusion that he was a 'bad man,' a gambler and a libertine. Not at all a good companion for Morris, though very popular with everybody. And there was Lili—

A smile fluttered about her mouth as Sally remembered how she had met Lili. How furious Morris would be if he knew about that! But it had happened so simply, so unexpectedly.

Looking away through the trees, flowing into infinity on every side, Sally could fancy she heard Lili singing in her light gay voice with a mournful cadence:

'Ma chandelle est morte,
Je n'ai pas de feu,
Ouvre moi ta porte
Pour l'amour de Dieu!

She glanced at Morris with a guilty feeling of having betrayed his confidence. That he should have something to forgive, inclined her to feel more forgiving towards him. Everybody made mistakes. It was impossible to be wise and cautious always. One must make allowances for differences of temperament which caused people to do inexplicable things.

She guessed how difficult it must have been for Morris to accommodate himself to life on the goldfields. He had done so in a way which surprised her, and yet in essentials he had not changed. Beneath his worn and dirty clothes, his beard and rough hair, he was still the Hon. Morris Fitz-Morris Gough, and expected her to remember it. Sally wished Morris could be on the same terms of easy friendliness with her, as he was with everybody else. But, evidently, it was not to be. She must treat him with becoming deference: allow him those dictatorial ways which he believed belonged to his birth and breeding, and to a husband who was several years older than his wife.

She thought desperation must have forced Morris to borrow and gamble. Of course, he would prefer to pay his debts; but cards had an irresistible fascination for Morris, it seemed. You could not blame him for seeking forgetfulness and a little distraction after hours of work in the broiling sun, long, lonely days prospecting in those grey distances along the horizon, and beyond, far and away beyond. What was there for men to do when they came in from dreary prospecting trips, or after working in the heat and the dust, all day, but drink or gamble? Morris was not a drunkard, thank goodness! She hoped she could persuade him not to gamble so much, or borrow money in the future.

He was still looking hurt and offended. Perhaps she had spoken too sharply. Of course, it was incredible that she could leave him! They were bound by so much more than the usual ties of husband and wife. They had been so much in love, and their marriage had been such a romantic affair: displeased both of their families. For a long time they had been cut off from all their relations.

There were obligations which bound her to Morris, Sally told herself, she could never forget. There were obligations, she thought, which bound Morris to her, he could not forget, although they might be pushed into the background of his consciousness for a time.

And yet, here they were sitting, side by side, silent and estranged, in this wilderness of trees and sky. So infinitesimal, they seemed, she and Morris, small dark animals, like ants, crawling on their way through the blinding light. Sally felt as if she were drowning in an unfathomable silence and solitude. She shrank against Morris, stricken with fear and an indefinable anguish.

Who else but Morris was there for her to cling to? Who to care for Morris in any disaster which might overtake him but herself? They two were alone in a world of strangers. Surely they could never forget all that bound them together?

Did Morris understand the panic which swept her, Sally wondered, as she gazed out over the grey unknown land before her. He said, on a gust of emotion:

'Swear to me, Sally, that you will not say such a thing again. That you will never leave me.'

'I swear it, Morris,' she murmured breathlessly. 'But you deserted me during the past few months.'

'You're the only person in the world I care about, Sally,' Morris replied, bitterly. 'How could I desert you? Up here, sometimes, a man loses himself. A dry rot sets in. He seems unable to throw off an apathy that acts like a drug. You'll understand, when you've been out-back longer.'

'I thought something like that was happening,' Sally said. 'That's why I came, Morris.'

CHAPTER XV

At sunset they drove towards a clutter of tents and bough sheds near the foot of a ridge broken by two or three bold hills. This was Hannans.

Brassy light painted the torn flank of the ridge and the mounds of rust-red and tawny earth. Here and there a windlass of bush timber stuck out against the clear sky, fading blue and green like clear water. Diggers were swarming about shacks on the main track, where a few tall, scraggy trees still stood: round the hotel, a ramshackle building of corrugated iron, and two or three stores built of scrap-iron and bags with brush-sheds alongside. Men were coming and going in a steady stream from a condenser further along the track. The smoke of camp fires, kindled to cook the evening meal, and the dust of dryblowing which had been going on all day, hung in the still air.

Morris pulled up before one of the stores. Some of the men standing about hailed him with lazy greetings and exclamations. They stared at the woman beside Morris, and strolled over to the buggy. Morris climbed down, handed out letters and newspapers, unloaded parcels of meat and vegetables, tools, and a pair of boots he had been commissioned to buy in Coolgardie.

He was bombarded for news of 'the old camp' and the Londonderry rush. As he gave it, diggers glanced curiously at Sally, sitting on the front seat of the buggy, dumb and unhappy at being ignored.

She was astounded that Morris did not introduce her to the diggers standing about, as Alf had introduced Laura at Coolgardie. Morris had made up his mind, she assumed, that she was not to be so friendly with the men on Hannans as she had been with everybody at Coolgardie.

A tall bearded man swung out from the store, his wide-brimmed felt hat, a certain swaggering grace and trimness distinguishing him in the crowd of men, unkempt and unwashed, their shirts and trousers red with dust, who surrounded Morris.

'Hullo, Morrey,' he called gaily, 'so you've brought the missus!'

His bold laughing glance flashed to Mrs. Gough, sitting in the buggy among her bundles.

'Welcome to Hannans, Mrs. Gough.' He lounged over towards her. 'I'd better introduce myself as Morrey's too busy to do the honours. Francisco Joséde Morfé, better known as Frisco Jo Murphy, at your service.'

93

He swept off his hat and bowed for the benefit of all observers.

'How do you do, Mr. de Morfé?' Sally replied.

'I do very well, ma'am,' Frisco mimicked her polite formality, though his eyes still laughed. He promised himself that this little lady would not always be so distant and dignified. He did not think much of her, sitting there looking tired and cross after her journey. She was no beauty, he considered, though she had fine eyes and a neat, sturdy figure.

'Guess you're dying for a cup of tea,' Frisco ventured shrewdly. 'I'll nick over to the camp and put on the billy.'

'Please do not bother.' Sally felt she was maintaining the matronly pose Morris expected of her.

Morris had disappeared into the store. He came out again and walked over to the buggy.

'So you brought your wife, after all, Morrey!' Frisco swung on Morris with a flash of derisive amusement. 'Thought you were going to leave her in Coolgardie.'

'Changed my mind,' Morris replied.

'I'll go along and straighten up the camp a bit,' Frisco volunteered, disregarding his ill-humour. 'How are we going to manage? I'll clear out, if you like, and Mrs. Gough can have my tent.'

'Thanks,' Morris did not sound grateful for the suggestion. 'I've fixed up with Mrs. Buggins to let us stay here for a while. There's a lean-to at the back of the shop we can have. It will be more comfortable for Mrs. Gough until I put up a shack for her.'

Frisco laughed. He perceived Morris was not welcoming friendly overtures towards his bright-eyed little pigeon. Installing her in the lean-to at the back of Buggins's store was a move to keep her out of his mate's way. There, old Monty and Ma Buggins were always on hand and could keep an eye on her. They ran a rough and ready dining-room in a shed made mostly of rusty kerosene tins, and there was a bunk house alongside.

'May I get down, now, Morris?' Mrs. Gough inquired.

'Wait, I'll help you,' Morris growled.

'No. I can manage.'

Sally passed her bulging handbag and two or three packages over the wheel to him, and Morris watched anxiously as she rose, turned her back and swung out her skirts. She stretched one leg to the buggy step and alighted nimbly, without exposing more than a slender ankle and one dusty black shoe to interested bystanders.

Morris looked quite pleased with her performance. He had dreaded perhaps, Sally thought, that her skirts would catch and she would make a display of legs and underclothing as she got out of the buggy. Morris insisted on carrying her bag and packages over to the store.

'But really,' Sally protested, 'they are not heavy!'

Frisco and several of the men grinned. They were tickled to death at the sight of Morrey Gough all uxorious importance.

Sally could not resist a smile and the flicker of a glance towards Mr. de Morfé as she followed Morris.

'Good evening,' she said primly.

Morris introduced his wife to the old couple who ran the store, and lived in it. The lean-to at the back was a shed of sapling posts covered with brushwood. Underneath its roof of dry leaves stood a dog-legged stretcher made of saplings and bags sewed together. There was a wooden box to sit on, but no other furniture. Morris promised to bring a rug from his camp and hang it over a rope across the entrance so that Sally might have a little privacy. She was to live here until Morris made other arrangements for her, Sally understood.

'What shall I do if it rains?' she queried, looking about her with dismay.

'Now for goodness sake don't start making trouble,' Morris replied testily. 'Though rain's never a trouble here. We don't get enough of it. I'll try to build a shack of some sort for you before it rains, anyhow.'

He went back to the buggy and brought in her tin trunk: said he must water his horses, turn them out for the night. Then Sally and he could go into the dining-room and get something to eat. Better to wait a bit: it was full of men now. He had warned Mrs. Buggins to keep them a bit of stew and boiled pudding.

Sally sat down on her tin trunk. She had a headache: felt tired and depressed.

'I only want a cup of tea,' she said wearily. 'Oh, Morris, why couldn't we have gone to your camp? I'd soon make it nice and tidy, and it would be more comfortable than to be stuck in this place with people about all the time. I could cook for you, and—'

'Allow me to know what is best for you on Hannans,' Morris replied coldly. 'You don't realize the scum of the earth is drifting about out here—and you're a woman.'

'But Morris,' Sally demurred, 'I was treated with the greatest respect in Coolgardie. Everybody says what fine men the prospectors are.'

'I know all that,' Morris frowned impatiently. 'You can't tell me anything I don't know about the goldfields, Sally. In the early days of Coolgardie that was so; but Hannans is different. It's a rougher mob here. The search for gold is more desperate —as time goes on it's bound to be like that with the riff-raff of the world pouring into the place. I wish to God you had stayed safe and sound at the 'Cross and not come after me up here.'

'You left me alone at the 'Cross for nearly two years,' Sally reminded him. 'Did you think I'd be safe and sound all that time?'

'Of course.'

'You never thought about it at all.'

'Oh, hang it all, Sally,' Morris flared, 'don't let's go over all that again. If you realized the tough times I've been through, you'd understand. I was out prospecting with Frisco for months at a time. Coming in once we nearly died of thirst—'

'Oh, Morris!'

'Listen, my dear,' Morris sat down on the box beside her. 'I've treated you badly. I know that. I should have written: should have gone back to the 'Cross to see how you were getting on. But this gold fever gets hold of a man: makes him do things he'd never dream of normally. We're a bit mad, all of us up here. We can't think or talk of anything but gold. After all, I've known hundreds of men pick up fortunes—and never had any decent luck. Oh, well, once, there was a share-out with Dinny Quin and Alf Brierly. But I bought camels and stores and went prospecting with Frisco, hoping to double what I'd got, and lost the lot. They say a man's only got to keep on prospecting and shovelling dirt to strike his. So some day I'll strike mine. Then we'll shake the dust of the goldfields off our feet, take a trip round the world—'

'It would be marvellous,' Sally breathed, following his dream.

'That's what I'm working for. That's what I want to do. Morris rose. He trembled in the throes of his repressed excitement. 'Go back to the old country; and live in comfort for the rest of our days. It's worth while to put up with hardships here, for awhile, isn't it, if in the end we can have money to play with? Show my old man that the prodigal sometimes comes back a millionaire and can redeem the family fortunes?'

'Oh, Morris!' Sally was dazzled by the prospect.

'Others have done it, why shouldn't I?'

Aglow with optimism, Morris looked years younger, vigorous and self-reliant.

'Here,' he said, 'look at this!' He pulled a wallet from his coat pocket and spread out a stiff paper. 'Shares in a new mine being opened up on Brookman's lease. An old miner, I know, says it's going to be one of the richest things on the fields.'

Sally glanced at the document he showed her. Morris folded it up and put it back in his wallet. He threw the wallet down on her tin trunk.

'Better put it away safely,' he said, with a glance at the door. 'You can't be too careful, these days.'

People were passing the open end of the shed all the time: miners and Afghans, surging in and out of the shop. A few gins came to look at the white missus: stood giggling and staring at her. Morris drove them away, shouting angrily, so that they scattered and fled like frightened birds. A boy hove out of the twilight, a weedy, ginger-haired lad, with a man's trousers hoisted over his legs, the remnants of a white shirt on his sunburnt body.

'Hey, Morrey,' he shouted, 'aren't you goin' to take your horses out to-night? They're lookin' tucked-up for a drop of water.'

'Take them over to the condenser, Paddy,' Morris called. 'I'll come along presently and fix up for the water.'

'This is Mrs. Gough,' he added. 'Paddy Cavan, Sally.'

'Pleased to meet you, ma'am!' The youngster gave a brisk neat little bow.

'You do anything you can for my wife, and you won't be the loser by it, Paddy,' Morris said.

'Shurre,' Paddy grinned. 'It'll be a pleasure to wait on the lady, Mr. Gough!'

'None of your cheek!' Morris called as Paddy whipped off.

'He's a smart kid,' he explained to Sally. 'Came up on the track with us—was cabin boy on an American sailing ship and deserted. Made his way to the 'Cross and out here. Has managed to keep himself by doing odd jobs. How, the Lord only knows—and Paddy doesn't care, so long as he can scrape together a few bob. But I must go and see the horses get some water. Young Paddy's quite capable of telling me he has watered them, and selling the water to somebody else.'

As Morris went out to the buggy, still standing in front of the store, Mrs. Buggins came into the lean-to with a mug of tea and thick slab of bread and butter on an enamel plate.

'Oh, thank you,' Sally said. 'I'm just dying for a cup of tea.'

'Don't thank me, thank Frisco,' Mrs. Buggins replied sourly. 'He made it worth me while. I haven't got time to be chasin' round after visitors.'

'It was very kind of him,' Sally murmured, sipping the hot strong tea, gratefully.

A middle-aged woman, tall, scraggy, with a squint in her washed-out grey eyes, buck teeth and a masterful air, Mrs. Buggins inspected her with disapprobation. Morris had said Ma

Buggins was a hard-doer, a good deal younger than her husband, bossed him and the business. Sally could believe it.

'If Morrey'd let us know you was comin', we could've fixed-up a tent for you, or the boys would've cleared out one of the shacks,' she grumbled.

'It doesn't matter,' Sally assured her. 'I'm used to camping out. And to-night, I could sleep anywhere. When I've had a good sleep, I'll be as fresh as a daisy.'

'Daisies don't flourish in these parts!' Ma Buggins snapped and strode away.

The poor woman was annoyed with Morris for dumping his wife on her, Sally thought. She was afraid, probably, of having a helpless and ailing female on her hands. That was why she had been so disagreeable. Sally promised herself to make friends with Mrs. Buggins, next day, and show her that she had no intention of airing ladylike graces on Hannans.

When she had finished drinking her tea, and eating the thick bread and butter Ma Buggins had brought, Sally sat on her trunk, looking out over the wide flat plains with their thick scrub under a clear green sky on which the first tinselly stars were glittering. She wondered at the fate which had driven Morris and her into this dreary, almost unexplored country.

Was it possible, that what Morris had said would some day come true? That they would strike gold—some of the vast stores of gold which this dark earth held—become rich and prosperous, travel round the world, visit his people 'in triumph,' as Morris said. It was almost unbelievable: sounded like a fairy tale. For other people, these things might happen; but for her and for Morris, Sally had a presentiment that good fortune would not come so easily.

Morris's optimism had betrayed her before, on the land and at the 'Cross. Here it might be different, she recognized. A man need not work very hard for his luck. He might stumble across it at any moment: break a rock that showed clots of gold and sell a claim for thousands of pounds. Then again there were hundreds of men who had left the fields after months of prospecting and dryblowing, convinced that the game was not worth the candle.

Sally had heard them say that the off-chance of making a fortune did not compensate for the hard and rough life a man had to lead to get it. Many men, too, put back into the ground, as they said, what they got out of it, spending money on camels and stores to go on a long prospecting trip, or sinking all they had to develop a mine. Already, Morris had been caught that way.

No, Sally told herself, she did not believe that she and Morris would shake the dust of the goldfields off their feet, very soon. She was prepared to make the best of things, become accustomed to living in a place like this; but she did hope Morris would take her soon to his own camp, or start building the shack about which he was talking. Meanwhile, it was absurd for him to think she could sit in this brushwood shed with idle hands. She must offer to help Mrs. Buggins as she had helped Mrs. Fogarty. To live on good terms with people one must share their work and interests. She had too much common sense, Sally assured herself, to play the lady with Ma Buggins.

When Morris came in with a lantern and rugs which he had brought from his camp, Sally was curled up on the stretcher, asleep. He hung a grey blanket on a rope across the entrance to the lean-to and wakened her to undress. She slipped off her clothes and put on a nightdress, surprised that Morris intended to sleep with her on that narrow bed. Morris threw off his clothes and stretched naked beside her under the dirty grey blanket.

CHAPTER XVI

LONG after Morris had fallen asleep, Sally lay awake, watching the crisp glitter of stars through gaps in dry leafy branches of the lean-to.

She was incensed that Morris could have behaved with so little decency. He had flung himself upon her while men kept passing only a few yards away. She could hear their guffaws and jokes about 'Morrey turning-in early' as if they were in the same room. It was humiliating for Morris to have been such a boor and exposed her to the lewd gossip of the camp.

Of course, she had longed to be folded in his arms and to find all the differences and bitterness between them swept away. Their reconciliation on the track had given her a sweet sense of peace and security. All that was broken now, and she had hoped that their re-union might be a second honeymoon.

Morris had been like a god in his first love-making; filled her with delight. Her whole being had thrilled to his touch. During those long months when she had been alone at the 'Cross, she had ached for him with a restless, terrifying desire. But this crude, vicious copulation meant nothing to her. It was an outrage he had committed against their love. Never again, Sally told herself, would she allow Morris to abuse their relationship in this way.

In the morning, she said firmly: 'I will not live in this wretched place, Morris. You must show me your tent and I'll arrange our things there.'

'Very well,' Morris agreed shamefacedly. 'But stay here, a day or two, until I can shift camp: pitch our tent out in the scrub a bit.'

At breakfast in Ma Buggins' dining-room, Sally made it clear she did not intend to respect Morris's wishes about being dignified and aloof on Hannans. She contrived to talk to men about her at the table; was interested in news of the field and passed on some information about the Londonderry rush.

Afterwards, she stopped at the kitchen door to say good-morning to Mrs. Buggins, assure her she had slept well and was thoroughly refreshed.

'If there's anything I can do for you,' Sally exclaimed cheerily, 'I'll be so pleased. I'm not used to being idle. And it will be nice to have something to do while Morris is at work.'

Mrs. Buggins invariably started the day with a sore head and a bad temper. She wondered what Mrs. Gough was getting at.

'You mind your own business,' she said sourly. 'And I'll mind mine.'

Sally wilted before her hostile gaze.

'There now,' Morris remarked, as he took Sally back to the lean-to. 'You can't say I didn't warn you what to expect if you will be so officious. Ma Buggins doesn't understand why you want to be sociable and a good sort.'

'But Morris,' Sally sat down on the stretcher, 'She must be a very ill-natured woman. Why shouldn't I want to help her?'

Morris smiled. 'Ma Buggins was the only woman on Hannans for a while and she's jealous of any other woman butting in on her, I suppose. Not above doing a line with the boys, now and then.'

'Oh!' Sally was horrified.

'Frisco says there's many a good tune played on an old fiddle, and I daresay he knows what he's talking about.' Morris rammed on his hat. 'But I can't stay here talking: must get along and shovel a bit of dirt.'

'I'll walk along with you. Can't sit here all day,' Sally said eagerly.

'Where's my wallet?' He glanced about him: felt in his coat pocket.

'Your wallet?' Sally queried, trying to remember what he had said to her about a wallet.

Morris stooped over the trunk: threw out the clothes. Sally searched. They turned over everything in the shed: hunted all over the ground for the wallet, but could not find it.

'I gave it to you to mind. Told you there was a fortune in those shares,' Morris stormed.

'Oh, Morris,' Sally wailed. 'I didn't touch the wallet. You threw it down on the trunk, yourself.'

'I told you to put it away safely,' Morris shouted. 'Didn't I tell you this place isn't the 'Cross or Coolgardie? You've got to watch your boots here, or somebody'll steal them. My God, if this mine turns out like Zeb Lane expects, I'll never forgive you.'

Almost in tears, Sally protested:

'If it is my fault, I'm sorry, Morris, but—'

Morris dashed out of the shed.

Sally heard him shouting in the store: old Monty and Mrs. Buggins shouting angrily back at him.

Mrs. Buggins came to the back door.

'Y'r can pack y'r traps and clear out,' she yelled. 'If you think I'm goin' to be called a thief to me face, y're bloody well mistaken, Mr. Gough. Get out—you and y'r lady wife. Comin' and puttin' it over decent people with y'r God-a'mighty airs! Been robbed, have y'r? Serves y'r right, if y'r ask me. Been robbin' us right and left for long enough. Never payin' a penny off y'r score and hoardin' gold. The boys ought to run yer out of the camp fer a lousy speilin' bastard. That's what they ought to do.'

'I just told you someone had pinched my wallet. Didn't suggest you had anything to do with it,' Morris explained, his rage abating before the storm it had brought about his head. 'There was no gold in it. Only a little money and—some shares.'

'Shares!' Ma Buggins screamed. 'Y'r didn't need money to buy shares, I suppose? But you couldn't pay me what y'r owed me for meals this last month. No. Y'r must go traipsin' off to Coolgardie and bring this hussy back with y'r. No better than she ought to be from the looks of her. You don't tell me any decent woman'd take up with a shyster like you, Morrey Gough!'

'Keep your tongue off my wife,' Morris said.

'Shut up,' old Monty growled. 'The lady ain't done nothin' to you.'

'Give it a bone, Ma!' a man's voice sang out, mocking and masterly. Sally knew it was Frisco's.

Several men followed Morris into the yard.

'Get out,' Ma Buggins yelled in a frenzy, 'and take that slut with yer! Y'r can turn out the place, boys, if y' think Monty or me had anything to do with his blasted wallet. I'm not standin'

for who ever took it. You can string him up for all I care—
starting this sort of a brawl on me. There ain't no man been
robbed in this store. And you chaps know it. I give you a fair
deal and a fair deal's all I'm asking for. But him—the lousy
bastard—that Gough, comin' here, and makin' a scene as if we
was to blame for him losin' his bloody wallet—the sooner he
makes tracks, the better pleased I'll be.'

Sally was trembling when Morris came into the shed. He
looked shaken and shamed by Mrs. Buggins' outburst.

'Pack up,' he said grimly. 'We're going over to the camp.'

Sally threw into her trunk the few things she had taken out
the night before. Morris folded his blankets. She put on her
dust coat and hat: picked up her handbag and parcels, and went
out into the bright sunshine.

Two or three men were standing near the shed talking over
what had occurred. She noticed Frisco and Paddy Cavan with
them.

'You don't have to worry about the shares, Morrey,' one of the
men remarked. 'All you have to do is notify the company you've
lost 'em. We'll start makin' inquiries who's been hangin' round
the yard, this mornin', and have a roll-up when we catch the
thief.'

'Where've you been, Young Paddy?' Frisco asked.

'Gee, Frisco!' the kid bristled indignantly. 'You wouldn't be
tryin' to fasten anything like this on to me? We was mates on
the track, me and Morrey. I wouldn't be doin' a dirty trick on
him. Besides, I took his horses over to Cassidy's last night, and
haven't been around this mornin'.'

'Well, keep y'r ears open, and let us know, if you hear anything,' Morrey said.

He was heaving Sally's tin trunk on to his shoulders when
Paddy darted forward.

'Shurre, I'll carry that fer y'r, Morrey,' he cried.

Morris relinquished the trunk with considerable relief. He
was walking away carrying his blankets, and Sally's parcels,
when Mrs. Buggins appeared again at the back of the store.

'How about settlin' up with me, before you go, Mr. Gough?'
she yelled. 'It's about fifty pound you owe me for meals and
stores.'

Morrey stood looking back at her, helplessly.

'All the cash I had was in my wallet,' he said.

Sally felt that she ought to defend him.

'I will see you get all the money we owe you, Mrs. Buggins,'
she said. 'I have never owed anybody a penny in my life.'

Ma Buggins' laughter cackled maliciously.

'Oh, yes?' she said. 'You'll make money, easy, I daresay. But I want a bit er spot cash.'

'You can't get what we haven't got,' Morris said.

Frisco strode forward, yanking a shammy leather bag from his belt.

'Come on, weigh-up and shut your mouth,' he shouted impatiently.

'The grass doesn't grow under your feet, Frisco,' Ma Buggins shrilled. ' 'Ope y'r get y'r money's worth.'

Sally's cheeks burned: her eyes sparkled with anger as she walked away beside Morris. She was glad to turn her back on the store and that evil-minded woman. Morris threaded his way among tents and shafts towards the hills behind the main track; but he was walking too quickly for Sally to keep up with him. She fell behind with Paddy who was stumbling along, her heavy trunk on his shoulders.

When Frisco caught up to them, she could not look at him, but murmured quickly: 'Thank you, Mr. de Morfé. My husband will repay you as soon as possible.'

'Don't worry about that, Mrs. Gough,' Frisco replied easily. 'Morrey'd do the same for me. If you've got gold, up here, and a mate hasn't, it's his if he wants it.'

He walked on and joined Morris.

Sally was as grateful for that as his assistance in placating Ma Buggins.

Young Paddy stopped for breath, and gazed after Frisco.

'Gosh, he's never short of a bit of gold, Frisco,' he gasped admiringly. 'We'll be the biggest men on the fields, him and me, one of these days, missus!'

CHAPTER XVII

Camps were scattered over the flat and along the back of the ridge, west towards the Great Boulder, and to the north end, beyond Hannans Reward as far as the broad bold slopes of Mount Charlotte. Morris and Frisco had pitched their tents in a row at the foot of Maritana, the steep hill which rose covered with small prickly scrub and grey furry bushes, mauve flowered, to thrust a blunt peak against the blue sky.

Tents, dust-stained and tawny, tents of bags sewed together, shelters of bags and rusty kerosene tins flattened out and nailed over a framework of saplings, and brushwood sheds spread everywhere through a scrub of thin spindling trees, with a frazzle of twigs at the top and a cap of dark leaves. Here and there a small thorny bush in blossom clotted the earth with pure gold.

Shakers rattled and a fume of red dust rose from the alluvial claims all day. Men moved along the ridge like strange sluggish insects working about the shafts, hauling dirt, opening up new ground. Windlasses squeaked. The drone and rattle of stones being thrown on the dumps, the rush of falling earth, went on monotonously, breaking the mysterious quiet of the surrounding country. Now and then a man's voice calling to his mate rang out like a song in the clear air. A crow ka-kaaed from deep blue of the sky, his note harsh and sinister, reminding everybody of the long summer when he would pick the bones of men who perished of thirst out there in the mulga, beyond the horizon.

It was very cold at night still. A dry bitter cold made the stars glitter like diamonds, and drove Sally early to bed. There was a thick rime of frost on the ground sometimes when she got up at dawn to light the fire and make Morris's breakfast. In an hour or two the bright sunshine warmed her blood; but sometimes an icy blast blew over the plains all day, and piercing the tent at night, made her teeth chatter under the blankets.

But she liked living in a tent, Sally told Morris. It was much pleasanter than running a boarding house, sweeping, scrubbing, cooking and washing dishes all day. What a dull weary business that had been! When one lived in a tent there was not much to do. A little tidying and straightening-up, that was all. It was easy enough to cook by an open fire and brush the earth round the camp with a broom of twigs, when the weather was good.

To be sure there were drawbacks. No washtubs, or cupboards, or closet. She had to walk off into the bush and make a little hole in the sand like a cat when it was necessary. And men tramped past the tent all day. Morris warned her to wash and undress with care behind its canvas wall, particularly at night when the kerosene lantern made a shadow play of every movement. But as yet it was winter. Dust, ants and flies not a serious complication to domestic arrangements. The days were all brilliant sunshine and blue skies, though the nights cold.

Flames crackled over the brushwood Sally had gathered the night before and stored in a tin box to start the fire in the morning, though often a log was still smouldering on the fireplace. All she had to do then was rake the embers together and pile on dry sticks. It was good to warm herself by their blaze, smell the fragrant smoke in the clear morning air and hear the birds calling. As she toasted stale damper, made porridge, and watched bacon frizzling in the pan, she was proud and happy to think she could give Morris a good meal before he started work. She cooked for him again at midday and in the evening.

Morris joked about the miracles she accomplished with tinned dog, a few onions and bits of bacon. Fresh meat was a luxury, vegetables, even in tins, rarely procurable, but Sally could make an appetizing soup or savoury hotpot from anything, Morris declared. She never plucked up sufficient courage to visit Ma Buggins' store, but made frequent excursions to the other store to buy groceries. A bottle of tomato sauce and a small tin of dried herbs were treasure trove.

Morris boasted that he could make better damper. It was true, Sally admitted. Morris made delicious damper, as crisp and light as baker's bread. She had to learn from him how to mix the flour and water with her hand, knead the dough quickly, stow a big scone away in the camp oven, and bed it down in the fire with a handful of embers on the lid. Frisco took breakfast and a midday dinner with Morris as he had been accustomed to, at first; but went off to Ma Buggins' for his evening meal.

It was an easy go-as-you-please existence. There was time to do everything in a casual, leisurely way as if nothing mattered very much, as indeed it did not, except to find gold and ensure supplies of food and water.

Sally left Morris to arrange for them. She was satisfied to enjoy the tranquil lethargy that had taken possession of her: sit gazing at the sky for hours or watch the men at work on the ridge.

She was amazed at the way Morris worked. He went off with his pick and shovel, soon after dawn, and came back from the claim during the late afternoon, red with dust: did not care how old and dirty his clothes were, or bother to change more than once a week.

Sally was conscious of a new respect for Morris: something that went deeper than the attachment which had thrown them together. She could forgive his neglect of her for so long, now that she saw how he lived. Even his carelessness about money seemed not to matter so much. It was part of a scheme of things shorn of all but the essentials of living and the search for gold. She understood better the lust for gold which obsessed and drove men.

Gold! Gold! Gold!

Nobody talked of anything else. Nobody thought of anything else. Gold was the centre of all activity. The life of the community depended on it. Every man dreamed of the fabulous wealth that one day would be his. Happy-go-lucky and dust-grimed miners and prospectors toiled and went short of food, rather than forfeit their hope of gold and a glorious future. Only the crows kaa-ed a warning through those bright spring days.

Men who understood it, hated them. Unk Tregurtha, an old Cornishman who had nearly done a perish out in the bush and lost a mate on the track, could not bear the sight of them: would take his rifle and blaze away, if the crows came flapping down from trees near his tent for a scrap of offal.

As the mild sunshiny days went on with unclouded skies and clear frosty nights, many men glanced upwards, cursing anxiously. Rain was needed. There had been a bad shortage of water last summer on Hannans, Morris explained. Every week, now, hundreds of prospectors, speculators and business men, with their horses and camels, were flocking to the field, and water would soon be a serious problem if there was not a good fall of rain.

For a day or two an icy blast whirled over the plains, driving a torn and dirty fleece of clouds before it. Then a tempestuous shower fell. The men shouted with joy. They capered about like lunatics, laughing and shouting boisterously. But how to cook by an open fire in the rain, Sally did not know.

Frisco rigged some pieces of kerosene tin over the fire and planted a sheet of corrugated iron along the back of the fireplace for a break-wind. Where he got the iron, nobody knew. Corrugated iron was almost as precious as gold on Hannans then. It was marvellous how Frisco could always obtain what he wanted.

'Beg, borrow, or steal, it's all the same to me, ma'am, so long as I get what I'm after,' he explained gaily.

Sally carried her cooking pots into the tent and Morris and she ate in their overcoats. Now and then, men dropped in as they passed to exclaim about the downpour. Drenched to the skin but in high spirits, they prophesied a good season, and the prospect of Hannans supporting as big a population as Coolgardie.

All night it rained, and huddled up under a 'possum skin rug, Sally lay listening to the rain beat against and drip through the roof of the tent. She was snug and warm and Morris snored peacefully beside her. She wondered that she could feel so happy and content: whether ever again she would be so happy and content, even if Morris sold the lease he and Frisco were working on, and they became quite rich; never again had any financial anxieties.

There were discomforts in this primitive way of life. Sally did not deceive herself. She would not always be satisfied to live in a tent and never take a bath. But for the time being, she could accept the days as they came and not worry. It was disquieting that Morris had heard nothing about his wallet. She did not know how he was paying his way. Of course, he shared with Frisco whatever gold their show produced, but Morris said that was not much. They wanted to sell their lease, or raise money to buy machinery. Other mines were doing well on the field, Cassidy's, the Maritana, Midas, Croesus, and Lake View and Star, and there were sensational rumours about the Great Boulder.

But of what use to fret about these matters? She must live as everybody else did on a mining camp. Like the birds that were picking up a meal as best they could, and not bothering about anything else. To be chirpy and resigned to the luck of the day was all anybody expected of you. Sally thought she was settling down to doing that, too easily, perhaps.

In the morning the rain had vanished. There were shining pools on the red earth. Mud clogged the men's boots and spattered their clothes. Wet blankets, trousers and shirts, were hung out on the bushes and tent stays to dry. They steamed in a brilliant sunshine. But everybody was still greedy for rain: not so pleased to see the clouds sweeping away inland.

'Nice morning for specking!' Morris pointed to men crawling along flanks of the ridge and out over the plain.

'I'll go specking, too,' Sally said.

She had seen men, women and children, at the 'Cross after rain, searching for small slugs. Usually, it took experienced eyes to single out lumps of gold from the dust-stained iron and sandstone pebbles thrown out on the dumps or scattered over the ground. But rain washed the dust off and the glint of gold might reward any mug on a morning like this.

Sally blamed the native cuckoo when she had no luck. Its long plaintive note came from the distant scrub, as if it were calling back the rain. The rain bird, the men called it, and Sally trailed it through the scrub hoping to catch a glimpse of this friend of her childhood. Even a few yards from the sprawling camps and scarred earth about them, the scrub was thick: here and there a tall salmon gum standing with coral stained column among the spindling snap and rattle, dwarf sandalwood and grey-leafed mulga.

Patches of herbage lay vivid green against the red earth, and thorn bushes were hung with downy yellow bobbles. Flocks of little green parrots flashed through the trees with a shrill sweet chattering. Fly-catching fan-tails in neat black and white suits danced crazily among the bushes, flirting their tails and snapping at midges. It was difficult to keep one's eyes on the ground, when the bush was so lovely that morning, and the birds so spritely and amusing.

But Sally did try looking for a nice little nugget. It would have been so exciting to find just the smallest and take it to Morris. She picked a big bunch of the thorn blossom and took that back to the camp instead.

'See,' she cried happily, when Morris came in at midday. 'I found lots of gold, Morris.'

Paddy Cavan had specked ten ounces within a stone's-throw of the camp, Morris said.

'Little devil,' he growled. 'Not the first time he's picked up a fat slug! What the hell does he do with his gold, though? That's what I'd like to know. Never seems to have a rag to his back and always cadging tucker.'

'Search me!' Frisco laughed. 'He's a shrewd 'un, young Paddy. Will be buyin' and sellin' us all one of these days.'

Every evening men strolled along to yarn to Frisco and Morris beside the camp fire. There was nothing Sally liked better than to sit on a box by the fire and listen to gossip of the fields. The firelight flared on rough rakish figures. All earth-stained and weather-beaten, they stood easily in groups, smoking and yarning, squatted on the ground, or sat on boxes. The ruddy glow caught faces full-blown, sun-scalded and bearded, or lean, brown and hard. Here the beak of a nose, there a crop of grey hair on end, a loose laughing mouth broken by barcoo, brawny arms, great gnarled hands, glittering eyes, broken boots.

Waistcoats, or coats, were slung over cotton shirts and grey flannels, sometimes two or three of them, with faded blue dungarees, worn moleskins or decayed tweed trousers strapped round a man's middle. His shammy hung there on his belt, to carry money or loose gold: his tin matchbox or tinder box was clipped on too. If he wasn't smoking, his pipe was stuck through the belt. His hat, a dilapidated felt, rarely left his head. There was nothing like an old felt to warm a man's brains in winter, and ward off a touch of the sun in summer, Frisco said.

'Hear the teams 're bogged all along the road from the 'Cross,' someone would remark.

Other voices cut in and carried on: 'There's been no rain outback—unless they got something out of the squall last week. Camels been carting water fifty miles to Siberia—'

'They say a reward claim's been applied for at Mount Margaret, out Lake Carey way, two hundred miles from the old camp. Thick scrub country. No water. One of Billy King's mates died on the track. The blacks're a bad lot round Lake Carey, speared Sandy Mac's horses. He and his party near done a perish: was three days without water when a camel team picked 'em up and took 'em on into the Ninety Mile.'

'What's this about Hobson's Hotel on the old Coolgardie road bein' burnt down—just after the gold escort got away?'

'It's a fact!'

'Gosh, somebody'll be kickin' himself—'

'Did y'r hear, Cassidy's Hill been floated in London for seven thousand pounds?'

'Nothin' to get excited about. Lord Fingal's payin' one hundred and eighty thousand pounds for the Londonderry.'

'Lake View and Ivanhoe battery's jest about ready to start operatin', Charley de Rose reckons.'

'Well, it took some doin'—cartin' that machinery up from the 'Cross. They brought a team of draughts over from Adelaide to do the job. The track was closed owing to the water shortage. Charley had to send fodder and water all the way along.'

'And now he's sore because the miners want a bit of feedin' up!'

'You bet they do. We're on strike for a rise of ten bob a week. Y' don't reckon three pound ten a fair wage for men workin' underground, what with the price of food and water on Hannans, do y'r, Sam?'

'Not me. Not on your life, Ted. Blunt Pick and me, we're not wages men. It'd take more 'n a lousy four quid to make us work on another man's mine.'

'Easy seen you haven't got a wife and kids to feed.'

'Not yet, but y'r never know when Blunt Pick'll be askin' Jiggledy Jane to name the day.'

A gust of laughter would drown Blunt Pick's cursing.

So the yarning went with a lazy desultory flow, sometimes warming to a heated argument; but fading out as the fire died down, and the men went off to the pubs, or decided it was time to turn in.

CHAPTER XVIII

SEVERAL of the men working alluvial claims nearby, or miners from Cassidy's and the open cut on Maritana, Sally knew quite well. They gave her a sheepish, respectful 'Good evening, Missus,' as they passed, or dropped into the circle about the fire.

There were Eli Nancarrow and his mate Parson Jarn, Sam Mullet, Blunt Pick Brown, Dynamite Dow and Yank Boteral, Camel Thompson, Dancing Dan O'Sullivan and Tassy Regan, as well as Big Jim. the Queensland drover. his mate Clary McClaren. and Unk Tregurtha. an old Cornishman with a square frill of fuzzy grey hair round his chin.

Eli and Parson Jarn were Cornishmen. too: shrewd. spare men who had a good claim on Brown Hill. Parson Jarn had been a lay preacher in the old country. 'Until the drink got him,' Unk said. Eli had stood by him in his disgrace and brought him out here to Australia. They were rarely seen apart: but all the Cornishmen stuck together on the fields.

Sam Mullet had a grand name. It was Samuel Wordsworth Mullet he reminded everybody when he was drunk; but Sam was a solid, solemn little man. not given to boozing, or talking over much. Usually he seemed to be wrapped in meditation: when he spoke had something to say worth listening to. Blunt Pick, his mate, could be depended on to do enough talking for both: was a wiry, energetic, garrulous man, with a shrill, squeaky voice, one eye and a broken nose. It was a blunt pick had saved his life in a brawl. he used to explain, 'and smashed up his handsome dial.' He was 'real grateful to that blunt pick!' Nobody bothered about the rest of his name.

Dan O'Sullivan. the big Irishman. with his full-blown, sun-scalded face and boisterous vitality, rushed in and out of the camp, always bursting with excitement. Camel Thompson came and went, square-cut and uncommunicative. a gleam in his iron-grey eyes giving a hint of how he worked camels and had weathered many a prospecting trip in dry country when other men would have perished. Yank Boteral looked like an American Indian: was tall and handsome with sleek black hair and black eyes. But had fought the Indians with Colonel Cody, he said: been a circus rider and had a sister in a nunnery. He and Frisco had known each other a long time: worked together on other fields, but Yank and Teddy Dow were mates now and getting good gold on their block south of Cassidy's.

The group was always changing, men coming in from a prospecting trip, or going off to rushes hundreds of miles away. Some like Eli Nancarrow and Parson Jarn, Sam Mullet and Blunt Pick, had taken up mining leases and were satisfied with their prospects on Hannans.

Sam and Blunt Pick could never get over the fact that they might have had the reward claim on the ridge. if they had prospected round when they were going out with the rush to Mount Youle. Blunt Pick was always willing to turn on the tale.

'There was me and a couple of hundred mugs, goin' off with teams and stores to look for a mountain of gold,' he would groan, and walkin' away from the best field in the country. First night out we camped near the Ninety Mile rocks. Tom Flannigan, Paddy Hannan and Dan Shea came in and wanted to know per-ticlers of the rush. They'd been out prospectin' and struck the old camp jest after we left. Grabbed four horses runnin' in the bush and came on after us. No foot sloggin' for them. They rode on ahead. We was camped on the flat here, a day or two later, havin' a game of nap in the evenin', when Paddy come back. Said his water bag had sprung a leak, he and his mates were short of water. He was goin' back to fill up at the Ninety Mile. We pushed on, never guessin' what had happened. Dan Shea says it was Flannigan picked up the first gold near Mount Charlotte—a small slug and some nice specimens.

'Dan says he liked the look of the country. "Never knew them sugar-loaf hills fail for gold," he says he told Paddy Hannan. Paddy decided to camp and do a bit of prospecting. Flannigan and Paddy Hannan went off lookin' for water, struck a soak a few miles further on, but didn't get more than a quart out of it. Paddy went back on his tracks towards Coolgardie, but it rained that night, and next morning when Paddy got back to camp Flannigan showed him a handful of gold he'd picked up in the gully there beside Maritana.

' "Plenty more where it come from," he says. He'd thrown a bush over the spot and gone off, so as not to arouse suspicions by speckin' around. There was still a few of us down on the flat, me and Sam among them. But we never tumbled why Paddy and his mates wasn't in a hurry to move on.

'They waited till we was out of sight before gettin' to work. Then shifted camp and pegged three men's ground. Got ninety-four ounces right away. Started dryblowin' and treatin' dirt. Paddy Hannan went off to apply for a reward claim. While he was away his mates picked up another hundred ounces—and there was me and Sam bustin' our guts to get to Mount Youle. We never seen colours on that trek, got wind of Paddy Hannan's reward on our way back, and Gord, did we whip the cat! It was the chance of a lifetime we missed, not prospectin' along the ridge here, before Paddy Hannan and his mates pegged.'

'There's some blokes has all the luck,' Sam mourned.

'Luck, be blowed,' Big Jim liked to say. 'I reckon they was good prospectors and you wasn't, not to keep your eyes open.'

Blunt Pick agreed. 'We was caught nappin'. But there's a lot of luck in the way some mugs 'll stumble on gold, and a good prospector walk over it.'

'That's how it was on the I.O.U.' Clary McClaren's lazy drawl might be heard as he smoked thoughtfully. 'Jack Mohr and his mates sunk a shaft and put in a lot of work on a reef there.

Decided she was a duffer, after a bit: pulled pegs and cleared out. Couple of months later, along comes an old moocher, drops his swag and starts to boil his billy. Sees a glim in one of the big rocks Jack'd rolled for a wind-break. Has a crack at it— and there she is, rich as blazes! He comes in with specimens, gets a syndicate together. They apply for a lease and sell for eighty thousand pounds.'

'God A'mighty!'

'Can y'r beat it?'

'That's the way she goes!'

Every man could see himself in Jack Mohr's shoes, or the old moocher's, cursing, or celebrating his luck.

'I'm not sayin' there's not a lot of luck in the game,' Big Jim maintained. 'But I'll back a good prospector to strike his sooner or later, if he keeps his nose to the ground and hangs on long enough.'

'Where she be, there she be,' Unk declared mournfully. 'And where she be, there baint I.'

The men's laughter streeled far out over the starlit plains. Harsh, resonant, derisive, with boisterous good humour, the voices clattered:

'Stick to 'er, Unk!'

'You'll strike her yet!'

'Be a rich man before you die. . . .'

'Like the rest of us.'

It was Bill Jehosaphat who came in from Kurnalpi with news of a sensational roll-up there.

'There was a snoozer, name of Winterbottom, had a show out be Merton's Gully,' he said. 'His mate was young Johnny Bull. They wasn't doing too well, but that old bumfreezer made out to Johnny he was sharin' equal. He started sneakin' a bit of gold over to the storekeeper: got eighty pound off of him for one slug and sent the money to his wife in Adelaide. Talks to Bull about slingin' the claim, because they was only makin' tucker, and gettin' a new mate.'

Bill paused for breath and dramatic effect: turned aside to blow his nose, grabbing it with a finger and thumb: wiped off the drips with a hairy forearm, and continued:

'The storekeeper smelt a rat. Tells Bull about that slug. Bull tackles Bum and the old skunk says Bull's been loafin' on the job, and he's not goin' to part up on the slug.'

The men muttered and swore indignantly. This was a crime. It struck at the fundamental principle of life on the goldfields, loyalty to a mate.

'There's about two thousand men on Kurnalpi, and you never

see such a mob as came along when we rattled the dishes for a roll-up. The boys was dancin' mad when they heard Bull's story.

'Well, they elected a judge and were the jury same as usual. Made Winterbottom stand in a buggy with a halter round his neck and the end swung over a rail stickin' out from the store. Some of 'em were so wrought-up they near pulled the rope on Bum when he pleaded "Not Guilty." The storekeeper and the man Bum'd been tryin' to get for partner gave evidence. The judge summed-up and asked the boys for their verdict.

' "Guilty!"

' "Guilty as Hell," we yelled. Every hand went up on the vote.

'And some of the hot heads shouted:

' "Hang him!"

' "Hang the bastard!"

'Great jumpin' Jehosaphat, y'r never seen a mob so worked-up at a roll-up! They rushed the cart Winterbottom was standin' on, and if they'd got hold of him, they'd 've strangled him alright. He was shakin' all over. Looked like his own ghost. And, by God, he'd been a ghost by now, if some of us had'n of got round that cart and made the boys listen to reason.

'There was a free fight for a while, then Ed. Joshua and Johnny Marshall got up and made them listen to reason. There'd never been a lynching on these fields, they said. We'd always been proud of diggers' justice. Did'n want to get a bad reputation on Kurnalpi. After a bit things quietened down. It was agreed Winterbottom had to hand out what he owed young Bull. Then the boys marched him off the camp with twenty-four hours' water and ration for the track, booin' and jeerin' so as you could hear them miles away.

'It'll be a long time,' Bill concluded with grim satisfaction, 'before anybody tries takin' his mate down on Kurnalpi again.'

Bill was going on into Coolgardie, to buy camels for a prospecting trip he and Speck intended to make north-east of Kurnalpi. But before he left, the camp was buzzing with the news that Jack Dunn had struck a reef, fifteen miles nor'-west of the Forty-Five Mile.

'Rich as the Londonderry, they say,' Bill chortled. 'Lumps of gold stickin' out all over her.'

He and Speck were making tracks for Dunn's Find right away. Packed their swags and went off to buy stores. Big Jim and Clary McClaren went out into the bush after their camels. Geordie James, Dynamite, and half a dozen other miners on strike, lost no time rolling their swags and getting ready to follow Speck and Bill. Morris fretted and fumed to join the rush, but Frisco was against it. The ground would be pegged for miles before they could get anywhere near it, he said, and they had to man their own lease. Jumping of leases was becoming a popular pastime. Warden Finnerty had heard a hundred cases recently, and a lease on Hannans was going to be worth more than a pothole on one of these flash-in-the-pan rushes.

Two or three nights later, a rumour of trouble on Dunn's Find was being discussed: of alluvial diggers rushing the lease and Jack Dunn flourishing firearms, bringing troopers to protect his property.

'Who the hell does Jack Dunn think he is?' the men demanded. 'Doesn't he know the mining laws? An alluvial digger's within his rights pegging to within twenty feet of the reef.'

Eli spat and smoked thoughtfully.

'But if some of these new choom diggers started samplin' reef —like Trooper Ryan says they were at—Jack Dunn was within his rights clearin' 'em off. By goom, if they come samplin' reef of mine, I'd bring out me bluderbus, too, and let 'em have summat to go on with—though thikky gun baint much use since Jarn blew barl out o' she.'

'That's alright,' Blunt Pick declared. 'But for why did Jack Dunn want to bring the police in on a diggers' rumpus? A roll-up 'd 've straightened things out and given Jack his dues.'

Sometimes Frisco would bring out his big steel guitar and start bawling a popular song. The men picked up the chorus, one after another the voices joining in, hoarse, harsh and melancholy, or flung out with boisterous vitality. Someone would call for Mullocky O'Dwyer to sing 'The Wearing of the Green.' Parson Jarn tune up with 'Shall We Gather at the River,' and the men carry on to a version of their own. Eli might break the silence that followed with a comic item in his cracked falsetto, or Frisco rattle off an interminable Mexican ditty with a lively refrain. He sang ribald chanties and airs from the operas, twanging out any sort of noise as an accompaniment.

Frisco's guitar strumming drove Morris nearly crazy. There was nothing he dreaded more than to see Frisco sit down to make a good fellow of himself and jangle away on that clumsy instrument which he boasted of having carted all round the world with him.

'But, Morris,' Sally protested, 'it's nice to have a little music round the camp fire, sometimes.'

'Music?' Morris howled. 'Do you call that row music? It makes me feel murderous.'

'Oh, well, the men like it,' Sally laughed. 'And so do I.'

Morris sat with nerves on edge, listening to Frisco's crashing discords, haphazard jingling and jangling on his guitar to a bawling of popular melodies mostly out of tune. It added to his exasperation to watch Sally applauding Frisco's performance, clapping her hands, laughing at any joke, and joining in the singing. Morris did not approve either of the way she talked to the men, addressing them by their nicknames and indulging in a mild badinage. They were beginning to lose their diffidence and to chat to her: refer to her as 'the little missus,' or 'Missus Sally.'

'You must refrain from hobnobbing with every Tom, Dick and Harry on the fields, Sally,' he said, irritably, after one of these sing-songs round the camp fire.

'Hobnobbing?' Sally raised her eyebrows. 'What exactly do you mean by that, Morris?'

'Well—' Morris had some difficulty in explaining exactly what he did mean. 'You must not be so free and easy in your manner.'

Sally's eyes lit-up as they held him with their direct gaze.

'Am I free and easy in my manner?'

'You address the men by their nicknames.' Morris replied uneasily.

'But I don't know their names—except the ones I hear you use, Morris. Parson Jarn, for instance, what's his other name?'

'I don't know,' Morris admitted grudgingly. 'But it's unseemly for you to sing and smile, and . . .'

'Unseemly to sing and smile?' Sally queried.

'. . . be so jolly with the men.' Morris added. 'On a mining camp. Yes. Your reputation won't be worth a straw, before long.'

'My reputation?' Sally's eyes sparkled to her anger. 'You should worry more about your own reputation, Morris.'

'Sally!' Morris looked hurt and deflated.

'Darling!' Sally's most beguiling smile glimmered. 'I'm sorry! But don't talk to me any more about hobnobbing. We must live on good terms with people here. Be as kind and friendly as they are. And as to unseemly behaviour—it's not necessary for you to tell me how to behave, Morris.'

CHAPTER XIX

THERE were always a few aborigines hanging round the camp dressed in cast-off clothing, trousers and shirt, an old skirt and dilapidated felt hat. Dirty sore-eyed scarecrows, they crouched in the dust round the stores or butcher's shop, cadging food and tobacco, doing odd jobs, or waiting to be picked up by a prospecting party. Morris warned Sally not to encourage the blacks to come to her for food or clothing.

'If you start giving them things, you'll never be rid of them,' he said; and chased off any natives he found near the tent.

Towards the end of the month, a tribe came in from the bush. Men and women, naked but for a hair-string belt or fur tassel. They stood in idle, curious groups, or stalked about as if this terrain belonged to them. Amazed and amused, they watched the white men scurrying about the ridge, digging and burrowing into the earth like great boudie rats. Their laughter clattered, and they called to each other with sharp, bird-like cries: at sunset, drifted away through the scrub and camped near the salt lake.

It was that night Sally heard the merry plangent note of native laughter near Frisco's camp fire, and saw a slim, dark figure moving about in the firelight.

Next morning the same young person was taking a bath behind the tent. With guileless grace, she stood there in the open, washing herself in one of Frisco's panning-off dishes.

'Frisco gib 'm chented chope. Tell 'm wash 'm all over,' she explained gleefully, lathering the soap into a white foam on her body and into her hair.

Never had she seen so attractive a native girl, Sally thought. The slim brown body with firm pointed breasts was like a statue in bronze: the girl had beautiful brown eyes, too, though her features were broad and coarse, the mouth barely defined by dingy coral. When she had finished with the soap, she stepped out of the dish, lifted it in her arms, and tipped the water over herself in a splashing shower.

As she did so Sam Mullet came whistling along the track, going down to his claim later than usual. Sally moved behind the tent; but Sam barely glanced at the girl as he passed, though he called, cheerily:

'My word, make'm bloody clean feller, this morning, Maritana.'

'My word, make'm bloody clean feller,' the girl echoed gaily.

She shook the water from her wet hair and pranced about in the sunshine to dry herself: dived into the tent, and reappeared in a few minutes in an old white shirt of Frisco's, with a piece of red and yellow figured print wrapped about her waist, and two or three necklaces of glass beads slung round her neck.

Sally found her presently at the opening of her own tent as she made the beds. The girl might have been a Mexican or a Spaniard, as she stood there with bright laughing eyes and bare

116

feet. Sally smiled a greeting, and all day the girl hovered about, shy and curious, exclaiming at the strange ways of a white woman, and asking questions in the pidgin of the fields.

'Who's the girl at Frisco's camp?' Sally asked Morris that evening.

'Maritana,' Morris growled. 'He swears she's a half-caste.'

'Maritana?' Sally smiled. That was why, she guessed, Mr. Frisco Jo Murphy had sung with such mocking braggadocio:

> 'Oh Maritana, wild wood flower,
> Did they but give thee a prouder name
> To place thee in a kingly bower,
> And deck thee with a gilded shame?'

'It's a lie, of course,' Morris said. 'Just one of his yarns.'

'But she looks different,' Sally demurred. 'Lighter in colour and more intelligent.'

'Rubbish!' Morris exclaimed emphatically. 'Maritana's an abo, and it's no use Frisco pretending she isn't. He picked her up in the usual way.'

'What's that?'

'The first night we camped here, at the foot of the hill, there was a blacks' camp further along. They sent a couple of girls over. Frisco wanted to keep one of them and sent the other back with a plug of tobacco and a tin of jam. The girl Frisco wanted was very young and scared, bit and scratched like a wild cat and cleared out. That's why he called her Maritana. The blacks sent other girls, but Frisco didn't like the look of them. The men chaffed him about that little black vixen and called the hill after her to rile him.

'A few weeks later Maritana came back. Tribal discipline, I suppose. Her father and prospective husband interviewed Frisco. It cost him a couple of bottles of wine and two plugs of tobacco to keep her. But to give him his dues, Frisco treated the kid kindly, fed her and dressed her up like a gipsy. She was quite happy for a while, then went bush again, mucked-up her clothes and distributed her necklaces. Now she comes and goes as she pleases, but she has to leave her clothes and gewgaws behind when she goes bush: wash and dress up when she comes back.'

All the same, Morris was indignant with Frisco for having Maritana at his camp while Mrs. Gough was living alongside. It was an insult to a white woman, this open and flagrant consorting with a gin, he said, and forbade Sally to have anything to do with Maritana.

'You must ignore her—and Frisco,' Morris said.

'How can I do that?' Sally objected. 'The girl is not to blame. I couldn't be unkind to her when she comes to me like a little wild animal out of the bush. And as for Mr. Murphy—we're still in his debt, I suppose?'

'Don't throw that up at me,' Morris growled.

'We can't ignore him, if it is so,' Sally persisted. 'But, please don't misunderstand me, Morris. I disapprove of this intercourse between white men and native women as much as you do.'

'That's one thing you'll never have against me,' Morris assured her. 'Dirty, stinking creatures, these aboriginal women, though not bad looking when they're young, sometimes. Beats me how a decent man can have anything to do with them. But the worst of it is, other men have to pay for the way some blackguards kidnap and abuse the gins.'

Sally knew that. It was a comfort to believe Morris had not associated with aboriginal women: they were repulsive to him. He had told her that before and that most of the trouble prospectors encountered with the blacks was due to some white men having interfered with their women.

Not that the natives seemed to have any objection to lending their women for sexual intercourse. It was holding of the women, and failure to share goods as a result, which caused hostility, raids on a prospector's camp, a shower of spears at dawn, shooting by the white men and the spilling of native blood. Then the feud was on. The natives regarded all white men as belonging to one tribe and guilty of the crimes any member of the tribe committed. It was tribal law: the only law they understood: 'an eye for an eye and a tooth for a tooth.'

In country where the blacks were known to be hostile, now, they sometimes sent girls as a decoy to the white men's camp. There were men who could not resist the lure of dusky damsels strolling into the camp at sundown. Others wiser, and more apprehensive of flying spears, would send the girls back to their people with a few tins of jam, or flour and sugar as goodwill offerings. They might go their way in peace. But men who slept with a native girl, on the track, out Lake Carey way, or towards the Arrow and the distant ranges, took their lives in their hands.

In big camps like Hannans where the blacks had degenerated to scavengers like the crows, intercourse with native women was fairly common, though most men were ashamed of the impulse which drove them to borrow a woman from the blacks. They kept her in the background, with some sense of decency. But Frisco flaunted this girl, because she belonged to a wild tribe, dressed

118

her up and made as much fuss of her as if she were a doxy to be proud of. That infuriated Morris.

Maritana's relations clustered like flies round Frisco's tent. They sat in the dust waiting for him to come from work: raised an excited jabbering when he appeared. Frisco strode among them, laughing and hailing them jocosely. He dispensed tins of jam, flour and sugar, a few old clothes, plugs of tobacco and pieces of coloured print. Kept a box of 'trade goods' for the purpose, he said, and argued with Morris it was worth while to be on good terms with 'the niggers.' He had learnt that as a sailor in the South Seas.

These Australian aborigines were a different proposition, in many ways, he admitted, less amenable to trading propositions, and then, too, they had nothing to trade—except water and women, or a knowledge of where gold might be found. To be sure, they were wary of contact with the strangers taking possession of their land until a taste for the white men's food, drink and tobacco had broken down their natural instincts. But Frisco maintained that the blacks could be very useful to a man out prospecting in waterless country: put him on to water—and gold —if they were friendly disposed to him. It was quite easy to get on with them, if you treated them well, gave them food, wine and tobacco, and knew how to manage them.

A costly business, Morris considered. Now and again a native had led prospectors to a likely outcrop, and guided them to water when otherwise they would have perished; but the wild tribes, these days, guarded the secret of their soaks and gnamma holes with fierce tenacity. Nothing would induce them to disclose the whereabouts of gold or water. They knew well enough that gold brought hordes of men and beasts which exhausted the water supplies and destroyed their hunting grounds. Frisco's generosity, Morris said, was merely an excuse for keeping Maritana.

CHAPTER XX

MARITANA moved so quietly that the pebbles scarcely clinked beneath her naked feet. The chinkle of her necklaces, those strings of beads Frisco had given her, or a gurgle of laughter announced her presence. Impossible not to smile and warm to her as she stood before you, a slight garish figure, with the wild, shy eyes of a young animal, long-lashed and beautiful. Sally told herself that, when Maritana came to see her soon after Frisco and Morris had gone off to work.

All the morning Maritana watched and exclaimed at what Sally was doing, studying her face and trying to read her thoughts as her people read tracks on the sand. So sensitive to every expression was she that she knew at once when Missus Sally was displeased, or had had enough of her: would drift away with obliging insouciance.

But she would return again next day, with naive merry laughter and her eyes asking questions. Sally found herself as interested in this aboriginal girl as Maritana was in her. Meeri, she liked to say, calling her by her native name. They tried to talk together in the ugly jargon of the fields, and quite naturally Maritana interspersed her queries and exclamations with filthy oaths she had heard the men use.

'You mustn't talk like that, Meeri!' Sally cried. Meeri understood that certain words were forbidden for women.

She was very intelligent: learnt quickly to imitate 'Missus Sally's' way of saying and doing things. Made herself a broom of brushwood and began to sweep and tidy-up round Frisco's tent just as she saw Sally doing round Morris's. Maritana washed the dishes too, and scrubbed out Frisco's dirty clothes; hung them on bushes to dry. Sally taught her to cook and sew. They made a full skirt of Maritana's length of red and yellow print, which she had been wearing like a sarong and which was liable to fall off at any moment, be picked up and carried nonchalantly over her arm. But Maritana was very proud of her new dress, the same sort of dress a white woman wore: realized that it must not be removed in public.

Frisco strolled over in the evening sometimes, carrying himself with derisive effrontery, but there were no more sing-songs by the camp fire. Frisco sang and strummed beside his own fire, and the men gathered there. Most of them. A few still continued to drop in and yarn to Morris, before Frisco started a two-up ring. But the spinning pennies lured even Morris to Frisco's fireside and the light of his kerosene flare.

Sally sat alone by her own camp fire then, although often Maritana would emerge from the surrounding darkness to crouch beside her, staring into the fire until she fell asleep, or Sally went to bed. Though not to sleep. The racket of gaffing over the spinning pennies went on into the small hours. She hated Frisco Jo Murphy, wondering how much money Morris had won or lost, dreading the effect on him either way, and a revival of his passion for gambling.

Morris had been very difficult and over-bearing of late. They had almost quarrelled about the way he played two-up nearly every night, and other matters. Maritana particularly. Sally could not understand what had come over Morris. He was so stubborn and churlish about the girl: scowled and chased her away whenever he found her with Sally.

Maritana did not wait to be chased, now. She fled when she saw Morris. Sally had tried to argue with him about Maritana; but Morris said Sally's attitude amounted to a tacit approval of Frisco's fornication with a gin. It lowered her prestige in the camp and was a serious embarrassment to him.

'I can't believe it, Morris,' Sally protested. 'It seems to me any woman would try to help a young thing like that—and I like to go for a walk in the bush with her.'

Frisco laughed boisterously when he found Maritana sewing a new blue patch on his working trousers, though they didn't need it, because Sally had put a patch on an old pair of Morris's pants. He said Mrs. Gough was making a domesticated tabby of his wild cat; but Maritana seemed very pleased with her new performances.

Not that she shed her old ways. Maritana had taught her a great deal, too, Sally liked to say. It was always exciting to go for a walk with her. Maritana had specked a small slug now and then, and showed her how to search the ground on a likely spot where water-worn pebbles were strewn about, or there were traces of decayed quartz and old rocks from the hills. It was fun, too, to watch her track a snake or goanna to its lair, kill it promptly and carry it back to the camp on the end of a stick.

Maritana would dump the reptiles in the embers of the fire, and share out the cooked white meat with Frisco. He said it was good eating, like fish; went well with a lump of melted butter. But Sally could not bring herself to try these delicacies, or the big white grubs Maritana pried from under the bark of old trees.

One day on a jaunt to the south of Mount Charlotte, they came across one of the queer, hideous, little creatures the men called 'a mountain devil.' It was a chameleon: in the sun turned yellow, spotted with brown; crawling among the rocks took on a protective brown and grey. Was quite harmless, but of an absurd ugliness: covered with tiny horns, and had bright beady eyes. Like a miniature dragon, Sally thought, or some evil beast out of a legend.

'Mingari!' Maritana exclaimed softly when she discovered it. She sat down on the ground, a little distance away, to watch the mingari and avoid disturbing it, as it basked in the sunshine. But the mingari glided away so quickly and quietly that Sally could not see where it went.

'Maybe she make cooboo' (baby), Maritana explained, and in an awed undertone told the story of how long, long time ago, when the first of all the black fellows came to live here, the mingari were women who would not have anything to do with men. Their law forbade them to speak or whistle in case men might hear, and fierce spirits guarded them as they moved about the hunting grounds. The mingari women had to make babies for all the tribes. Wherever they sat down to rest by a water hole or a big rock, they left many babies. But a mingari woman had cried out when she was captured by a young warrior, and so the fierce spirits had changed all her sisters into these little creatures, without a voice, and covered them with horns to protect them from their enemies.

But the mingari still made babies wherever they rested, and no doubt Maritana, or Sally, herself, would catch a baby if they sat on the ground where the mingari had been, Maritana explained hopefully.

'Let's go!' Sally cried, pretending to be alarmed. 'I don't want a baby just now, Meeri.'

Maritana's laughter burbled, though she eyed the white woman with curiosity and incredulity.

'Wiah! Not want catch'm cooboo?' she murmured.

On another of their excursions, they found the shining expanse of the salt lake swarming with wild duck. Maritana hurried back to tell Frisco. Morris and Frisco got up before dawn, next morning, and set out for the salt lake. They waded through marshy ground and into the lake, screened by bushes, like the blacks did, to get a shot at the birds. Maritana went with them, slipped off her dress and slid out into the icy cold water to retrieve the birds after they fell.

She was delighted to come back carrying scores of glossy little black bodies dangling from a stick over her shoulder. All day, she worked busily, covering the birds, feathers and all, with a plaster of mud, and scooped a native oven out of the ground in which to cook them whole.

'You can't beat wild duck à la Maritana,' Frisco boasted.

Morris preferred his wild duck plucked and cleaned, so Sally braised his share of the birds in the big black pot which was her camp oven. She and Morris had no guests for their dinner party. But half a dozen of Maritana's relations arrived mysteriously from nowhere to share her duck-feast. They sat in a semi-circle beyond Frisco's camp fire, as if they were entitled to share in the game Maritana's man brought in.

Frisco laughed when he saw them. Enjoyed posing as a mighty hunter, he said, and handed out roast duck with good-natured generosity. The natives drifted away when the meal was finished. But they were hanging about the camp when Frisco returned from work next evening: demanded flour, sugar, tea and tobacco. Frisco's temper flared and he drove them off with the foulest abuse, cursing and yelling until the last black form had vanished.

Maritana took his outburst as a matter of course. She went about as usual, with a bubbling merry little laugh and amused interest in the jobs she had learnt to do about the camp. But after two or three days, she disappeared. Had gone bush, Frisco said, and would wander about with her tribe until Bardook, the old man who was her aboriginal husband, wanted wine and tobacco. Then he would send Maritana to the white man's camp again.

CHAPTER XXI

THE days of golden sunshine, and skies of a blue so fine and intense that Sally thought it must be the most beautiful thing in the world, were passing with the approach of summer.

After the rains, and during the cold weather, the colour of earth and sky had been rich and crude. Terracotta the tracks and torn flanks of the ridge, emerald the herbage sprouting beside them and through the bush. Sapphire the cone of Mount Burgess standing up on the horizon, and the sea of the scrub stretching in every direction, dove-grey, almost hyacinth in the mists of evening and the glow of sunset.

The wild flowers seemed to hold the pigments for all that landscape painting. Yellow, scarlet, purple and blue, they tasselled prickly bushes and splurged over tough low-growing plants. White everlastings spread their snow, and wild pig-face its magentary silken flowers for miles beyond the lake. But as the breath of summer fanned them, flowers and herbage vanished, the lake dried up. The colours of earth and sky faded to dreary monotonous pastels of heat and dust. Only the sunsets remained a miraculous spectacle, a glory of rose and gold over purple dark of the earth; and the nights, when moonlight steeped the drab, ugly surroundings of the camp in its silver radiance.

Sally often sat watching the sunsets and moonlight, soothed and comforted by their mysterious beauty, when Morris had gone off to the two-up ring. A little distance away she could see men crowded round Frisco's camp, and hear the racket of the gambling.

Raucous and shrill, delirious with excitement, the voices rose and fell, blaspheming joyously or cursing gloomily.

'Am I set?'

'A quid he heads 'em!'

'Up they go!'

'Come on! Come on, me beauties!'

'Heads she is!'

'God A'mighty, it's rainin' heads!'

'Betyer dollar!'

'Ten bob!'

'A quid!'

'Up the lot!'

'Spin 'em, Yank!'

'Porca madonna!'

'Betyer he catches the grouter!'

'Tails she is!'

Whoops, groans, a frenzied babble, and another bout of betting. The noise became monotonous droning away through the quiet night.

Sally had seen and heard men playing two-up so often in the 'Cross and Coolgardie, she knew what every cry meant. The game had become so much part of the life of the fields that all sorts of issues were decided by the toss of a penny. 'Toss y'r for it!' the men said in any argument about paying for drinks, or going for water to the condenser.

On Sundays, they would stand, or squat, in a ring, all day, in the dust and blazing sun, watching two pennies chucked in the air, and gamble fiercely on how they might fall. Tough, bearded prospectors, old fossickers, hard-headed miners, hawk-eyed strangers and sawny youths, all wrought to a pitch of crazy excitement by the toss and fall of a pair of pennies. Usually the game was not played at night, out of doors. The uncertain light led to too many disputes. But when things were dull on a camp, time hung heavily, a ring might start among men who had confidence in each other, like this one of Frisco's, and the play last half the night, on a sandy patch under a kerosene flare.

You couldn't blame men whose life was hard and dreary, for taking any way of getting a little amusement, Sally told herself; and two-up gave them a brief, reckless forgetfulness of the grim struggle for existence they were engaged in. It was a queer, childish game to absorb their interest so completely, but Morris said that had nothing to do with it.

Two-up was a straight-out gamble. Fair enough; the fairest gambling game he knew. It offered a poor man the chance of winning quids. That was its attraction. But Morris, himself, admitted having lost fifty pounds and won more sometimes. Yank Boteral tossed for tenners when he was in luck. Sally had heard the men talk of a hundred pounds changing hands in the ring, and of many a man being cleaned out as a result of his play. Not that that seemed to matter! A digger could always borrow to play again, and get credit from the storekeepers for food.

When a crowd collected for a regular game, and the ring-keeper was a well-known man, with some money behind him, the betting ran high; but most of the diggers were wary of a flutter with strangers. Some of them had been fleeced by spielers 'ringing in the nob,' a two-headed penny, or 'the grey,' a penny with two tails. A crook discovered trying those tricks was roughly handled by a ringside crowd. One of them had been nearly kicked to death on Kurnalpi, but that did not prevent others from trying their skill occasionally.

Any man could walk into the centre of a ring to spin the pennies. Two were placed tail-up on the kip, a small wooden board, so that everybody could be sure a double-header was not being used. Betting began as soon as the spinner handed his bet to the ring-keeper, or put it down on the ground at his feet, five shillings, ten shillings, or a pound. The spinner backed himself to head 'em. The ring-keeper started the betting; got his bet set.

Men begging on tails laid their stakes on the ground before them. Others backing the spinner threw the money into the ring. Side bettors backed their fancy either way for smaller money, sixpences and shillings. If the spinner threw a head and a tail, 'a one and a one,' he could spin again. If he tossed tails, he flung down the kip and walked out of the ring, having lost his bet. If he tossed heads, he could stay and double his bet, spin the same pennies again, or change them. After a man had headed his pennies three times, he paid five shillings to the ring-keeper. If he was making a lot of money, he would hand out a pound or two and throw ten shillings to the picker-up.

Sometimes a successful bettor twisted, after backing heads, and backed tails. 'Catching the grouter,' that was called. But a grouter bettor could only have one or two bets a night. The ring-keeper might object to a spin, on the grounds that the kippy had put a 'gig' on it, or touched the kip with his fingers. A 'butterfly' fall was in order over a sandy patch, but not if there were any stones about on which she might bounce and start an argument.

Morris said that he did not like two-up. It was too crude and uproarious for his taste. He preferred a quiet game of poker or murrumbidgee. But two-up was a national institution and a man had to be sociable. He played to keep on a good footing with the men: couldn't afford to be thought uppish or close-fisted. It was only shrewd old skin-flints like Eli Nancarrow and Unk Tregurtha who steered clear of the two-up ring. Parson Jarn, too, of course, but it was generally recognized that he was entitled to inveigh against two-up as a trap for lost souls.

Sally was inclined to agree with him. She wished Morris would not go over to the ring so often. It depressed her to think he was wasting money, when they needed it to pay their debts, and build a house. She hated the idea of borrowing and living on credit. Surely Morris must realize they could not go on living for long in the haphazard way they were doing now?

It would be better to do any honest, ordinary work than give people like Ma Buggins an excuse for abusing them. Sally did not see why she should not try to earn her own living in Hannans as she had done in the 'Cross and at Coolgardie, and let Morris continue to work on the shaft he and Frisco were sinking, or go prospecting. Luke Geoghegan had built an hotel round the Black Swan bar which he had run in a tent. He needed a cook. Why couldn't she apply for the job? But Morris would not hear of it. And he resented Sally's attempts to dissuade him from playing poker and two-up, until they could afford 'to take the risk of losing money,' as she said.

'I make more money than I lose,' Morris declared impatiently.

'Then I hope we've paid Mr. Murphy what we owe him,' Sally replied.

Morris could give her no assurance on that score: requested her not to interfere in matters which did not concern her.

'But it does concern me, Morris,' Sally insisted.

'I am the business manager of this firm,' Morris said dourly. 'There was a time, perhaps, when I appeared to forget it; but I thought we had arrived at a satisfactory understanding on our way over from Coolgardie.'

'Oh, yes.' Sally had let the memory of their pact on that drive obliterate her protest.

She thought it had some effect, however, because Morris did not so often go over to the ring, and before long Frisco was running it only at the week-end.

'Hear Zeb Lane's floated the Great Boulder in London,' he remarked, strolling over one night when Blunt Pick and Sam Mullet had dropped in for a yarn with Morris.

'Got a lot of luck, that mob,' Blunt Pick piped up. 'They'd on'y got colours and were jest about stony when Brookman applied for twenty acres round the Boulder. Then Sam Pearce struck a leader further along, and Brookman tramps off into Coolgardie after another twenty out Lake View way. Forty acres—a nice swag of country to write home about.'

'Brookman says their last assay on the Lake View was higher than it's ever been,' Frisco said, impressed by that fact.

'The geologists and mining experts, up here recently, consider the Boulder mines won't live up to value at depth,' Morris observed.

'Gee-ologists and mining experts!' Blunt Pick spat emphatically. 'They give the Brookman shows a bad name. As good as say the Great Boulder's a "wild cat." But what did they say a few years ago? Gold would never be found in payable quantities in Western Australia. And there's Bayley's and the Wealth of Nations and the Carbine to prove 'em wrong—to say nothing of White Feather and Kurnalpi. Now they want to make out Hannans 'll never be a reefer's field and the alluvial is peterin' out. Well, I reckon they're wrong again.'

'T' hell with 'em!' Frisco cried gaily.

'Brookman's mines may not be as flash as Bayley's,' Sam remarked cautiously. 'But there's a lot of good gold in 'em, and the lead's running through a bigger stretch of country. We're hangin' on to the Boulder Half-mile South, 't any rate, Blunt Pick and me.'

'You bet we are,' Blunt Pick agreed.

'Till some mug comes along and buys you out for an English syndicate?' Morris queried: 'or you can float her in Adelaide?'

'Well, I'm no bloomin' capitalist to spend money on development,' Sam replied, somewhat aggrieved. 'And she's a good positional block. We been getting traces and I reckon she'll bring a fair price when things get goin' here.'

'They'll get goin',' Blunt Pick declared.

'That's what I've been telling Morrey,' Frisco explained, derisively. 'He wants to pull out and go off to White Feather. But I'm backin' Hannans to catch the eye of the big investor before long.'

'There's a good many men 've thrown up their claims here to go off to Menzies, White Feather, Kurnalpi or Dunn's, will be kicking themselves,' Sam spoke in his slow, practical way as if there could be no doubt of the matter.

'Zeb Lane's deal over the Great Boulder's not a good omen,' Morris remarked, drily. 'It was a smack in the eye for the Australian directors. No cash and only a third share in the English company. London investors are scared of mining propositions on this field since reports of the geological experts got round.'

Frisco flared: 'If the ore Charley de Rose was showin' me don't boost Lake View and Boulder East shares when the battery starts crushin', I'll sling the game. Meanwhile I'm buyin' as many as I can get hold of.'

'You got Lake View and Boulder Easts, Frisco?'

'Bet y'r bottom dollar I have—and hangin' on to 'em. Got two thousand from old Whitford at a shilling a piece.'

'It's obvious,' Morris stuck to his point, 'Brookman's syndicate is scratching dirt. Hard-up for money. The directors in Adelaide have reorganized into a limited liabilities company. The Coolgardie Gold Mining Prospecting Company, they're calling themselves now, with a hundred thousand shares at one and one.'

'Jesus God!' Frisco swung to his feet, yawning and stretching, 'she's not dead the Great Boulder, and if she's "a wild cat," I'm speckin' shares on her kittens.'

His laughter rang out, relieving the tension, although Morris sat tight in his grouch and gloom.

'That's the idea, Frisco!' Sam chuckled. 'Boost Hannans and we'll all be millionaires.'

'Might be alright for you blokes with mines in y'r pockets, and dough to gamble with on the share market,' Big Jim exclaimed. 'But it's no use to diggers chewin' the dust of the tailin's dumps. I reckon Morrey's right. Lost faith in Hannans, meself. But what's the odds? There's a lot of country worth prospectin' yet, and a man always runs the risk of pickin' up a fortune, out-back.'

He and Clary McClaren had returned from Dunn's Find, having done no good on the rush. Clary was in Coolgardie, trying to borrow money to buy a couple of extra camels for a long prospecting trip to the north-east, and Jim had strolled along with Yank and Ted Dow on their way to the pub.

'Come 'n-'ave-a drink!' Ted shouted breezily.

It was the way most arguments ended on the fields. The men scrambled up from the ground on which they had been sprawling, or sitting squatted back on their haunches.

They were all drunk, Frisco and Ted shouting and singing hilariously, as they made their way along the track to their camps, after midnight.

CHAPTER XXII

SALLY was surprised to find that she missed Maritana.

At home in the south-west, she had been accustomed to seeing natives about the place. Her father had taken a kindly interest

128

in them, unlike many pioneers. The dark people, he called them. Some of the young men worked for him as stockmen and clearers, and her mother had trained women and girls to help with the house work when she had two or three young children to look after. An old gin had been with her when Sally, herself, was born and it was impossible to get any other assistance. But dark and different the natives had remained to her family.

Sally could not remember ever before having become attached to an aboriginal girl, although she had been on good terms with old Polly and the house girls at home, laughing and joking with them, as the best means of getting work done. But Maritana was not like any other aboriginal girl she had known. More intelligent, and more eager to learn the ways of white people.

Her interest in Maritana had been a pleasant diversion, Sally confided to herself. There was so little to do in the camp during the long day when Morris was away at work on the claim, or in the evenings when he went off to the two-up ring. She thought there might be something in what Frisco said, that Maritana was a half-caste. Her skin was a clearer bronze than the skin of other women in her tribe, and her hair softer, woody-brown, with bright glints when she washed it.

Sam Mullet agreed with her. ' 'T any rate, I've seen other brindles older than Maritana, in these parts,' he said. 'Maybe men in Hunt's survey parties weren't all saints. There were soldiers and convicts among them, and one of those escaped convicts was never recaptured. The blacks say, when a gin walks in the shadow of a white man, she bears children not as dark as the rest. That's the on'y explanation they've got for Maritana. Kalgoorla, her mother, is scared stiff of white men: not walking in the shadow of any more if she can help it. And she hates Frisco: is always prowling round if Maritana is with him. Calls from the bush, when the visit has lasted long enough, and Maritana is gone like a bird.'

Frisco went off to Coolgardie, for a few days, soon after Maritana's disappearance. He came back driving a four-wheeled buggy and pair of brumbies he had bought from a lucky prospector leaving the fields. That was not all. When he jumped out of the buggy, leaving his fagged horses to stand in their tracks, he flourished two letters for Mrs. Gough, and from under the buggy seat produced a bottle of wine Mrs. Fogarty had sent her.

Sally exclaimed with pleasure at such surprises. She forgot to be disapproving of Mr. Murphy: thanked him delightedly, and sat down to read her letters. One from Laura and the other from Marie.

Laura's letter was full of descriptions of the house Alf had built for her near the mine. Not very big, but quite comfortable, with a latticed verandah and netted windows to keep out the flies. She had a cool safe, and a stove in the kitchen, linoleum on the floors, white lace curtains, and a bedroom suite with all the necessary crockery. A bathroom too, and two big water tanks, which were full at present. Sally must come soon and stay with her for a few days, Laura wrote, if only to enjoy the luxury of a bath.

As Sally sat on a box reading her letters, Frisco stood talking to Morris. She could see him out of the corner of her eye: a tall, rakish figure, and hear him explaining exuberantly:

'Went out to have a look at the Lady Laura. And Alf took me over to the house for a drink. Christ, it's a sight for sore eyes, the place he's put up there, Morrey, with a garden and all! Flowers and cabbages growin' all over the place. Alf says this country'll grow anything with a drop of water. Never think you were on the fields, sittin' in the parlour, and Mrs. Alf lookin' as pretty as a picture. Dinny's a bit worried about the mine though. Reckons she's peterin' out, and Alf's a fool to sink money in her. Dinny went off to Dunn's, brought in three hundred and seventy ounces and sold his claim to Lord Sudley. Been celebratin' at Fogarty's.'

Morris was more interested in the new find Jimmy Thompson and Carbine Smith had reported, twelve· miles to the north of Dunn's.

Frisco laughed as if that were a good joke.

'There was only a few good claims on Dunn's besides the Wealth,' he said. 'And trust Paddy Baker to strike one of 'em. He's been in Melbourne and Sydney splashin' up all the gold he won at Kurnalpi. Said he came back, broke, but started shovellin' dirt with a diamond ring on his hand. Collected a handful of slugs in three or four days, and sold for three thousand. But mostly it's poor country, the boys tell me. No true run of gold. A lot of 'em got fed up and cleared out, Jimmy Thompson and Carbine Smith among them.'

Frisco lit one of the cheroots he liked to smoke when he could get them and rattled on:

'Jimmy and Carbine pushed off to the north and cursed when blacks ratted their camp. They had to turn back to Coolgardie for stores. Jimmy went on prospectin', knappin' a rock here and there, as they travelled. Struck a bit of an outcrop, and was pokin' around when he sees what looks like a wombat's hole under a clump of bushes. Stoops down to find out if the little bugger's at home, and cripes, he nearly fell over when he sees the walls of that hole. They was fairly blazin'. That wombat sure liked a bit of colour. He'd scraped the rock clean and was livin' in a golden hole alright.'

Morris listened hungrily; his eyes moist and shining.

'Jimmy let out a yell and his mates run across,' Frisco grinned, enjoying his yarn. 'They packed the camels with specimens—most of 'em schisty quartz matted with gold—and headed for the Warden's office. Sold for ten thousand pounds. It's the flamin' truth, Morrey, there was more bloody gold than stone in some of those bloody specimens. They were on show at the bank. Jimmy reckons he's got a world-beater of a mine and a mate. So he's callin' the mine the Carbine—but she's lyin' in poor country. One of these rich pockets like the 'Derry and the Wealth, I reckon.'

'God, Frisco,' Morris cried, excitedly, 'what's the good of hanging on here. Hannans is done. And all the time they're picking up fortunes all round us.'

'A few of 'em are, and a lot aren't makin' tucker,' Frisco's voice steadied and hardened, though it still rollicked cheerily. 'No use droppin' a good bone to chase shadows, and we've got a good thing here, if we stick to it, Morrey. We'll cash in before long. These English investors are buyin' up everything they can float.'

'Not on Hannans,' Morris persisted. 'They're after ground alongside these flash shows where they can see gold for their money, and we're seeing mighty little these days.'

He poured water from the kerosene bucket into an old panning-off dish and went behind the tent to wash the grime of the day's work from his face and hands.

Frisco lounged over to where Sally was sitting, thinking over her letters, and listening at the same time to what Morris and Frisco were saying.

Marie's letter was not as exciting as Laura's. She had no very good news to report. They had given up their claim, she said. Mr. Bell was working as yardman at Fogarty's and Jean had taken a job on Bayley's. Marie was terrified every time he went underground; but he promised her that he would not work as a miner for long. Only until he had saved enough money to go prospecting again. Then he said he would go to White Feather, or somewhere beyond Hannans. Perhaps, if this happened, she would see her dear Sally again; but it was all uncertain, and not very cheerful living in Coolgardie, just now, although she had a small house near the mine, made of corrugated iron. Pleasanter to live in than a tent when it rained, but it was such a long time since it had rained, and on a hot day what an oven the small iron house could be!

Sally sighed, wondering how long it would be before Morris put up that shack for her he had been talking about ever since she arrived. If he was dissatisfied with Hannans, what would his next move be? Where would they go?

'If you wish to go over and see Mrs. Brierly, ma'am,' Frisco said, standing before her with his air of mocking gallantry, 'my carriage and horses are at your disposal.'

'Thank you, Mr. Murphy!' Sally met the challenge of those bold, inquisitive eyes, and relinquished any thought of paying Laura a visit. 'I do not wish to go.'

'I did not suggest that so disreputable a person as myself should accompany you,' Frisco remarked, his derisive smile playing. 'Morrey might be persuaded to, perhaps. Or you might even drive yourself.'

He turned and walked away, but swung back to look at her. As Sally's glance caught his, he drawled:

'By the way, another friend I met in Coolgardie sent her best respects—Mme. Marseilles.'

Sally flushed and her eyes brightened with anger. How dare the man say such a thing? How dare he presume to imply that— But Frisco appeared to enjoy her discomfiture. He went off to unharness and water his horses, laughing as if he had heard a good joke and it had put him in an excellent humour.

CHAPTER XXIII

FRISCO came back that evening to share out with Morris the proceeds of the gold he had sold in Coolgardie. Yank Boteral joined them, and before long, Sam Mullet and Blunt Pick strolled along to hear the news of the old camp. They had settled down comfortably, when Paddy Cavan dashed up, his eyes wild and his hair on end.

'Hey, Frisco,' he spluttered, 'did y'r know there's been a murder at Bardoc? Couple of blokes pulled-up at Ma Bugginses. They been out on a rush along the Sore Foot road. She's a duffer, they say. Men not makin' tucker. Comin' in, Ike Mogford and his mate was doin' a bit of prospectin' in the bush, eight miles out from Bardoc, when they see a cove shovellin' dirt like mad. Thought he was on a good thing: went along next mornin' to have a look. And there was a corpse, with his head bashed-in down the hole where the old cove'd been diggin'—'

Men round the camp fire muttered and swore. They wondered whether young Paddy was lying. How much of the yarn he had made up?

This was the first murder that had been heard of on the fields. Everybody was dumbfounded and uneasy. It struck at the principle on which their lives depended—loyalty to a mate.

'If y' don't believe me, go and ask those blokes,' Paddy squalled indignantly. 'They're camped down by the condenser.'

'Who was he?'

'Did they get the murderer?'

Paddy was bombarded with questions. He only knew the corpse was so battered nobody could recognize him, and that Bardoc diggers were out after a man suspected of the crime.

Sam and Blunt Pick hoisted themselves up from their seats by the fire. They hitched their pants and went off to have a word with the men Paddy had been talking to. Frisco and Yank followed, Paddy gabbling beside them.

It was true, Frisco told Morris next morning. For once in his life Young Paddy was not lying. Troopers had gone up to investigate. They were combing the country. But Ike Mogford said there was nothing to identify either the victim or the man who had killed him.

Every evening Morris went down to the condenser, taking his turn with hundreds of men waiting for a gallon, sometimes half a gallon of water. This had to provide for all needs. Since that one welcome downpour, in the spring, there had been no rain, and with the hot weather beginning, everybody was anxious about the threatened drought.

Coolgardie had been drawing on the condensers at the Hannans salt lake, carting water nearly thirty miles by spring cart and camel trains. In the camps, every drop had to be used sparingly: kept for rinsing dishes and clothes after washing face and hands. Water was a luxury, and costly for most prospectors who were barely making tucker on their claims round about Hannans. There was great indignation when a rumour went round that condenser holders were talking of putting up the price of water.

Morris was later than usual going down to the condenser, the evening Frisco strode into the camp without any of his usual swagger.

'Trouble down at the condenser, Morrey,' he said, in a way which indicated the gravity of his news. 'McDonald's raised the price of water from sixpence to a bob a gallon. The boys won't stand for it. There's going to be a roll-up.'

'About time.' Morris stood up. He had just finished his meal and Sally was clearing away. 'Jerry M'Auliffe was telling me, the other day, he and his mate and their horses were two days without water when they struck the condenser at Peake's Find. Cost him two pound a head for one drink for his horses. He paid fifteen pound for water before he could get a move on.'

'The condenser holders 've been holdin' a gun at our heads long enough,' Frisco said angrily. 'Remember our first summer on Hannans we were payin' five shillin's a gallon. Now McDonald's got bores on the lake, drawin' salt water and producin' eleven thousand gallons a day. Coolgardie's short, too, and he's been supplyin' the old camp. But the boys reckon he's makin' a fair profit at sixpence a gallon, and are sore about him organizin' a ring of condenser-holders not to sell at less than a bob a gallon.'

The rattle of tin dishes could be heard in the distance.

Morris and Frisco went off to the roll-up.

When they returned, late that night, Morris said there were more than a thousand men at the meeting, most of them unwashed and dust-grimed, because they were hard-up and already going short of water. Alluvial had petered out on Hannans and many men were hanging on to their claims and ekeing out a bare existence in the hope of selling when the big investors paid more attention to the mining prospects of the field.

Miners and prospectors were furious with the condenser-holders for taking advantage of the scarcity to slug them. The salt water, condensed for sale, was the property of the people, they contended; and the condenser-holders were making a fair profit on their plant and labour by selling it at the usual rate. Some of the smaller condenser-holders had climbed down, as a result of the roll-up; agreed not to join the ring, or support McDonald in putting up the price of water. A dour, stubborn man, the wealthiest and most powerful of the condenser-holders, McDonald held out for a bob a gallon and defied the roll-up.

Next day the diggers made a scarecrow, branded it McDonald and carried it along the main street and through outlying camps, to a chorus of jeers and curses. It was set on fire, and tempers were blazing when a second roll-up was called. Over a thousand five hundred men met and decided to march out to Hannans Lake and interview the man who was trying to corner water and make a fortune out of the diggers.

McDonald had a store in a canvas shack beside the lake, now a dry stretch of salt-encrusted earth shimmering in the hot sunshine. His condenser plant and tanks stood beside the store.

Morris said most of the men thought, when they started out,

that straight talk and a vigorous demonstration of their determination not to pay a bob a gallon for water would bring the old skinflint to his senses. But on the way out, some wild Irishmen and speilers who had been drinking and were itching for a brawl, fanned the men's anger and resentment to an ugly pitch. There was talk of rough-handling McDonald and burning down his store.

Sam Mullet, Blunt Pick, Eli Nancarrow, Frisco, and several others who had called the roll-up, feared there would be no holding the mob if McDonald refused to listen to reason.

When the diggers arrived at the lake-side, they found McDonald had cleared out to Coolgardie. The man he left in charge of the store was incapable of coping with the situation: did not know what to do. Frisco, Sam and some of the others realized that they had to take a hand and try to stop the diggers from running amok. Some of the craziest were preparing to burn down the store and smash up the plant.

Frisco made his way into the shack and barred the door. He found McDonald's wife and two children, sleeping in a room at the back: rushed them off into the bush, by the back door, and sent the storekeeper after them. When he returned, a battle was raging between the bunch trying to set fire to the store and smash up the plant, and the diggers determined to prevent a wanton destruction of food and water.

'Sam and Frisco yelled themselves hoarse trying to put a bit of sense into the mob,' Morris said, telling Sally about the shindy afterwards. 'They managed to calm most of the men down. But one young fool drove a pick into an eleven thousand gallon tank and there was the water we might all be dying for, running to waste. Blunt Pick tore off his shirt to plug up the hole and I used my coat to beat out the flames when the store started to blaze. We didn't discover till everything had settled down, what would've happened if we hadn't stopped that fire. There were ten cases of dynamite and three thousand detonators in the store.'

McDonald was sufficiently impressed by the bitter feeling against him, to attend the next roll-up and explain why he was raising the price of water. Cost of horse feed and carting wood to keep the condenser going were his chief excuse. Four delegates, appointed to investigate the plant and running expenses, reported that they were satisfied McDonald was making a decent profit on water at sixpence a gallon. The men pledged themselves not to buy water from him at a higher price.

Other condensers were set up. The ring McDonald had tried

135

to organize, collapsed. Water came down to one pound a hundred gallons.

Blunt Pick was jubilant.

'It's just like Dinny says,' he chuckled. 'When the workers stick together and organize, there's nothing they can't do. The chances are we'd all have been blown to blazes if the snake-headed mob runnin' with Billy King'd had their way and set fire to the store.'

CHAPTER XXIV

IT had been a hot, dusty day. Men were straggling back to their camps, after working on the ridge and on the claims at the foot of Maritana, the afternoon Sally looked up from the neat darn she was putting into one of Morris's grey flannel shirts, to see Dinny Quin coming towards her.

But a Dinny she had never met before. He wore a brand new slop suit, white shirt, collar and tie, big felt hat. A bunch of flowers wilted in one hand and he carried a sugar bag slung over his shoulder. Sally would scarcely have known him but for his limp and the shy grin reaching out to her from the thin withered face under that big hat.

'Dinny!' she cried with surprise and pleasure. For the first time she realized that she thought of Dinny Quin as a good friend: had a real affection for him.

Dinny understood she was glad to see him. He handed her the flowers, marigolds and geraniums and a few larkspurs, and dumped his sugar bag on the ground.

'Mrs. Alf sent 'em,' he explained ruefully, taking off his hat and wiping the sweat from his brow. 'I've just got in be the coach. Kept the flowers in a newspaper all the way over, but they look poorly. There's a bit of fruit in the bag, and some vegetables. We're getting so flash in the old camp, y' can buy almost anything y' want now. Ten pubs workin' overtime, and stores full of food and flash clothes.'

'Oranges and lemons, and a cabbage,' Sally exclaimed, opening the bag and looking into it. 'How kind of you to bring them, Mr. Quin!'

She was remembering to be polite, and that Morris would not like her to call him Dinny.

Dinny blushed like a schoolboy. His face, clean and well-shaven, looked years younger: his eyes were very blue and happy.

'How are you gettin' on?' he asked awkwardly. 'We've been worryin' about you, me and Mrs. Fogarty, and Alf and his missus. Frisco told us you was livin' up here on the claim with Morrey. Never been on Hannans, so thought I'd come over and have a look round—see how you was gettin' on.'

'Me? I'm well and I like it,' Sally said. 'It's nicer living in a tent than by myself at the 'Cross. But you're in luck, Mr. Quin! I'm so glad.'

'Great jumpin' Jehosaphat, it's Dinny!'

Bill was coming up the track with Morris and Frisco. He took a flying leap and grabbed Dinny's hand. Morris and Frisco closed in on him, as pleased to see Dinny as Bill. While they were all gabbing and teasing Dinny about his grand clothes, Sally put her flowers in water, threw some sticks on the fire and swung the billy over. In a few minutes she had mugs of black tea on the table and slabs of the currant damper she had made that morning.

The men sat on boxes or sprawled on the ground, to handle their mugs and dampers comfortably, and hear what Dinny had to say.

Other diggers stopped to hail Dinny as they passed. Sam and Blunt Pick, Speck and Eli Nancarrow among them. Sally rinsed the mugs and cut more damper, although there was not enough to go round. Dinny wanted to know what was doing on Hannans, Broad Arrow, Kurnalpi and Kanowna, as the old White Feather was being called now. He gave the news of Coolgardie and the nearby camps.

'There's been the divil of a row between Frank Vosper and Lord Percy Douglas,' he chuckled. 'Lord Percy's jest back from London and Vosper slung off at him in the *Coolgardie Miner*. "By courtesy," he ses, "Viscount Drumlanrigg and Baron Kilbeach," and called Percy a company monger. "There's a term to describe noble lords who join boards of advice and such like bodies for which they have no qualifications," Frank ses, "they call them guinea pigs. The *Miner* was not started to bolster up duffers and play the sycophant to aristocrats and capitalists!"'

'Gosh! that's the stuff,' Blunt Pick's squeaky voice cut in. 'He's been floatin' dud shows—Lord Percy—givin' the fields a bad name.'

'Good old Waspy!' Bill exclaimed.

'Vosper's all out for the workin' miners even if he does go round lookin' like a poet or a religious crank,' Dinny went on. 'Stood by the shearers in the big Queensland strikes and got gaoled for it. Lord Percy wanted to fight him, but Vosper's not a fighting man. Lord Percy went for him all the same and bashed him about till some of the boys hauled him off. He pretty near killed Frank!'

Frisco snorted contemptuously:

'Serves him right. A man can't go round with long hair and refuse to fight if he says things like that.'

'Fists never settled any argument,' remarked Sam in his solemn, meditative way.

'That's what Vosper says,' Dinny said. 'He reckons a man should fight with his brains. It's only when he's short of brains, or hasn't got a case, he has to try his fists. The boys think a lot of Frank Vosper in the old camp, Frisco. He's got guts alright. Stands by the prospectors and miners against the mineowners and speculators all the time. Is with us on the Anti-'Ghan committee, and this professional jumpin' business. The big bugs 've got their knife into him for that. All they want is cheap labour and to hold on to half the country by trickin' the minin' laws.'

They were discussing the forfeiture and jumping of claims when Smiler Hales strolled along with Yank Boteral. Smiler had come in from Kurnalpi the night before, and Yank had been showing him over the open-cut on Maritana, and his claim near Brown Hill. Smiler liked to be considered a prospector, and a journalist only when he was hard-up. His jokes travelled the length and breadth of the fields and made him a welcome visitor in any camp. He and Dinny greeted each other like long-lost brothers, and Smiler settled down, pipe between his teeth, to hear what Dinny had to say about the jumping of the Londonderry North and South Blocks.

'There's something rotten about the whole business! What's at the bottom of it, Dinny?' he asked. 'On Kurnalpi we'd know what to do with a rat sneaking on to the property of a hard-working miner and putting in his pegs in the dark. But it seems, the lawyers 've got professional jumpers working for them, in the interests of powerful syndicates.'

'That's about the strong of it,' Dinny replied. 'They hang round like crows waitin' to pick on a prospector for neglectin' some reg'lation and apply for forfeiture on behalf of rich men.'

'A man who jumps claims for a living 's the meanest skunk unhung,' Frisco shouted.

'No reason why we shouldn't make a pure angel out of the first professional jumper we can lay our hands on,' Smiler remarked. 'Even if we have to make a soiled corpse of him, first.'

A gust of laughter skirled and gurgled away.

'I wouldn't hesitate,' Smiler went on, blandly, 'to give a jumper a calm, christian greeting with a three-foot waddy, if I found him prowling round a claim I'd worked and watched.'

'Same here, Smiler, Frisco crowed.

'There's only one law for such vermin.' Smiler paused before making his point. 'And that's digger's law. A pick handle in the strong right hand of an indignant prospector's a better argument than any legal document.'

'The legal business in the Blocks' case proves that,' Dinny said. 'Stinks from beginning to end. First of all Finnerty recommends forfeiture, and refuses to state a case for the opinion of a judge. Huxley and Mills petitioned the government that they were entitled to hold the leases and the jumpers were not. Petition not answered. Executive Council advises the government to declare leases forfeited and the government brings in a bill to bolster the jumpers' case. Turns out it was a family affair, the jumpers acted for a syndicate, all friends or relatives of members of the Council.'

The men muttered and swore angrily.

'It's a rotten business, alright,' Morris agreed.

'George Leake has accused Sir John Forrest of gross injustice,' Dinny concluded. 'But the jumpers 've got a valuable property.'

'God pickle my soul in hell, if I see why we should take it sittin' down,' Blunt Pick cried shrilly. 'This hits every prospector on the fields. If Jack Mills and his mates 'll fight it out, we'd ought to get behind them.'

'They won't!' Dinny said. 'They've got enough gold out of the 'Derry to keep 'm quiet.'

He stood up. The men round him shifted and stretched, shaking the dust off their clothes. They eyed him expectantly. Dinny was in luck. The next move was his. But his gaze wandered to where Mrs. Gough was sitting on her three-legged bag chair, still darning Morris's shirt.

'Come 'n 'ave a drink!' Frisco took the words out of his mouth.

'My shout,' Dinny said, quickly. 'And dinner at the pub.'

Frisco followed Dinny's eyes to Mrs. Gough.

'Too bad you can't join us, ma'am,' he exclaimed. He derided the hope Dinny had not dared to express that Sally would come to dinner with them.

'Why not?' Smiler was very much a man of the world and charming to women. 'If Mrs. Gough will do us the honour of dining with us at the Club Hotel, we can see her home, afterwards, and proceed later with our evening's entertainment at Dinny's expense.'

Sally caught Morris's eye vetoing the suggestion.

'Thank you so much,' she replied. 'But I couldn't be such a spoil sport. Dinny'll come to see me again before he goes back to Coolgardie. Won't you, Mr. Quin?'

Sally played her most radiant smile for Dinny. She could not allow Mr. Francisco Jo Murphy to jeer at her and discomfort Dinny in his new suit and big hat. He had come to pay her a visit. Everybody must understand he was a special friend of hers, and that she was pleased to see him.

'Sure, Mrs. Gough!' Dinny beamed and glowed under Sally's smile. 'I've got all sorts of messages for you from Mrs. Fogarty, and Alf's wife. How about to-morrow afternoon?'

'I'll expect you,' Sally said.

The men surged round and Dinny went off with them.

But it was several days before Sally saw him again, and then, he shuffled away, shamefacedly, for fear she might stop and speak to him. Dinny had been drinking for a week after that first night's shout on Hannans, and looked it. Collarless, unshaven, his eyes red-rimmed and goggling, his brand new suit dirty and crumpled, he shrank back into the pub as Mrs. Gough came towards him.

CHAPTER XXV

'Kerosene tin full of gold!'

'Rich new field, somewhere south of the old camp!'

Sally heard the men exclaiming, asking questions, swearing with gusty excitement. She came out of the brushwood shed that hot morning, to see Clary McClaren on his big bay nag, just as he had ridden over from Coolgardie. The horse was blowing and lathered with sweat, and Clary's face ablaze. He had brought a newspaper.

Half a dozen men were clustered round, reading it. From every direction men were gathering, some loping along or breaking into a jog-trot, others just strolling as if no news on earth could put them out of their leisurely stride.

Morris and Frisco joined the group. Sally heard Clary tell them that one of the morning newspapers had published the report of a sensational find.

'A kerosene tin filled with gold was brought into town recently,' it stated, 'and everything points to a new and extraordinarily rich goldfield.' Coolgardie had gone mad with the news and a big rush was brewing. No details were known yet, but Clary had ridden over to tell Big Jim, collect their gear and stores, and make back so as to be with the first push into the dry shingly ridges away to the south.

He retrieved his paper and rode off, leaving turmoil behind him. Men who had been dryblowing on almost exhausted claims at the foot of Maritana and Cassidy's, already were packing their swags. Lease holders and diggers working shafts along the ridge made arrangements to get away, and rushed off to the town to buy stores, a horse and cart, or camels. Frisco went after his horses which were running in the bush, and Morris set about throwing their picks and shovels together, rolling his blankets and camp equipment, almost without a word. The blood seemed to have flown to his head: his eyes had a feverish brightness.

'Give me all the tinned stuff you've got, Sally,' he said shortly. 'A quart pot, tin plate, knife and fork. Oh, and tea and sugar! I'll take one of the billies too, that waterbag, and the small tank.'

Sally busied herself helping him to pack. Every camp along the track was in the throes of similar preparations. When Frisco returned with the horses he harnessed them into the buggy and drove off for a load of stores. Morris stowed the gear on board as soon as he got back, and Frisco went along to the mine.

He had to provide for manning of the lease while he and Morris were away. Reckoned he could persuade a couple of old fossickers and a miner who had several children to keep things going for a few days. He didn't intend to do more than have a look at the new field, he said, unless it was exceptionally promising. Morris could hold down any claim they might peg, and ensure they did not lose anything worthwhile if it was going begging. But he believed in hanging on to a good bone when you had one: wasn't so keen on shadow chasing, nowadays.

Frisco's swag was soon packed and flung into the back of the buggy. It was not until they were ready to leave that Morris said, as if it had just occurred to him:

'Stay here until you hear from me, Sally. If you don't hear in a day or two go to the Brierly's!'

'Don't worry about me, Morris,' Sally replied cheerily, knowing very well he had not thought twice about leaving her. 'I'll be alright.'

'God, you're game, ma'am,' Frisco laughed.

Morris hesitated and then kissed Sally.

'Of course she is,' he said. 'If I didn't know that—'

'Good luck!' Sally cried. 'And bring back a kerosene tin full of gold from the new field.'

The buggy whirled away in a cloud of red dust, already part of the cavalcade moving off towards Coolgardie.

News of the new find had spread through Hannans like wildfire, and from every direction men were tramping along the track out of the town. Camels and camel buggies heavily loaded, buckboards with old crocks harnessed to them, spring carts and

141

sulkies behind heavy draught horses, or sturdy brumbies, and donkey teams. Soon they were all streaming in the direction of the old camp. Men on horses and camels, men on bicycles, on foot, bowed under the weight of tools and swags, or pushing handcarts, all the afternoon and evening, they were trailing in from outlying camps and swelling the rush to that as yet unknown rich new field.

By evening a strange quiet had settled down on Hannans. All the noisy, riotous life seemed to have been drained out of it. No racket of gambling came from the two-up school: no gust of drunken singing from the pubs. Only a few camp fires glowed in the dusk. Sally found herself almost alone among the deserted dumps scattered below the darkening ridge.

She knew this madness of a rush too well to be surprised at the way men were being carried away by it. When the lust for gold was on them, they were conscious of nothing else, and it affected Morris more than most men. She was quite unconcerned, as a matter of fact, about being left alone in the camp, although she wished she had thought of asking Morris to take her into Coolgardie so that she could go to see Marie and Laura.

From day to day, Sally heard rumours about the rush, at the store, from Eli and Parson Jarn who were too satisfied with their mine to move. Hordes of miners and prospectors flocked to Coolgardie from as far out as Kurnalpi, Roaring Gimlet and Dead Finish; but no details of where this 'new, extraordinary rich field' might be located had come to light.

The law required that prospectors should declare any gold they found, within ten days, and the place where it was found. But no prospectors had declared a rich haul, or any place where it was likely to be made. Hundreds of enraged men, straining at the leash, demanded information from the *Golden Age*, which had published the paragraph about that 'kerosene tin filled with gold.'

After a week, Frisco came back to see whether arrangements for working the lease were going on satisfactorily. He said the rushers were going to wreck the *Age* offices and there would be the devil to pay if the newspaper did nothing to prove its statement. He went back to Coolgardie when word came through that a prospector named McCann had given the information, and he knew where the gold came from. But it wasn't until Morris returned that Sally heard the whole story.

He was as angry and sore about it as the rest of the men who drifted back to Hannans, and blamed the newspapers for taking the babbling of a drunken fool for gospel. McCann, himself, was a rotten dog, everybody considered, to stick to his yarn when he knew prospectors were scouring hundreds of miles of waterless country, and likely to die of thirst and starvation in the search for a goldfield which did not exist.

John Marshall, honorary secretary of the Diggers' Association, prevented the rush having tragic consequences, Morris said. Marshall discovered the way in which the newspapers had got their story, and was satisfied there was going to be serious trouble if the thousands of diggers hanging about Coolgardie for the rush found out they had been fooled.

An angry mob had started to knock McCann about when Marshall made his way to McCann's side and shouted:

'Look here, boys, you know who I am. It's time we did something to end this maddening doubt and uncertainty. Reports published by the newspapers appear to have no foundation. I'm determined to locate the alleged rush and find out whether McCann's report is true or not.'

The uproar subsided. Through hoots and groans, and shouts of approval, John Marshall continued:

'On behalf of the Association, I'll call a public meeting for this afternoon at three o'clock. McCann will have to speak and tell us what he knows, and then a party can be organized to go out with him and settle whether the find is a fraud or not. I'll take charge of McCann and see he turns up at the meeting.'

The bell-man went round, and a few hours later, a tremendous crowd gathered round the wagon outside the offices of the Diggers' Association. McCann spoke from the wagon. A tall, broad shouldered man, with a drooping black moustache, looking ghastly and hollow-eyed after a bout of heavy drinking, he faced hundreds of diggers vowing vengeance on him if he deceived them. The diggers greeted him with hisses, groans and jeering applause. But McCann stood up to the ordeal so well, many believed what he said.

McCann admitted that he had been on a bender. What the newspaper reporters got out of him when he was drunk, he said, he didn't know. No man could be blamed for what he said when he was drunk. The newspapers, and not he, were responsible for the rush that had occurred, but— The hopes of the rushers rose again as he offered to lead a party to the place where a rich deposit of alluvial gold had been found recently.

Funds were subscribed to equip the party, and two buggies started out, with four diggers chosen by the men. They were all tough and experienced prospectors, and well-armed, as there had been threats to get McCann if he did not prove the truth of his public statement. The police and the Warden had informed the men put in charge of McCann that they would be held responsible for his life. They were on oath to bring him back to face diggers' justice.

Reports of men who had set off along the track, in the first days of the rush, and were marooned without food or water in the ridges between Coolgardie and Widgiemooltha, kept anger and indignation simmering. Relief was being organized when a thunderstorm brought heavy rain. It saved many lives. As prospectors returned, with accounts of gruelling experiences and no sign of tracks, or new workings over a wide area, pessimism increased.

Bulletins about the progress of the search party were posted at the offices of the Diggers' Association. Diggers flocked to read and discuss them. But nothing was heard to encourage the hope that McCann would justify his promise. Plans to waylay the search party on the way back to Coolgardie and shoot or hang McCann by the roadside, were thwarted when Dinny and some of the older, more level-headed prospectors arranged for a watch to be kept, night and day, on the road by which the search party was expected to return.

It got back early one Sunday evening. The men in charge of McCann took him to Marshall's house and reported that he had led them on a wild goose chase: was not able to indicate gold-bearing country, much less any workings from which alluvial gold had been taken recently. Marshall took a short cut to the police camp through his back yard, and McCann was removed to the lock-up for his own protection.

There was some guts in the man, Marshall said, because he wanted to stay and face the diggers, and was only with difficulty induced to keep out of the way. He would never have survived had he not done so, Morris was sure. When Johnny Marshall met an infuriated mob at the door of his house, there were howls of: 'Where's McCann?'

'String him up!'
'Give the rotten cow his deserts!'
'Shoot him!'
'Shootin's too good for him!'
'So's hangin'!'
'Bash his head in!'
'Tear him limb from limb!'

It was a sickening demonstration, Morris said. He would never have believed men could lash themselves into such a mania. They wanted to revenge themselves on John Marshall also. Accused him of hiding McCann and threatened to wreck his house. But every man capable of reasoning knew how wisely and courageously Marshall had acted in refusing to surrender McCann.

The older, more stable prospectors rallied to Marshall and would have defended him with their lives when he jumped up on a packing case outside his house and addressed the crowd.

A fine figure of a man, he stood there, upright and handsome, and honest as the day, everybody knew. His nobility of bearing and his fearlessness, in opposing the madness which was dominating hundreds of men, undoubtedly had its effect. He did something which no other man could have done to abate the furore. The most savage howlers for McCann's blood shut up to listen to John Marshall. And Marshall spoke with a strength and simplicity which restored the sanity of every decent man.

Calmly and clearly, he outlined the circumstances which had led to the rush and pleaded with the diggers, despite their natural anger and indignation, not to be goaded into reckless deeds by some violent and vicious characters among them. John Marshall explained that the police and the Warden were holding him and the men who had accompanied McCann responsible for his safety; and that, in the interests of the diggers themselves, he had requested the police to remove McCann to the lock-up. On the track McCann had repeatedly begged the men in charge of him for a revolver to blow out his brains. Several times the search party had been held up by diggers anxious to revenge themselves on McCann.

Marshall ended with a plea for the poor, drunken fool who had been made the victim of newspaper sensationalism. McCann had tried to brazen his way out of a terrible situation and realized his guilt in this respect.

'But this man has been terribly punished already, by the horror and misery he has suffered,' John Marshall pointed out. 'He wanted to give himself up to the diggers to-night and make an end of the whole business! If the diggers wreak physical vengeance on McCann, many other men will have to bear the brunt of it. And, surely, no man in his senses wants the disastrous consequences of this rush to go any further.'

Marshall asked the crowd to disperse, and urged responsible diggers to prevent any disturbance which would prolong the tragic farce of the rush for which the publication of inaccurate information was chiefly responsible.

That demented, hostile crowd responded amazingly to his speech. It moved off, cheering, and convinced that John Marshall was right. He had saved many men from a murderous assault on McCann, and maybe from joining in a fight to punish Marshall himself for defending McCann.

There were some mutterers and blusterers still bursting to demonstrate their wrath; but they turned off in the direction of the newspaper offices. The police were there before them, and though windows were smashed, no great damage was done.

McCann made his escape at dawn next morning.

Morris had not returned to Hannans until the last act of the rush was played out by a party coming back from a futile trek in the southern ridges. It tramped into Coolgardie with an effigy of McCann swinging on a gallows.

Diggers still hanging about the town quickly fell into a procession behind the newcomers and marched towards the newspaper office which had started the rush. The effigy was soaked in oil and set alight. While it burned, a horde of diggers yelled curses and abuse at the newspaper and newspaper men generally. Then they flung the burning effigy into the frail wooden building.

That was the end of McCann's rush. Many prospectors had thrown up their claims, trudged from camps a hundred miles away, wasted time and money, almost died of thirst and starvation scouring the country. All because credence had been given to some drunken boasting about secret knowledge of a rich find which did not exist.

'Is it any wonder the diggers feel murderous about people who start a bogus rush?' Morris growled. 'Storekeepers and publicans have been known to do it because a rush is good for trade; but I hope I never get mixed up with a mob that's been hoaxed again. I was as mad as the rest of them, Sally.'

CHAPTER XXVI

MONTHS slipped away, with days of dry, withering heat, iron-grey skies, brilliant white light, dust storms and suffocating nights.

All day the camp shimmered in a blinding incandescence: the hot air quivered on iron roofs and whitewashed shacks of the township. Red dust fumed on the tracks beside the slowly moving strings of camels. Horse teams stood where they halted, the big Victorian draughts dead beat after their long pull from the 'Cross. Western scrubbers stood up to their loads better, and the donkey teams crawled stubbornly, in strings of fifty, over hundreds of miles to the outlying camps.

Clouds of dust overhung the alluvial claims where a few dry-blowers were still working. The rattle and clank of work on the mines along the ridge went on with dreary monotony, from dawn until late in the afternoon, although owing to the shortage of water, exemptions were granted and many leaseholders, miners and prospectors had left for the coast. Only those who had weathered the hot months before and could not afford to go south, hung on to their claims, working doggedly, sweating, cursing and defying the sun.

There was nothing to do about the heat but grin and bear it, they said, and Sally realized she must do likewise. She did not doubt her capacity for endurance. If Morris could stand this hot weather on the fields, she was sure that she could. After all, she told herself, she was 'a brumby, born and bred,' and surely could do as well as the bush-bred horses Cracker Jack swore were the best on the road during the summer.

So she went about, pretending to be as brisk and lively as ever, determined to keep up her spirits, and the men's when they came round the camp, though life often became just a gasping for breath and an anxious hoarding of food and water: a living from day to day in the heat and glare as if you were withering and drying up inside, but must crack hardy and joke about it to show your grit.

The scarcity of water and fresh food caused a lot of sickness. Festering sores, the men called barcoo rot, broke out on their arms and legs. Sandy blight bunged up their eyes. Typhoid was raging. Every day there was news of some man lying ill in his camp and others dying in the makeshift huts of bagging and tin, known as the hospital.

Things were no better at Coolgardie, where two trained nurses had been installed in the government hospital. But the hospital was still no more than a collection of hessian shacks through which the dust poured and the flies hung in swarms. There were funerals every day and the cemetery was in a terrible condition: the stench overpowering, and graves falling in over the hurriedly-interred dead.

The bush reeked with the ordures of men and beasts. Flies swarmed from it, polluting food and water. Afghans and camels, flies and filth were blamed for the fever. Everybody went in fear of it. An effort was made to clean up round the camps, and to get better arrangements at the hospital and the cemetery.

At Hannans the track to the cemetery meandered through scrub and the men joked about how a funeral sometimes got bushed. The horses could scarcely crawl along, and often had to stand in the sun for a couple of hours while his mates dug a man's grave.

'Did y'r hear about the corpse that disappeared?' Dinny asked cheerfully, one evening.

'Garn, Dinny, that's one of Smiler's yarns,' Blunt Pick objected.

'P'raps it is,' Dinny admitted. 'But I got it from a bloke who says his mate's brother told Smiler about how some of the boys tried to bury old Bobby Mofflin. And Smiler got it all wrong. Seems his mates thought Bobby was dead: got a death certificate and a coffin for him. But bein' new chums at the undertakin' they didn't fasten him down properly. On the way to the cemetery, came to a pub, and thought a drink wouldn't do them any harm. They had several, and when they went back to the cart where they'd left the coffin, in the broiling sun, the corpse was missin'! Gosh, did their hair stand on end!

'They didn't know whether it was the divil 'd snatched Bobby, or the undertaker, because he hadn't been paid for his coffin. But they didn't inform the police, like Smiler says, or advertise in the *Miner*: "Lost, stolen, or strayed, a pale-complected corpse, more or less deceased." They found Bobby in a camp near the pub, still alive enough to have a drink with 'em. "Here's to the late Robert Mofflin," says he. "God bless him. May his soul rest in peace." After which he stretched peaceable like, and died again. His mates postponed the funeral until next day. But they paid the undertaker and made him close down the coffin before they started out for the cemetery.'

The camp accepted Dinny's version of that story rather than Smiler's which rather slung off at the men's attempt to do their duty by an old mate.

Through the sweltering heat, dust storms, scarcity of water, shortage of food and raging fever, the lust for gold remained unabated. It drove men to slake their thirst at the pubs when they knocked off work towards sunset. There was beer even when water was rationed. It helped the men to forget the sun-blasted country about them, and their desperate struggle to survive: gave them a sense of the need for good fellowship and reckless gaiety in it all.

Stories of new finds, sensational discoveries on outlying fields were told and retold. Dick Eades had brought in two thousand ounces from a lease he was taking up west of the Brilliant Reward and calling the Break o' Day. The ground was being pegged in every direction. Bully Hayes and his mates were showing magnificent specimens from the Hit and Miss mine, twenty miles east of White Feather. The Great Fingal Blocks at Edjudina had been sold to an English syndicate for £175,000.

Goodenough Sharp was pegging forty-two acres north-east of Menzies.

Through the hot still nights, the men stretched yarning and smoking, and Sally lay on her back, looking up at stars, misty in the heat. The darkness and dim silvery light were balm after the blaze of the sun all day and an oven-atmosphere which seemed to sap all the moisture in her body. But even that brief peace was destroyed by the roaring of a bull camel, or the grunting and growling of beasts in Faiz and Tagh Mahommet's stinking camel yard.

After work, Morris usually went along with Frisco to the nearest pub for a drink. There was plenty of beer, even when water was scarce, and if he staggered up the track, drunk at sunset, Sally could not complain, or begrudge him anything that helped him to pull through the inferno of those days.

Rumours of a mountain of gold at Mount Catherine, and of a massacre of natives round about Pindinnie, were being discussed in all the camps.

Dinny, who had returned to Hannans after McCann's rush, and was camped with an old mate near Brown Hill, said Mick Gerald, one of the prospectors, had come in with specimens which started the mountain of gold yarn. Mick had gone out with the Parry boys and a small party making for Mount Margaret, he said. The party had split up. He and Bill and Syd Parry struck a big quartz hill, knapping it got nice shotty gold, and called the place Mount Catherine. They had not picked up a skerick of alluvial, but further on discovered another reef which they intended to register as the Daisy Bell.

While they were out prospecting, natives raided the camp, and speared the pack horses. They went out after the natives and met Ned Robbins who had struck the far end of the Daisy Bell reef and pegged a lease there. Ned went with them to settle with the natives.

Mick Gerald and Syd Parry lost no time getting into Hannans to apply for the lease of Mount Catherine. Robbins followed them. Gerald and Syd went on to Coolgardie. Robbins went after them and there was a great row. Gerald swore he had not applied for a lease of the Daisy Bell and Robbins took the coach back to Hannans to apply for the lease. Bill Parry jumped on his horse and beat him to the Warden's office. They fought it out when Robbins arrived, too late to claim the ground. Gerald and the Parrys had got away with a dirty trick, most of the men believed, by making Ned Robbins believe they would leave him in possession of the Daisy Bell, but Robbins swore to get even with them.

He gave information to the police about that massacre of the blacks. Gerald and Bill Parry· were arrested. Syd, when he heard what had happened, gave himself up.

The Coolgardie Miner came out with an article drawing attention to the ill-treatment of natives by certain unscrupulous prospectors.

'Blacks had been killed wholesale,' it declared, 'without regard to age or sex. Infants had been taken from their mothers and the brains battered out of their tiny bodies with rocks, innumerable outrages were perpetrated on the women and the unfortunate savages slaughtered ruthlessly.'

What could you make of it? Every man on the fields knew that the blacks got a raw deal from some prospectors. They had a pretty good idea why the Pindinnie tribes were considered a bad lot, fierce and hostile. It was a desperate struggle to survive in that area. Strange men and beasts, camels and horses, exhausted the native wells and soaks: deprived native game of feed and water. Spears flew to defend native rights. The white men shot and killed. If they stole a native's food and water, the natives considered they were entitled to steal the white man's food. Reprisals had been savage and every man knew that he carried his life in his hands, prospecting in the back country these days.

Speck Jones and Bill Jehosaphat said they had never had any trouble with the blacks because they gave them food and never interfered with their women. They kept their eyes skinned in country where the blacks were known to be hostile, all the same: slept a good way from their camp fire, and tethered the horses handy.

Big Jim and Clary McClaren agreed that the placatory method was all right if the blacks were not looking for vengeance. But it was an eye for an eye and a tooth for a tooth with them, and they didn't mind whose eye or tooth they got, so long as a white man paid for an injury to the tribe. A man had to shoot in self-defence. But this business of rounding-up a tribe and slaughtering men, women and children was something few men could stomach. Most of the diggers were shocked and condemned such brutality, convinced that other prospectors would have to pay for it.

Frisco and a few others defended Mick Gerald and the Parrys. 'The bloody niggers 've got to be taught a lesson,' he said. 'There'll be no living in the back country, if they get the upper hand. Think they can rat a man's camp and leave him without stores, a hundred miles from anywhere.'

No one doubted that Ned Robbins was telling the truth; but

they could not forgive him for telling it. Going to the police with it above all. There was a lot of personal gall in his action. The men did not blame him for being sore about being juggled out of the lease of the Daisy Bell; but after all, he should have been awake to what Mick Gerald was likely to put over him, in order to have a legal right to the ground.

It was one thing to have a grievance and be ready to air it, and another to send three men up for murder of a few blacks. No jury on the fields would convict the prospectors, everybody knew. Ned Robbins would be sorry he had spoken. He *was* at the end of the trial; got the thick end of the stick.

Warden Finnerty was on the bench when Mick Gerald and the Parrys were charged with murder 'in shooting a number of aboriginals.'

They pleaded not guilty.

Ned Robbins, as the chief witness for the prosecution, described a number of shots which had been fired and how several blacks had been killed. His evidence was lame and reluctant. His aboriginal boy, Ben, said he had heard shots fired and saw natives killed. Sergeant Stokes stated that he and a trooper found the remains of a native among some rocks and other remains nearby. Mick Gerald and the Parrys admitted the shooting, but pleaded that they had been forced to defend themselves.

'Not sufficient evidence to commit,' the Warden decided and discharged the prisoners. But Ned Robbins was remanded in custody for being *particeps criminis*. It was two or three days before he was released.

The Warden administered justice in a rough and ready fashion, as was expected of him, and with a grim sense of humour. It was a good joke that Ned Robbins had landed himself in the lock-up while the men he accused went scot free. Prospectors approved of the verdict, chuckling over it round the camps and in the hotel bars.

That was the way to deal with an informer, they agreed. Robbins had tried to get three men strung-up to work off a grudge against them. He cared as little about the niggers as Mick Gerald. It was tough luck Robbins should have been done out of a valuable property he had pegged, of course; but a man had to have his wits about him and apply for his lease as soon as he pegged, or be left in the lurch.

'A prospector must know the mining reg'lations and keep on the right side of 'em if he wants to hang on to auriferous ground,' Dinny said. 'It's all in the game. Remember how

Carr-Boyd and Bill Adams did Speakman and Ryan out of the Twenty-Five Mile?'

Some of the men grinned: others swore grimly.

'That was the rottenest jumping ever I heard of,' Sam Mullet said flatly.

'But Carr-Boyd got left all the same,' Blunt Pick chortled.

'You've said it, Sam,' Dinny smoked thoughtfully.

'Speakman and Ryan, and a bloke name of Erickson, went out prospectin' from the 'Cross in 'ninety-two before Bayley's was discovered. They struck gold at Ullaring, and further on at the Twenty-Five Mile: wanted to have a good look round before they applied for a lease. Then, one morning, they twigged a stray camel with a load on his back. Put the glasses on to him, and saw it was a man the camel was carryin'. Went after the camel and found Doc Schneider strapped to its back. He was all-in, 'd been without food or water for days and was jest about a gonner. But Speakman and his mates nursed him round, and then Schneider told them about the rush to Bayley's.

'Seems he and Adams and Carr-Boyd were on the Murchison when they got the news, and decided to ride overland to Coolgardie. But they had a row, and Adams and Carr-Boyd went off without Schneider. Schneider started out after 'em on the camel, but lost their tracks. When Speakman and Ryan started for the 'Cross to apply for their lease, Erickson and Doc Schneider decided to go along with a party which had come out from Coolgardie. They wanted to have a look at Bayley's. And who should Schneider run in to but Carr-Boyd and Adams. He started crowin' over them about the claim he'd struck and how Speakman and Ryan were making for the 'Cross by way of Ullaring, and were going to register a big find at the Twenty-Five, as well.

'Carr-Boyd tipped Adams the wink, while he hung on to Schneider, and Adams got away on a fast riding camel, marked off Speakman and Ryan's lease and applied for it before they got into the 'Cross. When the case was heard in the Warden's Court, Finnerty had to abide by the regulations and give the verdict to Adams. But Adams just told Carr-Boyd where to go, when he wanted to share the loot.'

'Cripes, can y'r beat it?' Sam muttered.

'Takes the goat's tail!' Blunt Pick agreed.

'Me, I'd like to put a bloke like that at the end of a long shovel in a hot end, for life,' Teddy Dow remarked.

'What's bitin' you all?' Frisco laughed. 'All's fair when a man's on gold, and he sticks to the regulations!'

CHAPTER XXVII

DURING those blistering summer months when typhoid was raging and every camp on the fields short of water, feeling against the 'Ghans ran high.

In arid country where the lives of men and beasts depended on some isolated soak or gnamma hole, it was a crime to pollute the water. Yet on the out-back tracks, Afghan camel drivers camped near the water holes and every dust storm blew their refuse down into the water. Not only that, but the 'Ghans were known to wash their feet and bodies in the water other men had to drink.

Dinny raved about it when he came in from a rush on the Ninety-Mile.

'Before the 'Ghans and their camels was usin' the tracks,' he said, 'you could depend on water bein' pure and wholesome— even if there wasn't much of it, anywhere you went in this country. Now, it's often liquid manure. We have to use it. There's no other. The 'Ghans say: "Allah provides the water" and they use it to wash with because washin's part of their religion. Don't care a damn if they make the water filthy for any Christian dogs who come along—though they won't eat or drink anything we've touched.'

'We've got to do something about it,' Morris agreed. 'Jim Sherry was telling me the other day, he pulled up near some rocks where he knew he could get water, about sixteen miles out of Menzies. Found three 'Ghans washing dirty clothes in one of the best rock holes. Argued the point with them and tried to make them understand they could take water, and wash their clothes away from the pool. But they came for him in a body and drove him off to a small hole where there wasn't enough water to give his horse a drink. He wasn't armed or he'd have stood up to them. Then they came along, flourishing a revolver and hurling lumps of rocks at him. He had to clear out, rode into Menzies and got some of the boys to go back with him. But the 'Ghans had disappeared.'

Frisco swore impatiently.

'I'd like to see a bloody 'Ghan move me off a water hole—or washin' his feet in water I had to drink,' he said.

'There was a teamster come in from Geraldton, couple of weeks ago,' Sam remarked, stoking his pipe. 'He says the dam on the stretch between Geraldton and Mullewa's no use now. 'Ghans been washing their camels in it, sores, mange, sore backs and all. The stench'd drive you off the track.'

'Sam and me tried to trick'm once,' Blunt Pick cut in. 'We was camped about fifty miles out from Dead Finish, but there was a nice water hole handy. When we see a 'Ghan washin' his camel's sore back in it, we'd shot a hole in him—if we'd had anything to shoot with. But we hadn't. So we hung a bit of salt pork on a stick over the hole so as the 'Ghans couldn't use the water—agen their religion to swallow anything pork has touched. But there was half a dozen 'Ghans and on'y two of us. They threatened to tie up and shoot any digger they found tryin' that stunt on 'm agen.'

'Christ,' Frisco shouted, 'are we standin' for that?'

'They're gettin' darn cheeky, the 'Ghans, Yank drawled. 'And they've got a new game—camel plantin'. If a man loses a camel, a 'Ghan 'll come along and say: "S'pose you give me money, me find 'm camel." "Right," says the prospector, "s'pose you find 'm camel me give you two pound." "S'pose you give money 'long storekeeper, now, me go find 'm," says the 'Ghan. He goes and finds the camel in a few hours: has had the beast tied down in the bush somewhere.'

'That's right,' Dinny said. 'There's been an epidemic of lost camels round about Coolgardie, lately, and 'Ghans claimin' the reward. Men comin' in from the bush have said they saw camels tied down and wondered what was up.

'Harry Vernon camped his camels at the Three-Mile. Next day, two of them was missin'. He tracked 'm for thirty miles. Met a prospector on the saltbush flat be Mount Burgess who told him he saw a 'Ghan takin' a couple of camels down to the Cattle Swamp. Harry went after 'em. Found his beasts there all right, tied down in the 'Ghans' yard. They refused to give up the camels. Said one of 'm had bitten a calf of theirs.

'They wanted compensation. Swarmed round, full of fight, but wouldn't produce the calf. Harry was unarmed. The 'Ghans made it clear they'd do for him if he didn't pay up, and they could've quite easy, out there, and nobody be the wiser. Harry gave them a couple of sovereigns he had on him, and they let him go. Him and the camels, but it's the last time he's goin' into a 'Ghans' camp unless he's got a gun on him, Harry says.'

'What are we goin' to do about it?' Frisco demanded. 'Let the 'Ghans boss the fields?'

'We've got an anti-Afghan Committee started in the old camp,' Dinny said. 'And it's goin' to clean things up. The storekeepers are dead against it, 'cause 'Ghan camel drivers are cheaper than white. The teamsters are with us. Say the 'Ghans are pushing them off the tracks. It's a working man's job to shift the 'Ghans. The big men like Faiz and Tagh Mahommet 've got freehold property. They're grabbing water rights and their slaves are gettin' jobs while our own mates are starvin'. Makes your blood boil. There's 'Ghans employed well-sinking, as police troopers, mending the roads. The 'Ghans' tender for any contract is always the lowest, because they don't pay the poor creatures workin' for 'em more than a miserable wage.'

'Captain Saunders, manager for Sultan Raj Mahommed, says the 'Ghans made provisions and water cheaper on the fields,' Morris murmured.

'That's a lie,' Dinny declared hotly. 'When white drivers showed they could handle camels as well as any 'Ghan, the 'Ghans had to bring down their prices. On Kurnalpi it was the white drivers brought down the prices of food. The 'Ghans got as much as they could.'

'Wherever there's slave owners, there's "mean whites," ' Yank's voice glided into the talking. 'That's how it was in America. The 'Ghans 've got the slaves to supply cheap labour. The working men on the goldfields 'll be "mean whites" before long, if we don't shift the 'Ghans.'

'We'll shift 'em,' Dinny said.

'It's "Hooshta!" for the 'Ghans, eh, Dinny?' Frisco laughed.

'One of the mineowners was sayin' the other day in Coolgardie,' Dinny went on, 'he didn't consider the miners overpaid on these fields, but "I can assert either Afghan or Chinese labour is much cheaper—" '

'Well, they're not doin' the workin' miner out of his rights for cheap labour, if we can help it,' Blunt Pick declared.

'That's the stuff, Blunt,' Dinny agreed. 'A 'Ghan's all right— if y'r can find a good 'Ghan—but we've got to make a stand against them grabbin' the water holes and gettin' away with this cheap labour racket.'

When Teddy Knowles was arrested and charged with killing an Afghan on one of the southern tracks, every prospector on the fields was prepared to defend Knowles. He was a quiet, decent little man, well-known and popular. Dinny went over to Coolgardie and got the facts from the anti-Afghan Committee which was taking up the case.

'Teddy Knowles and his mate, Hatfield, had a bullock wagon, and were making for the Esperence road,' he told Morris, Frisco, and the other men who gathered round him in the camp when he returned. 'They'd come overland from Oodnadatta, and pulled up near a tank, about fifteen miles nor'-west of Ponton's Station. There was a big camel camp in the bush, and about four o'clock in the afternoon, when the 'Ghans had got all the water they wanted, Teddy went down to get some, and saw a 'Ghan washing his feet in the tank. Shouted to him to stop.

' "No care," yells the 'Ghan. Teddy tells some of the 'Ghans standin' near to make him get a dish to wash his feet in because white men had to drink that water. They just cackled among themselves.'

'How do you know, Dinny?' Morris asked.

'That's what Teddy Knowles, himself, says in a letter to the Committee,' Dinny replied. He went on:

'Teddy went up to the 'Ghan and tried to hustle him away from the tank. The other 'Ghans came for him with sticks and stones and flourishing firearms. A stone struck Teddy on the face, and he drew his revolver and fired at a 'Ghan aiming another stone at him. The shot hit the 'Ghan in the shoulder, and the mob closed in on Teddy. In the struggle, his revolver went off again and caught another 'Ghan in the stomach. The 'Ghans grabbed the revolver, were kicking and beating Teddy, when Hatfield and another man came up with a rifle which was kept loaded on the wagon.

'The 'Ghans overpowered them, and carted all three men along to their camp; tied them up to trees. About three-quarters of an hour later, the boss 'Ghan came along and struck Hatfield with his whip several times. He threatened to burn the three white men if Noore Mahommet died.

'Teddy was tied-up so tightly he would've konked out if a chap named Thomas Boetcher, travellin' with the 'Ghans, hadn't made 'em loosen the ropes. Teddy and his mates were kept tied-up till three o'clock next day, when Ponton and Coleman came over from the station and persuaded the 'Ghans to release them. Teddy went on into Israelite Bay and reported the whole business to the police.'

The men's indignation burst in a confusion of oaths and angry queries.

'Hatfield says,' Dinny added, 'eight 'Ghans attacked Teddy in the first place, and the prospector who gave him a hand tryin' to save Teddy reckons there was a hundred and eight camels and their drivers in the 'Ghan camp.'

Knowles' trial at Albany was followed with deep concern by prospectors throughout the goldfields. Many a man could see himself in Teddy Knowles's shoes: had suffered by the Afghans' abuse of water and their aggressive attitude towards poorly-equipped white men travelling singly, or in pairs, in the back country.

Teddy Knowles's acquittal was hailed with excitement and rejoicing. The case intensified bad feeling between the 'Ghans and white men. But threatened with an embargo on their traffic, Faiz and Tagh Mahommet, owners of the big camel teams, issued instructions that their drivers on all the inland tracks must observe the law of the country and refrain from giving offence to other travellers using the scanty water supplies.

CHAPTER XXVIII

SALLY had just finished her odd jobs round the camp that hot morning, she looked up to see Maritana coming towards her from the scrub. She was quite naked, a supple brown figure in the blazing sunshine.

'Oh, it's you, Maritana,' Sally exclaimed, pleased to see the girl again.

'Eherm,' Maritana murmured, smiling.

'Why did you run away?' Sally asked.

Maritana gurgled shyly, shaking her head as if the reason for her comings and goings was a mystery to her also.

Sally remembered suddenly the joey she had kept as a pet at Southern Cross. Dinny had brought it to her from its mother's pouch. His dog had run down the mother and killed her. She was a rock wallaby, and the joey a beautiful little creature with straight-lashed brown eyes and a soft-brown and grey pelt. Sally had used a baby's bottle to feed it, and soon it was hopping about, nibbling bits of grass and vegetable leaves from her hand: followed her like a puppy.

Dinny fenced off a corner of the yard to keep the joey in; but a couple of stray mongrels had broken into the yard and savaged the joey before her eyes. Sally could never forget that sight and the horror and rage which overwhelmed her. She had beaten off the dogs, screaming crazily, until Morris ran out to her. But the joey was dead.

It was such a cruel thing to have happened to that gentle, helpless creature. Sally wept bitterly in Morris's arms. Morris said he had never known her to cry like that. It was a long time before she could get the sense of tragedy out of her mind. The joey's brown eyes and pretty futile little hands haunted her.

Maritana's eyes and hands, now, reminded her of the joey. She had the same wild, shy ways as the little rock wallaby. That sense of tragedy swirled again. Sally brushed it away. Maritana was not a girl like any other, standing there naked: so naive and defenceless in the bright sunshine. Sally flinched to a recurring vision of the dogs attacking her joey. She was panic-stricken for Maritana. It was so absurd.

Maritana understood that something had disturbed Missus Sally. The flurried gesture, and smile banishing her distress, indicated that it had passed. Sally hoped that none of the men would pass until Maritana was dressed. Maritana interpreted her glance towards the track.

It was not necessary to say: 'Go and put on your dress, Maritana!' Maritana had slipped away, and a moment later was busy with her ablutions. Frisco might shout angrily when he saw how much water she had used, Sally thought; but she could not bring herself to interfere as Maritana soaped and splashed herself, giggling happily.

Her hair was still wet, hanging round her head in glistening strings, when she came back to where Sally was sitting in her chair made from the three-pronged trunk of a tree with a bag slung across for a seat. Maritana had put on the dress Sally helped her to make. With jingling necklaces and smiling eyes, she waited for Missus Sally's word of approval.

'That's better!' Sally said, smiling too.

Maritana's burble spoke for her. She thought she had discovered the cause of the white woman's perturbation. 'Bin walkabout, walkabout,' she explained conversationally, squatting on the ground. 'Sun jump-up, fall down, plenty feller. Weary booger, me!'

That meant she had walked a long way and was hungry, Sally guessed.

'Oh, of course,' she said quickly. 'You must have a cup of tea and something to eat, Maritana.'

While Maritana was munching thick pieces of bread and jam, Sally stirred up the fire and hung a billy of water over it to make tea. There was nothing Maritana liked better than to have a cup of tea with her like a friend and an equal. And the girl was ravenously hungry, she could see. Maritana was not interested in anything until she had finished her meal and drunk two or three cups of tea.

Then she beamed and was ready to talk again.

'Yienda [you] catch 'm cooboo?' she asked cheerfully.

'Goodness gracious, no!' Sally looked startled. 'What on earth makes you ask such a question, Maritana?'

Maritana gurgled delightedly.

'Mine catch 'm,' she explained. 'That feller mingari leave 'm baby where we sit down in bush, one day. Bardook tell'm go camp. Plenty tucker camp. Black feller all weary booger. Tucker? Wiah [no]. Malga [water]? Wiah.'

158

'Oh!' Sally was filled with consternation. She realized that her tribe had sent Maritana back to Frisco, because it was short of food and water. But how would he take this news of the mingari baby? Was it his? Or the child of her native husband, Bardook?

Maritana was watching her, Sally knew. She tried to hide the feeling of apprehension and disgust her thoughts stirred. But Maritana's reaction was instantaneous. Her face became sullen and scowling. Presently she jumped up and walked away.

Frisco's was a rowdy camp that night. When he strolled up the track, late in the afternoon, there were several men with him. He greeted Maritana boisterously; but went off to the pub and did not return until after sunset. The men came back with him, and as the sky darkened they lighted the kerosene flare.

Sally could see Maritana's slight fantastic figure struck out by the garish light; hear the men teasing her and Maritana replying with a few filthy oaths at which they laughed in lazy amusement. Frisco strummed on his guitar and sang now and then.

As men collected for a game, the ring formed, and the usual racket over the betting began. Two newly arrived diggers appeared on the scene, bottles sticking out of their hip pockets. They had picked up a thirty ounce slug and were celebrating, they said: wanted to spin on their first luck at Hannans.

But one of the strangers was so drunk, he made a nuisance of himself: was hustled out of the ring. He lurched over to the fireplace where Maritana sat crooning to herself and playing with two or three dogs who had followed their masters to the two-up ring. He sat down beside her. Maritana sprang up, and was sliding away when he grabbed her and tried to pull her off into the scrub.

Maritana shrieked and the dogs sprang at her assailant. There was pandemonium for a few moments, an uproar of cursing, with Maritana screaming, the dogs yelping, and the drunken lout yelling: 'The black bitch led me on! What's a gin, anyhow, to make a fuss about?'

Frisco laid him out and turned on Maritana. He clouted her over the head, shook and bashed her about until Maritana dragged herself away and disappeared into the darkness. Sally could hear her whimpering nearby. The men laughed uproariously as Frisco strode back to the ring, having vindicated his honour. The gambling went on for hours.

In the morning, Sally found Maritana sleeping near her fireplace.

'Yukki!' she exclaimed, jumping up and blinking at the light. 'Bin make 'm big shut eye!'

She watched Sally rake over embers of the fire and put some brushwood over them, fill a billy with water and hang it on a hook over the flames.

'Jinkie [evil spirit] feller, grab 'm,' she explained, with a furtive glance towards Frisco's fireplace. 'Frisco badgee [cross] : kick'm be-'ind.'

'I know,' Sally replied. 'I'm cross-feller with Frisco about it.'

'Wiah?' Maritana looked surprised.

She sauntered across to Frisco's fireplace, and, as Sally had done, raked the ashes of the fire together, filled a blackened billy with water and swung it over the blaze. Then she washed her face and hands, as Missus Sally was doing, and set cups and saucers on the table in the bough shed beside Frisco's tent. She had learnt to make porridge, fry bacon and eggs, and went about getting Frisco's breakfast ready for him.

Morris had gone over to the ring the night before: said he wanted to turn-in early. Sally intended to follow him but sat brooding in the coolness of the starlit night for awhile. So she had seen the brawl over Maritana. Morris had only heard it: been annoyed and kept awake by the noise.

'We'll shift camp,' he told Sally, when he was eating his breakfast. 'I can't stand the way Frisco's carrying-on any longer.'

'Further along the track,' Sally agreed eagerly, 'we would have a little more privacy. It was terrible last night, Morris; I wanted to go to Maritana's assistance, but—'

'Good God!' Morris exclaimed harshly. 'You couldn't interfere! It's the sort of thing that's bound to happen if there's a gin about.'

'Oh, dear!' Sally wailed. 'But it wasn't Maritana's fault, and Frisco treated her brutally.'

'Never mind about that!' Morris was impatient of any opposition. 'Frisco's to blame for having Maritana at his camp. He knows what to expect; but I'm not going to have you mixed up with his gin-shepherding.'

'Oh, Morris!'

Sally's exclamation conveyed a reluctance to argue with him, and a suggestion of reproach that he was evading an obligation to defend Maritana from ill-usage. She had an uneasy presentiment it would not be so easy for her to evade that obligation; but she was beginning to understand the awkward situation into which Maritana might lead her. What was going to happen about Maritana's mingari baby, for example?

Maritana was crouching by the fireplace again next morning.

She looked dazed and miserable: like a dog that had been kicked by someone who usually fed and fondled it.

'Frisco tell 'm get-the-hell out of it,' she said, as if asking Sally how this could be. 'Not want 'm. Not want 'm bloody black bitch make 'm cooboo round camp.'

Sally was furious: sick and furious at the man's brutality, and Maritana's bewilderment. She did not know what to say. After a moment it came to her.

'Bardook want 'm cooboo?' she asked.

'Eherm!' Maritana's face brightened. 'Plenty laugh and jump about, that one. Old feller wife longa him no catch 'm cooboo.'

'You go back to Bardook, Meeri!' Sally said. 'Better for cooboo to be with your own people.'

'Wiah,' Maritana said flatly. 'No rain bin comin'. Black feller hungry feller. Frisco give 'm tucker.'

Sally reminded herself she had suspected Maritana was sent to Frisco, so that her relations might have a claim on his food supplies. She gave the girl a good breakfast and Maritana disappeared before Morris was stirring.

Bardook, his brother, and an old man of the tribe visited Frisco next evening. Frisco blustered and swore: refused to give them the usual presents. Morris told Sally afterwards that Frisco had tried to make the natives understand he was not going to take any responsibility for Maritana's baby.

There was a terrible hullabaloo when Bardook thought Frisco wanted to claim the baby. Bardook's brother, who had acted as guide for several prospecting parties, and understood the white man's language better than his tribesmen, straightened out the misunderstanding. He explained that Maritana was Bardook's woman, he would lend her to a white man; but not the child the mingari had given her, because the child was a spirit of one of the tribe's ancestors. Therefore it must always belong to the tribe, and to Bardook who was its tribal father.

Frisco roared with laughter when he realized that Bardook did not associate Maritana's condition with sexual relationship, either by himself or Frisco, and that he believed absolutely in the mingari yarn. Frisco handed out a generous supply of rations then, with the customary plug of tobacco and bottle of wine.

'Every aboriginal woman is supposed to have an immaculate conception of sorts, it seems,' he exclaimed, enjoying the joke of having escaped from an unpleasant obligation. 'She catches a baby from any rock or water hole haunted by ancestral spirits, and the mingari is one of 'em.'

Sally could not exonerate him so easily. Frisco found Mrs.

161

Gough's back carefully presented when he approached. She would not look at or speak to him. Morris said she was behaving absurdly. There was nothing else for Frisco to do.

'He can at least see Maritana doesn't starve because she's bearing his child,' Sally replied sharply.

The tribe camped down near the dry lake and hung round the town for some time. Water and game were so scarce in the back country, Dinny said, the natives were forced to live by cadging food from the white people.

Maritana brought her relations to visit Missus Sally, taking it for granted that she would be as kind and friendly to them as she had been to her. And it was not so easy, Sally discovered, to refuse an old gin a few handfuls of flour and sugar with Maritana's laughing eyes looking on, as it had been to say: 'No! No! Go away!' to other blacks who came begging round the camp.

Maritana was a little in awe of her own people: shrank away with becoming humility if there were men about, and deferred respectfully to the old women. But Sally had seen her strutting gaily among the younger gins and children, in her gaudy dress, now bedraggled and dirty. Maritana would send them into fits of laughter, by the way she walked over the rough pebbly ground, holding up her skirt, as if she were Missus Sally; or by giving an imitation of Ma Buggins as she trotted down to the condenser, wobbling her fat behind, and screaming at Paddy Cavan for helping a teamster with his horses, instead of coming to carry home two heavy kerosene buckets of water for her.

The break with Frisco had not troubled Maritana very much, Sally assured herself. She was as happy and carefree as she had always been: quite content to wander half-naked and hungry with her tribe, though she still wore her necklaces and the remnants of her white woman's dress.

Morris made no attempt to shift camp as he had talked of doing.

'What's the use?' he said. 'We may be moving on to Menzies or Kanowna before long.'

The drift from Hannans was beginning to depress everybody. And Morris was dissatisfied with the gold he and Frisco were getting. Menzies and Kanowna were attracting population. Prospectors and financiers discussed the possibility of one or the other becoming the centre of the goldfields.

Collapse of the Londonderry created a sensation. When the golden hole, which had been sealed down until large-scale operations could be undertaken, was opened up, Lord Fingal found that the rich deposits had been exhausted. Another shaft and

Cross-cut exposed the poverty of the mine beyond that first glittering chute. Shares fell disastrously, and although directors of the company made an attempt at restitution, many investors were ruined. Westralian gold mines became a drug on the overseas market.

Stores and pubs closed in Hannans. Only a few fossickers remained dryblowing in the gully beside Maritana and below Cassidy's. But Frisco believed that the Brookmans, Charley de Rose, and Zeb Lane were not hanging on to their mines on the Boulder ridge for nothing. They said these mines would 'justify the most sanguine expectations before long, and boost Hannans sky high.'

CHAPTER XXIX

MORRIS had become restless and dissatisfied with the show he and Frisco were working. He had lost faith in Hannans and it exasperated him to hear of men doing well on outlying fields while he was marking time on a proposition which might prove worthless.

Gold had petered out in the shaft he and Frisco had sunk on their lease south-west of Cassidy's. They had not been 'seein' her' for many weeks; but the block had a positional value and Frisco was holding on to it in the hope of selling to English speculators. In the depressed state of the market they were shy of mines which showed no immediate prospect of rich crushings. No buyers looked like being interested in Cassidy's South-West for a long time.

And Morris was short of cash. How Frisco contrived to be always in funds was a mystery, he said. Frisco had been lucky: made a few thousands when Coolgardie was booming, lost most of it prospecting and gambling in shares; but managed to keep ahead of things by buying and selling gold, raking off a commission on various deals, and running the two-up ring. Morris was in debt to the storekeepers and publicans Sally knew. There was every reason for him to be frantic about getting ready money.

When Con Mahaffy came in from Kanowna with news of a rush, to the south-east, Morris decided to go out with him. Con was an old man, but a good prospector. His mate had just died in the hospital, after a heavy bout of drinking, and Morris was able to fix up with Con to take him on as mate for the trip.

Frisco made no bones about dissolving partnership, and bought

163

out Morris's interest in their lease for £200, which Morris thought rather decent, considering he was prepared to dump it, and values were at such a low ebb in Hannans.

Kanowna was no more than twelve miles away; but as she trudged beside the spring cart that blazing day, on the road to Kanowna, they seemed the longest and weariest miles Sally had ever walked. Morris had bought a spring cart and an old crock of a white mare to transport his camp and prospecting gear. The cart was loaded up with them and all their worldly possessions: the tent, blankets, condensing plant, dryblower-shaker, picks, shovels, a small water tank, stores, Sally's tin trunk and his portmanteau.

'You can sit on the dashboard as soon as you get tired,' Morris said, when they started out at dawn.

He was no longer gloomy and depressed, but full of energy and good spirits, though the sun was hundreds in the shade as they tramped the long road, snaking away through the scrub. Con rode ahead on his rough-haired brumby with a pack horse behind. The dust fumed up round him and round their own cart and nag.

He was a surly old man, shaggy as a wild goat and stank like one. Not pleased that his new mate was bringing a woman with him and determined to ignore her; but he slewed off the main track, where the earth had been churned-up by the teamsters' wagons, and took the camel pad alongside, so that the dust should not blow back into Sally's face; and was first to pull up at midday.

Con had lit a fire by the track and swung a billy of water across before Morris and his horse halted, sweating and gasping after a tough pull through the sand.

'Might as well have a bit of tucker,' Con growled. 'No need to bust ourselves.'

'Take your word for it, Con,' Morris laughed, mopping his forehead with a dark blue handkerchief.

His face was sun-roasted and red with dust, but nothing seemed to diminish his good humour. Sally hauled the tucker bags off the cart, opened the food tins and began cutting off bread and corned beef.

'Easy seen you been in the bush before, missus,' Con muttered. 'A thumb piece'll do me.'

'Same here,' Morris grinned. 'None of your ladylike slices on the track, Sally. We like 'em thick and solid.'

Con took the knife. 'A hunk of bread and a lump of meat. Hold the meat with your thumb. That's the idea, missus. And

164

wash 'em down with a pot of hot tea. Best meal in the world,
I reckon.'

He had helped himself and started to eat. Morris followed
suit. Sally plastered a piece of meat on a piece of thick bread.

'Tastes good,' she agreed, stretching her mouth round it.

Con got up to make the tea, filled the quart pots with the hot
black brew, and cut himself another slab of meat and bread.

'Gosh,' he said, rising and stretching when he was satisfied.
'That's what I call a decent feed. A nice bit of corned beef and
baker's bread. It'll be damper and tinned dog where we're goin',
missus. The nearest store's ten miles away—though I daresay
you can take the spring cart and drive into Kanowna to do y'r
shoppin'.'

That was intended to be a joke. Sally laughed obligingly.

'A real flash camp, Kanowna,' Con added to reassure her.
'Couple of streets and half a dozen pubs. Plenty of money flyin'
round and more go in the place than Hannans.'

Morris would have liked to stretch for a midday snooze. The
trees threw a few rags of black shade, though the sun beat relent-
lessly on the red earth. But Con wanted to reach Kanowna
before sunset.

The horses had been given a spell in the shade while the meal
was in progress. Con saddled up again and was ready to move
off, while Morris was still yawning and stretching. Sally packed
away the food in the tucker bags and started to harness Queenie.
Con hobbled over to help her.

'Well, if that don't beat cock fightin',' he chuckled. 'I reckon'd
you was one of these lady janes, and it seems like y'r used to the
track, missus.'

'I was born and bred in the bush,' Sally told him. 'Know
more about horses than Morris. He'd never've bought this one,
if I'd had anything to say about it.'

'She's not much to look at,' Con agreed.

'Hollow-backed and spring-halted,' Sally said crisply. 'Going
a bit lame, already.'

'Jest as well we're not on a long stretch.' Con swore uneasily.
'Keep her goin' so as she doesn't knock up this side of the
Feather.'

They set off again, but before long Queenie was going very
lame: toiled slowly over the soft heavy track. Morris realized
that he had made a bad bargain when he bought her and the
spring cart from a prospector in from Kurnalpi. He thought
there was nothing to do but give the old mare a spell and a feed,
leave the cart by the roadside and walk into Kanowna; but Sally,
guessing such a breakdown in their plans would irritate Con,

took the mare in hand, kept her going by talking to her, cheering and urging her over a heavy pull, steering her on to the best parts of the road, singing to her, and giving her a whack on the rump now and then.

It was exhausting work in the heat and the blinding glare. Con looked back, occasionally, to see Mrs. Gough trudging along the dusty track and almost hauling the mare over a sandy patch, with Morris shoving behind.

'That's right, missus,' he called. 'Keep her at it. On'y a couple of miles to go now.'

But those last two miles were the worst. It took the combined efforts of Sally, tugging the mare on, and Morris belting her with a leafy branch, to keep her going. To have let her stop now would have been fatal, Sally knew. Nothing on earth would have induced Queenie to move again that night. She had to be forced to labour on at the slow mechanical gait which brought her at last to Kanowna.

CHAPTER XXX

KANOWNA spread out over the flat land, torn with potholes, and dumps of creamy rubble, pinkish and tawny clay. The scrub flung back a long way, flowed into the distance, grey as the sea, deepening to hyacinth and indigo as the sun set above it in a glory of crimson and gold, flaring and fading on the wide scoop of the sky.

Lights sparkled in the huts and shacks ranged beside the wide sprawling track. They were as ramshackle and dilapidated as the huts at Hannans or on the hill at Coolgardie, though here and there an hotel of desert sandstone, or store of corrugated iron, blue-grey or whitewashed, stood out among them. The main street, alive with diggers in the early evening, looked busy and prosperous. Men were trooping up from their claims, and swarmed about the open bars and stores, paying for their drinks and groceries with gold.

It was a rough and roistering crowd: rougher and richer than the mob on Hannans had ever been, Morris said. Alluvial followed the wide sweep of a subterranean river, and almost every man on the claims along its course was on gold. The ground had been pegged for miles in every direction, and although there were a few reefing propositions to tempt wealthy syndicates, Kanowna was flourishing as a poor man's field. Fine gold in the greasy grey pug, found at depth in the shafts, promised a fortune to those who could discover a profitable method of extraction.

Tom Doyle's was the biggest, most imposing pub, with a verandah straddling out from it on wooden legs; but Con had some objection to drinking there. He pulled up at Giotti's further along and Sally waited in the dining-room while Morris and he watered and fed their horses, and then went off to the bar to quench their own thirst.

Morris came presently to know whether she would like a glass of port wine. Con staggered after him, insisting that Morrey's missus should have one with him.

'Hey, Vi'let,' he called back into the bar, 'bring a bottle of champagne for my mate's missus.'

'But, Mr. Mahaffy—' Sally demurred.

She had a fiendish headache: felt worn out after walking in the heat all day and keeping the mare going. What she wanted more than anything in the world was a wash and a big glass of cold water. These she could not have, it seemed. But champagne, yes! An hysterical little laugh fluttered within her and died away. Morris scowled a warning. She understood that she must not refuse to drink with Con. He was Morris's mate. So much would depend on their getting on well together when they were out in the bush, and the chances were Con would take offence if she refused to drink with him.

'—that would be wonderful,' Sally finished weakly.

An out-back chandelier hung over the table: a triangle of deal sticks tied together with a tallow candle at each end. The grease dripped on the table and the candle flames flickered over the bare room. Sally caught glimpses of its earthen floor and walls of corrugated iron lined with dust, a fly specked calender on a nail and a vase of pink paper flowers at the far end of the table. The seats on either side were made of tree trunks set on posts in the ground.

'The teams're late and they're short of kerosene,' Con remarked, with a gurgle of amusement. 'Well, that don't matter so long as the booze and gold hold out. Are you makin' that champagne, Vi-let?'

'Coming,' the girl said quietly.

She was there, standing beside him: put the glasses and bottle on the table. A young thing with jet black hair and dark blue eyes in a grave white face. Almost as out of place as the champagne, she looked, in that hot dingy room.

'Tell the boss to score it up to me,' Con said grandly.

'That's all right, Mr. Mahaffy,' the girl replied, and was gone.

'Who is she?' Sally asked.

167

'That's Vi'let. Vi'let O'Brien. Got a bloody beautiful voice. She's Giotti's barmaid,' Con grunted, wrestling with the cork of the champagne bottle. 'Nice kid. Come over from Coolgardie, couple of months ago. Knew her old man. Went off prospectin' over a year ago and hasn't been heard of since. Left the missus with a swag of kids. Vi'let's the eldest.'

The noise from the bar almost drowned what he was saying. So many hoarse rough voices were shouting, laughing and talking with drunken hilarity. Sally could just see the girl in her white dress, standing beside a big swarthy Italian and handing out drinks.

Con had filled the tumblers with champagne. He handed one to Sally and passed another along the table to Morris.

'Here's how, missus—and good luck to us!'

'Oh, yes!' Sally forced herself to a flashy brightness. 'Lots of gold and quite soon!'

Con guffawed and tossed off his glass of the sparkling wine.

'The sooner the better, eh, Con? Morris drank at a gulp also.

It was good wine. The real thing, but lukewarm. Sally sipped it slowly. It made her feel sick at first. Its effervescence died quickly, but gradually the aches and pains in every part of her body subsided. A pleasant enervation permeated her. She laughed lightly and easily.

'Fill 'em up!' Con shouted. 'We're celebratin', Morrey and me. Hey, Vi'let! Bring us another bottle.'

'No! No!' Sally pleaded. 'I'm not used to drinking much wine, Mr. Mahaffy.'

'This is on me.' Morris jumped up to go and order the champagne.

'Sit down, me boy.' Con was drunk already and doing the honours: would allow no interference.

'Last time me and my mate were celebratin' at Giotti's,' he reminisced lugubriously, 'we was on top of the world—come in with four hundred and fifty ounces, and a thirst on us from here to Kingdom Come. Christ A'mighty, we near drunk Giotti out of business, and Barney went stone mad, started shootin' the heads off the bottles. There was wine, beer and whisky runnin' all over the floor. The boys grabbed the bottles and drank from 'em with their mouths cut and bleedin'. The barmaid here then was a big lump of a girl with a lot of common sense. "Let 'em go, Giotti," she said, "they'll pay for it." And we did. Cost us two hundred and fifty pounds that binge, but was worth it. Pore old Barney, he couldn't stand much booze. Got the horrors and kicked the bucket before we'd bust up that cheque. He was a great mate—Barney. Best mate ever I had.'

Big tears stood in Con's bloodshot eyes and coursed slowly down his furrowed, dust-stained face. Sally was glad to see Violet standing beside him with another bottle of champagne.

'You've got to humour him, Sally,' Morris muttered. 'I'll take him off to the bar presently.'

The tumblers were filled again. Sally pretended to drink; but already the room was swinging in a golden haze. The noise in the bar became a vague riotous uproar. She could hear herself talking wildly, gaily. She wanted to laugh and sing. Everything was so different than it had been a little while ago. She no longer felt tired and depressed, but pleased with everything and everybody. This funny, dirty, little pub, and old Con, so generous and good-hearted, though a little drunk, as she suspected she was herself.

But what did it matter? On a mining camp, apparently, one must get drunk and be jolly like everybody else. She hoped Morris would realize the wine had gone to her head: and that he would be able to look after her. He was nearly as drunk as Con; but not quite, she thought, because presently he coaxed Con back to the bar. She laughed until she cried as they staggered away, arguing and embracing each other. So absurd they looked, Morris and that shaggy, stinking old man, clawing at and clasping each other.

Then she was sleepy. She wished she could go to bed. The room whirled about her when she stood up to go and find somebody who would tell her where she could sleep. She was dismayed to find she could not walk; sank limply into the bag chair and sobbed drearily. The exhilaration of a little while ago was gone. She felt as flat and dull as the dregs of champagne in the thick tumblers still on the table. The last of the candles was guttering out.

Still the uproar in the bar went on. The rowdy chaffing, uproarious laughter and babble of men's voices was hushed suddenly and a girl's voice rose, singing like a bird. Sally remembered vaguely what Con had said: 'That's Vi'let. She's got a bloody beautiful voice.'

Through giddiness and the hot darkness, Sally heard the pure melody of that young voice and marvelled at it. She slumped into oblivion, and was aroused by the girl trying to awaken her, shaking her and saying impatiently:

'Come on. Mrs. Giotti says you'll have to sleep in my room.'

'Oh, dear,' Sally struggled to her feet, her head whirling, 'I had too . . . too much wine, Violet.'

'You're shickered, all right,' Violet agreed. 'Hang on to me, and I'll help you to get into bed.'

'I . . . I'll be all right,' Sally jumped up, ashamed to have this child looking after her. Violet caught her as she swayed, and led the way in the dark to a shed in the yard.

There was only one stretcher in it and a couple of sugar boxes set up for a dressing table. Violet lit the end of a candle and barred the door. Sally flumped on the bed.

Violet started to undress.

Sally stared at her stupidly.

'Better take off your dress and corsets,' Violet advised. 'You can sleep in your petticoat.'

She had slipped on a calico nightdress herself: looked younger than ever with her black hair in two long pigtails.

'I'll unlace your shoes.'

'Oh, no,' Sally protested, but Violet was undoing the knots of her shoe strings as she spoke.

'Just as well you're not fat,' Violet observed. 'When Mrs. Giotti and I had to sleep together, before he built on this room for me, it was a terrible squeeze. The last barmaid here had her own tent in the yard. She married Bob Pearse when he sold his claim on the lead, you know.'

Sally did not know; but Violet's chatter gave her a chance to unbutton her bodice and unfasten her corsets. It was a relief to take them off, and her dress and petticoat, too. She was pleased to show Violet that she was still capable of independent thought, and would sleep in her camisole and drawers.

There were no sheets on the bed. Violet slept on an old rug, and pulled another over her when she was cold, she said.

It was a heavenly relief to lie down and slip into blessed drowsiness, Sally found. She was grateful to Violet: wanted to explain to her that she was not used to drinking so much wine. It was the first time she had ever been drunk, although on the night of their wedding Morris had ordered a bottle of champagne. It had been a magical beverage, ice cold and glittering like liquid sunshine. They had been so much in love and so deliriously happy, Sally did not know whether it was the wine, then, or just being in love that had intoxicated her.

But to-night, she had drunk thirstily, desperately, to overcome her weariness and play up to Con's chivalrous intention. Tepid wine on an empty stomach might upset anyone, perhaps! She had been terribly tired, too. And so she had got 'shickered,' as Violet said, and was ashamed of herself. How Mr. Frisco Murphy would jeer if he knew. Sally hoped he never would hear of her discomfiture.

What would Morris say? What must this girl think? And how on earth would she ever hold up her head again. Sleep blotted out Sally's consternation and confused consciousness of disgraceful behaviour.

In the morning when she wakened with a throbbing head and black nausea, it all came back to her. She got up, went into the yard and was sick: crawled back into bed, and lay down feeling thoroughly miserable.

'You'll be all right, now,' Violet assured her, getting up. She dressed carefully under her nightgown: went out to the yard and came back with a panning-off dish and a little water.

'We'll have to share this between us, Mrs. Giotti says,' she remarked regretfully; poured half the water into a mug and washed her face and hands in the other half.

Then she undid her plaits, combed out her black hair and piled it on top of her head. Looking surprisingly fresh and attractive in her blue print dress, she glanced at Sally with an air of experience.

'A hair of the dog's what you need,' she said calmly. 'I'll ask Mr. Giotti to give me something. And then I'd get up, if I were you. You'll feel better when you've had a wash. It's a bit cooler this morning—and the men are harnessing up. You don't want them to know you were out to it last night, do you?'

'No.' Sally sat up. She felt ill. But she could not endure the idea of Morris, or anybody else, knowing how that champagne had upset her.

Violet went out of the room and presently returned with a nobbler of brandy. Sally drank it. Felt better: washed in the tin dish, making the most of this opportunity for an all-over scrub with a wet rag. She looked sick and sallow, when she glanced at herself in Violet's small cracked mirror; but not really the sort of woman who got drunk and was suffering from the after-effects. She wet her hair and it fell into loose waves. Her eyes laughed back at her from the mirror. She thought it was absurd to have worried so much about what had happened the night before.

'It was an accident, Violet,' she exclaimed lightly. 'But I'll have to be more careful about what I drink in future.'

'They all say that,' Violet replied. 'There are so few women about, and if a man's on gold, he thinks there's nothing good enough for her. You've got to drink with him or he gets offended.'

'I know.' Sally smiled. 'That's why—'

'Mum says, if you must drink, stick to whisky,' Violet volunteered. 'But Mr. Giotti won't let me drink at all yet. He's very strict with me—but kind, too. Charley says I might as well be in a convent as working here. It's not quite the same, though, is it?'

She smiled her slow, grave smile.

'It seems dreadful for a girl like you—' Sally hesitated. She was going to say: 'to work in a bar.'

Violet guessed that. 'I was lucky to get the job,' she said defensively. 'Mum needs the money just now. When Dad comes home I won't have to work here. Perhaps he'll have struck it rich and we'll go away. I can study to be a singer.'

'How old are you, Violet?'

Violet's deep blue eyes held a faint smile. 'I'm supposed to be eighteen, but I'm not really. I was fourteen last birthday. Don't tell anybody, will you? Even Charley doesn't know.'

'Who is Charley?'

'Charley? Charley Leigh.' Violet looked surprised, as if everybody should know Charley. 'He's my boy, at least he would be if I could have a boy; but Mr. Giotti won't let him speak to me, if he can help it. He says Charley's no good, because he's always loafing round the bar and drinks a lot. But I like Charley —and he wants to marry me.'

CHAPTER XXXI

Con and Morris were ready for the track before breakfast. They decided not to wait for it. Wanted to get a move on right away, they said: could boil a billy and have a bite when they felt inclined, later on in the morning.

They too had taken 'a hair of the dog,' Sally suspected. Morris looked bloated and bleary eyed, and Con's blue eyes still burned with the alcohol he had consumed. Both men were irritable, and avoided speaking to each other.

Mrs. Giotti and Violet came out to say good-bye to Mrs. Gough. Mrs. Giotti scolded and exclaimed at the men for being in such a hurry, but she was very affable and friendly with Sally: invited her to come and stay at Giotti's whenever she felt lonely or miserable with those bad men.

Giotti did not appear. The settling up with him had been more than Morris bargained for. Con's score, it seemed, could stand; but a stranger was expected to pay his way. Morris had paid, and handsomely, to hold his own in the bar.

That's what he said when he growled about it, as he and Sally walked beside the spring cart, following Con on a track which turned south and then east over a vast sun-scalded stretch of pinkish clay above which a mirage quivered, throwing an illusion of long stretches of tranquil water, fringed by misty trees along the distant horizon.

'Do you wonder prospectors can't bear the sight of a mirage?' Morris queried sourly. 'They've lured many a man, maddened with thirst, to his death, the mirages.'

So real that lovely vision of water and trees was. Sally could imagine its effect on the brain of a sun-crazed, desperate man in sterile, waterless country. Behind the mirage, eastwards, lay the roll of blue hills towards which Con was making. The mare, although still lame, plodded along staunchly. They could afford to let her take her own time, Morris said. It was easy going on the clay-pan: the ground baked hard and firm, and they hadn't far to go. Con reckoned it was only ten miles from Kanowna to the gully in the ridge where he and Barney Malone had struck a good patch a few months ago.

Con had changed his mind about it being worth while to try their luck on Tom Doyle and Bissenger's rush. Too many men on the ground already, and none of them making more than tucker, Busy Bugger himself had told Con.

The heat on the clay pan increased during the morning. It beat down on Morris and Sally crossing the bare shadeless expanse, on foot, as if the faded sky were made of metal, white hot; and rose from the earth, burning through the soles of their shoes, and sapping their energy, until they seemed to have only the strength to crawl after Con and his horses. It had been 110 in the shade the day before, but there was no shade on the clay pan. Nothing between her and Morris, and those fiery rays which poured down from the sun, Sally thought, frantically, except their clothes, and they seemed to be shrivelling on their bodies.

It was a relief to reach the rough broken ground of the ridge, where a few trees scattered a black lace of shade, and to halt finally in the gully where Con's old brushwood shed still stood. Con threw off his saddles, put a bell on one of the horses, and let them go.

The mare stood where she had come to a standstill, head dropped and blowing feebly. Sally unhooked the traces and took her out of the shafts, while Morris measured out her ration of water. Con was going to erect a condenser on the salt lake, a mile or so out on the clay pan below the ridge. The lake was dry now, but brakish water could still be got a few feet below the surface. Before they began to climb the ridge, Con inspected the hole he and Barney had dug on the lakeside, and found it would still make water.

But still it had to be used carefully. The condenser would convert the brakish water into drinking water for the camp; but wood had to be cut for fires beneath the condenser, and a new well dug for the water to seep into, in case an animal may have fallen into and fouled the old one. The boilers had to be cleaned frequently to prevent salt and other minerals corroding the boiler, so that water represented time and labour, as well as the basis of existence in this almost desert country.

Con and Morris took a walk over the ground before they unpacked and pitched their tents. Sally could see them squatting to scoop up the earth and rubble in their hands. 'Looks good, doesn't she? Tell y'r I can smell gold here,' she heard Con say. 'To-morrow I'll go looming along the ridge, and you can put up the shaker there be the mouth of the gully, Morrey.'

Sally busied herself piling stones together for a fireplace. She had the billies boiling and a meal ready when the men returned. They were glad enough to eat and sit smoking awhile, then in the leisurely way of bushmen set about pitching their tents. It was almost dark before they had finished, and the two shells of dust-stained, patched and dirty canvas gleamed white in the twilight, a few yards from each other on the ridge, overlooking the dead salt lake and the wide sweep of the clay pan.

Never had she slept as she did that night, Sally declared. At first, when she lay down every muscle in her body ached: every nerve twitched and jumped. But all her aches and pains passed away in the blessed unconsciousness of sleep; and in the morning she was as fit as usual. Morris had put their mattresses on the cart, as this was not a long trek. He promised to cut down three or four trees for timber to make stretchers, so that they would have a comforable bed next night.

Morris was up at dawn and searching the earth along the gully. Con laughed at his eagerness as he boiled his own billy. There was plenty of time for slug hunting, he said. The gold would not run away. Morris ate his breakfast in a fever of impatience and was off again. He set up his shaker, shovelled dirt and put it through the shaker all day.

Con refused to take a hand, and went off to search for traces of gold along the ridge. 'Looming,' he called it, and came back in the late afternoon with bags of samples to break up in his dolly pot and pan-off for traces of gold.

They were going down to the lake to dig for water and set up the condenser, next day, so decided they could afford a little water to wash the dirt. Put an empty kerosene tin aside for a 'poverty pot,' and poured the washing-off water into it to be kept and used again when the dregs had settled; also any gold there might be in the water.

Morris was luckier than Con with his panning-off. After care-

174

fully swirling water over dirt from the lowest tray of the shaker, until all the loose light stuff had been washed away, there was a nice fat tail of gold dust on the shining curve of his dish. The dish shone with the colours of a peacock's tail, and the gold glittered brightly. Morris trembled with excitement as he gazed at it: his face lighted with joy.

'Looks as if we were going to strike her, here, all right, Con!' he cried exultantly. 'I'm pegging, right away!'

'May as well make it four men's ground,' Con agreed, a twinkle in his eyes. 'There's three of us here, and we can ring in another mate, if we want to.'

'I've got a miner's right, at any rate,' Sally said. 'Mr. Quin says every woman on the fields ought to have a miner's right. You never know when it might come in handy.'

'Good on you, missus,' Con's cackle of laughter trailed after him as he followed Morris down to where the shaker was standing. Morris had his pegs ready with his name and the number of his miner's right attached. He was taking no chances with pegs which were not regulation size. Con used an old set that had served him on many other occasions.

'Time was,' he exclaimed indignantly, after the claims were marked off and he and Morris had settled down for their evening meal, 'when a man needn't be too fussy about his pegs. Twigs or a little heap of stones would do, and if y'r left y'r pick and shovel on a claim, no one would've thought of jumpin' it—knowin' the owner was sick or away on urgent business, so couldn't be complyin' with labour conditions. But now, there's so many crooks and spielers about, y'r can't be too careful, or they'll jump y'r and get a verdict if y'r don't stick to every bleedin' letter of the reg'lations.'

Morris worked in the broiling sun all the following day, and for two or three days on the shaker, with no more encouragement than a glittering crescent of gold dust in his panning-off dish each evening. He had knocked off only to help Con set up the condenser and cart water. Con, himself, had tramped the ridge and failed to locate a reef, so he was taking turns with Morris, shovelling dirt and rattling the shaker.

Morris was first to call: 'Slug-O!' And there was such triumph in his voice that Sally ran down the hillside to him, and Con dropped his shovel and was beside him in an instant. The lump of gold, covered with red dust, Morris held in his hand was not very big. Con reckoned it wouldn't go more than twenty ounces. Morris, his face beaming with pride and happiness, bet him ten bob she'd go thirty, at least. He spat on the gold and rubbed off the dust on his trousers, gazing at the slug admiringly.

'Take my oath she's not an orphan,' Con warbled.

They went up hill to the tent and Morris got out his scales: took the tiny delicate instrument from its velvet lined case and set it up on a box. The weights had to be adjusted with meticulous care and the slug balanced against them. Con chortled when he won his ten bob. The slug weighed twenty ounces, six pennyweights; but that did not diminish Morris's pleasure, or Con's satisfaction.

Almost every day, for the next few days, one or two slugs were gleaned from the top tray of the shaker, and several 'little beauts from the lower riffles.

'Must've struck a nest of 'em,' Con said.

He was more excited and cock-a-hoop than Morris had been over his first find, when he picked up the daddy of them all, on the ground lying a few yards from his tent. It was a crumpled piece of gold which looked as if it had been boiled in some prehistoric cauldron and tossed down here on the earth to cool. But it weighed sixty ounces, and that was all Con and Morris cared about.

They went on searching for the rest of the family, as they said; but had no more luck for two or three days. Stores were getting low. Somebody had to go into Kanowna for flour and tinned meat.

'Time we were reporting our gold, too,' Morris said.

'Wait a bit,' Con's eyes narrowed shrewdly. 'We might as well apply for twenty-four acres—a mining lease—while we're about it. It's a fact we haven't located the reef these beauties were shed down from, yet; but I reckon that outcrop where I got colours 'd pay for workin' round a bit. A lease'd give us a chance to work over more ground for alluvial, before the mob gets wind of it.'

'When we report these slugs there won't be any stoppin' a rush,' Morris said.

'That's right,' Con grinned, 'but we're not reportin' 'em, yet.'

'And risk forfeiture?' Morris growled.

'You don't have to worry about that,' Con's cackle of laughter was reassuring. 'Men on the 'Derry didn't. A man 'd be a mug not to hold back a bit of alluvial when it suits him.'

Morris was not satisfied; but willing enough to fall in with Con's scheme. He helped Con to dig a costeen and test the outcrop. They were delighted when they dollied a bag of stone for a few dwts. It was good enough to justify expectation of better results. Con decided to go into Kanowna for stores, apply for the mining lease he and Morris had pegged, and keep his mouth shut about the larger slugs.

'Do no harm to own-up to a bit of small stuff,' he said. 'Trust me to know how to handle the boys. Keep 'm quiet, and not suspectin' we're on a good thing.'

Sally had learnt to work the shaker. She got into the habit of going down to where Morris and Con were working, every day, and taking the shaker arm. It was easy enough to keep the shaker arm moving gently; but at first she had not been able to detect the sluggard who held back when all the other pebbles and scraps of rubble were dancing and jumping on the tray. Con had pounced gleefully when she did not see a nice little slug, red with dust. But soon, she understood the movement of the lighter stones and the way gold, being heavier, hung back or fell to lower trays, where the blower fanned off grit and dust.

Standing in the blazing sun and dust, just making that mechanical movement and watching those dancing brown and rust red pebbles, for hours, was tiring and trying work all the same. Sally marvelled at the way Morris worked: doggedly, indefatigably, as if his life depended on unearthing more of those elusive blobs of gold.

As he and Con slung a pick, breaking the hard ground, or shovelled rubble on to the dump, stopping every now and then to feed the shaker and keep an eye on Sally's manipulation of it, they were shrouded in hot red dust. Faces and arms were red with it. The sweat poured from them, leaving tracks in the thick grime.

Sally wished she could have worn the gossamer veil she usually put over her hat on hot dusty days, but it would have interfered with being able to see clearly and quickly. Besides, a veil would not have made much difference as protection from the dust. It penetrated one's clothes even. Eyes, ears, nose and mouth were filled with the dry, powdery red earth which rose from the men's picks and shovels, and from the dryblower, and hung in the air.

But while the men worked so hard, she could not sit about the camp doing nothing, Sally told herself. They said she must have got the gold fever to stick to her job so well. She did not tell them that she thought the gold was not worth all the discomfort they went through to get it. It was a compensation for her drudgery on the shaker, however, to be able to call: 'Slug-O!' occasionally, see Morris and Con drop shovel or pick and scramble towards her all curiosity and excitement.

While Con was in Kanowna, she cornered the biggest slug they had yet found. Morris was so jubilant when he saw it, that he kissed her until the sweat and grime on their faces mingled. They went up to the camp as excitedly as children to weigh the slug. When he found it tipped the scales at eighty-five ounces,

Morris said that was good enough to knock off for: celebrate by having a wash and loaf in the shade for the rest of the day.

Con returned just before sunset. But in his wake trailed a string of camels, horsemen, spring carts, and prospectors foot-slogging from Kanowna. Morris swore bitterly when he saw them. Con muttered shamefacedly that he'd been drinking: opened his mouth too wide—and now they'd got a rush to cope with.

There was no need to explain what that meant. Soon the ground would be pegged in every direction, and there would be no chance of cleaning up alluvial along the gully, as Con and Morris had intended before applying for a mining lease. Before leaving Kanowna, Con had gone over to the Warden's office and applied for the lease, they had already marked off, but there was small chance of it being granted now until the alluvial was exhausted.

CHAPTER XXXII

THERE was a good deal of bad feeling between the rushers and Con. After the first few days, a spokesman for the men who had followed Con out from Kanowna, accused Con and Morris of holding more ground than they were entitled to, and of hoarding gold which should have been reported as alluvial. They rushed the lease and pegged right up to the costeen which Con declared marked the line of his reef.

Con, in a frenzy, grabbed his gun and threatened any man who attempted to work a claim on the lease. Morris did his best to restrain Con and the Warden was sent for. At a rowdy Sunday morning roll-up the Warden gave a verdict for the men.

This meant that alluvial claims could be taken up all along the gully and over the flat stretching out from it. Con and Morris were left with a dud reef on their hands and lost promising alluvial ground lower down.

Con could not reconcile himself to being deprived of this ground. He became surly and vindictive in his attitude to the newcomers: refused to let a couple of them use his condenser, on the grounds that the plant was too small to supply the needs of more than himself and his mate and their horses. That was true enough; but the refusal added to the score against Con. Another prospector set up a condenser on the lake side and began to sell water to the men on Con's Gully, as the place was called.

Morris continued to work on the alluvial claims he and Con

still held, and on the claim they had pegged for Sally; but Con prowled restlessly, blackguarding everybody he came in contact with. He seemed unable to settle down or get over his grouch against the men who had rushed the lease. Two or three of them did quite well at first: could show several plugs weighing from ten to seventy ounces. But most of them pulled their pegs, and drifted away before long, satisfied that there was mighty little gold on Con's Gully, and that only a few men near the old water-way would have any luck there.

Sally drove into Kanowna for stores, next time they were needed. Morris was afraid to leave Con in case he might provoke another rumpus. He said that if she left early, Sally could make the trip and be back before sundown.

It was quite an adventure and pleasant to get away from the camp where there was so much bad blood between Con and men on the alluvial claims. Morris had been wonderful, she thought: taken charge of Con and prevented him from making a violent attack on the diggers who were on gold.

Morris had kept his temper: remained calm and good-humoured despite the sultry hostility towards Con and himself. He took no notice of scowling glances and abusive remarks. But Con was always shouting: 'Robbers, thieves and blackguards!' when Sam McGinn and some of the lucky diggers passed. McGinn and his mates came across to deal with Con, one night, and he would have got some rough handling had not Morris managed to placate them.

'Con's got a touch of the sun, boys,' Morris explained. 'He's just crazy. Doesn't know what he's saying. You don't have to kick an old man when he's down, do you?'

'That's all very well,' McGinn growled. 'But we're not goin' to stand for the way he's carryin' on. The pair of you tried to work a dirty trick on the alluvial diggers. We're within our rights. And you know it. If he doesn't shut up he'll be run out of the camp.'

Con shut up and behaved more reasonably after that. He knew the men were justified in resenting his crankiness. They could forgive him for trying to beat the regulations but not for being a bad loser. Con could only blame his own blabbing for bringing them to the gully, and that riled him most of all. It was no use whipping the cat about it now, Morris pointed out. When the alluvial was exhausted and the lease granted, they might sell out, and still make a few hundreds.

Sally enjoyed jogging along the almost imperceptible track of wheels on the claypan, in the cool of the morning. She was not afraid of losing her way, although there was no landmark for

179

miles across the dead level of sun-bleached clay. If she met 'Ghans or natives on the track, Morris said, she was to drive on: take no notice of anything they might say or do. Sally herself was not scared of natives; but she hoped she would not meet a camel team and its dusky drivers.

She drove all the morning without seeing another living thing, except a few crows flecking blue of the sky, until she approached the town. Then she passed two or three prospectors on bicycles going into Kanowna. They looked surprised to see a woman sitting in the spring cart behind her dusty white moke, gave her a respectful: 'Good-morning, missus,' and rode on. When she came abreast of an old man trudging along with a heavy swag on his back, and loaded down with gear, she stopped and asked whether he would like a lift.

'Is it the voice of an angel that speaks?' he queried, slung his swag into the back of the cart, and climbed up.

He was going north. There was a big rush to Lake Darlot, he said, as he sat beside Sally on the plank Morris had put in the cart for a seat. An old mate was up there and had sent word for him to make tracks right away. His name? Sure, it did not matter. The lady may have heard of Pigweed Harry. It was the name he was known by since he had near done a perish and managed to keep body and soul together by sucking the pigweed. Come into a camp with the green of it oozing all over him. So Pigweed, the boys called him, and grateful enough he was to the weed for saving his life. If he struck it rich on the Darlot, he would not forget this day when he had been hoofing it, footsore and weary, into Kanowna, and Mrs. Gough had given him a lift on the road.

They said good-bye at the store where Sally pulled up to make her purchases. The store was filled with prospectors: more men, horses and camels about the main street than was usual at that hour of the morning.

'Looks as if there's a rumour got around about the Darlot,' Pigweed chuckled, 'and a man won't be lonely on the track, missus.'

Sally had to wait to get her stores. The storekeeper was busy and flustered with so many customers to serve at once. She heard the men discussing the rush to Lake Darlot. That David Carnegie had come into Coolgardie with a nice swag of alluvial. And that Jimmy Ross, the original prospector of Lake Carey and Mount Margaret, was saying Lake Darlot and Bowden Range were the best reefing country he had seen, and he knew the lay of the land from Hall's Creek to Widgiemooltha. Cutmores had dollied a hundred ounces on their show in a few days; some of their rich specimens would probably yield a thousand ounces to the ton. Jimmy reckoned there was over a ton of rich specimens at grass on the block.

There had been thunderstorms and a good rain recently. But men must be well equipped for prospecting this area, and prepared to cart and pack water ten or twenty miles, most of the year. Lake Darlot was three hundred miles north of Hannans and the natives fierce and, hostile round about Pindinnie and Mount Catherine.

At last Sally was served: got her tank filled with fresh water and drove along to Giotti's to see Violet. It was quite exciting to be paying a visit. She thought she would have time to give Queenie a nose bag, and have a cup of tea before starting on her return journey.

Mr. Giotti, himself, came out to take Queenie over to the stables—no more than a roof of brushwood on four posts of bush timber—and give her a feed. Violet and Mrs. Giotti greeted her as if she were an old friend.

'Come in! Come in! We maka da cuppa tea,' Mrs. Giotti cried cordially. 'Violetta and me, we 'ave wonder about poor Mrs. Gough. How goes it with her? On campa with no womens about. Si. Si. I know it is hell'va life—and nice to come together with frien's.'

Chattering eagerly, with gurgles of laughter, Mrs. Giotti ushered Sally into a small kitchen, full of the smell of garlic and corn beef, cooking for dinner, the buzzing of blow flies, and hot sunshine. She fussed about her pots on the stove as she talked, relating her experiences and suffering in this damned country and sympathizing, inferentially, with Mrs. Gough over the hardships and discomforts she must be undergoing on a prospecting camp.

Mrs. Giotti was fat and good-natured: still attractive despite her slovenliness. Her hair, black as a crow's wing, was piled over a full face, flushed with the heat and too much wine. She had fine eyes and beautiful white teeth. Had been an opera singer. Not illustrious like her Alberto. He had sung Rigoletto for a season at La Scala, but in small parts Bianca had been quite a success. Yes. Until the babies came. But how was it possible to travel and bring up a family?

She had learnt to cook: was a better cook than a singer, Alberto said. Which was just as well when he lost his voice of a malady of the throat, because then she could open a little ristorante. But, for their sins the Blessed Mother of God had sent them to Australia where the brother of Alberto made much money on the goldfields. It was a purgatory to live in this Kanowna, but better than La Scala, or the ristorante, for making money. Some day they would return, she and Alberto and their children, and live well in their own country.

Violet made tea while Mrs. Giotti talked. She had scarcely spoken; but Sally caught her grave, unsmiling glance, and smiled to assure Violet that it was to see her she had come to Giotti's.

When Violet was called away to serve a customer in the bar, Mrs. Giotti explained that she was worried about the girl.

'Violetta, I am fond of her. She is good girl—has good voice.' Mrs. Giotti's voice dropped to a cautious whisper. 'It would be bloody shame if she maka mess of her life for da waster like Charley Leigh.'

Mrs. Giotti confessed that she liked Charley: everybody did. The men said he was a good mate, although he was just an English Johnny when he came to the fields a few years ago. He had had some luck for awhile and spent it all on booze and gambling. Now he was hard-up and in love with Violet, 'crazy mad about her,' and threatening to shoot himself if she would not marry him.

At first, Sally understood, Violet would take no notice of Charley. She was used to men in the bar flattering and 'kidding' her, as they said. Behaved like a little princess if anybody got too free and easy, or used bad language—though Giotti would not stand for that either. Men had to treat a girl in his bar with respect or get out. But Charley Leigh made love to Violet over the bar, and behaved so badly when he was drunk, that Giotti had warned him off the premises. Giotti was very angry with Violet because she would meet Charley and go for a walk with him on Sunday afternoon. Giotti refused to give her a singing lesson and said he would send her home if she did not drop Charley.

'Violetta is too good barmaid,' Mrs. Giotti said. 'Alberto will not send Violetta 'ome. But 'e is afraid da Charley will persuade 'er to marry 'im.'

Violet came back into the kitchen and Sally got up to go. Mrs. Giotti made a great outcry at the idea. It was impossible that Mrs. Gough should leave before dinner, she declared. Sally explained that she had promised her husband to return before sundown, so that she must be off. He would think she had lost her way, otherwise, and it would be quite easy to do that if she did not reach the camp before dark.

Mrs. Giotti was alarmed at the prospect. She was all eagerness then to hurry Sally on her way.

'But you will come again,' she urged hospitably, 'and sleep at Giotti's. Not maka long drive in da sun all day.'

It was Mrs. Giotti who suggested that Violet should take a little drive with Mrs. Gough. It would do Violet good and she could walk back in time for dinner.

Violet climbed into the cart and sat down beside Sally. Her face was sombre: her blue eyes dark and thoughtful. But presently she said shyly, a little aggressively:

'Mrs. Giotti's been telling you about Charley, I suppose.'

'Oh, yes!' Sally's smile made Violet feel that they were good friends: understood each other very well.

'I like Charley,' Violet said, frowning as she looked ahead of her over the bare dry plains. 'But I don't want to marry him.'

Sally did not know quite what to say to that. There was only the obvious thing: 'You're so young, Violet.'

'It's not that,' Violet exclaimed impatiently. 'If I'm old enough to be in love, I'm old enough to be married.'

'Of course—' Sally suspected that this child knew more about love and marriage than she did. On a mining camp, at any rate.

'I don't want to get married,' Violet exclaimed passionately. 'I don't want to have any man bossing me and giving me children. Mum says, they're all the same, the men. They'd do anything to get what they want. Then they clear out and leave you. Not caring what happens to you or the kid. A girl's got to get married some day, and put up with a man's nature, Mum says. But not me—I'm not going to put up with a man making love to me one minute and banging me about the next. That's Dad all over—though it's as much Mum's fault as his. She slings off when he comes home drunk and calling her lovey-dovey names. He gives her a black eye and a baby and goes off prospecting again. "But I love him," Mum says, "and you can't blame a man for what he does when the booze gets hold of him. . . ."'

The old horse plodded along the track, stirring the soft dust. As if it were a relief to pour out her angry troubled thoughts, Violet went on:

'She's right. I'm awfully fond of my Dad. He thinks the world of me, too—and the rest of us. When he's in luck, nothing's too good for us. Mum's the best-looking woman on the fields and we're the finest youngsters a man ever had. He splashes his money around, as good natured and generous as you please. But he just can't stand up to things when they go wrong. Starts boozing and rousing about everything. Mum's a god-damned slut and we're the worst horde of filthy brats a man was ever cursed with. That's what comes of being a gentleman, Mum says. Dad thinks he's got a right to the best of everything and goes to pieces when he can't get it.

'Mum must've been pretty when she was young, but you'd

never think so to look at her now. She was working at a pub when Dad married her. His family thought she wasn't good enough for him. That's why we've got no relations, and Mum's had a tough time trying to feed us all when Dad goes off prospecting. I've seen too much of married life to let myself in for it—before I've got to. Besides, there's my job. Mum couldn't manage just now if I didn't send her my wages. But Charley—'

The hard angry young voice changed to a tender, regretful note.

'I like Charley. Never thought I could get so struck on a man. But he's so good-looking—and different from the others. When he's had a shower, washed his blueys and put on a clean shirt, it makes me happy just to see him. My heart sort of turns over when he comes into the bar. And then, when he looks at me, it's like going to mass with the music and singing all going on inside of me, and little bells ringing. . . .

'Other chaps 've wanted me to go with them and marry them,' Violet brooded. 'But nobody's been so crazy about me as Charley —telling me I've got eyes like wet violets and all that, and making love to me before everybody. If I'll only promise to marry him, Charley says, he'll turn over a new leaf, stop drinking, save money and take me away from this blasted pub.

'We'll live in London, Paris or New York, and I can learn singing. His mother's a wealthy woman, Charley says, and wants him to go home, but he won't go without me. How could I leave Mum and the kids until Dad gets back? And how can I believe Charley's telling me the truth, Mrs. Gough, when the very next day he forgets the new leaf he was going to turn over, gets roaring drunk, is sick all over the floor and his mates have to drag him out of the bar? He looks horrible then and I hate him.'

What could one say? Sally asked herself.

'Oh, dear,' she exclaimed. 'It's very difficult for you, Violet. But it would be more difficult if . . .'

'I know,' Violet agreed. 'That's what I told Charley when I gave him another chance, a month ago. It would be worse if we were married. He tried. He did try to keep off the drink, Mrs. Gough. For nearly three weeks never touched a drop. Then, it was just the same, all over again, of course. . . .'

Latterly Charley had been hanging round the pub every weekend, boozing and making love to Violet, in a fury of jealousy and despair. He wanted to fight any man who breasted up to the bar and chatted to her with the familiarity she was accustomed to. Giotti had ordered Charley off the premises because he was making a damned nuisance of himself.

'And so he was,' Violet agreed. 'But Mr. Giotti didn't mind

so long as Charley was buying drinks. He's made a lot of money out of Charley. But now Charley's down on his luck, Mr. Giotti's got no time for him: says he'll send me home unless I break off with him. There was a terrible scene on Saturday night—and Charley went off, saying he'd do for himself.'

'Oh, dear!' Sally exclaimed, distressed that she could say nothing to help Violet.

'Mum says, a man never means it when he talks like that.' Violet scowled as she wrestled with her problem. 'But I am worried about Charley, Mrs. Gough. He looked so wild and desperate. And he said: "Life won't be worth living without you, Violet. If I can't see you and talk to you, the sooner it's over the better." '

'It's not fair to have made things so hard for you,' Sally said.

Violet was not the sort of girl who wept easily, she guessed. Her eyes held an awareness of tragedy, and her thoughts were too troubled for tears.

'He didn't think of that,' Violet said. 'I wish I didn't like Charley so much, Mrs. Gough. If it wasn't for the booze, I daresay I'd marry him. But I do want to be a singer and go away from this place when Dad gets back.

'A singer?' Sally queried, glad to think Violet's love affair had not obscured that dream. 'You've got a lovely voice, Violet.'

'Mr. Giotti says I'd be a world famous singer, like Melba,' Violet said quietly. 'He was giving me singing lessons until he got cross with me about Charley. But now, he says, if I'm going to muck-up my life for the first good-looking waster who comes along, I'm not worth bothering about.'

'I don't believe you're going to muck-up your life,' Sally said firmly. 'You've got too much strength of character and common sense to do that, Violet.'

'Do you think so? Do you really think so? Violet's eyes turned their brooding gaze on her.

'Sure of it,' Sally said.

Violet thought it was time for her to go back to Giotti's. She got down from the cart: stood a moment on the dusty track looking up at Sally.

'I hope you're right. I do hope you're right, Mrs. Gough,' she said, as if she doubted it.

Sally tried to think of something cheery and consoling to say.

'And remember,' she cried lightly, 'first love isn't last love, Violet.'

Why on earth had she said that? she asked herself as she drove on. Hadn't she loved Morris when she was not much older than Violet? And didn't she still love him? Was it possible that she could ever love anybody but Morris? No, of course not. And yet—she banished the thought that her love for Morris had passed into a prosaic affection. Married people got so used to each other, she told herself, it was quite natural they should be less amorous than they had once been; but that did not mean the bond between them was not as strong and valued. On the contrary, it meant— What did it mean?

Sally clucked to her old mare. She was anxious to get over the claypan before the light failed. As she talked with Violet, Queenie had been moving at a snail's pace, but now it would be a serious matter if Queenie went lame. Sally felt pleased that Violet had confided in her. She hoped she had helped Violet to avoid disaster. The girl was so young, and yet so mature, so disillusioned and yet bewildered by her love for Charley.

If only she got a chance, perhaps Violet would be a world-famous singer, Sally told herself. There was no doubt she had a beautiful voice and with opportunity might make good use of it. But was it possible she would ever escape from that ramshackle pub, and the passions this lonely, sun-blasted country bred?

Her mind was so full of Violet and her troubles, that Sally scarcely noticed the miles as Queenie lumbered over them. The sunset flamed, and the ridge in the distance was still a blurred mass, when she realized it would be dark before she pulled into the camp on Con's Gully; but she could see piled boulders against the skyline where the track ascended, and knew she must steer for them.

The sky faded to lilac and green as the first stars appeared, and Sally sang to herself as Queenie limped along, fagged now but pulling with a will, because she was near the end of her journey.

Sally felt at home and in harmony with this outstretched, mysterious country. After all, she told herself, it was part of Australia. Very different, of course, to the southern forests in which she had been brought up. But still her country and she belonged to it. She was glad to have proved to Morris that she could find her way about and had no fear of it. Sally thought eagerly of all the news she would have to give Morris about the rush to Lake Darlot and her visit to the Giotti's.

'But first love is not last love, Violet!' She wondered why she had said that. The phrase haunted her. What had put it into her head?

As Queenie stumbled on the rough track up hill and then down, Sally got down from the cart and led her. It would have been quite easy now to lose her way in the darkness. She coo-eed and Morris replied in the distance. She was pleased to see the

glow of camp fires in the gully ahead. Presently Morris came towards her with a lantern, and she cried:
'Oh, darling, it's nice to be home again!'

CHAPTER XXXIII

RUMOURS of the rush to Lake Darlot had reached Con's Gully while Sally was in Kanowna. Only half a dozen men still clung to their alluvial claims along the gully, and most of them, for weeks, had been shovelling dirt and dryblowing with only a few weights to show for their pains. They lost no time pulling pegs, rolling tents and blankets, and making ready for the track.

It was the agent for an overseas syndicate who brought the news. He had been inspecting Tom Doyle and Bissenberger's Hit-and-Miss Mine to the north-east, and ridden over to have a look at Con's Gully. Was sufficiently impressed with its prospects for flotation purposes to want to buy up the claims. He paid McGinn and his mates £100 for their claim; offered Morris and Con £100 for theirs, and another £300 for the right to take over the lease.

Con jumped at the offer. He wanted to go off to the Darlot, and although Morris thought they ought to have stuck out for a higher figure, he realized that they were doing pretty well on the reef which had given no indication of payable gold. Alluvial along the gully was just about played out, he suspected, and Morris, too, was hankering after Lake Darlot. Since Sally had told him about gossip in the store, and 'rich specimens at grass,' up north, he was reconciled to Con's deal and eager to be on their way.

Con was up early next morning and brought in the horses. Sally helped Morris to fall the tents, shift and hoist the shakers, load and pack tools and camp gear. She was glad to be leaving this barren, shadeless place of stark rocks, with the dead salt lake and long, sun-baked flats stretching out from it: as excited as the men to be shifting camp and off on the rush. In an hour or so, she and Morris were trailing after Con across the claypan.

He rode on ahead with his pack horse following. Sally and Morris walked beside the spring cart which was heavily loaded. They had stopped by the lakeside to dismantle the condenser and stow the tank: were apprehensive as to how Queenie was going to stand up to her load, after having covered the same distance the day before.

'She'll pull through!' Morris declared, optimistically. 'Got a lot of grit, the old girl. Like you, my dear.'

Sally laughed. 'Am I like Queenie?'

'Not quite so short winded and gone in the knees, perhaps,' Morris admitted. 'But as willing to pull your weight under difficulties.'

'Oh, Morris!' Sally was elated by his recognition that she could be a good mate.

'Con's Gully was about as rough a camp as ever I've been on,' Morris said. 'And I've never struck such rotten feeling among the men as we had to put up with there. It was my fault, and Con's, I suppose, for not sticking to the regulations. Not making a clean breast of the gold we had won. But we didn't do so badly after all. Next time we hear of Con's Gully it'll be a wild cat on the market, and some English company promoter 'll make thousands out of it, no doubt.'

'And others be ruined?'

'You can't tell. Maybe she'll turn out better than was expected, if they put down a shaft and start development work. Then we'll be cursing ourselves for selling.'

'I'm glad we're out of it.'

The sun was blazing down on them. The perspiration streamed from Sally's face as she trudged along. The dust rising from the cart wheels and her own feet, powdered her clothes and skin.

'Where we're going will be worse than Con's Gully,' Morris said, gruffly. 'In fact, you can't go.'

'But Morris—' Sally could not hide her dismay.

'You can go and stay with the Brierlys for a while, and Madame Robillard, or put up at Fogarty's, but not as a servant. I won't have any more of that nonsense.'

'No,' Sally said firmly. 'I could stay with Laura or Marie only for a week or so, and you may be away for months. Why can't I come with you up north, Morris? Con says I'm as good as a man in the camp.'

'I know,' Morris admitted grudgingly. 'You've stood up to things pretty well, Sally. Better than I thought any woman could.'

'Sandy Gallagher takes his wife everywhere with him,' Sally demurred. 'She was on Kurnalpi and Dead Finish.'

'I'm not Gallagher—and you're not a great raw-boned waler like God-save-us Sarah, as the men call her.'

They plodded on in silence. Then Morris, with a glance at Sally's downcast face and dejected figure, said quietly:

'It's bad enough to have brought you out here, Sally. Almost more than I can endure to see you dragging along like this, tired, dirty and trying to be cheery all the time.'

He turned on her that look which came from depths of passion and tenderness, rarely stirred. Sally's eyes widened to his gaze.

'Oh, Morris,' she cried, 'but I don't want you to leave me again. I'm happy just to be with you. No matter what happens. Even here in the heat and dust.'

Morris took her in his arms and kissed her. It was a delirious moment. Had Con looked back, he would have thought they were mad to stand wrapped in each other's arms under the broiling sun at midday. Never before, Sally reflected, had he been likely to detect any sentimental weakness between them. But it was delightful to know Morris could still forget time and place: want to kiss and hold her in his arms with loverlike ardour. Such an impulse had not moved him for many months.

The miles slipped away more quickly as they trudged along, after that. They walked, holding hands like children for a while, feeling ridiculously light-hearted and pleased with each other. Sally's long skirts trailed in the dust, and the sweat poured from Morris's face, streaking the dirt that caked on it. But they joked and made fun of everything. It was like being young and in love again to enjoy such foolishness, and be indifferent to the heat and glare.

Con pulled up at midday to boil the billy. Sally and Morris had a pannikin of tea and a snack to eat with him. Then they all went on again. Con had got over the grouch which drove him nearly demented at the gully: was in high spirits and looking forward to a booze up at Giotti's. He offered Morrey's missus a turn on his horse, but Sally said she would ride on the spring cart when she got tired.

'Morris and I are getting into our stride for Darlot,' she boasted gaily.

'We'll need camels for that trip,' Con replied, 'and good ones.'

Sally would not ride on the spring cart, although she was so leg-weary long before they reached Kanowna, she could scarcely crawl. She comforted herself that Morris and Queenie were just about knocked-up, too.

'A ten-mile walk with the sun hundreds in the shade, and an old crock with a heavy load to keep going, isn't quite the same thing as a stroll on a nice day, is it, darling?' she queried.

'It is not,' Morris agreed. 'And we've got twelve miles to do to-morrow, between Kanowna and Hannans, don't forget.'

Kanowna's main street was teeming with miners and prospectors, camels and horses, when they passed along it. Stores and pubs were thronged. Many of the men had come up from the claims which honeycombed the wide flats stretching out from the street, for their sundowner, as usual. Others had abandoned unsatisfactory workings on outlying camps and were tramping or riding into Hannans on their way to Lake Darlot.

Con made a beeline for Giotti's. It was the busiest time of the day and the small squalid hotel in an uproar.

'Let's camp by the road on the other side of the town, Morris,' Sally begged. 'We can sleep under the cart. It will be much nicer than spending the night in a stuffy pub, with all that noise going on.'

'Right. But we may as well have a meal first. I'll go and fix up with Mrs. Giotti.' Morris went into the hotel.

He reappeared a few minutes later.

'You never saw such chaos as the place is in,' he said, with an expression of disgust. 'Mrs. Giotti's drunk. And an old chap trying to cook, almost as bad. There won't be a meal in the place to-night, if you ask me. Your friend, Violet is in trouble. Her young man, Charley Leigh, was found lying dead at the bottom of a disused shaft at the old White Feather, this morning. Violet has gone home to her mother and Mrs. Giotti is all tears and maudlin sympathy; but blackguarding Violet for having left her in the lurch, with so many men going to the rush, wanting a meal, and Alberto needing Violet to help him in the bar. I didn't tell Mrs. Giotti you were here, so we can move on.'

'Poor child!' Sally grieved for Violet and the young Englishman whose death had made so little difference to the roistering life of the town that night.

Thought of them, and of the tragedy which could so swiftly descend and blot out all human relationships in this great indifferent land where the fear of death was less powerful than the lust for gold, oppressed her.

Morris went back to try to buy a piece of fresh meat and baker's bread in the township. He had a round of drinks with Con and men in the bar at Giotti's before he returned.

Sally made a fire by the roadside. They roasted the meat on the end of forked twigs, spread slices of bread with rancid butter and raspberry jam, drank black tea: 'dined well,' as Morris said.

He hauled a mattress off the cart and they stretched to sleep on it with a light blanket over them. Sally was glad Morris did not want to drink with Con at Giotti's: glad that he wanted to make love to her under the diamond-spread canopy of the blue dark sky. They must make the most of life: hold fast to their love and each other if they were to defeat death and any tragedy lurking for them, she thought. She could see herself, as if in a dream, plodding along like old Queenie beside Morris, through all the ups and downs, rushes and slumps, dust storms and mirages of their life on the fields.

CHAPTER XXXIV

THEY camped a mile out of Hannans next night. Con caught up to them during the day: said he must have feed and water for his horses, so went on. Morris had enough only to keep Queenie going and give her a start in the morning. She had plugged along stolidly, but was going to be no use on the long track to Darlot. He wanted to sell her, and tried to prevent her knocking up on the last stretch of the road into the township.

When they arrived in Hannans about midday, Morris took a room at McSweeney's. He and Con rode off to Coolgardie on Con's horses the same afternoon to buy camels. They returned two days later with a string of half a dozen and a camel buggy, very pleased to have got them from a prospector recovering from typhoid who wanted money to go south for a holiday.

The camels were a poor lot, mangy and sore-backed, and there was a bad brute among them who promised to give trouble. He had the Afghan's black mark on him; but Con reckoned he could handle the brute, and they were lucky to have got camels at any price while the rush to Lake Darlot was on.

Con went on a bender that night; but sobered up late next day to take the camels in hand, wash their backs and plaster them with sulphur and fat. Morris bought stores for three months, and they were ready to start.

Morris had spent all their money on the camels and stores, Sally knew. There was no question now of whether she should accompany him. It was understood that she would drive the camel buggy. She had never driven camels, but was a good enough horse-woman to manage a pair of old cow camels, Morris said.

Of course, she was, Sally agreed, pleased to have got her own way and to be going on the trip up north. After a few days' rest and idleness at McSweeney's, she was full of energy, and in good spirits, ready for any emergency.

It had been wonderful to have a bath, wash her hair, get into clean clothes; but she could not endure the idea of having to put in months of just sitting about and doing nothing at this squalid, rowdy little pub. She wished, though, that Con had not sold his horses. They were tough bush-bred brumbies. She would have been happier travelling with them, or with old Queenie and the spring cart, than with camels. But Queenie already was working on the whip-stick of a mine in which Frisco was interested.

Frisco had been one of the first to greet them on their return from Con's Gully. And his greeting had been as gay and boisterous as if Morris were really a long-lost brother, and Sally the light of his eyes. Those dark eyes which had always disturbed her. But Frisco was astounded to hear that Sally was going on the rush to Lake Darlot.

He tackled Morris about it.

'You're mad to be taking the missus with you, Morrey,' he said. 'It's bad country, the blacks hostile, and too far out for a woman to go.'

Morris as good as told him to mind his own business.

'Leave her here in Hannans. Let her stay on at McSweeney's. If you're short, I'll put up the cash,' Frisco urged.

'Thanks.' Frisco's advice increased Morris's decision that Sally should go with him. 'Mrs. Gough wants to come,' he said.

'But she doesn't know what she'll be up against,' Frisco argued. 'You do. You've got no right to let her go. It's downright criminal, if you ask me.'

'I don't,' Morris remarked dryly.

'As a matter of fact,' he added, 'things are so damned bad in Hannans just now, what with the typhoid and scum of the earth drifting round, I think she'll be safer with me. Jimmy Ross says there's good feed and water on the track. The weather'll be alright for a couple of months. And Con says the natives won't attack a camp if there's a woman about.'

'That's why you're taking Mrs. Gough,' Frisco jeered.

The blood rushed to Morris's head.

'God damn and blast you,' he stuttered. 'Sally's going because she wants to. Won't be left behind—and Con backs her up. Says she's as good as a man on the track.'

He walked off and Frisco stood staring after him. Frisco had a word with Con later.

'What sort of a bloody fool are you, lettin' Morrey take his wife to the Darlot?' he demanded.

Con roared laughing.

'Me? What've I got to do with it?' he queried jocosely. 'D' y'r think I want a bloody female tailin' after me? Or Morrey either? It's Mrs. Sally, herself's made up her mind she's comin' with us. And that's all there is to it. You fix it up with her to stay in Hannans, Frisco—and we'll crack a bottle on the strength of it.'

His wink and broadside made no impression on Frisco. It was one thing to have a reputation for being partial to women, but a horse of quite another colour to have his honest concern about Mrs. Gough being regarded as a pretext for amorous purposes.

She, herself, did him the justice of recognizing there was nothing of that in it. Frisco told Sally that he was not satisfied with reports about the track and the prospects of the field.

'I'm scared you'll have a tough time, ma'am, and not be able to stand up to it,' he said. 'Many a man can't. Con's a good bushman and the chances are he'll see you through—if anything goes wrong. But when men are on the scent of gold—have got the gold fever—their judgment's not to be trusted.'

'I know all that,' Sally's queer little smile flickered. 'Perhaps that's why I want to go with them.'

Their first days on the track had been uneventful: just following a dusty road through the scrub, with breaks at midday to eat and boil the billy, or to unload at sundown and camp for the night.

Con steered ahead with the camels. Morris rode one in the rear and Sally trailed along driving two cow camels in the buggy loaded with a water tank, prospecting gear and camp equipment. The heat was suffocating, and there were long stretches to cover between the water holes each day; but the camels swung along at their slow, even pace, eating up the miles bearing always north into the grey distances and pale blue sky, bleached of nearly all its colour by the hot sun.

Beyond the great Ninety Mile salt lakes a stretch of sandy country and shallow lakes made heavy going. Rains had fallen recently and further on the track ran through mulga and good grass. Huge boulders held gnamma holes and a soak stretched out from their rugged bases. It was here Morrey shot a turkey, and the rich smell of the roasted meat brought dingoes howling about the camp at night.

Con had a bad time with his warrigal camel. After a few good feeds, the brute started bucking, head down, and bolted, slewing off sideways and propping, in a way Con swore was murderous. He rode with a stout waddy in one hand to belabour the camel over the head when he played-up. Con's temper suffered as much as the camel's. Morrey suggested putting a bullet through the beast, but Con would not hear of that. He had never met the camel that could beat him, he said. He'd break the bastard or die in the attempt.

Sally was scared of that camel: he had attacked one of the cows in her buggy and savaged it cruelly. The way he roared in the night, and bared his long yellow teeth to bite whenever Con went near him, made her blood run cold. She had seen him bolting in hobbles and Con running after him, dragging on to his reins, and belabouring him with a pick handle. There was a vicious feud between the man and that great evil-smelling beast. Con remained the master only by a ruthless brutality and constant watchfulness.

Morris, too, was afraid of what this feud might lead to. He did not want Con to be disabled or have his mental equilibrium destroyed by the brute. Any such accident might mean disaster on a prospecting trip.

It was at the Eighteen Mile Rocks they met Parkes, the original discoverer of Lake Darlot, going down to the old camp. He boasted that he had won 700 ounces in three months, and that there was plenty more where it came from.

He talked of two new reefs he had pegged beyond Mount Catherine, which prospectors were calling a mountain of gold, the great quartz blow could be traced for two miles. It rose to fifty feet: was about fifteen feet thick on top: had been tested to thirty feet down and was showing fine and coarse gold which would keep a twenty-five head battery going for years. Hundreds of acres of auriferous country round about, and in the Black Range, had been picked over but never worked. Con and Morris were wild with excitement. They could think or talk of nothing but pushing on and pegging before all the likely ground on the new field was taken up.

For several days Sally had been suffering from an attack of dysentery. She tried to pretend that she was quite well: went about getting the meals, and driving all day as if she were in the best of spirits. But every day she felt weaker, a blinding headache made it impossible for her to see the road, and at night, as she lay in her blanket near the buggy, she was conscious of the fever raging in her blood, racking her with ague in the early hours of the morning. One morning she had found a yellow-bellied black snake in her blanket, and screamed with terror. It had slid away, and she could not be sure whether she had imagined seeing it.

She knew she was ill: desperately ill, but determined not to tell Morris. She could not bear to admit that she had failed to stand up to hardships of the track. It would be easier, she thought, to die than to spoil Morris's chances of striking gold. But could she go on?

If only Morris would let her stay here by the track and go back to Hannans with some prospector returning! But he would not do that. He would want to stay and look after her. Take her back to Hannans himself. And Con would curse at having their plans upset. Besides, it would be dangerous for him to go on alone with that bad camel and the chance of natives attacking the camp. They were in the country now where the massacres had occurred and the blacks were still fierce and hostile. Every passing party of prospectors had warned them not to sleep near their camp fire, to keep their guns loaded, hobble the camels beyond the light of the camp fire.

Sally's thoughts raced, whirling over each other, confused and distraught. How much longer could she go on? How much longer would Morris fail to see she was ill?

They had reached the Twenty-Five Mile Rocks when a party of prospectors pulled in. The jagged peaks of Mount Margaret were looming in the distance. There was a good soak here. Con had seen a group of blacks scatter into the scrub at sunset.

The prospectors brought news of another find to the north-east. There was a well-beaten track to the Flat Rocks and a donkey-pad to Mount Margaret, they said. Another track ran due east. It was rough spinifex country, water scarce, nothing but a dry lake and heavy sand for ten miles. Then you struck Menankily, the place of many skulls, the blacks called it. But that was where Goodenough Smith and his mates had pegged. That was where they had struck the rich specimens they were taking down to support their demand for a reward claim.

Sally, lying on her blanket a little distance from the camp fire, knew that this was the end of the journey for her. She was too ill and weary to move again.

Vaguely through the excited clatter of voices round the camp fire, she heard Con and Morris getting directions for this track through the spinifex and dry country.

She decided to ask the men going south to take her with them. But when she tried to get up and walk over to them, she swayed dizzily, her legs withered under her and she fell. She must have lain all night in a drugging stupor, she thought, because it was dawn and the camp stirring before she was conscious again. Then, as if in a dream, she could hear the men going south, move off with cheery exclamations. She wanted to call out and run after them, but was unable to stir or raise her voice.

'Well, s'long!'

'Good luck, Morrey!'

'See y'r in the old camp!'

'Keep goin' and y'r bound to strike her round about Menankily or the Darlot, Con.'

Con and Morris shouted back. They were in good heart, too, it seemed. Had decided to make for Goodenough's find and risk the dry stretch while they could still load up with water from the soak near which they had camped.

They brought in the camels, filled up the tanks and water bags:

began to reload. Sally lay faint with pain and misery. She was too weak to move: lost consciousness every now and then, but fought her way back to brief realization of what was going on round her.

She saw Con and Morris standing over her. They loomed huge, sinister figures one moment, the next they were gone in a black cloud. Then she heard Con cursing and Morris arguing with him. It was over a hundred miles back to the Ninety Mile, but Con said Morris would have to take his wife there and get the publican's wife to look after her. Morris was reluctant to leave Con in the lurch: abandon their plan of prospecting round about Menankily before going on to Darlot, still nearly two hundred miles distant.

'Maybe it's only dysentery Sally's got,' he said gloomily, 'and if she rests here she'll be alright and ready to go on again in a day or two. But if it's the fever—I'll have to take her back to Hannans.'

Con swore angrily.

'Comes of bringing a woman on a trip like this.'

'That's all very well,' Morris said bitterly. 'But you said yourself there was no need to worry about natives if there was a woman in the camp.'

They decided finally that Con should push on with the camels and try to pick up a native guide, or another prospector to accompany him. He would leave Morris one riding camel and the buggy, to follow as soon as he was able. But before Con was ready for the track, Morris went down to the soak for water. He found a couple of gins there.

Morris persuaded them to go back to the camp with him because his woman was 'sick feller—close-up finish 'm.'

Kalgoorla recognized him. She knew he was a white man from whom the blacks had nothing to fear—though she hated white men. A sullen, middle-aged woman, her eyes smouldered to undying rage as she looked at them. But Morris's distress, his appeal for help, made her curious that day. She went to see the white missus who was sick.

When Kalgoorla and the young gin walked into the camp behind Morris, Sally was lying unconscious in the shade of some bushes, babbling faintly about the heat and the flies, and the yellow-bellied black snake she had found in her blanket one morning. She was terrified of that snake and of Con's warrigal camel.

Morris bathed her face with the cold water he had brought from the soak. He laid wet rags on her head. Kalgoorla and the gin squatted down and watched him. When Morris went over to the fire to boil some water for Sally to drink, Kalgoorla broke off a branch of mulga and brushed the flies away from her face.

'Missus bloody sick-feller alright?' Morris asked anxiously.

'Eh-erm,' Kalgoorla replied.

Morris brought flour and sugar, a tin of jam and put them beside Kalgoorla. The young gin exclaimed delightedly when she saw them, but Kalgoorla's eyes did not swerve from the sick woman. She kept on gently waving the spray of mulga to keep the flies away, and presently began crooning a queer winding little melody. It went on and on, softly, eerily. Sally's breathless, weary chatter ceased. She fell asleep. Still Kalgoorla went on singing: singing and waving that branch of grey fragrant leaves.

When Sally wakened, it was the young gin she saw first. Her eyes cleared and she smiled.

'Oh, Meeri,' she whispered, 'have you come to look after me?'

The girl was not Maritana; but Kalgoorla muttered fiercely, and the young gin gasped:

'Eh-erm, Meeri.'

A moment later, at a word from Kalgoorla, she slipped away through the scrub. Before long several men of the tribe approached the camp. They carried their womeras and long hunting spears; but at a shrill cry from Kalgoorla, put them on the ground and advanced warily.

Eager and curious as children, they crowded round the sick woman, but Sally was sleeping again. Kalgoorla drove the men back with a few muttered words. They huddled together while she explained what had happened: how Morris had found her at the water hole and begged her to come to see his woman who was 'close-up finish 'm.'

Con sized-up the situation.

'Best thing we can do is clear out, and leave the missus with the blacks, Morrey,' he said. 'Kalgoorla'll look after her. We can leave 'em some stores. If we hang around the men'll clean us out, and there'll be trouble. Fix it up with the old bloke, and promise him the moon if he takes the missus back to Hannans safe and well. That's all you can do. And it's the best you can do.'

'Christ,' Morris groaned, 'I can't leave her, Con.'

But he knew that if he went back to Hannans with Sally, Con would have to shoot the bull camel and go on alone. It was a tough proposition for a man to handle a string of camels and go through this country on his own.

Failure of the trip would leave them both stony-broke. On the other hand, if they stuck to it and struck gold, Morris told himself, all his dreams might be realized. He believed that they would strike it. Every prospector coming down from the north was weighing in well. God, they couldn't miss a chance like this, and the prospect of locating a reef out Menankily or Mount Catherine way.

Morris was sorely tempted. The gold fever was as hot in him as the typhoid in Sally—though to give him his dues he did not know it was typhoid. Con declared Mrs. Gough was suffering from an attack of dysentery. 'The missus would be delirious and much weaker if it was the typhoid she was down with,' he said. All she needed was rest and boiled water, until she could get about again. If Kalgoorla could be persuaded to look after Sally, and take her back to Hannans, Morris decided he would go on with Con next day.

He talked to the old man of the tribe, promised to leave him some stores and that Missus Sally would give him flour, sugar, tobacco and wine if Kalgoorla looked after her while she was sick, and the tribe carried her back to Hannans in a day or two.

The old man agreed, though Kalgoorla scowled at him from under her heavy brows.

Sally heard something of what Morris said. She knew Con was raging at the delay and trouble her sickness had caused. She was too ill to care what happened. It was a relief to think she need not move. A relief, too, to realize that Con and Morris were going on, and would not have to fret about upsetting their plans.

'Oh, yes, Morris,' she said wearily, when he came to explain to her. 'It's the best thing to do. You must go on. I'll be all right. There's nothing to worry about. You know I always get on well with the natives.'

Morris cut down a couple of tough slender trees to make poles for a stretcher, covered it with bags and a blanket. He lifted Sally on to it, and showed the blacks how to carry it; got them to build a miah of mulga boughs over the spot where Sally was lying, and tried to explain to Kalgoorla that water must be boiled before Missus Sally drank it, and that wet rags must be kept on her head. A little weak tea and condensed milk, she could have when she asked for it. He swept round the miah with a leafy branch, telling Kalgoorla to keep the place clean and free from flies. Kalgoorla took her instructions in glowering silence.

When he came to say good-bye, Morris kissed Sally shame-facedly.

'It goes against the grain, leaving you, dear,' he said, as if he found it difficult to adhere to his resolution. 'But you know how it is. We can't afford to have this trip mucked-up. I wouldn't go, of course, if I thought you were very ill, but Con reckons it's only an attack of dysentery. You'll be all right in a day or two. And we've got to get a move on. Water'll be drying up on all the northern tracks, soon, and the chances are we'll miss something good if we don't get to Goodenough's Find before he passes the news on to other men on their way up here.'

'Of course,' Sally forced herself to speak cheerily, although she could hardly speak at all. 'It's bad enough to be such a crock. I'd never forgive myself if I—mucked-up the trip, Morris.'

CHAPTER XXXV

SALLY did not know how long she lay ill and helpless in the blacks' camp. As soon as Con and Morris went on their way, the tribe came and camped at a little distance from the miah they had made for her. Sally thought she must have slept, on and off, for days: been unconscious some of the time, perhaps.

She had a confused memory of being glad to lie still, and not have to keep going through the heat and the glare with a blinding headache and her bowels churning: of not having to drive those great lumbering camels and watch Con belabouring the vicious brute he was riding. It was a comfort to feel Kalgoorla or one of the gins brushing the flies away and putting wet rags on her head: to drink the water they brought her.

She was conscious sometimes of the blacks moving about in sunlight and shadow beyond the miah. Once she seemed to have been awakened by a row going on in the camp. Men's voices talked angrily, excitedly. Sally thought she heard Kalgoorla, taunting and abusing the men. She got an impression that the men wanted to abandon her; but Kalgoorla was fighting for her, talking about Morrey and Con, and the 'bacca, wine and jam Missus Sally would give them when they brought her to Hannans. After that she knew she was moving: the camp had broken up, and she was being carried for a few hours every day.

When the fever subsided and her brain cleared, Sally remembered seeing, through the leafy screen of the miah, those dark naked figures moving about in the bright sunlight: the men going off hunting in the morning and coming in later in the day with a kangaroo or some small game: the women squatting to pound seed on a flat stone: children laughing and playing near them. And at night, listening to the clicking of kylies and the mournful cadence of native singing, she thought she had been re-born into this primitive life.

It was as if she had been wrestling with death and was surprised to find herself still alive. Alive and feeling happy about it. Never before had just living seemed to be so wonderful! Her heart was full of gratitude for the blacks who had brought her back to life and this strange land of theirs that was like a milky opal shot with fire and all the colours of the rainbow.

The morning she sat up to smile and speak, Kalgoorla cried, 'Yukki!' with such joy that immediately men, women and children were crowding round the stretcher, grinning and clucking delightedly.

Everybody, Sally thought, was pleased and excited by her recovery. The blacks had shifted camp many times since they had taken charge of her, she realized; and presently two men lifted the stretcher and walked off with her. Others took turns during the day. They swung along at a slow, easy pace, resting for a sleep at midday, and camping before sundown. Fires were lighted, and the smell of bungara (a large species of iguana) or wild doves being cooked made Sally feel hungry. Kalgoorla brought her toasted bardies to eat. Sally recognized the fat white grubs Maritana used to devour with such relish. She ate them, thankfully, and found them delicious.

The tribe had long since finished all the provisions Morris left, she suspected, and she would have to subsist on any food the natives could share with her. She shuddered to think afterwards of what she might have eaten during those days, but at the time she did not care whether she was eating snake, goanna, or boudie rat. She was glad to eat anything, and there was little enough of it until they reached the districts where mining camps began to appear. Then Sally was able to get a little flour, sugar and tea from isolated prospectors. These she shared with the blacks, though there was never more than a day's supply.

Men at one of the camps would have driven her into Hannans in a buggy; but the natives, clearly, were opposed to this suggestion. Kalgoorla tried to explain that Morris had put his woman in their charge and that they must deliver her at Hannans. They expected there to receive their reward for having accomplished what they had agreed to do. Sally understood that, having brought her over the worst part of the journey, it would not be fair to deprive them of the satisfaction of having kept faith with Morris and earned what he had promised them. She was well enough now to know she would survive the last stages of the journey, and satisfied to let the natives have their way about it.

'They were so good to me,' she used to say, remembering that time. 'You wouldn't wonder I've always had a friendly feeling for abos, if you knew how good to me they were when I was ill on the track.'

'If they had cleared out and left you—'

'Oh, yes, there would've been a few bones for the crows to pick. But they carried me back to Hannans. Over a hundred and fifty miles. I daresay I wasn't very heavy, but still natives are used to travelling light, and it wasn't easy for them, yanking me and a stretcher all that distance. They took their time, never seemed to be in a hurry, except when the water holes were far apart. Every day we shifted camp, and the men, even the women, took turns carrying me. When they put the stretcher down on the spot where our tent used to be at Hannans, I nearly wept for joy. There was no tent, of course, but my brushwood shed was still standing.'

Men from the surrounding camps came round, and Sally told them what had happened. They wanted her to go to the hospital or to one of the hotels and convalesce in all the luxury available in the township. But Sally said it was her own place she needed: just to rest and feel 'at home' for a while.

In no time a tent was going up for her and a bed had been found. Somebody had brought Sally's boxes up from McSweeney's where they had been stored. A billy was boiled for tea. How good it tasted, and the bread and butter she ate with it!

Frisco and Sam Mullet escorted the blacks down to the store and piled them up with meat, flour, sugar, tobacco, jam, and a few bottles of wine. They camped down near the lake and feasted half the night.

Many miners had wives and children on the field by then. Most of them living on the flats stretching out from Hannans, or round about the Great Boulder. Mrs. Molloy, the wife of a miner working on the Croesus, was Sally's nearest neighbour. She and her husband had come up from Southern Cross in a spring cart with several children and a herd of goats. She had almost as many children as goats, the men said. But Mrs. Molloy did not mind how many children she had, so long as she had goats to feed the children. How she managed to feed the goats in dry weather was a mystery; but they nibbled thorn bushes, went scavenging round the camps, and survived on a meagre ration of bulled water.

'Mrs. Molloy's rough as bags, but so big-hearted she'd share her last crust with you, missus,' Sam Mullet explained when Frisco had gone to bring Mrs. Molloy to see Sally.

Mrs. Molloy came bringing sheets, a pillow and towel, a blanket and tin of fresh goats' milk. She bustled about doing everything to make the invalid comfortable, chattering cheerily as she hunted for clean things in Sally's trunk, washed her and helped her into a nightdress.

201

'I don't blame you for not wanting to go to the 'orspital, dearie,' Theresa Molloy exclaimed in her vigorous, downright way. 'It's a death-trap the place is—so many dyin' there of the typhoid every day. And you'll be better here than in one of the pubs, with nobody to look after you, but a woman has more on her hands to cook and clean for everybody in a place like that, than she can get through. Our camp's not a mile away, and I can run over and do for you every day. A pleasure it'll be for me, though it's out of the way of female society I've got, tramping about with Ted and looking after the children and goats.'

'It's very good of you,' Sally said, feeling she had found a friend in this big slatternly woman.

'Good, me foot!' Mrs. Molloy laughed heartily. 'Most of the miners' wives here 'll tell you I'm a bad lot. Living with Ted Molloy and not married to him. Ted's got another wife somewhere. Where, he doesn't know, and I don't worry about it now. We've been together for fourteen years, and nobody any the worse. So what does it matter?'

Other miners' wives, wearing their best dresses and hats, came to make friendly inquiries next day. Was there anything they could do for Mrs. Gough? They brought scones and soup, made tea, and sat gossiping and exclaiming at the hard life women led on the goldfields; but nobody offered to be of more assistance when it was known Mrs. Molloy was looking after the patient, and that Kalgoorla was learning from her to wash clothes, make a bed, and cook a little. At night Kalgoorla slept by the camp fire near Sally's tent, but she kept out of sight when white women came to visit: resented even Mrs. Molloy interfering with her services.

Sally had an idea that Kalgoorla would not leave her until Morris had returned. That's how it looked, anyhow. The family group which had taken charge of Sally visited her now and then, laughing and exclaiming in friendly fashion when she was able to stand up to greet them and walk about. If there was food in the cool-safe Sally felt bound to share it with them, because the blacks had shared all they had with her.

They would go off again, leaving Kalgoorla, although sometimes she disappeared; spent the day with her own people in the camp they had made down near the lake.

Kalgoorla never talked much, even among the blacks, although she understood well enough what Sally said. She seemed to resent being separated from her tribe; sat brooding over the camp fire at night, or stalked off into the bush when her few chores were done. There was a fierce, restless glitter in her eyes after her people had left her, and she would shrink away and hide in the brush-shed if Frisco and Eli Nancarrow, or Sam Mullet and Blunt Pick came round to see how Mrs. Gough was getting on, and whether they could do anything for her.

'They were fine men, the prospectors and miners, in those days,' Sally used to say. 'There was nothing they would not do for a sick woman. Later on, when there was a bad outbreak of typhoid on the Catherine and the water gave out, the coach brought down the women and children, all of them helpless with dysentery. The men did everything for them, fed them with boiled water and cleared away all the mess. One of the women told me about it. You couldn't believe, she said, how kind and gentle those men were. People may say what they like about the early prospectors. That they were a tough, hard-drinking lot, cared for nothing but booze and gold. But they had a rough chivalry where women were concerned—white women at least. God knows how I would have fared, but for that.'

Old mates on Hannans could not forgive Morris for having left his wife to the tender mercies of the blacks when she was so ill. They knew all about the gold fever and the madness which takes a man on the rush to a new field. But after all, they argued, it was Mrs. Gough's life that was at stake, and Morris took too big a risk gambling on the blacks looking after a sick woman. They were as likely as not to have cleared out and left her if they suspected she had the sickness which was spreading death through the country. They would never have encumbered themselves with one of their own women in such straits. Then, too, with game becoming scarce and wells drying up, they had to shift camp frequently, and the meagre food supplies of the tribe were jealously guarded.

From what Sally had told them, the men agreed that Kalgoorla had probably saved Mrs. Gough's life. For what reason, they could not imagine. She had no love for the white people and it was unusual for a gin, even one who evidently was regarded as of some importance, to oppose the will of the men.

Maritana solved the mystery when she came with her man to visit Mrs. Sally. He belonged to a group which hunted further west than Maritana's although it was part of the same tribal organization. Kalgoorla was her mother, Maritana explained. Kalgoorla would always be 'good feller alonga Missus Sally' because Missus Sally was 'good feller alonga Maritana.'

Maritana had a chubby, honey-coloured baby in her arms. She was very proud of and delighted with him. Her man, a skinny, elderly warrior, followed her about and ordered her back to camp when he thought the visit to Missus Sally had lasted long enough. He was as proprietorial as any white man towards his woman and child.   Maritana obeyed him with becoming docility.   There were lewd jokes at Frisco's expense, and Frisco promised to lay out the next man who asked him what he thought of Maritana's baby.

At any rate, it was no thanks to Morris his wife had not died out there in the bush, over a hundred miles from anywhere, the men said.   A man had been tarred and feathered for less than what he had done.   But Sally would not listen to any criticism of Morris.   She was so distressed when harsh and indignant comments were made, that the men shut up on the subject.

Mrs. Molloy told her Frisco, Sam Muller, Eli Nancarrow and Blunt Pick were going to let Morris know just what they thought of him, when he returned.   Sally pleaded with them not to blame Morris.

'What else could he do?' she asked eagerly.   'He couldn't let Con go on alone, with that bad camel, and the chance of hostile natives attacking him.   I suppose it was the fever I had, but Morris didn't know—and it was all my fault, being so stupid and obstinate, about going with him on this trip.   I'd 've been so upset if I had ruined his plans and Morris had stayed with me, or brought me back to Hannans, I could never have pulled through.   So, please, don't think of it any more, or make any unpleasantness for Morris when he gets back.'

'What you say goes, ma'am,' Frisco agreed.   'Though if it was any other man treated a woman like Morrey's treated you, he'd get a rough deal from the men on this field.'

CHAPTER XXXVI

As soon as she was well enough to get about, Sally began to think of some way to earn her living.   She had no money and felt she must not continue to be indebted to Frisco, Sam Mullet and two or three other men, for all the food and water she used.

And there were the blacks.   It was all very well for her to share what food she had with them; but too much to expect the miners and prospectors who put provisions in her cool safe, to keep her and Kalgoorla, and the horde of natives who still hung round her camp.

Morris sent word by a teamster coming down from Lake Darlot that he and Con had struck bad luck after leaving Sally.   The bull camel had slewed when Con was mounting, got him by the leg, and savaged it viciously.   Morris had to shoot the brute, and carry Con over to the buggy. Con managed to drive, but they had to abandon the idea of going to Menankily: turned back to the Darlot track, and reached the main camp towards the end of the month.

Con had had a bad time with his leg, but it was alright now. They were doing pretty well on an alluvial claim they had pegged on the Darlot; but there was talk of good reefing country further east and they were going out to have a look at it before long.

Morris added that a native coming in from Flat Rocks with a party of prospectors had told him the 'mindic [sick] white missus was close-up walk about feller.' Kalgoorla, he seemed to think, had driven her sickness away. Kalgoorla had gone to the big camp the natives called Kalgoorlarry, with the men who were carrying the white missus, the boy informed Morris.

Morris hoped that Sally was fit and well now, and said he would send a cheque as soon as he and Con cashed in on this deal with Carnegie's syndicate for the claim. Meanwhile he suggested that Sally should score up what she needed at Killington's store. Ned Killington had always been good for credit when a prospector required it, and would be honoured by Mrs. Gough's patronage.

Sally had no illusions as to Mr. Killington's good-natured rather than enthusiastic acceptance of Morris's proposal. His face brightened, however, when she confessed she was going to use the brushwood shed near her tent as a dining-room, and serve meals to the men round about, so in a few weeks expected to be paying for goods as she bought them.

Frisco objected that there was no need for Mrs. Gough to open a dining-room. She was not strong enough yet for all the hard work it would involve, and Morris would not like the idea. There was no need to worry about anything the men did for her. Morris would settle up with them when he returned, and, in any case, there was nothing any one of them did not feel it a privilege to do for Mrs. Gough on her own account.

'I am quite well, thank you, Mr. Murphy,' Sally said. 'I can never repay Morris's friends for all their kindness. But I must have something to do, and will be ever so much happier with my dining-room.'

Sam Mullet and Eli thought the dining-room was a good scheme. They promised to round-up the boys to have meals at Mrs. Gough's, and offered to help getting the bough-shed ready for customers. They fixed up a trestle and forms, put a sheet of corrugated iron round the open fireplace, and built a table from butter boxes, on which Sally could prepare and serve meals.

Hannans was beginning to enjoy the boom some of the hard heads had prophesied for her. There were over five hundred miners working on the Boulder mines, and leases all along the ridge from the old reward claim to Hannans Lake were selling for fancy prices. Land on which the colour of gold had never been seen was bought up and floated for hundreds of thousands on the London market. The agents of German and French firms had negotiated several purchases. The Stock Exchange and the Open Call were thronged with eager speculators. Every hotel in Hannans was crowded: meals and accommodation difficult to obtain. Newcomers, often, were forced to roll-up in a rug and sleep on a verandah, or on the ground under the stars.

Men from the camps round about Maritana willingly patronized Mrs. Gough's bush dining-room, because it was difficult to get any sort of meal in the township. Kalgoorla helped Sally to serve and wash-up afterwards; but even so, cooking breakfast and dinner in kerosene tins for from twenty to thirty men entailed more strenuous work than Sally had anticipated. She contrived to do it, during those summer months, only by careful planning and watchfulness. The flies and dust drove her nearly crazy. Flies swarmed over everything, blowing even the butter if it was left uncovered for a moment, and sometimes a willy-nilly would whirl along, deluging dinner and diners with red dust.

The men joked about these disadvantages of eating at the Café de Bush, as they called it. Their banter saved Sally a good deal of embarrassment, and drew her into easy back-chat. But Sally prided herself on giving her customers as appetizing a meal as they could get in Hannans. They were all good friends of hers and she did her best for them. It pleased her to see them stroll out of the shed, loosening their belts and blowing with satisfaction.

'Gosh, that was a good feed, missus,' she liked to hear them say. 'I'm as full as a tick!'

Or: 'The boys reckon we've got the best chef on the fields, Mrs. Gough. Don't mind how long it is before Morrey gets back.'

Often there were only scraps left over for Kalgoorla when the men had finished. Sally herself felt too tired to eat when her day's work was done. A cup of black tea and a piece of bread and butter was all she ate. Her stomach had been queer since her illness. She was sick nearly every morning. Even the thought of food became nauseating when she had to cook so much.

She had to have breakfast ready soon after dawn, before the men went off to their claims: hurried away afterwards to buy any fresh food that may have come in at the store: took a brief rest at midday, then busied herself with preparations for the evening meal. Her grit and energy were amazing. Thin as a rat, but always sprightly, she contrived to make a success of her dining-room and impress everybody by her good spirits.

Sometimes, in the evening, after the dishes were washed and the remains of the meal cleared away, Frisco would stroll back to give her a bit of news, and sprawl on the ground, smoking and yarning. Sam Mullet, Blunt Pick, Eli and his mates usually drifted along soon afterwards.

'Hear comes the guard of honour,' Frisco would say with a grin, enjoying Sally's discomfiture.

She still flinched at the thought of Ma Buggins's insinuations, and the fact of the matter was, Frisco's attentions did cause her some uneasiness. He was always doing something for which she could not help feeling grateful. He had brought over her three-legged chair with a bag seat, for example. Very comfortable it was, that chair, to lie back and rest in after rushing about all day. Frisco had taken it when she and Morris broke camp to go to Con's Gully. He returned it with an embarrassing compliment about its being his most valued possession.

And often there were grapes and oranges in the cool-safe without any explanation of how they got there. Sally tried to thank him, but Frisco protested laughingly that he did not know what she was talking about. The men treated her with such amazing kindness and chivalrous respect, she had come to expect nothing less from them.

She should not allow them to do so much for her, perhaps, Sally thought: bring a load of wood from the bush, and see that her water tank was filled. But it was difficult to get as much water and wood as she needed. What else could she do but rely on these services the men gave her so willingly? It was not necessary even to remind them when the tank had to be refilled, or some wood cut. They all took a hand at chopping the wood; but Frisco carted the water in his buggy, and, she suspected, was responsible for keeping an eye on all her other requirements.

She was perturbed about that, and about how much she owed to his help and concern for her comfort. 'The guard of honour' made her realize Sam and the others were uneasy also about where the growing warmth of her friendliness with Frisco Jo Murphy might lead. Sally tried to make Sam and Eli understand that she was as pleased to sit and yarn with them as with anybody else.

There was no denying, however, the evenings were more interesting when Frisco talked about his adventures, wandering about the world on a sailing ship, singing in opera in Mexico, or digging on the goldfields of California and in the Kimberleys. And she liked him to bring his guitar and start strumming and singing, while the other men discussed the news of the day.

It would have been lonely and depressing to sit by herself every night, although she always went to bed early because she had to be up at dawn and have breakfast ready before the men went off to their claims, soon after sunrise. They came along in the evening, occasionally, to cheer her up with gossip of what was happening in the township and on outlying camps she knew. No further word had come from Morris, although Blunt Pick said a party of prospectors, down from Lake Darlot, told him Morris and Con had sold their claim and gone off on a rush to the Black Range.

Young Paddy Cavan joined the group now and then. He was a gawky lad of fifteen or sixteen now, though he looked such a kid, squatting there on the ground among the men with a grin on his freckled sunburnt mug, his blue eyes screwed up and shining as he related some bit of news.

'Did y'r hear?' he would say, and launch into a lively account of a big new deal, the latest crushings on the Great Boulder, or the way a party of prospectors had put it all over the agent of a foreign company, who thought he could buy their lease for a couple of thousand, if he turned on the beer.

'Shure the boys had a few drinks wid 'm,' Paddy exclaimed gleefully. 'Signed up all the papers. But Porky Parsons wouldn't sign. Doesn't drink anything stronger than water. So the deal fell through. And the boys reckon they had a good booze-up for nothing, and it cost the furriner fifty quid!'

Paddy had come to see Sally while she was ill: brought her a bunch of wild cassia. Often before in the spring he had brought her wild flowers, and he knew she loved the cassia. Its tiny flowers, like golden boronia, had an exquisite fragrance, frail and musky. You could smell it for miles along the dry creek beds where it grew, and it bloomed most of the year. Paddy knew a spot, a couple of miles out, beyond Hannans Lake, where the cassia was plentiful.

He said he made a few bob selling it to flash barmaids in the pubs, and the girls at Madame Marseilles. She had come over from Coolgardie when the tide of prosperity turned towards Hannans. The Japanese prostitutes had moved over, too, and were living in box huts behind the main street. They were crazy about flowers; but had no money to buy them, Paddy lamented. They flocked round him, chattering and squealing like magpies. if he passed with a bunch of flowers. He had to give them a piece of scarlet desert pea, or a bit of cassia, to get away. Wild flowers were the only sort of flowers to be got on Hannans, and Paddy declared he had made a lot of money, last spring, selling wild flowers in the pubs and she-beens.

When he came along with his bunch of cassia and squatted on the ground for a chat, Sally could not believe all the yarns she had heard about the youngster. It was a case of give a dog a bad name, she thought; and Paddy had had a hard time fending for himself.

Sam Mullet said Paddy was as cunning as a monkey. Nobody knew more about everybody's business than Young Paddy, and he'd do anything for money. Had no scruples about doing any man out of a few dwts if he could. He had specked two or three nice slugs himself on various occasions and got his share when Old George sold the claim they were working together near Mount Charlotte.

The men didn't like him: never trusted him, though the miners used him to get rid of a bit of gym, which was what they called the gold they got out of a mine with the Gympie hammer. It was easy to get away with in their crib bags or billies.

When Paddy was working for Pa Buggins, he acted as go-between for the miners and Pa, collecting gym. There was no end of a row when it was discovered Paddy was deducting his own percentage of the gold before it reached the storekeeper. But Paddy knew how to defend himself. The row died down and Paddy won on his first round, when he threatened to give information as to how Pa Buggins was running his business.

He could put the screw on a number of 'big men,' he bragged, and did, when it suited him. He wasn't popular among miners or mineowners; but that didn't worry Paddy. Not in the least. He was always as cheeky and cocksure as if he were on the best terms with everyone.

Sally thought she might have a good influence on Paddy if she showed a motherly interest in him. So she offered to mend his pants, if he washed them and brought them to her nice and clean. He borrowed a pair of Frisco's while she patched his own in several places, and gave him a little sound advice at the same time.

'You've got a good brain, Paddy,' she said. 'You could be a fine man if you keep yourself clean and straight.'

'Think so, ma'am?' Paddy queried, wickedly. 'It's the cost of water on the fields stops many a man from being clean—and straight.'

You couldn't moralize with Paddy, Sally realized. He made you feel as if you were talking nonsense, and he knew better than you what a man had to do to survive on the goldfields in those days. How could a kid have knocked about and earned his own living, without having to use his wits?

He was a weedy, undersized youngster, never physically much to look at, so had had to make his way as best he could. Of course, he had taken all the short cuts and got many a kick for doing so. But that didn't worry Paddy. He was always 'as hard and shrewd as they make 'em,' the men said.

The next time Sally saw him, Paddy showed her a new pair of boots he was wearing and explained that he had lifted them from a toff staying at the Exchange Hotel, who put them out to be cleaned.

'A man had ought to clean his own boots,' Paddy declared indignantly. 'Or take the consequences.'

'You shouldn't do such a thing, Paddy,' Sally protested. 'You'll be run out of the town, some day, for light fingers, as the men say. That's what will happen to you.'

Paddy grinned.

'There's a lot more 'll be run out before I am, ma'am,' he said gaily. 'And I'd rather be run out for liftin' a pair of boots than go sore-foot, or ask for 'em. But nobody's goin' to make a fuss about liftin' a pair of boots from one of the toffs. They've got plenty more. If it was a mate, it'd be different. But you know how it is up here, if a mate's got what y' want, y' just take it and square up with him afterwards. It's the law of the fields, ma'am, like Frisco told you, the first day you was here.'

That was Paddy all over. Sharp as a needle and fighting back. Paddy wanted to remind her, Sally thought, of what she owed Frisco, and what Ma Buggins had said. It was his way of letting her know the pot could not call the kettle black. She was making her way by one method, he by another. What difference was there between letting a man give her more than she could repay, and stealing a pair of boots?

Yet she could not take offence, the way Paddy put it, with a deferential air, and sly innocence. She could not even be sure he intended to imply what she imagined. There was no doubt about it, Paddy had something which made the men say he would be able to buy and sell them all some day. But his grit and humour reconciled everybody to the young scamp. There was always a laugh when Paddy was about. He usually had some inside information about the mines, or a spicy bit of gossip to retail.

You couldn't be sorry for Paddy, Sally found. Not even when one of the miners gave him a hiding for pinching the gold he should have passed on to Pa Buggins. Paddy boasted of the way Big Bill had laid into him.

'But it was worth it,' he crowed, 'to hear Pa Bug and Big Bill exchangin' compliments as to which of 'em was the biggest thief and liar on the goldfields.'

Mrs. Gough said she understood what people meant when they talked later, about the magnetic charm of Sir Patrick Cavan. 'He had it even as a kid. A sort of beguiling impudence and instinct for pleasing people when he wanted to get something out of them—if it was only a laugh at his own expense.'

But even in those days, when he was a mere lad, Paddy's mind was set to one purpose. It was a good joke when he started haunting the Open Call and buying script. Where did he get his money? What did he do with it?

Paddy grinned and said he was learning the ropes. He had made up his mind to be a rich man, and the sooner he started, the better. He had got a few quid together by selling wild flowers, doing odd jobs round the pubs, and passin' on a bit of gold for the boys, on a commission basis, now, you bet.

'The little devil!' Frisco exclaimed. 'He goes round cadging old clothes, and pinching boots as if he were a poor boy willing to do anything for a crust. But Paddy Cavan's got an account runs into three figures, one of the bank clerks was tellin' me.'

The days and the weeks ran on. Days and weeks of blinding white light and breathless heat. When a dust storm swept up, the red dust filled the air, blotting out the sun and making it dark at midday. Shops in the township had to be closed and business was suspended. Sometimes a few drops of tepid rain fell after the wind passed, allaying the dust; but still no thunderstorm had brought a steady downpour and relief to the parched earth and sun-stricken settlement round about Hannans.

Sally was very weary always at the end of the day. It required incessant work and scheming to cook and serve meals in the open under such conditions. As she lay back in her chair at night, limp and exhausted, she wondered how much longer she would be able to carry on. She never would have been able to make a success of the dining-room but for the kindness and assistance of the men, she realized, particularly Frisco. He thought of innumerable ways to make things easier for her: had stores sent up from the township, sparing her many a long tramp, and talked of putting up a shed of corrugated iron for her to cook in. She had got into the habit of relying on him, and asking his advice.

When Frisco saw she had burnt her hand, one evening, he insisted on bandaging it: looked at the injured hand queerly. It was so rough and hard, ingrained with dirt, Sally was ashamed of it, pulled it away.

'My hands are awful,' she apologized quickly. 'I can't get them clean.'

Frisco had taken her free hand, held it to his lips and stood bowed over it.

'They're the bravest, most beautiful hands in the world,' he said.

The grace and homage of his bearing moved her. Surely Frisco could not be the unscrupulous blackguard she had once thought him if he were capable of such a gesture, Sally told herself. She did not believe half the yarns she had heard about him, any more than she believed the same sort of yarns about Paddy Cavan.

A few nights later, Frisco said, quietly:

'First time I set eyes on you, Missus Sally, I felt we weren't strangers.'

He was sitting on the ground near her as the rosy glow of sunset faded out of the sky, and the warm darkness gathered round them.

'Did you?' Sally queried, a little stiffly, surprised by the tone of his voice.

'You seemed to recognize me, too,' Frisco said. 'You did, didn't you?'

Off her guard and with her natural honesty, Sally replied: 'Yes. Funny, wasn't it?'

'Not so funny,' Frisco brooded a moment. 'It explains a great deal. Why I wanted to be different, afterwards, for example. And why I felt you knew the best and the worst of me from the word go.'

Sally sensed danger in this conversation and tried to avoid it. 'I didn't, of course.'

'But you do,' Frisco insisted. And laughed. His eyes held her with their derisive familiarity. 'Every time I look at you and laugh, you know why, and just what I'm thinking.'

Sally was glad Sam and Blunt Pick arrived then. It was true, what Frisco had said, although she dared not admit it. She was conscious of a secret understanding between herself and this man. It had been there when their eyes first met, although she was determined to deny it: afraid of what such a subtle intimacy might mean.

To be sure, never in words, before, had Frisco hinted at anything but a distant, respectful admiration and concern to help her over difficulties. It was his eyes that had done the damage, disturbing her with their gay recklessness, and forcing some response from the depths of her. It was not permissible and must be repressed, that altogether disgraceful feeling, Sally told herself.

After all, she had heard enough about Mr. Frisco Jo Murphy to be on her guard against him. There were Maritana and Lili. Of course he was a fine figure of a man, handsome and powerful, with a dash of that romantic gallantry which would be attractive to any woman. And he had been very kind and thoughtful. But she could not permit herself to be drawn into any sentimental weakness for Frisco, Sally assured herself. She must never let Mr. Murphy know what he had done to her, by arousing sensations which made her feel guilty towards Morris.

CHAPTER XXXVII

THERE was champagne with dinner in Mrs. Gough's brush-shed, the afternoon Frisco sold his lease to an English syndicate. Sally had to drink with the boys celebrating Frisco's luck. They went off to McSweeney's afterwards to make a night of it, and Frisco shouted all and sundry in the bar, as was to be expected.

He held forth about his plans, next day: was going for a trip round the world; intended to live like a lord in London, Paris and New York. But he was in no hurry to be off, it appeared. Hung round his camp for a week or so, and shouted old mates in the pubs every night.

'I'm waiting for a windjammer,' he told Sally, 'and she won't be in port till the end of the month. Worked before the mast on the *Loch Katrine* for a couple of years, and always promised myself I'd travel in the best quarters reserved for passengers, some day. God, she was a fine sight, stepping up to a stiff breeze with all sail spread! You never saw anything more beautiful, ma'am. And I'm longing for the sound and smell of the sea after scrounging in this blasted desert so long.'

'You can't complain. It hasn't treated you so badly, after all,' Sally reminded him.

'That's a fact,' Frisco agreed, jubilantly. 'Feel as if I could buy up the world, and be none the worse off. Maybe it would be better to go to the Old Country first class on a mail steamer; but I've got this hunch about a windjammer, wanting to feel as if I owned her and see the albatross swooping round, strong and sure of themselves, like a man ought to be.'

'Yes,' Sally murmured. She envied him that long journey on a sailing ship. 'It will be wonderful for you, Mr. Murphy.'

Frisco talked of the places he was going to visit: London, Paris, the Swiss Alps, Monte Carlo and Rome. Perhaps he would settle in London for a while, or Paris. He wanted to know all Mrs. Gough could tell him about them. But to Sally they were just names, scraps of geography, almost mythical places about which she had heard Morris and Marie Robillard talk.

'I'm a sand-groper,' she snapped, exasperated by Frisco's gloating over his good fortune. 'Don't know anything about London or Paris.'

It was the goldfields way of saying she was a West Australian, Frisco knew. That irritation in her voice was what he had been playing for as he painted his glowing pictures of the future which lay before him.

'Come with me, and you won't regret it. You can have anything in the world you want—and by God, you know I'll be good to you.'

Sally stared at him, dumbfounded. It had never occurred to her that he might make such a proposition. But there was no misunderstanding Frisco's eyes: the demand they made on her. She wanted to withdraw from them: to shake off the spell they put over her. In her confusion and dismay, the treacherous undertow of that 'disgraceful feeling for Frisco' surged tumultuously.

She stammered:

'How dare you, Mr. Murphy! How dare you say such a thing!'

'I'd dare anything to get you, Sally,' Frisco said bluntly. 'Christ, I'm mad about you. What's the use of all this money if I can't have you—if we can't be together for good. I've loved you from the first moment I saw you. And you know it. You know, too, you like me, though you won't admit it. Have fought against me, determined to stick to Morrey whatever happens. You've been afraid of me—afraid, all the time, of what there is between us.'

'Yes,' Sally felt as if the admission were wrung from her, 'but that doesn't mean—'

Frisco had her in his arms before she could say anything further. The blaze of the sunset behind the dark trees passed into them as they kissed. When Sally moved from him, she was horrified at the way she had yielded to Frisco's embrace.

'No, no!' she cried, as Frisco drew her back. 'You don't understand. I love Morris. I'll never leave him.'

She wrenched herself away, hating Frisco and herself, and the power he had of vitalizing and stirring her to this crazy state of body and mind.

'Don't be a fool, Sally,' Frisco pleaded. 'I love you more than

Morrey ever could. I'm a blackguard. Have never pretended to be anything else, but Morrey's worse. I'd never 've left you in the blacks' camp, and gone off prospecting when you were dying of fever. Why should you stay here working like a galley slave in the dust and heat, when you could come with me and live like a princess? Hell, we'd be happy. All the time it would be like it was a moment ago. We're the same sort of people. Have got the spirit and guts to keep on being alive. That's why I've been wanting you, and you've been fighting me. You're such a damn fine little lady, and I'm only a bloody prospector in luck. But it won't always be like that. I swear you'll be proud of me, Sally. I won't waste this money. We'd make a decent thing out of our life together.'

As she listened to him, Sally was swept by a desire to throw everything to the winds and go away with Frisco. He must have been a little in awe of her, she thought afterwards, not to realize that. He could not believe, perhaps, that his damn fine little lady would have been so easy to take possession of.

But he gave her time to reply, and in that moment of weakness she was conscious of a 'No' at the back of her mind, like a tribal taboo. What was it? Pride and obstinacy, or some primitive instinct of self-defence asserting itself? She did not know. The 'No' was stronger than her craving to be in Frisco's arms and forget this dreary existence and her duty to Morris.

She thought that she could be happy with Frisco. His vigour and gaiety were what drew her to him. Morris was so much older than she, and she missed in him the vigour and gaiety of her own disposition. Life looked like being a fascinating adventure with Frisco. But was that enough?

Were they the same sort of people, as he said? She would hate some of the things he did. Would this attraction for each other last? Frisco had loved many women. Could she break her word to Morris for something that seemed a fantastic dream? Sally remembered the promise she had given Morris when they were driving over from Coolgardie. Her marriage vows did not seem so binding. When she was married, she had been a blind innocent; but later, when she promised to stand by Morris, never to leave him, she knew what she was doing. To be sure, he had treated her badly of late. She would never reproach him for leaving her with the natives and going on with his prospecting trip; but she could not forgive him for failing to send her news or any money for so long. How did he think she was living?

Morris had done the same sort of thing when he first came to the goldfields. She had had to fend for herself as best she could at the 'Cross. But all that did not exonerate her, now. Her

215

obligations were the same whatever Morris might do about his. And she knew he still cared for her in the only way he was capable of caring: never doubted her loyalty and devotion.

Could she abandon Morris to his fate when they had embarked on their life together with such hope and joy? Morris's fate? She had always feared Morris would never have the luck which came to many other men so easily. It would be a hard and weary road they would have to tread perhaps. But could she leave Morris to travel it alone? They had come through so much together and something firmer and deeper than their first love had grown from companionship and the contact of their bodies. She had hoped that some day she would have a child and never again be lonely. Could she forget that, and break faith with herself and Morris? 'No! No! No!' Always the veto rang in her brain.

'It's no use,' she said quietly. 'I am bound to Morris in a way nothing can alter. And for you, there will always be other women, Mr. Murphy.'

'Other women?' Frisco swore angrily. 'Of course there'll be other women. But there'll never be another woman I want like I do you, Sally. It's not only that. It's something good and strong tells me you belong to me, and not Morrey Gough. God damn him!'

Frisco flung away into the bush as Eli Nancarrow and Parson Jarn came along the track. Sally cried after him, but he did not hear. In any case, it would have been no use for him to come back. There was chagrin in her triumph.

She had to sit for a while and talk to Eli and Parson Jarn. But she scarcely heard what they said. Her heart was pounding and her thoughts racing distractedly.

'Better turn in early, missus,' Eli said, after a while, tactful and compassionate. 'You be lookin' fair done-up wi' heat an' all.'

'If you don't mind, I will.' Sally got up to go to her tent. She thought they must have seen Frisco and guessed why she was so troubled.

When Eli and Parson Jarn had said good-night and gone off down the track, Sally sat on her bed, trying to understand what had happened to her. She was angry with herself and perplexed by the complexity of her emotions. Why had she been so crazy with Frisco? What had come over her?

She had thought she was so safe in her marriage to Morris that this sort of thing could never happen to her. She was not the kind of woman who made scandals for herself. She had lived and worked among the men on this camp, secure in the conviction they realized that.

But this wild fire had flamed in her, kindling every nerve and fibre. She was still in the throes of its lingering glow: wanted to go with Frisco, almost beside herself with grief because she must stay with Morris. It was outrageous, ridiculous, to have got herself into such a state of mind. How had it come about? Was it the country that had made her feel just a woman, and not merely Mrs. Morris Gough? In the loneliness, under this burning sun, it might be natural, perhaps, for a man and woman, thrown into each other's company, to desire that closer association which made everything else seem unimportant. And Frisco's virile devilry had overwhelmed her!

Or was there more in her impulse towards Frisco than a touch of the sun which would pass? Was that what she had meant when she said: 'But first love is not last love, you know, Violet'? Had there been a presentiment in her mind that some day she might love someone more than she loved Morris?

Sally was furious with herself for harbouring the suggestion. She scoffed at the idea that she was in love with Frisco Jo Murphy: thanked her stars she had sufficient common sense not to let Frisco make a fool of her. That was what it would have amounted to if she had believed what he said, and forfeited all she had in common with Morris, to go away with him.

It was unthinkable that she could have done such a thing. There was something fixed and final in her marriage to Morris, which she could not repudiate. No matter if it was not what she had imagined it would be, and Morris no longer the lover of her youth, at least it was a reality she was committed to and bound up with. The only sure thing in the world for them both, Morris had said.

The picture Frisco drew of an easy pleasant life with love and happiness always in the foreground, quivered before her eyes.

'A mirage,' Sally told herself contemptuously. 'Serve you right if you thought it was anything else. You're a respectable married woman, Mrs. Gough. Ought to be ashamed of yourself, behaving like this.'

She was pleased that she had straightened the matter out in her own mind. In the morning it was annoying to see her face in the silver-backed mirror Morris had given her when they were married. It looked woebegone, with heavy shadows under the eyes. She put on a pink print dress to smarten herself up, and sleeked her hair with a wet brush, hoping the men would not notice anything unusual in her appearence when they came along for breakfast.

Frisco did not come, nor did she see him all day. It was not until after the evening meal, she heard Sam and Blunt Pick talking about the great show Frisco had put on at McSweeney's the night before. He had got fighting drunk, they said: wanted to pick a quarrel with everybody. But he had started off on his grand tour that afternoon: driven over to Coolgardie in his buggy and taken one of the girls from Madame Marseilles along with him.

CHAPTER XXXVIII

IT had been 112 in the shade, a day of suffocating heat, with the dust swirling in sudden eddies, and Sally was serving out the evening meal when she looked up to see Alf Brierly and Dinny Quin coming towards her.

Hot and sweaty as she was, and flustered with the rush of feeding all the men in the shed, Sally felt more distressed than pleased to see Alf and Dinny. She knew her dress was soiled. Water too precious just then to spare for washing clothes. Her hair strayed in wet strings about her face, and out from the usually neat bob on her neck. She was so upset that the plate of hot soup she was handing to Kalgoorla slipped out of her hands and spilt over her dress. She could have cried with vexation.

'Well, I'm damned,' Alf said. 'Why on earth are you doing this, Mrs. Gough?'

'It's the only thing I can do,' Sally replied.

'Where's Morrey?'

'He's out prospecting round about Lake Darlot.' She added eagerly, 'You must stay and have dinner with me. We can have a talk then. I've got all these hungry men to feed, now.'

Alf and Dinny sat down on the ground to wait until Sally had served the men in the bough-shed.

She kept back some of her hotpot and the pie made with dried apples she had baked for the men, to give Mr. Brierly and Dinny. Eli, Sam Mullet, Blunt Pick and a few others, when they had finished their meal and strolled out of the shed, discovered Alf and Dinny: hailed them joyfully. They crowded round to hear the news of Coolgardie and what Alf and Dinny were doing on Hannans.

But when Sally was ready, she hustled Sam and the rest of the men off while Alf and Dinny went to have dinner with her in the shed. They were old friends, and she wanted to talk to them, everybody understood. Of course, she was tired and excited. It had been a trying day, so hot and dusty. That was the only explanation Sally could give for fainting when she lifted the heavy billy to make tea.

The next thing she knew, she was lying on the stretcher in her own tent with Dinny and Alf Brierly fussing beside her. They had got whisky from somewhere and made her drink it. Alf washed her face and hands with a wet rag.

Sally was furious with herself for having fainted. She had never done such a thing before, she said. Soon, she declared she was better; insisted on getting up and going to sit on her dog-legged chair. The air was cooler out of the tent; but still a red glow in the western sky warned of another sweltering day.

Kalgoorla had washed up and was sweeping round the dining-room.

'Kalgoorla,' Sally called.

The gin came to her.

'Put butter in cool safe, bread in big tin—all tucker away from flies and ants?' Sally asked.

'Eh-erm,' Kalgoorla murmured and turned away.

'You've got her well broken in, missus,' Dinny said.

'I don't think so,' Sally smiled. 'But I think she'll stay with me until Morris returns. She wants to be with her own people, though, and I wouldn't try to interfere with what she wants to do. She's been so good to me. And I owe her so much.'

Dinny and Alf had heard about her illness on the track to Lake Darlot from the men, Sally realized. They did not ask about it, and she, fearing their disapproval of Morris, talked hastily about other things. How the camp had grown all round her tent, and how Hannans was flourishing, with all the mines being opened up and speculation at fever heat.

Alf said he and Dinny were going to camp in the bush further along and have a look around. The Lady Laura had not fulfilled expectations. They had sunk all their money in her and she was closed down. Things were very dull in Coolgardie. Alf thought he might try to get a job on one of the Boulder mines or go out prospecting with Dinny.

'When Lord Fingall blew the bottom out of the Londonderry, Coolgardie was hard hit,' he said.

'English investors've been scared stiff of Coolgardie shows ever since.' Dinny explained. 'You can't blame 'em. The Londonderry was boosted as the richest show on earth, and Fingall paid a hundred and eighty thousand pounds for her. She was floated for seven hundred thousand pounds. But the original prospectors'd picked the golden hole clean before they sold out, and Fingall didn't get more'n a few ounces when he opened up and started sinkin'.'

'Investors've got their second wind with Hannans putting up records as a reefing field,' Alf pointed out. 'But I reckon Coolgardie'll come again. It's hard to lose faith in the old camp.'

'Faith's about the last thing y'd ought to invest in the minin' industry,' Dinny argued. 'I've got it in me bones Hannans is goin' ahead now. There's nothin' to stop it with a score of mines in full swing, prospectin' movin' out in every direction from the town as a centre, and the railway due in a couple of months.'

When men started talking gold and the prospects of various fields, there was no telling when they would stop. Sally turned the conversation, impatiently. She was sick to death of the talk about gold and the mining industry.

'How is Laura?' she asked. 'Will she come to live at Hannans too?'

Alf's eyes held a shy smile.

'She's well,' he said, 'but gone to the coast for a few months—until after the baby's born.'

Sally was caught into his awed happiness. Surprised, self-conscious, delighted, wondering, she exclaimed: 'I never thought of that! How lovely for you both, Mr. Brierly!'

'Laura didn't want to go,' Alf went on. 'It was hard to make her. But I couldn't take the risk of letting her stay on the fields for the summer. She must have the child in hygienic surroundings. Typhoid's raging in Coolgardie and the hospital's in a bad way. Sister O'Brien and Sister Miller have left. It's been almost impossible to get fresh food and water lately.'

'There's been as many as nine deaths a day,' Dinny added. 'The boys're scared to go into hospital. They're dyin' in their camps and the cemetery's so crowded y' can scarcely move between the graves. Undertaker's 're makin' a fortune, usin' any old boxes for a coffin, and blackin' 'em over. But even the blackin's given out. Bob Harden went to his last restin' place in a coffin made of packin' cases, branded, "Explosives, with care. Keep away from the boilers!"'

Dinny's whimsical grin faded.

'It don't seem right to make a joke about it. But we got to laugh to pull through tough times up here, missus.'

'I laugh, too, Mr. Quin,' Sally said.

'You'd ought to be goin' to the coast yourself, missus,' Dinny said.

Sally felt the hot colour flooding into her face.

'Me?' she queried, wondering if he thought she, too, was going to have a baby. 'My head has been very stupid since I was ill on the track,' she said slowly, 'and now I am so busy. Morris will make arrangements for me to go away for a little change—when he returns, no doubt.'

'Better not delay,' Dinny looked concerned. 'The mailman was tellin' me horses've been dyin' on the track between Boorabbin and Reens Soak. Water's short and likely to be shorter. You needn't worry about exes, missus. Alf and me'll look after that and Morrey can fix up with us later.'

So they did think it, Sally exclaimed to herself.

'Oh, no,' she cried, confused and curiously elated, 'I couldn't go away until Morris returns. But thank you—thank you both for suggesting it.'

'How is Marie—Madame Robillard?' she asked. 'Have you seen anything of her lately?'

'Saw Robbie, the other day,' Dinny told her. 'His mother died in the Old Country, recently, and the old man has come out to live with Robbie. He was talkin' of shiftin' over to Hannans, too.'

'Oh, I do hope they will,' Sally cried. 'Hannans will be quite different if Marie and Laura come to live here.'

Alf and Dinny sat with her a little longer, yarning about Coolgardie. A big fire had burnt out a block of buildings and threatened the whole township with destruction. Shacks of hessian and weatherboard burnt like matchwood. The blaze, leaping up into the sky, could be seen miles away. It had been touch and go to save the post office. Every man in the surrounding camps, including abos and Afghans, had turned out to fight the flames.

Fogarty's was in danger for a while. The sheds in the yard were burnt down. Bill and Mrs. Fogarty had fought like demons to save the pub. It was built of corrugated iron and that had helped it to survive. But the newspaper office and one of the banks were in ashes.

Alf thanked God Laura had gone down by the coach a few days before. She was living at a farm near Guildford: wrote to Alf every week, telling him how kind his friends with whom she was staying were, and what a beautiful place their farm was.

Alf took a bundle of Laura's letters from his pocket and read scraps from them describing fruit trees in blossom and grass so green that you wanted to eat it. Laura said she was drinking lots of milk and picking oranges whenever she felt inclined. She sewed and knitted little woolly garments all day. Sometimes she went for a walk by the river and picked wild flowers. It was wonderful to see so much water, all silver and tranquil, flowing through green paddocks. And the air was so fresh and invigorating, she felt years younger and as well as could be. 'If only you were with me, darling, how happy we would be—'

Mr. Brierly sighed and folded up the letters.

'It's rotten luck not being able to go down to her, now, when she needs me most.' he said. 'But I've got to stick it out here: try to make some money, so that things'll be easier for Laura and the kid.'

'Don't you worry, Alf,' Dinny cheered. 'We'll fix it. You'll get a job on the mines, and I'll go out prospectin' for both of us, so. as we can have a bit of extra cash handy.'

When they had gone, Sally lay back in her chair looking up into the great shallow bowl of the sky. The rosy glow of sunset was fading behind the darkening trees. The last light burnished shabby dust-stained tents, the dumps of rubble and the spindling poppet legs of mines on the ridge.

To her that glow and the golden glitter of stars in frail lavender and green of the evening sky meant only another hot day: the blinding glare of sunshine, hundreds in the shade. And there was so little shade. Only the black lace of shadows scraggy trees cast, or the brush-shed might weave. Noises of the camp came to her: the drunken shouting and singing of men down the track, the racket of a two-up school.

She was conscious of a strange new excitement, of fear and bewildering happiness. Could it be that what Dinny had suggested was true? How shameful that he should have awakened her mind to the possibility!

Sally stood up and looked down on her body under the greasy, dust-stained blue cotton frock she was wearing. She noted how tight it was over her bosom and at the waist: the bulge of her abdomen. Had thought that her figure was losing its shapeliness because she no longer wore corsets. It was so much easier to work without them in the hot weather. And then, too, corsets were a very precious possession: must be preserved for wearing on special occasions when an attractive appearance might be necessary. About other symptoms of maternity she knew very little and was disturbed by the realization of her ignorance.

'Kalgoorla!'

The gin was squatting on the ground and staring into the darkness, near the camp fire. She looked up when Sally stood beside her.

'You think me bin make'm baby?' Sally asked.

'Eh-erm,' Kalgoorla replied indifferently, her gaze returning to its sombre brooding.

Sally walked back to her chair. She was wildly excited, filled with an ineffable joy. She had been expecting this to happen ever since she and Morris were married, but for some unknown reason it never had. To be sure, Morris had not wanted children.

He had decided they must not have children until they had made their fortune. Well, here was the baby growing within her, and here she was going to be a mother, Sally told herself. She wondered how Morris would take the news. He would not be as pleased as she was, perhaps. But after he got used to the idea, he would be glad. How could it be otherwise?

After all, he could not blame her entirely for what had happened. The responsibility was his also. That first night on Hannans had to be remembered, and so many afterwards when Morris had taken her with a rough passion quite unlike the tender love making of their first years together. Smiling and exclaiming to herself over every phase of the marvellous revelation that had come to her, Sally was quite sure Morris could not be displeased by her news. It was very amusing to think of Morris as a father. He would feel so important and proprietorial: like Bardook with Maritana and her baby.

Of course when he knew, Morris would want her to go south so that the child could be born in 'hygienic surroundings,' as Mr. Brierly said. Doctors on the fields were often drunk when their services were required, and there were so many cases of typhoid. Some of the men were sure it was typhoid she had had herself on the track. They said she was lucky to have pulled through.

It was no wonder the fever spread in Hannans. Only the hotels had pans in backyard sheds. The ground in the scrub round the camps was filthy and swarmed with flies. Storms whirled the dust into water and food: the flies spread infection. On hot still nights like this, a stench hung in the air from the surrounding scrub. Even the dry, musky fragrance of mulga burning on the camp fires did not prevail against it.

Sally was panic-stricken at the thought of bringing a little life into this poisoned atmosphere: into the blazing sunshine which blasted and seared the whole countryside: into a world where it would have to fight for existence against drought and suffocating dust storms.

She would write to Morris immediately, she decided, inquire at the store about teams or prospecting parties going north. No doubt Morris would come soon when he knew how important it was for her to go away to some place where there was plenty of water and fresh food. If he was on gold, well and good: if not— still he must come and arrange somehow to provide for her and the child.

Sally wished that she need not make this demand on him. If only she had started her bush dining-room sooner, she thought she might have been able to save enough money to pay her own expenses for the long journey and a doctor, and living at a boarding house, down south, until the baby was born. But she had just paid for a month's stores, some crockery and cutlery, cooking utensils and a few sheets of corrugated iron to make a roof over the fireplace and bough-shed.

A thunderstorm might blow up any day and rain fall in torrents. She had prepared for them and no money was left to provide for going away. Surely Morris would realize that nothing was so important as the baby now. Sally believed that he would, and come soon, all eagerness to arrange for the safe arrival of his son. Of course Morris would want the baby to be a boy, and of course Sally was willing to oblige him in that way. Oh, yes, the baby would be a boy, and he would be her son!

A lullaby she used to hear the gins singing to their babies on the track was winding through her brain. When she went to bed Sally sang it softly to herself as if she were already crooning to her baby. Never had she been so happy, so full of a sense that she was no longer alone. There would always be this other person with her now. She thought of the baby like that: as a person coming miraculously to fulfil her secret longing for something to love absolutely, as she no longer loved Morris, and refused to love Frisco. How glad she was now that she had resisted the temptation to go away with him. He had taken Lili instead. There was bitterness in the thought. But nothing could hurt her now.

Life would be different with her son to think of. She must fight all the time so that he might be well and strong: have more of the good things of the world than she and Morris had been able to obtain for themselves. The delicious commotion within her fused into a drowsy reverie at last, and she fell asleep, thinking of Laura's letters: dreamed of a river flowing silvery through green paddocks and of fruit trees in blossom.

CHAPTER XXXIX

So pure and clear, those notes of the bell bird, as they dropped through the cooler air before dawn! Kalgoorla, curled beside the ashes of her fire, stirred. She always heard them and they were Sally's alarm clock.

There was no time to lose after the bell bird called. Although the sky was still dark, the first light just glimmered in the east. The sun rose quickly, and the men with it, in order to start work on their claims before the heat of the day began. Sally poured herself a little water to wash in, gave some to Kalgoorla, and was dressed in a few moments.

Kalgoorla, building up the fire, stared when she saw Missus Sally so brisk and smiling that morning. She had not been sick and was wearing a clean cotton frock: tied her black cooking apron over it, and bustled about stirring porridge in a big pot, and moulding rissoles of bully beef with a sprinkling of dried herbs. Soon the rissoles were frizzling in pans made of kerosene tins cut lengthwise, and set on bars over the embers. The blackened billies Kalgoorla had filled with water, steamed on hooks slung at either end of the fireplace.

The sky blushed and light glittered from a gash in the sky. In every direction, the camps were awaking to activity: men calling to each other, mine whistles shrilling, the smoky incense of burning wood drifting into the air still flat and stale with the heat of the previous day.

When the men trooped up for their breakfast, Sally was ready for them with porridge, rissoles and pannikins of hot tea. A dab of tomato sauce went with the rissoles. Tins of jam in their gaudy jackets stood on the table in the bough-shed: biscuit tins shining like silver held cut bread.

Sam Mullet and Blunt Pick were surprised to see Mrs. Sally looking so bright and well. They knew she had been seedy the night before; and had exchanged confidences about her with Alf Brierly and Dinny Quin.

'How are y'r, missus? Sam inquired, his round owl's eyes quite grave.

'Good,' Sally replied, blithely. 'I'm feeling as good as gold, thank you. How's yourself, Mr. Mullet?'

She liked talking to the men in the idiom of the fields now.

Sam hung back after breakfast, as if he had something on his mind.

'The boys are a bit worried you're overdin' things, Missus Sally,' he said awkwardly. 'Don't like the way you knocked-up last night. Think you ought to go to the coast for a bit. Want to put in for it. Morrey can fix up with them later, if he likes.'

Sally blushed, and then, angry with herself for being self-conscious, laughed happily.

'It's very kind of them,' she said, 'but Morris himself will make arrangements for me when it's necessary.'

It was a relief to get rid of the men and clear up after breakfast. First of all there was that letter to write to Morris, and then shopping to do at the store. Inquiries must be made about a teamster or prospecting party going north. She intended to prepare the evening meal when she returned and use those hours of rest at midday to visit Mrs. Molloy. If there was anybody who could tell her all she wanted to know about a baby, Mrs. Molloy was that person, Sally was sure.

Kalgoorla went with her to help carry back the food she bought at the store and the butcher's shop. It was a lucky day. The butcher had killed the night before and was in a good humour. Sally bargained successfully with him for beef which could be braised in her camp oven. She found a pumpkin, potatoes and onions at the store, and Ned Killington said a mail was leaving the post office for Darlot next morning. So with great satisfaction Sally dispatched her letter in the safest way from the shack of corrugated iron and bagging that was the post office in Hannans.

She was hot and breathless after lugging heavy parcels of bread and meat from the store to the camp. Kalgoorla had gasped and grumbled a good deal, plugging along beside her with a bag of onions and potatoes slung on her back. But Sally had no time 'to waste humouring her that morning. She set Kalgoorla to peel potatoes while she herself cut up the beef and put it in the camp oven; stood the big pot in embers of the fire, put a shovelful on the lid, and told Kalgoorla to renew them when they died down.

It was midday, and she was sweaty and tired with rushing about all the morning, when she explained:

'I'm going to see Missus Molloy. Back plenty time cook dinner. You make'm fire, hot water, all ready, Kalgoorla?'

'Eh-erm,' the gin murmured, her eyes wondering at Missus Sally's air of suppressed excitement.

'Yukki,' she exclaimed smiling, when Sally came from her tent in a white muslin frock with close fitting bodice and full skirt. The dress was creased with having been packed away in a trunk for a long time, and there was nothing new about the big straw hat Sally wore round the camp, except the scarlet ribbon she had tied on it. Before Kalgoorla's astonished gaze she unfurled a scarlet parasol.

'It's such an important visit. I must look nice for it, Kalgoorla,' Sally explained, light-heartedly, and went off down the track.

Ted Molloy had built a shack for his wife and children on a slope near the Great Boulder Mine where he was working, and Sally had a long walk before she reached it. The sky was like a sheath of dim luminous metal overhead: all the colour bleached out of it. The corrugated iron roofs of buildings round the mines, she passed on the way, threw off a quivering haze of heat. The earth, baked red and hard as a brick, burned through the soles of her white canvas shoes.

After the blinding glare, and breath of what the goldfields people called a 'scorcher,' Sally was glad to drop into a chair at the Molloy's and fan herself with her hat.

She was red in the face and perspiring, rather breathless, and her heart fluttering; but it was pleasant to be greeted with such friendliness by Mrs. Molloy and to be gazed at by the admiring eyes of all the young Molloys.

They had pelted downhill to meet her as soon as they saw her toiling up the rough track from the Boulder road. A few goats scattered among the rocks. So many children, bare-footed, bare-headed, with scraps of cotton pants and skirts flying about their thin brown bodies, that Sally gasped:

'Are they all yours?'

'Lord love y'r, of course they are, darlin'. Every divil of a one of them,' Theresa Molloy exclaimed, all exuberance and good humour, as she bustled about on broad bare feet, making tea, a baby in her arms and a toddler clinging to her skirts. 'And called after the big cities of Australia with a saint's name for luck. Shake hands with Mrs. Gough, Sydy, and you Mel and Brissy, and Perthy, you bring me some sticks for the fire. Adey, see if there's a drop of goat's milk in the cool-safe—'

Sally shook hands with Sydy, Mel and Brissy, though they hung back, staring at her shyly, tongue-tied and curious.

'They've never seen a lady with a red umbrella before,' Mrs. Molloy burbled on, 'and sure, y'r a sight for sore eyes, looking so cool and iligant on this hot day, dearie.'

'I want to have a talk to you,' Sally said nervously. 'That's why I've come.'

Mrs. Molloy sent the children off out of doors, with various instructions to bring in the goats, gather some brushwood for the fire, and not to get into mischief. She handed the baby over to the eldest girl and sat down to drink a cup of tea with Sally.

How Mrs. Molloy laughed when Sally told her that she thought she was going to have a baby!

'I could 'ave told you that months ago, darlin',' she said, comfortingly, and drew on her own experiences to assure Sally that there was nothing in having a baby to make a fuss about. In fact, the less fuss the better.

'My kids were all born wherever I happened to be at the time,' she said complacently. 'Ted, himself, had to give a hand when young Perth arrived a couple of weeks too soon. Once or twice I'd only a gin with me—and very good they were, too. Better than some of these drunken doctors a woman has to put up with on the fields.'

She thought Mrs. Gough was probably six months gone, and

if she were going to the coast she ought to go at once. Mrs. Molloy decided it would be better for Sally and the child to go south for her confinement, as she was still poorly after the fever. But, in another month it would be risky for her to be bumped about in the coach for a week, and then have to face a day or two in the train from the 'Cross.

'There's a chance you'd be havin' your baby beside the track, like I had Perthy,' she said, cheerfully. 'And that'd be hard on you, dearie. Only men about, and maybe you'd lose the baby.'

'I could go to the hospital, here,' Sally said slowly. 'But there's so much fever about.'

'If the worst comes to the worst,' Mrs. Molloy volunteered, 'y'r can always come to me, dearie. I'll look after y'r.'

Sally thanked her, trying to hide her dismay at the prospect. This big, fat, slatternly woman, for all her good will and experience, was ignorant of much a midwife ought to know, she thought. And the shack had only this one room for kitchen and sitting-room, with an end screened off by a hessian curtain where Mr. and Mrs. Molloy slept. The children's beds, stretchers of bush timber and bags, stood on the narrow verandahs, back and front. It seemed impossible to think of a baby being born in such surroundings.

'Morris will come as soon as he gets my letter, I'm sure,' Sally said, firmly. 'I'll go to the coast as soon as he does.'

Walking back to Hannans in the blaze of the afternoon sun, she was not sure she believed what she had said. That Morris would come as soon as he received her letter. The exhilaration with which she had set out to visit Mrs. Molloy gave way to a vague depression. What assurance had she Morris would react to her news as she hoped? If he were on gold, he would be unwilling to tear himself away from the fascination of each day's yield. If not, he would still be dissatisfied to return without any gold, or very little. Was it possible that thought of the child and any hardships she might have to bear bringing him into the world, would not penetrate the obsession of his search for gold?

Sally put the idea from her. She accused herself of being unfair to Morris imagining that he could be so indifferent to his responsibilities. Of course he would want to be with her when his son was born. Insist on her having proper care, a nurse and capable doctor in attendance. No one would be more fussy than Morris to ensure that the youngest of the Fitz-Morris Goughs had suitable attention. He was still a man of his family and traditions, though you would never think it to look at him. What did he want gold for but to go home and live as he had once done?

His son, Sally thought, would be the only thing in the world more important to Morris than gold. He would come. Of course he would come. She would never forgive him if he did not.

The men liked their dinner soon after they stopped work. If they were working their own claims they knocked off at about four o'clock, had a few pots at the nearest pub, back in their camps washed begrimed faces and hands, and strolled into the town for water, stores or a meal. Sally hurried back that afternoon, hoping Kalgoorla had kept an eye on the camp oven, and that none of her tribe had arrived to raid the food boxes.

But all was well: the camp oven still buried in warm ashes, and Kalgoorla going about setting the table in her leisurely way. It was a bit of a rush to cook the pumpkin and potatoes, make a custard with condensed milk and egg powder to go with the dried apricots she had stewed; but Sally was ready for her customers at five o'clock as usual.

She carried on pluckily during the next month. Had never felt better in her life, she assured Mrs. Molloy: got a little flustered and weary now and then: but Kalgoorla was doing all the heavy work, carrying water and wood. No word had come from Morris.

Prospectors coming down from Darlot said he had gone out with a rush, taking a track eighty miles east, towards the Black Range.

The weeks of blazing sun and sweltering heat passed slowly. Sally worked with flagging strength. Her face became drawn and haggard as her body swelled. She knew now she would not be able to go away: that her baby would be born on the fields. She and the child would have to take their chance in the wretched hospital, built of hessian and corrugated iron and filled with fever patients, or depend on the kindness of Mrs. Molloy.

'Don't worry, dearie,' Mrs. Molloy cheered. 'You'll be as right as rain. You can come to me and I'll look after you like I have many another woman lately. I'll springclean the whole place, and Ted and the kids can camp out for a day or two when young Gough comes to town.'

That's how it happened after all. Kalgoorla went for Mrs. Molloy, the night Sally found herself racked with pain and terrified now her time had come, sooner than she expected. Ted Molloy and Sam Mullet came back with Kalgoorla. They carried Sally to the Molloy's cottage on the stretcher they had got ready for such an emergency.

There, Mrs. Molloy met her with open arms, full of excitement and importance. She even looked like a nurse, very clean and capable, in a print dress with a white handkerchief pinned over her head for a cap.

'Sure, darlin',' she said afterwards, 'I thought it would comfort you if I dressed up for the job.'

'It did,' Sally assured her.

She heard Mrs. Molloy tell Ted to go for the doctor, and all through the hours of pain she was conscious of the big kindly woman fussing about, cheering and encouraging her; and of Kalgoorla standing near, holding her in the last cruel struggle through which she screamed helplessly.

And then, in the early hours of the morning, Mrs. Molloy bent over her to say:

'It's a son you have, Mrs. Gough. A fine boy, God bless him! See, here he is.'

A son. Sally emerged from the coma of her exhaustion to look at the bundle beside her. A small dark head nestled against her bosom. The tears welled in her eyes and coursed slowly down her cheeks.

'My son! My son!' she whispered. It was exquisite happiness to know he was there beside her.

CHAPTER XL

THE whole Molloy family escorted Sally and her baby back to her own camp. Ted Molloy trudged ahead with her suitcase. Mrs. Molloy walked beside Sally carrying her son. Dick, the young Molloys called him, already. He had been registered as Richard Fitz-Morris Gough. A grand name, Mrs. Molloy declared.

She had given all her kids grand names, she said, to make up for their having no legal right to their father's. Sydy Patrick, Mel Anthony and Brissy Xavier, like lively young scarecrows, trailed along behind, each carrying something, and taking turns to give Vicky, still a toddler, a ride on their shoulders. Adey Cecilia trundled the Molloy baby in a cart made from a box on wheels.

Most important of all was the little nanny goat which was a present from Mrs. Molloy and kept Perthy and Bart, who were trying to lead her, running off into the scrub. Everybody went into shrieks of laughter as she dragged the boys after her, got her rope tangled in a thorn bush, or sent them sprawling.

She was a pretty creature, white, with dainty hooves, and horns curved like the crescent moon: frisky but gentle. Sally felt so well and happy, she laughed as gaily as the children at the nanny's antics. She had learnt to milk the little goat and Dick guzzled her milk contentedly now: was beginning to thrive on it. Sally had been horrified to find she had no milk for her baby, and to feel his mouth straining at her empty breast. She had wept and gazed at his small, ugly face despairingly.

'There, there, darlin',' Mrs. Molloy comforted, you must not upset y'rself. With your illness, and the hard life y've had lately, it's no wonder at all you're not able to feed the child y'rself. He'll be all right when we get him on to the goat's milk, and there's a little nanny come in, will be just the thing for him. . . .'

Sally felt that she owed her life and her baby's to Mrs. Molloy and that goat. But all the Molloys seemed to have had a share in pulling Dick and her through those first difficult days.

How good they had been! Ted Molloy turning out of his bed and getting Sam Mullet to help him carry her to the cottage, fetching the doctor and keeping hot water going in kerosene tins on the fire all night. The doctor had looked in after the baby was born and congratulated Mrs. Molloy on her work. He couldn't have done better himself, he said.

'Nor half as well,' Ted growled. 'And him in the drink, the way he was, I had to drag him out of the Exchange bar, and stand over him with a basin of hot water to wash his hands, before I'd let him near ye, missus.'

Ted and the children had camped out in the scrub for a few days, and it had been extraordinarily pleasant in the cottage. Sally could not express what it meant to her, just to lie in bed and be looked after with such loving care, her baby beside her: sleeping and dreaming of what this new association was going to mean in all the years ahead.

When the young Molloys came trooping in to see her and the baby, they brought all manner of small gifts. One of the boys had made a little cart from a wooden box for Dick, another had tied a number of bright parrot feathers together on the end of a long string, and Adey had sewed a bib for him, all by herself. Tears filled Sally's eyes as she thought of those gifts and all Mrs. Molloy had done for her.

Soon she had insisted that Mr. and Mrs. Molloy must have their own bed, and she could sleep on a stretcher in the sitting-room. The children came back to the house. They swarmed everywhere, noisy and curious, and their mother bustled about, cooking and sweeping, washing and ironing. So many people in such a tiny house! Sometimes it seemed they were all chattering at once, quarrelling and screaming, laughing and singing;

and the din went on all day, with the sudden bawl of a child being slapped or a baby crying.

After a few days, Sally decided she was well enough to go home. It was odd to think of her tent and a bough-shed as home; but she was longing to be there and have her baby to herself: to be able to wash and dress him without an eager little crowd looking on.

So this procession on a Sunday morning brought her back to her tent near the foot of Maritana Hill. It had to stop on the way, every now and then, to show her baby to old friends like Sam Mullet and Blunt Pick, Eli Nancarrow and Parson Jarn.

While Mrs. Molloy bustled about unpacking Sally's and the baby's things, Ted went down to the store for food. One of the boys lit a fire: another tethered the goat, and Adey swept away the leaves and dust which had silted up in the bough-shed and about the tent.

When Ted returned he said he had met a teamster down from Lake Darlot who had seen Morris and Con. They were making out towards the Black Range with a rush that had started when the alluvial on Darlot began to peter out. The chances were, Morris had not received Mrs. Gough's letter about the baby. Men coming down from the north had all heard reports of good gold on the Black Range, although it was tough country for prospectors.

'Don't you be worryin', Mrs. Gough,' Ted said, in his bluff, hearty way. 'Morrey'll be strollin' in one of these fine days, with a fortune in his pocket, maybe.'

'I am not worrying,' Sally said, quietly, looking down on her baby.

She had thought very little about Morris since her son was born, she realized. Her mind was full of the child, his hourly and daily needs, and how she was going to provide for him when he was older. Very soon she must open the dining-room again and begin to earn money. She had still a little saved from those months of toil before Dick was born; but it would not last long, and she told herself she must always be able to provide for both of them.

It seemed as if Morris had forfeited his right to the child. He had not come to share with her the joy of knowing he was on his way, or the anxieties and ordeal of his birth. Dick was hers as if Morris had disowned him, and she must be responsible for having brought him into the world.

Kalgoorla had disappeared after Dick was born. All that night Sally was conscious of the dark figure beside her, moving quietly, exclaiming softly to soothe and reassure her. Mrs.

Molloy said Kalgoorla had been a godsend, and helped at the birth, doing just as she was told with steady hands, very gentle and clever. She had taken charge of the baby while Mrs. Molloy did all that was necessary for the mother. But in the morning Kalgoorla was gone, and no one had seen anything of her since.

'When Kalgoorla comes back, we'll open the dining-room again,' Sally told Ted Molloy. She was sure Kalgoorla would come back.

'Now, now, dearie, don't start doing too much—and fretting about money,' Mrs. Molloy scolded. 'The boys won't see you stuck. Besides, while Ted's earning good wages, what's the need? Wisher, wisher, God bless us, aren't we proud and pleased to have had the pleasure of your company this last week or so, and to have brought His Honour into the world? Look at him there now with a smile all over his face for his aunt Theresa!'

In the evening the men came round to welcome Young Gough, they said. Eli explained that the boys did not know what to buy as a present for him. But seeing he was a real goldfields baby, they'd each put in a few 'weights, and he handed Sally a new shammy with the gold in to buy something for Dick.

Everybody swore he was a fine child and the dead spit of Morris. Sally herself knew her son was a poor weedy scrap of humanity; but promised herself that he would grow to be strong and good-looking.

The men told her the news of the fields as if she had been away for months. Hannans was booming. Mines changing hands at big figures, so much machinery on the roads and arriving daily there was not enough labour to handle it, and Cracker Jack said it was lying piled up at the 'Cross: more teams needed to cope with the loads, though the railway was nearing Coolgardie and great doings being planned for the opening day.

The contractors reckoned they'd reach Hannans a few months later and there was talk of changing the name of the town to Kalgurli, or Kalgoolarry, which was the name the natives had for the locality. New shops and pubs were going up everywhere. The bag shanties which had held the post office and the Warden's court were being pulled down and imposing buildings of desert sandstone being erected. The town was to be lit by electricity within a year. Condensers had been installed on the Government bore east of Hannans Reward; but a move was on foot to demand an adequate water supply.

And Frisco was making a great name for himself in London. He was Mr. Francisco José de Morfé now, if you please, dashing round with Lord Percy Douglas, floating companies and telling the newspapers that Hannans was the centre of the richest gold-mining area in the world.

Alf Brierly had got a job on the Midas and was building a house. Yes, they'd put him in as manager, and his missus was expected up any day. Didn't Mrs. Gough know? Look at that now! Mrs. Brierly had a baby, too. A girl, and Alf had got as drunk as a fiddler's bitch wetting the baby's head.

Not often Alf took more than he could carry, but he went clean off his head with excitement when the telegram came: 'You have a bonny daughter. Mother and child both doing well.' He showed it to everybody, and of course there were drinks all round. Seeing he was manager of the Midas, now, too, he did the right thing, had a barrel of beer sent round for men on the mine.

Dinny was out prospecting, but Alf sent a native to find him and tell him the good news.

'Has anybody heard Morris's whereabouts?' Sally asked. 'I sent him word about Dick to Lake Darlot, but Ted Molloy says Con and Morris went off with a rush to Black Range.'

There was an awkward silence. Bad news about that rush had come through, and nobody wanted to pass it on to Mrs. Gough. Then, it seemed, all the men were talking at once:

'Chances are Morris hasn't got word from you, yet, missus.'

'It's over a hundred miles from Darlot to the Black Range.'

'He'll be walkin' in on us, any day, I reckon, with some decent specimens.

'You bet. Morrey 'll be makin' tracks when he gets news of young Gough.'

Alf himself came to see her next day, bringing some oranges and lemons. He was full of pride and happiness about Laura and his daughter, and the new house he was building for them. It was almost finished, had a verandah back and front, fly-wired doors and a bathroom. Alf complained about the cost of freights and labour, but congratulated himself on having got the materials for his house at any price. He wanted Laura to have all the comfort and conveniences possible on the goldfields, he said; and his job on the Midas had made it possible for him to raise money and get the cottage run up quickly.

Sally was surprised to see a girl in white muslin and a big shady hat with a frill of goffered muslin round the brim, coming towards her a few days later. She looked like a Dana Gibson girl taking a walk along the dusty track, among the dust raddled tents.

But it was Violet O'Brien. A Violet so changed from the grave and shabbily dressed young barmaid at Giotti's pub, that at first glance Sally did not recognize her. Violet's eyes were the same, though, eyes of such a dark blue you could not forget them. They still had a rather sombre expression, despite the smile hovering about her mouth, as if she were amused at her fashionable appearance.

'Is it really you, Violet?' Sally cried, going to meet her.

'I can hardly believe it myself,' Violet said. 'But I heard you were here, Mrs. Gough, and wanted to see you before I go away. Oh, yes.' Her eyes lighted. 'I'm going to Melbourne to study singing. Dad came home a few weeks ago. Struck a good show, up north, and has just sold it for ten thousand pounds. At least that's Dad's share.'

'Oh, I am so glad!' Sally felt as delighted and excited as if she were sharing in this good fortune. 'Fairy tale things like this can happen after all!'

Violet nodded, still grave and marvelling at the realization of her dream.

'It seems too good to be true, doesn't it? Of course, I don't like leaving Mum and the kids. But it's my chance, the chance I've been always wanting. And Dad says I've earned it. And he's proud of me: doesn't want me to waste my life here on the fields—marry some miner or prospector, and have half a dozen kids in no time.'

'I've only got one, but I like him,' Sally laughed.

She took Violet over to the box in which Dick was sleeping, lifted the fly net, and let her look at him. 'He's very small and ugly, isn't he? But I'm as happy as larry because he's here!'

Violet had seen too many babies to be enthusiastic about them.

'That's all very well for you,' she said firmly. 'But I want to be a singer. Hope I'll never be in love again—or broken up, like I was about Charley.'

'It was dreadful for you, all that,' Sally agreed. 'But now you've got your chance, I hope nothing will interfere with it. You're young and beautiful, Violet; and you've got the strength of character that will help you to succeed.'

'Do you think I will? Oh, do you think I really will escape from all this?' Violet looked about the dead dry earth and the ramshackle camps, as if she feared they could still hold her back from achieving her purpose. 'Sometimes, I tell myself, I won't let anything stand in my way; and sometimes I'm afraid, if Dad runs through all this money—he's made as much and lost it before.'

'You mustn't think of that!' Sally said, as Dick began to cry and she picked him up.

'No.' Violet's voice hardened. 'Mum wants Dad to put his money into a pub, or land, before it's all gone in shares and mining investments. Anyhow, I won't come back to the fields, Mrs. Gough. I won't come back, though I'll be worried about Mum and the kids, if anything goes wrong.'

Sally felt as if the shadow of Violet's foreboding had touched her also.

'Don't come back, whatever you do,' she said. 'I'll think of you often, and be clapping in the distance when you're a world-famous singer, my dear.'

Violet went away then, swinging along the track. Her white-clad figure merged with the red dust rising about her as she walked. Slight, straight and self-reliant, as she disappeared through the dust and blaze of the sunshine, the girl seemed to be a part of her environment.

Sally wondered whether she would escape from its subtle influences. Violet was young, had an austere beauty and a voice of unusual quality, very pure and mellifluous, like the bell bird's. Surely, she would win what she was seeking? Not only self-expression through her voice, but independence, and the fulfilment of some standard of personal integrity. Sally almost prayed that it might be so. There was something about Violet, too rare and valuable to be wasted in the sordid atmosphere of a gold-fields pub.

Sally, herself, was quite content for a while to enjoy becoming acquainted with her son, washing and feeding him, taking him for walks in the bush, singing him to sleep. Summer had passed into cooler days, without rain, and there was the usual fear of water shortage. Stories from the far-out camps were all of a scarcity of food and water. Alarming reports had come down from Darlot about the rush to Black Range. In and out of her happiness and looking after the baby, Sally was anxious about Morris. She asked Sam Mullet and Eli Nancarrow to try and get news of him for her: made inquiries at the stores and from teamsters coming down from the north. But nobody seemed to have heard of Morris or Con after they set out on the rush.

The teamsters said the rush was the most disastrous that had ever been known in the West. There were over two thousand prospectors on the Darlot field at the time, and rumours about gold at Mount Black struck the camp when the alluvial was just about exhausted. In one night a thousand men pulled pegs and were off. Many just tramping along with swags on their backs, or harnessed to loads of gear and stores on rough sledges. The first horsemen, and men riding camels, to cover the hundred and ten miles had reached Mount Black, to find neither workings nor indications that any prospecting had been done there.

The country was not even auriferous and there was no water.

They turned back, or made for the Murchison. But rushers who had been foot-slogging, ill-equipped with food and water, had little hope of surviving on the tramp back to the Darlot. There was a wild stampede, as the men, trapped in that barren wilderness, threw away blankets and camp gear, every ounce of stuff they had been carrying, and started back on their long journey. Many perished. How many would never be known.

A prospector, riding a camel at its last gasp, brought the news to Darlot, and a relief party was arranged. Dinny Quin went out with it. Several men had been picked up in the last stages of exhaustion and brought back to the camp. A string of camels had been sent out after the relief party, with water and food. It was still searching for stragglers and prospectors who may have collapsed further along the track.

Sam and Eli tried to reassure Sally.

'Con and Morrey 'll be all right, missus,' they told her. 'Chances are they've made for the Murchison. Had camels, and Con 'd get about this country, anywhere he wanted to go. Y'r couldn't kill Con in the bush. He's too tough—and a good mate. He'll stick to Morrey. You see, they'll be walkin' in on us, one of these days, none the worse, and cursin' duffer rushes.'

CHAPTER XLI

KALGOORLA was there sitting by the fire, the morning Sally came out of her tent, later than usual. Very gaunt and dejected Kalgoorla looked, crouched beside the smouldering embers. A little uncertain of what her reception would be, too; but as Sally's greeting was all pleasure and excitement, Kalgoorla smiled and lost her air of a runaway dog, expecting a rough rather than friendly greeting.

She exclaimed at the baby. Quickly fell in with Missus Sally's joy and pride in him, though she understood he was not to be touched until she had washed. Missus Sally pointed to the wash basin and soap.

'You have a good wash and I'll find you a gina-gina, Kalgoorla,' she said; but guessed Kalgoorla was hungry.

She made tea and gave Kalgoorla some bread and meat. After Kalgoorla had eaten ravenously, Sally found an old dress for her and Kalgoorla went off to the bough-shed with a dish of water and a large piece of soap.

She reappeared, with wet hair, looking clean and pleased with herself in Sally's blue print dress: picked up the baby, and stood watching as Sally brought the goat in from the scrub where she was tethered. Kalgoorla exclaimed in amazement when Missus Sally started to milk the nanny, and again when she used a bottle with a teat on it to give her son a drink of goat's milk.

Sally explained that she had no milk herself to give the baby. Kalgoorla's face became heavy and sombre. She spread her hand over her stomach and touched her breast in an expressive gesture. It was like that with her own people, too, Sally gathered. The aboriginal women were hungry and their breasts empty. Kalgoorla had come to her, not for any sentimental reason, but because the natives were short of food.

Later in the day, Kalgoorla's relations arrived. Men and women. They had been begging round the township, Sally guessed, but were still hungry. She gave them most of the food in her cool safe. The men had learnt the use of money. She could give them money to buy food, they intimated. Sally showed them the purse in which she kept her small change, and Kalgoorla explained that Missus Sally also had been short of food. She produced Dick's bottle with the teat, and demonstrated how Sally milked the goat: put goat's milk in the bottle to give her child.

'Yukki!' Men and women crowded round with merry laughter, exclaiming their amazement. They were convinced that Missus Sally was as hard hit by the drought as themselves to take milk from that little white beast, like a dog with horns, to feed her child.

Sally knew she had only to send for some of the men working on their claims, and they would have driven the blacks away with angry threats as to what would happen to them if ever they bothered her again. But she could not forget these people had shared their food with her when she was helpless and at their mercy. It seemed reasonable enough that she should share what she had with them. She understood their point of view and was conscious of a moral obligation; but how to make the blacks understand one person could not feed so many?

Kalgoorla, it seemed, had done that for the moment; but there was no knowing what further demands they might make. Sally decided she must be prepared for them: have more money to buy food supplies.

With Kalgoorla's help she could open the dining-room again. She took Kalgoorla with her when she went down to the store. They came back laden with groceries, meat and potatoes; and Sally sent word to Sam Muller that the Café de Bush would be serving meals again next day. She asked him to round up old customers.

There was a good muster, and Mrs. Gough got a cheering welcome when the men saw her at her bench, serving out hot soup, as brisk and lively as she had ever been.

'Haven't had a decent meal since the last you cooked for us, missus!'

'Gosh, it's great to see you on the job again, Mrs. Gough, ma'am!'

Sally thrilled to the kindly intention of these remarks. She knew the men realized how worried she was about Morris, and that she must do something to provide for herself and Dick. It was their way of expressing sympathy with her in her trouble and assuring her of their help and support.

She was busy all day now, and had not so much time to spend nursing and walking her baby about. To be sure, she did not neglect him. His needs came first; but she could no longer run and pick him up whenever he cried, and sometimes he yelled lustily all through the evening meal. Not often, because Kalgoorla would hoist him on to one arm and carry plates to the table with the other. Sometimes a grim bearded miner would pick up young Gough and dandle him alarmingly, just to show he knew all about youngsters: was a father himself. Sally looked on, frightened that Dick might be dropped and injured for life. But the great rough hands which held him were strong and gentle. Dick seemed to like the feeling of them: crowed and gurgled into the faces of the men as they bent over him.

'Oh, they were so good and kind: you'd never believe how good and kind everybody was to me,' Mrs. Gough used to say, remembering that time.

Mrs. Molloy came along to see Sally once or twice every week: liked to sit and gossip over a cup of tea, and give good advice about Dick. The young Molloys chopped wood and went messages on Saturdays. Syd was working at a store now, and the other children who were old enough, going to school.

The school had just been opened, and Mrs. Molloy was very pleased about it.

'Hannans is goin' ahead like a house afire,' she commented affably. 'What with the school and the railway comin' and all the shops and pubs goin' up, we won't know ourselves soon. And you should see the house Mr. Brierly's put up for his wife, darlin'. A fair treat, it is! No more than corrugated iron whitewashed, with a lattice in front of the verandah, painted green; but he's got it fixed up so comfortable, with wash-house and troughs and all, and pretty flowered stuff for curtains and pinnies on the furniture. I reckon Mrs. Brierly 'll be the first woman on the goldfields not to do her washin' in a kerosene tin over a fire in the back yard.'

A day or two later, Mrs. Molloy was full of excitement. Mr. Brierly had borrowed a buggy and horses and driven over to Coolgardie to meet Mrs. Brierly.

Sally heard from the men, as they talked over their dinner, how Alf had driven through Hannans that afternoon he brought Laura home—though he was Mr. Brierly now to all but old mates, being manager of the Midas.

You never saw a man look so proud and happy as Alf when he drove through Hannans with his wife and child beside him, they said. He beamed on everybody and people stood in the street to cheer as the buggy passed.

Sally was looking forward to seeing Laura and her baby; but it was a pleasant surprise when Marie Robillard rushed into the camp and embraced her.

'My darling Sally,' she cried. 'I am so 'appy to see you. La! la! Me, I was so lonely at Coolgardie—and I worried much about you when Mrs. Fogarty tell me you 'ave bébé coming. Quick! quick! I must see 'im—and then we will talk.'

After Marie had seen Dick as he lay asleep in his box cradle, and exclaimed rapturously over him, she chattered eagerly, giving Sally her news.

'But, yes, we come to live at 'Annans now,' she said. 'Mr. Brierly, 'e will find the job for my Jean on the Midas. But I do not like that mon mari work underground in the mine, Sally. 'E is not well, my Jean. Always 'e cough, cough, cough—and I fear that 'e 'ave the miner's sickness. The papa of my Jean is with us now, also, and 'e does not wish Jean to work in the mine. 'E says 'e will work, the poor old man! Moi même, I can work also—sew shirts and dresses. But, yes, I am very good—how you say it? Seamstress? And will be the succés fou in 'Annans.'

They were going to camp near the mine, and Marie had left her men to put up the tents while she came to find Sally. She had to hurry back to help them unpack and put things in order. But what a joy it was to know she could run over to see Sally and talk to her again soon!

Marie had heard that Morris had gone out on the disastrous rush to Black Range, and that Sally was waiting for news of him.

'Mr. Brierly told us,' she said, gently. 'Mon Dieu, it is terrible for you, this anxiety, darrling! But try not to think the worst until you must.'

'I do,' Sally said. Marie's warm sympathy and affection were very sweet. It was like having been given a bunch of fragrant flowers, to think of them. Hannans would be a different place, she felt, with Marie there—and Laura. She was fond of them both, but Marie and she were more temperamentally alike. They had struggled against hardships, laughed and thought the same way about most things. Laura had lived more softly and easily. She was such a young lady, very charming and friendly; but rather stupid, and a little patronizing in her manner sometimes.

All the same, Sally was glad to see her when Alf drove Laura over one afternoon. He went on into Hannans to buy stores, leaving the two women 'to talk babies to their heart's content,' he said.

Laura was blooming, so plump and jolly that she seemed quite a different person to the rather shy girl who had come to the fields as Alf's bride. Her baby was chubby and rosy, too, a lovely scrap in her fine dainty clothes, woollen bootees, and bonnet embroidered with tiny roses.

She had christened her daughter Aimée, Laura said, though she supposed nobody would call her anything but Amy on the goldfields. Aimée had a lot of other names, too, as many as a princess, Alf declared. There was Elizabeth for his mother and Marianne for an aunt Laura was very fond of, and Laura's second name, Maud, because Alf insisted the child should have something of her in its name.

It was very absurd! Laura laughed happily, but Aimée did not seem to mind. She was a good baby. Nurse had said she was one of the best babies they had had in the hospital for a long time. She said it was because her mother had such an equable disposition and could feed her child from the first. Laura was thankful she could.

'It must have been dreadful to have to depend on goat's milk, Sally,' she added.

'I was glad to get even that,' Sally said.

'Oh, my dear,' Laura was overcome with regret at her tactlessness, 'you've no idea how I worried about you. It didn't seem fair that I should have all that comfort and care—and you up here in the heat and dust, struggling along as best you could. I begged Alf to send you down—no matter what it cost. We could have arranged about that; but he said you wouldn't come.'

'It was very good of you to make the suggestion.' Sally's heart welled to her appreciation of Laura's concern. 'But I couldn't let you and Mr. Brierly do so much for me. There were good friends here who made everything easy. Mrs. Molloy was goodness itself to me, and very capable.'

Sally confessed that Dick had been a miserable looking little creature at first; but he was doing well now. Really thriving and she was quite content.

She had a twinge of envy, though, when Aimée began to wail and Laura unfastened her dress to give the child a drink. Laura looked lovely, nursing her baby. Her soft white bosom was swollen with milk. Aimée snuggled into it and slept peacefully afterwards.

Sally talked about her anxiety for Morris.

'He would have sent me word, or returned by now, if he were alright,' she said.

'Alf says Dinny's up at the Darlot, and he's sure will make inquiries about Mr. Gough,' Laura consoled her. 'Alf thinks Dinny and Con may have struck out for the Murchison when they found water was so short on the track to Darlot. Con Mahaffey came down from the Murchison when Coolgardie was discovered, Alf says, and would make back there. Couldn't you come over and stay with us until Mr. Gough returns? There isn't a spare room, of course, but we could make you quite comfortable on the verandah. And I'd love to have you, Sally.'

She was like that, Laura, very generous and lovable, but Mrs. Gough, as Dinny said, always had her 'stinking pride.' She could not accept favours easily. She liked to be independent and carry her own burdens. She was grateful to Laura; but she could not endure the idea of dumping herself and a baby in the little home Alf had made for Laura and himself. It was not built to accommodate more people.

On Sunday afternoon, sometimes, Sally went over to have tea with Laura; but never felt quite at her ease. Everything looked so clean and brand new, she was afraid of leaving a mark on the oilcloth or soiling one of the chintz covered chairs when she sat in it. Laura kept the house in apple-pie order.

Alf had persuaded Mrs. Molloy to let her eldest girl go over to wash and scrub for Laura. There was nothing he did not do to make life easy and pleasant for his wife and child. He had built cupboards and a dresser: planted a quickly growing creeper beside the trellis: was digging rough earth behind the cottage for a garden. Toiled in it every day for an hour or two before going along to the mine.

She had never seen two people so happy and wrapped up in each other as Alf and Laura at that time, Sally thought. Laura laughed and sang as she went about the house, and Alf was so full of satisfaction and pleasure in his wife and child and home, that he could talk of nothing else, even gold, although he put in most of his days and nights on the Midas: was proud of the way he had opened up new workings and increased production on the mine.

CHAPTER XLII

When two men came stumbling along the track from the township towards her, Sally thought they were drunk. One of them was guiding the other. She merely glanced at them in the gathering dusk and hoped they would not want a meal. Dinner was finished in the bough-shed and she was clearing away after it: Kalgoorla still washing dishes.

Sally's mind worked quickly. If the men asked for food, she would have to give it to them: open a tin of meat: make some fresh tea. One of the men slumped on the ground, a little distance away, the other came on. And then she saw it was Dinny.

'Dinny!' she cried, and her thoughts flew to Morris. Dinny must have just got back from Darlot and could tell her—

'I've got bad news for you, missus,' Dinny said.

'Morris?' Sally gasped. 'He's—'

'No. He's not dead,' Dinny said gently. 'But he near done a perish on the track from the Black Range. I went out with water and stores when I heard things were so bad up that way: brought him in. Con went off his head, though, and cleared out. How Morrey pulled through, I don't know. He was jest about all in when we found him lyin' beside the soak where he'd been diggin' for water and not a drop there. He's alright now—he'll be alright—but he's a bit queer in his head. Doesn't remember anything. You'll have to go easy with him: let him come round in his own time.'

'Where is he?' Sally's voice was no more than a whisper.

Dinny jerked his head to the man sitting on the ground. Sally ran to him.

'Morris,' she cried, kneeling beside that derelict figure. Morris lifted his head and looked at her with dull, bloodshot eyes. But he knew her. There was a quiver of recognition on his face at the sound of her voice.

Sally put her arms round him. She drew Morris's head against her breast, and kissed it, murmuring:

'Oh, darling, darling! I'm so glad you've come. Everything will be alright now.'

As he watched, Dinny was satisfied Morris knew where he was and that Sally was with him. He could not throw off the heavy torpor which had taken possession of him; but that would pass. Dinny remembered how he himself had felt after his thirst on the Siberia track.

243

'We'd be glad of a bite to eat, if it's not puttin' you to too much trouble, missus,' he said. 'Had plenty of tucker on the way down; but I reckoned it'd be better to bring Morrey straight here than take him into one of the pubs or cafés for a feed. All he needs now is a bit of lookin' after and gettin' used to the idea he's not doin' a perish still, out there in the Black Range. God, it's the roughest damned country ever I was in. And scarcely a skerek of gold has anybody got out of it for their pains! Morrey's had about as bad a time as a man could have and pull through. It'll be a while before he gets over it. But he'll pull through, don't you worry.'

Sally hurried to get a meal ready, while Dinny had a wash: helped Morris to wash his face and hands and took him over to the bough-shed.

For the first few days Morris did not speak. He had to be told and helped to do everything, get up, dress, wash, eat his food. He moved feebly like an old man, stood staring vacantly before him, or sat in the bag chair, indifferent to whatever was going on. It was heart breaking to see him, but Sally talked to him and treated him as if he understood all she said. The men, too, tried to rouse and cheer him as they came and went for their meals, always stopping to say:

'Hullo, Morrey, how's things?'

'Gosh, it's good to see you back in the old camp, Morrey!'

Or give him some bit of news:

'Hannans is booming alright, these days, Morrey. Four thousand miners workin' on the field.'

Morris did not reply, although sometimes he grunted as though he were trying to speak. And Sally thanked the men with a smile and eager appreciation.

'Every day he's better, I'm sure,' she said. 'Soon Morris will be himself again.'

She had showed him the baby: told him how Mrs. Molloy had taken care of her; and was a little disappointed that Morris gave no indication of the slightest interest in their son. The first sign of returning consciousness, she noticed, was the way he glowered at the men going into the bough-shed, watched her every movement as she served a meal, and the men settled up with her on pay day.

She and Kalgoorla were busy, rushing their dinner to the men, and Dick had been yelling lustily, when Sally glanced across to see why he had stopped crying. And there was Morris, walking up and down with the child in his arms.

'Look, look, Kalgoorla!' she exclaimed. 'Boss mind 'm baby.'

Kalgoorla's chuckle was confirmation of her hope that Morris at last knew his son.

The dry weather continued; but in the strange stillness of an evening when the sun was setting behind a streel of dark clouds, and a queer lurid light painted the ridge and wide plains, Kalgoorla said suddenly:

'Big feller rain bin comin'.'

Kalgoorla was usually right about the weather. When thunder was rumbling in the distance, and lightning whipping and cracking across the sky, Sally put as much of her foodstuff as possible into tins. She stowed clothing away in her trunk and wooden boxes, and looked anxiously at the tent.

It was old and sun-rotted. She had patched it with new canvas and reinforced it with bagging in various places: but the roof had leaked so badly during the last rains, that she had been drenched as she lay in bed. Now there was her baby to think of. She kept a tarpaulin handy to rig some sort of shelter over Dick if there were a heavy downpour.

She had gone to bed, and Morris, too, was asleep, when the storm swept the camp with cyclonic fury. The tent ripped and was torn from its ground pegs. Sheets of corrugated iron and the branches of trees sailed through the air and crashed into the scrub. Then the rain descended in torrents, thrashing and blinding her as she stood exposed to it.

Sally scrambled into a coat and shoes, as the first blast struck the camp. She was battling with the wind and trying to wrap Dick in a rug, when Morris took the rug from her, wrapped the child in it, and lifted him out of her arms. Morris looked half naked himself, wearing only old moleskins and a thin shirt that flapped and flew about him. But he was quite calm and self-possessed.

Through the roar of the wind and the driving rain, Sally heard him say:

'You can't stay here all night. We'll go to the open cut.'

He strode off into the darkness and Sally followed him, terrified, scarcely realizing that Morris had spoken for the first time since his return. Already water was lying on the ground everywhere, and she splashed after him, not having heard distinctly what he said. The open cut was like a cave on the far side of Maritana Hill, but when Morris turned towards the hill, Sally screamed:

'No! No! Morris, not that way!'

There were so many shafts and pot holes between the camp and the hill, and the tracks that ran between them were so narrow, she was afraid Morris would take the wrong track, or make a false step and fall into one of those death traps with his precious burden. Sally sobbed distractedly, battling with the wind and rain and stumbling after him. She knew Kalgoorla was padding along behind her.

'Let Kalgoorla go first,' she begged, catching up to Morris, and believing that Kalgoorla's instinct would be a surer guide than Morris's memory of the track.

'I know this track better than Kalgoorla,' Morris shouted.

He should surely, Sally told herself, remembering all the times Morris and Frisco had tramped along this very track when they were working their lease on the Maritana boundary.

Morris remembered every inch of the way, it seemed. He called back, once or twice, and warned Sally to keep close behind him when the track narrowed, and led them at last to where lights were twinkling in the open side of the hill.

A crowd had collected there and got a fire going. Men were sitting round it in their rain-sodden clothes, or lying sprawled further back in the cave, trying to sleep. These first workings on the mine, where the gold had been torn off the surface with gad and hammer, appeared to be the only dry spot in the rain-swept countryside. But nobody complained about the deluge, or the storm which had blown away their frail dwellings. An old fossicker, who had been camping in the open cut for some time, produced a box for Mrs. Gough to sit on, and presently a billy of tea.

'That'll warm the cockles of y'r heart, missus,' he chortled, handing Sally a pannikin of the scalding black brew.

It did, Sally assured him, as she sat nursing Dick and watching the rain descending in a thick grey veil beyond the firelight and the walls of raw red earth which surrounded her. She could rejoice with everybody else over the storm, because it had restored Morris to normality.

He sat on the ground near her and listened to all the good-humoured cursing and joking about the behaviour of the elements, one day burning and blasting the whole country to a desert with scarcely a drop of water for man or beast, the next nearly drowning them with the rain they had been praying for. The storm and the tricks it had played on everybody, by slapping down their shacks and tents as if they had been made of paper and scattering all their worldly possessions, was treated as a joke. This rain promised renewed zest, plenty of food and water for the next few months and a good season for prospecting in the back country. Yarns were told of flooded creeks, teams bogged on the roads, and the luck a man might have specking for alluvial after rain.

Morris joined in the talking, quietly and as a matter of course. The men understood what had happened, and Sally encountered many a kindly nod and grin on Morris's account. Towards morning everybody dropped and dozed. Kalgoorla had curled up with her back to the fire, and Morris slept leaning against Sally's knees. Some of the men snored peacefully. Sally herself lost consciousness for a while.

Then it was dawn and the men stirring. Rain still fell steadily, but some of them went off to get a meal and see what had happened in the township. Morris went with them. He must try to find the goat, or get a drink for Dick from Mrs. Molloy, Sally told him. Morris brought the goat with him when he returned.

Not a tent was left standing on the open ground at the foot of the ridge, he said. Almost every shack and tent between Hannans and the Boulder mines had disappeared overnight. Only a few of the more solidly built huts remained standing, and some of them were roofless. The wind had carried sheets of corrugated iron for half a mile sometimes. Every house and pub was gorged with men, women and children who had taken refuge in them during the storm.

Sally had thought of going to Mrs. Molloy until the rain stopped; but Morris said the Molloys already had two families in their shack, which was one of the few with a roof still intact. The Brierlys' was another. He wanted Sally to go there: she did not want to. Then Dinny arrived and declared Mrs. Brierly had sent him to bring Mr. and Mrs. Gough to her place.

Dinny helped Morris to carry the tin trunk in which Sally had stowed a few of their clothes before the storm burst, and they trudged off, like drowned rats, with Kalgoorla tagging along behind, to the neat whitewashed cottage Alf had built on rising ground near the Midas mine.

Laura gave them the warmest of welcomes, though she looked dismayed to see Kalgoorla. Alf had finished breakfast and gone off to work, she said; but he had told her to say that it was an ill wind that blew nobody any good and he hoped they would have the pleasure of Sally's and Mr. Gough's company for a few days. She rushed about finding dry clothes, and then getting another breakfast ready, commiserating with Sally over the damage done by the storm to all her belongings, and congratulating herself on having escaped similar consequences.

'It was wise of Alf to get this place built,' she chirruped happily, 'though it cost a lot of money, and we don't know when we'll be able to pay it all off. But at least we can live in some comfort. Alf suggests that we put a tarpaulin along the back verandah, and if you and Mr. Gough could sleep there, Sally dear, we can fit in nicely. Kalgoorla can camp in the wash-house. It's not the way I like to treat guests, but the best we can do, under the circumstances.'

'It will be marvellous, Laura,' Sally said wearily. 'And it's very good of you to take us in like this.'

Laura did her best to make her small, well-ordered house accommodate two families in the days that followed. And it was not easy with only one bedroom, one sitting-room and a kitchen for them to share. Particularly when the two babies were screaming at the same time, or one wakened the other and upset both their mothers. Fortunately Alf was away most of the day, and Morris had decided to look for work, so took himself off early in the morning also.

Living with Alf and Laura, Morris tried to be the sort of guest they would ordinarily like to entertain. He shaved off his beard and had a hair cut: made an effort to spruce up his clothes and be agreeable. It was as if he had remembered that he was the Hon. Morris Fitz-Morris Gough, and not merely a prospector down on his luck.

'Goodness, Sally,' Laura exclaimed. 'I'd no idea Mr. Gough could be so charming.'

'He's had nobody to practise on for a long time,' Sally laughed. 'Feels he owes it to you and Mr. Brierly, I suppose, to show he knows how to behave.'

But she was troubled by Morris's failure to get a job, any sort of a job, that would tide them over this difficult time. They were really destitute. The tent had been torn to ribbons in the storm and the weather was now cold and squally. A freezing wind swept the plains in the early morning and at night, making the miners huddle under their coats when they came off shift. The best place to be, at this time of the year, they declared, was underground, where many men were still sweating, half-naked, as they worked in a temperature of 80 degrees.

Even if they could get another tent, Sally dreaded living in the open again, just now, for her baby's sake. Yet, after the first week, she realized she must not take advantage of the Brierlys' hospitality much longer. Where to go, though, or what to do next, she could not think.

With all the goodwill in the world, Laura was beginning to be irked by the way her house was cluttered up because so many people were living in it, and so many small garments were always drying in the sitting-room before the fire. Sally washed the baby's clothes, and tried to help her; but Laura liked to do almost everything herself. She seemed to be cooking, cleaning and tidying up all day. Was fussier and not so sweet-tempered as she had been at first.

Kalgoorla had gone bush the morning after the storm. The rains would mean a good season for her people, and there was no knowing when she would return. That's the way it always is with a gin, Laura said. You can never depend on her for long at a time. Sally thought that she understood Kalgoorla's flitting. Kalgoorla knew well enough she was not very welcome at the Brierlys. Laura could not get over her aversion from the blacks. She did not like Kalgoorla to come into the house, or touch her baby, although Sally assured her that Kalgoorla was a wonderful nurse.

Sally herself usually took the babies for a walk after lunch, while Laura was resting. She packed them both into the little box cart the Molloys had made for Dick, and sometimes went along to see Mrs. Molloy. The Molloy youngsters, if they were at home, crowded round to admire Aimée. She was the prettiest baby they had ever seen. As plump and rosy as a doll, always fresh and sweet and prinked out in the daintiest white clothes. But Theresa Molloy was concerned about Aimée.

'She's too soft and pink-and-white for the fields,' she said anxiously. 'They'll have trouble to rear her through the summer. But him'—she beamed at Sally's ugly brown little grub—'he's bred on the dust of the goldfields. He'll be alright.'

Alf would not hear of their leaving at the end of a week, when Sally suggested it.

'Wait till Morrey gets a job,' he said cordially. 'Wish I could offer him something. But we're over-staffed as it is on the Midas, and the directors demanding a reduction of expenses. Damn them!'

'It's very good of you,' Sally demurred, 'but we couldn't do that.'

'Nonsense!' Alf declared. 'We love to have you, don't we, dearest?'

'Of course,' Laura replied, without any enthusiasm.

'Besides,' Alf went on, as if apologizing to her for his persistence, 'this is just a slight return for many kindnesses in the past. I can never repay you for what you did for me when I was down and out, Mrs. Gough.'

Dinny had dropped in that evening and heard the end of this conversation.

'Same here,' he chuckled. 'Remember, Alf, how I chewed the lug of nearly every man in the 'Cross for a fiver, that day Art Bayley rode in with the first gold from Coolgardie? We was jest about givin' up hope of swampin' on the track, when Mrs. Gough ups and says: "But I can lend you five pounds, Mr. Quin: And you, too, Mr. Brierly, if you wish.'

'Cripes!' Alf laughed. 'Sweeter words were never spoken, were they, Dinny?'

'Ever pay back that fiver?' Dinny asked.

'Well, I'm blest! Don't believe I ever did.'

'Nor me, neither,' Dinny chortled. 'Nice pair of blackguards we are, Mrs. Gough. Clean forgot we owed you a fiver apiece.'

'So did I,' Sally admitted gaily.

But next morning Dinny came to see her and talk over what he described as 'a business proposition.'

He had made a bit of money on the Darlot, he said, and wanted to invest it in some solid security. So he thought of building a house. Not a flash cottage like this place of Alf's; but something bigger and more profitable that could be let as a miners' boarding house. There was a crying need for places of the sort, and good money to be made if a capable woman took charge of such a boarding house. Dinny himself wanted a home he could come back to after prospecting trips; and he reckoned on building on a block of land he had bought, a few days ago, from a mate who needed the money.

Sally suspected that Dinny's business proposition was intended to give her a roof over her head; but she thought she could make a good investment for him. She went to see Dinny's block of land about half-way between Hannans and the Boulder. They talked over plans for the house: chose the spot where it would stand, a little back from the road, with a garden in front and a vegetable patch behind.

Dinny squatted on the ground to draw his design of a long, narrow shell, with a verandah in front and a trellis on which they could grow creepers, or maybe a vine. At one end there would be a dining-room, kitchen, and bedroom for Mr. and Mrs. Gough. Opening on to the verandah, four small rooms which could be let to boarders. The room at the end Dinny would keep for himself.

He explained, all innocent exuberance:

'Dream of me life, missus! A place of me own, a home to come back to—if only you'll take on the proposition. You can make a going concern of the boarding house—sell the goodwill when Morris gets a job and you want a cottage like the Brierlys or go to the old country.'

'Oh, Dinny, you're a good liar,' Sally could not resist saying. 'It will be heaven to have a house to live in. I can't tell you how worried I've been at the thought of having to go back to a tent in this weather, with Dick to look after. I'll make a success of the boarding house. Be able to pay you rent. You'll see!'

Dinny decided that he and Morris could start building the house at once. There was a shortage of labour and materials; but he set to work buying all the corrugated iron, old and new, he could lay his hands on: collected bush timber and scantlings for the framework, and took his camels over to Coolgardie to see if any suitable odds and ends were for sale among the deserted shops and houses on the old camp. It was his house, and Morrey doing him a favour by giving a hand, Dinny asserted. So he put Morris on the wages of a builder's labourer.

There was nothing Dinny had not done in his time. He had run up many a shack before this, he said. In a week or so one end of the corrugated iron walls was roofed. Sally moved in. She had watched every stage of the building, from the moment Dinny and Morris dug holes for the foundations and bound the house's legs with galvanized iron bandages to protect them from the ravages of white ants. She could be of more use to Dinny and Morris if she were on the spot, she explained to Laura.

Laura was loth to let her go before the house was finished; but Sally as anxious to relieve Laura of the domestic difficulties so many guests had caused, as to have a place of her own again.

She had planned to clear the stony ground and start digging for a garden while the soil was still moist with rain. Already she could see the long iron shack, whitewashed and screened by vines, a garden flourishing before it in the springtime, and fruit trees in the back yard.

Alf had proved that anything would grow in the rich red earth beneath the rough shingle. In the winter and spring, at least, and by saving every drop of water from the washing of dishes and clothes a few plants could be kept alive during the summer. White ants were the worst problem, he had discovered. They devoured the roots of orange and peach trees, but were not so partial to figs, grape vines and lemons.

'You've been wonderful, Laura, to put up with us so long,' Sally said, gratefully. 'But it's time, I think, for the Goughs to move into their new home.'

CHAPTER XLIII

THERE was plenty to do during the fresh bright days after the rains. Dinny and Morris went on with the house, fixing the windows and doors, partitioning off the interior, setting a stove and putting a ready-made chimney of galzanized iron over it. Until that was done Sally cooked over a fire in the yard.

Dinny had bought a big water tank in Coolgardie and erected a platform for it. He built a wash-house in the yard and installed troughs and a copper: put a bath in the shower shed: made cupboards for the kitchen and bedrooms.

'It's a real up-to date modern residence, Dinny!' Sally exclaimed delightedly, when the place was finished.

'No good spoilin' the ship for a ha'p'orth of tar,' Dinny insisted when it was a question of furnishing. 'Get what you need from the stores, ma'am. We can settle-up after the boarders are payin' their way.'

It was no use arguing, Sally knew. Morris brought her table and forms and their stretchers from the old camp, and she bought all the extra things required to make her boarding house look pleasant and comfortable, keeping a frugal eye on the cost, but determined to make the most of this opportunity to have a home about her at last.

She was quite excited to go shopping, ransack the stores for material to make curtains and cretonne covers for a sofa and the easy chairs Dinny had picked up at a sale in Coolgardie. Marie went with her and helped with all the planning and sewing there was to do. Marie's husband and his father had put up a shack for her on the Brown Hill lease where Jean was working. Soon they hoped to build a better home, but meanwhile she was quite satisfied to have some shelter from the freezing winds, and a fireplace indoors to cook by and warm the place at night.

As soon as her rooms were ready, Sally let three of them to young miners working on the Midas and Great Boulder. Decent steady lads Dinny brought along and recommended as likely to pay regularly and not give Mrs. Gough too much trouble. She would have to do their washing and cut cribs for them, as other boarding house keepers did. But Sally was prepared for that: had done the same sort of things for men at the 'Cross, and was quite happy in the launching of her new enterprise.

Dinny, himself, was itching to go off prospecting again. He could never stand living in a town for long, he said, and the rush and bustle of Hannans, these days, with every pub crowded and the streets swarming with strangers, was more than he could endure. He loved the wild open country, loaming for gold where no one had ever found it before, beyond the furthest horizon, long quiet days with the zest of the chase in his blood, and nights of yarning beside the camp fire with a good mate: starry skies overhead and nothing to worry about.

Barney Gipps, his mate then, wanted to try a stretch of country to the south-east he had heard about from a native, so **Dinny** brought in his camels and they set out.

Dinny had tried to persuade Morris to go with them. He said: 'I'll work for wages, any sort of wages, Dinny, but I'm not going prospecting again.'

Oh, well, it was the way a man felt when he'd been through the sort of time Morris had on the track, Dinny admitted. But when Dinny had gone, and there was no more carpentering to do round the house, Morris was at a loose end. He went looking for work in the town and round the mines again. For young men, labourers, miners and mechanics there were plenty of jobs; but for a middle-aged man with no particular qualifications, it was not so easy to find employment.

Sometimes on a Sunday Alf and Laura would come over and take the Goughs for a ride to the Salt Lake. While Alf and Morrey had a shot at the black duck on quiet backwaters, Laura and Sally sat on a rug under a tree and talked about their babies.

It was an easy, peaceful time. Wild flowers spread a bright carpet round them. They gathered pink everlastings, tiny blue and yellow stars on long stalks, and curdy white wild candytuft. There were masses of mauve and white blossom on tall bushes, which put a delicate fragrance of turpentine into the air, shawls of magentary silk thrown by the pig-weed beside the track, and here and there thickets of cassia with its tiny golden cups and exquisite perfume. Most of the wild flowers withered quickly; but Sally and Laura usually took a big bunch of turpentine bush and cassia home with them.

But soon the flowers vanished: the herbage withered: the dust began to blow in freakish willy-willies. Summer was on the way, and they both knew what that meant. Laura had weaned Amy and the child was not doing so well on goat's milk. She had lost weight: was fretful and restless. Laura was going south again for the summer and thought Sally should go, too.

There was no prospect that she would be able to, Sally knew. She had to make her boarding house pay and find the rent for Dinny. She had bought many things for the house which were not paid for yet. There was oilcloth on the floor now, new crockery and cooking utensils in her cupboards. She and Morris had a nice bed, and the boarders new stretchers with sheets and blankets on them. It had cost a lot of money to buy these things at the stores, or have them sent up from the 'Cross, and although she was paying for them gradually, Sally felt that her obligations to Dinny must be met.

Morris had been pleased with the house, and to live in some

comfort, though he hated the boarders: kept out of their way as much as possible.

'When I get a decent job we'll have a home of our own,' he said irritably. 'It's almost more than I can bear to see you fetching and carrying for these hobbledehoys.'

'But they're not much bother,' Sally protested. 'And this way we can provide for ourselves and have a house to live in.'

Morris had been very gentle and considerate since the storm. As if he were trying to make amends for those months of silence and indifference when the gold lust was on him and he was beating about on the rushes up north. He was a different man now. Something had gone out of him. Perhaps it was the hope of ever making a fortune, prospecting, as he had dreamed of doing. He no longer talked of gold and what he would do when his luck turned.

Since his return from the north he had slept alone: even after the storm, when his health was normal again. Sally appreciated that he did not attempt to resume their old relationship as a matter of course. Morris understood, she thought, that her feeling for him had changed. She could not easily forgive him for having failed to share the responsibility of her pregnancy and the birth of their child. Then, too, there had been the disturbing wild fire of that episode with Frisco.

But it was impossible to see Morris so broken and humble and not try to restore his self-respect and assurance. The only thing left to him seemed to be her love and understanding. Surely she could not deny him these, Sally argued with herself. After all, she did love him. She did understand what the gold fever did to a man; and she, herself, had been in danger of being swept away by another fever, which this country bred, as devastating and obliterating of all moral considerations. There was nothing for her, or for Morris, she thought, but to hold fast to each other and make the best of their lives together.

It was necessary, too, to protect herself from the spell which Frisco had put over her. She quailed at the thought of it, her nerves stirring to 'that disgraceful sensation,' her brain swimming as if she had been breathing some strange narcotic perfume. This weakness must be exorcised, she told herself. She must root it out of her system.

And so she had made love to Morris: seduced him from his gloomy aloofness and convinced him of her desire to be not only a good wife but his lover, as in the days when they were first married. Their reunion brought them both a new lease of life and happiness.

Morris, it seemed, could hold up his head again: face the world with some pride and secret satisfaction. After all, he had something which so many men lacked on the fields. And Sally found herself singing as she washed dishes, swept and tidied the house. She no longer harboured any grouch against Morris, and the restless undertow of her feeling for Frisco ceased to trouble her. Morris was taking more notice of Dick now: often minded him or took him for a walk, though he was a little jealous of Sally's absorption with the child.

'Never heard such nonsense!' he exclaimed when Sally chattered and laughed with her baby as if he really understood what she was saying.

'Oh, well, he likes it,' she replied. 'And I like making a fuss over him, because he really is a darling little curmudgeon, Morris, and I'm crazy about him.'

When Morris came in after one of his tramps looking for work and said that he had got a job, Sally exclaimed eagerly: 'Oh, I am glad, Morris!'

She thought that regular employment would help him to regain confidence in himself. But Morris was very mysterious about his job: refused to talk about it. He asked her to cut a crib for him, and it was not until she saw him going off, in his working clothes, with one of the boarders who was a miner on the Great Boulder, that she suspected Morris was going to work underground.

She was filled with consternation when he came home in the evening, splashed with grey sludge and scarcely able to drag himself along. Oh, yes, he was bogging on the Boulder, and the first day shovelling ore took the stiffening out of a man. But he would get used to it, Morris declared. Men older than he were working on the same shift.

'Oh, Morris, you shouldn't do it,' Sally cried. 'You're not strong enough yet—and there's no need, really. We can manage quite well, now that we've got the boarders.'

'I've let you manage long enough, Sally,' Morris said dourly. 'I've got some guts left. Must earn a crust. If this is the only way I can do it, well, I'm a bogger for the rest of my life.'

A bogger was known by the men as a 'miner with his brains bashed out.' Sally knew how galling it had been for Morris to take this job. She understood he wanted to show her that he would do any work rather than leave all the responsibility of earning a living to her. She begged him not to risk a breakdown in health by this back-breaking toil in the heavy atmosphere underground. But Morris was obdurate about sticking to his job now that he had got one.

Day after day he plodded off, joining the stream of men going to work on the mines, and returning with them in the evening, as bowed and ghastly as any of them, slouching along the wide dusty road in their mud-splashed moleskins and flannel shirts, carrying their blackened billies and crib bags. Every time the mine whistles shrilled after an accident, Sally ran to the gate and watched the road anxiously.

But when Morris was carried home on a stretcher, it wasn't an accident, the men said. He had collapsed at work. Damned lucky he hadn't been alongside the ore pass with the ore shifting under him! The doctor said it was his heart and he'd have to rest-up for a bit. By rights he shouldn't have been working underground. But he'd be alright.

'Nothin' to worry about, missus,' the men exclaimed in their kindly, casual way, and went back to work.

'Sorry to be such a crock, Sally,' Morris groaned.

'Oh, my dear,' she wept, 'I'm so glad that you're here.'

She sent for the doctor. He told her that Morris had probably strained his heart and would never be able to do heavy manual work again; but with rest and care, there was no reason why his heart should not recover a fairly normal action before long.

Morris fretted and fumed at having to lie in bed and do nothing for several weeks. But gradually he was able to move without 'that pounding of the battery,' as he said, and the paralysing weakness which had overwhelmed him in the mine.

There had been great celebrations in Coolgardie for the opening of the railway. Nearly all the men who had tramped up from the 'Cross on the first rush came in from the bush for the occasion and took part in the procession. No end of a row blew up when the Afghans with their gaily caparisoned camels wanted to lead the procession. They refused to walk behind Christian dogs; but the Railway Reception Committee was not to be bluffed.

A Highlander led off with his pipes skirling. Dinny, Alf, Sam Mullet, Blunt Pick, Bill Jehosaphat, Speck Jones, and some of the original prospectors of the field followed in drags drawn by gaily beribboned horses. A brass band and the fire brigade swung along before the Mayor and Councillors. His Excellency, the Governor of the State, Sir Gerald Smith, and the parliamentary representatives had an imposing escort of mounted troopers. Sulky and disgruntled, the Afghans in their white flowing robes strode beside their camels, and a few miserable looking scarecrows of natives brought up the rear.

Coolgardie was en fête for a week: beflagged and gaily decorated with coloured streamers! A sports meeting, grand dinner, innumerable sprees and a ball were included in the festivities.

'S'elp me, if ever I see such a turn-out,' Dinny exclaimed telling Morris and Sally about it. 'Five hundred of us sat down to dinner in a big shed, built for the purpose. The Mayor, himself, told me the celebrations was costin' Coolgardie five thousand pounds. The Wilkie brothers, who built the railway, spent one thousand pounds on champagne alone. And so they might. They made a fortune when they got the contract for layin' a line to the goldfields.'

Hannans was preparing for its greeting to the railway. Not to be outdone by Coolgardie, Hannans also was going to spend £5,000 on the celebrations. With the coming of the railway it was going to shed its old name and become Kalgoorlie. Already arrangements were being made for the procession, banquet, race meeting, ball, sports, goat races, camel races, and all manner of junketing for young and old.

The railway was regarded as a guarantee of the future prosperity of these goldfields towns. It would ensure supplies of food and water, transport building material and mining machinery to keep pace with the demands of the mines and a population that was growing by leaps and bounds. The railway, everybody believed, would make the isolation of these mining settlements a thing of the past; bring them all the comforts of civilization. Its advent was a matter for general rejoicing.

Laura went down to the coast soon after the railway was opened. Alf drove her over to Coolgardie and put her on the train. The red dust penetrated even his neat little bandbox of a house. It lay in a film over everything, water, food and clothing, despite cupboards and cool safes. Aimée had lost weight: become sickly and peevish in the hot weather, and Alf was taking no chances with his precious family.

Before Laura went away, Sally knew that she was going to have another child. Morris was appalled: wanted her to go to the coast at all costs. Swore he would find the money. That it must be done. Sally realized it would be almost impossible for them to face such expense. She assured Morris she had confidence in Mrs. Molloy. With such a good friend to look after her, and a new doctor at the hospital, a nurse and matron there, now, also, there was no earthly reason to go away.

Morris started to look for work again: any work he was physically fit for, and that would enable him to send Sally away before her second baby was born. Dick was just toddling, and how she was going to do all the work of a boarding house with another baby to look after he could not imagine.

CHAPTER XLIV

DINNY disapproved of Morris having taken a job underground.

'You was lookin' for trouble, Morrey,' he said. 'A man's got to be pretty fit and used to the game to stand boggin' at your age.'

When Noah Coates, the undertaker, gave Morris a job, helping him with his accounts and interviewing customers, Dinny thought he was making a mistake.

'You'd do much better if you came out prospectin' with me, Morrey,' he said.

'I'm finished with prospecting,' Morris repeated. 'It's wages and a steady job I want now.'

Morris learnt the business and made himself useful to old Noah Coates, who was ill. The carpentering he had picked up from Dinny, building the house, came in handy, and he became quite accustomed to measuring the dead and making coffins. When Noah died, Morris carried on for his widow.

'If only I could buy her out,' he exclaimed to Dinny, 'I'd do it like a shot. There's money in undertaking, Dinny. It'd be a good investment—if you've got any cash to spare.'

Dinny was impressed with the figures Morris showed him. He mortgaged the house and bought the business from Mrs. Coates, on the understanding that Morris was to manage it and take over from him as soon as profits made it possible.

Being an undertaker was a grim joke to Morris; but he got a certain amount of satisfaction out of having found something he could do effectively. He threw himself into making a success of his business, cleaned up and painted the dusty old hearse: fed and groomed his scraggy horses.

A funeral often passed the house on its way to the cemetery, the procession headed by the hearse and mourning coach, with a few buggies and sulkies behind, and men and women trudging along the dusty road in the hot sunshine.

Sally almost wept when she saw Morris walking beside the hearse, in his shabby frock coat and tall hat with black weepers round the crown. Morris and the driver wore white weepers on their hats if a baby was being buried, and dingy, moth-eaten white plumes waved on the hearse. There were black and white ones for young people, and for girls, coffins lined in cheap white satin with frills to enfold the body.

It was a point of honour for bereaved families, or miners burying a mate, to spare no expense in order to give the deceased what was called a 'slap-up funeral.' Morris had to make his arrangements accordingly and satisfy the desire of grief-stricken friends and relatives to do honour to their dead in the only way they could. Incidentally, he made a handsome profit on these extra trappings of a funeral: a coffin of English oak with a silver plate and electroplated fixings, the plumed hearse, and assistants wearing weepers.

Only the destitute and friendless were packed away in a plain deal coffin, or Jews, whose religion demanded austerity in their last rites. Jewish women would come to tire their dead, being careful not to touch the body as they washed and prepared it for sliding into its wooden resting place. Sally had seen them sometimes when Morris was very busy and could not come home for his evening meal. She took it to the shed where he worked behind the shop, which was also a mortuary.

Often he had to work all night, because burials could not be delayed in the hot weather. She wondered how Morris endured the depressing atmosphere of the place, and this constant association with death. He seemed to have immured himself to it: to have acquired an undertaker's professional imperturbability.

Only once had she seen him disturbed and horror stricken. That was the night when Sally had been sitting with him a while and he was finishing a coffin for a dead baby. The child had been brought to him, and was lying under a white cloth on the bench.

'Just wait until I've fixed up this poor little brat, and I'll walk home with you, Sally,' he said.

As he put the baby in its coffin, he uttered a cry of dismay. The sweat dripped from his face.

'It opened its eyes,' he exclaimed hoarsely.

'Don't be silly!' Sally went over to look at the baby, and saw its face quiver.

She lifted the child out of the coffin and held it while Morris brought a bottle of brandy from one of his cupboards. They bathed the baby in brandy, smacked it, breathed into it, and Morris ran for the doctor. The baby lived for a few minutes, but died before the doctor arrived.

It was a nerve-wracking experience; but that baby made him the most cautious undertaker on the fields, Morris said. Never again would he risk burying anybody alive, man, woman or child. He could joke about the fright he had got afterwards; but Sally was sick for days, remembering how she had tried to fan the flame of life flickering in that tiny body.

Kalgoorlie had its great day when the first train steamed into the splendid new railway station. There was a good deal of heart-burning and back-biting, to be sure, as to who should have been, and who should not have been, invited to the celebration banquet which lasted until midnight. It was much more an official and big-wigs' party than the dinner at Coolgardie had been. Alf Brierly, as a mine manager, was invited to attend, but not Sam Mullet or Blunt Pick, who were pioneer prospectors of the district.

There had been no social distinction on Hannans in the early days. Every man stood on his merits, and the women, miners' wives and the wives of storekeepers and publicans, foregathered occasionally for a sports meeting or party without any thought of personal importance. To maintain some sort of friendly relationship in their isolation was the chief purpose of all and sundry in those days.

A man might be a down-and-out prospector one morning and a millionaire the next, and new comers were pleased to be admitted to the free and easy camaraderie of the fields. Few men cared to be known as Mister when all men were scouring the country, going dirty, bearded, and often short of a feed, for the same reason. Men addressed each other by their christian names or nicknames, with a bloody or two thrown in as a mark of affection.

But with buying-up of the mining leases by English, foreign and Eastern States companies, and flooding of the field by financial magnates and their agents, speculators and spielers of all sorts, the hail-fellow-well-met, go-as-you-please social relationship changed. In the hotels the wealthy strangers demanded the best of everything. They had to be waited on and given a good impression of the resources of the town. The interests they represented had to be considered. Mine owners and mine managers drew together to see that they were. Miners and working prospectors held aloof from the big bugs, realizing a difference in their interests.

This difference had always existed, no doubt; but in the rough and tumble of the search for gold, when men had to depend on each other as mates on long prospecting trips into the unknown wilderness of grey scrub and stark ridges, English lords and foreign notabilities had been glad enough to forget any claim to superiority. They had hob-nobbed, gratefully, and roughed it with miners and prospectors then.

Dinny remembered when Lord Salisbury, in moleskins and a dirty shirt, had worked like any other prospector, and jumped up on a barrel sometimes to have a word at a roll-up. Lord Henry Lock, too, he said, had boiled his own billy and shovelled a bit of dirt.

When Kalgoorlie became a flourishing centre for mining investment and speculation, however, the conflicting interests of the mine owners and mine managers and those of the mine workers and prospectors, grew more apparent. There had been strikes on the first Boulder mines and the working miners were still struggling for better working conditions and higher pay.

The great railway dinner marked the cleavage of these interests. While the mine owners and government officials, bank managers and distinguished visitors feasted and swilled champagne, toasting the prosperity of the town, the miners and many of the old prospectors excluded from the banquet shrugged their shoulders and laughed: 'Where'd they've been without us?'

Celebrations in honour of the railway had subsided and everybody who could afford to had gone off to the coast for the summer, when Alf went down with typhoid. He had insisted on going to the hospital where a new matron and doctor were installed, for fear of leaving any infection about his own house. His chief concern was to keep Laura from knowing about his illness and worrying about it.

Dinny was demented with anxiety: plagued the hospital authorities to give Alf a tent to himself and insisted on his having all the comfort and attention that money could buy. He, himself, sat with Alf, watched over him, fanning the flies away and hosing the tent to keep it cool. The hospital was full of fever patients, as usual, and the doctor and nurses relieved to have anybody who would help with the necessary jobs. Dinny nursed Alf under their direction, and as soon as he was well enough, took him home and looked after him there.

Sally's second baby was born that summer: a solid, sturdy boy. more like Morris than Dick. In her own home, with a doctor in attendance, Sally found Tom's birth was not such an ordeal as Dick's had been. She suckled him proudly for three months, then had to fall back on goat's milk; but by that time the summer was over.

Kalgoorla had appeared again a few weeks before Tom was born. As a matter of course, she took charge of Dick and set about doing all her old chores. Marie Robillard was a godsend, too, coming to cook meals for the boarders and take Mrs. Molloy's place when she had to go home and attend to her own family. Theresa Molloy, herself, was going to have another child, treating the event as a great joke, and wondering when she was going to cease adding to the population of the fields.

'Reckon I've done my bit, dearie,' she said. 'Don't you? Jest about time I went on strike. The worst of it is, Ted says I start havin' a baby if he hangs his pants on the end of the bed, so what can you do about it?'

When Laura came back, she was upset to find that Alf had not weathered the summer as well as she. He was as thin as a rake, still weak after his bout of typhoid, and not fit to be working again, she said. Why had nobody told her when Alf was down with the fever?

Laura looked very smart and pretty in the frocks and hats she had bought in Perth. She was concerned about getting fat and tucked herself into long, tight corsets which Alf said was absurd. He liked her plump, she explained contentedly. All the same, she wished she could keep her figure as Sally did. With two children, Mrs. Gough still looked slight and girlish, though her hands were rough and work-worn.

She had had a marvellous time, down south, this summer, Laura said. The Honourable Margaret Summers had been very kind: taken her to the races and parties at Government House. She had been able to leave Aimée with friends where she was staying and go out a good deal. It was surprising how many people were in Perth for the summer: the Brookmans and Zeb Lane, Lord Percy—and, of all people, Frisco, who was Mr. Francisco de Morfé now, if you please, and a great swell.

The Hon. Margaret Summers had come to the fields with her husband, who was buying for a syndicate. She had taken quite a fancy to Laura, it seemed: thought it was a tragedy for so charming a girl to be living in such a god-forsaken hole as Kalgoorlie. Alf was annoyed with the way the Hon. Margaret took possession of, flattered and patronized Laura; but he had to be civil to her. Her husband was one of the directors of the Midas Goldmining Company and had come out to inspect the mine. The Hon. Margaret was really master in that partnership, though, a wealthy woman in her own right, and a shrewd speculator in mining properties.

Kalgoorlie was booming. All along the ridge from Mount Charlotte to the far end where it dipped into Hannans Lake, mines were working. There were nearly five miles of workings and round about the Boulder township a square mile of mines. The richest square mile of golden ground in the world, the boomsters were saying. The Golden Mile, they called it.

The railway could not cope with the traffic and transport required to feed the mines with plant and machinery of all sorts. Horse teams, camel teams and donkey teams still hauled stores of gear from Esperance and Southern Cross. They thronged the streets, discharging burdens and loading up for outlying camps. Menzies, Broad Arrow, Kanowna were all flourishing and attracted the interest of foreign speculators. They used Kalgoorlie as a centre for investigations further afield.

At the same time there was a tremendous growth of wild-cat schemes. The demand for mining leases increased. Ground in the vicinity of Kalgoorlie, without the sign of a reef or lode, was as easy to dispose of at fancy figures as properties with actual gold values. 'Salting' was not necessary even, and important men lent their names to companies floating blocks or leases on which not a tap of work had been done or a pennyweight of gold found. Reputations were at a discount. Scribes calling themselves mining experts cropped up everywhere, prepared to write glowing reports of any mining property for a fee of £30. Some of these men, who tacked M.E. on to their names, did not know one kind of rock from another.

'We used to say there was the "lie," positive,' Dinny said. 'The comparative of the word was liar, and the superlative, mining expert.'

But genuine prospectors and decent mine managers did not stoop to this form of robbery. They maintained there was enough gold on the field for sound development. Men like Alf Brierly feared that wild cats and mad speculation would sooner or later bring the Kalgoorlie mines into bad odour, and destroy the growing importance and prosperity of the town.

Alf was an important man these days, dashing about with mine owners and mining magnates; but he looked care-worn and worried. Laura complained that he worked too hard on the mine, and was out almost every night at meetings of the hospital board, the race club, or the committee which was trying to make the town council clean up brothels and shypoo dens behind the main streets and improve the sanitary arrangements of the township.

To be sure, she and Alf went out a good deal. They were invited to dinner parties and luncheons on the mines to celebrate the installation of a new battery, or a change of ownership: met distinguished foreign visitors and entertained them sometimes in their own home.

Sally and Morris were not invited to these parties of the mine managers and their wives. They remained somewhere on the outer fringe of this select society of the fields. Morris, of course, had been a working miner: was the local undertaker now, and Sally kept a boarding house for miners. Morris smiled as Laura described some of the functions she had attended. Sally minded Aimée when Laura and Alf were going to a dinner party.

'It's too bad you're not coming too, dear,' Laura exclaimed when Zeb Lane was giving a dinner to the Summers. 'Mr. Lane always does things in style, and the Summers are charming people, really.'

'Morris and I know our place,' Sally remarked.

'Nonsense,' Laura laughed. 'Everybody knows you've got more social position than most of us, if it comes to that. But, you know, you always refuse when I ask you to dinner, and want you to meet these people.'

To old mates Alf was as genial as ever. Stopped for a word and shouted them a drink when he ran across them unexpectedly. At the sight of Dinny his eyes would light up and his thin, tired face break into a glad, boyish smile.

'Where the blazes have you been, and what the hell've you been doing, you old devil?' he could cry. 'God, it's good to see you, Dinny. Come and have tucker with us this evening. The missus'll be pleased and there'll be a couple of bottles in the cool-safe.'

With Morris, too, Alf was on the same easy friendly terms as ever. On week days Alf might be just part of the working machinery of the Midas Goldmining Company; but on Sundays, sometimes after the rains, he and Morris would go off duck shooting; or to see if they could bring down a scrub turkey in open country out towards Mount Hope, which stood as if it had been dipped in a blue bag, against the horizon.

But, with the growth of the mining industry, new ways and ideas were taking charge. Mines had changed hands. New managers were being installed: men with engineering experiences and technical qualifications, from all parts of the world. The old type of managers, who had acquired all their knowledge of mine management from work on the field, were being shoved aside: becoming a drug on the market. That was the fate Alf feared if the Midas were sold and he found himself looking for a job again. Meanwhile, he put all his energy into proving his value as a man whose experience produced practical results.

Laura's enjoyment of social amenities with the managerial set did not make any difference to her friendship with Sally at first. Often in the afternoon she went to see Sally and tell her all about them. Aimée was toddling then, and loved these excursions to the long verandah where she could sit and play with another child. Dick and she fought and played together hilariously. With another baby on her hands, Sally found it difficult to visit anybody herself, although Tom was a good child, easier to rear than Dick had been. Marie came nearly every day to take him for a walk, and sometimes Mrs. Molloy trundled along for a gossip and cup of tea, bringing two or three children.

She was there one afternoon when Laura arrived, and very soon, by a slightly distant and patronizing manner, Laura managed to embarrass and dislodge Mrs. Molloy.

'How on earth can you stand that woman, Sally?' she asked

impatiently, after Mrs. Molloy had gone. 'She's so vulgar and familiar.'

'I like her that way,' Sally said quietly. 'In fact, I'm very fond of her.' She was doing some mending, and stitched deliberately to restrain her annoyance.

'I know she's kindness and good nature itself,' Laura confessed. 'And of course I want to be friendly with everybody up here. But Mrs. Molloy is rather a trial. The other day, when Mrs. Summers was having tea with me, she burst into the sitting-room. Just shouted: "Is anybody at home?" walked in and sat down.'

'Custom of the country,' Sally murmured.

'She had come to apologize about her goats breaking into the garden and eating all those cabbages Alf's been watching so tenderly,' Laura went on. 'But the way she did it! Swearing and laughing, and spluttering, and spreading herself all over the sofa.

' "Those bloody goats'll be the death of me! Soon as I see where they'd got to I sent the kids down to drive 'em away, but it was too late and I was that upset, Mrs. Brierly, the way I am too, expectin' any minute, as you may say. I had to come at once, and tell you how sorry I am the little bastards have et up the Boss's cabbages. It's a god-damn shame, that's what it is, and I give Perthy a good 'iding for letting 'em out of his sight. I could've cried when he told me them bloody goats had et up the Boss's cabbages after all the trouble he's took to grow 'em." '

'The poor thing!' Sally exclaimed sympathetically.

'That's all very well,' Laura protested. 'But as Mrs. Summers said: "There's a time and a place for everything." And for a mountain of flesh to go rushing round like that when she's "expectin' any minute," as she says herself, it isn't decent, Sally. It really isn't. I had to make it clear to Mrs. Molloy I don't like people bursting into my house like that.'

'I must remember,' Sally smiled.

'Don't be absurd,' Laura exclaimed, 'that doesn't apply to you, Sally.'

'Well,' Sally reminded her, 'Mrs. Molloy is a good friend of mine. What on earth I would have done without her when Dick was born, I don't know, and I don't like you treating her like that, Laura. Please don't make her uncomfortable if she is here when you come to see me again.'

Laura was offended.

'If that's the way you feel about it,' she said, 'perhaps I had better not call so often.'

'Oh, my dear—' Sally put down her sewing, intending to smooth down Laura's ruffled feathers.

But Laura flounced out of the room. 'Come along, Aimée,' she called sharply. 'We're going home now.'

The child shrieked furiously at being torn from the game she was playing with Dick.

Sally watched Laura going down the garden path and along the track, carrying the child, still struggling and screaming. She was sorry for Laura, but angry, too; could not forgive her for snubbing Mrs. Molloy, and being so carried away by her own importance.

CHAPTER XLV

WHEN Mr. Francisco José de Morfé returned to Hannans with Lord Percy it was understood that Frisco Jo Murphy had ceased to exist.

Old mates chuckled in the pubs and round the camp fires about the metamorphosis. They had been impressed with Frisco Jo's rise to fame when local newspapers quoted the English press, giving Mr. Francisco de Morfé's views on the future of gold mining in Western Australia. Dinny, Sam Mullet and some of the others thought it even more of a joke when mine owners in Kalgoorlie began to regard Mr. Francisco de Morfé as an asset in London, and to refer to him with respect.

But old mates had no faults to find with Mr. de Morfé when he returned because he continued to display some of the late Frisco's most amiable qualities: was as generous and hail-fellow-well-met with them as ever; shouted all and sundry in the bars and sat round the camp fires, gossiping and turning over the news of the country, as he had always done. He even brought out his steel guitar and sang 'She was a good girl' to restore the atmosphere of the past.

To be sure, he looked different when he was getting round with English visitors and mine owners: more like an elder brother of his former self, preoccupied with weightier matters than had ever concerned Frisco Jo. Mr. de Morfé was always well dressed, too: had acquired the most elegant manners, an assurance and poise which even the English visitors could not equal. They were often like fish out of water on the goldfields, at a disadvantage trying to foregather with miners and prospectors: come to terms with them over the sale of a lease or inspection of mining properties.

266

But Frisco held his own with either crowd. He knew the world of the wealthy investors and the world of the prospectors and working miners: could speak the language of both. He was popular with the prospectors because they believed he was still sufficiently one of them to stand by them for a fair deal with overseas speculators. Frisco took care to reassure them on that score. And investors had confidence in him because they believed he knew all the tricks of the game: had his own interests to protect as well as theirs, and would prevent them from being deluded by brilliant prospects as Lord Fingall had been over the Londonderry deal.

There was no doubt Frisco worked hard to maintain his new reputation: shed his reckless and dashing ways: lived at the best hotel in town and made himself indispensable to the visitors. He arranged for them to visit outlying mining camps with all the comfort available: kept a pair of blood horses and a smart buggy to drive them about the mines, and a string of camels and Afghan drivers for trips further out.

Every train arriving from the south brought consignments of fresh fruit and foreign delicacies for Mr. de Morfé. The dinners Frisco gave at the Western Star became a topic. Mine managers and their wives accepted invitations to dine with Mr. de Morfé, not so much to meet the distinguished strangers as to enjoy the good food Frisco procured as if by magic. His dinners were luxurious feasts with soups and entrées served under French names, and wines for each course.

Foreign guests said Mr. de Morfé was a connoisseur of wine and food. It was rumoured that Mr. de Morfé superintended cooking of some of the dishes himself. Old mates declared they wouldn't put it past Frisco. He was a good cook, and fed the toffs like fighting cocks for reasons of his own, you could bet on that. Few visitors or local worthies, who had been subsisting for some time on the rough and ready fare of Kalgoorlie pubs, failed to appreciate an invitation to dine with Mr. de Morfé.

Despite his good dinners and champagne, however, some of the mine owners who had known Frisco before he went abroad were chary of doing business with him. There was a certain amount of jealous apprehension in their attitude. They resented the significance Frisco had managed to achieve in financial circles abroad. Because of that, they could not afford to ignore Mr. de Morfé. He had the confidence of an influential section of British and French investors, and what was needed at the moment was capital to exploit the resources of mines whose production was not being maintained at depth. Local proprietors did not forget, however, that Frisco Jo had not been too scrupulous as to how he made money in the past.

Disquieting rumours were rife about the exhaustion of rich oxidized ores on the Lake View and the Great Boulder. In fact on all mines in the Boulder area. The persistence of sulphide ores at from two hundred to three hundred feet did not reassure English directors. They imported American and South African managers to take charge of their properties; but although these men criticized wasteful methods of extraction, they did not immediately provide a solution to the problems connected with the economic treatment of sulphide ores. Collapse of the boom was being foreshadowed when telluride came to the rescue.

A. E. Holroyd, an Australian metallurgist, had first published the discovery of sulphide ore containing telluride of gold in 1896, although Octavius Watkins claimed to have discovered it a year earlier.

'Tellurium is an unimportant mineral from every point of view except the boomsters,' said some would-be authorities. But Mr. Modest Maryanski, the urbane Polish geologist, smiled at such a statement, and promised a long lease of prosperity to any field so rich in telluride.

Mr. de Morfé was backing Maryanski's forecast and boosting telluride: pointing out that the existence of telluride invariably indicated richness of stone and that, in some cases, ore which would go thirteen or fourteen ounces to the ton had been thrown out on the dumps as valueless. Mr. de Morfé's reports to his principals were likely to sway decisions of immense importance to the future of the field, mining men realized. In fact, de Morfé, despite past practices, was a man whose power had to be reckoned with.

Frisco was aware of this: as hard and ruthless in his business deals as any foreign speculator and more clear-sighted and confident than many. He had visited other goldfields on his trips abroad, Alaska and South Africa: was satisfied, he said, that there was more gold worth mining in Western Australia than anywhere in the world. He went on buying mines in which the rich lodes had petered out, floating companies to work them with modern machinery and up-to-date methods, installing new managers, and generally refusing to listen to croakers about an impending slump.

Alf and Laura had been Mr. de Morfé's guests on several occasions and he had visited them in their home. Sally was a little surprised that Frisco did not come to see her. Laura explained, one day, that Mr. de Morfé always inquired about her, very kindly, and asked to be remembered to her.

Sally's brows lifted.

'Does he really?'

Laura exclaimed, a little petulantly:

'Why don't you like him, Sally? You're as bad as Alf. It's as if you can't forgive Mr. de Morfé for being such a success, and knowing how to behave like a gentleman.'

Sally's eyes widened: a sly, enigmatic smile crept about her mouth.

'Perhaps,' she said.

She wondered whether one day Frisco would come, and the conflict between them begin again. It was possible that he would not. No doubt he had found plenty of women to make love to while he was away. Among Lord Percy's friends there were sure to be beautiful and charming young ladies who would not be indifferent to so good-looking and wealthy an admirer. Oh, yes, Sally persuaded herself, when months passed and Frisco had made no attempt to see her, it was obvious that Mr. de Morfé was as anxious to forget a brief embarrassing insanity as she was.

She heard a good deal about him from Mrs. Molloy and Marie. Theresa said: 'For the life of me I couldn't make out what in the name er blazes had struck Frisco, when his smart buggy pulled up at our place, and he told the boys to haul a case of apples from under the back seat.'

He had come into the house, sat down, drunk a cup of tea and yarned to Theresa about the old days, asking how this one and that one was getting on. 'As affable as never was,' according to Theresa.

' "And how's Mrs. Gough?" he asks, off-hand like,' she related. 'Don't mind tellin' you, dearie, I was a bit worried, one time, thinkin' Frisco had his eye on you, so thought I might as well let him know it was no use tryin' that game again.'

' "She's bloomin', now Morrey's back and she's got a home of her own," ses me.'

' "To say nothing of two children," ses he, laughin'.'

' "And another comin'," ses me.'

'Oh, Mrs. Molloy!' Sally flushed, perturbed in spite of herself, by the thought of being a topic for discussion with Frisco.

'Nothing to be ashamed of, dearie,' Theresa burbled on. 'You been showin' this last month or so, and Tom's eleven months old now.'

'But it's too soon,' Sally protested. 'I didn't want another baby so soon.'

'What we want, and what we got to put up with's never the same thing, love,' Theresa reminded her.

Marie, too, had talked of the reputation Frisco was making for himself, not only as a good sort among old friends, but as 'a great favourite with the ladies.'

'As for me, chèrie,' she cried, amused at the idea, 'I am not on the list of Mr. de Morfé's admirers. He is very agreeable, all the same. Brings to my Jean a bottle of good wine, sometimes, and likes to talk French with us; but the French, mon Dieu, of a vache espagnole.'

Marie had established herself as a dressmaker: made and altered frocks for the wives of several of the mine managers, and it was from the chatter of her customers she heard scraps of scandal about Mr. de Morfé and his lady friends.

Most of the men, Marie discovered, warned their wives that de Morfé was an adventurer and a blackguard. But he was the handsomest man in town, the women said, and if he was a blackguard, a very fascinating one. Few of them could resist his gifts of grapes and peaches in hot weather, or the deferential courtesy of his innumerable small services. Quite flattering when few men had the time or inclination for lovely attentions to their wives! Gold, the problems of production, and fluctuations of the share market, occupied the men most of the day and night. Women were expected to put up with boredom and discomfort; be entirely wrapped up in the financial interests of their husbands. Usually they were; but two or three young wives found the attentions of Mr. de Morfé a very pleasant diversion from domestic duty.

Laura among them, to Sally's amazement, although she could not believe that Laura was more than a little elated to drive with the great man, and be the recipient of his fruit and flowers.

Morris told her Frisco had asked them to dine with him, several times, but he had refused. Could not endure the idea of being patronized by Mr. de Morfé, and had excused himself on the grounds that Sally was not able to leave the children, and he did not accept invitations for dinner unless she could accompany him.

Frisco had roared with laughter at this explanation: bustled Morris into the Palace for a drink, and infuriated him by introducing him to some English business men as the Hon. Morris Fitz-Morris Gough, better known on the fields as Morrey Gough.

Frisco wanted to impress these strangers with the social standing of his friends, Morris said; and humiliate him by arousing their curiosity as to what he was doing in Kalgoorlie. It was so long since he had used that name, Morris felt it was an offence to drag his family into his affairs now. Sally hated Frisco for doing it.

But she forgot that when she opened the front door to see

Frisco standing there with a basket of fruit and the gay, impudent air of an impertinent prodigal.

'Hullo, Sally,' he said, 'you see I couldn't keep away. As a matter of fact, I've been aching for a sight of you. Have never caught a glimpse of you on the road or in town. Let me come in and talk for a while.'

'No,' Sally said firmly. 'I have nothing to say to you, Mr. de Morfé.'

'Don't be silly, Sally.' He pushed past her and put his basket on the table. 'People will wonder and gossip, if I don't pay you a visit. I've done the rounds, been to see the Brierlys and Molloys. Why shouldn't I come to see you?'

Sally was conscious of the old bewildering power this man exerted over her.

'Sit down,' she said quickly. And trying a little formal politeness: 'It's very kind of you to bring us the fruit. Morris told me you were being the fairy godfather to so many people.'

Frisco sat in one of her easy chairs and Sally seated herself on a stiff-backed one beside the table.

'You don't have to rub it in, Sally,' Frisco said with a wry smile. 'I've done what I said I would: showed you I could rise in the world, as they say. But it's not what I wanted, or the way I wanted it.'

'All the same, you're rather enjoying it.' Sally's voice was crisp and impersonal.

Frisco laughed.

'It's been fun playing the big mugs at their own game. I met Percy in London and he showed me round. I was just what he needed at the time, a man who'd made money on the fields and was a practical miner. We floated two or three mines, and he started the rumour I was the long-lost son of a French aristocrat. Found out the story went with my name—and it is my name as far as I know. So there I was, launched in London society with a pedigree and money to burn. What was there to do but make the most of 'em. I did, you bet, and Percy did, and we came back here as representatives of a syndicate that's got half a million to play with.'

'What are you going to do with it?' Sally asked.

'Buy up the Golden Mile,' Frisco cried gaily. 'That's a good name for the mines on the god damned dreary stretch of country round about the Boulder, isn't it?

'It tickled the imagination of the big men, anyhow. They put their money into our syndicate on the strength of it—though that's confidential, my dear. We don't want any leakage of information till the deal we're negotiating, at present, is fixed.'

He went on talking in a lazy, confidential way, taking Sally's interest for granted and making no attempt to pick up old threads.

'We may do some crook things on the fields, sometimes, Sally, but, God, they're nothing to what English company promoters are putting over the people. When I arrived in London I had some properties to offer buyers, for mates here. Put up at a flash hotel, got meself a decent turn-out, silk hat and kid gloves; went off in a four-wheeled growler with plans and specimens, to interview one of the big men. Showed the specimens on a piece of velvet and sold the Golden Cluster to Whitaker Wright for thirty thousand pounds, straight away.

'Then all sorts of sharks came round, offering me big money to write up a mine for 'em. One firm had bought a show on a bit of a salt bush flat. The vendor asked four thousand pounds for it and shares. Between ourselves, it wasn't worth four bob; but the firm requested the vendor to put his price up to ten thousand pounds, in order to give the public more confidence in the proposition. And you should've seen the prospectus they got out with a map showin' the Big Boulder, White Feather, Hannans and Bayley's Reward, all within a stone's-throw of each other—though the nearest of 'em was forty-five miles away at least. I told that bunch of rogues where to go and walked out on 'em.

'Percy introduced me to a mob of his friends, men with money and an interest in acquiring properties showing genuine values. We went to Paris: had a great time there, with wine, women and song thrown in, launched the Parisian Gold Mining Syndicate, and came out to do some more buying.'

When Tom cried, Sally went to his cradle, lifted him up and returned to her seat with the child in her arms. Then Dick wakened and came running in, all flushed and tousled from his afternoon sleep.

Frisco jumped up when he saw her with Tom in her arms and Dick clinging to her knees.

'Now you're thoroughly barricaded,' he said lightly. 'You're not afraid of me any more. But it doesn't make any difference to me, Sally. You're still the woman I want—more than all the others.'

He stood staring at her a moment: looking down through her eyes to the truth which lay at the bottom of their dark wells. There was still a flicker of that will-o'-the-wisp passion for him in the depths of her, Sally knew, and Frisco realized it. In that instant he seemed to claim her, mock her loyalty to Morris and the children, then thrust her aside, realizing she was pregnant.

He went off laughing in a way which made Sally's blood boil. How dared he laugh at her like that?

She wept with rage and grief when he had gone. It was so humiliating to have had to meet Frisco looking like a brood mare, and so work-worn and weary. How could he help hating her: being disgusted with her? And yet the magic between them had stirred again, giving Frisco his fleeting triumph, and Sally the memory of laughter that was like the lash of a whip.

CHAPTER XLVI

SALLY's third son was born early in December. Morris had made arrangements for her to go to the coast, and Marie Robillard was to have looked after Dick and Tom. But when it was time for Sally to go away, Dick had a touch of the dreaded summer diarrhoea and nothing would induce Sally to leave him.

'If I can't take the children with me, I won't go at all,' she said cantankerously.

Summer had swooped down on the fields with its scorching days, hot winds and whirling dust. Sally went about the work of her house, heavy and unwieldy with the burden of her child. She had never been so restless and irritable as she was just before Larry was born, she used to say.

'Never again,' she told Marie, desperately.

'But, Sally,' Marie expostulated, 'you are so lucky! Me, I would like many babies, and cannot have one.'

'That's all very well,' Sally said. 'But a baby a year's no joke. I've told Morris I'm not going to have any more—for a long time.'

'If you were a good Chinese wife, you would choose a concubine for your husband,' Marie laughed. 'But me, I would not be very 'appy with such an arrangement.'

'Why should a woman have to put up with a man's nature all the time?' Sally demanded, angrily. 'It's all very well when you're willing and want a baby. But when you're not, and already have two or three children, it's not fair for a husband to take advantage of marriage to be so—so overbearing.'

Marie understood that Sally was in some mental distress. They were fond of each other, but reticent; did not often exchange such personal confidences. Marie wondered whether Mr. de Morfé had something to do with Sally's unrest.

There had been gossip about Mrs. Gough and Frisco when

273

Morris was up north, Marie knew. She had heard it: could not believe Sally had been unfaithful to Morris; but it was not difficult to imagine Frisco's love-making had had some effect on her. Marie, herself, never took his whispered compliments and admiring glances seriously. But then he had never made love to her seriously, and she suspected there had been more than his usual philandering in Frisco's caring for Sally. She thought she understood what that look in his eyes meant when he spoke of Mrs. Gough, or her name was mentioned.

Despite her devotion to Morris and determination to do her duty by him, Marie guessed Sally was not indifferent to Mr. de Morfé. She looked like that woman in the legend who was haunted by the voice of a demon lover, longed to go to him, but baked the bread, brewed the beer, and bore the children of her good man. Marie wished her dear Sally were not so unsophisticated. So naïve and lovable, she was, for all her common sense and hardihood. Because of her honesty and simplicity, a sitting dove to a sharpshooter like Frisco. Marie wished she could cure Sally of any tendress for Mr. de Morfé. She tried by laughing at him and his attentions to various women in the town; his absurd swagger and new grandeur.

But her sweetness and sympathy helped Sally through those trying days before her baby was born. Kalgoorla had come, as usual, to do the housework, and Mrs. Molloy took charge of the birth. Marie cooked for the boarders and fussed happily when Sally's youngest son lay beside her.

Morris showed more interest in him than he had done in his other sons: chose his name, Lawrence, and decided that he was to be called Larry for short, after his own brother. Sally said she was getting so used to having babies that she could not be excited about this one. She was only glad when her discomfort and pain were over, and she could be up and move about freely again.

Dick was still sick and she was more anxious about him than the new baby. She was able to nurse Larry, and he was a fine healthy specimen, according to Mrs. Molloy, although not as heavy as Tom had been. Tom was her favourite of Sally's children and she lost no opportunity to let Sally know it. Perhaps, because Sally was so wrapped up in Dick, and Theresa thought Tom did not get his fair share of attention.

Morris still growled about the rooms Sally let to miners. He said she wore herself out cooking and washing for so many men, and 'the game wasn't worth the candle.' She would be glad to have the house to themselves, Sally assured Morris, when he had established himself in the undertaking business. But he had not yet been able to make an allowance for housekeeping expenses, and she felt too much indebted to Dinny to risk not being able to pay the rent regularly.

At first Morris had handed her two or three pounds a week. Latterly, sometimes he had forgotten to give her any money, or explained he had had a lot of expenses that week. Someone hadn't paid for a funeral and there were a lot of bad debts on his books. But Sally discovered he had been playing poker at the Western Star, at night sometimes, when she thought he was working, and that he had lost heavily in a recent fall of Associated stocks.

Morris said he had learnt his lesson: would not get into financial difficulties again by rash buying. But how could a man resist the chance of making easy money when the mines were booming? Who would have thought that rumours about petering out of the oxidized ores would have set in so quickly, and cause such havoc on the market?

Sally understood well enough the temptation to have a flutter on the Stock Exchange, or Open Call, when every man in town was gambling in shares; but with the children to think of, she could not risk losing her only means of providing for them. She was afraid to rely on Morris; must keep her boarders until his position was more assured, Sally told herself.

As she recovered her energy and good spirits, she was better able to look after her children and keep the house in order.

'You are so capable, darling,' Marie exclaimed. 'How on earth you get through so much work, I do not know!'

'Neither do I,' Sally replied.

Sometimes the children seemed to be all squalling at once, and a dust storm raging, when she had most to do. Now and then it swept all the clean clothes from the line and slammed them in the dirt, just after they had been washed. And often the whole house was deluged with red dust as soon as it had been swept and tidied. While Kalgoorla was with her, she could manage quite well, Sally said. Kalgoorla helped with the washing and ironing, scrubbed the floors and washed dishes. Sally dreaded the time when Kalgoorla would vanish with the first rains, and she would have everything to do.

The railway had increased the population of Kalgoorlie and the shortage of water was more acute than ever. But Mr. C. Y. O'Connor, the government engineer, had visited the town, and already Sally was dreaming of 'the river of pure water' Sir John Forrest, the premier, promised he 'would cause to flow through the goldfields.'

The danger of fires and fever had been increased also by the pressure of population. The hospital was filled and overflowing with fever patients. Fires were frequent and clanging of the fire bell a terror of summer nights. Blocks of shops and houses blazed and quickly fell into blackened ruins. There was little water to spare for putting out a fire, and a kerosene lamp accidentally knocked over had destroyed many a home, all the possessions of a family, and done thousands of pounds' worth of damage to business premises. Citizens were demanding a system of electric lighting to stop the destruction caused by 'the kerosene fiend.'

A few street lamps cast a feeble glow in the main thoroughfares, and better lighting of the streets and roads was becoming a necessity. There had been several cases of robbery and garrotting on the Boulder road, for which the riff-raff brought by the railway was blamed. But these civic improvements were held in abeyance by those disquieting rumours about the mines along the Golden Mile. Reports persisted that the gold in them was freakish, appearing and disappearing mysteriously, or giving way to low-grade ores of little value. Shares had fallen, although the prevailing tone was still one of optimism. Few mining men who knew the field could believe that the brilliant bubble of Kalgoorlie's prosperity was evaporating.

Mr. de Morfé laughed at the idea. He said that there was more gold on the field than had ever come out of it. Telluride was a guarantee for the future.

Sally and Marie gossiped over the news of the day as they sat on the verandah, during the hot, still evenings. Dinny was away prospecting somewhere beyond Kanowna, and they missed the yarns he could always be depended on to add to a verandah gossip.

Usually other men dropped in to see him when he was at home, and the women learnt more of what was happening in the countryside then than they did ordinarily. The miners who had rooms on the back verandah were quiet, sober men who went to their work and came from it, unobtrusively. If Dinny was there they would sit about, yarning with him on the verandah; but otherwise kept to their own quarters, knowing that was what Morris expected.

They had been indignant lately about the death of two of their mates on the Great Boulder. The men had been working at the hundred feet level, with dangerous ground overhead. Tons of earth came down on them. Both were killed.

'Men are cheap,' Pete McKay said gloomily, 'cheaper than timber.'

A few weeks later five men were killed by an explosion at the North End. Marie was always terrified when the mine whistle shrilled for a serious accident, because Jean was still working underground, though his cough was so bad he had promised not to go below if he could get any job on the surface in the new year.

Every woman whose man was a miner knew that pang of anguish when the mine whistle blew for an accident; ran to the gate, waited and watched anxiously until the ambulance passed. She never knew when it would stop before her, or one of her husband's mates come to break bad news.

But accidents on the mines were part of the normal life of the place. They cast a gloom over any conversation. Women avoided talking about them when they exchanged the scraps of news which stirred the monotony of their everyday lives.

Earlier in the year, the shooting of May Waine had been a topic. Jim Connelly was arrested for murder, and Sally knew Jim. He had often come to her bush dining-room, and she could not believe he intended to shoot the woman.

Jim Connelly was a kindly, good-natured bloke, the men said, but too fond of showing off what a good shot he was. Would pull out his revolver to shoot a blow-fly. May Waine kept what was supposed to be a cool drink shop on the Ninety Mile road, and Jim and Bob Reid had been on a bender when they pulled up there, one Sunday afternoon. They had a row with some 'Ghans about moving their camels, and Jim fired a few shots to make them move on. A bullet got May as she came to the door. Everybody was glad when he was acquitted, but Jim Connelly left the fields, overwhelmed with remorse to have been the cause of her death.

The murder of Tagh Mahomet, the wealthy Afghan merchant, in the mosque at Coolgardie, was a more cold-blooded affair. He had been stabbed by another Afghan, in the early morning, as he knelt at his prayers. For what reason was never known. Goulam Mahomet confessed proudly to what he had done, and went to his death like a man who had vindicated his honour.

Several months later the Mohammedan high priest, Hadji Moola Mirbon, an old man of nearly a hundred, died, and Afghans assembled from all over the country for his funeral ceremonies.

The funeral of a Japanese prostitute happened about the same time. Sally had watched it pass along the dusty road to the cemetery, wondering at the gaily-decked coffin and the Japanese women following it, like gaudy butterflies in their bright kimonos. Morris said the dead girl had been dressed in her best clothes, painted and adorned as if for a festival. Her friends had escorted her to her grave with shrill singing, a tinkling of silver bells and the chirping of eastern fiddles.

Such a commentary on their life, Sally thought: the sordid, wretched existence they led in the brothels behind the main streets. This girl had been killed in a brawl when the Frenchman who kept two or three Japanese prostitutes in an iron shack on one of the outlying camps, put up the price for admission. Her friends brought the body into Kalgoorlie and had arranged to bury it according to their national custom.

But these incidents, revealing as they did strange, sinister undercurrents in the life of the community, passed without leaving a ripple on the surface. The future of the mines and the fate of the city was concerning everybody, and pessimism growing. Many people who usually went to the coast for the hot weather that year remained to watch over their business interests, or because they could not afford to take a holiday.

Laura said Alf had promised to go away with her, but now he was worried about the mine and would not leave Kalgoorlie. She refused to go without him, though she had sent Aimée south for a month or two.

Looking across to the Boulder ridge, Sally often marvelled at the mines on which so much depended. Their poppet legs and sky shafts rose out of the sultry haze: surface works, machinery sheds, batteries and offices, roofed with corrugated iron, squatting against the bare red earth. The Croesus, Midas, Iron Duke, Hainault, Kalgurli, Australia, Great Boulder, Associated, Perseverance, Ivanhoe, Golden Horseshoe, Lake View and Star. There was magic in the names. Names which had made Kalgoorlie! And yet, there, like great beasts they grovelled, burrowing for miles beneath the surface, spewing out ore, feeding the batteries to produce gold. Gold that meant wealth and luxury for the mine owners; but not for the miners who hacked and tore it from the dark, tortuous workings underground.

It was amazing how this sprawling city of Kalgoorlie, and the new township of Boulder spreading out across the flat beneath the ridge, had grown to serve the mines. Tons of gold had come out of them: millions of pounds' worth of gold. You would have thought that the producers of so much wealth and power might have had impressive quarters: be surrounded by splendid buildings. But only a forest of poppet legs, drab and ramshackle sheds, marked the site of the richest mines, as if some poverty-stricken wretch had run them up in a hurry and trusted to luck that the next willy-willy would not blow them all away.

The life of Kalgoorlie now surged round the mines. Thousands of men and women depended for their existence on the sweating, toiling, hazardous industry which kept the mines in production, although alluvial miners continued to be an important factor in local prosperity. Mine owners were jealous of the rights of alluvial miners, and as the rumours of diminishing high-grade ores in some of the big mines continued to circulate, alluvial miners were being forced to protect their rights.

A meeting of alluvial diggers had been held to protest against the decision of Warden Hare that the manager of the Ivanhoe Venture lease was entitled to deprive men of the right to peg alluvial claims. Fear of the impending slump made miners and prospectors apprehensive of any interference with their alluvial rights.

But forebodings were thrust aside as Christmas approached. Everybody was looking forward to the two or three days' holiday which goldfields' folk had made the most of, since the first celebrations in the old camp at Coolgardie: shouting each other in the bars, foregathering at a big sports meeting, and finishing up with socials and dances which overflowed into the street in the early hours of the morning.

Sally, herself, was so busy making puddings and cakes, and preparing to feed all the men in her house over the holidays, she had no time to think of much else. Now and then, though, an anxious thought fluttered, and she wondered if disaster were really threatening Kalgoorlie, and what would happen if working miners lost their right to alluvial gold.

CHAPTER XLVII

Once or twice a week Marie persuaded Sally to let Kalgoorla mind the children, and to get away from the house for an hour or two.

They walked into Kalgoorlie to see whether any fresh fruit or vegetables had arrived by the train. This walk had become quite an important event. They dressed for it, carefully, and set out, usually in long white starched dresses with waists clipped by a neat belt, the gem hats, which were fashionable when they first came to the fields, perched on top of their heads, white cotton gloves, parasol and shopping basket indicating that they were sedate young matrons, in spite of their youthful appearance. Usually they promised themselves a cool drink at one of the fruit shops after their dusty walk, and that was the most exciting thing which could be expected to happen on one of these excursions.

Sally wanted to do some Christmas shopping, the afternoon Frisco passed in his spanking buggy with flash horses, going out to the mines. There was a big, fat foreigner in a light silk suit and black chimney-pot hat, sitting beside him.

'That is Monsieur Malon, the French millionaire, I suppose.' Marie said. 'Mr. de Morfé told Jean the other day that Malon was coming to inspect properties he 'ad been buying for the Parisian Gold Mining Company. And who do you think he 'as married, this so rich Monsieur Paul Malon, my dear?'

Sally could not imagine, and Marie chattered on:

'Why, Lili! You remember Lili—the girl who was singing that day when we visited Madame Marseilles?'

Sally smiled. 'We were lucky Morris and your husband never heard about it.'

'But yes!' Marie's eyes danced. 'It was very indiscreet. And poor Laura, she was so shocked. As for me, I found it very pleasant to talk to madame and Lili. If one did not know, one would not have guessed they were improper persons, Sally?'

'No.'

'What has 'appened to them all, those girls who were with Madame Marseilles, I wonder?' Marie mused. 'She promised to find them all good 'usbands.'

'Lili went away with Frisco, somebody told me,' Sally said.

'I remember,' Marie's eyes had their sympathetic raillery, 'but it is Mr. de Morfé we must say now, darling! And if Lili is Madame Malon, she has the bonne chance. It is not usual among the French bourgeoisie for a man's family to permit such a marriage. Perhaps we will meet her at Mr. de Morfé's party. La! La! it will be amusing to see some of our grandes dames meet Madame Malon!'

Frisco was giving a New Year's party. It was to be a gathering of all sorts and conditions of people in the best traditions of the goldfields, he said. He particularly wanted old timers to be present, and Morris had promised that he and Sally would go. Laura and Alf, the Robillards and the Molloys were going, too, and Marie had remade her own and Sally's old evening dress, since new ones were out of the question. She could not endure the idea of their being at a disadvantage among Frisco's smart friends, some of whom were sure to be there.

As they turned the corner by the new imposing Palace Hotel, into Hannan Street, Marie exclaimed as a buggy from the livery stables pulled up and a young woman alighted. Such a radiant vision in flowing skirts of pale blue sprigged muslin, with a blue ostrich feather flaunting from a small blue hat, that both Sally and Marie stopped automatically to gaze at her. The vision's fair, pretty face broke into smiles when she saw them. She rushed towards them, crying:

'But it is you, dear Madame Robillard, and you, Mrs. Gough! I am so 'appy to see you. It is Lili. You remember me? Yes! But now, I am Madame Malon, and 'ave the big fat pig of a 'usban'; but so rich and so kind. Ma foi, it is the miracle that 'as 'appen. And we are just arrive to buy gold mines. Quelle horreur, these days! I forget it could be so 'ot on the fields. You will come and 'ave a drink with me? Yes, and I will tell you how I am zis Madame Paul Malon.'

There was no resisting such a whirlwind of joyous excitement. Marie and Sally found themselves whisked into the hotel in the wake of Lili's billowing skirts and waving plume, upstairs, and into her private sitting-room. She subsided into a chair, still chattering gaily; but had forgotten to order the drinks, jumped up and ran back to the staircase calling Charley, the waiter.

Bells there were in this new, up-to-date hotel. Lili rang and called alternately, until the old waiter in a dirty white shirt bloused out over dingy professional black trousers, appeared with champagne and glasses. He had been quenching his thirst frequently, as was excusable on such a scorching day, and spilt half the wine when he opened the bottle.

Lili ordered another, and he went off mumbling about having to climb the stairs again, while she threw off her hat, drank to her guests and started immediately on the story of her adventures from the day she left the fields with Frisco, as if Sally and Marie were old friends dying to hear every detail.

There was no need for them to do more than exclaim, or murmur vaguely as Lili rattled on.

'But, no,' she cried dramatically, 'I did not go to Paris with Frisco, as everybody thinks. It is true 'e fix-up with madame to release me and we leave the fields together. But in Pert' we 'ave big quarrel and Frisco go away on 'is sailing ship. Me, I will not travel on zis dirty old tub, so I take passage by ze mail boat. Naturellement, Frisco give me the cheque, not so nice as I like. 'E is un peu stingy, zis Frisco! But I 'ave a good time on the boat. Oh, yes, and fall in love with a sous-officer: verry young, and be-yootiful in ze white and gold uniform. I weep much when we say adieu at Marseilles.'

Sally sipped her champagne warily. It was cold and refreshing: Lili's sitting-room with blinds down to shut out the glare, half dark, and degrees cooler than the atmosphere out of doors. She felt as if she had been wafted into another world, far from the bare, red earth with its breath of a furnace and the dirty, whitewashed and dust-raddled goldfields town, lying out there in the hot sunlight. Lili's room was furnished with big easy chairs. A cloying perfume of musk and roses drifted from her clothing, and her light gay voice went on and on with the tale of how she had met an old friend in Paris, and lived with him for a while. He had got her an engagement to sing and dance at a café chantant.

There was a clamour of women's voices on the stairs, a rustle of silk and starched petticoats, and Belle, Bertha and Nina rushed in. Lili flew to Bertha and was clasped to her great bosom. She threw her arms round the other girls: kissed and hugged them in turn, while everybody chattered, squealed and laughed delightedly.

Sally and Marie, a trifle embarrassed by this addition to the party, tried all the same to appear friendly and at ease.

'Oh, Madame Robillard and Mrs. Gough, how nice to see you again,' Belle greeted them affably. 'And on such an occasion. To welcome Lili and congratulate her on her good fortune.'

Lili was busy with the bell and calling Charley frantically. She ordered more champagne, and explained to the girls how she had met Madame Robillard and Mrs. Gough in the street. Was so delighted and excited to see them, that they had come up for a drink with her, and she had been telling them how she came to be Madame Paul Malon and such a thoroughly respectable person, enfin.

'Tell us! Tell us, Lili,' Belle and Nina cried.

So Lili went all over the story again.

'And then, one night, when I am so miserable with zis cochon of a Reval,' she explained, 'I see Frisco in the café, and we meet, and I tell 'im my troubles. "Hell, Lili," he says, "you must leave zis Reval." And I do, and Frisco tell me about his bizness, and how I can 'elp 'im to make some big man put money in a gold mining company.'

'Did you see anything of madame in Paris, Lili?' Belle asked.

'Madame Marseilles?' Lili's laughter skirled. 'But she is Madame d'Aunay now, you understand. Verry pious and respectable. Ze widow of a docteur who died in zis terrible Australie, helàs—but not before 'e 'ave made much money in gold mines and leave 'is pauvre Matilde a nice fortune.'

Bertha and Nina shrieked at the idea; but Belle was angry.

'The old bitch,' she cried, letting herself go. 'She knew I wanted to get a house of me own, and she always promised to let me have her place when she went away. But she sold it over our heads, and wanted to pass us over to that damned I-talian who said in the court the other day he'd bought a girl for sixty-five pounds. But Bertha and Nina came with me, and we're working together now. Times aren't what they were, though, Lili. The boys aren't as generous as they used to be. And there's a lot of toughs and spielers hangin' round the fields these days.'

'But Archie still says she's the finest woman in town,' Nina said slyly.

'Shut up,' Belle growled. 'Archie's got a wife and children to think of, and I don't want any scandal getting round about me and my place.'

Her eyes shifted uneasily to Sally and Marie.

'But we're all friends here, Belle,' Lili chirruped. 'We do not make the scandale.'

'And did the big man put money in Frisco's company, Lili?' Nina queried.

'Oui—dà,' Lili replied gaily. 'Frisco brought ce Monsieur Malon to see me at "Les 'Tites Folies" where I sing and dance. 'E laugh and laugh. Every night 'e come and laugh and make love to me. And I kiss ze bald head and tell 'im I adore 'im. because 'e is so fat and 'ave ze 'eart of gold. And 'e tell me 'e is so lonely since 'is wife die. So zere is an apartement—oh très élégant for la Lili, and Frisco is pleased because Monsieur Malon will put much money into ze Parisian Gold Mining Company.'

Lili paused to refill her glass. 'Voyons, we forget the wine,' she cried. 'Fill up, mes chères!' And continued in the same breath:

'Alors, my Paul, now is so jealouse, 'e does not wish me to sing and dance at ze café chantant. Me, I say I cannot give up my work. Some day 'e will leave me, and what then? D'ailleurs, I am the succès fou with my new song and dance! It is about ze little Coq aux Indes who came to ze farm in France and 'ave many affaires with ladies of the 'en-yard. Un peu mèchant mais très amusant. I am ce petit coq. I wear only ze bandeau of feathers and a big tail. Mais, attendez, I will show you.'

As she stripped off her dress, petticoat and long lacy drawers, Lili went on triumphantly:

'It was too much for my Paul. 'E was enragé! But yes. a madman. "Marry me," 'e say, "and sing and dance only for me, chèrie." And I say: "But willingly, mon chou," and so I am Madame Malon. The family Malon is furieux. But that does not matter. My Paul is ze big boss. 'E is 'appy with me, as never before, 'e tell everybody. And 'e pleases 'imself, sacré bleu!'

In a moment, Lili was standing in pink brocaded corsets and high-heeled shoes, stockings rolled round garters at her knees. Snatching the blue ostrich plume from her hat, she tucked it into the lacing of her corset. When she began to sing and dance, the blue plume sticking out from her plump buttocks nodded and waved provocatively. She strutted and pranced with irresistible gaminerie, demonstrating the antics which had captivated patrons of the 'Les Petites Folies,' and her Paul.

The party in the hotel sitting-room that afternoon was reduced almost to hysterics. Belle and Nina giggled and screamed helplessly. Marie laughed until the tears streamed down her face, and Sally laughed as she had never done in her life before, although she didn't understand the words of the song, or know quite why she was laughing. She felt a little dizzy but so light-hearted that she couldn't help laughing. Lili's capering seemed the funniest thing she had ever seen.

Belle looked as if she were going to have a fit, her big mouth was gaping and her blue eyes popping over the rolls of her fat red cheeks, when she gasped:

'Stop, Lili, stop! You'll be the death of me!'

And Nina cried:

'It's like when you used to do the can-can at Madame Marseilles, Lili.'

Lili dropped into a chair, breathless and wet with perspiration. She wanted more champagne, rang and called Charley. But Marie thought the party had lasted long enough. It was time she and Sally were going. She caught Sally's eye and they stood up, wondering if they had been drinking too much and whether they could walk straight.

'Oh, but you are not going?' Lili protested. 'Paul will come soon, and you must dine with us.'

Marie apologized gracefully: said she and Mrs. Gough had had a delightful afternoon. But they must go home and prepare a meal for their families. Already they were late. There would be angry men and hungry children clamouring for food if they delayed longer. Terrible scenes, in fact!

Lili kissed them energetically. No! No! She did not wish to be responsible for domestic infelicity, but she hoped they and their husbands and children would all dine with her and her Paul, some evening, soon. Sally and Marie extricated themselves from her embraces and walked to the door.

They found the staircase and went down it, clinging to each other: pulled themselves together to cross the lobby, hoping they would not meet anybody they knew. In the blinding glare of the street, they turned homewards, unsteadily, but with all the dignity they could muster. Not until they were a safe distance from the shops and passers by did they allow themselves to laugh over their escapade and slightly intoxicated condition.

'Oh, la! la!' Marie exclaimed, 'but life is not so dull on the goldfields after all, Sally. It is true, as Mr. de Morfé says: "Anything can happen here!" And we have been to a matinée at a café chantant.'

CHAPTER XLVIII

FRISCO's New Year's Eve party was never forgotten by those who were there. In the early days, these new year gatherings of all and sundry had been boisterous and care-free. Prejudices and conventions were forgotten in a go-as-you-please among miners and prospectors, store-keepers, their wives and daughters, barmaids and publicans, and the few mine managers or wealthy visitors who happened to be about. There was something in the air of the fields in those days which broke down social distinctions, people used to say.

The fact of the matter was, miners and prospectors were a law unto themselves then: the law that mattered most in the scattered camps cut off from the rest of the world, the unwritten law of the fields. And wealthy strangers, wandering aristocrats and mining magnates, who depended on the goodwill of the working miners and prospectors, knew it. They were glad to fraternize with these men who could make their way through the grey seas of scrub flowing beyond the horizon in every direction: men who could discover gold in the great red bluffs and stark ridges, hundreds of miles away.

Gold was the god everybody served. If a man was on gold, nobody bothered about his manners or who his father was. He might be a down-and-out prospector one day, and worth thousands the next, spending money like water. No, not water. Water always had an uncanny value in this country where men perished for the lack of it. So at Christmas and New Year miners and mine-owners, prospectors and prospective buyers of their luck, foregathered and enjoyed a common jollification.

But times had changed. The men who owned the mines were now on top and could make their own terms with the mine-owners and prospectors. As their interests diverged, the two groups had held aloof from each other. They did at Frisco's party, until the champagne, beer and whisky, flowing freely, broke down social barriers and his guests mingled in the sort of convivial orgy that had been held, all through the ages, at this time of the year.

Everything was quite formal and proper at first. The big dining-room at the Western Star where Frisco was staying had been cleared for dancing, the floor waxed and polished. Frisco had got together a brass band for the music, and drinks were on tap in the bar. Miners' and prospectors' wives sat on forms against the wall: some of them with babies in their arms and toddlers beside them. Their men hovered near, spruced up for the occasion.

Distinguished visitors, mine-managers and their wives, collected at the far end of the ballroom. Angora Davies, with his flowing white beard neatly brushed and combed, stood pompously among them. Paddy Cavan, in a new slop suit, his ginger hair slapped down with a cow's lick, fidgeted beside him. This was Paddy's first appearance at a social event of such importance, and everybody laughed at his planting himself among the swells.

Old friends thought Frisco wanted to intimate that he did not intend to turn them down because he had risen in the social scale: could associate with mine-owners and company promoters on equal terms. And his new friends thought de Morfé had put on this show to prove to them his good relations with all sections of the community.

These men had come to the party in swallow-tails and stiff shirts and the managers' wives wore evening dress. Several of them had been living in bungalows near the mines for some time. Mrs. Dowsett, a fat, fair woman with lovely shoulders, resplendent in mauve satin, bustled about vivaciously. The men used to say they would go anywhere to see Mrs. Dowsett's shoulders. And she made the most of them. Her dress was cut so low, on the night of Frisco's party, that her huge white bosom bulged over the top of her corsage.

Mrs. Archie Malleson's shabby gown of maroon silk revealed only yellow skin and bones. She was a tall, scraggy woman with buck teeth and a neighing laugh which could be heard everywhere as she chatted with Lord Percy, Charley de Rose, Dorrie Doolette, M. and Mme. Malon, or Frobisher of the North End.

Frobisher had brought his English wife, a beautiful girl, blue-eyed, buxom and golden haired. He was a great rough brute: had been living by himself near the mine, going about half-naked, with a bushranger's beard, until she arrived. He had shaved off the beard to meet his bride and become more civilized; but was madly jealous. Wouldn't leave her in the house when he went to work. She had to follow him and sit in the office all day until he was ready to go home. Mrs. Frobisher, in a white satin dress she might have worn for her wedding, was considered the belle of the ball, although she was so drunk before long that when her long golden hair tumbled down, Laura had to pin it up for her.

Lili, in black gauze, diamonds flashing in her ears, looked a demure and clinging little creature as she entered on the arm of her portly husband. She was not to revive old acquaintances, it was evident. M. Malon played the amiable dragon: did not move from her side and she did not dance.

Sally sent a smile towards her as she passed, dancing with Jean Robillard.

Lili bowed and smiled sweetly, one eyelid flickering in a sly wink.

Early in the evening the mine managers danced with their wives and with the wives of other mine-managers or local notabilities. The women kept to their own set, and Frisco went dodging about among them, dancing with one and another. Very dashing and gallant doing his duty as host, he danced with the miners' wives as well: took Mrs. Molloy for a polka and led out prim and shrewish little Mrs. Nesbit, in a high-necked, starched print dress, for a schottische.

Sally saw him dancing with Marie and Laura, and although she caught his glance now and then, he did not come near her. She danced with Morris and Alf and Jean Robillard, and Sam Mullet and Blunt Pick, as if she were very gay and excited by the unusual pleasure of being at a party.

There were not enough women to go round. Men from camps in the bush, who had come into town for a spree, hung round the door, staring hungry-eyed at the bare-shouldered women and the toffs hopping round with women in their arms. As free drinks emboldened them, they took the floor, dancing together in their dust-stained moleskins, rough dried shirts, old felt hats and hobnailed boots. The M.C. tried to chase them off. But Frisco shouted, with genial good humour:

'Come on, boys! Come on!' And, 'Let her go, Gallagher!' he called to the band.

The band blazed away conscientiously, and after a few rounds of drinks, just blazed, scarcely keeping track of a tune. Everybody was drunk before long, musicians and dancers, and the dancing went faster and more furiously. Frisco had sent for some of the girls from the brothels to provide his guests with more partners. They mingled with the throng, dancing with whoever seized them.

Archie Malleson could be seen cavorting with Belle, and little Bob Dowsett swinging Battleaxe Bertha in a riotous set of lancers. Their wives did not seem to mind. Mrs. Dowsett was making love to every man she danced with, one great white breast flopping out over the top of her dress. She pushed it back, but most of the time was unconscious of whether it was exposed or not. There was a howl of laughter when the M.C.

put a ring of white chalk round a pool.on the floor. And nearly a brawl when Mrs. Frobisher screamed: 'Somebody pinched my bottom!' Frobisher wanted to fight half a dozen men standing near her; but the crowd roared laughing, and Frisco took Frobisher off to the bar.

Morris had retired to the card-room with Lord Percy and some of the older mining men after the first two or three dances.

M. Malon removed Lili early in the evening, and Alf and Laura left when the roistering was in full swing. The heat and excitement were too much for Jean, Marie said. He had had a bad fit of coughing, so they, too, disappeared before supper.

Sally wished she had not come to Frisco's party. She was piqued because he had not asked her to dance, and angry with herself for feeling like that. As she sat by the wall, watching the riot of the dancing, she hoped Morris would come soon to take her home. It was humiliating to think she had worn her yellow satin dress and a Spanish comb in her hair to please Frisco, and he had taken no notice of her.

The last time she had worn them was at Government House, soon after she and Morris were married. But she had been young and attractive then, and now, although she was still in her twenties, she thought she must have lost any charm she ever possessed. It had been quite thrilling when Marie said, 'You look ravissante to-night, darrling!' Mr. de Morfé did not think so, apparently. Serve her right for letting him disturb her, Sally told herself. And she had forgotten her baby!

Tom McSweeney, the publican, had put his own bedroom at the disposal of mothers with young children, so Sally had left Larry asleep there, with half a dozen other babies, when she went down to the ballroom. The noise of the music, singing and dancing wakened the babies and they yelled lustily for awhile. One of the miners' wives had gone up to pacify them and was sitting asleep in a chair, beside the big bed on which the babies lay, when Sally went into the room.

She picked up Larry and took him out to the narrow balcony verandah to give him a drink. It was a hot, still night, with the stars dim in misty radiance of the sky. When Larry had ceased to suck and fallen asleep in her arms, Sally remained, sitting on the steps which led down to the yard, glad to have escaped the rowdy, drunken rampage downstairs.

Frisco found her there.

'Well, Sally,' he said, and sat down beside her, 'how do you like my party?'

'I don't like it,' Sally said.

288

Frisco laughed in the devilish way he had of delighting in her disapproval.

'That's because you're sober,' he said. 'We're the only people here to-night quite unhappily sober, Sally. That's one of the things I learnt abroad: to keep a clear head when others are drinking.'

'It's disgusting to see people lose all sense of decency,' Sally flared. 'Alf has taken Laura home.'

'Poor old Alf,' Frisco stretched lazily, 'he's lost his sense of humour. Takes his domestic responsibilities too seriously. Laura, now—she didn't want to go. Was rather enjoying herself. The fact of the matter is, my dear, I get on quite well with Laura.'

'For God's sake, leave Laura alone,' Sally begged. 'It would be the end of Alf if—'

'—if I tried to run away with Laura, as I did with you, eh? The trouble is, she'd come. And I don't really want to run away with her.'

'You're a blackguard,' Sally stormed. 'Just an unscrupulous blackguard.'

'Of course,' Frisco said, smiling into her eyes. 'That's why I make love to any good-looking woman who wants me to make love to her, even though she pretends she doesn't.'

'If you think—' Sally began, but he cut her short.

'You're a model of all the virtues, Sally,' he said, bitterly. 'I didn't dare even to dance with you to-night. Put that brat down and come back here for a moment. I've got some good news for you.'

Sally took Larry to the bedroom and laid him down on the bed again.

When she went back to the verandah, Frisco was standing against the railing, looking grave and gloomy.

'It's the last day of the old year, Sally,' he said. 'The last day of all the old years, for me, unless you'll change your mind.'

'I won't change my mind,' Sally said.

'Thought not.' Frisco's voice had taken a harsher note, despite his air of derisive banter. 'You haven't got the guts to. You'd rather grub along with Morrey to the end of your days than have anything to do with me and my love. Well, I'm cutting you out, too, my dear. I'm going to marry a beautiful bitch like Laura, or Betty Frobisher, raise a family, and be a great man in the financial world. It's so easy when you know how.'

'Is it?' Sally was holding herself on a tight rein. 'Just float a few wild cats, I suppose!'

'Wild cats or telluride, what does it matter to you?' Frisco taunted. 'I don't care how I make money if I can't have you, Sally.'

'Oh, I hate you, and all the men who talk like you do,' Sally cried, desperately. 'You don't care what happens to anybody else so long as you get what you want. But I've believed in you, Frisco. Thought you were different than you pretended to be. I wanted to show you I had the guts—but now, I don't want to. I want to love Morris, and be a good wife to him always.'

Suddenly she was weeping and his arms were round her. There was magic in his voice as he assuaged her pain and anger. The passion that flowed between them was too strong to be denied.

As they kissed, Sally was conscious of yielding to an infinite desire for this moment, and for the dissolution of her conflict with Frisco. It seemed that there was no resisting the spate of glorious madness which swept her. A guffaw startled her. Looking down, she saw the moon-white faces of men in the yard. Frisco drew her back into the shadow of the verandah.

Pandemonium was raging in the ballroom. It was nearly midnight. His guests were howling for Frisco. 'Frisco! Frisco!' They yelled and shouted. There was a surge to the stairs.

'Where is he, the bastard?'

'With a dame on the balcony!'

'It's no time to be canoodlin' when old mates are celebratin'!'

'Bring him along, the damned old renegger!'

'Ye'd better go down, Mr. de Morfé.' It was Tim McSweeney standing in the doorway to the verandah. 'They're after comin' to fetch ye.'

Frisco cursed beneath his breath.

'Right, Tim,' he called. 'Hold 'em. I'll be there right away.'

'Stay here,' he whispered to Sally. 'You can't leave me now, my love.'

When he had gone, Sally heard the riotous chorus of 'Auld Lang Syne,' and the romping gallop of scores of feet stampeding round the ballroom. A shrilling of mine whistles and banging of kerosene tins greeted the new year from the township. Sally sat dazed and oblivious to everything except the fury and exhilaration of the passion for Frisco which possessed her. Then through the din downstairs she caught the frail cry of a baby. With a gasp of dismay she realized that it was her baby, crying, and horror overwhelmed her.

She ran along to the room where she had left Larry, picked him up and fled down the steps into the backyard of the hotel and out on to the road.

Walking along the road in the silvery waning light, carrying her baby, Sally could scarcely believe that she had been on the brink of abandoning herself to Frisco's love-making. The thought appalled her. With a baby by one man still on the breast, how could she let another man be her lover? It would have been shameful. Never again could she have held up her head: had any respect for herself.

But it was the irony of circumstances that had saved her, not any strength of mind, she realized. She could never explain her passion for Frisco to herself: was ashamed of it. Never intended to let it run away with her, or interfere with her devotion to Morris. But there it was, something she would always have to fight and be on her guard against—though this would be the end as far as Frisco was concerned. He would never forgive her for having failed him to-night.

But Sally was glad she had not broken faith with herself or the way of life to which she was committed: Morris and the children, and providing for them. That was the job she had undertaken to do. Did she love Frisco? No! No! Sally told herself. It was Morris and the children she loved and must hold to. She felt free of the crazy desire to lose herself in Frisco's arms now. Free, and at peace, with a sense of reprieve from disaster.

The shabby iron, wood and hessian houses, whitewashed, rusty, dust-raddled, and looking as if they were made of cards stacked together as they spread out over the flat below the ridge and workings of the mines, were transformed: mysteriously beautiful in the wan silver light. The moon had a rainbow nimbus.

Trampling of the stamps vibrated through the night air, reminding her of the grim, sordid struggle for existence which never ceased: the days of toil which would stretch across the year, all the years, for people like herself, bound to it. The mining industry might make wealth and power for a few men and women, but the many would always be smashed and battered beneath its giant treads, as the batteries were breaking stone, to-night. She could not escape from her place beneath those treads, Sally knew, though for a few moments she had forgotten that with Frisco.

CHAPTER XLIX

Dinny came in from Kanowna while the Ivanhoe trouble was brewing.

He had been prospecting to the south-east when reports of

alluvial won on claims near the cemetery reserve at Kanowna drew a swarm of diggers. The bed of an old creek ran under the cemetery, and it was from this wash dirt the gold was coming. Diggers demanded throwing open of the reserve, and ten acres were made available; but the ground had to be re-surveyed and the scattered graves protected.

A rumour got round that pegging would be legal at midnight on a certain date. In the darkness, by the flickering light of candles and lanterns, hundreds of prospectors rushed the ground, measured off and pegged. But in the morning a telegram from the Minister of Mines announced that pegging would not be lawful until half-past two that day, so pegs had to be drawn.

Three thousand men lined up to wait for the sergeant of police who was to open the reserve. When he rode into the cemetery and stood with a watch in one hand and a white handkerchief in the other, there was a breathless silence. Dropping of this handkerchief was to be the signal for action.

Diggers broke through the fence, at the same instant, in the wildest stampede. Claims were pegged and over-pegged. Fists and picks flew: dust and oaths whirled in fierce brawls everywhere, as attempts were made to mark off a claim. There were a dozen claimants for almost every block pegged. The Warden's Court sat for three weeks dealing with disputes about the ownership of these claims.

Dinny and his mate reckoned they had been done out of a good block by a shark for one of the syndicates who found fault with their pegs.

'I'll swear me pegs was reg'lation, Morrey,' Dinny mourned, 'though I've scratched out the angles of a claim and pegged with twigs in me day. But times is changed. There's a different mob on the fields now than there was in the early days. You never saw such a murderous gang as got goin' in the cemetery rush. A man was lucky to get out of it with whole bones, and in nearly every case the Warden gave a verdict to some bloke workin' for a syndicate.'

' "The freedom and safety of a State," says Socrates,' Dinny's mate muttered, ' "consists in the impartial elocution of the laws. When the laws are otherwise elocuted, magistrates are held up to contempt!" '

He was a big quiet man with bowed shoulders, beard and hair almost as white as Angora Davies's, but not old, this mate Dinny had picked up on a prospecting trip out near Lake Yindargoorla. In the fifties, he might be, perhaps, but he was as tough and strong as a bullock, Dinny said. Could do a day's work with any man, Chris, though he was not fond of hard work. Christopher

Crowe, he called himself, but was generally known as Dinny's old Crow. Chris seemed to be always wrapped in a gloomy thoughtfulness, rarely spoke, and then, as a rule, only to quote some poet or philosopher.

Dinny had found him living by himself in a humpy of bag and tin, far out in the bush, just keeping body and soul together by fossicking on the dumps of a deserted rush, and swapping a few weights of gold for flour, sugar and tea when he went into Kanowna.

'There he was,' Dinny said, 'livin' like an old hatter, miles from anywhere, with a few pets, when Barney and me came across him. We'd struck a bit of alluvial near the lake and were cleanin' it up; used to stroll along to see Chris sometimes. He'd tamed some birds, a couple of doves, a butcher-bird, a few lizards and one of these little horney mountain devils. Mingari, the blacks call 'em. Ugly as sin they are, and change colour wherever you put 'em. Chris used to have all his animals drinking out of one dish, and the devil'd crawl all over him.

'One day the butcher-bird made a swipe at the devil and nearly killed him. Chris set a trap for the butcher. Caught him and plucked all the feathers off of his neck.

' "If you see a butcher-bird flyin' round with only a tuft of feathers on his head," he ses to us one day, "have nothing to do with him. He's a rogue." And quotes a bit of Latin to prove it.

'Barney thought he was gone in the upper storey, but I reck'n he's got more there, Chris, than most of us. When Barney got the dysentery so bad he couldn't stand, we made a stretcher, and Chris helped me carry him into Kanowna. It was near on fifty miles. God, I was glad he was with me when Barney passed out. It fair broke me up for a while. Chris has stuck to me ever since.'

Dinny's room was always ready for him, and Sally said Dinny's mate was welcome to a shakedown in the bunkhouse in the yard. She had had this built to provide extra accommodation for boarders when Morris was ill. So Chris hovered about the place for a few days, following Dinny, or sat on the verandah talking to himself.

Morris discovered that he was reciting Greek verse sometimes, and Sally heard him making speeches about citizens and democracy. But Chris never talked of himself, where he came from, or why he had come to the goldfields. Dinny said all he knew was that Chris had been a bit of a radical in the old country, and been driven out of some university for expressing his opinions too freely. Often he went on, when they were sitting beside the camp fire in the evening, as if he were arguing and discussing things with old friends of his. One night he introduced them to Dinny.

'Mr. William Morris, Mr. Hyndman and Mr. Frederick Engels,' he said. 'Mr. Denis Quin!'

'Pleased to meet y'r!' Dinny said, bowing to the ghosts round the camp fire. But Dinny was concerned about what was happening on the Ivanhoe Venture Lease.

'What's the strong of it, Morrey?' he asked as soon as he had given the news of the cemetery rush and introduced Chris.

'Some of the boys got wind of alluvial on the Ivanhoe Venture,' Morris said. 'They made up their minds to peg alluvial claims: asked the manager to define his reef so as they could comply with provisions of the 'ninety-five Mines Regulation Act. Carlisle pointed to the four corners of the Syndicate's lease. "Everything within those four pegs is lode matter," he said. The boys laughed at him.'

'You bet they did.' Dinny grinned. 'We got the right to work alluvial gold to within fifty feet of the reef. Used to be twenty. Remember how sore Art Bayley was when he found the boys working up to his reef? Rode in for the Warden, but Finnerty knew what he was doin'. "Well, what's it to be, boys?" ses he. "D'y reckon twenty feet's a fair thing?" And we did—but the 'ninety-five regulations pushed us back to fifty.'

'Carlisle can't define his reef because he hasn't got one,' Morris said. 'He's working on deep alluvial. The men have pegged right up to his shaft. One party got a fifteen-ounce slug. Some of the men've been getting from fifty to sixty ounces a week.'

'They're within their rights,' Dinny declared. 'These John Bull companies are tryin' to buy up the country and do the alluvial miners out of their rights.'

'Carlisle's applied to the Warden for injunctions,' Morris said dryly. 'The alluvial diggers refused to quit: are going on working. Alluvial claims've been pegged on the Golden Key and Hannans Central. There's going to be a dust-up, Dinny. The mine-owners will move heaven and earth to smash the alluvial regulations, and according to Mr. de Morfé the government's behind them.

'But they can't do it,' Dinny declared. 'Look here.' He rummaged in the pockets of his coat and brought out a bundle of papers, picked out a scrap torn from the *Kalgoorlie Miner,* and read triumphantly:

' "It has been a principle on the goldfields of all the colonies that the alluvial gold, the easily obtained gold, is the property of the nomadic population who will get it out quickly and distribute it, while the reef or lode gold, entailing heavy expense and machinery, could be leased to the mining companies. Clause 36 of the Mining Act was framed to perpetuate that principle." '

'I know the Act,' Morris reminded him. 'It gives working miners the right to dig for alluvial within fifty feet of a reef.'

'The big investors are scared about what they call the dual title.' Morris sucked his pipe thoughtfully. 'They don't like the idea of any man with a miner's right being entitled to peg for alluvial when they hold a mining lease. They're saying the Act was framed before deep alluvial was discovered.'

'Me eye!' Dinny exclaimed wrathfully. 'We were workin' deep alluvial on Nannine, Lake Austin and the Gascoyne in 'ninety two. At Kanowna they're down more than a hundred feet now. On Hannans it's always been from surface scratchin' to anything from sixteen to thirty feet.'

'The member for the district is a shareholder in the Ivanhoe Venture Syndicate,' Morris observed. 'And hand in glove with Carlisle, so you can't put all the blame on Cockney stock jobbers.'

'Charley Moran?' Dinny swore. 'He'll be out on his ear at the next elections. The boys'll see to that. Harry Gregory puts the thing in a nutshell, and he's member for North Coolgardie. I've got another bit out of the *Miner* about what he's been sayin.'

He hunted through his papers, and produced another torn fragment of newsprint.

'Listen to this: "Are we going to allow large companies, holding possibly from seventy to a hundred acres in which alluvial gold may be found, to work a gutter, which may run through the property, under the present labour conditions for leases? Such a course would be antagonistic to all our old ideals, and I sincerely hope will never become law in this country. We have always looked upon alluvial gold as the heritage of the miner, and under the Mining Act the State has entered into a contract with him, and that contract should not be annulled except by the sanction of Parliament.

' "It is said that a dual title is inconsistent and frightens the capitalist, but if we allow the capitalist all he requires, mainly the fee simple after the expenditure of a certain sum, and no labour covenants, our wisest course would be to sell him the country and leave it to nigger labour." '

'I'm not denying that the alluvial diggers are right as the law stands.' Morris said slowly. 'And it's obvious overseas financiers and mining proprietaries are out to get a firmer grip of the resources of this country. What can you do about it? That's the question. The Warden's backing the Ivanhoe Venture.'

'Twelve months ago Warden Davis said in Kalgoorlie,' Dinny

295

declared indignantly, 'that he had to "administer the law according to instructions." '

'It was a feather that shows which way the wind's blowing.' Morris stuck to his point.

Dinny and Chris pegged an alluvial claim on the Ivanhoe Venture lease. Not so much because Dinny wanted to work that bit of ground, but because he could not bear to be out of this fight to defend the rights of alluvial miners.

The fat was in the fire when the Minister for Mines rushed through a regulation amending Section 103 of the Mining Act. This new regulation prohibited alluvial diggers from sinking below ten feet. Smouldering resentment at the Warden's support of the Ivanhoe Venture Syndicate blazed at such action by a Minister to defeat the claims of working men.

Alluvial diggers flocked to the Workers' Hall, headquarters of the Amalgamated Workers' Association in Boulder. Most of the older generation of prospectors knew the Mining Act and just what rights it conferred on them. They had to know it in order to protect their interests. The size of a man's pegs, or any failure to comply with working conditions, might entitle a jumper to deprive the prospector of his claim, and there were plenty of sharks working for the big companies who were on the look-out for any pretext to grab a promising show. This attack on the rights of alluvial diggers threatened the livelihood of thousands of men. It aroused a storm of indignation, the like of which had never been known on the fields.

The question of what was and what was not alluvial had been thrashed out on every camp. Gill Maitland, the government geologist, gave his verdict when he stated that the Ivanhoe Venture Lease held alluvial ground, and that alluvial gold was to be found at 114 feet.

The Minister said: 'It may be geologically alluvial, but that is not alluvial.'

The men laughed angrily at this quibble. 'Can y'r beat it?' they asked each other.

They understood by alluvial, any loose soil, earth, or rocky substance containing, or supposed to contain, gold not running in a lode or quartz vein. Cement was considered alluvial because it held free gold without lode or definite veins. Most of the diggers objected to the definition of gold found in seams as non-alluvial. Alluvial gold was usually associated with the action of water on mineral deposits in the dim ages. Water-worn pebbles had led to the pegging of alluvial claims on the Ivanhoe Lease.

The Ivanhoe Venture Lease had been recommended but not

yet granted. It was an alluvial flat which should never be granted as a reefing proposition, the diggers contended, or at least not until the alluvial had been worked out and there was some indications of a reef.

'It looks,' Dinny said, 'as if the company wants to grab the alluvial, and then float the show as a reef: swindle a few more poor mugs on the share market.'

On every goldfield in Australia, the diggers maintained, the right of working miners to prospect for alluvial gold had been recognized. In Victoria a lease was not granted for eleven years, and men were still working alluvial on it. In Queensland, after two years, a lease was granted if the alluvial was worked out, but the time could be extended if diggers were not satisfied the alluvial was exhausted.

The law all over Australia had been that land containing alluvial gold could not be leased until it became costly and difficult to work through great depth, wetness or some other natural cause. But on this youngest and richest field the people's birthright was being snatched from them by a state government of Swan River settlers and their supporters. Alluvial diggers of the West refused to submit to such barefaced repudiation of a national principle and the common right of working men throughout Australia.

That was the spirit behind the Alluvial Diggers' Rights Association which prepared to fight the Forrest government on this issue. It was the spirit of men who had prospected the fields, pioneered settlement of the far-flung mining camps, in this still only half-explored wilderness of mulga scrub and shingly ridges. These men had made possible establishment of the mining industry and thriving cities. Were they going to allow their fundamental rights to be filched from them in the interest of foreign speculators and a few political traitors?

Sally heard miners and alluvial diggers discussing every phase of the situation with Dinny. She understood their indignation: her sympathies were with them. She could not separate herself from this struggle in which they were involved. It seemed her struggle as much as theirs.

Frisco had laughed at her partisanship when he came to see her one morning, soon after the New Year's Eve party. But he had been angry, too: angry and resentful to find Sally had moved a long way from him since that night on the balcony. She would not let him touch her, or listen to his plans for a holiday at the coast. He was prepared for her to cart her children with her, he said; would take a cottage and behave with the utmost discretion.

There would be no expenses in connection with the trip. But Sally remained stubborn and aloof.

'I couldn't do it,' she said, quietly. 'Not only because of Morris and the children, but because of the people here. I stand with them and you don't.'

Frisco was furious that the question of alluvial rights should have had anything to do with her decision. He went away vowing no woman would ever again make a fool of him.

CHAPTER L

At a roll-up on the lease, a drag was used for the speakers to stand on. Mick Mannion had driven Frank Vosper and another member of parliament over in it, and the diggers gathered round, six or seven hundred of them, to discuss the situation.

It was a dull, sultry afternoon after a hot day. Light still played with a blinding glare over the wide flat below the Boulder ridge, and over whitewashed buildings of the town and workers' huts crouched against the earth. Here and there on the lease the crooked stick of a dead tree accentuated the dreary sun-blasted prospect of bare, red earth, dumps of mullock, windlasses over shafts and dust-raddled tents.

The temper of the men was as sultry as the late afternoon. There was not a doubt in anybody's mind as to the seriousness of the position. The diggers were angry: their anger smouldering under a sense of gross injustice. They knew well enough that they were up against powerful financial interests seeking to deprive them of rights which had been theirs ever since Australia was prospected.

They realized, too, that one of those conflicts lay before them in which there were going to be victims and perhaps loss of life. But their blood was up. The spirit of working men who had struggled against injustice and oppression all through the ages, burning in them, refused to consider any other course than resistance to those who would ride rough-shod over them in order to favour the rich and powerful.

There were men in the muster who had taken part in the great shearing strikes, a few years before, in Queensland and New South Wales. Men who remembered with rage and bitterness how the workers could be slugged into subservience, no matter how just their cause. There were men who remembered Eureka, and had stood behind the stockade when the government of the day sent troops to fire on the miners forced to rebel against its autocratic measures.

Talk of Eureka was in the air, and a sober realization of where this fight might lead. The men, it seemed, were ready for any action to preserve the conditions under which alluvial miners had worked in Western Australia. But the Alluvial Diggers' Rights Protection Association was discouraging all suggestions of violence, or any movement likely to prejudice legal aspects of the struggle.

Mick Mannion, president of the Association, made that clear when he spoke. He was voted to the chair and outlined the purpose of the meeting. A little whipper-snapper of a bloke, Dinny said, it was remarkable how Mick controlled the meeting. There was never any disorder when Mick was in the chair. He had a way with him when he was speaking. You could have heard a pin drop. He wasn't an orator like Frank Vosper at his best, or a fiery, rousing speaker like Charley McCarthy, or Mullocky O'Dwyer, giving the boys something to laugh about and making them crazy with enthusiasm for whatever he said. But he had a good head on him, Mick, and the men believed in him. They knew he had guts and brains and they trusted him to steer things in their interests.

Mick knew that, and he knew what he had to do if the alluvial men were to gain the support of the whole community for their cause.

'Legislation of the character of the Ten Foot Amendment,' he pointed out, 'led to trouble at Ballarat. The diggers of 1845 rebelled, and rightly, against injustice. But we are not lawbreakers but upholders of the law. The government of the day is the law-breaker. And it has made a law to defend its own law-breaking.'

The men broke into an angry bawl of agreement, but there was silence again when Mick raised his hand and went on:

'The Association has engaged the best authority on mining law available, and Mr. Jones is confident that the alluvial diggers can win on the merits of their case. But we've got to keep the fight orderly, boys. There's got to be no loose violence. Nothing would suit the Ivanhoe Syndicate better than to give the police an excuse for making arrests for disorderly conduct and destruction of property—or for any other reasons than the injunctions. Remember that! We've got to fight legally, because it's the Ivanhoe Syndicate, Warden Hare, and the government who have been acting illegally!'

A volley of groans, hoots and jeers for the Warden, Ten-Foot Ned and the government drowned his voice for a moment. Then

Mick said: 'Stand solid, boys! Keep the fight clean and we'll show the government, the mining magnates and all the big companies that they can't buy up this country. Not while the alluvial diggers are willing to defend their rights!'

'We'll stick to it, Mick,' the men shouted.

'You bet we will!'

'Let 'em give us a fair go!'

'That's all we want!'

Hand-clapping and cheers gave vent to the confidence and enthusiasm Mick's speech had aroused. When the applause subsided an old miner shouted:

'It's alright what Mick says, but if we want to keep the rights we've got on this field, we must be ready to fight for 'em like we did at Eureka.'

'We'll fight like they did at Eureka—if we've got to, Scotty,' somebody yelled.

A delegate from Kanowna spoke.

'Ten-Foot Ned may be a good judge of fat bacon and champagne,' he said. 'That's his job—but he doesn't know anything about mining. This "irregulation" of his will chase him and his ministry where they belong.'

'T'hell with 'em,' several men yelled.

'We made a scarecrow of him at Bulong and burnt it!'

'Pity it wasn't himself, begorra!'

'There's been a lot of talk about land reform lately,' the speaker continued, 'and the government's been making a song about it. Now it's aiding and abetting the London stock gamblers to get a monopoly of mineral leases. The worst kind of monopoly. We've got to stand shoulder to shoulder, boys, and see this fight through. I reckon it's best, as Mick says, to fight on the basis of the law, at this stage. If that fails—no need to forget we've got another card up our sleeve.'

The diggers laughed and applauded.

Then Frank Vosper stood up and was greeted with shouts of goodwill, a storm of hand-clapping and cheers. He was member for Kanowna in the Legislative Assembly now; but everybody knew he had supported the men in the Queensland shearing strikes, and suffered for it. His courage and championship of the workers could be depended on.

As he stood there on the drag in his parliamentary frock coat and black pants, the men knew he was one of them, though he looked more like 'a god-damned poet' with his flowing hair and fine intellectual face, Dinny said.

Vosper began by saying he was proud to be with the alluvial diggers in this struggle. In the opinion of the Association's legal adviser, the amendment was *ultra vires,* and Mr. Wittenoom, the Minister of Mines, exceeded his powers in having promulgated it.

'Alluvial mining would be absolutely doomed,' Vosper continued, 'if the alluvial miner is to be at the tender mercies of the lease-holder and the capitalist. The government geologist, Gill Maitland, had declared that auriferous dirt obtained at 128 feet was alluvial. The amendment had been passed after this statement.'

'Shame!'

'To hell with it.'

'Three groans for Ten-Foot Ned!'

The men hooted and groaned their anger and resentment.

'I did not come to inflame you,' Vosper declared, 'the government has done that!'

'Hear! Hear!'

'It's done that alright.'

'You bet it has!'

'Down with the Forrest government!'

The men's voices subsided and Vosper went on:

'But I want to advise you to go about this business of defending your rights in a quiet, orderly manner. Take up your claims, and if an order comes to leave them, do it. That need not hinder you from going back. When a policeman comes to shift you, be sure he is doing it under the law. But stand firm on your rights! If you do that, as you should, and are determined, this regulation will be swept away. The men of these goldfields will demonstrate that such a flagrant abuse of justice cannot be tolerated, and go on to organize so that all the wrongs suffered by the people of this vast territory will be removed!'

When the applause for Vosper had died down, Oldham, another member of parliament Vosper had brought with him, spoke. He said he was not a miner; but was satisfied from what he knew of this dispute that the alluvial diggers had a good case and must fight it on constitutional lines. Otherwise, he pointed out, the opposition would use any disorder, or violent resistance on the part of the diggers, to cloud the main issue.

The men were in no mood for passive resistance and fighting within the bonds of legal action, but a majority had been convinced by Mick Mannion and Vosper. They recognized that the strength of their position lay in the Goldfields Act, and the way in which the Warden and the government were trying to thwart its provisions by favouring the mining companies.

A resolution was put which became a declaration of rights for diggers on the goldfields of Western Australia.

It was carried with a thunderous chorus of ayes that startled the sleek, well-conditioned horses of troopers on the outskirts of the crowd. The troopers, too, were impressed by the forces held in leash by the diggers' organization. They were not looking forward to duty on the fields during the next few months, as they rode back to the police station in Kalgoorlie.

CHAPTER LI

THE manager's house on the Ivanhoe Venture lease, a bare cottage of galvanized iron, stood a little distance from the shaft, with a yard for his horses and a wind-break of bushes behind.

There was a whip over the shaft, and an old horse padded backwards and forwards all day in the blazing sun, hauling water from the depths of the mine. The main shaft was making seven thousand gallons a day, the men said. A good enough indication of what it was working on, though the dumps gave that away, too: big dumps of wash-dirt alongside the shaft which Carlisle had put a man on to guard from the alluvial diggers. Their claims spread out from the main shaft, with shafts, windlasses, dumps and pot-holes making the flat look as if a horde of boudie rats had taken possession of the ground.

Dinny said a hundred and fifty men were working on the lease the morning word got round that injunctions were to be served on five parties working below ten feet. At a roll up, a few nights before, the men had decided by a show of hands to go on working, and not to resist should there be an attempt to arrest any of them for refusing to obey the injunctions.

Everybody knew that police reinforcements had arrived from the south. But Mick Mannion warned the men not to be provoked. He reminded them that the Alluvial Diggers' Rights Association was going to fight on legal aspects of their case, and any violence at this stage of the struggle would prejudice their interests.

'Let's stick to it, boys,' Mick said. 'Show the government what a body of working men battling for their rights can do to maintain discipline. It's not going to be easy to keep our hands off the cops if they start arresting our mates—but we've got to do it. Not put ourselves in the wrong. Nothing would suit the Ivanhoe Syndicate better than a dust up with the police; but see they don't get it—and we'll win all along the line.'

Early in the afternoon, the bailiff, 'in a silk shirt and knickers,' Dinny said, came along and served his writs on five parties. He had to yell down the shafts and ask the men what they were working on, and usually got his answer: 'Twenty feet!'

The writ was lowered in a hide bucket, but the men went on working. Then the police arrived. Bill Bray and Pat Hughes were arrested. There were enough diggers on the lease to have given the police a bad time and they were sorely tempted. But Bill and Pat themselves kept their heads.

'It's alright, boys,' they said. 'We expected this. Don't get rattled. Stick together and keep things going, orderly, like Mick said.'

The police buggy drove off while the diggers stood watching, restless and agitated, itching to smash the buggy to matchwood and rescue their mates; but held back by Dinny and a few others who kept reminding them that this was the test of the decision they had made.

'It was a miracle,' Dinny said, 'how the boys managed to keep their hands off the troopers. Any moment they could've mobbed 'em and pulled their mates off the buggy. But Mick had made us understand that was just what would queer our pitch and play into the hands of the Syndicate.'

The men's rage boiled that night when they heard bail had been refused. Bill Bray and Pat Hughes were to spend the night within the stinking, sweltering walls of the lock-up. The diggers were ready to storm the lock-up and release their mates. It took all Mick Mannion's powers of persuasion, all the arguments he, Bob Gorry, Dinny and half a dozen others were capable of, to keep hundreds of angry men from demonstrating their power.

In the Warden's Court next morning, Bill Bray and Pat Hughes were sentenced.

'For what term?' Jones, their lawyer, inquired.

Warden Hare replied: 'There is no necessity for me to limit any time: when the defendant considers that the contempt is purged, he can apply to the Court for release.'

It was unheard of! Unbelievable! The men cursed and fretted. They could scarcely endure this outrage. Two of their mates had been given an indeterminate sentence, on the ground that their refusal to obey an unjust order of the Court, illegal in essence, constituted contempt of that Court. They could only be released by admitting the error of their ways and begging to be pardoned. That Bill Bray and Pat Hughes were to be removed to Fremantle gaol was the last straw to their anger and indignation.

When the news reached the Ivanhoe, the men knocked off work. They were in a dangerous mood as they stood round discussing their next move.

'We've got to hold 'em,' Dinny!' Mick Mannion said.

The suggestion of a procession to the railway station to see their mates off was hailed with enthusiasm. Alluvial diggers from the Golden Key lease joined the Ivanhoe men.

'Keep it orderly! Keep it orderly, boys!' Mick Mannion begged, hopping about like an old hen with a batch of chicks several sizes too large for her.

The men set out, marching three abreast, a digger on a brumby saddled with a bran bag, leading them. In their working clothes, sleeves rolled up, dilapidated felts slammed down on their heads, they marched five miles into the railway station, every now and then cheering for Bray and Hughes, breaking into a volley of hoots and groans for Blowfly Hare and Ten-Foot Ned. Diggers from other claims, fossickers and dry-blowers joined them all along the long, dusty road. They were over six hundred strong when they swung down Hannan Street, cheered by crowds in the street.

A buggy came down from the lock-up and turned towards the station. Two troopers were sitting on the front seat, Bill Bray and Pat Hughes behind them.

It seemed as if the procession would break up and mob the police buggy.

'Come on, boys, pull 'em off!' a hot-head called. But there were others who shouted him down. 'Shut up, you bloody fool! Stick to it, boys! Keep her orderly! Don't let 'em put us in the wrong!'

On the station, when hundreds of men milled round the carriage where Bill Bray and Pat Hughes were standing, it was touch and go several times as to whether the discipline the diggers had imposed on themselves would hold.

'God!' Dinny exclaimed, 'it was almost more than we could bear, lettin' the police get away with Bill and Pat. There was a riot brewing that afternoon if ever there was. And there'd have been plenty of broken heads if it'd started. The men were fighting mad, and just dyin' for the word to pull Pat and Bill off the train.'

'Pat and Bill, themselves, more than anything else stopped 'em. They kept sayin': "Steady, boys! We've got law and justice on our side. Don't do anything which will prejudice our cause. Anybody who acts reckless and violent will spoil all we're fighting for. We're not a lot of hooligans. We're honest, decent men, and we've got to show the government we can organize against injustice and any attempt to do the alluvial diggers on these fields out of their rights."'

The *Kalgoorlie Miner* pointed out next morning: 'The spectacle of a thousand diggers bidding farewell to two of their fellow workmen who had become the victims of an illegal act committed by the very person sworn to uphold the law, was a unique one, and we may say unparalleled in the history of any goldfields. No attempt at violence was shown: the men knew they had law and justice on their side and they were determined to set a good example to those who, regardless of consequences, had so recklessly set the very worst example.'

After the train left, the diggers surged to a meeting in the street, near the railway station.

'The first two of our mates have been sent below,' Bob Gorry said. 'If they lock up one, they'll have to lock up the lot of us. Others will take the place of every man arrested. We'll go on working alluvial ground on this field. And if it's contempt of court to refuse to obey the injunctions of Warden Hare's court, well, there are thirty thousand alluvial diggers they'll have to take proceedings against.'

There were cheers for Bill Bray and Pat Hughes. Several men volunteered to work their claims while they were in gaol. Hundreds shouted their willingness to stand by their mates as Bill Bray and Pat Hughes had done.

The crowd moved off to interview Mr. Moran, member for the district, and one of the principals in the Ivanhoe Syndicate. They pulled up outside his hotel, singing the song which Charley Moran usually sang at smoke socials and on convivial occasions:

'Oh, Molly Riley, Oh,
I love you.
Tell me, Molly Riley,
Does your heart beat true?'

The diggers called on Mr. Moran to come out and address his constituents. Moran refused.

Police tried to clear the streets, but local constables knew better than to interfere with the diggers that afternoon. Somebody had rigged up a guy which was supposed to be the Minister for Mines. It was hanged on a lamp-post in Maritana Street while the crowd roared approval.

Then the guy was set alight and burned. The tumult subsided in an hour or two. It was boisterous and uncontrollable while it lasted, a demonstration of mob madness no one dared to interfere with, but not destructive. No damage was done, except to the effigy of the Minister for Mines, Dinny said, and the outburst did the men good: gave them a chance to let off steam, and at the same time show the government what forces were seething beneath the Alluvial Diggers' Rights Association, and its policy of passive resistance.

Vosper went to see the men in Fremantle gaol.

After a while it was suggested, in ministerial circles, that Bray and Hughes had only to express regret for their action and apply to the Warden to be released immediately. Vosper reported to Mick Mannion that both men 'were prepared to regard it as a life sentence' rather than comply with such conditions.

Pat Hughes had said: 'To do so would be to admit that we were wrong and trying to rob the Venture Syndicate. On the contrary, we were the victims of an attempt to despoil us, and though we submit to force, we will not compromise ourselves by any retreat.'

'Let the government keep on filling the gaols,' Vosper wrote. 'They will soon be glutted by men suffering willingly and displaying courage and fortitude. The ministry cannot keep on making martyrs for ever.'

Diggers on the Ivanhoe Venture went on working their claims. Two others were arrested and imprisoned. Two men at Bulong, also, were sentenced and sent to gaol at Fremantle.

CHAPTER LII

DINNY and Alf quarrelled bitterly over the Ivanhoe trouble.

'You can't mean it, Alf,' Dinny exclaimed. 'You're not askin' me to believe because you're manager of the Midas you're goin' to support these blackguards havin' men arrested and gaoled for defending their rights?'

'The Act was framed before deep alluvial was found in the West,' Alf said.

'It's a lie,' Dinny declared. 'Deep alluvial was worked at Lake Austin and on Nannine in 'ninety-two. But that's got nothing to do with it. You know as well as I do alluvial's been recognized as poor man's gold on every field in the colonies. The alluvial miner's got a right to work alluvial gold. It's all very well to lease twenty-four acres for reefin' and goldmining with a big set-up of machinery and engineerin'. But what's goin' to happen if the big bugs can grab all the land like that and keep the alluvial men off of it? Old prospectors and alluvial diggers are goin' to be starved off the fields, and you know it.'

'You can't have a dual title,' Alf said irritably. 'You can't have mine-owners holding a lease, and alluvial diggers with a miner's right to peg claims of twenty-five by twenty-five feet within fifty feet of the reef.'

'Why not?' Dinny argued. 'We've had it until now. You haven't done so bad out of the arrangements y'rself now and again. All the mining companies've got any right to is the reef gold.'

'There's more to it than that,' Alf said doggedly. 'English investors don't understand our mining laws. They don't understand all the gold on a lease isn't theirs. They won't stand for the dual title. They're threatening to pull their money out of the country if the government lets the alluvial men get away with this business. Stocks'll fall: everything'll go to pieces on this field if they do.'

'Stocks've been falling these last few months,' Dinny said angrily. 'And it's not because the alluvial diggers've been putting up a fight for their rights. It's mining trickery on the Associated and Great Boulder, peterin' out of the oxidized ores, and the way the wild-cat speculators've been fleecin' British shareholders, has more to do with it. You don't see the big men gettin' out. If somebody's "bearin'" the market they'll buy low and sell when she's "bullin'." No. They'll stay where the money is and let the gover'ment stew in its own juice. Capital looks after itself. You don't have to worry about the mine-owners and the gover'ment, Alf.'

'I'm a servant of the Midas Gold Mining Company, and I've got to play its game,' Alf said. He could not look Dinny in the face.

'D'y' mean,' Dinny demanded, 'if alluvial men pegged on your lease you'd apply for injunctions?'

'Those are my instructions,' Alf said.

'Christ,' Dinny implored, 'don't do it! Don't go against the boys in this, Alf. They'll never forgive you. It's different with some of these jumped-up jackanapes like Frisco. Nobody expected him to be anything but a boss's man. But you can't rat on your mates, Alf. You can't go back on the men you tramped up from the 'Cross with. You can't see the alluvial diggers squeezed off the fields by a lot of greedy blackguards who'd sell up the whole country to live like millionaires in England and France.'

Dinny was almost weeping in his consternation.

'It goes against the grain, Dinny.' Alf's voice broke, too, but he had made up his mind. 'I had to give my word I'd stand by the mine-owners if there's alluvial trouble on the Midas. It was the boot if I didn't—and there's Laura and the child to think of.'

'The alluvial men've got wives and children,' Dinny flared. 'If they have the guts to fight for what they know's right, haven't you?'

'God, I haven't. And that's the truth,' Alf groaned. 'I can't face being out of a job again. Not the way things are now—and everybody talking about the need for qualified men to take the place of mine-managers with nothing but a rough and ready knowledge of the job to recommend them.'

'I'm not broke, Alf,' Dinny said, all his concern for this man he had loved like a brother uppermost again. 'I'd see you through any hard times. Money don't matter between mates.'

'No,' Alf said desperately. 'It's no use talking like that, Dinny. I've taken enough from you in the past. We've made money together. I've spent or lost mine. You've hung on to your dough. I can't afford to play ducks and drakes with my chances in life any longer. I've got to hold on to what I've got—and make the best of it.'

'Right.' Dinny's anger blazed. 'We've been mates a long time, Alf, but this is the end. If you go against the alluvial diggers in this fight, you go against me. I got no time for a man who'll swallow any injustice, and doesn't care what happens to anybody else so long as his own belly's full. He's a skunk—and that's what you are.'

Dinny turned and walked off down the road to the Boulder township. They had been talking by the roadside, the bare sun-baked earth throwing a glare all round them. Alf stood looking after Dinny, as he limped away, kicking up his own dust and as full of fight as a gamecock. He could not be angry with Dinny: could not resent what he had said. Skunk! From no other man would Alf have taken that word.

'I agree with Dinny, all the same,' he told Morris, calling on him at the shop on his way into town. 'I feel a skunk not to be fighting with the alluvial men on this issue. I'd rather be with them on the claims than playing the game of the mining pro-prietaries. But I can't afford to lose my job.'

Lean and haggard Alf looked that day in the white ducks and straw hat he was wearing to attend a meeting of the Institute of Mine-Managers. Laura liked Alf to wear his white suit on such occasions. She laundered it herself: never minded how she sweated and toiled, washing and ironing for him, so long as he could keep up his end among the other mine-managers and visit-ing magnates. Frisco and the Americans were always well turned out in tussore or white suits during the summer months, and Laura prided herself that Alf looked as smart as any of them.

Usually Alf's working clothes were as shabby and dust-stained as any other man's. He only consented to dress up when he was interviewing directors, or his pride demanded equal status with managers of the big mines. But there was no pride in him the day Dinny broke with him. He was as miserable as a bandicoot, Morris guessed. When the two men had been as close to each other for many years, as Dinny and Alf, it hurt when they quarrelled. Hurt like hell, when it was like this, with accusations of cowardice and treachery.

Dinny cared for Alf more than anyone in the world, Morris knew, and Alf cared for Dinny more than anyone, except his wife and child. But for them, he would never have gone against Dinny and the diggers.

'You can't blame Alf,' Morris told Sally. 'I'd do the same if I were in his position.'

'Thank goodness you're not!' Sally said sharply. 'It will be better for your business interests to remain friendly with the alluvial diggers. As for me, I can't support injustice, as Dinny says. I must help the men all I can, Morris.'

There was no arguing with Sally when she talked like that. Morris did not try; but he insisted on defending Alf.

It was easy enough to see Alf's point of view, Morris said. Alf had never regained his strength after that attack of typhoid the previous summer: was a wreck of his former self. He didn't look as if he could handle a pick and shovel as he had once done. His days of prospecting and chasing a fortune were over. All he wanted now was a job and a regular salary.

Alf had told Morris he was beginning to loathe the fields: to long for the time when he could go south, buy a farm or an orchard and live more easily. In all the years he had worked on the fields he had never been free from financial anxieties, except during those first months when the Lady Laura was floated. He had lived then in a happy dream, never doubting each year would build up his position, re-insure his investments.

His optimism had received many shocks. After the collapse of the Lady Laura, out of work and hard up, he had gone prospecting again with Dinny: taken any job on the mines when his luck was out. Management of one mine after another had given him another chance to come back among the bosses. But mines were being bought and sold and managements changing hands quickly. Alf found himself battered from pillar to post, never sure from one day to the next who his directors were going to be, or when his services would be dispensed with.

Gambling in script, he had made and lost money, striving always for that margin which would give him economic security: enable him to shake the dust of the goldfields off his feet and look forward to an old age of peace and comfort. The margin had never materialized. It had hovered like a mirage on the horizon of his prospects and vanished a dozen times. Alf blamed vicissitudes of the industry and the market. They kept him on tenterhooks all the time. In the end he had dropped gambling in shares: was stacking on this job with the Midas and a steady income to give him what he had worked for all his life.

He was afraid now of old age and poverty. He could see himself like some of the old-timers, broken and derelict, drifting about the town, scrounging for work, or dry-blowing round the mines.

And there were Laura and the child to think of. Always he came back to that. For them, he kept his mind on his job and refused to be drawn into the diggers' struggle for alluvial rights. Morris realized Alf was determined to demonstrate to the Midas Gold Mining Proprietary Ltd. that they had a good man, a reliable and able manager, and a faithful servant in Mr. A. E. Brierly.

That was all very well, Sally agreed; but she could not believe Alf was justified in claiming for himself better conditions than other men and their wives and families had to put up with, or in being false to his own standard of honour. He knew the men were right, yet was going to work against them, in order not to risk his own position and comfort. It was disgraceful!

Sally felt about Alf as Dinny and the alluvial diggers did, though she contrived to say 'good morning' or 'good afternoon' when she met him occasionally. Laura came to see her as usual.

Laura was very plump and pretty at about this time. She liked being a manager's wife, going about with the wives of other mine-managers and distinguished visitors, dining with them and entertaining them. At balls or social functions Mrs. Alfred Brierly was always popular. She sang at concerts and played the accompaniments for other performers.

Frequently, Mr. de Morfé cavaliered her when Alf was too busy, or away inspecting mines for the Midas Company. Laura had many admirers: quite enjoyed life on the fields: gave herself all manner of fashionable airs and graces when she fluttered in the new, exclusive social set which had sprung up in Kalgoorlie.

She dropped those airs and graces when she visited Sally. That was not so often these days. But sometimes she came, bringing Aimée, and the children played in the backyard where Sally was trying to grow vegetables and make a garden.

Dick and Tom spread out pebbles and sticks there in a complicated arrangement of what were supposed to be mines and railways. Aimée had been initiated into the mystery of their games; but now and then, with mischievous glee, mussed them up, and there was a scrimmage, with all three children scratching and screaming at each other. Sally's boys hated this imperious little person in a sunbonnet and dainty frock, who wanted to play with them and wrecked their mines and railways. When Aimée was a little older, though, they forgave her these youthful indiscretions, because she could run as fast and kick a tin as far as they could. They even forgot she was a girl when she looked as dirty and harum-scarum an urchin as either of them.

Sally usually had Larry near her in his cradle while she and Laura sewed and gossiped. Laura was very lovable and kind-hearted, if somewhat tactless and exasperating, now and then. She took on the ways and manners of people with whom she associated: like a mingari, changed colour to suit her surroundings.

Her assumption of a slightly patronizing air irritated Sally, but Laura enjoyed strutting a little, preening her feathers, and talking about her social successes. What Mr. Zabina Lane had said to her, or Mr. Modest Maryanski, and Mr. de Morfé. How one of the American managers, Mr. Herbert Hoover, when he came to dinner, exclaimed: 'Waal, I never would have thought there was such a cute and comfortable little home as yours on the goldfields, Mrs. Brierly!' And the French engineer with him had added: 'Or such a charming hostess!'

'You ought to go out more, Sally,' she said. 'There are so many dinner-parties and interesting people to meet in Kalgoorlie these days, one lives in quite a social whirl.'

'Does one?' Sally inquired.

'Oh, my dear, if Morris is an undertaker,' Laura exclaimed quite seriously, 'what does that matter? Everybody knows you and Morris could hold your own in any society. But you've so buried yourselves among the miners here. Never get away from them.'

Was that why she felt so differently to Laura when the struggle for alluvial rights began? Sally wondered. She had lived and worked among prospectors and miners for so long: been on the same footing with them as a woman earning her living: knew so well the hardships of their lives, that she seemed to have adopted their point of view as a matter of course.

It amazed her when Laura talked foolishly about the miners 'never being satisfied,' always wanting 'more wages and shorter hours of work.' How 'ill-advised and unreasonable' this fuss over alluvial rights was! Laura sat, one afternoon, looking smug and complacent, as she parroted the phrases current among mine-managers, and men like Mr. Lane and Frisco: 'absurdity of a dual title,' companies having 'to consider the interests of shareholders,' 'what we owe British capitalists who have opened up the mines on the Golden Mile.'

It was more than Sally could endure when she babbled on:

'And Alf says it's a few agitators and lazy blackguards who won't work in the mines who are to blame. Why, they even hoisted a red flag on one of the shafts when they were down twenty feet!'

'If Alf says that, he's a worse coward than I thought he was,' Sally cried indignantly. 'Alf knows the men are right. He's lost all sense of decency. Mr. Bray was taken away without being allowed even to say good-bye to his wife and children. He's ready to suffer for his convictions. But Alf—he's as rotten as any of the mine-owners trying to rob men of their rights!'

Laura stared at her, hurt and offended.

'Oh, Sally,' she gasped, 'how can you say such a thing?'

'It's the truth,' Sally replied.

Laura went to the door and called Aimée. Aimée objected to being taken away from her game with the boys: kicked and screamed furiously as Laura bundled her off. Laura did not speak as she turned away, and Sally could not bring herself to retract anything she had said or to apologize.

The coolness between her and Laura lasted a long time. They passed like casual acquaintances if they met in the street. Sally saw Laura driving with the wife of a mine-manager, or Mr. de Morfé, sometimes; but Laura did not always see her, and Mr. de Morfé usually appeared entirely engrossed by her amiable conversation.

CHAPTER LIII

THE riot that 'might have been' gave the diggers many a laugh in the weeks which followed, although they were in no mood for laughter when Sir John Forrest turned down the demands of their committee and refused to address the deputation of ten thousand.

It had happened when the Alluvial Rights Association decided to interview Sir John as he passed through Kalgoorlie. Dinny liked to browse and chuckle over his newspaper cuttings and reminiscences of that day. A ministerial party had been to Menzies for the opening of the railway, and their special train was expected to arrive early in the afternoon.

The day before, hundreds of men tramped the twenty miles in from Bulong. Miners and prospectors came in from all the outlying camps. Over a thousand from Kanowna. When they mustered at the railway station to demonstrate to the leaders of the government the strength behind their protest against the Ten Feet Regulation, and the imprisonment of alluvial diggers, there was no thought of disorderliness or creating a disturbance. The men's leaders had given a guarantee to the inspector of police nothing of the sort would occur.

But before the train was due, the crowd had become so dense that the police cleared a passage for Sir John, and patrolled it with mounted troopers. As far as you could see from the station and round about Wilkie's hotel, where the interview with the diggers' committee was to be held, a seething mass of diggers, citizens and derelicts of the town had congregated. Women, children, councillors, justices of the peace, natives, 'Ghans, girls from the brothels and spielers from the shypoo dens, mingled in the multitude, sweltering together under the sun, wrapped in its glare and the red dust which rose from their restless feet. A sweating, excited throng, agog with curiosity to see the great man, they stood waiting patiently, chattering and speculating about the outcome of this meeting.

John Forrest had been regarded as something of a popular hero. An explorer and good bushman, a bluff, hearty and kindly old boy who, despite the fact that he had been given a title recently, could be hail-fellow well-met with goldfields folk when he met them in the city. But now Sir John was suspected of having become so puffed-up with his own importance and political power, that he thought he could run the goldfields for the benefit of a few old southern families and mining magnates.

Everybody wanted to hear what he had to say. How he would answer the demands of the alluvial diggers. Whether he would promise to restore the diggers' rights, as many who knew him believed, and release the men who had been imprisoned in their struggle for justice. Or whether he would support the Warden and Wittenoom and let the diggers take the consequences. Few of the men's leaders thought he could, or would, fail to promise a sympathetic hearing to their grievances, on behalf of the government. Expressed in the suave, vague terms of a shrewd politician, of course.

When a stray goat wandered into the passage reserved for Sir John, there was an outburst of amused cackling and laughter.

'Who is it?'

'Wittenoom!'

The police laughed, too, as they led the scapegoat away.

Mr. Moran had been advised not to meet the Premier and accompany him to the hotel.

'The diggers will hoot you, and Sir John will think the hoots are meant for him,' Dinny said he had told Moran. 'We don't want to rub his nibs up the wrong way and prejudice our discussion from the start.'

Some said it was Moran himself who tried to start a cheer for Sir John when he arrived, and got hoots and yells of derision instead. It was not the sort of reception John Forrest was accustomed to, and disconcerted him. He raised his hat and smiled affably, however, as he walked down the aisle through that clamourous throng, escorted by the Warden, police officials and the diggers' committee.

The men said afterwards that the discussion opened well enough, although Sir John was in anything but a good humour when he sat down in an upstairs room which had been reserved for the interview at Wilkie's. The crowd, locked-out, waited, buzzing and yelling impatiently round the hotel. One of the men's leaders appealed from the balcony to the diggers to maintain order and not allow a few unruly spirits to destroy the purpose of the demonstration.

Two of the town councillors, Byrne and Rutter, put before Sir John the facts of the position with regard to the Ivanhoe Leases, and the Ten Feet Regulation. He admitted to being impressed and that he saw the matter in a different light than he had previously done. He had been out of the Colony for two months and had not yet discussed the matter with his minister. It was almost an apology, but at the same time, he said:

'I have not the slightest doubt in my mind that the law is considered by the minister to be a good one, and if you will permit me to give an opinion, I will say that I believe the Ten Feet Regulation is a good one.'

The diggers' committee growled their dissent.

'I mean that it is good in that it is a valid regulation,' the Premier revised hastily. 'And I think the Supreme Court will say it is within the Act. A very wide power is given to the minister to frame regulations.'

When Mick Mannion made it clear that the Alluvial Rights Association was demanding withdrawal of the regulation and release of the imprisoned diggers, Sir John's attempt to talk his way out of an awkward situation with conversational pleasantness broke down. He looked baffled but stubborn.

After nearly two hours, the men had got nothing from him but: 'I think your arguments with regard to the regulation are very good and deserve careful consideration by the government.'

'A manifest injustice has been done to the alluvial diggers by the government,' said Huggins of Bulong.

'I think that a very strong remark,' Sir John snapped.

'Yes.'

'I have not come here to be insulted, but to talk to you as a friend.'

Sir John went on to make a long speech assuring the men that he wanted to see the country prospected from end to end, and that he realized alluvial men were necessary for this work. 'But also,' he added, 'we must do all we can to encourage those who are willing with their energy, pluck and capital to develop the country . . .

'I assure you that no one desires to have your goodwill more than I do,' Sir John said. 'I want it. I long for it, but at the same time I will not do what is not right in law, and every member of the community, I'm sure, will agree I am perfectly right in that respect.'

There was nothing anybody disagreed with in all this, but it was far from the matters under discussion.

The din out of doors had become terrific. It was as if thousands of wild dervishes were yelling: 'Come on, John.' 'Let's hear what you've got to say!' 'Trot him out, boys!' 'Alluvial rights for alluvial miners!'

'You all know nobody likes to give in at the point of the bayonet,' Sir John said, pouting like a fat, sulky schoolboy. 'If I held a bayonet up to you and said, "You've got to give in!" you wouldn't like it . . . In the meantime, let me advise you not to allow yourselves to be made "cat's-paws" of by anyone. Let none of you go to gaol to gratify anyone who writes leading articles. Be true to yourselves, and depend on it everything will come right in the end.'

The men stared at him dumbfounded. Was there ever such a mixture of obstinate stupidity, hypocrisy and platitudinous guff as this speech? they asked themselves.

A delegate who had butted in half-way through the conference stuttered hoarsely: 'We are dissatisfied with your reply, Sir John.'

'Are you a member of this deputation and authorized to speak?' Sir John demanded.

'Never mind about that! I say your reply is not satisfactory,' the digger replied.

Sir John jumped up from his chair, strode out of the room, and made his way downstairs. He refused to speak from the balcony: ignored the advice of the diggers' committee to say something, if only a few words which would pacify the crowd. With his bodyguard of police officials, the Warden, and one or two members of the Association who stuck to him, Sir John forced his way into the street.

315

But the man from Bulong was calling from the balcony:
'He refuses to speak to you! Won't release the prisoners!'

The crowd went mad. Howling and shouting, booing and hissing, men who had been standing in the sun for hours, expecting to hear the leader of the government speak and give them some hope of a fair deal, let themselves be carried along by their rage and indignation.

'Where is he?' they yelled.

'Make the bloody old hypocrite speak!'

'Stick up for your rights, boys!'

'Why are you robbing the diggers, John?'

'Pull him back!'

'Don't let him skedaddle!'

'Release the boys in prison!'

'Down with the Ten Feet Regulation!'

'Alluvial gold for the alluvial miners!'

The crowd surged round the party escorting the Premier to the station. Mounted troopers rode the men back, screams and curses arose as the horses trampled in on them; but shoving, jostling and bearing past the police, the crowd swung in on Sir John.

Angry oaths and exultant shouts defied the bawling of the troopers: 'Keep back! Keep back, blast ye!'

There was boisterous jocularity in the scrimmage. Only a few drunks fought savagely when their mates held on to them. The diggers' committee, going about among the men, tried to restore order. In the struggle round him, an umbrella carried by one of his own party jabbed Sir John in the ribs. Warden Hare pulled the Riot Act from his pocket. In the din not many people heard him read it. He sent three troopers off to the police station for firearms. But when mounted constable Whelan galloped up with a Martini Henry rifle on his saddle, Sir John had reached the station and been bundled into his train.

The crowd roared with laughter at the sight of the trooper with that blunderbus, and a nettlesome horse playing up at the way it flapped against his withers.

'Put that bloody thing away,' his chief called. Cheers and groans resounded as the discomforted trooper rode off with his weapon.

It was all over in a few minutes. The rowdiest and wildest of the demonstrators melted away before the displeasure of their leaders. The diggers' representatives contended that the crowd was justified in giving Sir John a piece of its mind, and an inkling of the anger and disgust which had been created by the raw deal his government had given the alluvial miners. But they repudiated the scrimmage which had provided the Warden with

a pretext for reading the Riot Act. The Alluvial Diggers'
Rights Association apologized to Sir John and protested that it
was not responsible for any disorder that had occurred.

Nothing of the sort would have arisen, Mick Mannion pointed
out, had Sir John addressed the men, and made even the usual
vague, political concessions to their grievances. After grilling
in the sun for hours to hear him speak, it was not unnatural that
the crowd had reacted as it did, and insisted on its right to hear
from the leader of the government why the alluvial diggers were
being persecuted and made to suffer by extraordinary legislation.

Most of the diggers chortled over the episode. They were
satisfied Sir John had got no more than he deserved; and they
had enjoyed the unexpected drama of bluffing the proud, corpu-
lent old fox into scuttling for his train, and the troopers into
turning out with their rifles. It had been good fun: given them
something to yarn and guffaw about for days.

But the best part of the joke was the coastal newspapers. They
came out with sensational headlines: 'Alarming Riot at Kalgoorlie.' 'The Premier Attacked and Seriously Injured.' 'Ribs
Shoved In With Umbrella.' Sir John was congratulated on his
heroic bearing and refusal to concede anything to an infuriated
mob. Mr. Maitland Brown's telegram: 'My God, I'm proud of
you,' became the toast of the goldfields.

Sir John's denial of injury, the police inspector's report that
the demonstration had never reached the proportions of a riot,
and that, in his opinion, it was an error of judgment on the part
of the Warden to have read the Riot Act, overwhelmed the affair
with ridicule. Not a hair of anyone's head had been hurt: no one
received a scratch. The most serious casualty was Johnny John-
son, an old one-legged bell-ringer, charged with alleged riotous
conduct. To wit, yelling:

'Stick to your colours, boys!'

'To hell with Sir John Forrest and any other animals like him!'

'Three groans for Blowfly Hare and Moran!'

Johnny was accused also of striking mounted constable Whelan's horse with his crutch. He got nine months' hard labour in
Fremantle gaol. Four other men also were charged with inciting
to riot or riotous conduct. When one of them asked for time to
prove an alibi, the magistrate, Warden Hare, said: 'I saw you
myself.' He convicted two other men with the same remark.
Tom Doyle and Billy King were acquitted on a similar charge.

But before the end of the month, the Ten Feet Regulation was
rescinded. A week or so later the diggers in gaol in Fremantle
were released; and on the appeal in connection with the Ivanhoe

Venture injunction cases the Supreme Court completely vindicated the alluvial diggers.

It was a great triumph, celebrated with much rejoicing in every mine and camp on the fields. The diggers went about in droves shouting to each other. Episodes of the campaign, the arrests, trials and the famous riot in which no one was hurt, were recounted with gusto and roaring laughter. Meetings and speeches honoured the heroes who had done time in Fremantle for the cause. The men went back to work on their claims during the day, but at sundown the streets and the pubs resounded to laughter, singing and cheers. Pots of beer rattled to: 'My God, I'm proud of you!'

There was only one cause for uneasiness: only one snag in the successful conclusion of this conflict with the mining companies and the government. Sir John Forrest had announced his intention of introducing a bill to give leaseholders control of all the mineral on their leases, with power to sub-let any portion on tribute.

'By gosh, if he does that,' Dinny swore, and thousands of alluvial miners and prospectors swore with him, 'the fight will be on again!'

But they had won the first round, and could afford to rejoice for a while.

CHAPTER LIV

THE new bill duly appeared, with a section providing that after one year a leaseholder could obtain a certificate freeing his land from the entry of alluvial miners.

Under the old Act the lessee acquired the reef gold: alluvial remained for the man with a miner's right. The intention of the new Act was to placate lease gamblers and London stock jobbers, the men believed. It snatched from the alluvial diggers the fruits of their victory: sought to deprive them of alluvial rights ultimately, and threw them back into the struggle for preservation of those rights.

The diggers were bitter and resolute. They did not intend to submit to such autocratic legislation. The fight was on again.

At a meeting of the Alluvial Rights Association, Mick Mannion quoted the Supreme Court decision in the recent case against Pat Hughes and Bill Bray. 'When a leaseholder or his representatives are called by the holder of a miner's right under Clause 36 of the Act to define his line of reef, it will not be sufficient for him to point to an imaginary line, but he must show that of an actual reef. Should the leaseholder fail to do this within forty-eight hours of being requested in writing, then the holder of the miner's right can enter on the lease, subject to Regulation 119, which says that if his taking possession be disputed, the Warden may be called to decide the point at issue.'

'This decision and the old Act made it clear,' Mick said, 'that the holder of a miner's right may safely search for and remove alluvial gold from a lease, but he must not in any way interfere with the actual rights of the lessee. The first attempt to wipe out the rights of alluvial diggers manifested itself in an attempt to ride rough-shod over the law. The next attempt is a law to override the existing law.'

'Abraham Lincoln said there was no law against human rights,' Chris Crowe, Dinny's mate, called.

'That's what we're fighting for—human rights,' Mick agreed. 'But the government goes behind the backs of the diggers and gives the big John Bull companies the right to all the gold on the lease. Thanks to the government, they can sit on velvet. An alluvial man will have to go cap in hand to leaseholders and ask to be allowed to work the ground on tribute. If they want a lease prospected and manned, they may say yes. If they don't, they can tell us to get to hell.'

There were meetings of protest against the new Mines Act everywhere. Hundreds of diggers gathered for the roll-ups on the camps: five thousand at Kanowna. Indignation rose to boiling point when it was announced that the Legislative Assembly, on the motion of the Premier, Sir John Forrest, had decided to compensate the Ivanhoe Venture Syndicate for its losses in connection with the recent dispute, to the tune of £2,500.

Several weeks earlier, following the Supreme Court decisions that the men had been acting throughout in accordance with their legal rights, that injunctions should not have been granted against them, and that they should never have been sentenced and imprisoned for disobeying those injunctions, Vosper had moved for the appointment of a commission to consider the compensation of diggers who had been imprisoned. This had been rejected; but soon afterwards a motion to appoint a commission to consider compensation of the Ivanhoe Venture Syndicate was carried by an overwhelming majority. Sir John's motion was a consequence of this decision.

'These honourable legislators are more concerned to safeguard their own property and class interests than the rights of the goldfields community,' Mullocky O'Dwyer declared indignantly. 'The diggers, who broke no law, were torn from their families, lost their means of livelihood and suffered all manner of indignities in order to educate administrators as to the meaning of their own laws. It is infamous that working men should have to bear the cost and the real criminals be compensated for having been frustrated in their illegal intentions.'

Not only the alluvial diggers were incensed by this outrageous action of the southern parliament. Business men and workers all over the fields denounced the government. The goldfields press voiced this indignation:

One of Dinny's cuttings from the *Western Argus* said:

'In the case of the Ivanhoe Venture Syndicate, it was the diggers who were cruelly wronged, as was shown by the Supreme Court, but it was the persecuting companies that a partisan government compensated. The Government was able to find £2,500 for this monstrous piece of iniquity, although its members have pleaded poverty when asked to explain the cutting down of the miserable pittance allowed to hospital nurses, telephone girls and other under-paid civil servants.'

The raw deal alluvial diggers had received stimulated dissatisfaction with the government. It was recognized that the right to alluvial gold of thousands of diggers and prospectors constituted the basis of local prosperity. Gold won from the big mines and leases flowed away to enrich shareholders in Perth or overseas.

Publicans, shopkeepers, teamsters and contractors, as well as prospectors and miners—all the people who depended for their living on the progress and development of these struggling goldfields towns—resented the way their interests were ignored by southern politicians with axes to grind on the mining industry. Prospectors and miners, in the first instance, had opened up the back country and brought wealth to an almost bankrupt State. It was argued that the goldfields were entitled to representation commensurate with their population and importance.

Roll-ups and mass meetings to protest against the new Mines Act, discussed also the electoral disabilities of the goldfields. The need for a broader franchise, redistribution of seats, direct labour representation and payment of members, was asserted. Dinny, himself, spoke at many of these meetings. 'Thirteen members,' he said, 'are returned to the Legislative Assembly by thirteen electorates whose combined voters do not equal one-third on the roll for Kalgoorlie and Boulder.

'Two of the north-west electorates contain thousands of cattle but only one hundred and fifty human votes,' Mullocky O'Dwyer used to say. 'They return two members, twice as many as Kalgoorlie and Boulder with six thousand voters, but not one bullock and only a couple of cows in the district.'

'The people of the goldfields are considered of less importance than cattle in the Kimberley electorates,' Dinny told his audiences. 'It looks as if cattle were being allowed to legislate for us. That's why the government's been able to defeat the diggers. Well, the men on these fields aren't goin' to put up with that state of things. I agree with Mullocky O'Dwyer, it's home rule for the goldfields we want!'

Sir John Forrest brought a hornet's nest about his ears with his new Mines Act. It had far-reaching consequences. Those hornets buzzed angrily during the next few months.

Agitation for effective representation developed into a movement for separation from the southern part of the colony and from control by the Forrest Government.

For many years the dream of a united Australia as the foundation of nationhood had haunted the minds of men and women who loved their country. It was proposed to unite the colonies which had grown into states, more or less independent of each other, under a federal constitution. A convention had been held, at which the delegates from all states agreed to support the idea of federation. Sir John Forrest had promised to submit a referendum to the people of West Australia on the subject when New South Wales adopted the federal proposals by a referendum. But he had now discovered reasons for opposing federation, and was stalling to prevent a referendum being taken.

This was regarded as a move on the part of the old landholding conservative minority of West Australians to retain control of the new wealth of the state. The prospect was anything but pleasing to the goldfields community. The goldfields declared for federation, and Sir John was denounced as a traitor to the ideal of a Commonwealth of Australia. When the suggestion that a goldfields state, which would be part of the federation, could be formed, it took root and thrived immediately.

As the struggle of the alluvial diggers grew in bitterness and intensity, Sally was drawn more and more into it. She went to meetings of diggers and citizens, and stood in the street with her children beside her to cheer demonstrations. She provided meals for many a digger in need of a good feed, and tramped miles collecting money from shopkeepers and publicans for the families of men in prison. Morris could not understand why she had espoused the men's cause with such fervour. He was inclined to be impatient and irritable about it.

'Hang it all, Sally,' he said, 'there's no need to get so worked-up over this business.'

'What do you mean?' Sally flared. 'That I should sit still and do nothing while men are being sent to gaol for defending their rights, and all this injustice is going on?'

'Don't snap my head off,' Morris growled. 'I object to you wearing yourself out, going to meetings and collecting money. That's all.'

'Oh, Lord!' Sally was tired and knew she had been bad-tempered. 'Didn't the men stand by me when I needed help? And how could I refuse to help them in any way that I can, Morris? After all, it's not only themselves they're fighting for, but all of us who live here on the fields.'

'I know all that,' Morris grumbled. 'I'm supporting the diggers financially, and no more is required of us.'

'Everything we can do, is required of us, I think,' Sally said, heatedly. 'Dinny says it's mean and cowardly to sit back and take things easy when other people are fighting for you.'

'What Dinny says matters more than what I say, it seems.'

'Don't be silly, Morris!' Sally's smile fluttered to appease him. 'But he's right about this.'

She had thrown herself into the struggle of the alluvial diggers, Sally told herself, because she felt as they did and as Dinny did. Their interests were hers, and the interests of everybody who worked for a living.

The alluvial diggers, too, helped to drive Frisco from her mind. Everybody knew he was working with the mine-owners and powerful financial interests to defeat the alluvial diggers and prospectors. Sally could not forgive him for that. She hated Frisco and hated herself for having yielded to his kisses: burned to them. She felt as guilty as if she had been in communication with the enemy: could not do enough for the diggers to overcome that sense of secret disloyalty. So when Paddy Cavan was ill, she nursed him as she would have any other working miner, during those months.

Paddy had stumbled on to the verandah, after one of the demonstrations, and said he had a bit of a gut's ache. Could Mrs. Gough give him something for it? Sally had given him a dose of chlorodyne. Paddy lay down on a stretcher on the back verandah and went to sleep there. Sally did not like to disturb him. She threw a rug over him when she and Morris went to bed, but all night she could hear Paddy moving about restlessly. In the morning she found him on a bed in the bunkhouse.

He was very sick, she could see, though Paddy declared it was only an attack of dysentery. He'd had it often before.

'Looks to me as if you ought to go to hospital, Paddy,' Sally said.

'For Chris-sakes, don't send me there, ma'am,' Paddy groaned. 'I'll die for sure. Let me lay here, and I'll be alright in a day or two.'

Sally was worried when the day or two passed and Paddy was no better. She realized that probably he had typhoid. But the hospital was full, and she was afraid he would die if she sent him there now.

Like so many other diggers, Paddy had a superstitious dread of the hospital. So many typhoid patients had died there that often a man would rather take his chance with the rough and ready nursing of some mate than go to the hospital. But Paddy had no mate he could rely on, at present, apparently. He had come to her, Sally thought, because she was the only person he knew likely to be kindly disposed towards him. And he looked such a pitiful sight, the big, gawky lad, in his pain and fear, that she could not turn him away. If one of her own boys was ever in such a plight and nobody willing to look after him, how would she feel, Sally asked herself.

'Don't send me to 'orspital, ma'am! For the love o' Gord, don't send me to 'orspital,' Paddy implored.

'It's alright. I won't, Paddy,' Sally promised.

Morris was furious when she told him she was going to nurse Paddy herself, and that Marie had come over and taken the two elder boys to stay with her. Sally had decided to keep Larry at home. There was not so much danger of infection for a baby, she assured Morris. She was sure she could do what was necessary for Paddy, and would take every precaution to avoid risk for the rest of her household. After all, Paddy was in the bunkhouse, and the two men sleeping there could camp on the verandah for the time being.

The weeks of Paddy's illness had been a nightmare of weariness and anxiety. But he had pulled through, and after a month was ready to return to his own shack on the Golden Feather lease, looking pale and shaky, but very pleased to find himself still alive. He was full of gratitude to Sally for what she had done for him, though quite unconcerned about all the inconvenience he had caused her.

It was a dirty trick Paddy had played Mrs. Gough, Dinny and the men declared, dumping himself on her instead of going to hospital when he knew he had the fever. But Sally did not believe Paddy had intended to play her a dirty trick.

'He was like a sick dog, the poor boy,' she said. 'Didn't know what was the matter with him.'

But when he was going, Paddy had said something which startled and angered her.

'Oh, well, ma'am, one good turn deserves another, I suppose,' he remarked, with his air of guileless impudence. 'And I reck'n I did you a good turn, holdin' me tongue about who was with Frisco, when the mob was lookin' for him, on New Year's Eve.'

CHAPTER LV

EVERY day Alf walked from his whitewashed cottage, half hidden by pepper trees, to the mine. Its sky-shaft and rickety poppet legs raked the blue sky from the brow of the ridge. The ramshackle buildings cluttered about the main shaft included the corrugated iron shed he called his office.

It was there he worked most of the day. Grey mud-splashed overalls and an old felt hat hung on a peg near the door, ready to be worn when he went underground. There was no knowing when that might be necessary; or when the urge to inspect work on the new drive would take him.

That iron shed was as hot as an oven, and the glare of the sun blinding on the bare red earth beyond the open door. But Alf threw himself into his correspondence, reports and accounts with a concentration which excluded every consideration from his mind except the mine and its interests. To return home, where Laura and Aimée were waiting for him, was all the happiness he needed, he assured himself.

He had come to a decision on the question of alluvial rights and would stick to it, he informed the secretary of the Alluvial Rights Association. If any men pegged alluvial claims on the Midas lease, he would carry out the Company's instructions and apply for injunctions against them. After his quarrel with Dinny, there was no need for Alf to explain his attitude.

He did not meet any of the diggers, men he had known, unless he had business in Kalgoorlie, passed them in the street or was having a drink in one of the pubs. Dinny refused to drink with him when they ran into each other one evening. Alf was going about with mine-owners and mine-managers these days: drinking with Zeb Lane, Callanan of the Lake View, Carlisle of the Ivanhoe Venture and Dorrie Doolette. His old mates would have nothing to do with him.

Of the old bunch Frisco was the only one who could stand with the bosses and keep on apparently good terms with the diggers. But he went to the coast when tempers were rising after the first arrests: spent the rest of the summer yachting and sea bathing.

324

He did not return until the Supreme Court upheld the action of the diggers and the imprisoned men were released. Frisco threw money about then and joined in the celebrations, although everybody knew it was no more than an armed truce that was being observed.

Alf was bitter about the way old friends cold-shouldered and ignored him during those months.

'They'll crack a joke with Frisco, who's pulling strings behind their back all the time, but they won't pass the time of day with me,' he complained to Morris.

Morris understood well enough why that was. Old mates expected nothing from Frisco. They knew he would stand with the Ivanhoe Venture Syndicate and the mining companies. Frisco had never disguised his policy of grab and be damned to everybody else. But Alf, the men had believed in him. They remembered the honest, good-natured lad they had known: the kindly, popular man who had always tried to give the men working for him a fair deal. That he should side with those guilty of gross injustice towards the alluvial diggers was more than they could stomach. Alf had been an alluvial digger himself. He wasn't a jumped-up poppinjay like Mr. de Morfé, they said; or some foreign capitalist trying to run the country and ride rough shod over the rights of Australian workers. They could not forgive Alf Brierly.

He was playing a dastardly part, the men considered, not only condoning injustice, but willing himself to send men to gaol for defending their rights.

Alf's face became drawn and haggard when he realized where this conflict had landed him. Men whom he had regarded as friends among the alluvial diggers looked straight through him when they met: spat as he passed, exclaiming contemptuously. Alf never had the nerve to resent it. He knew they were right: went about ashamed and miserable, trying not to see anybody, passing Dinny in the street with a curt: 'Good-day!' to which Dinny never replied. With the mine-owners he was stiff and cool, as though he, and not they, were conferring a favour by this contact.

Morris had come to have a warm affection for Alf. Alf's kindness after the storm had helped him to pull himself together and tackle the undertaking proposition when it turned up. They had more in common than most of the men with whom either of them associated; and in this crisis Alf turned to Morris as the only man he could talk to.

Morris made no bones about it. He could see Alf's point of view: confessed that in Alf's position he would do precisely what

Alf was doing, and not feel so badly about it. Morris defended Alf to Dinny, Mick Mannion, Mike Burke, Mullocky O'Dwyer and other members of the Alluvial Diggers' Association, who collected at the house sometimes to talk things over with Dinny.

The fact of the matter was, Morris pointed out, Alf Brierly could not face the prospect of losing his job. He knew what his chances of getting another would be if he went against the mining companies, and they won. Alf reckoned they would win, and it looked as if he was right. The big men had the government and the police on their side. They could pull strings to get the mining regulations altered to suit them. Hadn't they done so?

The alluvial diggers agreed that Alf had only acted as most men in his position would have done. He had stuck to his class and personal interests. That was all there was to it. But Alf knew the mine-owners were slugging the prospectors and alluvial diggers. He knew the men were right. He had been a prospector: understood what alluvial rights meant to thousands of men and their wives and families on the goldfields. But he didn't care what happened to them so long as he saved his own skin.

What respect could decent men have for a man who was prepared to see old mates suffer outrageous injustices, and do nothing about it for fear of losing his job? Worse than that, side with the enemy committing those injustices and trying to starve alluvial diggers off the fields!

Vosper, Gregory and some other well-known citizens who had come out in defence of the diggers were not counting the cost. But Alf Brierly slunk behind the Mine Managers' Association and talked about carrying out the instructions of his directors, if alluvial diggers pegged on the Midas lease—which they were not likely to do. The Midas lease had been granted when the alluvial was exhausted.

The alluvial men could forgive some of the bosses who had never made any secret of what they were in the country for: to use any and every means for getting all the gold they could out of it and live in luxury on the other side of the world. But they could not forgive Alf Brierly for combining with the big capitalist to defeat men who had been mates on the old diggings, and who were fighting to preserve the rights of Australian working people. Besides Morris, only one of the crowd who had swamped along the track from the 'Cross, expressed any sympathy with Alf. That was Paddy Cavan.

Young Paddy was becoming quite a person of importance. He could run with the hare and hunt with the hounds, though nobody trusted him further than he could be seen. Paddy pretended to be with the diggers in this struggle over alluvial rights; but it was rumoured he had various interests in mining properties. That was hard to believe. Not so hard, Dinny said, when you'd watched him bidding in the Open Call for years. He was willing to bet Paddy held stock which would make him a rich man some day.

Paddy treated the idea as a joke.

'It's me firm intention to buy up the Great Boulder, Dinny,' he said. 'But not to-morrow.'

He was working as a miner on the Golden Feather, a mine in the bush a mile out from Maritana. Paddy went about, most of the time, dirty and unshaven in old moles and a dilapidated felt hat; but was sometimes seen breasting-up to Frisco and Zeb Lane as if he had a right to talk with them.

Alf was not particularly pleased when Paddy bowled up to him one afternoon on his way home, grabbed his hand and assured him:

'The present troubles make no difference to me regard for you, Mr. Brierly!'

'Thanks, Paddy,' Alf said dryly, wondering what had moved the young blackguard.

He was vaguely irritated by Paddy's assurance and the sharp smiling glance of his pale blue eyes. It was as if Paddy were investigating and summing-up for himself just what effect the diggers' hostility was having on Alf.

Paddy had thickened out: looked a husky young chap now. Not very prepossessing. His pudgy face was still blotched with big freckles. His gingery hair rose in a coarse mop through a broken hat, his light-lashed eyes had a shrewd, measuring stare; but there was no getting away from an impression of ability and latent power the lad gave. He was talking now like a man and an equal.

Alf's irritation changed to interest, a slightly cynical amusement.

'It's this way, Mr. Brierly,' Paddy said. 'I reckon a man's got to battle for himself. And no man on the field's done it fairer or straighter than you. I got a fine opinion of you, Mr. Brierly, but you're not seein' far enough in this alluvial business. It's all right. It's good for the country. I am all for the local capitalist and keeping money on the fields. Where'd we be if the foreign speculators ruled the roost? Sure, life wouldn't be worth livin' in these parts, and there'd be no place for honest men like y'self and yours truly.'

Alf laughed. Was his honesty on a par with Paddy's? 'I'm only thinking of the Midas, and my job,' he said harshly.

'Yah!' Paddy swung off along the track to the township. 'They're sellin' out on you. Frisco's after her for a French syndicate. If y're lookin' for work in the near future, Mr. Brierly, let me know—and maybe I can put something in y'r way.'

CHAPTER LVI

'WEIGHIN' a hundred pounds?'

'Begorra, it'd be the bobby-dazzler of a slug to be weighin' that,' said Tassy.

Paddy Cavan had just pushed back the gate and rushed up the garden path to Gough's verandah. He was bursting with the news: all mud-splashed and touseled as he had come from work.

'What comes off of Paddy, when he has a scrub, is good alluvial,' Dinny remarked once. 'You could get tailin's in any dish where he's been cleanin' himself. That's why he don't wash too often. Scared of losin' something.'

Dinny and Tassy Regan were sitting on the edge of the verandah, smoking and yarning with two or three other men over a temporary lull in the alluvial rights struggle, that evening Paddy blew in on them. Chris, on one of the bag chairs in the background, made an occasional muttered comment. Paddy, with his red hair on end and his eyes wild, jerked them out of their peaceful cogitation. There was great news about when a man looked like that: news of a big find and a rush. The nerves of every prospector prickled and stirred responsively. Old timers like Dinny and Tassy were no exception, though they pretended to take Paddy's news soberly.

'Where'd it hail from?'

'Who got it?'

'Divil a bit anybody knows,' Paddy declared. 'It's Father Long is over from Kanowna and says two prospectors brought in the big slug; but his reverence will give no particulars. Says he's pledged to secrecy!'

Tassy stood up, hitching his pants. 'He can't get away with that, Dinny. We'd better see what's doin', and pack our swags, if—'

'The rush is on all right,' Paddy interrupted. 'There's a mob on the road to Kanowna, already. Me and my mate's makin' tracks right away.'

'Sorry, ma'am,' Dinny yelled to Sally, 'but we won't be wantin' any dinner to-night.' In a split second, every man on the verandah was gone.

'Well—I'll be damned,' Sally came to the door and saw them streaking along the road into the township: Dinny, Tassy Regan and Paddy, with the other men and Chris Crowe in the rear. Hot and exasperated, a big dinner left on her hands, she cursed rushes and madness they put over men. She had heard Paddy blaring his news and knew what to expect.

Morris came in later: curiously unmoved by Father Long's story, and all the commotion of the rush setting out for Kanowna, where it was thought further particulars might be picked up. He had his doubts about the whole business. Neither the police nor the Mines Department could give any information about the new find, he said. If it had actually occurred, the gold should have been declared and new claims been applied for.

It was realized, of course, that a lot of gold won was never declared; but prospectors kept a sharp eye on the law in this respect. The penalty for failure to declare gold was forfeiture of a claim. And no man on gold wanted to risk that. So, usually, big and important finds were reported. Only minor leakages found their way to unlicensed gold-buyers and the illicit dealers in snide ore.

Sally marvelled at the change which had come over Morris. Before that gruelling experience at Mount Black he would have been first to catch fire and whirl off with a rush. Since then, and particularly since he had taken on the undertaking business, he seemed quite unconcerned by the rumours of rushes and gossip about rich alluvial on new fields.

Morris had forced himself to do this job, she knew. He had deadened his first repugnance, and was more or less pleased that he could make a success of undertaking. It was something to be able to measure corpses, make coffins or drive the hearse in a funeral procession to the distant cemetery, he thought. And he could do that now without nausea and shamefacedness: as a matter of course, or a rather grim joke. The joke paid. That was the best part of it.

'It's a little gold mine,' Morris told Alf. 'Who would have thought I'd strike it rich burying corpses? But you never know your luck, Brierly, my métier seems to be undertaking.'

He was quite competent and preoccupied with his shop, carpenter's shed and stables: took some pride in his funeral arrangements, solicitude for the bereaved family, a generous display of crepe, memorial cards and verses he wrote himself. He even asked Sally to make wreaths of white everlastings for one of his customers.

'I assure you, my dear, I seek to give satisfaction,' he remarked sardonically.

Sally did not know quite what to make of Morris and his absorption in this business. Had he abandoned hope and decided to settle down to a humdrum existence? She almost wished he were stirred by heated arguments over the rush and fuming to be off with the rest of the men. But Morris remained unperturbed and disinterested.

Dinny and Tassy, carried away by the high fever raging, went off to Kanowna. They could not believe the priest was lying. It was a sure thing he had seen the big lump of gold, if he said he had. And he did; but refused to divulge a sacred confidence. A secret of the confessional, everybody imagined, was involved: theft or murder, or both.

Hundreds of men went off with their picks and shovels, on camels and horses, in donkey carts and drays, on bicycles, and on foot, swags on their backs, to scour the outskirts of Kanowna. In a few days they were drifting back: nothing had been heard of the big slug in Kanowna. No news could be gleaned of alluvial diggers on the claims round about, or prospectors coming in from further out, who had been celebrating their luck or making any suspicious moves recently.

In fact, the old White Feather lead and other once rich shows in the district were petering out: storekeepers and publicans complaining of a slump. They greeted Father Long's news with jubilation. Not so the men toiling in the sun, with nothing to show for their pains; and not making tucker as they slung pick and shovel all day, without knowing even whether they were in the vicinity of the sacred slug's birthplace.

Prospectors arrived from the eastern states to join in the search, and an ugly situation developed after nearly three weeks' desperate activity.

Dinny remembered the McCann rush and the fury of the men who had been led on a wild-goose chase by the boasting of a drunken fool. He warned the police and the Warden that they would not be able to protect Father Long unless they did something to allay the hardships the rush was causing thousands of penniless and hungry diggers. If there was truth in his story, Father Long must defend himself by telling the locality in which the slug was found. Otherwise the men would believe he had been talking too freely with the drink in him, or that a deliberate fraud was being worked off on them for the benefit of certain storekeepers and publicans.

Father Long agreed to tell where the nugget had been found. An announcement was made that he would give his information publicly from the balcony of a Kanowna hotel on a certain day at two o'clock in the afternoon.

It was an ill-tempered crowd collected round that pub, Dinny said. Enough to scare the guts and the gizzard out of any man.

'There must've been six or seven thousand rushers, most of 'em foot-sore and shaggy with the beards that had grown on 'em. Wild-eyed and half-starved they looked, ready to tear the priest limb from limb if he did not keep his word. All who owned horses or camels, bicycles or buggies had brought 'em along, and stood or sat ready to make a dash in the direction Father Long might say the big slug had come from.'

There was a dangerous quiet about them, when the young priest appeared; the sort of oppressive stillness you feel before a thunderstorm.

'A few tried to cheer as he stood there pale and tremblin', tryin' to put a brave face on it,' Dinny said. 'God knows what would have happened if he hadn't said something definite. And at first I was shakin' in me shoes, the way he went on talkin' about the unenviable position he was in, and apologisin' for not realizin' the way the gold fever took us. Then he asked the boys to promise not to ask any more questions if he told 'em where the slug was found. Some promised, gettin' impatient, and arms went up like as if we were sproutin' broomsticks.

' "And now," says Father Long, "I will tell you where I think the nugget was found and the truth about it. I cannot tell you the names of the men who found it, because I have not got their permission. The nugget is at present unsullied and untouched. It is not in this town, but perhaps in one of the other towns and will be brought back to Kanowna. . . .

' "The nugget was found—," you could've heard a pin drop as the men held their breath to hear the next words. And then he said slowly: "a quarter of a mile on this side of the nearest lake on the Kurnalpi road."

'The crowd roared and plunged, men surgin' off, crashing and smashin' into each other, with horses rearin', camel-buggies tearin' a way for themselves. Shoutin', yellin', cursin', bawlin' with crazy laughter and cheers, the rush stampeded off towards the Kurnalpi road. You never saw such a mix-up. It was hell let loose and no mistake, and the wonder was nobody was trampled to death.'

Dinny said that he and a couple of hundred diggers waited to see if Father Long had anything further to say. When the uproar died down, he had said: 'The nugget was found not far from the road at a depth of five or six feet, and it weighed from ninety-five to a hundred pounds.' Then he walked off the balcony.

There was a feeble attempt at cheering, and somebody moved

a vote of thanks to Father Long for his statement. But a growling undertone made itself heard also. Many old hard-headed prospectors like Dinny and Tassy Regan were not impressed by the way the priest gave his information. It was no more than an 'I think' after all—and 'perhaps.' He had talked not so much like a man defending a sacred principle, but like one who was afraid 'he had been made the victim of a dirty trick.'

A number of diggers slung their gear together and turned back to Kalgoorlie. They were satisfied nothing would ever come of the rush: that Father Long's big slug was a myth. Hundreds of men, however, continued to peg and tear up the ground for miles round that dry lake on the Kurnalpi road; but without getting any indications of gold-bearing country for their pains.

The yarn went round that Father Long had been drinking with a well-known publican and some of his cronies who were boasting about the richness of the field. Under the influence of their whisky and tall tales he had either been shown a lump of something supposed to be gold, or he had had a vision of the glorious slug, and mentioned it in an unguarded moment, not realizing the danger in a whisper of any such find, and that a rush might be a matter of life or death for thousands of men. To those responsible for talking like that also, when his lies were exposed, McCann had just escaped with his life.

The rushers thirsted for vengeance against the men guilty of misleading Father Long. Tom Doyle, the big publican, and most popular man in Kanowna, was suspected of having something to do with it. Everybody knew his fondness for playing practical jokes. But Tom, six foot of a powerful wild Irishman, promised to pound the liver and lights out of any man harbouring such an idea.

Besides, he reminded a group of prospectors who tried to cross-question him, he was a prospector himself. Every penny he had was made on the fields. He was too long in the tooth to fool round with dynamite, like talking about a big slug that did not exist. He swore by the mother of God and all the saints he was with the boys in wanting to discover the hoaxers—because there wasn't much doubt in his mind that the priest had been deceived by some blackguards for their own purposes—whatever they were.

Not a word would he hear against Father Long, who, it must be understood, was under his protection. And wasn't Tom Doyle with the alluvial diggers in their struggle for justice? Of course he was! And hadn't he raised his voice for the diggers when John Forrest thought he could treat them like dirt? By God and so he had, and been arrested for it and charged with disorderly behaviour, inciting to revolt and what not—though there was no evidence, when it came to the point, that Tom Doyle had been doing any more than exercise his rights as a citizen to defend the alluvial diggers.

Sure, the men said, they knew all that. They did not believe Tom was in league with a gang of crooks who would start a rush for fun, or to make money out of it; but they had to let him know what was being said and investigate any such gossip.

Tom agreed with them and there were drinks on the house. Minor rushes to Golden Valley, Broad Arrow and Mulline carried off the backwash of Father Long's indiscretion. It was said he narrowly escaped rough-handling on more than one occasion.

Though Father Long continued to live on the fields, he looked like a ghost of himself. That fabulous nugget and the effects of the rush preyed on his mind and killed him, most people believed, rather than the typhoid fever he died of in Perth a few months later.

Tom Doyle was elected Mayor of Kanowna soon afterwards. But not before the alluvial diggers' struggle had entered a new phase.

It began when Mike Burke, Jimmy Miller, Ed ·Burns and Tassy Regan were arrested and charged with stealing ore, bagged and removed from the claims on the Ivanhoe Venture lease.

CHAPTER LVII

THE alluvial diggers went on working their claims on the Ivanhoe Venture lease. The Syndicate had been bagging and removing auriferous wash dirt from the dumps. Michael Burke, whose claim overlapped the Syndicate's main shaft, started work on the dump. His mates helped him to shovel and bag dirt, cart it to the battery. They contended that alluvial wash on that dump belonged to them.

A few days later Mike Burke, Tassy Regan, Jim Miller and Ed Burns were arrested and charged with bagging and stealing ore which was the property of the Ivanhoe Syndicate. The case was remanded, pending decision of the Full Court in a similar case at Peak Hill.

At a roll-up after the remand, diggers pointed out that they could not afford to hang round doing nothing meanwhile. They went back to work. Reports of good gold being won on many of the claims stoked their determination not to be deprived of it.

Burke's ore yielded two hundred and ten ounces at the battery. It had to be banked until the legal aspects of possession were cleared up. The men waited with growing excitement and assurance for the verdict in the Peak Hill case.

When it was announced their hopes were dashed to the ground. 'Can y'r beat it?' they exclaimed, flabbergasted.

The verdict was to the effect that alluvial miners may enter upon a goldmining lease to search for gold, but may not remove gold from the lease.

Such a pronouncement, in the opinion of the diggers, outraged justice and common sense. Who could be expected to support it? Not alluvial diggers on any goldfield in Australia. Only lease-holders and the mining companies greeted the verdict gleefully.

To be sure, the decision of the Court was not unanimous. There was talk of appeal to the Privy Council; but the alluvial diggers already had spent thousands in an attempt to have the law interpreted. If the case were taken to the Privy Council, the Government would have to bear the costs, they maintained.

The alluvial diggers announced their intention of fighting the issue on the spot. Prosecutions and imprisonment, they declared, would not induce them to surrender their right to alluvial gold. They knew that they were legally and morally right. Corrupt politicians had demonstrated their capacity to override the law and suborn its officers to their purposes. Nothing remained for workers on the goldfields but to demonstrate the power which lay behind their resistance to such measures.

The diggers went to work as usual. Burke and his mates continued removing ore from dumps on the claim. When a constable strolled across from the manager's house one morning and ordered them to stop work, they asked for his authority. He could not produce any. Diggers chaffed him good-humouredly and went on shovelling and bagging dirt.

Towards midday, Sub-inspector Holmes and Corporal Nicholls came out in a buggy. They took Mike Burke, Tassy Regan, Jimmy Miller and Ed Burns off to the lock-up. The men could have put up a fight, but they followed instructions and made no resistance.

They had expected that Mike Burke and his mates would be arrested again, made a joke of it, cheering them as they drove off in the police buggy and giving lusty curses and groans for the Warden and the government.

Acting all the time on the best legal advice to be got on the fields, the men faithfully carried out instructions, and on this skirmish, the Alluvial Diggers' Association scored another victory.

Judge Hensman in the Supreme Court, on the appeal in connection with the case, decided that as Jodrell, the original holder of the Ivanhoe Venture Syndicate lease had died without providing for a successor in his trust, and no steps had been taken for any person to establish a title, the lease was without a holder, and 'all actions subsequent to his death in connection with alleged trespass were beyond the powers of persons nominally prosecuting.'

It was stated that, in ordinary circumstances, Burke's action would have been theft from the leaseholders, because his claim overlapped the lessee's; but Judge Hensman ruled that the property had been allowed to lapse and Burke was as fully entitled as any other holder of a miner's right to seek for alluvial gold and remove ore from a dump, or from any other place within fifty feet of the defined reef. No attempt had been made to prove the existence of a reef on the Ivanhoe Venture lease.

In law, since the Peak Hill decision, an alluvial digger may be wrong to remove ore from a company's lease, it was argued, but in the equity of common sense and reason, Burke was proved to be well within his rights, removing gold carrying alluvial wash from what the judge declared to be an illegally held area.

There was great rejoicing over this judgment, although the new Mines Act and the Peak Hill decision still remained to obstruct progress.

CHAPTER LVIII

INCIDENTS continued fanning the men's anger and indignation. Alluvial ground which should never have been leased was being granted to leaseholders. At Slug Hill and Broad Arrow there were roll-ups protesting against leaseholders pegging over the claims of alluvial miners. The Ivanhoe Syndicate continued to obtain injunctions against the diggers: the diggers continued to work their claims.

Many old chaps, incapable of hard work, were fossicking and dryblowing round about Cassidy's Maritana and the Boulder. They eked out a miserable existence with the few 'dwts' they managed to glean now and then. The police started suddenly to demand their miners' rights, and hustled them off the claims when they could not produce up-to-date documents.

'Everybody knew the poor old b's hadn't a penny to bless themselves with,' Dinny said. 'It was a damned shame.'

A group of alluvial diggers on the Adeline lease, one of the Boulder group, had been doing well. When the lease was rushed and a hundred men pegged, there was a resurge of hostility to alluvialists. Tributors suspected of dummying for the company began to move ore from dumps claimed by the alluvial diggers.

In no time twenty diggers from the Adeline lease were in Fremantle gaol, Dinny among them.

Roll-ups on the claims, and mass meetings in the streets and halls of towns all over the fields were the order of the day again.

'There was no end to the dirty tricks the companies were ready to play against the men,' Dinny declared. 'Switching the test case against the Boulder tributors was one of them.' When the alluvial diggers got wind the case was to be Hannans Proprietary versus Cowly, the men's leaders pricked up their ears.

They began to make inquiries, declared that they had given their lawyer no instructions with regard to this man Cowly. Cowly had left a claim when the injunctions were issued. The men he had been mates with said they had seen nothing of him since, and he had no longer any interest in the claim.

Cowly had got a job with the Hannans Proprietary. That was all they knew about him. Yet this was the case taken to the Supreme Court before McCarthy's, Horan's or others, which had been heard in the Warden's Court some time before. Cowly's case had been accepted on the authority of the Warden, it transpired. The Association refused to have anything to do with either Cowly or his case.

Alluvial diggers were awake to the trap. The mining companies backing the tributors had got the Association cases deferred, hoping to get a decision on Cowly which would bind the diggers. The men laughed at the idea. They weren't going to be caught by such stinking cheese.

Not many men had recognized the new mining law and agreed to pay tribute to the mining companies for their right to mine alluvial gold. Under the new act most of them who had were regarded as dummies for the companies. The game they were playing was soon clear.

When a tributor on the Boulder backed his dray up to Dan Shea's dumps, Dan asked him what he thought he was doing. The tributor said he was working dumps on the lease and going to cart off the ore.

'You haven't got a hope,' Shea replied. 'The dump's mine. The ore came from my shaft.'

Shea admitted when he was charged that he took the horse's head, led it away, undid the slip and tipped the dray.

The tributor swore Shea had abused and threatened him, shoved him out of the way; and a couple of constables, standing handy to witness the episode, corroborated his evidence. Every-

336

body knew it was a put-up job. But Shea went to gaol for it.

The diggers decided to cart the ore on Shea's dump. In the morning, when dishes rattled for a roll-up, men mustered from all over the claims. The men's leaders explained the position. The time had come for action.

Four drays were driven up and backed against Shea's dump, loaded and driven off to the puddling machine at the back of Brown Hill. Several hundred diggers followed as an escort. Near the top of the hill troopers were waiting with a sergeant in charge. One of the Boulder tributors demanded that the police should arrest the drivers of the drays. Sergeant Smith played for time. He asked the diggers to wait until the Warden and Inspector Newlands arrived. They were on their way out and wanted to hear the facts.

The Warden did not come, but Newlands and Detective Kavanagh presently rode up. It was obvious that they intended to commandeer the drays and arrest the drivers. But the men were in a dangerous mood that morning. Troopers found themselves hustled to and fro as they tried to reach the drays, grab the reins and unseat the drivers. They were helpless among hundreds of angry and exasperated diggers, withdrew, and the drays drove on amid exulting cheers.

When they had emptied their loads, the drays returned to the dumps again, filled-up, and carted off another load of wash. All day the men worked doggedly, keeping to their plan of action. Inspector Newlands warned Mike Burke that it was likely to have serious consequences.

These consequences were deferred by return of the first batch of the Adeline men who had served their term of imprisonment at Fremantle.

A great reception was arranged in their honour. Thousands of men and women met them at the railway station. Sally went to welcome Dinny. The released diggers drove off in a four-in-hand drag, with banners flying and bands playing. A folded umbrella, carried like a sacred relic at the head of the procession, provoked laughter and hilarious booing from the crowd which lined the road. The townsfolk cheered enthusiastically as the returned men and marching diggers passed, in the brilliant sunshine of that sweltering afternoon.

At the intersection of Maritana and Hannan streets, a halt was made for speeches. One after another diggers declared their pride in the cause they were fighting for, and in the men who had suffered for their convictions. The spirit of the alluvial diggers remained undaunted. They said the Alluvial Diggers' Rights Association would continue to fight for the right of working miners to alluvial gold. Applause drowned the hoarse, passionate voice of the speakers.

'We know the people of Coolgardie, Kalgoorlie, Kanowna, Menzies—every camp on the fields—are with us,' Dinny, himself, said, when he spoke from the drag. 'The Alluvial Diggers' Association has obtained the best legal advice and we follow instructions. We've acted with care for two years: surrendered men peaceably to test our case.

'The places of prisoners are being taken by their mates in order to preserve every man's right to his claim. Accordin' to legal advice the Association's been given, tribute is an illegal tax. It's hittin' below the belt. But nothing's been too mean and unscrupulous for the legislators in Perth to try, in order to beat the diggers. They have not succeeded. They will never succeed in breaking the spirit of the men who've prospected and pioneered this country. The Alluvial Diggers' Association stands for justice for all and favour to none.'

Cheers resounded. Cheers for Dinny Quin, the Adeline heroes, 'the cause we fight for,' and the Alluvial Diggers' Association. Then the procession moved on with its bands and banners, trailing away down the long dusty road to the Boulder, where drinks and a great feed were to regale the returned men at the Exchange Hotel.

This demonstration was chiefly responsible for the patching-up of a truce between the Adeline men and the Boulder tributors. Well-known citizens were busy trying to overcome the causes for conflict. Alluvial diggers could not afford to stop work. They were living on tick at the stores, they explained. But they agreed not to remove ore from the disputed dumps until the test case approved by the Alluvial Rights' Association had been heard, on condition that the companies' men also agreed not to remove ore from these dumps.

'How do we know we can rely on you?' the citizens' committee asked.

'The alluvial diggers have never yet broken their word,' Pat McGrath replied, proudly.

After a week or so, when the diggers discovered that tributors were working the dumps, they reported the matter to the Warden. He warned the tributors that if they worked, the alluvial diggers would do likewise. The tributors continued to remove ore, a roll up was called, and the diggers decided to start work immediately.

But this time five hundred diggers stood by to help while their mates took possession of the dumps. Four drays drove up and were loaded.

They set out for the puddling machine at the back of Brown

Hill, escorted by hundreds of diggers. A squad of troopers under Inspector Newlands met them on the road. He harangued the diggers: told them that they must obey the law. The men's leaders replied that the ore belonged to the men who were handling it. They intended to keep what was theirs. There would be resistance if the police interfered.

Newlands ordered the arrest of the carters. The diggers closed round the drays. In the scuffle the troopers were driven back. The drays drove on, with the diggers following, exultant, and aroused to renewed energy and determination by this first demonstration of their power. All day they worked on their dumps and carted ore.

Police reinforcements, twenty troopers and fifty foot-police, arrived from the south and were camped on the Boulder lease.

Over a thousand diggers mustered to shift and cart ore after that. The police watched but did not interfere. There were roll-ups in the morning to discuss operations and big meetings at night. Discipline and loyalty were insisted on as essential to the carrying out of tactics. Everybody realized that a crisis was looming. But the diggers were more determined than ever to assert their right to take possession of the alluvial gold won on their claims.

Then one morning, soon after dawn, before the diggers assembled to start work, troopers and foot-police raided the claims and arrested a handful of men.

The *Kalgoorlie Miner* informed the townsfolk what had happened.

Dinny read a comment on the news aloud:

'The opinion is freely expressed that the police acted with remarkable bravery and dash. They raided the ground in the early morning; but still there were fully a dozen diggers at work, and the fact that it only took seventy police to overawe them redounds highly to the credit of the force. The police were armed with rifles, revolvers, swords, but were not supported by artillery. Such a deed can never be forgotten . . . It is confidently believed that the seventy can hold their own until reinforcements arrive.'

CHAPTER LIX

FIVE thousand diggers mustered on the Boulder lease, the following Sunday morning, to assist in the bagging and carting of dirt. Fifteen drays lined up to convey the ore to the Ivanhoe Venture where the men had a puddling machine.

There was a lot of wild talk. The policy of non-violence and allowing the law to take its course began to lose ground. But the Association kept a firm hand on the situation, urging members and supporters not to despair or play into the hands of the enemy by indulging in destructive acts and personal violence.

'The men's leaders held the organization together by inspiring a sense of discipline and loyalty which amazed all who saw that army of fearless and angry men,' Dinny said, as if he were addressing a public meeting on the subject, as he had often done. 'The men were as hot-headed and physically powerful as any who ever battled for their rights. Every citizen of the goldfields, knowin' the injustice and ill-treatment the diggers had suffered, understood the volcano the government was sittin' on. The arrogance and stupidity of the ministry was past understanding.'

Even mine-owners and the agents of foreign financiers on the fields, aware of the influences busy with the government behind the scenes, and the voices tempting old Sir John to play the strong man, marvelled at the patience of the alluvial diggers, as well as at the soundness of their organization. These men were frankly apprehensive of the situation: feared it could not last. And what of the riots and disorders in which the weight of numbers would be with the diggers? The foreigners were all for reinforcing the police and even for having a corps of militia on the spot. But people who knew the alluvial diggers realized that any such demonstration of force would drive the men to assert their heroic quality. Some might achieve the aura of martyrdom. And then the game was up. This was a disadvantage that capital had to contend with. There was no way to beat a body of men united to organize dauntlessly for their democratic rights.

Singing at a smoke social, Wallace Brownlow had added a verse to 'The Harp That Once Through Tara's Halls.' The diggers took it up. They could be heard, beefing the song out in the pubs and at roll-ups:

> 'And here in Freedom's cause we'll stand
>   And win in honest fight
> Against the laws that keep the land
>   Back from each miner's right.
> We'll rally round and keep our ground
>   And then with heart and might
> We'll make the very hills resound—
>   "Protect each miner's right!"'

The diggers sang as they drove their dray loads of disputed wash to the battery; cursed Blow-fly Hare, and the tin-pot legislators in Perth; swore cheerfully over every pot of beer in the pubs to stand by their cause and each other, until every man with a miner's right could work alluvial gold as he had been accustomed to.

'They've gaoled a few of our mates,' the diggers declared exuberantly. 'But there's twenty or thirty thousand of us waitin' to be dealt with. What's Sir John goin' to do about that?'

Those who were on gold contributed nuggets to the fighting fund of the Alluvial Diggers' Rights Association. Every man put a few shillings into a kitty for the wives and children of mates arrested and imprisoned. Many business men and well-known citizens donated large sums to pay legal expenses, others gave £1 weekly to keep the diggers in food and tobacco.

Every day made a clash between the diggers and the police seem inevitable. Well-known business men and leading citizens got together to stave it off. At a quickly arranged conference, Father O'Gorman, the Mayor, the Warden, John Kirwan and delegates of the Alluvial Diggers' Rights Association, drew up a scheme for settlement of the trouble. A truce was declared until the government should be given an opportunity to sanction the terms of this settlement.

The government's reply did nothing to reassure the alluvial diggers. A deputation from the conference interviewed the Premier and achieved nothing.

Mick Mannion's application for forfeiture of the Ivanhoe Venture lease brought a new factor into the stormy atmosphere.

Mick's grounds for making the application were non-compliance with labour conditions for working the lease, and the fact that the lease had been put on the list for forfeitable non-payment of rent. Mick's evidence went to prove that no work had been done on three days specified, that the ladder was broken on the company's shaft and that a man running a condenser plant was not an employee of the company.

Charley Moran, opposing the application, claimed that the Minister of Mines had removed the lease from the list of holdings forfeitable for non-payment of rent. The government's expressed intention of compensating the company was a recognition of its legal position. Mick lost, of course. The Warden decided that the leaseholder could not work the lease, owing to the presence of alluvial diggers on the ground. It would be unfair, therefore, to penalize him for non-compliance with labour conditions, and deprive the Ivanhoe Venture Syndicate of the lease.

The men howled their derision of such a verdict. It was just another example, they contended, of the way the law was being used against alluvial diggers and in favour of the leaseholders.

Opposition was growing to the Association's policy of legal action and non-violent resistance to the police.

The Alluvial Diggers' Association still urged the need for giving the government no pretext to deal with the diggers as a disorderly mob.

'We're fighting for a grand principle,' Pat McGrath said. 'We're not crooks or larrikins, ashamed of what we're doing. That's why we gave our names to the police the other day. We're seeking an opportunity to justify ourselves before an impartial tribunal. We must get laws for the benefit of the people and not for a few boodlers.'

That was all very well, the men agreed. But many had become restive and dissatisfied. The police were armed. If they used their arms—if any diggers were killed or wounded—it would be more than some of the boys could stand. What would happen in the madness of such a moment no one could foresee. A man was entitled to defend himself. He could not see his mates shot down in cold blood, and be unprepared to shoot back. But for a digger to start the shooting would be fatal to the cause they were fighting for. Every man recognized that: swore on oath not to reveal he had any means of defending himself, or to use a weapon until the police had opened fire.

'But,' Mike Burke said impressively, 'we show the spirit that is in us when we take the drays past the police. We will never stop now until this new law which favours the monopolist and capitalist, and hinders honest working men from earning their living, is wiped off the statute book.'

CHAPTER LX

A CLASH was expected on the following Sunday morning. The diggers mustered in force to protect the men shovelling ore on the dumps and driving the drays. There were cheers when they started off, eighteen of them, moving slowly in single file against the blue sky and red earth. Dinny was driving one, and Chris Crowe on another behind him.

Eight thousand men had gathered to take part in any conflict, if the police attempted to stop the cavalcade, or arrest the drivers. No names were to be given if they were asked for. It was rumoured that several of the men's leaders had revolvers and that rifles were hidden near the spot where trouble was expected. If the police interfered with what the men were determined to do, everybody knew there was going to be violence and bloodshed that morning.

Mounted troopers watching the men at work from the outskirts of the crowd remained alert but inactive.

Before beginning operations, and at knock-off time for crib, Pat McGrath and other speakers warned the diggers not to touch any but their own ore, and to go about their business in a disciplined and orderly way. The diggers were told to avoid hostility to the police; but if the police attempted to interfere, the diggers must carry on with their business as had been decided. Every man must be prepared to suffer the consequences of the day's work. It might mean years of imprisonment.

'We'll risk it!' the men yelled.

'We're ready to show 'em we mean what we say, Pat.'

'It's a great fight for a grand principle we're in, boys,' Pat McGrath shouted. 'We've endeavoured to get justice by quiet ways, we must use the only other way in our power, now. Demonstrate we intend to keep what is ours.'

Work continued all day without any disturbance; but the municipal elections were being held next day, and most of the men went into town to vote.

That afternoon, when only two or three diggers remained on the claims, twenty-eight armed troopers with Sergeant Smith, Inspector Connolly and several plain-clothes policemen stationed themselves behind the stable yard, near the manager's house on the Ivanhoe lease. Plain-clothes men went among the diggers and arrested them. The men could make no resistance. They were packed into a cart and driven off to the Kalgoorlie lock-up with an escort of twelve mounted troopers.

The cart, driven by a black tracker with a policeman beside him, returned to the stable yard on the Ivanhoe Venture lease. Four more men were arrested by the same ruse, among them Mike Burke, Dan Shea and Paddy McGrath.

When the diggers heard what had happened they flocked to the police station. Hundreds stood hooting and jeering at the police and the government, cheering the arrested men. Stones rattled on the roof of the police station. Bill King and some of the Kanowna men were ready to rush the ramshackle buildings and release their mates. Mullocky O'Dwyer, on behalf of the Association, held them back: called on them to remember their oath of loyalty to decisions of the organization.

The police were called out to guard the police barracks and

gaol. They stood with fixed bayonets facing the diggers. Nothing was more calculated to break the last straw of the men's sanity and patience. They howled their derision and defiance. For a moment it was touch and go whether the incitement of that display of force, or the desperate appeals of the men's leaders would prevail.

Mullocky won by carrying the diggers off to a meeting in the town. Standing on a cart at the cross streets, he made a speech full of natural eloquence, wit, noble sentiments, and hell-fire for the government. Mullocky O'Dwyer was a grand speaker and a fine figure of a man, six feet, with a mane of golden hair and a great golden beard, like a legendary hero of old Ireland. As a mob orator he was unequalled: could do anything with a crowd.

He urged the men that evening not to let themselves become tools of the enemy, by wrecking the gaol, or getting into holts with the police. Nothing would suit the government better than to bring charges of riotous behaviour against the diggers, he pointed out, reminding them that they stood for right and justice, and that all decent men who were capable of judging between right and wrong supported them.

Under great provocation the alluvial diggers had remained a disciplined body of men, acting in accordance with decisions agreed upon. Let them do nothing hot-headed or foolhardy which would destroy their organization, or ability to fight on. They must fight more resolutely than ever, now that so many of their leaders had been arrested. They must fight until the political cockerels in Perth were defeated and every digger had won his miner's right to alluvial gold.

Mullocky O'Dwyer was now regarded as the men's leader. An escort of two or three hundred followed him about that night. When he heard a crowd had gathered round the gaol again, he went along to keep any boozers out of mischief. A few drinks had made some of the lads noisy and obstreperous. The police were still lined-up facing the crowd with fixed bayonets. When Inspector Connell came out to give instructions, the diggers howled him down and surged forward. Connolly ordered the police to clear the streets and they charged, driving the people before them.

'It was a sight a man's not likely to forget,' Dinny said. 'The police with their swords flashin', drawn up in a line facin' Maritana Street and the mounted constables behind. They drove the people off the streets: off their own land as though they were a rabble and had no right there. God! There was murder in every digger's heart that night. We were unarmed. But we could've stood up to the police and wiped them out, if we'd used

344

the rifles we did have stowed away. Some of us begged Mullocky to give the order, but Mick Mannion and John Reside held him back. And Mullocky was no wild Irishman, but a good leader. He would have led the men into any organized resistance, but he would not let them rush madly into a shindy that night.'

Bail was refused the imprisoned men, though Father O'Gorman and several well-known citizens applied for it on behalf of the Association.

At seven o'clock next morning, after an early session of the Warden's Court, the prisoners were packed off by special train to Fremantle. This prevented local justices from sitting on the bench during hearing of their case. The men's lawyer was not informed and deprived of an opportunity to advise them.

Such a flagrant abuse of authority created furious indignation.

At a meeting of diggers and citizens held in Boulder, a resolution was carried that 'the introduction of a semi-military element on to the fields is dangerous and repugnant to a self-governing community.' Speakers pointed out that in no other Australian colony were police kept under arms to coerce the people.

Dinny voiced the anger and resentment of the meeting when he said:

'The alluvial man's birthright has been given away, and now the Gover'ment is goin' to bayonet the people to make them submit to robbery. In Victoria, no lease would be granted on a goldfield for eleven years, and in Queensland for two; but if the alluvial is not worked out, the time can be extended. The West Australian Mines Act was based on the Queensland Act; but two years is too long for the speculators wantin' to float their claims in London, so they'd made a bargain with the Forrest Government. If they were given the reefs and lodes, the mine owners agreed to let the alluvial men take the alluvial. But that was only the thin end of the wedge. As soon as they got the reefs and lodes, they wanted the alluvial as well, and in an evil hour the government broke faith with the people. The Perth policemen would have to dragoon the fields to make people submit to such iniquitous injustice.

Everywhere this attempt at 'government by fixed bayonet' was being discussed. Citizens and diggers reminded each other of Sir John Forrest's remark to representatives of the Alluvial Diggers' Rights Association, only a few months ago:

'If I held a bayonet up to you and said: "You've got to give in!" you wouldn't like it.'

The whole town boiled over in criticism of the Warden, the

police and the government. A protest meeting was organized to be held on the Kalgoorlie Recreation Reserve.

Men, women and children turned out to cheer the procession, which with three bands and many banners, led by Patrick Whelan, J.P., on a grey charger, marched from the Adeline leases through the town. The crowd took up the texts on the banners and shouted them lustily: 'Alluvial Rights and Alluvial Gold for the Alluvial Men!'

'Fair Play, Fair Laws, Justice for All.'

Ten thousand people followed the procession to the reserve and stood in the hot sunshine, listening to the speeches.

Two platforms had been erected. Among others, the Mayor, Fimister, Frank Vosper, John Kirwin, Father O'Gorman and John Reside spoke from them. Volleys of applause interrupted their speeches, putting the case for the diggers and denouncing the government. Mr. William Burton, one of the justices of the peace, impressed everybody when he said:

'I did not come here, on this Sabbath afternoon, to incite people to revolution.' His voice shook with emotion. 'But there is a reason why our feelings should be stirred to the utmost, and for us to resolve that, unless the wrongs the goldfields people have to bear now are remedied, strong action should be taken.'

Everybody knew the goldfields had saved Western Australia when it was on the verge of bankruptcy. Yet with a population more than a half that of the rest of the State, the goldfields had practically no voice in the government. Heavily taxed, and still struggling against water shortage, the most primitive lighting, hospital, sanitary and educational arrangements, continually ravaged by fire and typhoid, the goldfields towns which provided the financial sinews of the state treasury, were fobbed off with only an infinitesimal fraction of the representation to which a democratic community was entitled.

'Kalgoorlie's the town that lays the golden egg,' people were saying. 'And what do we get for it? Less consideration than Cockney stock jobbers and land sharks. Half a dozen families down south think they can run the country for their own benefit. With a monopoly of the vote make laws to suit themselves and try to rule the goldfields by armed force!'

What William Burton had said was an indication of how serious the situation had become. When a mild and pious old chap like that could speak so strongly, no wonder the diggers were straining at the leash. But Mr. Burton had only said what people were thinking. It was surprising that the diggers had not broken into open revolt before this. The marvel was how the Association had held them. Nothing but the discipline and loyalty to their organization, which the men's leaders required from every member, had prevented conflict with the police.

The arrogance, stupidity and corruption of the Forrest government would be held responsible for any violence and bloodshed which occurred, that was certain. The diggers had behaved with remarkable self-restraint, considering their numbers, and that they were for the most part tough and powerful men who were bursting to let off steam in a violent skirmish.

Since the recent arrests and shanghai-ing of the men off to Fremantle without trial, keeping them herded in railway carriages without proper food, or sleep, for thirty-six hours, nobody could blame the diggers if they resisted further arrests and defended their mates by any means in their power. After the way armed police had chased citizens off the streets, hustled and jostled them as if they were cattle, the townsfolk understood very well how such a brutal threat to human life maddened men, and drove them to accept the challenge with a reckless indifference to consequences.

Every bayonet in a policeman's hand had meant: 'Get out of my way or I'll kill you!'

People on the goldfields could not forgive that. They could not condone the use of armed troopers against their own people: against the alluvial diggers who had suffered such injustices, against women and children in the crowd, and against the rights of citizens in their own town. This Kalgoorlie which they had raised from a ramshackle mining camp in a drought-stricken wilderness to a fine city, and regarded with such possessive pride!

The whole affair outraged democratic instincts. It brought many people who had been more or less passive supporters of the diggers into active co-operation with them, because it was realized the diggers' struggle had become part of a struggle for better living conditions which all dwellers on the goldfields would share. The wave of indignation and sympathy rose to full tide, that day, and swept everybody into a maelstrom of wrath and resentment.

When Vosper began to speak, he was greeted with cheering which could be heard miles away. He stood before the people as their champion: a champion of the rights and liberties of the working-class, a tall, black-coated figure with long hair flowing back from his noble, clear-cut face. In a calm, ringing voice, he addressed that angry, excited assembly, bringing reason and logic to bear on the chaos of many minds. He was all for maintaining resistance to the government's oppressive measures by organization and the avoidance of physical violence.

There were still means, he maintained, by which the wrongs of people of the goldfields could be redressed. Public opinion in all the states of Australia was with them: funds were being dispatched to aid the alluvial diggers, and more adequate political representation for the goldfields could be won. Although Mr. Justice Hensman's latest decision on the basis of the new Mines Act had gone against the diggers, and in favour of the lease-holders, the legal fight was by no means over.

The judges admitted there was a big doubt, even yet, as to whether alluvial gold did not belong legally as well as morally to the diggers. Chief Justice Onslow had remarked on the absence of positive language in the Act, to provide for giving the gold to the leaseholders. Mr. Justice Stone was even more dubious about an interpretation which did so. Who could blame the alluvial diggers, then, if they refused to be bound by such a ruling? Or by an Act designed to defeat the purposes of their struggle.

When the government lost a case in the Full Court, recently, it proposed an appeal to the Privy Council—at the people's cost. The diggers were prevented from making such an appeal because of the heavy costs involved. How could they be expected to accept such a state of things!

The crowd roared its answer:

'They never will!'

'Alluvial gold for the alluvial diggers!'

'To hell with the Forrest government!'

'Home rule for the goldfields!'

Vosper moved the resolution which declared: 'That the present crisis is due to the vague laws and maladministration, and it is imperative on the government to introduce comprehensive measures which will comprise justice to the alluvial men.' This resolution was carried with enthusiasm, but did not satisfy the expectations of an audience hungry for a plan of drastic action.

Father O'Gorman, the young Irish priest, captured the spirit of the day when he said: 'There is only one way to allay the present unrest; and that is to give back to the alluvial digger his God-given right, and let the leaseholders keep the reefs and lodes.'

It was rumoured that in the anger of the moment, after the arrest of Mike Burke, Dan Shea, Tassy Regan and the others, Father O'Gorman had cried to Mullocky O'Dwyer:

'What are ye goin' to do about it?'

'I don't know,' said Mullocky.

'Don't know?' the priest exclaimed heatedly. 'Y're great hulking carcase is all y're thinking of. In Ireland y'd know what to do: but here in Australia, where the oppression is worse, ye don't know what to do!'

Mullocky had to persuade Father O'Gorman, the yarn went,

that he was bound to act in accordance with decisions of the Alluvial Rights Association, and that when the workers had a powerful organization to achieve their ends, more was to be gained by working through it than by raiding the gaol and taking the men out of the hands of the police. Father O'Gorman had come round to that point of view: done all he could to get bail for the arrested diggers and arouse support for them among the townsfolk.

Dinny chuckled when he explained how a letter had arrived from the Bishop asking Father O'Gorman to refrain from taking part in political activity. It was intimated that his activity in connection with the alluvial diggers' struggle had become displeasing to the Premier, Sir John Forrest.

'Who is this man, John Forrest?' O'Gorman inquired. 'I am not acquainted with him. This letter did not emanate from the brain of His Reverence. It emanated from the brain of this man, John Forrest. Therefore I am disregarding it.'

O'Gorman belonged to an order which could afford to disregard local dignitaries of the Church, it was said. He continued to identify himself with the cause of the diggers. There was never a more popular priest on the goldfields.

The news that a warrant was out for Mullocky O'Dwyer's arrest whetted the anger of the crowd. At the same time everybody was delighted to know Mullocky was dodging the police.

'Did y'r hear how Mullocky gave the troopers the slip last night?' someone would say. 'There he was, sitting in the barparlour at McSweeney's, goin' over a bit of business with the boys, when he noticed somebody tamperin' with the skylight. Mullocky waited till that rat crawled away and then did the disappearin' trick. When the troopers surrounded the house, he wasn't there.

'They thought they'd got him having a drink with some of us at the Exchange. A whole squad of troopers lined up to lay hold of him; but all of a sudden, Mullocky wasn't there at all, and there was the police, stompin' round, ransackin' the place, and cursin' to be makin' such fools of themselves, and the boys mockin' and givin' 'm hell all the time!'

The story went the rounds: gurgling laughter and outbursts of jubilation accompanying every account of Mullocky's exploits. His jokes and sayings, the verses and songs he made for the diggers, passed from one to another, stimulating confidence, good-humour and a bold adoption of the purposes for which this great open-air meeting had been called.

Its significance was contained in the last resolution, which Dinny still treasured and read with pride:

'That, in the event of the government refusing to deal justly with the diggers or to redress their wrongs, this meeting pledges itself to take immediate action to shake off once and for all the intolerable tyranny inflicted on the goldfields residents by the Perth parliament.

Thousands of people who had passed that resolution with a great singing roar of 'Ayes,' with shouts of exhaltation and a mighty swinging outburst of enthusiasm, went home, intoxicated with excitement and the stirring sense of a new, vigorous life before them.

It was impossible now for southern politicians to talk of 'a turbulent, worthless and accursed minority' on the fields, stirring up strife and fomenting disaffection. Or for Sir John Forrest to pretend that the 'poisonous and disreputable' goldfields press was exaggerating reports of seething discontent and a movement for separation.

All sections of the community had spoken at that historic Kalgoorlie meeting. The voice of people living on the goldfields had made itself heard. Loudly and clearly it spoke, announcing that the cause of the alluvial diggers was the cause of the people, and that a separate goldfields state was not the wild dream of a few malcontents. It had been adopted as an objective for which residents on the goldfields could work, to attain a full measure of democratic representation, and remain an integral unit of the federation of Australian States.

There was the rub, and there the big stick which people of the goldfields held over the Forrest Government.

CHAPTER LXI

No time was lost in giving effect to the resolutions by the Kalgoorlie meeting. Almost immediately a conference was summoned which met in Coolgardie. Delegates from representative bodies all over the fields attended it and carried a vote for separation by sixty to one.

A plan was drawn up to establish a separate state with Esperance as its port, and railways connecting the port with inland towns of the mining area. These would make Coolgardie, Kalgoorlie, and all the far camps independent of Perth and Fremantle, besides providing a shorter route for travellers and food supplies. The idea spread like wildfire. It was adopted by mass meetings everywhere, and a petition presented to parliament.

This was treated rather as a joke by the people down south who did not understand the grievances of goldfields residents. The government, of course, promptly rejected the petition.

The separation movement gained strength from the Forrest Government's continued opposition to federation. Sir John was proposing at last to take a referendum on an adulterated and confusing version of the Commonwealth Bill. This manoeuvre deceived no one.

Mr. A. E. Morgans, the mining magnate, who represented Coolgardie in the Legislative Assembly, was anti-federation and anti-separation. His constituents called upon him to resign. He kept his seat and abused the separation movement as 'grovelling and treacherous.' Miners and prospectors hooted derisively. Could anything better describe the behaviour of the honourable member, they asked.

Father O'Gorman had got his walking papers by this time. He was going to London and promised to bring the wrongs and grievances of people of the goldfields before members of the House of Commons with whom he was acquainted.

It was remembered that John Morley had said to the Secretary of State for the colonies, Mr. Joseph Chamberlain, in the House of Commons, before the Boer War:

'In the name of paramountcy, you are going to impose conditions on the Transvaal Republic which, for the life of you, you dare not impose upon any self-governing colony you have got.'

To which Chamberlain had replied:

'If a self-governing British colony should impose upon British subjects such conditions as are imposed upon British subjects in the Transvaal, I say we should interfere to cut the connection.'

That was plain enough, Dinny argued. The Goldfields Separation Movement had got in touch with members of the House of Commons who were prepared to remind Mr. Chamberlain of this statement in connection with the goldfields petition.

A handsome casket was ordered and thousands of signatures collected for a petition to Her Majesty Queen Victoria. Pasted on white calico, they were a mile long and appealed that the British Government should accede to the request of loyal subjects on the goldfields for incorporation in a separate state: a state separate from Western Australia, but part of the federation of Australian states.

The people of the goldfields had the support of the other states in their resistance to the Forrest Government. Their demand for separation, and federation, became a vital factor in the campaign for federation.

Each of the other states by a referendum had accepted the

proposals for federation. Only the people of Western Australia were being deprived of an opportunity to vote in a referendum for that specific purpose.

What the Secretary of State for the Colonies did in the matter was not known for some time. Then it was ascertained that he had communicated with Sir Alexander Onslow, the Governor and Queen's representative in Western Australia, by telegram, requesting him to impress on the Forrest Government the urgent need for Western Australia to join the federation of Australian colonies. The possibility of the goldfields being granted separation, if Western Australia failed to become part of the union, was emphasized.

The bunglers in Perth had fallen into the fire they, themselves, started. For Sir John it became a question of lose the goldfields or federate. A measure was rushed through both houses of parliament, enabling men and women, who had been in the colony twelve months, to vote, thus freeing the goldfields population from a restricted franchise and ensuring success of the referendum.

Alluvial diggers congratulated themselves on having forced the issue: given the Forrest Government a taste of democratic discipline and won the day for federation in the West.

Vosper, Mick Mannion and most of the first organizers of the Alluvial Diggers' Rights Association regarded what had been accomplished as a vindication of their policy of 'calmly and firmly executed passive resistance.'

But Dinny, Paddy McGrath, Mike Burke, Mullocky O'Dwyer and some of the men who had fought all through the campaign, said that was all very well in the beginning. It had enabled the diggers to organize: have a powerful, well-disciplined body of men behind them. But it was only when the policy of passive resistance had failed to have results, and the men were prepared for militant action, whatever the cost, that the government had been forced to capitulate. Public feeling had been aroused and the fear of another Eureka. To be sure, the principle the men were fighting for strengthened their position. But that had not affected the Forrest Government. It was sound organization, plus a militant spirit, which had won the day and moved the Colonial Office to take action.

Dinny's old Crowe muttered now and then as the discussion raged round him one night at Mick Mannion's.

'What's that y're sayin', Chris?' Mick asked.

Chris's quotations from poets, prophets and ancient philosophers, were regarded almost as oracles.

'It was stated by Cleobalus,' Chris said, 'that "the great state is where the citizens fear blame more than punishment." '

At the same time as the politicians in Perth were scuttling about like ants whose dump has been knocked about their ears, the alluvial diggers were standing trial.

They had been brought back to Kalgoorlie and committed to the Quarter Sessions at Coolgardie. It was understood that no jury on the goldfields would convict them and the charges must be dropped.

The government was all out now to save face and avoid arousing further demonstrations of hostility. Under the circumstances, Mullocky O'Dwyer was advised to allow himself to be arrested and have the charge against him disposed of when the others were heard.

It was a great day when the Crown Prosecutor entered a *nolle prosequi*, which meant that no proceedings should be taken against the alluvial diggers, and they came home in triumph.

CHAPTER LXII

THROUGH the ferment of the roll-ups, meetings, arrests, court cases, demonstrations, Alf contrived to occupy himself with the daily business of running his mine. He had come to think of it like that. As his mine, though he jeered at himself for doing so. Not a pennyweight of gold in the Midas belonged to him: not the screw of a machine. Neither script, nor contract, entitled him to any share in its production.

And yet the mine, as it moved now, was his creature, his ship, the complicated mechanism which he forced to function producing wealth. The underground boss, constructional engineer, engineer, metallurgist, miners, mechanics and clerks cursed Mr. Brierly for the way he drove them to serve the mine.

Primitive methods had damaged the Midas in its infancy. It was one of the oldest mines on the field: the guts had been torn out of it and it had been left derelict for nearly two years. When it was reopened, the mine showed a loss of nearly a thousand a month for three months.

Nobody denied that Brierly had worked wonders with the Midas. He was able to show a profit the first month after he took charge: within the next few months had opened up a new lode and brought the mine into the first line of producers.

It had been a tough proposition, crawling through the dark

wet bowels of the mine, inspecting ground that had been worked over and abandoned, probing with the new diamond drill for prospects to develop. He thanked his stars when he struck a rich lode, at the hundred and twenty feet level: opened it up and stoped. Those stopes were still feeding the ore bins.

Alf held the mine in his consciousness like a clockwork toy, a rather old-fashioned and rusty toy which he had oiled, cleaned, and made to work. He was familiar now with every twist and turn of its haphazard underground burrowings, every rise and winze, every rough and ready device for hauling and crushing ore. He had overhauled gear and machinery, repairing and improvising, until he knew the strength and weakness of every link in the chain of its production processes.

As he sat in his office, with maps of the mine on the wall and the blue prints of machinery he wanted to buy lying on the table beside him, he was acutely conscious of the work going on all round.

He could see the main shaft from his window: watch the winchman lowering the men going on shift. Almost unconsciously followed the cage as it bumped and slobbered against the wet walls of the shaft, descending to the lowest levels. In his mind's eye he saw miners slouching through the stopes, their candles flickering in the damp, foul darkness: watched them start work in dangerous rises, apprehensive and cursing, heard the buzz and roar of the drills, and the clatter of stone falling as the machine-man's mate cleared away after the last firing.

Ore was rattling down the ore passes, in his brain, night and day: the stampers pounding with their heavy, hungry, trampling tread. He swore at the boggers shifting mullock and loafing over the job: fretted impatiently about work which had started on a drive south of the lode to make connection with a winze coming down from the surface. He was anxious about the progress of that work. It should insure increased production.

That was the worst of these old mines. They weren't any better than the Cornish mines which had been worked hundreds of years ago, the American engineers said. Alf was ashamed of the way his mine had grown, without planning, without any regard for ventilation or the safety of men who worked in it. The old workings had fallen in, in some places, and the earth creaked in untimbered stopes. No wonder the men refused to work in them. He had timbered to a certain extent and improved conditions; but they remained insanitary, dangerous and a constant source of breakdowns and stoppages.

Mr. Brierly had urged on his directors the need for a comprehensive scheme of reorganization, ventilation and timbering.

They informed him they were not prepared to embark on any plan which would require such expenditure in the immediate future.

Alf thought he knew what that meant. Paddy Cavan had confirmed his suspicions: sale of the mine was on the cards, although he rejected the idea of attaching any importance to what Paddy said. Alf realized that all he had done was to satisfy his employers the mine was an asset and not a liability. The chances were they would sell while production was on the up-grade.

Meanwhile, to steer the mine on an even keel was his responsibility. He accepted it, though the burden became increasingly heavy. His pride and prestige demanded that the Midas should maintain the position which he had given her.

Alf had earned a reputation for being a shrewd and capable manager 'of the old school,' honest and scrupulous in the service he gave his employers. It had not been easy to acquire that reputation. His methods were based on the experience of a practical miner, and the smattering of engineering, geology and metallurgy he had picked up from specialists in the various phases of mine development, with whom he had worked. No one was more conscious of his limitations: no one more envious of the brilliant young men with university degrees, arriving from America and Germany, under contract to the big firms. Some importance was still attached to men of his type: men who knew the country: had learnt their mining on the fields. But more and more the mines were being handed over to technically competent newcomers.

They talked loudly of the waste and inefficiency of mining on the Boulder and everywhere around Kalgoorlie, although they declared more mines had been ruined by bad mill management than by bad mining. They were introducing the open stope, although Australian mine-managers favoured the mullocking-up of stopes to prevent disintegration in the mine.

Alf was sure the Yanks were wrong in this and that time would show the advantage of the Australian practice. But the miners were still working with candle, hammer and drill: dry-boring with old-fashioned piston machines, dust flying all the time. The men worked in the smoke from fractures. Hundreds of lives were lost through miners' phthisis. Defective timbering, worn out gear, caused many accidents. In almost every mine where soft ground stoping was carried on, falls of earth were continually occurring.

There had been a heavy fall in the Midas recently. Two men were killed. Of course, the Midas Gold Mining Company got a verdict of 'no blame attachable.' And, of course, blame was attachable. Alf writhed when he thought of it: could not get the sight of those men out of his mind, or the way their mates had toiled to get the bodies from under a pile of shifting earth and rubble, with the overhanging wall threatening all the time to come down on them. Sheer grit and a courage the average miner displayed as a matter of course!

Alf felt sore about that accident because he had drawn up an estimate for ventilating and timbering the stope a year ago. Only to be told expenses must be kept down and profits maintained for the present.

'Production will improve if men are not afraid the ground they're working is likely to come away on them,' Alf had pointed out. 'A man doubles his output in safe ground.'

But it was no use. Men were cheaper than timber: could easily be replaced, although something would have to be done about that stope now. The Americans gaped at some of the places men were working in, underground, on the Boulder!

'Get me outa this, quick,' the big Texan, who Alf was showing round the Midas, exclaimed. He made no attempt to disguise his panic when he discovered the state of the roof over a lode formation he had been examining.

'Garsh,' he breathed, out of the danger zone, 'the whole caboose is liable to come down on you any minute.'

'It's good for a few months yet, we think,' Alf replied carelessly, not relishing his visitor's assumption of superior knowledge.

'Waal, I guess Gard put the gold in the ground, and all you guys reckon you gotta do is haul it out and run it through an old stamp mill,' the American remarked. 'Of all the gol-darn, infernal, prehistoric relics! Wastes almost as much as it turns over. Why, there's fortunes in y'r tailing dumps! And Modest Maryanski tells me y'r've been throwing y'r telluride on to the dumps—'

'To say nothing of paving our streets with gold,' Alf added. 'Maryanski never forgets to mention he found a few decent specimens in road metal.'

The American grinned:

'And some of the big men are sayin' the future of this town depends on solving the problem of sulphide ores. I'm stackin' on our new mills to eliminate waste.'

Alf was impressed with these mills which pulverized by both the dry and wet processes, breaking the ore into fine particles suitable for cyaniding or chlorination. He wanted them installed on the Midas. The old-fashioned stamper battery was slower, but simple, his directors contended. They preferred to stick to it until the new American mill had proved itself.

Mr. Brierly and his directors had had some differences of opinion about this. The occurrence of sulphide ores at depth and their treatment was disquieting the directors.

What was known as 'the sulphide bugbear' had been perturbing mining men for some time. Because of the persistence of sulphide ores the Great Boulder and Associated Mines were in a bad way. Although the group of mines along the Boulder ridge had been proclaimed the richest gold producers in the world, it was being rumoured now that their oxidized ores were limited. Only the schists, or country rock near the surface, bore the lodes impregnated with high-grade gold: the sulphide ores, containing telluride of gold, obtained at depth were of less value.

Zeb Lane's contract with the Boulder Milling Company to treat Great Boulder tailings and sulphide ores gave colour to this rumour. The contract provided the Milling Company with handsome terms. Investigation supplied the reason. Money to finance the Milling Company had been found by the Great Boulder. The chairman, some of the directors and officers of the Great Boulder were also shareholders in the Milling Company. The scandal created a sensation, but passed as one of the tricks to bleed shareholders regarded as legitimate business. The problem of sulphide ores remained, depressing the share market and worrying producers.

Alluvial diggers saw in the sulphide difficulties of the mine proprietors another reason for the move to deprive working men of alluvial gold. But Alf was sure the problem of treating sulphide ores would be solved, and give a new lease of life to the mining industry. He had been interested in Callanan's experiments at the Lake View: watched him treating the ore by crushing, cyaniding and filter presses, preparing the sulphides for roasting.

'Gold may be richest where the sun shines on it,' he said, 'but the wealth of the mines is not going to rot because we have not yet learnt the most effective way to handle it. Sulphide won't wreck Kalgoorlie.'

It did not. But Alf did not live to see the tall smoke-stacks belching their yellow, evil-smelling fumes along the Golden Mile, clouding the starry sky at night, and making millions for the men who had bought shares during the sulphide slump.

CHAPTER LXIII

ALTHOUGH he had foreseen it might happen, it was a shock to Alf Brierly when he received a letter from his directors, informing him that the mine had been sold to a French syndicate, and that their representative, M. Paul Malon, who was in Kalgoorlie, would immediately take possession of the property. Mr. Brierly was thanked for his valuable services to the company and requested to facilitate transfer of the mine and its offices to the new proprietors.

Alf lost no time in calling on M. Malon, who had a room in Frisco's offices. But it was Frisco who met him on behalf of Malon and his syndicate.

Oh, hullo, Alf,' he exclaimed, all geniality as usual. 'Have a cigar?'

Frisco opened and handed over the box of cigars. Without waiting for Alf to help himself, he went on:

'Malon asked me to get in touch with you. He's mighty pleased with himself about bringing off this deal with the Midas Company. They're tough customers—stuck out for a cool £20,000. Big figure in the present state of the market. But I advised Malon to stump up. We've got a lot of money behind us in this syndicate. Have bought the Gloria and the South-West Extended. Will be floating 'em in the near future.'

Frisco would have gone on talking breezily about Malon, the Parisian Gold Mining Company, its plans, and Mr. de Morfé's association with it as agent and local adviser, but for Alf's suspicion that Frisco was keeping him in suspense, and was rather enjoying the position of being the power behind Malon and his syndicate.

'What I want to know,' Alf said, bluntly, 'is where I stand in the new set-up?'

'Of course!' Frisco was immediately apologetic and concerned. 'Sorry, old chap, but you know how it is with these foreigners. They want to put their own men in charge, install up-to-date machinery, and show us just how a goldmine ought to be run.'

'Christ!' Alf protested. 'Nobody could've done more with that warren than I've done!'

'That's what I told Malon,' Frisco said, soothingly. 'As a matter of fact, I urged him to keep you on—even as underground boss. But the syndicate's committed to place a couple of its own men, qualified mining engineers, and, strictly between ourselves,

Alf, I know one of them has been engaged already to take over from you.'

'Thanks,' Alf replied dryly. 'I'm not admitting incompetence for management to please this damned syndicate of yours. Goodday.'

He clapped on his hat and walked out of Frisco's office.

It was not going to be so easy to find another mine on which he could prove his competence, he realized. The field was facing the worst slump it had ever known. Kalgoorlie leading stocks had been falling steadily during the last month. Large selling orders were being dumped on the market and had almost created a panic.

When the Associated closed down, several smaller mines followed suit. Others, like the Maritana, were being let out on tribute: men going over them with gad and hammer, picking out old leaders. It was said the Great Boulder had seen its best days: would never again dazzle the world with its output of pure gold. The future of low-grade ores, as one commentator remarked, 'was a glittering uncertainty.' Telluride and solution of the sulphide bugbear might work the miracle. Meanwhile there was talk of amalgamation of the Ivanhoe and Horseshoe, as well as of several other mines. And in all this, men were being thrown out of work: bankruptcies and suicides cast an ominous gloom over business men and the mining industry.

No wonder Frisco congratulated himself on having brought off the Midas deal for Malon and his French syndicate, Alf thought bitterly. Few mining properties were changing hands just now, and Frisco would be making a tidy commission.

His mouth twisted to a wry smile at the thought that he had made a good thing of the Midas for Frisco's benefit, while he himself got the boot. Fortunes of war, Alf told himself, and mining was as rotten a game as war. This campaign at present being waged against the Boers, for example! Mining had become a war of the big financial interests against smallholders of all sorts.

The mine-owners were blaming the struggle over alluvial rights for depression of the market and the falling off of buyers for Westralian goldmines. But there was more in it than that.

Since discovery of the field, small investors overseas and in Australia had been victimized by fraudulent companies, wild-cat schemes, stock exchange manipulation of their shares. Mining trickery might be regarded as legitimate business by the big men, but the public was beginning to demand legislation to safeguard its interests: make robbery of a shareholder, by concealing information he had a right to, as much a felony as picking a man's pocket.

It was well known that most directors were using special information supplied by their mine-managers to enrich themselves and cheat shareholders. With good news in their possession they would allow some damaging information to leak out, disquieting rumours to be circulated. Then they would buy up all shares thrown on the market, and garner the harvest when reports of a new rich lode, or phenomenal crushing, were released. It had been done over and over again: become a common practice.

So much so that a board of directors in London, recently, had protested indignantly because local shareholders heard of a rich crushing as soon as themselves. The manager was warned that such a thing must not occur again. Men had been sacked as dishonest who gave inside information to local shareholders which English directors regarded as their exclusive property.

The worms in London had turned on one occasion, Alf remembered with grim satisfaction. Suspicious of the tactics of their directors, and on the strength of a cable from the manager of the mine to his brother, a group of shareholders had called a general meeting and ousted the shoal of sharks posing as directors of the company.

The Associated scandal and the Great Boulder Milling Contract opened the eyes of the public to the fact that even men with big reputations in the mining world were not above swindling ordinary shareholders when opportunity offered.

Could you beat the Great Boulder Milling Contract as a confidence trick?

The Great Boulder was in a bad way, the yarn went round: oxidized ores almost exhausted. Zeb Lane had advised the board of directors to enter into a contract with the Boulder Milling Company for treatment of the mines' tailings and sulphide ore. The contract provided that the Milling Company would first take 3 dwts. per ton from the gold recovered and 40 per cent. of the balance, turning the remainder over to the Great Boulder Company. This worked out so that on 26 dwt. ore the Great Boulder crushed the ore and divided profits in sulphides and tailings with the Milling Company. On low-grade ore the Milling Company would make a handsome profit, and the Great Boulder Company find itself in debt.

Meanwhile Great Boulder shares and the shares of half a dozen other mines along the Boulder lead were falling. Quotations were half what they were six months ago. One or two shrewd shareholders had started an investigation and blown the gaff.

The Great Boulder Company had found the money, £20,000, to finance the Milling Company. Zeb Lane, and several other directors of the Great Boulder, were also directors of the Milling Company. They held big wads of shares, and were using the Milling Company to bleed shareholders of the Great Boulder.

At the same time, directors of the Great Boulder, as trustees for the shareholders, were drawing £4,500 a year between them, and were well supplied with vendor shares which cost them little or nothing.

'The Great Boulder is regarded as the pioneer Mining Company of Western Australia,' said Billy Barnett when it came to a showdown. 'It has paid magnificent dividends, and although the directors have been given great credit for this personally, I believe that God Almighty made the mine, and all the directors have done is put a thirty stamp battery on it.'

He was prepared to admit that 'our directors may have been animated by the highest and noblest motives that could animate a board of directors,' but to put it mildly, he considered they had made an 'indefensible bargain' at the expense of shareholders.

'Might as well have given the mine to the Milling Company while they were about it,' another shareholder shouted. And roused a gust of jeering laughter when he pointed out a clause in the contract to the effect that 'the Milling Company should take all precautions to prevent loss of gold by theft or dishonesty.'

Collapse of the Associated had exposed another scandal.

It amounted to this, control of the big mining properties by overseas boards of directors was responsible for scrip mining rather than the development of gold resources. It meant that fortunes had been made by directors, their families and friends, on inside information, withheld from ordinary shareholders. It meant that as much money had been made by 'a few in the know' from the flotation of properties on which no gold had been won, as from some of the richest mines on the fields. It meant that mining had become a pretext for swindling great numbers of people by rigging the share market, while the mines themselves were worked like racehorses by unscrupulous owners: permitted to do a sprint now and then, and their performances kept dark for gambling purposes, as it suited the book of certain managing directors.

Fluctuations of the market were controlled by a powerful group of financiers in London. It was difficult to follow their game, but Alf had seen enough of it to suspect that they were 'bearing' the market at present, and creating a depression in order to tighten their hold on all worthwhile mining properties on the field. 'Australian investors are a damned nuisance to British operators,' he had heard a visiting magnate say. The policy seemed to be to freeze out the small independent Australian investor and buy up his shares. Then engineer a renaissance, boosting of stocks, and another boom for Kalgoorlie.

What was it Zeb Lane had said at a luncheon on the South Kalgurli, a few days ago? Oh, yes, that: 'The field was under a cloud just now, but he was confident prosperity would shortly reign over the whole district.' Richard Hamilton, manager of the Great Boulder, had backed him up about the cloud, but suggested the road to recovery lay through 'cheap treatment of large quantities of low and medium grade ores.'

Straws which showed the way the wind was blowing, Alf thought. But meanwhile people on the goldfields would have to scrounge for a living as best they could. The alluvial diggers had probably saved the goldfields towns from disaster by their fight for alluvial gold. It gave the people a certain amount of power: kept money in the country and circulating. There was no doubt that wages on the mines would have fallen also had the diggers been beaten.

Dinny said the workers had a sense like ants of hard times approaching. They fought to defend their rights against the predatory designs of the British capitalists because of that. But they had been up against the interests of their own ruling class at the same time. Putting personal gain before national and democratic advantage, a few rich men were ready to mortgage the country to preserve their mining investments with the big overseas financiers. From this treachery, only the courage and determination of the alluvial diggers had saved Western Australia.

But legislation was needed to curb the abuses of scripping and make an honest business of mining: give the goldfields a chance to develop their mines and let the country gain some real advantage from the wealth it produced.

There was nothing wrong with the mines. Alf believed in the wealth of the mines, and the country. Those old rocks along the ridge before him, disrupted slowly through the evolution of centuries, had produced the richest gold in the world.

The lowest levels of almost every mine on the Boulder ridge held almost inexhaustible deposits of low-grade ores. The value of these was being discounted, at present; but he was sure, as various metallurgists had insisted, the economic treatment of telluride and sulphide ores was only a matter of time.

He believed that they held so much gold, they could provide abundantly for the health and comfort of the whole goldfields community. Instead of these miserable shacks cluttering the flats and the slopes of the ridge below the mines, instead of the stinking lanes with their open backyard pans oozing filth into the ground and contaminating the air, give the people pleasant homes and decent sanitary arrangements. Light, water, hospitals, schools and parks, the town needed.

Already tons of gold had been torn out of the ground and sent overseas. Millions of pounds had been squandered in luxurious living by people who had no conception of the hardships prospectors endured to pioneer these goldfields, or what a battle for existence life still was through a slump and the long summer.

Alf realized all this, with a bitter sense of his own culpability in having backed the mine-owners against the diggers. He did not excuse himself. He cursed his own weakness, and fear of losing his job: told himself he deserved what had happened. Who could have faith in a man who had let down his mates, no matter whether his circumstances were different from theirs or not?

What had he done? Been willing to pile up profits for the Midas Company and rob the alluvial diggers, knowing he was wrong: knowing the diggers were right. He had loathed himself all the time for what he was doing: been unable to disguise his partisanship with the diggers from the mine-managers and mine-owners with whom he associated, and so had lost with them and with the diggers. It was going to be difficult to get another job on the mines, or to go prospecting, since Dinny had turned him down, and no decent prospector would take on as a mate a man who had ratted on the alluvial diggers.

CHAPTER LXIV

LAURA hated to leave the home Alf had made for her, in the green shade of pepper trees beside the mine; but the Midas Company required it for their manager's quarters, so Alf and Laura moved to an unsightly shack on the Boulder Road. It was made of rusty iron, falling to pieces. They could find no other empty house, Laura explained light-heartedly. She would have to put up with it until Alf got another job.

She did not doubt that Alf would soon be installed as manager of another mine. Every day he went into Kalgoorlie, hung round the clubs and pubs, hoping to meet some mining magnate who could employ him. But there were other men in the same position, he found. Men who had learned all they knew about mining on the field: had no scientific training or degrees, and plenty of new young men with both, prepared to accept any terms which would give them practical experience.

The Mine Managers' Association, in control now of more highly qualified men, was demanding inclusion in the Mining Act of a clause which would make it impossible for a man without adequate certificates to obtain a job as mine-manager. Alf realized this was bound to come: that the men with superior qualifications were going to be of more value to the industry than those who had merely a smattering of mining technique.

But he believed that men like himself, with years of experience, could still be trusted to develop a mine. He had demonstrated his ability on the Midas. Some of the smaller companies stacked on the old type of mine-manager, Australians who knew the country and had worked underground with and without diplomas in geology and engineering. The big English and American proprietaries preferred to import their own men: were cold-shouldering Australian engineers and metallurgists.

They blamed petering out of the oxidized ores, the alluvial trouble and fall of shares, for closing down of the mines and unemployment; but other issues were involved, Alf suspected. He could not get out of his mind the idea that a conspiracy to obtain more effective control of the mining industry was on foot. The mining magnates and the mine-managers with whom he still came in contact, in the hope of impressing them with his ability, abused the alluvial diggers and colonial governments as incapable of dealing drastically with an unruly mob.

Day after day, for months, Alf walked back along the dusty road from the township, looking weary and dispirited. At first, he had seemed anxious to keep up appearances, turned out in whites and a straw hat; but lately was wearing his suits until they were limp and soiled. Occasionally, he swung along unsteadily: had taken to drinking more than usual, in an attempt to overcome his despondency.

Laura fretted a good deal. Alf was not sleeping, she said. He walked up and down the verandah half the night: was so nervy and irritable, she could scarcely speak to him.

'Of course he's worried about being out of work,' she exclaimed. 'I don't know what to do.'

In her distress, she had come to see Sally again, and they forgot there had ever been any break in their friendship. The children played together and Laura talked about Alf: how restless and depressed he was.

'I spoke to Mr. de Morfé about it when I met him in town the other afternoon,' she confessed. 'He promised to find something for Alf. "Tell him not to worry," he said. "I'll find a job for him."'

Laura was very upset when Alf wanted her to go home on a long visit. 'Before all their money was spent,' he had said. Laura was hurt and annoyed with him for making such a suggestion. Her people had not approved of her marriage, although Alf's good luck in the early days of the goldfields reconciled them to it.

Laura had written to her mother, now and then, telling her of Alf's successes, and of the birth of a granddaughter. But she could not endure to let her family know when things were not going well. Her parents would be only too pleased to say she had 'made a mess of her life,' and blame Alf. She could never let them say that. Laura wept as she thought of such a thing. She would never go back and let her father and mother think Alf was a failure, she protested: that he wanted them to keep her and Aimée until his prospects were brighter.

She could do something to earn money, herself. Of course she could. There was no reason why she should not do as Sally had done, start a boarding house or teach music and singing—even play at the hotels. Paddy Whelan at the Shamrock and McSweeney of the Western Star were crazy about music, and often, after a dinner party, she had played Mr. Brownlow's accompaniments. Alf was furious when she suggested it: said she just wanted to humiliate him, talking like that. He threatened to blow his brains out before he would let Laura slave for any Tom, Dick and Harry in the town, like Mrs. Gough had done, or play for drunks in a pub.

And then, when she told him what Mr. de Morfé had said, Alf accused her of flirting with Frisco, of being willing to—to be immoral with him. Oh dear, it was dreadful! Poor Laura, she shed all her airs and graces, trying to make the most of the little money Alf gave her to buy food: scrubbed and cleaned to keep the dirty little shack in order, washing, ironing and mending continuously so that she, Alf and Aimée would always look spic and span, and nobody guess what a struggle she was having. At the same time, she did her best to be cheerful, in order to keep up Alf's spirits, and prevent him from imagining that she could not endure hardships when it was necessary.

Frisco seemed in no hurry to find Alf the job he had promised. Alf put his pride in his pocket and went to ask him if he knew of anything available, prepared to take any job Frisco might offer. Frisco had been full of goodwill promises that day and forgotten them the next, although whenever he saw Alf, he exclaimed boisterously:

'Don't worry, old man! Something will turn up. I'll let you know as soon as I can fossick out something good for you.'

'Blast him,' Alf groaned. 'He likes to think he can come the big man over me.'

Morris had heard that Frisco himself was in deep water. He had been involved in a duel between two rival groups of company promoters, and come a cropper. Although he bluffed out his losses and continued to live like a millionaire on commissions from the Parisian Gold Mining Company, it was rumoured that Mr. de Morfé's bank had asked him to reduce his overdraft.

Morris, himself, was one of the busiest men in town, that summer. Death stalked the fields brazenly, carrying off mothers and babies, and many young men. The hospital was full, a particularly virulent type of typhoid prevalent.

Undertaking, however, was not as lucrative a business as it had been. People did not have the money to pay for an elaborate coffin and the showy turn-out for a funeral, on which Morris had made his profit.

Morris had to carry many of his customers, now, as the storekeepers and publicans were doing. There were so many unemployed, so many alluvial diggers not working, or working under difficulties owing to injunctions, arrests, demonstrations, the turmoil of the conflict. Debts accumulated.

If he could have collected all the money owing to him he would have nothing to growl about, Morris said. But he had become too much a man of the fields to do that when everybody was having a bad time. Old mates helped each other as a matter of course, and many took advantage of this principle of life on the fields.

Morris had been glad to give Alf a few days' work, putting his books in order: was wondering how he could provide him with some other means of earning a few pounds, when Alf announced that he had got a job.

Yes, it was a fact. And Alf was a different man because of it. More like his old self, good-natured and confident of his ability to run a mine, organize its production and finances.

'But you'll never guess who my new boss is,' he told Morris laughingly. 'Strictly in confidence, I can tell you, Morrey, though it's got to be kept under your hat.'

'Daresay my hat'll stand the strain,' Morris replied.

'Paddy Cavan!'

Morris had his misgivings.

'Felt the same way myself,' Alf confessed. 'But I've seen his papers, and they're in order, Morrey.'

He told Morris how Paddy had waylaid him on his way home from the Midas, a few months ago, and intimated that if ever Alf wanted a job, he, Paddy, might be able to do something about it. Alf had not attached any importance to the incident: thought young Paddy was just skiting. It never entered his head to apply to him when the Midas changed hands and he was dumped, although Paddy had warned him the deal was in the offing before he knew about it himself.

Paddy had come to the house the other evening and offered Alf the management of the Golden Feather. He was working on the mine, himself; but also satisfied Alf that he held a dominating interest in the show. Pete Watkins was dummying for Paddy, and they had got a croney of Pete's as manager. But Ike Pepper had had a stroke, wanted to go to the coast and live with his daughter. The mine was in a bad way: production going to pot and she was a good little mine. The gold was there all right. And Frisco was after her, but Paddy did not want to sell. What he needed, he said, was a man he could trust to develop the mine and watch over his interests.

'You and Dinny Quin, I reckon, Alf, are the straightest men I know,' Paddy had explained. 'But Dinny's more of a prospector than a miner: doesn't understand mine management, and you do. I'd like to have both of you with me on the Feather; but I'd reckon my luck was in if you took on this job.'

Alf promised to think it over, and after some preliminary investigation, which proved to him that Patrick Aloysius Cavan practically owned the Golden Feather and an amazing amount of script in other mining properties, he signed the contract Paddy had drawn up.

Paddy's terms were not generous; but they weren't bad—what the manager of a small mine could usually expect. Alf was too pleased at the prospect of getting back to work, and having a steady income behind him, to bargain with Paddy, though he did demand accommodation near the mine. There was a corrugated iron hut, with a water tank and bath-room, which Ike Pepper had lived in, and Laura was content to make the best of that for the time being.

'Well, I'm blest!' Morris could not get over the idea of Paddy as a mine-owner and monied man. Alf said on paper Paddy stood behind £100,000 at least, though probably that was not the full extent of his holdings. But Paddy, it seemed, did not want to figure in the mining world: thought he could make his way better if he did not attract attention.

'Says he's had a bit of luck, gambling in shares, and put it into the Feather,' Alf said. 'But that doesn't mean he hasn't got to work like hell to hang on to it and keep out of the way of the big sharks.'

'You wouldn't've thought he was worth two bob when he was down with typhoid last year,' Morris growled. 'He begged Sally not to send him to hospital. A man always dies when he goes to hospital, he said. Sally nursed him herself because she said she couldn't bear to think of one of her own boys being ill like that, and nobody caring whether he lived or died. She thought Paddy was hard-up and would want to pay his expense as soon as he started work again. But not him, not Paddy! And he must've been well in, then, the rotten dog.'

'I reckon I'll have to keep my eyes open working for Mr. Cavan,' Alf spoke slowly, thoughtfully. 'We always knew he was sharp as a needle, Morrey: bound to get somewhere. Remember we used to say that on the track.'

Morris remembered. 'Paddy's been hanging round the Open Call for years,' he said. 'Couldn't've been more than sixteen when he was buying and selling stock like an old hand.'

Alf smiled ruefully: 'Seems to have done better at the game than you or I, Morrey.'

'And don't forget,' Morris said, 'the trick he put over Ma and Pa Buggins when he was supposed to be collecting store accounts for them. The miners were paying in gym. Pa Buggins buying from them. But young Paddy extracted a percentage of all the gold he collected. When the boys kicked up a row about the price they got from Pa Buggins, Pa Buggins showed them his weights, and young Paddy was caught. But neither the boys nor Pa Buggins could squeal because Paddy could've squealed louder.'

Alf laughed. He was glad to defend Paddy. 'You can't blame him for getting even with the Bugginses. Some of the boys gave him the father of a hiding, too, if I remember rightly. Most of the big men on the field to-day have started out with a bit of shrewd robbery, I reckon. Can you beat the jerrymandering of shares to-day, and the way the big companies are doing their shareholders in the eye?'

Morris admitted that he could not blame Paddy. Paddy had only swum with the tide. The marvel was he had done it so successfully. But that did not mean Alf could afford to have too much confidence in his new employer.

'You might say the same of any man on the mines,' Alf remarked.

'That's a fact,' Morris agreed.

'Oh God, Morrey, I'm as happy as larry to be on the job again,' Alf exclaimed eagerly. 'I'd rather build a mine—put her in decent working order—get the gold out of her and make her pay her way, than do anything else in the world. I suppose it's the same as building a ship, or running a farm. There's a fascination in creating something: the adventure of overcoming natural obstacles: the triumph of human ingenuity in working out all the details in connection with a project. It's this damned script mining which is destroying the industry. Overseas control and share mongering. There's nothing wrong with the Boulder mines, I'm convinced. Enough gold in them to keep us going for ages. What we want is legislation to put a stop to mining trickery, and give a country with good mines the advantage of the mining industry and the gold it produces.'

'Interfere with the sacred rights of capital?' Morris queried dryly. 'You can't do that, sir. By God, that's anti-British, treason, indefensible. Better not let anybody hear you saying that, Alf, or they'll think you're one of these socialist windbags like Dinny and Chris Crowe, stirring up trouble on the fields.'

Alf groaned. 'I wish I were, Morrey. I wish I'd stuck to Dinny and the boys on the alluvial rights question. Wouldn't feel so like a broken-down old nag on the whip stick of a mine now!'

CHAPTER LXV

THE races were always an event of the year. With pioneer prospectors, and the first publicans and shopkeepers on Hannans, it was a point of honour to attend. They remembered the day when a rough course marked out on a flat near the lake had been the scene of their first social gathering and gallivanting.

After Kalgoorlie emerged from the chrysalis of the old mining camp, and became a city of butterfly prosperity with wide streets, from which the tree stumps were removed, with a railway station and post office of desert sandstone, shop fronts with glass windows and brick pubs, the race-course was fenced and a grand stand erected. Gone were the days when a hessian shack held the post office and the Warden's Court met in a dilapidated tent. Gone, too, something of the old spirit which had held the scattered community together when food and water were scarce and diggers' law dealt severely with offenders against the common welfare.

Although old-timers blamed the mining industry and coming of the railway for the bad reputation Kalgoorlie had got recently,

369

they were proud of that fringe of poppet heads along the Boulder ridge, and the townships of Boulder and Kalgoorlie sprawling out from it: townships whose streets were paved with gold, according to Mr. Modest Maryanski, when he found colours in the road metal. He had toddled off to Germany soon after the slump began, to consult with his principals who held mining properties on the fields. No one was more optimistic about the solution of the sulphide problem and the future of low-grade ores.

Maryanski had boomed telluride. It was he who drew attention to the enormous value of the rich telluride ore in the Kalgoorlie mine. When he inspected the jeweller's shop at the hundred feet level, on the Kalgurli, he fairly danced with excitement, it was said. He declared there was nothing like it in the mines of Colorado.

And on the Kalgurli and the Australia they had been throwing telluride out on the dumps. Thought it was iron pyrites. A prospector camped over there used to boil his billy on a couple of lumps of this ore: found the fire roasted out the gold. He and his mates had been helping themselves.

Telluride, it was prophesied, would bring about a new era of prosperity for Kalgoorlie. There were still problems to be solved in connection with its treatment. The future of the mining industry lay in the solution of these problems. Maryanski and most of the foreign metallurgists were confident that they could and would be solved before long. They said that the oxidized ore in upper levels of most of the big mines was accompanied by sulpho-telluride at from two hundred to three hundred feet.

Dinny himself had yarned with Maryanski.

'No refractory minerals are associated with these ores, Maryanski says,' Dinny explained. 'The rock's made up of gold, silver, tellurium, iron and sulphur. By roasting, the tellurium is thrown off with the sulphur, leaving the gold content ready for treatment both by amalgamation or cyanidation. The bulk of the gold can be obtained before usin' the cyanide process. The only serious trouble is the recovery of gold from slimes. Filter presses make it possible to secure a close extraction of gold from the coarser particles of crushed ore, and promise to revolutionize the mining industry. But there is still the problem of residues of gold in the slimes to be solved.'

So that, despite the depression and financial difficulties of that year, men who had prospected this field, made these towns, maintained a sturdy optimism. They believed in the mines and that the wealth of the lower levels would be exploited when the confidence of investors was restored, and when the big men got over their sulking because they could not grab all the alluvial gold in the country.

Slump or no slump, miners and prospectors were going to the races. They came in from all the outlying camps for the Kalgoorlie Cup, prepared to make a day of it. No one would have thought, to see the gay holiday crowd, that there was any depression hanging over the fields, any shortage of money, or prospect of more mines closing down.

Men, women and children flocked to the course, taking lunch-baskets and bottles of cold tea. Buggies, sulkies and drags, with spanking horses, dashed along the dusty road. Men in white suits and women dressed up like fashion plates, indicated that the swells of goldfields' society were going to be represented on the course. They would preen themselves in the enclosure and on the grandstand, and family parties, not wanting to pay for admission, settle down near the fence, further along. The thimble-riggers and three-card tricksters tried their luck there, and it was good fun to watch them and listen to their patter.

Morris insisted on going to the grandstand. He took his betting seriously: liked to spend most of his time in the saddling paddock and bookmakers' ring, but he was pleased that, this year, Sally had decided to accompany him to the races. They started off in a flutter of excitement, Morris because he was going to enjoy a day's gambling, and Sally because she had on a new dress.

Marie had made it for her, and it was very becoming: grass lawn, with a tight bodice and full skirt and rose-coloured pipings. Sally was a little uncomfortable in the new corsets Marie had persuaded her to wear, but what did that matter? Marie had trimmed a hat for her, too: put a wreath of roses on an old burnt straw, and made it look quite fashionable.

Every miner's wife tried to have a new dress for the races; but it was so long since Sally had bought one, she felt somewhat self-conscious about looking so smart. It had been quite reassuring to hear Marie say: 'You look adorable, darrling!' Marie herself had re-made an old dress, because her husband had lost his job when the Associated closed down, and their funds were low. As usual, though, she contrived to look cool and elegant in her frock of green foulard, and a black hat with 'follow me Charlies' of green ribbon.

Kalgoorla was minding the children, and Laura had called during the week to inquire whether she might leave Aimée with Kalgoorla. Laura did not want to go to the races, she said, but Alf thought they ought to put in an appearance. People would think they were still having a bad time if they did not, and Alf had to keep in with the mine-managers: let them know he was making a good thing out of the Golden Feather. Laura did not look happy. She was still worried about Alf.

'He works so hard,' she told Sally. 'Is doing the work of two or three men, and something's upset him about the mine. I don't know what it is. He hasn't told me. I only hope it doesn't mean he'll be out of work again.'

Sally and Marie sat in the grandstand while their husbands went off to the saddling paddock and betting ring, under the few tall, graceful salmon gums left standing. Well-known bookies came up from Perth now for the goldfields race meetings. Their gabble, calling the odds, almost drowned popular melodies blared out by the band. It was amusing to watch the crowd swarming over the stretch of sun-dried grass, prospectors in dirty moles and slouch hats, their faces and boots red with dust; and others, spruced up in brand new reach-me downs and cheap cabbage-tree hats. They rubbed shoulders with mining magnates and bank managers in white ducks, or flannels girded by a red cummerbund. A panama, straw decker, or Stanley-in-darkest-Africa sun helmet might be perched on august heads, though sometimes an old native was to be seen getting round in a dilapidated specimen of the white man's glory. The wives and daughters of minemanagers, shopkeepers, publicans and miners, mingled with the throng in flowing skirts and bright colours, and there was always a pretty barmaid in some ultra stylish dress to exclaim at.

That year it was Madame Malon who created a sensation. She trailed about in a Parisian toilette of grey chiffon, close-fitting as a glove and embroidered with silver sequins. They flashed and glittered as she moved, and her diamond ear-rings, brooch and bracelet threw a dazzle about her. But Lili spent most of her time talking to Bertha, Belle and Nina.

Sally and Marie were afraid she might see them, and greet them enthusiastically before their husbands, after which those awkward and so long delayed explanations would have to be made. But Lili only glanced once in their direction, smiled, and blew them a kiss from the tips of her fingers, sheathed in long, dove-grey suède gloves. Laura, who had been sitting with Mrs. Finnerty and some of the mine-managers' wives, came over to exclaim:

'Everybody's scandalized at the way that woman's behaving. Of course, everybody knows she was one of Madame Marseilles' girls, not so long ago; but some of the managers' wives have had to dine with Malon and meet her. He's a millionaire, they say: buying up mines all over the place—and she twists him round her little finger.'

'Quite a feat, considering his size,' Sally remarked.

'Of course,' Laura agreed. 'But I wish Malon hadn't bought the Midas. Mr. de Morfé says, if I told Lili what a blow it was to Alf having to leave the mine, he was sure she would have made Malon keep Alf on. But I couldn't do that, could I? I couldn't ask favours of that sort of person?'

'Why not?' Marie queried. 'As for me, I would have asked her—under the circumstances.'

'I couldn't. That's all,' Laura replied, irritably.

She went back to her seat beside Mrs. Finnerty. When her husband took Marie off to meet a French metallurgist who had arrived recently, Sally strolled down to the tree where she was to meet Morris for lunch.

While she was standing there, Frisco passed with a tall, handsome girl. Sally's pulses stirred when she saw him, although he had become almost a stranger. Frisco looked as jaunty and debonair in a white suit and panama hat as he had done when he first returned from abroad. Having been associated with a fraudulent English company, and narrowly escaped gaol, did not seem to have affected him in the least. It was hard to believe, too, that he had come to grief, lately, on the Stock Exchange. He carried himself with as much swagger and gay assurance as ever. The girl glanced round and came back.

'Hullo, Mrs. Gough,' she said.

'Why, Violet,' Sally exclaimed. 'What are you doing here? I thought you were in Melbourne, studying singing.'

Frisco replied with flattering unction: 'She has been singing in opera.'

'In the chorus,' Violet added.

'I'm so glad,' Sally smiled, wondering why Violet did not glow responsively.

'It was a beginning,' Violet said, gravely. 'I might've gone on from that. But Mum wrote to say Dad had lost everything gambling in shares. He'd gone off prospecting again. And she was ill—couldn't manage without me. I had to come back. I'm working in the bar at the Exchange now.'

'Oh, Violet!' Sally explained afterwards that she could have cried at the way Violet said that.

'Perhaps I'll get another chance.' Violet's eyes were dark with her disappointment. 'But it will be too late now, I think.'

Frisco interrupted, impatiently:

'Nonsense, Vi! You can go all over the world from this town. Come along, or we'll miss the next race. Sorry, Mrs. Gough, but we're backing Telluride. Must whip him up the straight.'

'I'd rather stay and talk to Mrs. Gough, if you don't mind,

Mr. de Morfé,' Violet replied, coolly. 'Come for me after the race.'

Frisco's eyes flashed to Sally with mocking laughter.

'I cannot compete with you, ma'am. But don't deprive me altogether of the company of my charming companion.'

He turned away and walked off to the course.

'It was kind of Mr. de Morfé to bring me,' Violet explained. 'I'm only off for four hours. He promised to drive me back to the pub.'

'Frisco's always kind to a good-looking girl,' Sally answered lightly, although she guessed it was unnecessary to attempt anything in the nature of a warning to Violet. Violet was too accustomed to the admiring gallantry of men to attach any importance to it. She was quite cynical about men still, Sally sensed, and as indifferent to their blandishments as she had been in the bar at Giotti's.

'I studied at the Melba Conservatorium,' Violet told her with repressed eagerness. 'It was wonderful, Mrs. Gough. Madame said she was pleased with me, because I worked hard—and she promised to help me with introductions when I went abroad. Then I got a job in the chorus of the Opera Company. All the principals were famous foreign singers. It was a marvellous experience. I understudied Marta in *Faust*. Then Mum's telegram came: "Desperately ill, come at once." I knew she was going to have another baby, and that Dad was broke: had gone off prospecting. What could I do? I thought Mum was dying, at least, and the children would be left without anyone to look after them. They wouldn't give me leave at the theatre. So I had to break my contract.

' "You'll never get another job here, my girl," the stage manager said. But I felt I'd never forgive myself if Mum died. She's had such a hard life, Mrs. Gough, and I knew it wasn't going to be easy having another baby at her age.

'But when I got home, she was up and quite well. The baby had died. There wasn't any reason at all for me to have come, except that Mum was lonely and miserable and needed money. She said my place was here, helping her, and I thought only of myself, wanting to be a singer, and leaving her to bear the burden of everything. I was angry at first; but I've got over that now. Dare say she's right. You don't seem able to do the things you want to in this life. Just what you must.'

'Oh, my dear, don't talk like that,' Sally pleaded. 'You mustn't lose hope, Violet. You're young yet—'

'I'm getting too old for the stage, and training as an opera singer,' Violet replied. 'Besides, they'll never give me another chance in Melbourne because I cleared out like that at a moment's notice. Even if I could take it— and I can't. Mum really can't provide for half a dozen children, no matter how hard she tries. All I've got to do is pull beer and everybody's happy. So there's nothing else for it.'

Frisco returned to claim Violet. His horse had won and he was in high spirits.

'Come and let's celebrate, Mrs. Gough,' he cried. 'They've got champagne in the bar, though I warn you it's lukewarm.'

Sally excused herself. She had promised to wait here for Morris, she said, and must not deprive Mr. de Morfé any longer of the society of his 'charming companion.'

It was a very self-possessed young woman who turned away with Frisco. Tall and graceful, she was, in a well-made dress of dark blue silk, almost the colour of her eyes. Her stage experience had given Violet that light, easy carriage and assurance, Sally thought. Violet did not seem in the least impressed to have Mr. de Morfé as an escort, although obviously he was quite delighted to be cavaliering such a lovely girl.

Nothing touched the core of Violet's being, Sally imagined. It was wrapped in her dream of being a singer. She had maintained herself apart from the demoralizing influences about her because of it. The tragedy was that she should have been forced back among them and would probably lose her unique poise with the hope of her dream ever being realized.

How could her mother have brought Violet back to work in the bar of a goldfields' hotel when her career was opening with such promise? She would never escape now. Sally had a presentiment of the doom hanging over the girl. She would be caught in the hungry life force surging beneath the surface of this race-course crowd. But Violet—her spirit would always demand something more than ephemeral excitement.

Would she ever find a happiness to compensate for the loss of her desire for self-expression? She was a child of the fields. More or less at home in the dust and heat, among all these rough, hard-drinking men, mine-managers as well as miners. A star now in the community; but so easily she might fade into obscurity: become as withered and care-worn, or blowsy and besotted as the wife of any man who depended on the mines, alluvial gold, or fluctuations of the share market, for a living.

The bright blue morning had changed into the blazing noon and blinding glare of a day in early summer. In brief kaleidoscope horses raced over the dusty oval track: the red, blue, pink, purple, green and yellow of their jockeys' jackets flashing through the delirium of the onlookers. So soon it was over, this one gala day in the dreary monotony of life for so many people.

A dust storm deluged the crowd before the last race. Women, afraid of a downpour, induced their husbands to drive them home early. A stream of buggies turned back towards the town; but the rain caught them, and thousands of miners and their families trudging along the road. Nobody minded the rain, except the women whose dresses were ruined, including Sally. If a man had won a few shillings on a race, he was satisfied it had been a good day, although he might be a few pounds out of pocket. He had got his fun in the gamble, in the hilarious excitement of being in the race with the horse he was backing. What did it matter if the bookies went away licking their chops? A goldfields' crowd always meant easy money for them. But even they couldn't beat a goldfields' judge when local interests were at stake.

Everybody knew old Belcher's son had a horse in the Goldfields Stakes, and everybody knew old Belcher.

'The boys backed "Bobby Dazzler" pretty solidly,' Dinny said. 'He came third, and didn't the bookies howl when the judge declared him the winner. But old Belcher stands pat. "I'm the judge of these races," ses he, "and I say 'Bobby Dazzler' won that race." '

A Boulder kid had beaten the bookies, too: a youngster taken from school to train as a jockey.

'Young Billy's a smart boy and a good rider. He was goin' to ride a local dark horse,' Dinny chuckled. 'But the bookies got to the trainer and he told the kid he was not to win. It was a blow because this was his first race, and Young Bill had been boastin' to all his schoolmates how he was going to beat the field. The horse started at ten to one; and the books couldn't make out why, just before the race, they were rushed by kids making two-bob and five-bob bets. Young Billy's horse won!'

CHAPTER LXVI

DINNY and Alf had steered clear of each other since the Ivanhoe trouble. They became almost strangers, passing with a nod and a stiffening of features if they met in the street, or in a pub. Both were miserable about their estrangement, but Alf knew that Dinny would never forgive him for letting down old mates in the alluvial rights struggle. He threw all his energy into his job on the Golden Feather.

Things were in a bad way when he took over, he told Morris: Production almost at a standstill and accounts in an awful mess. Paddy gave him a free hand to straighten up: agreed to a scheme for reorganization and development, though he could not be induced to spend money on timber and machinery until the share market recovered.

'My boss,' Alf would say, referring to Paddy, a faint, quizzical smile in his eyes, and exclaim sometimes at the way that shrewd, uncouth young man was going about the business of learning how to run a mine.

Alf himself had learnt all he knew by associating with mining engineers, geologists and metallurgists, reading the books they read, discussing with them every phase and process of the mining industry. Paddy was educating himself on the same lines. He had been almost illiterate: could write his own name and that was about all, when Alf took over management of the Golden Feather. Now Paddy was studying book-keeping and accountancy and reading any book on finance he could lay his hands on. All that year he was working in the mine, Alf helped and advised Paddy with his studies.

He was amazed by the common sense and stubborn ability Paddy displayed in analysing financial theories and problems. Paddy was satisfied to shelve some and measure others by his own experience; but refused to waste time studying geology and metallurgy.

'That's for specialists, Alf, I reckon,' he said. 'Maybe they'll be of use some day, but they don't know enough about these fields yet.'

Paddy professed great contempt for the imported mine-managers.

'It's men like you we want in the mining industry, Alf,' he said. 'Practical men—men with experience of this country and a good general knowledge of mining practice. I reckon you're one of the best practical men on the field. Degrees and deeplomas, yah! Let 'em have 'em on the Associated, Lake View and Boulder, if they like. You and me, Alf, we've got brains and experience. We'll make more money on the Golden Feather—if we use our nouse, and don't let the mug scientists run away with our cash.

'Why, the scientists said a few years ago there was no auri-furious rock in the country. Then they tried to make out this is an alluvial field. Now they want us to believe the oxidized ore's peterin' out, and there's no future for sulphides. Me bloody foot! I don't mind makin' a bit out of oxidized and alluvial, but it's the big stuff I'm after—buyin' scrip, not sellin'. Now's the time to buy, Alf, and buy big. All the gold I can get's goin' into scrip.'

'Auriferous rock, not "aurifurious," Paddy,' Alf remarked.

'Thanks,' Paddy grinned. 'Pick me up when I don't say things right, Alf.'

He worked on the Golden Feather and drew his wages like the rest of the miners. To all intents and purposes he was underground manager. Few of the men knew Paddy was the biggest shareholder in the mine. Those who did know kept their mouths shut. They had reasons for doing so. Paddy had bought gold from them, was still buying, Alf suspected.

Every man on a good patch knew that his best plan was to square up with Paddy. He might not give as good a price as some of the buyers, but it was safer to do business with him than quarrel about a few bob. Paddy they understood was working for the big gang dealing in illicit gold, and the ramifications of the gang were awe-inspiring. Included were some of the police, and the Big Five could protect any of their clients if they got into difficulties. That was well known.

Alf found himself taking an interest in Paddy's development: wished he could influence him to make a fine thing of his life.

'Look here, Paddy,' he said, 'you'll be worth a lot of money some day, if you go on the way you're doing.'

'My oath,' Paddy agreed.

'Well, you'll have to learn a lot, besides how to gamble in scrip, if you want to hold your own among the big men by and by.'

'Plenty of time for that,' Paddy replied. 'Though I dare say it wouldn't do any harm if you put me up to a few tricks, Alf.'

'You could start,' Alf suggested, 'by getting a hair cut and a decent suit.'

'Cripes, y'll have the d's thinkin' I'm in the gold, if I start lookin' slick and prosperous.'

'Aren't you?' For the first time Alf tried a direct question.

'Now, y'r fergettin' yerself, Mr. Brierly.' Paddy chuckled, as if this were a good joke. 'In the perlite society of Kalgoorlie there's two things you don't ask, I'm told: where a man gets his love or his money.'

Alf laughed, too.

'Oh, well, Paddy, it's your own business, I suppose. You've got all your life before you, and a good chance of becoming a successful man. Why not cut out the crook stuff and run straight?'

'Like you've done?' Paddy hit in adroitly.

Alf winced.

'Like I've done. It hasn't got me very far, I admit. But, after all, there's something in having a reputation for being honest and reliable, even in a town like this.'

'Not much,' Paddy jibed. 'Not enough to keep you from pub crawlin' when you can't get a job. I want a few thousand before I start.'

'God!' Alf groaned. 'Perhaps you're right. But I'm not made that way. I've got to go straight—or go under.'

'Don't be a mug, Alf.' Paddy leaned forward, his pudgy, freckled face set to a mask that was old and grave. 'Everybody's in on the gold, here—'

'You mean the gold stealing and illicit buying?'

'You know what I mean. And if you're not in on it, they'll think you are. So what the odds?'

'I'm not. That's all.'

'Have it y'r own way,' Paddy grinned. 'But where'd you have been now, if I hadn't given you this job?'

'Where'd your blasted mine've been?' Alf blazed. 'You said you wanted me to take over because I was straight—'

'And a man with practical experience of mine management.'

'Well, aren't you satisfied? Haven't I cleared up the hell of a mess on your mine and increased production? The management was a damned disgrace till I got to work. Your accounts are in order now. Something like a decent statement of affairs can go to shareholders. You can pay a dividend this year—'

'Yees,' Paddy chortled, 'Mr. de Morfé offered a couple of thousand down, for his client, on the strength of that.'

The vitality drained away from Alf's lean, careworn face. His hands clenched and unclenched nervously.

'That means my services will be dispensed with, I suppose,' he said bitterly.

'You bet they will,' Paddy agreed. 'Frisco's never forgiven you for the hiding you give him comin' up on the track, Alf. Besides, he's always got one of these minin' engineers with a fancy degree hangin' round. On the other hand, I might hold on to the Feather a bit longer, seein' we're makin' a pretty good thing out of the mine—if you wasn't so keen about checkin' up on every bit of gold comin' out of her.'

'What do you mean by that?'

'Well,' Paddy was eager at last to come down to tin tacks. 'It's no use objectin' to the boys gettin' away with a bit of gym. Most of the mine-managers don't. They know what's goin' on —and wink at it. For the good of the order. Keeps the men quiet and satisfied, and the gold stays in the country. Keeps trade flourishin' in this town. Better than sendin' it all overseas to let some English swells live in luxury. All we got to do is give the boys a bit for their gold. That's alright. That's fair enough.

'The men who're doin' the work on this here mine don't get away with too much. That's where you come in, Alf, and me. I'm not workin' underground for the good of me health, or pokin' round the battery—except to see what's goin' on. I want to know just what's the leakage on the mine and who's handling it. I reckon I do know and it suits me not to interfere. I get my whack, and if you don't—well, more fool you.'

'I see,' Alf's voice was flat and tired. Paddy thought he was beaten, beginning to see reason. 'What do you suggest?'

'That's easy,' Paddy crowed. 'You don't have to see any more than you been seein' these last few months. I'll make it worth your while, Alf. You don't have to check up on every bit of gold comin' out of the mine or off of the plates. If there's a crack in 'em, now and then, no need to worry.'

'Swindling your own shareholders. It's a pretty low-down game, Paddy. I'm not blaming the men. But you get it both ways: slugging them and the shareholders.'

Alf had taken up his pen and was writing. He spoke, firmly, uncompromisingly, as if the matter no longer interested him, and he did not care what Paddy thought of his comment.

Paddy's face crumpled to sudden rage.

'You can't stop me,' he snarled. 'You can't do anything about it, Mr. Brierly. I wouldn't've talked if I didn't know that. I've been talkin' to you for your own good. Come off your perch if you don't want to go to gaol. What have you been doin', sitting on the bones of your behind, and lettin' the shareholders be robbed of a third of the gold in this mine for nearly a year? You're guilty of gross negligence in the discharge of your duties, a magistrate would say. And so I'll swear you have been.'

'Go ahead.' Alf rose from his chair. 'Here's my resignation. I wrote it while you were giving me inside information—for my own good.'

CHAPTER LXVII

DINNY and Chris Crowe were working on a claim near Binduli, three or four miles west of the Boulder, but they came into the township for stores, and spent the week-end at Mrs. Gough's. Sally said she could never forget the Sunday morning Alf Brierly came to see Dinny.

380

She was surprised when Alf pushed back the gate and walked up the garden path. Alf walked in a slow, slack way, as if he could scarcely drag himself along. He looked ill and wretched, Sally thought, when he jerked up his head as she greeted him.

'Where's Dinny?' he asked.

'He's in his room,' Sally said.

'Dinny!' she called. 'Here's Mr. Brierly to see you.'

'He won't want to see me,' Alf said, 'but I've got to have a word with him.'

Alf went along to Dinny's room. It was a couple of hours before he came out again, and Dinny with him. They walked to the garden gate together and stood talking. Dinny looked upset: there was fear in his eyes. He talked as if all the differences between Alf and himself had been wiped out, and he was trying to cheer Alf up.

Sally heard Dinny saying:

'Things are never as bad as they seem to be when you're down on y'r luck, Alf. You and me, we could go out prospectin' again and maybe strike something good like we did on the Lady Laura. There's as much gold in the country as ever came out of it; and we're just the men to prove it.'

Alf seemed impervious to Dinny's pleading: as if he were blind and deaf in his own misery. He slouched away down the road and Dinny stood looking after him.

'My God, ma'am,' he exclaimed, when Sally called him to dinner, and he came into the hot kitchen, full of the smell of roast beef and buzzing flies, 'he's in a bad way, Alf. We got to do something about it.'

'What's the matter?' Sally asked, whisking away the flies as she carved.

She knew that Alf had resigned from managership of the Golden Feather, and that Laura was upset because he had done so.

'Alf had a row with Paddy Cavan about some crook business on the Feather, it seems,' Dinny said. 'And Paddy threatens to make him responsible. Don't see how he can, meself, and risk exposure. But that's not the worst of it. Alf's gone to pieces: dumping his swag.'

Sally's mind was torn between fear that the flies would blow the meat she had put on the plates, irritation with Morris for not coming when she called him, and concern for Alf.

'Oh, no,' she exclaimed. 'He wouldn't do that. Mr. Brierly's not that sort, Dinny.'

'I'm not so sure,' Dinny replied, as Morris came in and they sat down to their meal. 'He says there's no place for him in Kalgoorlie. He's been whipping the cat because he didn't stand by the men in the alluvial trouble: says he knew all along he was wrong. Just hadn't the guts to stand by the men. Didn't realize the mining game was so rotten. Can't suffer it any longer. And his boss is as crooked as a dog's hind leg.'

'Paddy Cavan?' Morris had started on his dinner. 'You could bet on that.'

'Can you beat it?' Dinny began to eat too, still worrying about Alf. 'Young Paddy, givin' orders to Alf Brierly, and Alf so up against it, he's got to play Paddy's game, or throw in his hand, he says.'

'We'll have a word with Paddy,' Morris said. 'He can't get away with all he thinks he can. And in spite of all Alf did, siding with the mine-owners in the alluvial rights struggle, I think a good many of the old-timers would stick to Alf, if Paddy tried any dirty trick.'

'Maybe you're right, Morrey,' Dinny said, dubiously. 'But the best thing we can do, seems to me, is get Alf out of town. I put it up to him we'd go out prospectin', and the sooner we start the better, I reckon.'

Their plans were too late to help Alf. The same evening he was found lying dead in the bush near the Golden Feather. There was a revolver beside him and a letter for Laura in his coat pocket.

In his letter, Alf asked Laura to forgive him. This was the only way he could provide for her and their child, he wrote. There would be enough money from an insurance policy to pay their fares to Victoria and keep them going for a little while. He hoped she would return to her own people. Dinny would make arrangements for her and settle up his affairs.

The shock of Alf's death was too much for Dinny. Morris had to take the responsibility of doing all that was necessary during those first few days. Sally went to Laura, who was quite helpless with grief. She could not understand how Alf had made up his mind to do such a thing: lost his sense of their common bond and desire to live.

'Why?' she sobbed. 'Why did he do it, Sally? How could he leave me? Didn't he know this would be worse for me to bear than any hardships we might have to face together?'

'He thought it would be better for you, this way,' Sally tried to defend Alf. 'Was so ill and worried, perhaps he wasn't able to weigh all the consequences.'

'Don't say it!' Laura cried passionately. 'It's my fault, really. I was so cross and upset when he threw up his job on the Golden Feather. Didn't understand why he was doing it. I don't know now—except that Alf said Paddy Cavan was a rotten dog and he couldn't work for him any longer. Oh, Alf, my love, why didn't you tell me what was the matter? Why was I so blind and stupid? Why didn't I know how you were feeling? If only I could explain to him, Sally, that it wasn't necessary. He shouldn't have done it. Anything would have been easier than such a thing happening to us.'

That was the way she talked, distraught and worn-out with weeping, saying the same things over and over again, finding no solution to the shock and tragedy of Alf's death: the breakdown of all her illusions about their life together and the bright future they had promised themselves.

The very men who had made it difficult for Alf to live, mining magnates and mine-owners who could have given him a job, were loudest in their expressions of regret and sympathy at his death. Obituary tributes, published in the *Kalgoorlie Miner* and *Western Argus*, referred to Mr. A. E. Brierly as 'the type of man the goldfields could ill afford to lose,' 'the soul of honour, a courteous, kindly and true-hearted gentleman, beloved and respected by all who knew him.' Old mates who had tramped from the 'Cross to Coolgardie with Alf on the first rush, insisted on paying the funeral expenses. They wanted to 'put in' to a fund which would help Mrs. Brierly.

Laura could not endure the idea, and Dinny had to tell the men that Mrs. Brierly appreciated their kind thought; but did not need their assistance because Alf had provided for her immediate necessities. He had left a small sum of money with Dinny, it was true, and Dinny was anxious to let Laura have any money she needed to go home to her people in Victoria.

Laura refused to go. She said that she intended to remain on the fields and after a while would try to earn her living by teaching music and playing at concerts, or in the hotels. Nothing Sally and Dinny could say to dissuade her made any difference. Laura told them she wanted to prove to herself, and to Alf, she was not the soft, helpless creature he thought her: and that there was no necessity for him to have killed himself.

She continued to live in the shack on the Boulder road which had been her last home with Alf: for months went about dressed in black, pale and sorrowful. No one looked lovelier than Laura in mourning, though she no longer bothered about her appearance; wore her honey-coloured hair drawn back tightly from her forehead, and her eyes filled with tears whenever Alf's name was mentioned. Nobody doubted that she would marry again if she remained on the fields, although she was so heart-broken just now.

'If her heart was not broken, it was never the same again,' Sally said. 'Her eyes always held the hurt of Alf's death.'

The gossips imagined Frisco might be one of the first to pay court to Alf Brierly's widow. He had been seen about a good deal with Mrs. Brierly when she was a plump, sedate little matron. Sally knew he had tempted her to many mild indiscretions, but she knew also that Frisco had failed to seduce Laura from any wifely devotion to Alf. But although it was obvious before long that several men were anxious to befriend Mrs. Brierly, Frisco was not among them.

Laura was naturally the sort of woman men felt it their duty to protect and advise. She made it quite clear that she did not wish to be protected or advised: was horrified when two or three men, without any love-making, made her proposals of marriage, that year.

'I will never marry again,' she told Sally. 'How could I? My heart is in Alf's grave.'

'That's all very well,' Sally said. 'But your body isn't!'

When her resources were almost spent, Laura started to teach music in the neighbourhood; but it was impossible to make a living this way. Most of the people who could afford to pay well for their children to learn music were sending them to the convent in Coolgardie. The few shillings Laura earned by teaching Mrs. Molloy's Vicky, Dick Gough, and two or three miners' children, did not cover the cost of rent and food for herself and Aimée. She earned a guinea now and then by playing accompaniments at concerts, and it seemed a godsend when Tim McSweeney offered her a good salary to play in the evening at the Western Star.

Leading hotel keepers vied with each other in the musical attractions they could offer patrons. Mick Mannion, who had bought the Exchange, was known as the musical publican. He had Wallace Brownlow singing in the bar quite often. Paddy Whalan liked to serve whisky to special customers in crystal goblets; and boasted three pianos in his establishment.

Violet O'Brien sang and played there now when she was not busy in the bar. The barmaid, known as Clara Butt because of her fine contralto voice, was McSweeney's chief draw card, until Laura began to play at the piano in the sitting-room beside the bar.

Dinny was opposed to her doing so; tried to induce her not to accept McSweeney's offer. He begged Laura to let him provide for her, as Alf's old mate should, he said. He had promised Alf to look after her and Aimée, and he wanted to fulfil that last promise to Alf. But Laura had her own pride and was very mulish about doing as she pleased.

'You needn't be afraid. I can look after myself, Mr. Quin,' she said.

Dinny was not so sure of that. But he was pleased to hear Tim McSweeney had taken precautions to have Laura treated with proper respect. Most of the miners and prospectors treated any woman with exaggerated courtesy. It was part of their code. In the early days a bully or bounder was hauled out of a bar and given a taste of powerful fists if he made offensive remarks to a barmaid. But these days, there were so many spielers and wild tykes about, a man never knew what they might do when they got over the fence, boozing, and took a fancy to a woman.

'Now boys,' Tim McSweeney explained the first night Laura played at the Star, 'Mrs. Brierly has consented to play for us for an hour or so every night. Ye're welcome to listen here in the parlour or in the bar as ye plaise. But no bad language in a lady's presence, mind. If ye can't behave y'rselves ye can keep out of the parlour.'

'That's alright, Tim,' a smart Alec piped up. 'Prospectors on this field always respect a woman. But you wouldn't object to a man tryin' his luck with such a likely-lookin' little mare?'

McSweeney's fist answered him with a wallop which sent him to the floor. Men round the bar cocked an eye and winked at each other. So that was the way the wind was blowing! McSweeney himself was pegging a claim on Alf Brierly's widow, they suspected, and he wasn't going to stand any interference with his privileges as protector of the lady's fair name and future.

He was a good sort, Tim McSweeney, Dinny admitted. Middle aged, porky and red-faced, with thin hair turning grey, but generous and kindly. A reputation for honesty and square dealing made him popular with all sorts and conditions of men, and he was well-in. Had spent thousands on making his hotel as well-equipped and well-furnished as any on the fields. Distinguished visitors and mine-managers put up there as a matter of course, and any man with a big cheque to bust knew he would get value for his money at McSweeney's.

Tim prided himself on the attractions of his hotel: its up-to-date bath rooms, the quality of his liquor and barmaids. Clara's voice and Jessie Grey's red hair were topics from Lake Way to Esperance. But Dinny did not like the idea of Alf's wife being included among those attractions, or her name being coupled with McSweeney's. The gossips were bound to make the most of Laura's playing at the pub, he knew; but he never dreamed she would marry McSweeney.

CHAPTER LXVIII

THERE had been many a wild night and big spree in Hannans, although never such spectacular shows as some lucky prospectors put on in the roaring days of Coolgardie. Dinny remembered the day when Big Mac and his mates sold their mine for £20,000 and went round the town in a six-in-hand, raked up a brass band and took Elliott's pub by storm with a champagne shout that lasted till morning.

Dinny had been in on the Londonderry boy's shout when they sold the Golden Hole and gave Flo Robins, the popular barmaid, a bath in champagne; but he doubted that many men even in their maddest moments had lit a pipe or cigar with a five-pound note. It might have been done out of bravado, by some fool wanting to show he had money to burn, he admitted, but he had never seen it.

Old Mat Lavers, who was yardman at the Rising Sun, boasted that he had washed his feet in champagne when he struck it rich. He had married a barmaid, settled all his money on her, after which she eloped with a young Englishman. A faithless woman, not the drink, had been the ruin of him, Mat swore, though he was drinking himself to death when his wife cleared out, Dinny said.

On Kurnalpi and Kanowna a prospector had sometimes run amok and started shooting the heads off bottles behind the bar. But for a long time no such roistering, damn-the-cost exuberance had marked a celebration on Hannans. The days when a prospector got big money for a promising show seemed to be over. Petering out of the Londonderry, the Wealth of Nations and the Carbine had brought about a more cautious attitude on the part of prospective buyers. During the slump there was little confidence in mining propositions of any sort.

Two or three mines changed hands and a few prospectors from out back cashed in on their gold; but the general depression had made most prospectors chary of extravagance: more inclined to put their money into some sound investment like a block of land or a pub, and less likely to squander a few hundreds on a night out with the boys in the rorty old style.

But when Bill King and Buck Quartz came in from Mulgabbie, after having sold their claim to an English syndicate for £6,000, the news got round that Bill was going to make a night of it at McSweeney's. The pub was packed on the strength of the rumour.

Most of the oldtimers were there. Dinny among them; Sam Mullet and Blunt Pick, Big Jim and Clary McClaren, Yank Boteral, Tassy Regan and a host of others.

Bill King was well known for putting on a show whenever he got a chance. He had come up to the fields as a teamster in 1893, struck a good patch at Kookynie, and ruled the roost there with a revolver on his belt and a crack on the jaw for anybody who did not recognize his authority. Liked to be called the King of Kookynie and keep order in the camp as Kurnalpi Mills did on his stamping ground.

Jack Mills had won the respect of the diggers on Kurnalpi. He was straight as a gun-barrel, they said, and could be depended on to give any man a fair go in an argument over the cards or a claim. But Bill King was as wild as a hawk and a bit of a bully. Too fond of showing off what a good shot he was: would send a bullet past a man's ear just to warn him who was boss if a stranger was making a nuisance of himself on the camp.

It was the ricochet of a bullet like that which got him into trouble, when a man was killed in a brawl on the two-up ring at Kookynie. A spieler had been caught ringing in the grey, a two-headed penny, and the boys were giving him a rough time when Bill tried to restore order, it seemed. Though that was not admitted when Bill was charged with murder.

Buck Quartz came to his aid: took charge of the case and proved that Bill had been miles from the camp on the afternoon of the tragedy. In fact, he had been out prospecting with a couple of mates, who swore they had got bushed, and did not get back to the main camp until morning. Not a single witness could be found to admit he had seen Bill King fire the shot that killed the crook who had been fleecing the camp for days. Bill was acquitted and returned to Kookynie in triumph.

But somehow his prestige waned. Buck Quartz had something to do with it. Nobody liked Buck, and after that accident Buck stuck to Bill like a leech. Bill's other two mates decided to square-up and go off on their own.

The claim was worked out, Kookynie almost deserted when Bill and Buck pulled pegs and came into Kanowna just about the time the rush to Death Valley was in full swing.

It was Bill King and his following who roused bitter feeling against Father Long and forced him to tell something of what he knew about the 'sacred' nugget. They were ready to make the priest bear the consequences, when no gold was found to justify his story, had not Tom Doyle shouted drinks and persuaded them to respect the cloth.

Tom congratulated Bill on having cleaned up the town, when

Bill led an attack on the French bludger who kept three or four Japanese women in miserable shacks at Kanowna. Bill said the boys would not stand for the way the swine lived on the little women, half-starved them and never did an honest day's work himself. So the boys smashed the windows and doors of the shacks and Bill put a few bullets round the monsoo. He made tracks, leaving the women to do business on their own account. But not for long. Tom took his mayoral duties seriously. The police moved the Japs on when they were becoming 'a menace to the good health of the town,' he explained.

There was no end of a commotion when the mayor, himself, was arrested for murder. He, Charley Cutbush and Dan Alves, had been mixed up in a brawl in which Doug Howard was killed. Buck Quartz again had given the accused valuable advice, it seemed, and claimed the credit when they were acquitted. He was something more than a bush lawyer, everybody knew: had been a light of the legal profession, struck off the rolls for misappropriating trust funds, before he came to the fields in 1893.

Buck was known as Charley Quarterman then, and turned on the manners of a gentleman when he wanted to. But no one would have thought to look at the bald-headed, parrot-beaked, dirty old codger who was Bill King's mate that he had ever worn a decent suit of clothes, or been an ornament of respectable society. He had a good brain, a gift of the gab and the hide of a camel, most men agreed, and was about as likeable as one of those beasts.

Buck Quartz, it was a good name for him, Dinny said. He had earned it for deserting a mate on the track: making off with their water and food. That was a crime which had never been forgotten or forgiven. Buck swore, of course, he had shared out the food and water supplies when he went off to get help. His mate, Jack Bell, was so feeble from dysentery he couldn't walk. He had left Jack beside a big outcrop of buck quartz, one hundred and fifty miles from Dead Finish; but natives who found the dying man said his water bag was empty, and the tracks of the white man who had left him not a day old.

Charley Quarterman swore the natives had stolen the food and water he put beside Jack. They looked surprised, explained that they had hidden gnamma hole in the rocks not far away; did not need the white man's water.

Nobody believed Charley Quarterman. He had to be given the benefit of the doubt, though; could not be convicted by a roll-up on the evidence of two or three natives. But Buck Quartz, Charley Quarterman was dubbed that day and the name stuck. There was nothing more unpopular among the early prospectors than the cold, unkindly white stone which had betrayed their hopes so often in a likely-looking outcrop.

Bill King might be a bit of a warrigal, but he had always been a good mate to any man down on his luck: warm-hearted and generous. The men only suffered Buck because he was Bill King's mate.

When Bill started to shout, everybody knew he was going to put up a record. Champagne was the only stuff considered worthy of such an event. Early in the evening the barmaids could not serve the stuff quickly enough. Bill began shooting the corks off the bottles. Corks and bullets flew. The girls got out of range. There was a scramble for glasses and bottles. A man grabbed what he could get and Bill went on shooting glee-fully, a devil in him: his only concern to play merry blazes and show he was on top of the world.

'For Chris' sakes, don't be such a bloody fool, Bill,' Buck implored when the racket was at its height.

'What's that? What are y'r sayin', y'r lousy old skinflint?' Bill yelled. 'D'y'r hear what he says, boys? Calls me a fool to be shoutin' me mates. Fill 'em up, miss. Hammer it down, boys!' And as McSweeney swung back the door of the bar: 'Y'r don't have to worry, Mister McSweeney. Buck'll pay the damage. Yaow, how's that for a bull's-eye?'

The glass door behind McSweeney splintered and the publican ducked back into the safety of the parlour where Laura was sitting beside the piano, a little tipsy and scared by the racket. One of the barmaids had brought her a bottle of champagne with Mr. King's compliments when the spree started. He wanted Laura to play and sing for his party. The uproar in the bar soon drowned Laura's banging out of popular favourites; her attempts to sing.

When Tim McSweeney stumbled back into the parlour, his face cut and bleeding from the broken glass of the door, Bill came after him.

'It's alright, Tim,' he bawled hilariously. 'We'll pay up, me and my mate. We'll pay the bleeding damage—beggin' your pard'n, missus.'

'Go ahead, Bill. You'll pay alright,' McSweeney said grimly, mopping his face.

'How's it for a song and dance, missus?' Bill queried.

Laura began to play again. Presently the men were all bawl-ing in the bar and Bill appeared with the big good-looking bar-maid they called Clara Butt. Clara had to sing for Bill. The men streamed out after him.

For lack of women they danced with each other. Clara frollicked off in a bear's hug with Bill. They stumbled and fell over each other, howling with laughter, and roaring out the chorus of 'Daisy, Daisy, for I'm half crazy all for the love of you.'

A fight started when two men wanted to dance with Jessie Gray, and a third grabbed and waltzed off with her. Half a dozen men were scrapping, and the girls giggling, and screaming in the rough-up, when McSweeney hustled them back to the bar with a round on the house to start the drinking again. He had an eye to business, Tim McSweeney, and the boys were easier to manage, he said, after they had had a skinful and a few of them had passed out.

'Y'd better go home now,' he said to Laura, when things were getting out of hand. 'This is no place for you, ma'am. I can't get away meself, but I'll tell the stable boy to put the mare in the buggy and drive ye home.'

But Bill had his eyes on Laura.

'Here's Len Minogue, he'll play a polka for us,' he roared, dragging a little man with an accordion, over to the piano. 'And I'm having it with you, missus?'

Laura was whisked off her seat and bounced away down the room, with Bill. She found herself caught up in the whirl of the gay, crazy excitement, being bumped and whirled through the crowd of drunken men. All the time Bill was muttering that he wanted to sleep with her: didn't care what it cost. Would she stay at the hotel? Where did she live? He would come to her house? There was nothing on earth could stop him when he was mad for a woman like he was for her. Laura felt helpless in the grip of the man's powerful arms, under his blazing eyes.

'No! No!' she cried, mechanically, struggling to free herself from his close embrace, but conscious of a wild inclination to say: 'Yes! Yes!'

The men McSweeney had shepherded back into the bar were clamouring for Bill. 'Hey, Bill!' they yelled. 'You reneggin'? What's struck him? McSweeney's shoutin' and closin' down on us!'

That got Bill. As if his interest in her had passed, he dropped Laura and went off to the bar. He couldn't afford to have his thunder stolen that night. Not by McSweeney.

Just to show who was shouting, Bill swept all the glasses from the bar and ordered another case of champagne. He started shooting the corks from the bottles again when the barmaids were not serving the stuff quickly enough. It frothed and spilled in every direction: was running over the floor, drenching the beards and dust-soaked shirts of the diggers who grabbed a broken bottle and poured the contents down their throats.

The bar was wrecked when Bill himself passed out. McSweeney cleared the house and shut up in the early hours of the morning. Bill squared with him next day for a dozen cases of champagne, and the damages. Cost him a few hundreds and was worth it, he said. But there was another account with Bill King which McSweeney settled in his own way.

Laura had not gone home that night. McSweeney gave her his room and made himself up a bed on the sofa downstairs.

'What happened last night must never happen again, me dear,' he said when they were having lunch together. 'Ye can't afford it—and it was murder lay in me heart for that blackguard, draggin' ye off your feet to dance wit' 'm. It's a man ye must have beside ye, a man to take care of ye and protect ye. I'm a rough, common sod, at the best of times—not a mate for the like of ye. But it's a good husband I'd be and there's nothin' y'd be wantin' ye couldn't have, if ye set your heart on it. Let ye make up y'r mind to marry me, Laura, and y'll not regret it. I swear by the Holy Virgin and all the saints, I'll trate ye like the queen herself, and ye'll have no need to worry about money for the rest of y'r days.'

'It's very kind of you, Mr. McSweeney,' Laura faltered. 'But I could never marry again—'

'It's just what ye must do,' Tim McSweeney insisted. 'Ye can see y'rself, now, the way it will be—and there's the child to think of.'

Laura blushed. She was ashamed and conscience stricken: unable to explain to herself the impulse which had overwhelmed her in that riotous dance with Bill King. McSweeney seemed aware of it and that she was not in a fit state to go home: so drunk, as a matter of fact, McSweeney had to help her to walk upstairs. She had slept in her clothes and been very sick in the morning. It was disgusting to think she had taken part in Bill King's orgy. But for McSweeney's ruse to get him back into the bar, she quailed at the thought of what might have happened.

McSweeney had tried to warn her about drinking, although it was good business to let the men buy drinks for her. He had put her up to the tricks: told the girls to serve her from the bottle of cold tea he kept for himself, or the water in a gin bottle that might be put into ginger beer; but Laura had learned to like brandy and the giddy exhilaration of champagne. She knew better than McSweeney how far she had gone in her taste for alcohol and feared what would come of it. She could see herself, a broken-down, destitute old woman like Meg Ryan, who cadged drinks all over the town.

'Oh, no,' she sobbed to herself. 'It won't come to that, it can't.' But it could, if she continued to live as she was doing, she feared. Laura could not escape a sense of her own weakness, her need for love and companionship. In the hothouse atmosphere of the hotel, among men starved of physical relationship, she had sensed the awakening of a new crude sexual desire.

She could have allowed herself to be kissed, drawn into the lingering embraces of some of these men; but the thought horrified her. She was still the well-brought-up girl who regarded all such casual intercourse as vulgar and immoral: the vain, complacent little woman who had been Alf's wife and prided herself on her virtue. Loose love, sex affairs without marriage, she considered degrading.

Laura was ashamed of this sensation, the chance brushing against a man stirred: the disturbance which went on in her under the lustful gaze of drunken men. She had tried to ignore it: met the suggestions of several well-known citizens and distinguished visitors with quiet dignity; but it was a pose now to pretend she was unmoved by amorous overtures. She did not deceive herself. As a matter of fact, they pleased and excited her: gave her a feeling of being physically alive again.

For a long time after Alf's death she had existed in a freezing isolation, cut off from the laughing and smiling eyes that communicated more than words. The shock she thought had stunned her, almost unhinged her brain. She could never have imagined Alf would hurt her so cruelly as to leave her like that. For a while she could not think or feel. It was surprising to find her body still moved: that she could stretch out and fold her fingers, see and hear. Even Aimée meant nothing to her. Later she had persuaded herself that she did not love the child, although she must be a good mother to her: do her duty and give their daughter all Alf wanted her to have.

She had sent the child as a boarder to the convent at Coolgardie when she began to play at the Western Star.

'I can't always be leaving her with you, when I have to be out at night,' she explained to Sally. 'And it's better for her not to be running wild with all the urchins in the neighbourhood after school hours.'

Laura had been so stiff and quiet, at first, playing in the bar parlour at McSweeney's. Mr. McSweeney had been very good to Mrs. Brierly, considerate in every way. The men respected her sorrow and the black dress she had worn for months. She could no longer remember when she had begun to be friendly with the barmaids, Big Clara in particular, because she had a good voice. A deep mellow contralto, very powerful and moving. Laura had played Clara's accompaniments when the men urged her to sing. Clara believed that brandy was a cure for all the woes in the world and so she had drunk brandy with Clara.

Gradually, she had become acclimatized to the atmosphere at McSweeney's: the rough kindness and friendliness. Now she liked it. Was interested in, and tolerant of, the miners and prospectors who crowded round to hear her play and sing. Even when they were drunk she could talk to them and listen to yarns about their good luck or misfortunes. Sometimes she had let them buy her drinks, finding it pleasant to relax and forget Alf was dead.

That weighed on her with increasing bitterness. It was a desertion, his death, a betrayal of their love she could not forgive him. It was as if he had not cared what became of her when he left her willingly and for ever. She was angry with him. Angry with a dull, resentful passion. This drinking with strange, uncouth men flouted his memory. There was a subtle satisfaction in treachery equal to his.

How could she live? How could she go on being the woman she had been, the happy and loving little creature with absolute confidence in her husband's wisdom and ability? Nothing, nobody could have destroyed her faith in Alf but his own act, and that had destroyed everything: not only their lives, but all her illusions. It was as if they had been strangers and he had never really loved her. But she had loved him; would never love any man but Alf, Laura assured herself.

Perhaps, unconsciously, she had been trying to demonstrate to him she could do without him; stand on her own feet and support herself by her work. She had a vague belief that somehow he would know what she was doing. She felt like saying to him when she looked at his photograph: 'See, I can do it. I can earn my own living.' But after all she was just the weak, helpless creature he had thought her.

Bitterness tinged her grief and self-abasement. But all the time her heart was crying for Alf. She longed to hear the sound of his voice; to feel the sweet comfort of his presence. It was the lack of this warm, close contact which made her so lonely and desperate now. As if she would be grateful to any man who put his arms round her and gave her that sense of living warmth again. She was so cold and empty without the happy glow she had lived in with Alf.

McSweeney clucked and fussed about her like an old hen with one chick when she came to play at the hotel. She had taken his attention more or less for granted, at first: been flattered when he hovered about the parlour to hear her play: sat listening with tears in his eyes when she sang 'The Last Rose of Summer,' or some other sentimental ditty. The signs and tokens were that McSweeney was in love; but Laura had not noticed them, and he made no move to disclose his hand, cultivating a friendly and mildly protective attitude, ordering a buggy to drive her home at night, and playing good natured watch-dog when any too ardent admirers were about.

But as the months passed, after the night of Bill King's record shout, and McSweeney had made his declaration, his devotion became more obvious and embarrassing. The barmaids teased her about it, and although Laura laughed and protested that nothing on earth would induce her to marry McSweeney, she became accustomed to the idea: even found something comforting in the thought that somebody cared for her as McSweeney did.

If she dined with Frisco, or some other man, McSweeney always sat a little way off, watching his gallantries with jealous, miserable eyes. Frisco found her better company than he had ever done. Laura had come to an easy familiarity with him, almost unconsciously imitated the gay, jesting manner of the barmaids in her association with men; could deal as lightly with their improprieties, unless she had been drinking. A hot kiss or a daring hand on her breast were not so easily resisted then. It had happened more than once when she had gone to a supper party, after hours, in a private room, with the girls and some of their friends.

McSweeney warned her about several men. He was gloomy and sore when he heard that she had been at a rowdy party in the house of one of the mine-managers.

'It's not good enough for ye—that sort of thing, ma'am,' he said simply. 'Y're too beautiful and sweet a lady to have anything to do with those lecherous dogs. It's the pains of hell I suffer when they look at ye, knowin' they're not worthy to dust the dirt off y'r shoes.'

Laura was moved by the sincerity of his distress.

'God knows, I'm not worthy either,' McSweeney went on, seizing this opportunity when she seemed willing to listen. 'But I love ye, ma'am. I worship the ground ye walk on. I'd be a good husband and look after ye.'

'No, no, it's out of the question, Mr. McSweeney,' Laura replied hurriedly. 'I told you, I'll never marry again. I loved Alf. I won't ever love anyone else.'

'Love?' McSweeney exclaimed gruffly. 'I'm not askin' ye to love me. I'm askin' ye to marry me, and give me the right to look after ye. If ye like me well enough to live wit' me I'll be satisfied.'

'I won't bother ye again, for a while,' he added, 'I won't say a worrd to displease ye. But me mind's made up and I'm a hard man to shift from me purpose. Ye'll be my wife some day, and ye'll not regret it. If the body and soul of a man are any use to ye, y've got mine when ye want them, me gurrl.'

Laura was shaken and a good deal stirred. McSweeney was right, she knew. She wanted what he could give her. It was a relief to think she need not pretend with him. At that moment she felt she might have agreed to marry him and regain the self-respect she was losing. But she could not bring herself to tell him.

CHAPTER LXIX

That cloud lowering over the goldfields became darker during the next few months.

'Kalgoorlie's done!' the speculators said, gloomily. They prophesied that like Coolgardie, Kalgoorlie would soon become an almost deserted out-back town, with a few mining camps scattered about. Already there were mines along the Golden Mile, whose wealth had been blazoned all over the world by the boomsters, standing idle, looking like derelicts, with machinery rusting alongside, and scores of unemployed miners loafing in the streets, round the pubs and the two-up rings.

Many had taken up alluvial claims or gone out prospecting. One group of miners was working an abandoned mine and doing quite well out of it. Every miner, every prospector, every man who knew the country, and every local business man who understood something of the causes behind the slump, believed in the mines: was confident that Kalgoorlie would come again, and that the gold was there in the underground lodes and in still vast unexplored tracts of country.

Kalgoorlie was suffering, they said, from mining trickery, unscrupulous flotations and financial corruption which had brought the industry into disrepute, and was still holding back the successful exploitation of low-grade ores.

The life of men and women who made their home in the mining towns went on much as usual. Women like Sally and Marie Robillard cooked and washed for their families, fighting the red dust with which the air was always heavy, and the swarming black flies, using their scanty water supply sparingly, and worrying about the rare visits of the sanitary man.

To get any fresh food or vegetables was still difficult, although they kept goats now, and had a cool-safe over which water dripped slowly. The same water was used to scrub the floors, and afterwards to run round the roots of a vine, or a few spindly tomato plants growing in the shade of bag screens.

Sally's days were spent in a ceaseless struggle to keep the house clean, cook and sew for her children. In the evening she and Marie visited each other occasionally, and sat on their verandahs, in the hot stillness, sewing or crocheting, and gossiping together.

The trouble over alluvial rights had dragged on for over two years. Dick and Tom were going to school, and Larry was two years old, when Sally knew she was going to have another child. She was glad about this baby: thought it would symbolize the reunion with Morris and all that their present way of life implied. They no longer dreamed of leaving the fields and were satisfied to have found a means of livelihood for themselves and their children.

When Dinny and Chris Crowe were in town, men were always dropping in to see them. They sat smoking and yarning until all hours. If Mullocky O'Dwyer was there, and some of the men who had taken part in the alluvial struggle, the discussion might be political and about current affairs. If some of the old-timers came, the talk drifted to yarns and reminiscences.

The trial of A. C. Bailey and De Stedingk in London, and liquidation of the West Australian Development Corporation, exposed the methods by which bogus companies had fleeced hundreds of small shareholders. The fraudulent practices of these scoundrels who induced people to invest in goldmines which did not exist, who declared a dividend of a hundred per cent. to inspire confidence when they had nothing to pay out, aroused a storm of indignation.

Frisco had been associated with the West Australian Development Corporation and got a lot of the backwash when Bailey was charged with having obtained £60,000 on false pretences. Bailey's assets were quoted as twopence in the bank and about a thousand in called-up shares. After ten remands he was sentenced to five years' penal servitude.

'Fat lot of good that does the poor mugs he swindled,' Dinny said, yarning with Mullocky O'Dwyer, Mike Burke, Bill Bray and Pat Hughes, one evening. 'Any spieler'd think it was worth doin' at the price.'

'There's others've made more, big men among the company

promoters and mine managers, and got off scot free,' Mike reminded him.

'Can ye beat the Boulder Milling Contract—although it's been cancelled, now?'

'And the stink on the Associated?'

'The directors are blamin' the manager for exaggerated reports and extravagance,' Mullocky commented sardonically. 'And he's blamin' the directors for tellin' him to tear all the high-grade ore out of the mine. They say they've been spendin' from twenty to twenty-five thousand a month, and he's worked her to a standstill.'

'Landau, the new French chairman, reckons two hundred thousand ounces has been extracted,' Bill Bray added. 'But shareholders can whistle for their share.'

'Somebody's made a pile!'

'Y'r can bet your sweet life about that!'

'But the Great Boulder keeps going,' Pat Hughes pointed out. 'Bit of a mystery about a new strike at the four hundred feet level. Rich reef, sort of golden hole, one of the men working on her was tellin' me. But the bosses are keepin' it dark. Shares still fallin'. They'll jump presently—and then we'll be boomin' again.'

'In the old days, when the Brookmans pegged blind, the Great Boulder was as much a wild cat as anything ever thrown on the market,' Dinny remembered, 'and turned out one of the richest mines. Shares jumped from a pound to seventeen, all of a sudden. Over three million's been made out of her.'

'Could've bought G.B.'s for five bob, a few months ago—'

'Saw a couple of hundred thrown into a two-up ring, the other day, against a fiver.'

'Wish I had 'em!' Mike laughed. 'The Great Boulder's alright, take my word for it. She's always been the bell wether of this field. And y' can't tell me the big boys aren't goin' to boost her again as soon as it suits 'em. There's another rumour goin' round about important developments at the thirteen hundred feet level, and shares movin' up—Lake View Consols followin' suit. Soon stocks'll be hoppin' again like 'roos.'

'Bah!' Dinny spat. 'Much good that'll do us. There's only one thing'll give Kalgoorlie a future. That's a clean-up of mining roguery. There's nothing wrong with the mines. The mines could carry twice the population we've got to-day, and give the men working in 'em decent living conditions, if they were run honestly, to let the damned capitalists have a fair profit on the loan of their money and develop this country, not just tear the guts out of it, and leave the people who live here to swelter and starve when it suits 'em.

' "Government," says Voltaire,' Chris muttered, ' "consists in taking from one part of the citizens to give to the others." '

'Where would we be now, but for alluvial gold?' Pat Hughes queried.

'That's right,' Mike agreed. 'It's alluvial gold—and a bit of gym—keeps the town goin' now: money in circulation. The big bugs thought they could turn this slump into a knock-out, and make their own terms with the government about carryin' on. But they're findin' they can't have things all their own way on these fields.'

The men chuckled and smiled, congratulating themselves and each other on their struggle and victory, as they smoked, meditatively.

'They're raisin' a great howl now,' somebody said, 'about gold stealin', illicit gold-buying—millions of gold lost on the mines, through the men bringin' up a few specimens in their crib bags. Talk of strippin' a man to his birthday suit to search him, when he comes off shift.'

'The boys won't stand for that!'

'By gosh they won't!'

In the prospecting and pioneering period, crimes of violence were almost unknown on the goldfields of Western Australia, old-timers said. It was not until the mining industry broke the morale imposed by diggers' law, and the railway made it easy for all manner of spielers and riff-raff to reach the mining towns that robbery under arms occurred, or cases of garrotting and vicious assault were heard in the Warden's Court.

During the slump they were many and frequent. The manager of Hannans Proprietary Ltd. was gagged by masked men in his own house: the assay room burst open. At Brown Hill, the watchman had been bailed up and gold-bearing sludge stolen. The battery house at the Royal Standard was raided and a large quantity of gold removed. But no arrests were made.

Kalgoorlie was becoming a hot-bed of lawlessness, corruption and vice, the southern press declared. Kalgoorlie folk repudiated the idea. They knew that the big companies had raked millions out of the mines, swindled shareholders with impunity and were strangling the town now to demonstrate their power. The wealthy men behind the mines saw no connection between their crimes and the crimes committed against them. The miners and alluvial diggers did. Although they denied having anything to do with the hold-ups, there was something of a grim joke for them in exploits which relieved the mining companies of some of the wealth they owed the people.

Gloom there might be in the Chamber of Mines and on the Stock Exchange, but in the homes of men and women who had seen Hannans grow from a rough and tumble mining camp to an imposing city, whatever hardships they were battling against, there was always a yarn and laugh to keep sturdy spirits going.

Tom Doyle was still Mayor of Kanowna and full of pleasure and pride in this position.

Dinny liked to tell how, bursting with importance, when he was first elected, he had broken the news to his wife.

'Glory be to God, Kate, I'm Mayor of this town now, and y're the Lady Mayoress,' said Tom.

'Tare 'n ages,' gasped Kate, 'what relation does that make me to the Queen?'

They gave a great party to the people of Kanowna. A ball it was called, and Tom, having been told how such things ought to be done, borrowed a dress suit for the occasion. He was a great strapping Irishman, six feet and handsome as a brigand chief, with a black beard showing a streak of grey, and flashing eyes, but beginning to put on flesh. The suit was so tight on him he couldn't wear anything underneath.

'Be jaysus, it's the truth, I'm tellin' y'r,' Dinny said. 'There was Tom half-full, sweatin' like a pig and prancin' round with the Warden's lady when he slips on the floor the boys'd polished-up with candle grease, and whack—crack—down he came with a wallop and the lady on top of him, and there's a great split in his pants. Kate rushes over and says she'll sew 'em up. Hustles him into the ladies' room and makes Tom peel off while she does the trick. But the women troop in after the dance, so she shoves Tom out by another door she thinks leads to the back premises. But it's into the ballroom she's shoved him, and there's Tom standing like an old rooster, with bare hairy legs, minus his pants, for all the town to gape at.

' "For Chris' sakes, let me in Kate," he bawls. "I'm in the ballroom!" The crowd roared, laughing so as Kate couldn't hear for a bit—and Tom had to stand there with his long legs shakin' under him, until she chased the women away, let him in and dressed him up again.'

But it took more than a little misfortune like that to destroy the gusto Tom Doyle put into being Mayor of Kanowna. He strode round the town as if he owned it: had a mighty fine time ruling the roost.

'I was drivin' over for the races with him, last year,' Blunt

Pick remembered, 'when we came across a man working on the road, and Bob Finey, the town clerk, giving him instructions.

' "Hey, Mr. Town Clerk," says Tom, "what's that parrty doin' diggin' up the road?"

' "He's makin' a culvert, Tom," says Bob.

' "Culvert, what sort of culvert does he think he's makin'? Put him off and have a decent culvert made."

' "But I can't do that," says Bob, "I've got an agreement with him."

' "What sort of an agreement?"

' "A verbal agreement."

' "A verbal agreement," says Tom, all high and mighty. "It's not worth the paper it's written on. Put him off. I want decent bloody culverts on my roads." '

It was always a good night when Sam Mullet and Blunt Pick, Jean Robillard, Eli Nancarrow, or Tassy Regan happened to be there together.

Sam had a story about Tom Doyle and Paddy Cavan, when Tom was acting manager of a mine alongside the old White Feather, between whiles of running his pub, and young Paddy wanted a job on the mine.

'Paddy used to stroll into Tom's office, about every second day,' Sam said. 'Sit down, stretch his legs under the table and say: "Got a job?" Tom'd say: "No," and clear Paddy out, pretty sharp. But it got his goat, the way Paddy'd turn up again, cheeky and grinning, with his: "Got a job?"

' "Now see here, young man," ses Tom, "if I had a job I wouldn't give it to you, askin' like that."

' "How'd you ask?" ses Paddy.

' "Well," ses Tom, getting up from his chair, "I'll show ye, if I was seekin' employment how I'd do it."

'He goes out of the room and Paddy takes his chair: helps himself to a cigar. Tom comes in.

' "Good mornin', sor," ses he, smilin' brightly. "May I inquire if there's any chance of pickin' up a job, here?"

' "No, you silly old cow," ses Paddy, puffin' at his cigar. "Y're too old and fat. Hook it!" '

Which would remind Jean Robillard how he got his first job on Hannans. He was a quiet chap, rarely spoke, and everybody knew he was doomed. 'Dusted,' the men said, and coughing his lungs out in the early hours of the morning.

There was no help for it. Hundreds of the men who had worked underground on the first mines were paying the penalty for dry-boring and lack of ventilation. Ted Molloy among them. He had been helpless for eight months, haemorrhaging and scaring the wits out of Mrs. Molloy and the children. Every dusted miner knew the long wasting illness he had to suffer; but Robbie was still on his feet, defying death—and looking for some light work. He had been machine minding on the Associated, until a few weeks ago.

'I come over from the old camp,' Robbie said, in his husky voice, with a slightly foreign inflection, 'when things were dull there. And I must have a job. It was Blunt Pick tell me, there is a good chance at the Brown Hill.'

'They were all Cousin Jacks on Brown Hill,' Blunt Pick butted in, to save Robbie's voice as much as anything. 'Salvo Jo struck a good thing there—real little jeweller's shop. He was boss, and so keen on savin' souls he wouldn't have anybody workin' in the mine who didn't go to his prayer meetings.'

'So Blunt Pick say to me: "Can you sing a hymn?"' Robbie went on. '"No, I could not sing a hymn." "Well, sit in at a prayer meeting," says Blunt Pick, "and say 'Praise the Lord' when you think of it." So I go to the prayer meeting two or three times and say "Praise the Lord," when I think of it. Then I ask Salvo Jo for a job, and get it alright.'

Robbie's breath came in gasps, with a dry rasp, but he carried on gamely:

'Next morning, I go below. It was not a big mine: not many men working on her. I see an old bloke with a square goaty beard like all Cornishmen wear, squatting back and knapping on the face where there was a rich patch. I squat down beside him and start knapping too. Presently, the boss comes along:

'"Praise the Lord, brother, how's she goin'?" says Salvo Jo.

'"Goin' good, brother, praise the Lord," says the old bloke, and goes on knapping. But I notice, he puts aside a nice specimen now and then. He had a sample bag full of nice specimens stowed away with his crib.

'"Thought you so re-ligious blokes would not do that," I say.

'"What?" says he.

'"Why, pinch a bit of gold," I say.

'"What the Lord put into the ground," the old bloke says, "the Lord meant the multitude to take out of the ground. I got as much right to the gold as Brother Jo."'

The men's laughter and Robbie's coughing mingled until somebody struck up with another yarn. Many a hot, quiet evening passed like that on Gough's verandah.

CHAPTER LXX

ALF had been dead two years when Laura decided to marry Tim McSweeney.

She went to see Sally a week or so after he had given her a ring. Tim was already announcing that he and Mrs. Brierly were going to be married at the end of the month.

'He's a good man and fond of me,' Laura said apologetically. 'I think it's the best thing I can do, Sally. I'm not the sort of woman who can look after herself, it seems. Too many men want to look after me—and when one starts drinking, goodness knows where it will end.'

Laura had put on flesh in those two years. She was buxom and well-corseted; handsomely dressed in blue brocaded satin. Her beauty had become rather full-blown. Her fair skin had lost its fresh colour: was of a sickly whiteness, suffused only by a dull flush with the heat. There was a puffiness beneath her blue-grey eyes, still mourning for Alf, and her breath smelt of brandy. Diamonds in the ring Tim McSweeney had given her sparkled on the white hands lying on her lap, like lost souls.

Having made her explanation, Laura wept a little.

'Who would have thought it could end like this between Alf and me?' she cried. 'We were so much in love with each other when we were married, and it was the same afterwards. I never thought anything could happen to separate us. How could he leave me? How could he do what he did?'

'There, there,' Sally tried to soothe and comfort her. 'It's like that with most of us. We're so romantic when we're young, and then—we have to do the best we can with things, the way they turn out.'

'That's it,' Laura agreed eagerly. 'You do understand, don't you, Sally? I love Alf. I'll always love him. I'll never love anyone but Alf; but it's better to marry Tim McSweeney than to go to pieces in a place like this. Oh, God, Sally, I never thought I could be a bad woman: really, loose and disreputable. But that's how it would be, if I don't marry someone and pull up. I don't know what would become of me. And there's Aimée to think of.'

'Why McSweeney rather than Frisco, Lloyd Carson, or one of the others?' Sally asked.

Laura's face twitched to impatience and disgust. 'Frisco doesn't want to marry me. You're the only woman he really cares for, if you ask me, Sally. He's always talking about you.

And Lloyd Carson's a sanctimonious old hypocrite. McSweeney's the best and kindest man I've had anything to do with since Alf died. He's really devoted to me. I feel I could live with him and get some peace and quietness into my life.'

'If that's the way you feel, it's best to marry Mr. McSweeney,' Sally said.

'He's very fond of Aimée, too,' Laura added, weakly. 'Promises to leave her some money when he dies.'

'That's good,' Sally declared. 'Don't cry, Laura. It will turn out alright, I'm sure.'

'Oh, Alf! Alf! Laura sobbed. 'How can I ever get over his death, Sally? If only he hadn't left me. It seems as if he were to blame that I've got to marry Tim McSweeney. But you do understand, don't you, Sally? You won't let this make any difference to our friendship? You'll always keep an eye on Aimée, for Alf's sake, won't you?'

'It won't make any difference to me, Laura,' Sally assured her. 'And my place will always be another home for Aimée when she wants one.'

Laura blew her nose and wiped away her tears with a small crumpled handkerchief. As she did so, she caught sight of herself in the mirror opposite.

'Oh, God, what a wreck I look,' she wailed. 'Who'd ever have thought that fat blowsy female with holes under her eyes, is me, Laura Brierly? What on earth Tim wants to marry me for, I don't know. But he does—and I'm going to oblige him. Not so much for his money and a comfortable home, as because he "worships the ground I walk on," he says. I can't live without somebody loving me, Sally. But I wish I needn't be Mrs. McSweeney.'

CHAPTER LXXI

THEY were sitting on the verandah at Gough's, Dinny and Morris, and Sally, with Dennis, a baby only a few weeks old, in her arms, the night McSweeney celebrated his wedding with a dinner party and free drinks at the Western Star. Dinny's old Crowe sat hunched up in the background as usual. Neither Dinny nor Morris could bring themselves to go to the dinner party, and Sally had a good excuse in the baby.

The men sat in the mute, comfortable thoughtfulness of old mates who don't have to talk to each other, though they looked depressed: were brooding over the past and their association with Alf, Sally guessed.

It was a still, hot evening, with a taste of dust in the air. The moon in its last quarter, tarnished and dingy, lurched across a dim sky sheening like silk. A few plants in the garden stood on dry sticks with brown paperish leaves.

Away across the flat, the earth stretched, bare and parched, to the slope of the ridge. The dry creek bed which wound across it could not be seen; but a few tobago bushes, relics of an Afghan camel camp, smeared its banks. In the distance the white shacks of Boulder township were clear in the wan light. Golden lights sparkled among them, and on mine buildings along the dark wall of the ridge. Poppet heads of the mines looked like a dead forest scraping the sky. White fumes from a tall smoke stack trailed across it, poisoning the air. Beyond the picket fence the Boulder road went on into Kalgoorlie city, squatted against the earth below the site of Paddy Hannan's first claim. Its crowded buildings, scores of pubs and street lamps cast a glow into the sky.

Several of the mines had closed down, but somewhere along the ridge a battery was working. The thud of the stamps, the rattle of ore, the grinding rush and roar of ore under the giant treads of the mill vibrated through the stillness, disturbing the rhythmic beat of quiet pulses, driving thought before it in a flurry of fear at the revelation of such relentless power. But the noise was far enough away that night to be no more than a remote thunder to those accustomed to it. The tinkle of goat bells drifted in from the flat, and nearer, from the backyard, an eerie wailing and clicking of sticks.

'Kalgoorla wants to go bush,' Sally remarked. 'She always does when she sings that little song about how the white men have brought death to her people.'

'Dirty old swab,' Morris growled. 'Don't know how on earth you can stand having her about.'

'She always comes when I'm having a baby,' Sally said wearily. 'And I'm glad enough to have her to do the washing and the cleaning.'

'That floggin' of abos on a station up be Marble Bar was one of the worst things I've heard of—barrin' the shootin' out at Menankily,' Dinny said slowly.

'What happened?' Sally asked.

'Seems the natives ran away from a cattle station owned by a couple of brothers, name of Anderson,' Dinny replied. 'The Andersons went out after the abos and drove them back: kept them without water, and thrashed 'em with a knotted rope, men,

404

women and children. Two of the women and one man died. Six of 'em were so badly flogged they nearly passed out. One man got away and informed the police.'

'I remember,' Morris said, 'the case was heard a few months ago.'

'That's right,' Dinny went on. 'One of the brothers died of fever before it came on, and the other got "penal servitude for life." D'y' remember what the judge said about "the inhuman flogging of mere girls"? And what he said to the accused? "Your crime was the deliberate, brutal, base, cruel murder of a man and two women."'

'"The native races know us chiefly by our crimes," as Mr. Engels said,' Chris muttered.

'What's happened to Maritana?' Dinny asked, out of the brooding silence which had captured everybody again.

'Oh, she comes into town sometimes,' Sally lifted the baby to her other breast. 'Kalgoorla says she's living proper white feller out at Mount Burgess with Fred Cairns. Got plenty kids and a horse and trap.'

'Fred Cairns? Long slab of fellow, looks like a dried shark?'

'That's Fred!' Morris said grimly. 'He's no good.'

'Poor Maritana!' Sally was thinking of the time when Maritana had been like a young wild animal, as shy and graceful, with beautiful brown eyes. 'She calls herself a half-caste now, Morris. And I'm sure she is. Maritana, herself, told me once two white men had caught her mother, and that's why she was different from the other native women.'

'Daresay the soldiers with Hunt's survey party or those escaped convicts took a woman when they could get one,' Dinny said.

'That was years before the rush to Coolgardie,' Morris remembered.

The talk lapsed, Morris and Dinny went on smoking and brooding. Sally wondered what they were thinking. How different everything was to when they had tramped out from the 'Cross with the first team, and gone off prospecting in every direction, no doubt. The whole countryside was an unexplored wilderness of waterless scrub then. It was difficult to believe that in such a short time cities had been built, and become almost as deserted as Coolgardie was now.

Kalgoorlie, threatened with the same fate, despite the railway and promise of a water scheme which would cause 'a river of pure water' to flow through the goldfields, was still suffering from the slump, though Morris said business on the Stock Exchange showed signs of looking up. So many mines had ceased production that hundreds of miners were unemployed, their wives and families living in hovels on the leases in the most poverty-stricken conditions. Hundreds of prospectors, too, had left the field and gone off to Klondyke.

Some people doubted that the depression would ever lift. They prophesied that before long Kalgoorlie would become a deserted mining camp like Coolgardie; that nothing would remain of 'the queen city' of the goldfields except streets of gutted buildings, a pub or two, and a few derelict mines. But not the old-timers. They scoffed at pessimism, and despite the gloomy forebodings which affected everybody, clung to their faith in the Boulder mines and the ridge which threw a long arm round Kalgoorlie.

Morris, as if to reassure Sally, pointed to the trail of fumes fouling the night air and drifting across the moonlit sky.

'Zeb Lane says that's solving the sulphide bugbear and the Boulder'll be booming again before long!'

'He ought to know,' Dinny said dryly. 'I reckon it'll be as soon as the mine-owners are ready. But things will never be the same again, Morrey. Times have changed.'

'And we've changed with them,' Sally said.

'That's right, ma'am, we've changed with them.' Dinny's eyes were compassionate as he looked at her. 'Some of the early prospectors had the sense to clear out when they sold a good claim: bought farms and businesses near their home towns. They tell me Bill Jehosaphat's gone on the land. Went east when Speck and him sold their show at Leonora. He's got a station in the Riverina now.'

'The old prospecting period on this field has passed.' Morris said. 'And a new one is beginning. A period when the mining industry will be stabilized: take a firmer grip of the country. To a certain extent we need the prosperity it will create. Growth of the mining industry built Kalgoorlie: gave us the mines and the railway.'

'That's right,' Dinny retorted hotly, 'but the trickery and rottenness behind the industry landed us where we are now. There had to be a clean up—and we'll have to fight always to see the people on these fields get a fair deal. I don't mean only men like you and me, Morrey, pioneer prospectors and miners, but the men and women who live and work here: have made their home on the fields, kept things going, and are treated like dirt by the mining companies.

Chris croaked in the background:

' "Agitation is the marshalling of the conscience of a nation," Sir Robert Peel said. "The people must keep agitating until they mould the laws to justice." '

'No need to argue about that,' Morris growled. 'God. when

406

you think of all the gold that's come out of this country, the millions of money it's turned over, it's hard to believe the people living here have got so little out of it! In spite of corruption, mismanagement, Stock Exchange thuggery, those mines along the Boulder ridge. The Associated, Great Boulder. Perseverance. Horse Shoe, Ivanhoe, Lake View and the rest of them, have paid over three million in dividends. And we live in a sun-blasted desert, most of the year, without a proper water supply, without decent sanitary arrangements. The hospital's still half a dozen weatherboard and hessian shacks, full of typhoid patients every summer. And the humpies of tin and bagging people live in round the mines are a damned disgrace.'

'You're comin' on, Morrey,' Dinney grinned. 'Not such a dyed-in-the-wool Tory as y'r used to be.'

'I'm a working man like the rest of you,' Morris said. 'A pick and shovel taught me all the politics I need.'

'But some of you who made money in the early days, squandered it,' Sally murmured.

'Course we did,' Dinny cried. 'It was just the crazy way we let off steam. Art Bayley drank himself to death in a few years, and many a man's on the scrap heap now, who struck it rich and lived like a lord for a few months.'

'Much good the gold did them,' Sally said waspishly. 'It was the mirage you all chased, thinking it would give you everything worth while.'

In the background, as if talking to himself, Chris chanted:

'This yellow slave,
Will knit and break religions; bless the accursed;
make the hoar leprosy adored; place thieves and give
them title, knee and approbation,
with senators on the bench.'

'Too much or too little, both are bad for you, ma'am,' Dinny mourned. 'Remember when the Londonderry men came in with a cartload of gold, Morrey, and hundreds of men on that rush were jest about starving?'

Morris nodded.

'But actually,' Dinny went on, 'a bloke never went short of a feed, when another man had the price of one on him, or enough rations to share. The Londonderry boys were free enough with their cash when they got it. Great, the spirit of the old camp, Morrey, when y'r come to think of it!'

'Finest bunch of men who ever trod shoe-leather, the early

407

prospectors!' Sally's exclamation was tinged with irony. She had heard it so often.

'So they were. ma'am,' Dinny declared. 'Not a rogue among them, or if one was discovered, now and then, a roll-up knew what to do with him.'

'Remember how thousands of pounds' worth of gold from Bayley's Reward used to lie in the old bag shack which was the post office and butcher's shop?' Morris queried. 'And no one ever thought of getting away with it.'

Dinny chuckled.

'They wouldn't 've had much chance if they'd tried! It wasn't until the mining industry got under way and the spielers and riff-raff began to arrive, there were hold-ups and shootin's to kill. Though things got pretty willin' at times when there was a 'booze-up.'

'God, will y'r ever forget the night the Warden and old Cruickshanks were run in by a new constable for bein' drunk and disorderly? The Warden managed to straighten things out with the constable in the morning, left Cruickshanks in bed at the pub when he went over to the court. And there he was sitting in the old tent we called the court, tryin' drunks, when along comes Cruickshanks, with only a shirt flappin' round him, and a bottle in one hand. "Leave those poor bastards alone, and come and 've a drink, you silly old bugger!" he calls to the Warden. And the Warden adjourned the court and went and had a drink with him.'

Morrey laughed over this yarn, as if it was still a good joke, though he had heard it, with variations, many times.

'And there was the time two Wardens happened to be passing through the same town, Kurnalpi was it, or Kanowna?' Dinny always enjoyed reminiscing like this. 'They were makin' a night of it at the pub and started fightin'. The local constable, not knowin' who they were, arrested 'em; but there was nobody to hear the case against 'em in the morning. So to avoid it goin' any further, and let each other off lightly, the Wardens decided to try each other.

'The Warden for the district had the first innings and thought he'd make the most of it. "How do you explain such behaviour," he asks his cobber. "You, a highly respected citizen, ought to give an example of good behaviour, not disgrace yourself brawling in this unseemly fashion. I'm going to fine you two pounds, in default fourteen days."

'Then the visiting Warden took the chair. "Well, I must say I'm surprised at the charge brought against you, of being drunk and disorderly, my friend," he says. "Under the circumstances,

I'm forced to take a serious view of the charge. This is the second of the same sort heard this morning. The town will be getting a bad name. I propose, therefore, to make an example of you, with the object of deterring others. You're fined five pounds, in default twenty-eight days!"'

Morris knew that yarn, too, but he laughed with Dinny as if he had never heard it before.

'What a magnet the fields were for all sorts and conditions of men,' Morris mused. 'English aristocrats and Irish rebels rubbing shoulders in the pubs and shovelling dirt on the claims.'

'Men who fought on the barricades of the Paris Commune, like old Fabre, too,' Dinny added. 'But Australians held their own, Morrey. They were always the best bushmen and prospectors.'

'Even if they let the overseas sharks commandeer the gold and grab the mines,' Morris remarked.

'Oh, well,' Dinny apologized, 'we had to develop the fields.'

'Could have done that with a sound national policy.'

'Y're right there, Morrey,' Dinny agreed. 'But we didn't have it. Pickin' up gold and mines has been a go-as-you-please for foreign investors. Still is, of course, but I reckon federation will make a difference and safeguard Australian interests.'

Morris paused, his thoughts reverting to the past.

'Worst bit of luck I ever had was losing that scrip in the Great Boulder. God, I'd like to know who the swine was got away with it.'

'Things were always rougher on Hannans than they were on the old camp,' Dinny said.

'They were,' Morris agreed. 'And there was no chance of checking up on scrip. It changed hands so often. Some crook did me out of the chance of a lifetime when he rooked me of those original shares, and I daresay he's sitting pretty, now.'

Dinny knew how sore Morris was on the subject. Though Morris still gambled in shares, he believed he would have made a fortune out of his interest in the Great Boulder.

'Queer,' Morris went on, 'how a few of us who've stuck together all these years, have never had much luck. You and I, Dinny, and Sally, the Robillards and the Brierlys.'

'Alf's the first casualty,' Dinny said bitterly—'And his missus.'

'You can't blame Laura,' Sally protested.

'I'm not blaming her,' Dinny said.

'I am.' Morris spoke with flat disapproval. 'She sent Aimée to the convent school in Coolgardie when she should've been looking after her. It's an outrage to Alf's memory for her to have married McSweeney.'

'You're very hard, Morris,' Sally murmured.

'Would you have done it?' he asked.

'I don't know. I might have,' Sally confessed.

Dinny thought it time to talk of something else.

'Frisco's been going the pace in London again.' he said, not conscious of having given the conversation a wrong twist. 'They say he's floated a big company and married a rich woman.'

Sally was glad of the darkness about her. Otherwise, she thought Morris must have noticed how she winced at this news.

'I heard that,' she said quietly.

'Paddy Cavan's sold him the Golden Feather,' Dinny added.

'Frisco and Paddy Cavan, can you beat it?' Morris exclaimed. 'Who'd ever have dreamed they would be big men on the fields?'

Dinny spat contemptuously.

'Big men? They've made money. But I'd rather chase 'weights all me days, than do the things they've done to be where they are.'

'Same here,' said Morris.

A long silence was broken only by the distant rumble and tramp of the battery. Kalgoorla's wailing had died away. Sally went into the house to put down the baby. When she returned to the verandah, Morris and Dinny were talking, and stopped, as if they were discussing some subject not for her ears.

'Morrey says he'll never go prospecting again.' Dinny said, when Sally sat down beside them.

'Won't you, Morris?' she asked.

'Gold,' Morris said, repressed bitterness in his voice, 'I don't dream of it any more, or hope my luck will change.'

'You've had a tough spin, and no mistake, Morrey.' Dinny agreed. 'But once a prospector always a prospector, I reckon. There's as much gold in the country as ever was found in it! Come out with me to the Laverton Ranges—and we'll strike her yet.'

'No.' Morris said. 'I'll stick to burying corpses.'

'Well,' Dinny replied slowly, 'there's nothing for me in this town now. I hate the smell of it, and that blasted row of the stamps! Happiest days of me life were when Alf and me was on the track and you never knew what glorious prospects any day'd bring. The mining industry got Alf; but I'll never work for wages again. Daresay y're right about the mines boomin' and a new bout of prosperity for Boulder and Kal, Morrey. But I've got in me bones there'll never be a fair deal for the working man until we rule the roost, like Chris says.'

He rose and stretched, as if throwing off the depression, which had been hanging over him all the evening.

'What can you do about it?' Morris demanded cynically.

'Me?' Dinny's query flew with a little dry laugh. 'Not much. But I reckon the workers will fix it some day like they did the question of alluvial rights. That was one of the best fights ever put up by the Australian working class, Morrey. It affected the whole future of the country, forced the Forrest Government to drop its opposition to federation and brought the West into the Commonwealth. Everybody admits, now, my dad and his mates did a good job for Australia at Eureka, and I reckon the diggers on this field did as much when they stood up for their rights in the alluvial troubles.'

'You had something to do with that, Dinny,' Sally said.

'You bet I did,' Dinny cried, his spirits rising to the implied compliment. 'But there's nothing doin' jest now, ma'am, and I'm stony. Goin' off prospectin' again in the morning.'

He stood for a moment, a slight, intrepid figure, looking out over the moonlit plains to where the grey-dark scrub stretched away inland and the mirages quivered on endless horizons. Then he turned, the quirk of a smile on his wizened face, jerked his head, and limped away. 'S'long!'

Other VIRAGO MODERN CLASSICS

EMILY EDEN
The Semi-Attached House &
  The Semi-Detached Couple

MILES FRANKLIN
My Brilliant Career
My Career Goes Bung

GEORGE GISSING
The Odd Women

ELLEN GLASGOW
The Sheltered Life
Virginia

SARAH GRAND
The Beth Book

RADCLYFFE HALL
The Well of Loneliness
The Unlit Lamp

WINIFRED HOLTBY
Anderby Wold
The Crowded Street

MARGARET KENNEDY
The Ladies of Lyndon
Together and Apart

F. M. MAYOR
The Third Miss Symons

GEORGE MEREDITH
Diana of the Crossways

EDITH OLIVIER
The Love Child

**CHARLOTTE PERKINS
GILMAN**
The Yellow Wallpaper

DOROTHY RICHARDSON
Pilgrimage (4 volumes)

**HENRY HANDEL
RICHARDSON**
The Getting of Wisdom
Maurice Guest

BERNARD SHAW
An Unsocial Socialist

MAY SINCLAIR
Life & Death of Harriett Frean
Mary Olivier
The Three Sisters

F. TENNYSON JESSE
A Pin to See The Peepshow
The Lacquer Lady
Moonraker

MARY WEBB
Gone to Earth
The House in Dormer Forest
Precious Bane

H. G. WELLS
Ann Veronica

REBECCA WEST
Harriet Hume
The Judge
The Return of the Soldier

ANTONIA WHITE
Frost in May
The Lost Traveller
The Sugar House
Beyond the Glass
Strangers

Other VIRAGO MODERN CLASSICS

PHYLLIS SHAND ALLFREY
The Orchid House

SYLVIA ASHTON WARNER
Spinster

MARGARET ATWOOD
The Edible Woman
Life Before Man
Surfacing

DOROTHY BAKER
Cassandra at the Wedding

JANE BOWLES
Two Serious Ladies

KAY BOYLE
Plagued by the Nightingale

ANGELA CARTER
The Magic Toyshop

WILLA CATHER
Death Comes for the Archbishop
A Lost Lady
My Antonia
The Professor's House

BARBARA COMYNS
The Vet's Daughter

ELIZABETH HARDWICK
Sleepless Nights

EMILY HOLMES COLEMAN
The Shutter of Snow

ROSAMOND LEHMANN
Invitation to the Waltz
The Weather in the Streets

TILLIE OLSEN
Tell Me a Riddle
Yonnondio

GRACE PALEY
Enormous Changes at
    the Last Minute
The Little Disturbances of Man

STEVIE SMITH
The Holiday
Novel on Yellow Paper
Over the Frontier

CHRISTINA STEAD
Cotters' England
For Love Alone
Letty Fox: Her Luck
A Little Tea, A Little Chat
The People with the Dogs

**SYLVIA TOWNSEND
    WARNER**
Mr Fortune's Maggot
The True Heart

REBECCA WEST
Harriet Hume
The Judge
The Return of the Soldier

ANTONIA WHITE
Frost in May
The Lost Traveller
The Sugar House
Beyond the Glass
Strangers